THE LEGEND OF
ZERO

ZERO'S RETURN

SARA KING

DISCLAIMER

(a.k.a. If You Don't Realize This Is A Work Of Fiction, Please Go Find Something Else To Do)

So you're about to read about badasses with plasma pistols, a devastating alien apocalypse, and people who move stuff with their minds. In case you're still confused, yes, this book is a complete work of fiction. Nobody contained within these pages actually exists. If there are any similarities between the people or places of *The Legend of ZERO* and the people or places of Good Ol' Planet Earth, you've just gotta trust me. It's not real, people. Really. Yet.

Also! Unlike in ZERO1 and ZERO2, this book contains profanity, namely because it deals with the people of Earth, and people on Earth use profanity, especially people on Earth involved in the criminal element, or, coincidentally, brilliant-yet-reclusive Alaskan writers. If you can't stand profanity, or likewise, if you want to bitch about it, this probably isn't the book for you.
You have been warned.

BOOKS IN THE LEGEND OF ZERO SERIES:

DEDICATION

I owe this one to Kim Burling, the Muse behind the story of S.H.A.E.L. Without you, her tale would have never been told.

AUTHOR'S NOTE

WARNING: Unlike the first two ZERO novels, Zero's Return is not a stand-alone. As you know, this book was 'finished' about eight months ago. Despite my valiant attempts to contain it, however, Book 3 ended up being so overwhelmingly huge in the 'edit' (A.K.A. The Perfectionist Obsessive Streak That Would Never End) that I had to break the story arc into two parts (what is now Zero's Return and Zero's Redemption). To give you an idea of just how mind-numbingly huge ZERO3 got before I split it, each of these 'parts' ended up being substantially larger than any other novel I've ever published. Generally, this wouldn't have stopped me from gleefully publishing a novel bigger than The Stand, but for my own sanity, I'm moving on to Redemption before I edit Return into the next *Collected Works of Shakespeare*.

For those of you who hung around while I obsessed for months over silly crap, I really appreciate your patience. And please. Do me a favor. The next time I say I want to 'edit' one of my books, please just haul off and slap me.

THE PARASITE PUBLICATIONS GLOSSARY
(BECAUSE SOMEBODY'S GOTTA TELL YOU THIS STUFF!)

Character author – That rare beast who lets his or her characters tell the story. (And often run completely wild.)

Character fiction – Stories that center around the characters; their thoughts, their emotions, their actions, and their goals.

Character sci fi – Stories about the future that focus on the characters, rather than explaining every new theory and technology with the (silly) assumption that we, as present-day 21st centurians, know enough to analyze and predict the far future with any accuracy whatsoever. I.e. character sci-fi is fun and entertaining, not your next college Physics textbook.

Parasite – The Everyday Joe (or Jane) who enjoys crawling inside a character's head while reading a book; i.e. someone who enjoys character fiction.

Poddite – Someone who allows other people to tell them what they like.

Furg – Generally a poddite who believes the best fiction makes your eyes glaze over…unless the glazing happens because you stayed up all night reading it and you can't keep your eyes open the next day. ;)

TABLE OF CONTENTS

1

TWELVE-A

*T*his is our future.

Though their bodies were naked, their minds empty, the fearful, half-mad faces that followed Marie from behind the sanitized bars of their cages were Humanity's hope.

Marie hurried her step. Despite almost thirty years on the project, the depraved gazes never ceased to bother her. They haunted her dreams, peeked at her from beneath her floorboards, watched her from the other side of her shower curtain, looked up at her from her morning cup of coffee, stared at her from between the lines of her medical charts. Unlike the other experts on the project, Marie had never been able to see past the source material they had used for the project, and every day, it ate at her.

A familiar voice entered her head, unbidden. *It will be over soon, Marie.*

Marie shuddered and gripped her pen, her eyes unconsciously drawn to the slender, blue-eyed experiment in the corner cell. His drip-bag had run out again and he was awake. Her heart started to pound as she met the deep cerulean eyes tucked behind the useless titanium bars. She knew, better than anyone, that Twelve-A could kill them all, should it ever cross his mind.

The slender experiment said nothing more, merely watched her from his thin, military-issue mattress.

Fighting the gut-deep urge to drop her charts and run, Marie hurried back through the foot-thick leaden doors separating the holding area from the lab and slapped the glowing red button inside the monitoring room. She allowed herself a soft breath of relief as the massive hydraulics of the holding area hissed shut, locking the experiments in their silent bunker of lead and concrete.

"Twelve-A needs another dose," she told the techs at their stations, trying not to sound as unnerved as she felt. "He's awake again."

"Colonel Codgson wants him awake," Sunny Carter, a young blonde Army lieutenant, said. The woman gave the holding area a nervous glance, then her eyes flickered back to her vitals monitor. "Codgson's got us monitoring him, making sure his patterns stay level—he's scheduled another demonstration for this afternoon."

Marie cursed. Codgson was a bureaucratic furg. Ever since he had discovered their prodigy's unique talents, the man had made every attempt to show him off to the board in every brutal way possible. Twelve-A had been pitted against everything the other labs could throw at him again and again—and had lived.

"Do you think Twelve-A will survive this one?" Lieutenant Carter asked, her face etched with worry. She cocked her head at the monitor that showed him hunched around his knees in one corner of his cell, staring at the wall. "What if they find a better minder and he doesn't survive? Don't we need him?"

Marie knew the lieutenant was partial to the handsome, blue-eyed young man in the last cage on the right. She didn't think of him as a killer. Marie, having seen the lifeless bodies Twelve-A left behind in the Dark Room, knew better. She also knew there was nothing that could stand against Twelve-A. By some luck of the draw, it was *their* lab, of all of them, that had hit upon the lucky combination that no amount of desperate cloning had been able to reproduce.

"He's survived all the others," Marie said. Still, Marie felt dread creeping into her soul. Twelve-A hated the Dark Room. If left awake after he was pitted against another experiment, Twelve-A would go broody and silent—or sometimes just curl into a ball and cry for hours. Ridiculously, 'Mental Fortitude' was Codgson's lowest rating for Twelve-A, just under 'Emotional Resilience.' What if, one day, their star performer just decided not to cooperate? What if he one day sat down and let the inferior creatures Codgson pitted him against simply end his misery? What if he just stopped caring? What if he grew angry? Or worse…what if he grew *vengeful*? Just the tiniest slip by the technicians monitoring him and he could wreak destruction on the whole lab. He could *escape*.

That, right there, introduced a whole new wave of horror to Marie's nightmares.

"I know," Lieutenant Carter said, observing the rows of monitors displaying the experiment wing. "That's what bothers me. He doesn't like it…it *hurts* him. What if he doesn't—"

A male voice behind her interrupted them. "We have his DNA. We can always make another, if he fails to cooperate."

Marie stiffened and turned. The colonel stood in the hall, his perfectly crisp blue uniform accenting a bored demeanor, as if they were talking about cloning rats.

You don't have a clue, you stupid furg, Marie thought. "We've tried that," she reminded him, having to physically stop herself from adding something unpleasant. The colonel's dull black eyes reminded her of the rodents they used in the early days of the project. Though she had said it a thousand times to the gun-happy thugs running the military side of the project, she explained it again. "Even an exact genetic match is no assurance of the same abilities manifesting in a clone. There is something more at work here, something that makes it all the more important to protect Twelve-A until we can figure it out."

The colonel caught her gaze and smiled, a wormlike twisting of his lips that chilled her to the core. "The first rule of this project is not to become attached to the subjects, Doctor."

Marie's anger spiked, as it always did around the colonel. As usual, he had completely disregarded that there was more to their project than simple genetics, as it didn't fit within his tiny mental box. Despite the outrageous and ingenious successes of the project, he had written off their failure to reproduce Twelve-A's...unique... capabilities as simple Human error and fired a few technicians. Then, when the second, third, and fourth clone batches had failed to manifest more of Twelve-A's special abilities, only telekinetics or telemorphs instead, he had reported it as 'mechanical malfunction' and ordered more equipment.

They were on the eighth and ninth batches now, though they were still in the pre-fetal stages. Several times, when walking past the incubation tubes, Marie had considered sabotaging them herself, to spare them the fate she knew awaited them if they disappointed their benefactor. Several months ago, after the seventh batch had been tested and confirmed negative for Twelve-A's minder qualities, Codgson spent a night in the lab destroying all the previous clone batches—after Marie had made a specific request to keep them alive for study. Eighty-four blond, blue-eyed young men, some only five years of age, most with the strongest mover or maker abilities they had ever seen. Dead.

Security footage had shown Codgson stalking from the building that night drenched in red because the sadistic shit had used a combat knife, sort of a manly coup he could tell his drinking buddies about in the Officers' Club. The next morning, because there were too many bodies for the technicians to take care of before they began to stink, Marie had been one of the ones on her knees mopping blood from their cells with a crimson rag.

For months, Marie had wanted to kill him.

Looking into Codgson's glinting, hollow eyes, she still did. It took all of Marie's control to keep her anger in check as she said, "You shouldn't leave Twelve-A awake. He could kill us all right now if he wanted to. He could empty our minds, make us all stop breathing just like he does in your Dark Room."

The colonel snorted in complete disdain. "I doubt that. My techs—"

"—would die too," Marie interrupted coldly. "You're playing with fire, Colonel."

The colonel laughed and rapped sharply on the thick leaden door separating them from the containment area. The sound diffused with the sheer density of the metal. The colonel gave her a smug look. "He doesn't even know we're here."

Marie glared, but said nothing.

"If he did," the colonel said. "He would have killed us a long time ago."

"You don't know that," Marie said, remembering the curled ball of misery she had found so many times after a visit to the Dark Room. "Maybe he doesn't like to kill."

The colonel's gaze sharpened, as if he were a hound breeder and she had suggested his dogs didn't like to hunt. He turned to Lieutenant Carter abruptly. "Collect the experiment and take him to the Dark Room. Our visitors are waiting in the observation booth."

As the tech went to get the necessary equipment, Marie fought another wave of dread. Reluctantly, she asked, "What's he going to fight this time?"

The colonel's wormy lips twisted again. "An experiment from another lab."

Marie had expected as much, but she stiffened anyway. "Twelve-A represents thirty-two turns of work. If you want a friendly competition for the generals' viewing pleasure, go get one of the Eleven-series to be your gladiator. Anything Twelve-series and above shouldn't be risked."

The colonel gave her a humorless smile. "There is nothing friendly about it. The lab that fails today loses its funding. If we lose our funding, every experiment will be killed and our data destroyed. We need to win. That's why I chose him."

For a moment, she thought the humorless, hardass shit was joking. When Marie blinked and saw the sincerity in his beady black eyes, however, it suddenly felt like all the energy of her body rushed out her feet. Softly, she whispered, "They would kill them all?"

The colonel inclined his head. "Now you see why it must be Twelve-A."

"Why?" she whispered.

The colonel gave her a long look before he shrugged and said, "The bureaucrats got cold feet. We had someone hack into our system. We're pretty sure it was Peacemakers. The board hopes we can stall them for a few years, and the fewer active labs we have, the better our chances will be of going undiscovered."

"Can't we combine the labs?" Marie blurted. "Throw them all into one building?"

The colonel shook his head. "We've established the genetic lines won't fight each other if they're kept in the same building."

Remembering the horrible child deathmatches and psychopathic mind-screwing that Colonel Codgson had used to determine that, Marie felt sick. In all, Codgson and his military fuck-ups had killed over three quarters of their non-cull subjects, more or less as target practice for the others. "Then maybe we could find some other means to determine the success of the experiments," Marie said quickly. Her chest was aching now. To lose so many lives, so many years of work…"Surely we can figure something out. Something that does not endanger their lives. There is evidence that latent brain activity is a clear indicator of—"

"We're constructing a *war*, Doctor," the colonel bit out, bristling like an angry dog. "The alien Congress will bathe in its own blood before it realizes it can no longer hold us. Twelve-A and his kind represent Earth's hope for independence, and it will take many of their deaths to see it happen." He gave her his zealot's smile—the one that had made her so excited at her interview—and said, "*I'm* willing to make the sacrifice. Are you?"

What kind of stupid question is that? Marie thought, appalled. With the colonel, everything was either black or white. In his mind, there *was* no other alternative. She bit down the urge to tell him he wasn't sacrificing anything, then decided to try a different tack, while she still had time to salvage her life's work. "You've used Twelve-A three times in the last month. Why not Ten-F?"

Colonel Codgson gave her a flat look full of patronizing amusement. "You want to place all of their lives on *her*?"

Marie licked her lips. Ten-F, though potent, was insane. She had fingernail scars down her face from where she'd tried to take out her own eyes, and she was missing her pinkie fingers from where she'd gnawed them off after her last visit to the Dark Room.

"Colonel," she began tentatively, "you don't stay to see them after their experiences in the Dark Room. It's obviously very traumatic for the minders, and you've already used Twelve-A many more times than my recommendations allow. I want you to retire him. He's too valuable to the project for any more games."

The colonel's eyes narrowed. "This…" he flicked lint off of his uniform jacket, "…is not a game." He gave her a glacial smile. "It's war." When Marie started to retort, he cut her off with a big, upraised hand. "Go find out what's taking Lieutenant Carter so long. I told them noon sharp." The colonel glanced at his big gold wristwatch and his mouth twisted in irritation. "We're two minutes behind already." Without another word, he turned sharply and strode off in the direction of the Dark Room, hard black boot-heels clicking briskly on the white tile as he departed.

Frustrated, Marie went looking for Carter.

She found the lieutenant slumped on the floor of the containment corridor outside Twelve-A's cage, the behavioral adaptor still clasped in her limp hand, unused.

"You *killed* her?!" Marie cried, rushing up to kneel beside the fallen woman.

Dr. Carter had a pulse. Relieved, Marie turned back to the experiment, intending to grab the adaptor and make her displeasure known.

Cold blue eyes met her stare, unwavering. Twelve-A was only two feet away, squatting naked behind the bars, watching her. He was angry.

I'm not fighting.

Marie stumbled away from him, her own vulnerability in the situation hitting her like a sledgehammer. She automatically glanced at the fallen behavioral adaptor, then froze when she saw the young blond man following her motions with his eyes, a grim twist to his lips. Twelve-A knew what she was thinking. He'd never let her use it.

Marie pulled her hand away slowly, so he could see it. Twelve-A watched her in silence, his intelligent blue eyes sliding back up her arm to rest on her face. Like most of the other experiments, the inbreeding and line-breeding required to emphasize the Army's desired traits—as well as the small infusions of alien blood—had left him with deformities. Most apparent on Twelve-A were the unsightly, almost Vulcan ears that seemed to stand out from his head in defiance.

At least he wasn't missing feet, or born with his legs fused together. Marie had seen those, and it had been on her orders they had been destroyed, just as it had been her orders to let Twelve-A live at infancy, despite his physical irregularities.

I like my ears, Twelve-A told her, frowning. He touched one with a slender finger.

They almost got you killed, Marie thought, watching the minder. *I saw them and almost culled you like the rest.*

Twelve-A snorted and released his ear. *I wouldn't have let you.*

Once again reminded that he could hear everything as crystal-clear as if she'd spoken her thoughts aloud, Marie swallowed. Carefully, she said, "You need to fight. If our lab fails this match, they'll all die." She gestured at the other experiments. "Codgson says there's some sort of funding shortage. Do you want them all to die?"

Twelve-A's childlike blue eyes darkened immediately. They flickered toward the other experiments, then back at her, full of accusation. *They're miserable. You treat them like animals. They're better off dead.*

In that moment, Marie realized that Twelve-A, out of all of the experiments they kept down here in the dark, actually *knew* what it meant to be Human. And, with that realization, she understood that he could not only kill her and her comrades, but he could also kill his own kind. With a thought.

A thought he was even then debating.

"No!" After twenty-seven years of living her work, foregoing her personal life for long hours at the lab, overseeing the births of each and every batch, the experiments had become Marie's children. At the thought of losing them, she completely forgot the history of the man in front of her as her heart rushed out to them. On instinct, she reached through the bars to touch his knee. "Things will get better, Twelve-A," she begged of him. "Please don't hurt them."

As soon as she touched his leg, Twelve-A recoiled, drawing deeper into his cell to glare at her. *You can't lie to me.*

"I'm not," Marie promised. "Just one more time. I'll make sure you won't have to do it again. Ever. You understand? Just one more time. We'll secure the funding and I'll put in a request directly to the Board. They won't make you fight anymore. You're too important to them, and I can make them see that. I just need some time."

Twelve-A glanced to the side, away from her, pain etched in his young face. For long moments, he said nothing. His eyes fell on the other cages once more, and for what felt like ages, he seemed to consider.

One thought, Marie thought, her heart pounding. *It would just take him one thought…*

Then, with great reluctance, Twelve-A turned back to her with a look that chilled her to the bone. *Take me to the Dark Room.*

● ● ●

"Watch closely," Colonel Codgson said, addressing the visitors. "See how he paces? Our experiments show an innate aggression…a drive to fight. He's anticipating the kill."

Marie watched with her back to the colonel, recognizing Twelve-A's pacing for what it really was—anger.

"Is the experiment contained?" one of the visitors demanded. A nasal, gray-haired woman pointed at the large observation station in the corner, indicating the two technicians monitoring it. "Are they all that stand between us and that monster?"

In the Dark Room, Twelve-A stopped and gave the observation booth a small frown before continuing to pace. The others did not notice, but Marie's heart clenched.

He knows we're here, she thought, horrified. *And he's listening.* Two things that, with the specially-treated glass and billions of credits of electronics shielding the place, shouldn't have been possible.

"We're in absolutely no danger," Colonel Codgson replied, with the surety of the truly mad. As he had done to Marie, he rapped his precious leaded walls with a knuckle. "The walls are a foot and a half of lead-ceramic composite. Even the windows are leaded. His abilities cannot penetrate."

"Has this been proven?" a woman in a sharp black pantsuit demanded, watching Twelve-A closely.

"Beyond a doubt," Colonel Codgson replied, beaming her that sociopathic smile. He had tousled his thick silvered hair—his one concession to his bible of 'regulations'—in the bathroom a few minutes before, and the room stank of his freshly-applied cologne. Seeing the handsome, chiseled face that had won over a hundred female officials before her, the pantsuit woman's rigid face melted a little and she gave him a shy grin. Seeing it, Marie thought she would be sick.

On the other side of the glass, the Dark Room doors opened and a second experiment, a naked redheaded woman, was thrust inside.

The fight ended as swiftly and undramatically as they always did with Twelve-A. He simply walked up to the other experiment, gently took her trembling chin into his hands, brushed the tears from her cheeks, touched his forehead to hers, and his opponent collapsed.

"Amazing," the nasal woman said, though she did not sound very amazed. "That's it? Why didn't they fight?"

"No one can fight Twelve-A," Colonel Codgson said, pride seeping through his voice, coating the walls of the room. "He is our finest creation."

Again, Marie thought she saw Twelve-A glance in their direction, but a shaking Lieutenant Carter was already leading the experiment from the room, her fist wrapped so tightly around her portable behavioral adaptor that her knuckles were white. The moment Twelve-A looked at her with something akin to apology, Lieutenant Carter twisted the dial and made him scream.

"He takes the behavior modification well," the pantsuit woman noted, as Twelve-A's naked body twisted on the smooth white floor in agony. "What's the range on his chip?"

"Two miles," Colonel Codgson replied. "More with a booster."

"We'll need more distance," the pantsuit woman noted. She gave Codgson a sideways look. "You have a personal number I can use to contact you for funding logistics?"

"I'm *very* busy," Codgson replied. "But I might have an hour or two tonight to discuss…logistics."

The pantsuit woman's face brightened before she quickly hid it with a cough. "I've got another night here in town before I fly back to DC. Perhaps we could discuss it in person…?"

"I definitely prefer face-to-face," Codgson replied, with that winning smile.

The pantsuit woman blushed.

Marie ignored the revolting interchange that followed, her eyes instead fixed on the naked figure writhing on the floor before dozens of indifferent faces, a sickness pooling in her stomach. Lieutenant Carter had never used the behavioral unit before, but now she used it longer than necessary, keeping Twelve-A screaming for long minutes as she panted, an almost triumphant look on her face. Only after Twelve-A had stopped struggling and simply devolved into unintelligible sobs did she switch off the unit and end his torment.

As Marie watched the other technicians rush in to help Carter carry the experiment from the room, she felt undefinable sadness. After two years of near crush-like status towards the 'cutie in cell 5', the lieutenant's good will had officially ended.

She and I were his only two friends in this place, she thought sadly, watching his limp body as it was carried out.

Afterwards, Colonel Codgson hosted a celebration to commemorate their continued research, but Marie could not bring herself to stay. She left the restaurant and drove back to the lab, thinking about the look of anguish she'd seen on Twelve-A's face as Carter had used the modifier. It had remained even after she had led him back to his cell and reattached the driplines, that lifeless pall of someone who had lost all hope.

Even though she got chills thinking of it, Marie wanted to see him. Console him. Assure him things would get better. She was in her car, driving back to the lab before she realized what she was doing.

When she got there, the lab was cold and dark, the monitoring booths empty. Marie flicked on the lights and moved to the holding area, then swiped her card and waited as the hydraulics pushed one of the thick leaden doors open. Inside, a sixth of the lights remained permanently on, more for the technicians' comfort than the experiments'—no one wanted to be alone in the dark with the monsters they had created.

Somewhere, near the back of the room, Marie heard crying. She frowned, thinking the sobs sounded as if they were coming from Cell 5, though knowing Twelve-A couldn't possibly be awake. She had seen the drip-bag Carter had given him. She had watched the woman add extra sedative. Deep down, Marie had actually hoped it would OD and kill him.

The sobbing continued, despondent and alone.

Though she carried no restraining devices, had followed none of the pre-entry assessment protocol, Marie stepped inside the corridor.

"Hello?" she whispered.

Though she knew her words had not been loud enough to carry beyond her own ears, the sobbing cut off instantly.

Cold prickles crawled across Marie's arms and back. She had *seen* Twelve-A get drugged.

Had Lieutenant Carter forgotten to actually attach the bag? Or had Twelve-A made her forget? Could he have done that, while bawling and shaking? They had always assumed the distraction of pain was enough to keep him from utilizing his abilities…

Marie knew right then she should hurry back behind the protective leaden walls and lock the containment area down to wait for assistance.

She knew…and yet, with the echoes of his misery still staining the walls around her, she found herself rooted in place, unable to leave. Guilt welled in her gut like a moldy sack, weighing on her soul. More than Carter, more than even Codgson, she was responsible for this lab. She had been with these young men and women every day of their short lives. She had decided on their exact genetic sequences, had implanted their modified embryos, made the gut-wrenching call of which fifteen from each batch could survive to puberty.

They don't deserve this, she thought, eying the other experiments in their beds. All slept, either naturally or by drugs, splayed out in naked disregard like animals.

The crying had not begun again, and Marie got the eerie impression that Twelve-A waited for her in the darkness. Realizing how blithely she'd stepped into his trap, Marie's pulse began to race. She had no behavioral unit with her, no way of mediating his rage. Like a farmer standing feet from a tiger hidden in the undergrowth, she had entered his realm, and her continued existence was solely at his discretion. Running was no longer an option, as much as her panicked thoughts screamed at her to do so.

Though it took every ounce of willpower she had, she made herself move deeper into the corridor of cages.

Twelve-A was tucked into a fetal position on his bed, knees to his chest, back against the corner where two walls joined. There was no drip-bag hanging from the stand inside his cell. A cold wash of goosebumps prickled Marie's body in a wave, seeing that, knowing that she *had* seen a drip-bag earlier.

He tinkered with our minds, Marie thought. She wondered how many times he had done that before, and for what purpose.

As soon as Twelve-A saw her, he stopped rocking and met her eyes. *I know their fear before I kill them,* he said in a whimper. *I have to.*

The self-loathing that emanated from Twelve-A in that thick mental wave drove Marie into an uncontrolled stumble against his cell. Panting, she struggled to keep from bursting into tears at the sheer *power* of the emotional barrage. Knowing that this was how he felt, that this was *him,* Marie's instincts screamed at her to help him. Before she could talk herself out of it, she opened the gate to his cell and went to sit down on the thin mattress beside him.

"Everything's fine," she said, touching his knee. "You're done. You'll never have to do that again."

Her touch made Twelve-A jerk, and for the first time, Marie realized that the experiment had never been allowed to touch another Human being before, other than those he meant to kill. Yet, before Marie could correct her mistake, he unfolded and threw himself into her arms like a frightened child.

There, the lab's most dangerous creation cried into her shoulder.

Marie froze, terrified of his presence, terrified of what she'd done. She felt Twelve-A's body tremble against her, wracked by an emotional torment whose very residues still left her weak and nauseous. Despite her fears, she felt tears coming to her own eyes and softly began stroking Twelve-A's shaven head.

"Everything's going to be fine," she whispered, again.

He shook his head against her chest and sobbed. Pent-up breaths exploded from him in tortured spasms, and the emotional barrage—anguish, unhappiness, despair, self-loathing—hit her in wave after crashing wave that left her shaking. His grip on her back began to hurt. Realizing he needed her touch more than her words, Marie said nothing more and wrapped her arms around him.

Biologically, Twelve-A was a healthy twenty-two-year-old man. Mentally, however, he was as vulnerable as a small child. Like all the experiments, they had kept his every stimulation to the barest necessary for survival, sedating him with drugs for most of his life, punishing him for basic Human urges like curiosity or attempting to talk, never speaking more than their experiment numbers or basic orders within hearing range, never giving him a chance to *think*.

The reason was simple; undrugged and unhindered—like he was now—he could execute his keepers with a thought. Unrestrained, his cell open, he could cast Marie aside and simply leave the lab. He could walk through the open containment area doors, all the way to the reception area, where it would be a small thing to get the guard to open the door for him and escape, never to be seen again. Like with Carter and the drip-bag, he could probably even make them all forget he had even existed.

Marie considered all these things as she sat there, holding him, but found she did not care. He needed her, and that was all that mattered.

Thank you, came his mental whisper in her mind. Twelve-A's body had calmed somewhat, leaving only an underlying shuddering, like someone who'd spent too much time in the cold.

"I'm going to help you," Marie said, before she realized it was true. "I'm going to help you escape this place."

Twelve-A looked her in the eyes and said, *I could escape any time I want.*

She froze, seeing the truth there. "Then why don't you?" Marie whispered back.

The others, Twelve-A replied. *If I took them with me, they'd all be caught and brought back here.*

She watched him closely. "But you wouldn't."

His face tightened almost imperceptibly and he shook his head once. The gesture gave Marie chills. She wondered just how powerful their experiment was, just how much he'd been hiding from them.

Tentatively, she said, "You know what's outside the complex, don't you? Can you actually feel beyond the walls?"

Twelve-A looked away. His silence was answer enough. All of their precautions, all of their procedures, all their efforts to keep him ignorant of his Humanity...all had been for naught. Twelve-A had been in contact with the real world since the moment he'd been born.

"I'll get you out of here," Marie said, on impulse. "I promise."

Twelve-A's blue eyes flickered to her for a moment of desperate hope, then, reluctantly, he nodded.

• • •

That night, Marie drafted an anonymous letter to the funding committee, to three separate civil rights groups, to eight government officials, to six leading scientists, and to three different news agencies. She knew it would end her career. She knew she and her colleagues would spend the rest of their lives in prison. But, after everything she'd done, it seemed a fitting demise.

She told them of kidnapping three hundred and thirteen of the planet's best 'psychics' and installing them in cells deep beneath the mountain. She told of measuring their capabilities, charting their genomes, harvesting their genetic material, then, once the first batch was successful, ridding themselves of the hosts. She told of traveling to alien planets to steal naturally-evolved telekinetic, telepathic, or telemorphic genetics. She told of killing six Jahul they had lured to Earth with whispers of oregano trade, then dissecting them to examine their sivvet. She told them of the over sixteen hundred culls. She told them of Codgson's cruelties, the deathmatches, the mind-wipes, the drugs, the nakedness, the child-soldiers, Phil's Jreet experiment, the alien genetics...She told them everything.

To Marie's surprise, her letter was not published the next day. Nor the next. Not even a whisper of it came in the weeks that followed. Her only indication that something had happened was the colonel's increasingly terse attitude, his shortening temper.

"Get Twelve-A," Codgson finally snapped upon entering the lab almost a month later. "He has another demonstration to make."

Lieutenant Carter left her desk and immediately went to do as she was told.

"No!" Marie cried, stepping between the iron-faced Lieutenant Carter and the holding area. "You promised, Colonel." Even as she said it, she knew it sounded weak, desperate. Like a child begging for a reprieve.

Codgson's eyes were cold, chipped obsidian as he said, "Someone betrayed us to Congress. Confirmed their suspicions. Their ships are coming. The committee is here to decide which specimens to use in the fight against the Dhasha commander. One of Representative Mekkval's own nephews. We put some alien captives in the Dark Room so Twelve-A can show those pencil-pushing bureaucrats what he can *really* do."

Marie froze. Congress was coming. By experimenting with genetics, in creating *weapons*, they had broken the Second Law of Congress. And now they would kill them all.

"Let me do it," Marie said, desperate, now. "Let me retrieve him."

The colonel glanced back to frown at her. "Why?"

Before she could override the aching in her chest with the logic that had ruled her life the last twenty turns, she blurted, "He is like a son to me."

Codgson's face flashed with superior disdain as he looked her over. "He is an animal, Doctor."

It took all of Marie's willpower to say, "It's not a crime to be fond of one's dog, Colonel."

Codgson gave a bitter laugh. "Whatever. Hell, screw the skinny prick if you want to. Just make sure he's in the Dark Room in six minutes."

Marie was shaking with a mixture of rage and terror as she walked down the corridor. Congress was coming, and Earth would feel its wrath for ages to come. She and every other scientist who worked on the experiments would be executed. The experiments themselves would be murdered, the labs destroyed. Their only hope of avoiding the coming apocalypse was if the experiments could do what they were created to do.

Defend Earth.

Defend their home and their people against a power so great it spanned the entire universe.

But *would* they?

Marie felt helpless as she approached Twelve-A's cell. She'd tried to help, but she'd brought the aliens to their doorstep, instead. It was her fault. All of it.

It wasn't you, Twelve-A told her, looking up from his cot to meet her gaze with solemn blue eyes. *I never let you send that letter.*

Marie clearly remembered sending it. She remembered checking her Sent files and getting Delivery Confirmation on the physical drafts, just to make sure.

Then Marie gasped at what the minder was trying to tell her. She had been in her own home when she drafted and sent those letters, twenty miles from the lab. His influence couldn't possibly reach that far. But if it had…

What was the limit?

Fearful, Marie began backing away. Twelve-A watched her soberly through the bars. He was huddled in one corner, his lanky knees tucked under his chin. She felt like she was caught in the tiger's stare, but this time the tiger was debating.

After a moment, Twelve-A looked away.

Marie sank down to her knees in front of him, so relieved she was shaking. Softly, she said, "I can help you all get out of here. I can help you start new lives on the surface."

Twelve-A's blue eyes flickered back toward her. *We can't go now. The aliens will kill us.*

Marie felt like she'd been struck. "You know about the aliens?"

I've been watching them. They're hunting down the other labs. This is the only one they don't know about.

Marie blinked at him, once again shocked by how much he had managed to hide from them.

"We need you to fight," Marie whispered. "We need you to stop the—"

Twelve-A looked up at her sharply. *I'm not killing the aliens.*

"But you've got to help us defend the—"

No, Twelve-A thought. *I don't.*

Coldness settled in the pit of Marie's stomach. "You're going to kill us, aren't you?"

I'm killing everyone who knows about this place, Twelve-A said, his voice cold and final. *It's the only way the People are going to survive.*

Marie met the deep blue of his gaze and sweat slid like ice down her back as she began to bargain for her life. "Once we're dead, then what? Where will you go? What will you do?"

Twelve-A's gaze lost its certainty and he reluctantly looked away, but not before she saw nervousness and anxiety tightening his thin face. For all of his talents, Twelve-A had lived in a cage. He had no idea how to survive on the surface.

Seeing her opportunity, Marie pushed on. "You don't know anything about the real world," she insisted. "You've had everything handed to you. You don't know how to *survive*. I can help you create new lives for yourselves. I can help you *adapt*. I'm your *friend*, Twelve-A. I can help you."

He didn't answer her. Looking drained, Twelve-A got to his feet. *Come with me to the Dark Room. I want you to watch something.*

Marie hesitated, wanting to say more, but Twelve-A was already getting to his feet, waiting for her to open his cage. Reluctantly, because she didn't really have a choice, Marie swiped her card and entered her code. Her skin prickled as the minder smoothly stepped past her and led her out of the holding area, through abandoned rooms and unmanned monitoring stations. Everyone, she noted, was gone. Every tech had left his or her post, every doctor had found somewhere else to be.

Once they stood outside the small green door to the Dark Room, Twelve-A gave Marie a gentle nudge to continue further down the hall, toward the observation booth. Confused, she went.

The inside of the booth was packed, the occupants were milling in obvious agitation. Every face she had ever seen inside the lab was there, checking their watches, grimacing at the blond experiment pacing in the Dark Room. As more staff filtered into the observation booth, Marie anxiously glanced from Twelve-A to the group of observers and back, wondering what he planned for them. Her entire body trembled with fear and adrenaline. She'd heard the minder's death was painless, like falling asleep. She was terrified she was about to find out.

"So what are we waiting for, Colonel?" one of the generals finally demanded. The group had become more and more aggravated as nothing happened in the room before them.

"We're waiting for your test subjects," the colonel replied briskly. "You said you had Dhasha. I don't see a damn Dhasha."

The general's face went slack. "What test subjects? We're here because you told us your famous Twelve-A could do something that would save billions of lives."

At Colonel Codgson's frown, a man in a pristine black suit bitterly snapped, "Do *not* tell us you brought us all together to waste our time, Colonel."

The colonel stared back at them in complete confusion. "I never sent for you, you diddling furg."

A thin woman with short-cropped brown hair entered the room and shut the door behind her, but paused on the colonel's last words. Frowning, she said, "You didn't? Then who did?"

In the center of the Dark Room, Twelve-A stopped pacing. He turned, his ice-blue eyes cold beyond the leaded glass.

Me.

It was like a mental thunderclap.

I brought you all here. To kill you.

Several members of the committee screamed and staggered toward the door. Only Colonel Codgson remained where he stood, staring at Twelve-A through the glass with a queer little smile.

Twelve-A looked at them through the glass, meeting each of their eyes, though Marie knew he couldn't possibly see through the tinted windows.

I want you to know, Twelve-A said in another resounding mental boom, *that I killed them because they didn't want to live, not because you told me to.*

Every expert and government official in the room was screaming and rushing for the door, throwing each other aside as they wrestled for the exit. Marie stayed where she was against the back wall, knowing that there was nowhere to run, nowhere she could hide from the telepath's mental barrage.

But with you, Twelve-A continued, *it's because you deserve it.*

Desperate men and women were making it out into the hallway, and Marie heard their frantic footsteps on the tiles of the corridor outside. Back in the Dark Room, the telepath shut his eyes and inclined his head slightly. As one, the dozens of uniformed men and women occupying the room around her collapsed in a silent, falling wave of flesh that thudded lifelessly to the floor.

Except for Marie. She kept breathing, waiting for it to happen, but it never did. Minutes after her companions' wide eyes began to glaze, she was stunned to find herself still standing amidst the corpses. Alive.

She looked at Twelve-A. Beyond the glass in the center of the Dark Room, his body had slumped to the floor along with his victims. He was now lying on his side, half-curled into a fetal position, arms pulled in towards his chest. Heart thundering, Marie climbed over the bodies to see if he lived.

Put me back in my cell, Twelve-A whimpered when she entered the room and knelt beside him.

Marie recoiled. "Your cell? Why?"

He squeezed his blue eyes shut, face creased in obvious agony. *I want to die.*

"No!"

Do it.

The mental boom allowed no argument, and Marie felt her body responding to the command before she realized what was happening. In a daze, Marie drew him to his feet and helped him back into the containment area. As she settled him onto his bed, Twelve-A grabbed her by the forearm with a white-knuckled fist. *Please kill me.*

The mental whimper was infused with so much emotional despair that it left Marie fighting to breathe. Her eyes flickered toward the IV rack they used to keep the experiments sedate. "I'll go get the drugs. They'll make you feel better." She turned to go.

Twelve-A continued to hold her arm, stopping her, his blue gaze intense. *You should kill me, Marie.*

"No," she said, finding strength in the words, "I shouldn't. I should get you and all your friends out of here like I said I would." She patted his warm, slender hand and Twelve-A reluctantly released his hold. She went to the labs, got the drugs, and hooked them to the rack. As she was connecting his IV line to the bag, however, the minder stopped her again. This time, his cerulean eyes were angry.

If you're not going to kill me, leave.

She winced at the force of his words, like sledgehammers that pounded against the aluminum walls of her brain. "What about your friends?"

Don't worry about us. Leave. Lock the doors and never come back.

Marie met his deep blue stare, saw the danger there, then dropped everything and ran from his cell. She heard the gate to Twelve-A's cage slam behind her as she went to the containment doors and set them to shut. She used her card to lock them, then rushed through the facility, gaining speed as she realized she was the only one left alive. The only one who knew about the experiments. The only one who could help them create new lives on the surface.

The only one who could keep them *alive*.

She could rehabilitate them. Find them jobs. Find them friends.

The guard was not at his booth. She remembered his fat corpse in the observation deck, still jiggling after it collapsed to the floor. Buoyed by her new mission, Marie hurried past, pushed through the bullet-proof glass doors, and locked them behind her with another swipe of her card. She followed the corridor upwards out of the mountain and exited through the single door at the top. Facing it, the entrance looked like the door to a decrepit coffee shop, with the Coffee House Express sign hanging askew and the paint peeling on the CLOSED FOR BUSINESS notice.

Under the façade, however, the door was tank-proof, the walls behind it bomb-proof. It would take nukes to get inside. Or get out.

Marie locked the entrance with her card, sliding it through an inconspicuous crack in the wooden trim.

Thank you, Twelve-A told her. *That should keep them out.*

"Yes," Marie said, hurrying toward her car. "But don't worry—you won't be in there long. I'll find somewhere to keep you. The war will make it harder, but once I've got living quarters and food, I'll come back for you."

You don't understand, Marie.

She stuck her key into her Ford. "Don't understand what?"

Once it's safe, we're going to get ourselves out.

"But I can—" Terror infused Marie's soul as she realized why Twelve-A had left her alive. Babbling, Marie said, "Please, Twelve-A. I can help you. I won't tell anyone. *Please*—you don't need to kill me."

Twelve-A gave a mental shudder, buoyed on a wave of self-loathing. *It's always so hard.*

Even as she opened her mouth to scream, a wave of calmness overpowered her. Her eyes drifted shut and she slid to the concrete beside her car, the keys tumbling from her hands to clatter on the cement. Trapped in the darkness of her own body, Marie felt her heart stop.

Somewhere, deep underground, Twelve-A replaced the IV line and closed his eyes. His shoulders began to shake as he waited for oblivion to take him.

2

A HUMAN MISTAKE

Earth Representative Fred Mullich was scowling at the latest—alarming—reports from his home planet when the Watcher activated a node in his apartment without his permission.

"Representative Mullich, the Regency requests your presence in its chambers immediately for a Regency-wide disciplinary action. Shall I take you there now?" The Watcher's voice was perfectly Human, lacking any of the metallic or artificial quality of other AIs. Of course, there were plenty of whispers that the Watcher *wasn't* an AI, but to say as much anywhere within the gravitational pull of Koliinaat was political suicide, at least for a Representative as politically impotent as Fred Mullich.

Today the Watcher was using the London dialect, sharp and crisp. Fred wasn't sure if the Watcher knew it, but it switched to a British accent whenever it wanted Fred to take him seriously.

More than a little spooked by the idiots back on Earth, Fred glanced at his call log. Whoever was behind the Watcher's request was influential enough not to have to use the CALL feature, which would have required Fred's acknowledgement before the Watcher could speak to him. Which meant a Board chair or a Tribunal member. Which meant that Fred would create an interplanetary incident if he ignored it.

"Give me a moment to finish what I was doing," Fred said, still desperately trying to make sense of the disturbing numbers on his screen. He needed to send a courier to Earth immediately. Get some sort of explanation. And, for the love of God, convince them to cease and desist. This was the sort of crap that got planets pummeled back into their Stone Age for hundreds of turns, to give them a chance to serve penance.

The Watcher's irritation was palpable, but it said nothing more. Instead, it merely hovered somewhere in the alien circuitry at the edges of his room, watching.

His nervousness increasing, Fred continued flipping through the files he had been examining. He *really* didn't like what he was seeing. Back home, military and scientific expenditures had quadrupled in the last three turns.

It almost looked as if Earth was preparing for a war.

He needed to deal with this, and fast. Before the other species' Representatives were given the same numbers he was reading. If they got wind of them, the insignificant planet Earth and its single sentient species would be obliterated. Like a Dhasha ripping apart a vaghi.

"This is important, Mullich," the Watcher interrupted.

"The Regency can go on without me," Fred snapped. "The attendance of any one Representative is not required for a session to progress."

"It is not in your best interest to deny this call to attendance, Representative," the Watcher replied.

"I'm not denying it, you inbred mass of circuitry," Fred said. "I said give me a *moment*."

He could almost feel the Watcher giving him a flat look through the sensors. *"For someone who depends upon my cooperation and perfection for every single transportational transaction on this planet, you have a... unique...view of my capabilities, Representative."*

Fred ignored him. As with any newly-drafted planet, Earth was at the very bottom rung of the political hierarchy. With only one planet and only nine billion people, Earth had no clout compared to the founding member species like the Ooreiki, the Jahul, and the Huouyt, each of which had trillions of citizens and thousands of planets. As long as Earth paid its tithes and supplied bodies for the Draft, nobody cared.

But this...He bit his lip, looking at the screen. This was different. This was *suicide*. The jenfurglings back home couldn't *possibly* think to start a war.

Yet, remembering the numbers, Fred had the gut-sinking feeling that they could. Because they didn't *understand*. They didn't realize what they were up against. They hadn't seen the armadas, hadn't been invited to the military expositions, hadn't watched the weapons demonstrations, hadn't toured the carriers. They hadn't seen the *Dhasha*.

Realizing that his anxiety was making him sweat, Fred retrieved a tissue from the dispenser on his desk and dabbed at his forehead. He hated sweating. Hair and sweating were both signs of a lower evolutionary life-form, one that could not consciously regulate its own body temperature. And Fred was hairy. And he sweated. A lot. He shaved religiously, keeping himself bald except for his eyebrows, but every time he started sweating in the Regency, it felt like every alien eye was upon him, judging him. Which only made him sweat worse.

Damn his short, hairy, slick-skinned furg of a grandfather. Oftentimes, Fred heard it whispered behind his back that Humans were certifiably the closest relatives to the furry, stupid little ape-like creatures that loved to pound their stunted faces against rocks and eat their own excrement. It was whispered that, based on that evidence alone, Humankind barely qualified for its seat in the Regency. And, worse, the physical similarities between Humans and furgs were *unmistakable*. Both were bipedal, upright-standing, with mostly hairless bodies, big skulls, and flat, ovoid faces. When compared to a computer-generated image of a Neanderthal, furgs were almost identical, if only half the size. Which, of course, made it even harder for Fred to face his more-evolved peers with any confidence or dignity. So they were *large* furgs…

"*Representative Mullich, if you need to bring tissues with you, I can arrange it,*" the Watcher said dryly.

"Just give me a moment to think," Fred muttered, irritated.

"*Don't think too hard,*" the Watcher replied…amused? "*I'm told you might rupture something.*"

Fred narrowed his eyes. Not even the *Watcher* respected him. The Watcher, who was supposed to be an impartial mediator between all species, a personal servant to every official on Koliinaat, insulted his intelligence to his face.

…and Fred knew he wasn't going to do a damn thing about it. Knowing he was a chickenshit, knowing the *Watcher* knew he was a chickenshit, Fred went back to reviewing the documents in front of him, unable to shake the nagging feeling that Earth was about to do something incredibly stupid.

The numbers bothered him. A lot. Earth had never wanted to join the vast alien Congress, but like every other newly-discovered life-bearing planet, it had been given no choice. Now, even eleven turns after undergoing the mandatory sixty-three turn trial phase and becoming a full member, Earth constantly tested the gray area of Congressional laws, seeing how far it could go.

And, as if Fred's job wasn't hard enough, Earthlings—the petulant little shits that they were—made no attempt to hide their disdain for Congress. They were constantly breaking trade agreements, stealing energy-pods, imposing sanctions, illegally harvesting planets, and raising tariffs. There were even whispers that Earth had hired space-pirates to harass neighboring solar systems, a major offense that usually brought with it three-sixths of probation and higher enlistment quotas.

It was as if they had completely forgotten why they submitted to Congressional rule in the first place.

Fred's written and video-feed warnings never seemed to make an impact in the number of Earth's violations, either. The furgs back at home considered his position ceremonial at best and were oblivious to the danger of angering the Regency. They had not seen the devastation Congress could wreak upon a rebel member. To them, Eeloir and Neskfaat were just myths.

Yet Fred had taken the mandatory tours after each war. He had walked the corpse-ridden continents. He had seen the slaver colonies, the factories, and the work-camps. He'd seen the misery, the unspeakable ruin. He *knew*.

As soon as a planet went rogue, it was utterly crushed by the Ground Force and Planetary Ops. Once it had been crushed so thoroughly that it could no longer resist, it became free game to the rest of Congress. Anything on it could be exploited by any enterprising species interested in claiming more land, free work, or limited resources. If Earth actually took the step and declared war, Fred had no doubt in his mind that alien races, especially the slave-hungry Dhasha, would set up trading colonies on Earth's surface after the Congressional Army wiped out all of Earth's resistance. It was no secret that the Dhasha had been harvesting unlucky Humans for their breeding programs for the last seventy-four turns. They now had their own home-bred populations on dozens of Dhasha planets, and illicit Human slaves were now in higher demand than Nansaba.

And, once again, Fred was powerless to stop it. That the Dhasha were enslaving free, sentient species was quietly overlooked by Congress, because the Dhasha were the single most dangerous species in Congress, even outstripping the Jreet due to their sheer numbers.

"*The Regency is waiting, Representative Mullich,*" the Watcher reminded him.

"Just screw the Regency a moment, all right?" Fred snapped. "I have an important diplomatic issue to deal with."

The Watcher sighed.

Fred ignored it. If Earth ever got reprimanded, the Dhasha would take over. They would use its incredibly high life-supporting resources to transform the planet into a breeding ground for slaves, which they would then ship back to their home planets for sale.

War. It looked like Humans were preparing for war.

They could *not* be that stupid.

"Representative Mullich, I understand that you have limited resources from which to draw, but generally, if an esteemed Representative such as yourself is summoned through direct-node, it is a reasonable assumption that someone on the Tribunal is demanding their presence." The Watcher paused for that to sink in. *"Further, it can be assumed that if the summonee does not respond appropriately in…fifteen seconds, now…the messenger—that would be me—has been given special instructions to retrieve said Representative for the sake of expediency and not displeasing the Tribunal."*

Frustrated, Fred closed the file and said, "Fine, goddamn it." He shoved his chair away from his desk. He hated going to the Regency. Nothing ever *happened* at the Regency. The alien equivalent of fat old men in suits would sit around and argue for hours on end and not accomplish anything. There *was* nothing to accomplish. Every political breakthrough that could have been worked out by Fred and his peers had been worked out millions of turns before he was born. The system was already perfect. There was no *point*. Especially not for *him*, a Representative of a species of absolutely no import. The Bajna ran the banking. The Jreet ran security. The Ooreiki made art. The Jahul traded. The Ueshi ran the Space Force. The Dhasha ran the Ground Force. The Huouyt stole property, lied casually, ran an Assassins' Guild that the Regency was too terrified to shut down, stole people's identities, made and smuggled illicit weapons, defrauded the government, stole patents, randomly poisoned strangers, and collectively made an ass out of themselves—but were balanced out by the rest of Congress. It was sheer formalities, and it bored him to tears.

"Five seconds, Representative," the Watcher said pleasantly.

Irritated, now, Fred growled, "Let's get this over with."

No sooner had he finished voicing the words than his vision grayed out and he felt an instant of pinprick discomfort throughout his body as the Watcher transferred him into the Congressional seat of power.

Built by the legendary Geuji, the Regency was an enormous spherical room whose interior was completely covered in seats, over seven thousand of them, only half of which were occupied in the anticipation of finding more members. Though it was unnerving to Humans, this had been the standard Congressional meeting-place for over one and a half million years, since it left no member higher than any other member. It was much like the mythical Round Table, except taken one step further. A specialized hologram hovered in the center of the room, made to be right-side-up to every creature in the room. Right now, the picture showed that of First Citizen Aliphei, who was older than some planets.

The First Citizen was the very last of his race. He was about the size of an elephant, with wrinkled, furry blue skin covering his body. If it weren't for his red eyes and four sharp black tusks, he would almost have looked much like a cross between an elephant and a polar bear. Fred could pick him out amongst the seats, his revered chair taking up the space of a dozen.

The fact that the First Citizen had taken it upon himself to make an appearance did not bode well for whatever poor planet had broken Congress's laws this time. Fred sat down and made himself comfortable, vaguely excited at the prospect of seeing a member planet chastised, since that always spiced up the usual humdrum discussion of intergalactic politics.

When the First Citizen's image turned to *him*, however, Fred felt the blood drain from his face. He glanced at the seats nearest him, trying to determine if possibly the hologram only *looked* like it was facing him.

All doubts faded when the First Citizen's alien snarl filled the room.

"*Representative Mullich.*" The speaker inset in the small lectern in front of Fred made him jump. His heart began to pound and he swallowed convulsively.

The alien hologram began to snarl again.

"*We have received reports that your planet has begun stockpiling weapons. Are your people preparing for a war against Congress?*"

Weapons? Shit! Sweat broke out on Fred's face in a warm sheen as he quickly said, "No, Representative Aliphei, Earth has no intentions of attacking any member of Congress. Humans are loyal members."

The hologram made a snort and what sounded like a high-pitched giggle, followed by several guttural clicks.

There was no translation from the Watcher, which meant Aliphei had intentionally switched his translator off as he conferred with his Bajnan assistants. Knowing what that meant, Fred broke out in goosebumps. *Oh God*, he thought, in growing panic. *They found something. Those furgs back home got caught!*

Aliphei spoke again, and this time it was translated. *"Not only is your planet stockpiling ships and weapons, but it has radically increased its science funding."*

"For peaceful uses," Fred said quickly. Too quickly. He winced, biting back the rest of what he had been going to say.

Aliphei spoke, and there was an iciness to his voice that even the Watcher managed to translate. *"We have reason to believe that Earth has instituted a breeding program for genetically-enhanced Human foot-soldiers."*

Fred's jaw dropped. The First Citizen was accusing Earth of breaking the Second Law of Congress, the most damning thing a member planet could do, other than attacking another member planet.

"Well, Mullich?" Aliphei's hologram demanded.

"That's not possible," Fred babbled. "Genetics experiments… you misunderstand the reports!"

The Shadyi's snort of disdain was translated impeccably. *"I misunderstand nothing. My information is much better than your own, Mullich. See for yourself."*

At that, a Human girl appeared in the center of the room, suspended in air like a rag doll. Even from that distance, Fred could tell that her eyes were glazed over almost as if she were drugged. Immediately, an image appeared on his lectern, and on every other lectern in the Regency. It was a scan of a Human brain. Embedded deep within the tissue, a square cube of white rested like a cyst. A chip, much too bulky to be Congressional-made. Fred felt bile rising in his throat.

"She is one of many we have captured," Aliphei growled. *"Human generals forced her to do their bidding by triggering the pain response through the rudimentary chip in her brain."*

"That doesn't prove…" Fred began.

"*She has the ability to move objects and matter,*" Aliphei interrupted. "*Human scientists also experimented with telepathy and energy manipulation, as well as dabbled in a failed shapeshifting project, and Earth's military is openly combating our patrols with the telekinetics and telemorphs as we speak. We already lost three ships to these mutated abominations.*"

There was a roar of outrage from those gathered in the Regency. Fred suddenly wished he could shrink out of sight.

"*Representative of Earth,*" Aliphei's voice boomed, "*I demand a Trial.*"

Fred's mouth was suddenly dry. The entire Regency was a resounding clash of noise, three thousand different alien languages demanding justice.

"*Watcher,*" Aliphei continued, "*secure Representative Mullich in his room until we are ready for him.*"

Before he knew what had happened, Fred had been teleported back to his room.

"Watcher," Fred said, in desperation, "I need to confer with my colleagues." He went to the door, but found it locked.

The Watcher remained silent to his pleas. When Fred went to the wall in desperation, he found that his incoming feeds were blank.

As the Representative of Earth, he was, until he could prove otherwise, guilty.

3

THE LEGEND OF ZERO

Joe cracked his eyes open to the stale taste of vomit and the sour stench of partially-digested whiskey. He stared up at the dirty ceiling through a pounding headache and listened to himself breathe. The ache in his temples reminded him of Jane. He'd bought her illicit body seven turns ago on the Jahul blackmarket prior to landing on Der'ru, and not even Daviin knew of her existence. Joe had purchased her dangerous curves and cold, sexy beauty for one purpose, and *only* one purpose, and Joe could almost *feel* her impatience with each day he put her off. Even then, she called to him from the other side of the bed, begging him to slide his hand over her ebony lines, wrap his fingers around her, tug her out into the light…

Not this morning, he thought. *This morning, you've gotta give a pep-talk to a bunch of jenfurgling kids.*

Which was true enough. He couldn't easily kill himself on a new batch of recruits' first day in PlanOps and die with a clear conscience. Talk about an excellent way to traumatize the starry-eyed furgs. Yeah, Jane could wait.

Then that jaded, smartass side of him kicked into gear and gave a bitter laugh. *You're just putting off the inevitable. Who cares if you blow your brains out on their first day or their tenth day? You're just being an*

33

ashing slavesoul again. Get it over with, Joe. You've served your time. You shouldn't have to deal with this soot anymore. Stop being a Takki skulker and get it over with.

And he was, too. It was the two thousand and eleventh standard day that he'd left Jane under her pillow instead of letting her serve her purpose. Two thousand and eleven days. Just over six turns.

Joe continued to stare at the ceiling. He didn't need to look at the clock to know it said 05:31. He always woke six tics before his alarm went off, to the second. It was a habit leftover from his training in Planetary Ops, one that he'd done his damndest to shake, but to no avail.

The bed beside him was cold, the soulmate that the lying vaghi of a fortuneteller had promised him still not making herself known. He squeezed his eyes shut as he heard the conversation in that tent once more.

"You will have a soulmate."

"Really? What's her name?"

"She doesn't have a name."

"O-kaaay. Uh. Where's she live?"

"She hasn't been born yet."

Remembering that, Joe felt his left hand shaking under the covers. After seventy-four turns of fighting and bleeding for Congress, she still hadn't shown up. He still spent his nights alone, his days trailed by a dozen soulless furgs with cameras, with Overseers and Directors by the hundreds smiling to his face while they secretly wondered how they could best position themselves to get a good picture with the universe's beloved Zero. Drinking buddy—and former ward—of a Jreet Representative. Personal friend to the Peacemaster himself. Survivor of two unsurvivable battles. The monkey who shat gold and killed Dhasha.

Joe clenched his shaking hand into a fist, aching inside. He'd never felt so isolated in his life. Even with every new Human recruit taught to memorize his every battle, his every inane comment, his every stupid thing he'd ever done, Joe had never felt more alone than he did right then. It was like a pall that was settling over his soul, darkening it.

She lied, he thought, in anguish. It had been one of the few things he'd hoped for, one of the few things he'd allowed himself to look forward to in the damned prophecy that had come to rule his life. Those five simple words. *You will have a soulmate.*

He'd ushered in a new Age. He'd had a Jreet rip out his still-beating heart. He'd befriended an assassin. He'd even shown mercy to a Geuji.

And he was still alone, twenty turns later. He hadn't seen any dragons or any innocents. Though he was well on his way to dying in shame, he was pretty sure that wasn't what the patch-wearing, two-faced bitch was talking about.

And while you shall die in a cave, shamed and surrounded by dragon-slaying innocents, your deeds will crush the unbreakable, and your name will never be forgotten.

Congress. She, the Trith, the Huouyt—they all wanted him to crush Congress.

It gave Joe a little bit of comfort that he could screw up the entire pretty picture they all had painted for him just by pulling Jane out of hiding and pulling the trigger. The satisfaction, however, was short-lived. Because he was still alone.

Joe took another shallow breath and wondered what it would be like to be a Huouyt. To be able to shed his face and live someone else's life. To become a different person.

That's what he wanted. To be a different person. He hated the monster that Zero had become. He hated the constant flash of the cameras. He hated the fake smiles and starry-eyed awe. He hated the power-struggles, the vying for his favor. He hated the posters, the motivational vids, the documentaries with his name splayed across the front cover in bold letters. He hated the random gifts, the desperate attempts at seduction, the awed stares. Lying there, staring at the ceiling, an unregistered plasma pistol within arm's reach, Joe would have given anything to be a Huouyt. To be able to take on a different face for a week. Or a lifetime.

Reluctantly, he pulled himself out of bed. He stared at the floor between his bare feet for several minutes, just breathing in the smell of his own stink. He hadn't rinsed his mouth after vomiting last night. His clothes were the same ones he'd worn the last six days. He couldn't remember the last time he'd bathed.

Like any woman in her right mind would want me now, he thought, miserable. *You probably scared her off already, you greasy-skinned furg.*

But that was the problem. It didn't matter what Joe did—the Congies loved him. If he wore his shirt untucked, the next week, it became the latest fad. If he stopped rolling his sleeves, the whole Human Ground Force stopped rolling theirs. He'd become a mascot. A figurehead. A shiny, gilded god that they could prop up in front of everyone and make smile for the camera. He could have literally any Congie woman he wanted—Human or not—just by twitching a brow of interest.

Joe dropped his head into his hands and stared at the floor. Beside him on the dresser, the alarm went off. He ignored it, studying the dirt and old clothes scattered over his mats. He had more than enough money to hire someone to take care of it, but he didn't bother with a maid anymore because the last one had hidden a camera in his bathroom to get pictures of him showering to sell on the net.

Alone. He was totally goddamn alone.

Joe twisted to turn off the alarm. Jane called to him again at the motion; a sweet, seductive melody in the back of his mind, begging him to twist a little further, to pick her up, to caress her deadly body…

Joe got out of bed and stumbled over to the bathroom entrance, catching himself on the wall. He took a deep breath, let it out in a shudder, then, fully intending to straighten and walk into the shower, Joe lowered his forehead to the doorframe and cried.

Alone. His every move studied, watched, and analyzed. Never had he been known by so many people, his face on every billboard, his picture revered on every Human recruitment poster ever made… and never had he been so totally alone.

I can't take it anymore, he thought, leaning into the wall. The false smiles, the politics, the subtle comments…Jane's melody was like a siren's song in the back of his head. Not for the first time, he wondered if she was his soulmate. He wondered when she had been made. She was not too old. Probably 'born' sometime in the last seventy-four turns.

Burning psychics, he thought, in despair. *They speak in riddles.*

Miserable, Joe tore his forehead from against the wall and took a long look at the shower. It only would have taken a few minutes to sluice off all the dirt and grime, all the stink of the last week of lonely nights with Jim Beam.

Joe caught his image in the mirror and grimaced. He had dark rings under his eyes. His face looked hollow, like something from an Eeloiran death-camp. His skin was dull with grime. It was his eyes, though, that gave him pause.

They'd given up. He realized it with a start that made him blink. The strength in their mountainous brown depths was…flat. Tired. Gone.

Looking at himself, Joe was once again aware that one of the Jreet's most feared hells was the hell of Solitude. Six hundred and sixty-six turns of loneliness. A Sacred Turn of isolation that every Jreet warrior had to face before he could enter the afterlife.

Twenty down, six hundred forty-six to go, Joe thought, with a bitter laugh. Not for the first time, he wondered if he'd actually died on that operating table on Jeelsiht. He wondered if he was actually wandering the Jreet hells even now, looking blindly for the afterlife. He realized he had a surefire way to find out.

Those kids need me, Joe thought, miserable, staring at the rim of the sink. *Have to get them through training.* But he wasn't fooling anyone. They didn't need him. He wasn't the one who led them in the tunnels or taught them how to properly put down a Dhasha. Their commanders and Overseers did that. Joe just gave speeches.

…Just like every other useless figurehead in the universe.

They need me, Joe told himself again. *A speech by Zero will make their millenniums.* He looked up again and peered into his own image. *Just one more speech, then I can finish the job.*

That actually gave him enough strength to pull on his boots and jacket and splash alcohol over his face before heading to the door.

Taking the knob in his hand, he straightened, took a deep breath, and tugged the door open.

Immediately, a mass of Congie and civilian photographers crowded him, their flashes going off in his face. They shouted questions at him, asking things like how he'd slept, what he'd eaten, whether he was planning on having kids.

Joe fought the urge to grab the closest camera and smash it into the side of the building. He'd learned long ago that just made him look like a sootbag in front of billions of people—and made the photographers more crazed to get him to do it again, prodding him like a stubborn animal that wasn't cooperating, *trying* to piss him off.

Ignoring the cameras, Joe stepped through the paparazzi and over to his haauk. Someone had yanked the key from the console and left it on the ground beside the machine, doubtless so Joe would have to bend over to retrieve it, giving two dozen reporters a good picture of his muscular ass.

Burning furgs, Joe thought, hating them. Instead of bending to grab the key, as they wanted, he pulled a new one out of his pocket— the trick wasn't new, and he'd shipped in a package of fifty of them from the haauk company upon his arrival on Torat. Behind him, reporters made sounds of frustration and jeered at him as he climbed onto the haauk, put his key into the console, and powered it up.

Just one more speech, Joe told himself, lifting up over the rooftop. Eight haauks followed him, each filled with five to six cameramen. They loved the haauk pics. Easy to make him look like he was soaring into the future, head held high, ready to take on Congress's enemies the moment they reared their ugly faces. Joe hunched down against his console and tried to ignore them. He'd only been on Torat for thirteen days, and he still hadn't had the opportunity to get a customized, locked, shielded haauk.

The civilian haauks had to stop at the edge of the Congie training base, but the Peacemaker and Congie crews continued to follow him as he crossed the training grounds and landed on the main square in front of a formation of nine hundred Human recruits. It was obvious that the kids had been waiting for him there for a while, even though he told their instructors eighteen tics from now, which meant their battlemasters had probably had them standing there since dawn. Sighing, Joe yanked the key from his haauk and disembarked. He tried to ignore the mass of black-clad cameramen as they positioned themselves around the parade grounds, ignoring the Congie commanders and Overseers waiting in a formation of their own a few rods away, aiming to get that next multi-million-credit motivational poster pic.

When they got in his way, crouching on the ground to look up and snap shots of him with the rising sun to his back, Joe suppressed another urge to kick the cameras out of their hands. They loved that, too. Showed his innate aggression, his fighting spirit.

Joe closed his eyes and swallowed.

His left hand had begun trembling of its own accord again. Fisting it, ignoring the reporters, he walked around them, up to the first rank of Human PlanOps recruits—all Battlemasters and above, as was required for application—and paused to give them a long look.

To their credit, they didn't fidget. The only sound was that of the wind whipping in their battalion colors and the scuffs and clicks of the photographers getting their pics of Zero 'training' yet another wave of Human recruits.

Joe took a deep breath, put on his Zero mask, and barked, "I hear you furgs wanna be PlanOps!"

Immediately, nine hundred voices shouted, "Kkee oora!"

"Oh yeah?" Joe started stalking down the line, looking them up and down with every ounce of disapproval he could muster. "What'd they do, send me *niish*?"

Like thunder, his response was, "Anan oora!"

"Yeah, well." Joe did a circuit, then went down the lines, taking time to look at every face. "We'll see." This was the part that was legendary about his speeches. He made them all sweat. Every single one of them. And with good reason. If they couldn't cut it, he wasn't going to pass them on to go get their comrades killed.

"You're missing teeth, furg," Joe said, stopping to peer at a smaller, freckled male recruit. "You ain't grown in your adult ones yet?"

"Anan oora," the kid mumbled, still staring straight ahead.

Great, Joe thought. Human teeth, unlike the rest of a body's anatomy, stubbornly stuck to a more normal growth schedule, despite Congressional attempts to bypass it. He was probably looking at an eight-year-old. *Burning great.*

"How old are you?" Joe demanded.

That made the kid flinch. "Seven turns, sir."

Ash. Joe would have asked more, but he heard a snicker from somewhere down the line.

"You," Joe snapped, swiveling on a massive, burly recruit with a smug grin on his face. "Get your sootbag ass out of my line."

The burly kid's grin dropped. For a moment, he just stood there.

"You *deaf?*" Joe demanded. "Go clean toilets, furg. PlanOps doesn't want you."

The startled, bull-necked kid gave Joe a look of panic. "But I was the best rifleman in my regiment—"

"You think I give a Dhasha flake how well you shoot?" Joe barked. "PlanOps works as a *team.* You can't work with the team, you get yourself and everyone else killed. Now get outta here. I can teach people how to shoot. I can't teach them not to be stupid."

And so it went, Joe wandering the ranks, weeding out the ones who snickered or twitched or just gave Joe a bad feeling. The Overseer and commanders never questioned his decisions, just grabbed the kids and led them off, utterly secure in their faith that Zero knew what he was doing. And Joe, because he could get away with it, sent home the ones who reminded him of people he had once known. He sent home the innocent kids that reminded him of Maggie, the nervous ones who had scared hazel eyes like Elf, the happy ones who had laugh-dimples like Scott, the stubborn ones who challenged him like Monk. He left the ones who reminded him of Libby, though. Those got to stay every time.

When Joe was finally finished, he went back to face the front of the now much-thinned ranks.

"So. You think you're worthy of PlanOps just 'cause some bureaucrat liked your paperwork?" he demanded at those who remained. Joe looked the perfectly straight columns of black-clad recruits up and down in open disgust. "You're not. Take a look at the Congies in front of you." He gestured to the Overseer and commanders in charge of his PlanOps regiment. "These unlucky furglings volunteered to train you. *They* are worthy of wearing the PlanOps tattoo. *You* undisciplined sootbags are just boots who wanted to be heroes." Joe stopped pacing and rounded suddenly to face the straight-faced ranks of kids. To their credit, they never flinched when the legendary Zero scowled at them like they'd just stolen his favorite PPU. Inwardly, Joe felt a pang of regret, knowing that most of these grounders weren't going to make it past their first battle.

Kids, he thought. *They're just kids.* He forced that down and went on, "The men and women behind me have been through hell and survived. Some have even spent forty, fifty, even sixty turns burning up Congress's enemies. They were generous enough to want to share their knowledge with you pathetic, useless furgs. So pay attention. Watch your superior officers. Do what they tell you. Learn what they have to teach, and maybe you'll come out of your first battle alive." Joe looked them all over one last time, then said, "Now go to chow, get signed into the barracks, and find something productive to do with your inadequate asses until 05:00 tomorrow morning, when your real work begins. Dismissed."

It wasn't his most graceful speech, but by the way the starry-eyed Battlemasters he'd 'passed' broke up in an awed daze afterwards, he guessed it had worked anyway. It was a running joke in the Human Ground Corps that Commander Zero could go into any Congressional cafeteria, unbutton his fly, piss in the nuajan machine, and Congress would rush to charge extra. Joe, who spent each night alienated and alone, who had no close friends to share drinks with because he couldn't stand the outright hero-worship, no lovers because every possible candidate had seen his picture heroically stomping on Dhasha skulls or squashing Huouyt zora with his boot, was fighting the urge to test the cafeteria theory just about daily. In fact, he felt so far removed from the legend of Zero that it didn't even seem like the same person to him anymore, just some usurper that had stolen his life and made him miserable.

"Excellent speech, Director Zero!" a man with three inner circles of a Secondary Overseer said to him, beaming with a huge, official smile. All around them, cameras flashed as he approached and, with exaggerated care and pause, held out his hand for Joe to shake.

Prick, Joe thought immediately. He hated to be called 'Director' anything. After Forgotten blew up Aez, Joe had been assigned to 'lead' an interspecies kill-squad composed mainly of Dhasha and Jreet tasked to take out the Aezi Prime Sentinel Raavor ga Aez and his misdirected—and fiercely loyal—crew of renegade Sentinels. Somehow, Joe had not only inexplicably stayed alive, but had kept some of the Dhasha *and* Jreet on his own team alive, as well, and that feat had apparently impressed the bureaucrats enough that they had belatedly offered him Phoenix's ill-begotten Corps Directorship. The *kasja* that came with it hadn't mentioned subduing the Aezi rebels or helping Flea uncover yet another Huouyt conspiracy—it had been given to him for 'uniting great warriors with extreme differences using pitiable natural resources.' Something that, of course, had only added to his legend. He hadn't received his commendation for stopping a Congress-wide war or saving the Ze'laa family or the surviving Aezi from extermination. He had gotten it because he managed to convince a Dhasha and a Jreet not to kill each other over who got to sleep on which side of the transport ship.

Accepting his Corps Directorship had been done with more than a little righteous vindication—and it was the worst mistake Joe had ever made. He had hated the office, and after one and a half turns of driving a desk while his friends and peers were off fighting battles and getting themselves killed, Joe had gone to the Galactic Corps Director and asked her nicely for a demotion. When that hadn't worked—and she'd given him a line of soot about Congress needing its heroes to lead the next generation—Joe had punched her in the face.

They probably would have left him driving a desk after that, anyway, but Joe had then intercepted and disabled a four-member Jreet Directorate squad that had been sent to babysit him under the guise of 'bodyguards,' stolen a ship at gunpoint, gone AWOL, shown up on Rastari with a biosuit and plasma rifle, and had incapacitated or assimilated the first, second, and third Peacemaker team that had been sent to retrieve him. All the while, he was killing renegade Jikaln, Hebbut, and Dreit; leading a hand-picked multi-species groundteam through the mountainous woodlands of Rastari; and taking over and commanding a besieged Congressional outpost in his spare time, holding it against all odds and turning the tide on yet another war.

After that, Congress left him alone. Joe wasn't quite sure what his official rank was anymore, since they had stopped paying him around the same time he'd busted the Galactic Corps Director's prissy snub nose, but everyone except the hardcore bureaucrats simply called him 'Commander Zero.' To the people who drove desks or spent their time rubbing elbows with fame and fortune, however, he was always 'Director Zero.' It was one of the first and easiest ways for Joe to tell if he was dealing with honest-to-God hero worship or an ambitious sleazeball looking for a leg up.

The man standing in front of him, as if the fake grin, posing for the cameras, and plaster-cast courtesy wasn't a dead giveaway, had already named himself the scum of the Corps with his officially-brisk-but-oozing-fake-cheerfulness 'Director Zero,' spoken in the overly friendly tone that made Joe's guts twist with the need to punch something. Joe continued to ignore the Secondary Overseer, pretending to analyze the recruits as they departed, hoping the leech would take a hint and go away.

He didn't. The man continued standing there, hand out like he expected Joe to take it, a stupid, sycophantic smile on his face. Because Joe had *ascended*. Because he'd left the Corps behind. Because he'd survived two unsurvivable wars. Because he'd road-burned a Dhasha and lived to tell about it. Because he'd turned three squads of Peacemakers to fight with him. Because he was *alive*.

Joe wasn't a mortal to them anymore. Mortals died. Mortals got paid. Gods got worshipped.

When he was bored, Joe wondered what kind of robotic Joe Dobbs Congress would fabricate to continue his legend once he finally put Jane to good use. Congress, after all, couldn't have its legends dying on it. Bad publicity. When he was really bored, Joe wondered if his double was already built, and whether it was getting his paycheck.

Though, aside from a little bitterness that he was perpetually stuck doing Congress's work for free, the lack of rank and pay didn't affect Joe overly much. Three billion credits went a long way, especially when he'd finally wised up and put his last billion into the hands of a Bajnan stockbroker. Now, effectively rankless and jobless, Joe took whatever Human assignment he wanted, whenever he wanted it, with Congress kissing his ass every step of the way. He was actually doing an old friend from Rastari a favor in going back to Torat and taking on the current load of recruits, since she had a younger sister in the batch and she wanted Joe to help get the kid up to snuff before they shipped her off somewhere nasty, like Dravus or L-4.

Yet another reason Joe had to keep putting Jane off. Some friend's little sister. Great. He wondered how many little sisters there were out there, and how many of them he was going to end up 'training' in order to put off the inevitable.

Apparently, the Secondary Overseer organizing that morning's formation didn't notice Joe's dismissive grunt or the fact Joe never took his hand, because the man's sycophantic smile never twitched. He dropped his arm back to his side. "Will you be coming to join us for dinner in the officer's club tonight?" the grinning furg asked.

"I eat alone, Overseer…" Joe squinted at the guy's nametag. "Death." He blinked and raised a brow. "Death? Really?"

The sycophantic smile slipped a little at the sarcasm in Joe's voice. "It is customary for Overseers and above to choose their own monikers."

"Yeah," Joe snorted. "But *Death*? Come on, man. You got raisins for balls?"

Even as the Secondary Overseer was bristling, a curvy Prime Commander stepped up to him and said, "Nothing escapes Death." She winked at Joe. "Unless you're the burning First Citizen. Death's got some good stories, if you care to hear them. Join us for chow, Commander?"

Joe gave her voluptuous body a less-than-polite once-over, then grunted at her, too. "I eat alone."

The Secondary Overseer muttered something impolite and turned to leave. Joe thought he heard 'drunken asher' under the guy's breath, but he wasn't sure. And, frankly, didn't care.

"How about dinner for two, then?" the woman asked, once the Overseer was out of earshot. Her smile had broken and there was curiosity in her eyes more than anything else.

"Sorry," Joe said. "Not interested." He'd actually come to enjoy his quiet-time at night. It was one of the few times he didn't have to worry about turning a corner and running into the paparazzi. Peacemaker propagandists *loved* his ass, and paid top dollar for a good pic.

Then, at the woman's flicker of disappointment, he realized he was turning down a date with a pretty lady because he wanted to play yet another game of solitaire with Jim Beam. *I'm getting to be an old man*, he thought, with a start. Congressional drugs and rejuvenation put his body physiologically at about thirty to thirty-five Earth-years of age, but after so many pretty young girls with hero-worship in their eyes hadn't even so much as made his cock twitch, he'd long ago begun to wonder if he even still had charges in his pistol.

Still, he'd learned the hard way—again and again—that Congie women just couldn't see past the motivational vids, the heroic poses, the recruitment posters, the legends. They didn't care about *him*. They cared about his friend in the Tribunal. They cared that he had once been Prime to the current Peacemaster, who still visited him whenever his duties brought him through the area. They cared that he had been one of only two legendary Humans to have survived Eeloir *and* Neskfaat, and was the only one officially still alive. They cared that he owned a yacht, and had Bajnan brokers overlooking a dozen different bank accounts on Eeloir.

They didn't care about *Joe*. They wanted to take him out in public and get their picture taken with the legend so they could send it back home to their Aunt Jenny—or tell the tabloids about the size of his cock during an hour-long exposé on his lovemaking skills, after which they quit the Army and retire to Kaleu to live on the royalties.

Not for the first time, Joe cursed himself for going back to Torat, rather than finding another war to get lost in. He was turning to leave when the Prime Commander touched his arm.

"Sir," she said sincerely, her face a picture of innocence, "you don't have to go at it alone."

Joe knew it wasn't kind, but he snorted anyway. "No offense, lady, but shows what you know." He tugged his arm out of her grip and turned to stalk across the parade grounds to the place where he'd left his haauk. He wasn't sure if she was actually sincere or not, but he'd had way too many innocent-looking girls grab him by the arm and look up at him with those same soulful doe-eyes and say something similar, only to find a new documentary about him on the news-feeds a couple weeks later, narrated by the very girls he'd taken to bed—undercover reporters for one of the Peacemaker news agen-cies—after his 'innocent' young playmate had left him one morning without even a note.

'Jaded' didn't even begin to describe Joe's outlook on life. He knew as much, but he didn't really care. Not anymore. He didn't care about much of *anything* anymore. He woke up each morning, forced himself to leave Jane under his pillow, got out of bed, went to the mirror, and recited to himself what he had to live for.

War.

That was pretty much the extent of it. He lived for war. He lived for the buzz of plasma, the scent of ozone and burned flesh. He used the legend of Zero to scare a few recruits into shaping up, then went home to drink himself into another stupor.

Pretty burning pathetic.

As Joe got on his haauk and drove himself home, he wondered what Daviin would have thought, seeing him now. Without even looking at himself in a mirror, Joe doubted Daviin would approve. He knew his uniform was rumpled, his boots laced haphazardly, his sleeves loose and baggy. He had permanent rings under his eyes from an increasingly chronic insomnia, his gut was starting to pooch from twenty turns of being able to eat whatever he wanted, and his left hand started to shake again whenever he didn't have a good, stiff drink, so he drank whenever he was alone.

And, as the man wearing Zero's legend, Joe was always alone.

He really wasn't looking forward to his next chat with Daviin, but he had the nagging feeling it was coming soon. He hadn't even spoken to the Jreet in a couple rotations, but he saw his old buddy making waves in Congress just about every time he turned on the newsfeeds. The last time he'd talked to his former Sentinel, Joe had been busting up yet another Huouyt takeover on Telastus, and he hadn't had time to talk. Joe, PlanOps had quickly learned, had a better sense for Huouyt than an Ayhi-manufactured zora scanner, and they'd put him to work combing his way through all the government positions on Telastus, finding plants.

After all, scanners were wrong twenty percent of the time. Joe had only ever been wrong once.

Well, twice, Joe amended, thinking of Galek. But Peacemakers had interfered on that one, and had given Galek's chip to his assassin, so that, mentally, the Huouyt continued to register to Joe as the Ooreiki. Joe liked to think he would've been able to tell the difference if he hadn't been chipped—and talking to him in his mind—as Galek.

Excuses, he thought, miserable. *So many died for you and you have nothing but excuses.*

God, he wished he'd stayed on Telastus. In a war, with death around every corner, slipping up to him in the darkness, wearing the faces of friends, he hadn't had the time to think. Now, when his only real duties were to show up once a week to dress down a few PlanOps hopefuls, he had nothing *but* time. It had quickly become apparent to him that taking the recruiting job on Torat was one of the worst decisions he'd ever made. Every time he looked those young faces in the eye, he felt Jim Beam calling to him in the back of his head. And, raising her seductive voice with his, Jane.

Joe dropped the haauk to the roof of his private apartment, ignored the flashes from nearby roofs as the paparazzi got their pics, and unlocked the door to his pad. Once he was inside, he shut the door, leaned his back against it, and tilted his head back to rest against the cheap metal as he stared up at the dusty ceiling.

Just a couple more turns, he thought. *I can go a couple more turns.*

For the thousandth time since leaving the Geuji sprawled over that box on Koliinaat, Joe heard the muffled, tinny words, *"But with great responsibility, one finds great loneliness."* His hand started to tremble again, and Joe squeezed it into a fist. Not for the first time, he wondered what would have happened if he'd accepted the Geuji's plea for friendship. He hadn't understood Forgotten's meaning before—had been too narrow-minded and self-centered to even begin to comprehend—but now he did. He understood it all too well. Every soul-wrenching second, he understood it.

He needed a friend. Someone who wasn't stuck debating with fat old sootbags or hunting down intergalactic criminals or making babies while detonating Huouyt ships. Someone who could sit across from him over dinner and listen to him pour out his woes, or take him out for target-practice when he felt that spirit-smothering urge to use Jane. Joe found himself wondering—again—if he could find Forgotten and get on his knees and ask him for a second chance.

No, Joe thought, the bitterness returning in an acrid wave. *He would have used you, and you would have danced to his tune. You're an amoeba to his space station. You can't be friends with something like that.*

And yet, sometimes, when Joe was staring into that mirror, after waking up alone and hung over yet again, the stale taste of old alcohol or bile burning his throat, he wondered if Forgotten could have helped him.

He was still standing there, yet again trying to convince himself not to go seek out the pistol under his pillow, when the call feature started buzzing on his wrist-com. Joe reluctantly glanced down at the device, then winced when he read the origin ID.

Old Territory, Koliinaat, Headquarters of His Excellency, Daviin ga Vora, Representative of the Jreet.

"Burn me," Joe muttered. He dropped his arm and leaned his head back against the wall to again stare at the ceiling. The last thing he wanted to do was to get lectured on honor and duty by a self-righteous prick on his lunch break.

A few moments later, his wrist-com activated, without his consent. One of the bennies of being a Tribunal member, one that Daviin made use of shamelessly, was the Tribunal's right to commandeer private technology for the Regency's purposes.

"It says you're alive and conscious," Daviin's irritated voice said from the device around Joe's wrist. "And that you're not being tortured or otherwise detained, nor are you in the middle of excellent sex—something my assistant tells me you haven't had in six turns—which makes me wonder why you would ignore another call from your best friend in this miserable world. Are you drinking again?"

"None of your damn business," Joe muttered, still not bringing the unit to his face. "What do you want, you unlovable furg?"

The Jreet Representative went quiet for so long that Joe brought the wristcom up, thinking Daviin had hung up on him. To his surprise, the Jreet was there, but his expression was grave.

Upon seeing Joe's face, Daviin grimaced. "You look like something a Dhasha shat out," he muttered, but it was halfhearted, at best.

Joe narrowed his eyes. Usually, Daviin would spend at least an hour lecturing him on the different hells he would enter for his lack of discipline. Never before had he just let it go with a single line. "All right," Joe growled, "what the hell's wrong? Another Neskfaat? Dhasha allied with the Jreet? Forgotten side with the Huouyt? What?"

His old friend looked extremely uncomfortable. "Forgotten gained the recognition he wanted for his species and then disappeared. We've heard nothing more from him since the captured Geuji were granted communications amongst themselves."

Recognizing the Jreet way of beating around the bush, Joe muttered, "Spit it out, Daviin. I'm missing an important meeting. J.B.. I'm sure you've heard of him."

Joe knew the call was serious when threats of intentional inebriation didn't even get a twitch of response from the Jreet. Instead, Daviin gave him a look of...apology? He straightened, obviously steeling himself, then said, "Joe, Earth is about to get convicted of violating the Second Law of Congress, with intent to violate the First."

Joe froze, the smirk sliding from his face. "Excuse me?"

Daviin continued to look uncomfortable. "I'm calling to invite you to Koliinaat. To stay. As my guest."

"Just hold up a second," Joe snapped, shoving himself away from the door. "What the ash are you saying?! Earth was burning around with genetics? Was it that flake my brother got mixed up in?"

Daviin grimaced. "Not just that. They uncovered an entire program. Shapeshifting, telemorphosis, telekinesis, telepathy…" The Jreet's scaly ruby head turned away for a moment before reluctantly returning to face Joe. "Mekkval and Aliphei have already made up their minds. The Humans will lose the Trial. And since Humans only have one planet, they're all being branded as traitors."

Joe's heart stammered at the word 'traitors.' He swallowed, his chest suddenly afire with adrenaline. "Did you just say they're killing all Humans?"

"No," Daviin said reluctantly. "A total recall. One of Mekkval's nephews died in rooting out the secret installations."

As soon as Joe heard the word 'nephew,' he knew who it had been. "Keval," he whispered, his heart stammering for his old friend.

Daviin nodded his ruby head in commiseration. "Your Second in hunting down the Prime Sentinel Raavor ga Aez, yes."

"Soot," Joe managed. Keval, like his father, Bagkhal, had been one of the good guys. One of the only Dhasha that didn't take slaves, or eat sentient creatures. One of the only ones Joe had been able to call a friend.

Seeing Joe's reaction, Daviin gave him a moment of silence before he went on. "It just took *one* of the Human experiments to kill Keval and twenty others. All war-hardened Dhasha, some with hundreds of turns in service. Dead by one *single* Human, you understand? The Dhasha want blood. I'm pushing for penance, instead."

Joe's heart was hammering like a miscalibrated engine drive. "Define 'penance,' Jreet."

Daviin's scaly ruby face again grimaced. "It is not my place to say. I've already violated a few dozen non-disclosure laws with this call. But I wanted you to know I'm sending my fastest ship—"

"Now *hold on* a minute," Joe snapped. "Sending your fastest ship for *what*?"

Daviin hesitated. "To pick you up."

"To move me to Koliinaat," Joe said.

"As my guest," Daviin agreed.

"Because they think I was somehow involved with the experiments and they're recalling me to Earth."

Daviin's reluctance was enough to send a cold chill down Joe's spine. "Because they're recalling the entire Human Ground Force and disbanding the Human section of the Army," the Jreet replied.

"Fuck me," Joe whispered, Bruce Thomson's colorful Earthling vernacular still coming to Joe's tongue even four turns after the Scot had served as Joe's Second on Der'ru.

"I've told you a hundred times you wouldn't like it if I did, Human," Daviin said, a ghost of his old playfulness back. Then his golden eyes sharpened. "You don't have much time. Aliphei is calling for a Trial. He's giving the Human Representative one rotation to prove Earth's innocence, but there is no defense. The proof is irrefutable."

"What are you saying," Joe said slowly. "All Congies are getting recalled?"

"All *Humans*," Daviin replied, almost unwillingly. "You only have one planet, and it was that planet that broke the laws. Therefore, you will all be sent home."

"Earth is not my home!" Joe snapped. "Last time I was there, the ashsoul furgs didn't even want me there. One of them spat in my whiskey right before I rearranged his face."

"Get on a ship," Daviin said. "Head for Koliinaat. My ship will rendezvous with you. If we can get you to Koliinaat in time, you'll have diplomatic immunity."

But Joe just stared at Daviin's picture, unable to believe what he was being told. "They're gonna take almost a quarter billion Congies and just throw them back on a planet that hates 'em? And what? Ask them to play nice?"

Daviin gave him a long, uncomfortable stare. "Joe…If Mekkval gets what he wants, they're going to bomb all the bases, tech centers, and universities, drop kreenit on the major cities, then leave Earth to serve penance for a Sacred Turn. It's quite possible the Congies are going to be the only ones to survive."

Joe felt his blood burning in his veins. Kreenit, the ancestral predators of *Dhasha*, were installed on the worst rebel planets as a way of making sure conquered races couldn't rebound and rebuild immediately, giving their populaces a chance to learn their 'lesson' before being allowed to rejoin Congress. All he could think to say was, "Female Congies are *sterile*, Daviin."

The Jreet's lack of reply was all Joe needed. Swallowing hard, he said, "You think Humans might not make it."

Daviin looked uncomfortable. "Compared to kreenit, Humans are…" The Jreet obviously struggled with a polite way to say 'insignificant weaklings,' a sign that he was actually learning some decorum from his last twenty turns moderating interspecies incidents in the Regency.

"Meat," Joe said. "Humans are meat."

Daviin glanced away. "The Watcher has a complete genetic profile of every Human Congie to enter the Congressional Army. If your species dies off, it can be resurrected."

"Burn that!" Joe snapped. "Goddamn it, Daviin, you've gotta *do* something! We had *nothing to do* with those sootwad furgs back on Earth."

"I *have* done something, you Ayhi-loving biped!" Daviin roared back, rearing up his serpentine body to glare at the screen. "I've spent the last twenty turns arguing with fat, complacent morons who quote rules and legislation made a thousand generations ago as somehow applicable to our current situation. I'm arguing for *leniency* instead of total annihilation." Then he lowered his head in a Jreet appeal for accord. "I'm also sending a ship for my best friend. The life of a Representative is lonely. Will you join me?"

But with great responsibility comes great loneliness. Joe took a deep breath and glanced at the ceiling. He thought of all the Humans who were going to die—and all the Humans he could save with a well-placed plasma round to the back of a kreenit skull. He took another breath and watched an unidentified desert pest crawl across his ceiling. Softly, he said, "You're saying they're dropping kreenit on the planet? You're sure?"

Daviin nodded once, wary. "Mekkval insisted. Why do you care about—" Then his scaly brows tightened. "Human, don't tell me you're thinking about—"

"Thanks for the warning, Daviin," Joe said. "You have always been a good and honorable soul. If the Sisters are kind, we'll walk the ninety hells together and I'll see you on the other side."

Daviin flinched and stared at him for a full minute, his small golden eyes startled. Then, very softly, he said, "Human, when did you learn Voran Jreet?"

Joe frowned. "I don't know what you're talking about."

But Daviin was staring at him as if he'd suddenly grown mandibles. For a long, awkward moment, the Representative said nothing, just stared. Then, in a whisper, the Jreet said, "I see now why she told me to find you. Good luck, my friend. It was an honor serving with you."

Joe felt his frown deepen. "Who said to find me? Phoenix?" When Daviin said nothing, he growled, "Daviin, the Ayhi smite you, I have no idea what you're—" Then he realized that the Jreet had not spoken in Congie—and that he had responded in kind. Joe felt a chill go up his spine.

Daviin was staring at him. For several heartbeats, nothing but silence reigned between them. Then, "I revoke my offer of asylum," the Jreet said softly. "You are not meant to rot on Koliinaat. You have better things to do, Human." And, at that, the feed cut off and Joe was left staring at his wrist like a furg.

4

EARTH ON TRIAL

Earth's trial came a rotation later. The Tribunal consisted of three elected Representatives, including Aliphei. The First Citizen sat all the way on the right, with the Jreet Representative's massive ruby coils taking up the center, and a mastodon-sized, iridescent-scaled Dhasha that had just celebrated its thousandth turn—sitting on the left. Representative Mekkval's lectern had been removed, and the huge, bobcat-like Dhasha sat on his haunches in all of his rainbow-colored glory. The predator's cold green eyes watched Fred unblinkingly as Fred fidgeted on his glass dais in the center of the Regency. Beside Mekkval, his Huouyt slave—once a fellow Representative of Congress—held a datapad for his master with quiet devotion, a vivid reminder of what happened to those who crossed the Dhasha prince.

Like the Ze'laa slave, Fred wore no chains, but like the Huouyt, he was no less a prisoner of the Tribunal than if he were still locked within his room. The Watcher would instantly teleport him right back to the podium if he tried to flee. That, or Mekkval would catch him and tear him to pieces. The Dhasha looked like nothing would make him happier.

Fred ducked his head and kept his gaze fixed on the meager evidence he had managed to drum up from his weeks in solitary.

He could feel thousands of alien eyes on him, boring into him from all directions, even below. The transparent dais Fred stood on had a small speaker set into the bottom, and it boomed with Aliphei's translated voice.

"Representative Mullich, we bring you here today as a spokesperson for your planet, which stands accused of violating the Second Law of Congress. Humankind has engaged in genetic manipulations of its own species, with the intent to use those mutants as weapons. Second, and perhaps even more importantly, Earth was planning an attack on its closest neighbor, the resource-rich planet of Rkaathia, a member of our great Congress."

"What proof do you have against us?" Fred managed. It was purely ceremonial—he had no defense. Earth was already convicted.

This time, it was the Dhasha that spoke. Resplendent in his rainbow-colored scales, Representative Mekkval looked down at Fred like some disgusting substance that might get stuck to one of his razored ebony talons. "We captured your ships and interrogated your scientists. We found seven experimental dens, each with more than three hundred living test subjects. Slave, packet A-1." He gestured with a scythelike black claw at the hologram screen, then waited for the former Huouyt Representative to project the required evidence packet before continuing with a sneer. "The scientists attempted to use these test subjects against Congressional forces and we responded in kind."

Fred swallowed. "Responded in kind?"

"The scientists and test subjects are now dead." The long pause the Dhasha left at the end of his words left no question he thought Fred should suffer the same fate.

Still, Fred breathed a sigh of relief. If a few dead scientists was all the damage they were going to do, Earth had gotten off ridiculously easy.

The First Citizen, however, was not through. Aliphei's voice boomed in the speaker at his feet, making Fred jump. *"Fred Mullich, Earth stands accused of violating the Second Law of Congress, with intent to violate the First. How does Earth plead?"*

This was Fred's most important role in the entire Trial. If he said guilty, then the Trial would end and justice would be dealt. If he said not guilty, then he would be given a chance to try to prove his case.

In the last few weeks, however, it had become appallingly clear that Aliphei had been right. During Fred's imprisonment, Earth had taken over the airwaves in a way unseen since the Peacemakers' capers with Ghost over twenty turns before. The Galactic News Service, one of the few stations that Fred had been allowed to access during his confinement, had been there as the Congressional armies uncovered the secret compounds buried deep within their mountain bunkers. They had recorded the dazed states of the experimental Humans, noting the fact that the experimentees did not even seem to have a language, but were manipulated like animals with the pain-chips that Human scientists had installed in their brains. There had even been coverage of a famous Dhasha commander getting mur-dered by one of the Human experiments, his entire rainbow-scaled body jerking violently as something inside his brain went horribly wrong, then falling limply to the ground with purple blood leaking from his nostrils.

That very same commander, Keval, was a nephew to the Dhasha now sitting before him on the Tribunal, a well-loved prince who had helped Zero put down the Prime Sentinel Raavor ga Aez before Raavor and his Huouyt backers could set off an ekhta towards Koliinaat. A damned Congressional hero. And Humans had killed him and twenty-three others on live broadcast. About the only ones *not* calling for an ekhta were the Jreet, mostly due to the fact Earth had spawned the hero that had led their much-loved Representative and other Sentinels to victory, time and again. The Jreet loved a good hero.

Yet, Daviin ga Vora was only one of three. Looking from the Dhasha's stony gaze to the First Citizen's unreadable boar-like snout, even then twisted in disgust, Fred knew that the only mercy they might show Earth was if he pled guilty and spared them the drama of a centuries-long trial. Sure, during that time Earth would be allowed to conduct its business on a probationary basis, but eventually, the farce would end and Earth would be punished even more harshly for its crimes. Nothing Fred could do was going to change the Tribunal's decision. He could only hope to curry some favor by making the Representatives' lives easier.

"How does Earth plead?" Mekkval snarled. His tone had the challenge of someone who was looking forward to a fight—and the disemboweling that would come afterwards.

"Guilty," Fred whispered.

Mekkval flinched. The Jreet lifted his head startledly, obviously having expected him to plead innocent. All around them, the Regency fell into uproar so loud it threatened Fred's eardrums. In the chaos that followed, Aliphei raised one shaggy blue paw. "*You realize you will be given no trial?*"

Fred felt himself sweating again. "Yes, your Excellency. Earth deserves no Trial. We have failed Congress and humiliated ourselves before the Regency. It is not my place to make excuses for furgs."

Immediately, the Regency burst into alien laughter, as Fred had hoped it would.

The First Citizen eyed him a moment, his tiny red eyes hard, then turned to confer with the Dhasha and the Jreet. The Justices argued amongst themselves at length, their microphones switched off. When they finally pulled away, the Dhasha was clacking his obsidian teeth with rage. Ignoring him, Aliphei said, "*Your wise decision has convinced Daviin and I to allow Earth to remain within the Congress.*"

Fred let out a pent-up breath.

"*However,*" the First Citizen continued, "*Earth's crimes cannot be ignored. Congress's rules are not made to be broken. You Humans act like spoiled children. You swore to obey our laws and you broke your oaths. You must be punished.*"

Fred fought his relieved grin and schooled his face into a picture of concerned attentiveness, knowing that the punishment would be something as simple as trade embargoes, maybe a few extra children drawn away each year for the Congressional Army. No big deal.

Because of this, he had to ask Aliphei to repeat himself when the First Citizen recited Earth's punishment.

"You are hereby given a sentence of a Sacred Turn to consider your wrongdoings," the First Citizen intoned again. *"Your technology will be destroyed with electromagnetic pulse. Your cities, your universities, your centers of culture and science will all be annihilated. Your ships will be confiscated, your armies returned without equipment of any kind. You will start over, and perhaps when Congress returns to Earth after you are done serving your penance in six hundred and sixty-six turns, Earth will take its vows seriously."*

Fred couldn't believe what he was hearing. For long moments, he just stared. When he found the breath to speak again, it was a horrified whisper. "You're going to throw us back into the Dark Ages?!"

"Stone Age, more like," Representative Mekkval snapped. "And if it weren't for the sentimental worm, you wouldn't even be allowed that."

"If you'd like to settle this out of court," the massive ruby-scaled Jreet said calmly, "I would be happy to strangle myself another prince."

Mekkval snarled something in the Dhasha tongue and the Jreet chuckled and settled back into his huge serpentine coil.

Ignoring the other two Representatives, Aliphei held Fred in place with cold red eyes. *"Representative Daviin has convinced us to give you Humans time to think about your crimes. You discovered all of your sciences once before, so you can discover them again. Maybe in a Sacred Turn, you will further discover how to honor your oaths. This, as witnessed this day before your peers, is our Judgement."*

He was being merciful, Fred knew, but Fred still trembled with despair. Everything Humans had learned, everything they had accomplished...gone. Almost eight hundred and twenty Earth-years in intellectual squalor. All because some ambitious Human politician had decided he wanted more land.

"Do you have any questions before we mete out justice?" Aliphei demanded.

A thousand questions ran through Fred's head, questions of war, of politics, of death, of mercy, of weaponry, of genetics, of technology. But all Fred could say was, "What about me?"

Aliphei laughed. *"You will remain here as Representative of Earth until Earth sends another delegate."*

Fred blinked. "It will take hundreds of turns. Thousands."

Aliphei's sneer was unmistakable. *"Then I suggest you take up an interesting hobby to pass the time."* At that, Aliphei nodded his tusked blue head at the Watcher, who immediately transported Fred to his room. This time, his door was open and his outgoing feeds were back online.

The Trial was over.

Rat froze. She had spent the last twenty turns sworn to Mekkval, and she trusted him with her life. He had become one of her greatest friends. Though she hadn't trusted him at first—had actually fought the idea of working for him—he had proven to be a wise and benevolent leader, something she never would have guessed from a Dhasha. After the first tense two turns of dispatching rogue Dhasha for him, she had eventually begun to see the depth of his empathy and understanding for the universe. Never once after her initial capture had she questioned his requests, disobeyed his orders, questioned his directives.

"No."

The word left her lips before she realized what had happened. Once said, however, she did not take it back.

Instead of responding with anger, Mekkval gave her a long, unhappy look, his green eyes like dying, egg-shaped emeralds set into his rainbow-scaled head. "You can no longer work for me, Human. After Earth begins its Sacred Turn for penance, any Human caught off Koliinaat will be killed."

"Let them try!" Rat snapped. "I follow you to death, my prince."

"I would be breaking Congressional law if I brought you back afterwards," Mekkval said. "The same laws I am tasked to uphold." He twisted to face her, lowering his massive head to touch her chest with his scaly lips in a gesture of Dhasha friendship. "And I would be tossed from the Tribunal if I sent non-native species back to Earth at the start of its Sacred Turn. What if your Jreet or Huouyt found a mate and bred? I can't have that on my conscience. But the abominations and their stewards *will* die. You understand?"

Shaking, Rat looked away. She lived for her prince. She had blood-bound to him, in a ritual overseen by her Sentinel. She had chosen to serve, and, as the turns had passed, she had been able to imagine no other life for herself.

"These experiments that escaped must be killed," Mckkval said. "If they live, it could…change everything."

Frowning, Rat jerked her head back up to look at Mekkval. The enormous Dhasha was once again watching the video of his nephew's death forever playing out on the wall behind her, examining the way a single, shaking, naked female Human had stepped up to the lines of Dhasha and closed her eyes. A moment later, Keval and two dozen other Dhasha commanders simply jerked and collapsed in lifeless piles of flesh and scales.

The perfect weapon, Rat thought. *With one of those at our backs, the Dhasha would never rise again.*

Then, belatedly, she realized that *nothing* would ever rise again—because there could be no freedom. Personal choice, individual thought, all of it would be gone. The weapons, once loosed, would take over. The telepaths would kill their way to the top of the Congressional hierarchy...

...and stay there.

Mekkval was right. It would change everything. She swallowed down bile.

"You see how important this is?" her prince asked softly.

Watching the scene of his nephew's death continue to replay on the wall, Rat slowly nodded.

"My vote was to annihilate the planet," Mekkval said. "Start over. Aliphei was with me. But the soft-hearted Ayhi petitioned Daviin and the damned Jreet refused to put in his vote."

Rat frowned. "The *Ayhi* backed Earth? Why do they even *care*?" She knew from her decades with Benva that the Jreet believed, wholeheartedly, that the Ayhi—the gentle, harmless, algae-eating Ayhi—were living demons of their ninety hells. Aside from the black Jreet herself, there was nothing that could calm a room of warring Jreet faster than a single Ayhi raising its proboscis for silence. That they had taken Humanity's side was odd enough it made her spine prickle.

But Mekkval wasn't paying attention. Instead, he was gnashing his teeth again at the screen. "Cowardly worms. Takes three votes to authorize an ekhta, and Daviin instead insists on leniency due to that stupid Jreet legend. First time in ten thousand turns the Ayhi raise a single voice of dissent in the Regency, and it's over *this*." Mekkval made a frustrated backhanded swipe at a priceless piece of Ooreiki yeeri pottery, shattering it and scattering head-sized pieces across the filthy room in a spray of colorful glass shards. Most of the room was in similar disarray, as Mekkval hadn't allowed any of his Takki inside to clean it up.

Rat watched the pieces of priceless artifact glitter and spin where they had fallen in smears and clumps of Dhasha shit for a moment before she said, "Do you know where the installation is?"

Mekkval hesitated and gave her a long look. "The North American continent. Between the western coast and the desert."

Rat took a shaky breath and let it out between her teeth. "I'll need coordinates. Best that you can provide."

Mekkval, who obviously hadn't expected her to agree, hesitated. "It's your last mission. If you go, you will die on Earth."

"Then I will die in your service, as was my oath," Rat replied. "How do you plan to get me past the telepath?"

For a long moment, Mekkval just peered at her. Then, almost suspiciously, he said, "It took my Bajnan team three rotations to hack enough files to come to that conclusion. How did you know there's a telepath?"

She smiled at him. "How else would an entire installation go unnoticed? It paid off a Geuji?"

Mekkval grunted. Then, almost reluctantly, he said, "I had a device made. It imitates random human brain-waves. Thousands of them at once."

"To blank out my signal," Rat agreed.

"We can't black you out completely, but we can make you a mite in a refuse heap," Mekkval replied. "It will be hard for a telepath to single you out, but it could be possible, so kill them before they have a chance."

Rat grunted. "And you want them all dead? Not just the telepaths?"

"*All* of them," Mekkval growled. "The experiment documentation listed out three types: Movers, minders, and makers—telekinetics, telepaths, and telemorphs. There were even some attempts at making Huouyt-Human hybrids, though we found only one living example of it, and he escaped."

Rat's brow creased in a frown. "Escaped."

Her prince tightened his ebony claws into the floor, carving holes into the expensive tile. "Zero's team freed him, after Neskfaat," Mekkval growled. "It was quietly overlooked because that same team consisted of a Tribunal member, the Peacemaster, a Bagan hive-lord, and a living legend. The hybrid is not important, though. He'll die in time, and his sexual organs are non-functioning."

Rat froze, picks of ice suddenly carving away at her veins. Thinking of Forgotten—and how nothing the damn Geuji had done had been happenstance—she said, "Why would Zero and his team free a Huouyt-Human hybrid?"

"Because the Mothers hate us." Mekkval made an irritated clack of his triangular black teeth. "The experiment was Zero's brother."

Rat felt a sudden wash of tingles up her spine. "The genius? I thought he was dead." She had *seen* the video of his execution.

Mekkval grunted. "Faked. My agents wanted to interrogate him out of the public eye, figure out where he'd gotten the experiment schematics."

"What did he say?" Rat asked.

Mekkval gave an irritated bat of his paw. "The maggot claims he got drunk, hacked into the computer of one of the installations, downloaded the technology, and experimented on himself because he was *bored*. They say he was a genius before, but now he's...something else."

"Half Huouyt," Rat breathed. She would have no problem putting a round through something like that, even if it *was* Zero's brother.

"If you catch a sniff of him down there, be careful," Mekkval commanded. "There's reports he might read minds."

Rat's frown deepened. "You're joking."

"Would I *joke* about something like this?" Mekkval snapped, slamming a paw into a support pillar. The hollow titanium alloy shredded, cutting the lights to one section of the room and leaving electrical cables sizzling in the open air. The Dhasha had begun to pant, neon-orange drool slipping from between his razor-sharp teeth to spatter upon the shit-covered floor.

"And Zero freed him. After he was already dead." Meaning they could no longer officially look for the hybrid without admitting they had faked *another* death in front of the masses. Public perception was already at an all-time low with rumors of mind-control chips and Regency corruption, and revealing another fraud like Forgotten's public 'confession' would have only increased tensions.

As she considered that, dread built in Rat's gut, spawned by the knowledge that the Geuji's plan must have taken one more unseen step twenty turns ago, something they could not have predicted. That the same multi-species groundteam Forgotten had hand-picked for Neskfaat had released Zero's brother, a *genetic hybrid*, could not be chance. The idea that they were about to yet again take part in a Geuji's game was so unnerving to Rat that her back prickled. That gut-deep feeling of danger she always got before attempting to do something that would get her killed started to send throbbing tendrils of anxiety through her lungs and spine. "You realize Forgotten is part of this somehow."

"Yes!" her prince snarled, hurling another priceless artifact across the room in voiceless rage. "And he killed my nephew!" He started to pace again.

"But he *specifically* wanted this hybrid—Zero's brother—to live. Why? What's special about him, other than he's a genius?"

The prince sneered. "The hybrid is a secondary concern. An itch, nothing more. The main concern is finding the telepath."

Rat found Mekkval's dismissal somewhat odd. The telepath could not possibly have been involved in his nephew's death, and according to Congressional law, *all* of the genetic experiments were equally in need of extermination to prevent the spread of artificial genes. More importantly, Forgotten had obviously taken a personal interest in Zero's brother. That bothered her. The last time the Geuji had taken a personal interest in something, a planet had been obliterated, a Tribunal member died, and a hundred and thirty-four Dhasha princes were executed.

Considering the Geuji had somehow worked himself into a mess that even without his intervention could mean even more devastating wars for Congress, Rat knew that the most important thing for them to do, right now, was to figure out the Geuji's game. To do that, they needed to figure out why he spared a Huouyt hybrid.

Why a Huouyt? she wondered. All the psychotic burners could do was shapeshift and out-think—

"Wait," Rat said, her neck prickling. "Zero's brother was a genius *before* the experiment. Like, everybody called him the Tesla of the Congressional Era. What was he *after?*"

"I don't care about the hybrid!" Mekkval snapped. "I want the telepath."

"Humor me, milord," Rat insisted.

Looking annoyed, Mekkval said, "Impotent and insane."

"Can he shapeshift?"

"No," Mekkval growled. "The scientists running the experiments overlooked the fact that a Huouyt needs zora to shift. He has no zora. They checked."

She frowned. "But he could out-think a Huouyt?"

Mekkval snorted. "If Forgotten's plan was to infect the Human race with alien genetics during their Sacred Turn of penance, there would be no need to out-think a Huouyt. The only beings allowed on Earth right now are Humans."

But Rat's experience dancing to the Geuji's tune on Neskfaat had taught her to think, rethink, and over-think every single piece of the puzzle she found, and she was certain that the Huouyt hybrid was part of the puzzle. The more Rat thought about the circumstances of the brother's escape, the more she was sure that it had been part of Forgotten's plan. Forgotten *never* did anything by mistake. Which made her even more leery of what was to come. "Milord, have you…?" She swallowed, trying to decide how to ask such a sensitive question without insulting her master.

Mekkval gave her a sharp look. "Have I what?"

"Already sent Huouyt to find them, master?"

Mekkval's scales tightened with anger. "I took an oath to uphold the law."

"So you *didn't*?" Rat pressed. "To hedge your bets?"

Orange saliva started to dribble from between his teeth, and glacial fury iced his words when her prince said, "If it were anyone else to have asked me such a thing, Leila, he would be dead right now. No. I did not. Ask me such a shameful thing again and our friendship will not save you a second time."

Sensing how truly close she had come to meeting her death on her prince's claws, Rat lowered her head in acknowledgement, burning with shame. "My humble regrets, milord."

Mekkval grunted. "Find the telepath for me and we shall consider the debt forgiven."

The telepath again. Rat frowned, but said nothing. Personally, if she were in Mekkval's place, she would be more interested in making sure Zero's brother was neutralized first. Ignorant, scared Human weapons, she could handle, but if Zero's brother were anything like *Zero*...

"So Zero's brother," she hedged. "Do you know where he might be? Do you have an address? A picture?"

"The hybrid is a *secondary priority*," Mekkval barked. "His existence is annoying, but scientists confirmed the experiment had made him impotent, so he's really of little importance to our goals. It's the ones with the capability to *reproduce* that you need to concern yourself with. The telepath and his friends. We don't want the worms *breeding*." He swung his head back to again become transfixed by the gruesome images on the screen.

"Understood," Rat said softly, even though her mind was churning with the exact opposite conclusion. "I just need to know what I'm looking for." She knew from experience that the more innocuous Forgotten made something look, the more important it was.

Mekkval grunted, still watching the screen. "The hybrid is tall for a human. All documents on him were purged by a system error a few months after his escape, but witnesses said his eyes glowed and his hair writhed."

"Glowed." Rat frowned. Huouyt eyes didn't glow. They just… made observers uneasy. Like looking into a mirror. A flat, psychotic mirror.

"An exaggeration, obviously," Mekkval said, sounding impatient.

"Obviously." She glanced again at the grisly death-scene that had been replaying on Mekkval's wall for eight days. Knowing the familial ties of Dhasha, she understood Mekkval's strategic lapse, and decided not to push it.

Rat took a deep breath, the truth of what she was about to do beginning to sink in. Mekkval had given his vow to his brother Bagkhal to raise Bagkhal's son as his own. She knew Mekkval would board a ship to Earth to kill the experiments himself if she refused him. His honor would allow nothing else. In fact, she was surprised Mekkval hadn't killed her for her comment earlier. All a worthy Dhasha prince would be able to think of, at this point, was honor. And she'd bruised it. Badly.

Rat gave a nod of acquiescence. "I'll find them, my prince." She reached out and switched off the video that had been haunting him for a week. As Mekkval grunted and rounded on her, his indestructible scales rattling as they clamped down in anger, Rat looked up to meet his eyes, gently placed a hand on the cold, glassy slickness of his shoulder, and said, "You have my word. I'll kill them all."

6

NEW BASIL HARMONIOUS

"They're *leaving* us here! The ailo fuckers are *leaving* us here!" The enraged thuggish scream echoed down the concrete corridors to the chorus of men shouting and beating their Bibles to pieces against the bars. Slade sighed and continued to stare at the ceiling. Of course they were leaving them there. They were *criminals*. Why should the pious, God-fearing men and women with their self-righteous attitudes and handy lead-fortified nightsticks let *criminals* out of their cells when the Earth was about to be rendered back into the Stone Age? That just set a bad precedent. After all, Earth would be lucky to wind up with a couple million survivors by the time Congress returned in its Sacred Turn. Why should those survivors be the descendants of *criminals*?

When the hooting and chanting continued, Slade sighed and rolled onto his side to face the opposite wall. His bunkmate had been replaced by a graphic brass rendition of the Crucifixion, bolted to the concrete with concussion guns. Slade, the wardens had quickly learned, could not have bunkmates. Either he liked them, or he didn't, and either way, it turned out poorly for New Basil Harmonious.

If he liked them, Slade would turn them into his lackeys and begin yet another carefully-designed institution-wide conspiracy to escape, four of which had already worked…for other people. Dammit.

If he *didn't* like them—i.e. if they were especially arrogant, obtuse, or otherwise distasteful—he would patiently take the time to give them long, highly logical monologues on their own lacking self-worth and safety until they ended up hugging themselves in a corner, rocking quietly, and shaking like one of those tiny pet dogs in a blizzard.

The last one who ended up in the straight jacket had earned that honor for rooting through Slade's stuff while Slade was in yet another mandatory interview with the government shrinks, then stealing— and chewing—Slade's last illicit stick of gum in front of him, which Slade had been saving to ease his headaches after spending hours explaining to shrinks the mechanisms behind their own personality flaws. The one he'd straight-jacketed before that had been a gerbil-brained furg who loved to slap Slade's ass while he peed, then giggle when he sprayed the floor and wall. The one before that, Trent, had snored at night.

Had that been Trent's only failing, Slade would have simply turned the corpulent dimwit into another lackey, but he'd been a chronic child molester before his 'repentance' at New Basil Harmonious, and Slade hated child molesters.

Thus, Slade was alone in his room, staring at his friend the Pinioned Dead-Man Statue, listening to the indignant roar of rapists, murderers, and thieves, when he heard the telltale *click* of someone throwing his cell lock. Frowning, Slade lifted his head to look.

A tall, blond, blue-eyed prisoner that Slade recognized from Third Lunch was standing inside the door to his cell, gripping the bloody, broken handle of a mop with all the reverence of a twelve-million-credit plasma rifle. Slade was pretty sure he saw hair and scalp clinging to the jagged end.

"Yes?" Slade asked, sitting up carefully. He hadn't *remembered* pissing this guy off, though maybe he'd hypnotized his little brother into thinking he was a vagina or something.

"You the Ghost?" the man demanded, peering at Slade. His voice had a distinct Southern twang to it, probably Alabama or Louisiana.

Aw, hell. I probably hired his sister to escort for me or something... Knowing it was gonna hurt—if he survived it at all—Slade put on his best look of horrified innocence and gave the guy's 'weapon' a dramatically terrified look, trying to calculate whether or not he could take it from him. Probably not. He was a computer geek, not a barfighter, and this guy was *definitely* six-foot-four-bash-your-face-in goon material. "*Me?*" Slade scoffed, exercising that geekish whine, "I wish." He had managed to keep that particular nugget of information from his wardens and shrinks, but he knew that, as a famous criminal overlord, the criminal underlings—who were usually smarter than their captors by a factor of twelve—would start to put A and B together.

The blond dude blinked, then glanced at the gruesome statue on his wall. "I'm lookin' for Ghost."

Apparently, this one should have been given a nightstick, Slade thought, exasperated. "Well, he isn't here," Slade said, "but if you're lookin' to pound some dude's face in, there's a big guy down the hall who likes to read haiku at night."

The guy gave him a long look, then, surprisingly, turned and walked back outside his cell in silence. All along the corridor, inmates were howling and throwing their belongings at the blond through the bars, demanding his attention. Slade frowned when the guy again reached for his lock, to seal him back inside. "Why are you asking?" Slade called, curious. Most of the guys in here would have beat the crap out of him anyway, just because.

"Got a computer to hack," the blond said, hitting the lock and sealing Slade back inside. "Got a tip on accessing the warden's account through a secret terminal behind the painting in the janitor's office, but can't get past security. Locked me out on the third try."

Slade sat up so quickly he hit his head on the empty bunk above him. "I can help!" he shrieked, grabbing his head and dancing out of bed so hastily he hit his head again. "I can help I can help!" He hurried up to the bars to face the blond on the other side, still hissing as he held his bruised skull with one hand. "Come on, dude. Let me out. I can do that. I can hack. No sweat. I'm Ghost."

His would-be savior gave him a flat look. "You said you weren't Ghost." He started to turn away.

"You were holding a *bloody mop handle!*" Slade cried. "I thought you were gonna kill me. Take me to this secret terminal. I'll do it. For the love of God, I'll do it."

The man hesitated, then turned slowly back to face him. "I'm Tyson."

Slade bit down the urge to tell him he didn't give a crap who he was, just give him something with pixels and lines of code. He smiled and held his hand out through the bars. "I'm Ghost."

"Your jumpsuit says Slade Gardner," Tyson said. It was pretty obvious he wasn't going to let him out again. Or shake his hand. Especially shake his hand.

Slade's smile faded and he dropped his hand. "Listen, you ill-bred inebriate. If you are somehow smart enough to get your incompetent ass to a backdoor into the system, you know damn well you can get us out if you can crack the code. But you can't, because you're an under-educated monkey with a Pleistocene fetish. You *need* me, because you don't have the processing capacity to work through complex mathematical algorithms in your woefully inadequate little brain."

Tyson stared at him blankly for some time. Finally, he said, "A what?"

"You *need* me," Slade repeated for him.

The thug cocked his head. "No, I mean that word you said. Plyyy…"

Slade blinked at him. Their lives or deaths were hanging upon the blundering orangutan's next action and he was standing there trying to get him to pronounce geological epochs. "Pleistocene."

"Yeah, that." Tyson scratched at his cheek, obviously struggling. "So that's like, what…Dinosaur time or something?"

Slade squinted and considered walking away and letting the nice primate play with his bloody stick. But, because he *really* didn't want to starve to death—he'd heard that was a miserable way to go—he reluctantly said, "It's a geological epoch that lasted from about 2,588,000 to 11,700 years ago, spanning the Earth's most recent period of glaciations." When the idiot just peered at him like he'd spoken ancient Jreet, Slade sighed, deeply. "It roughly correlates with the Stone Age, give or take about six hundred thousand years."

The tiny, rusted gears in the guy's head started turning. "So you called me a Neanderthal? He pronounced it 'Nander-thawl.'

Slade sighed and lowered his cranium to the bars, his last little flicker of hope going out upon that halfwit drawl. "Never mind."

Tyson tapped the bars by Slade's head, looking curious. "So you called me a Nander-thawl."

Slade lifted his head, eyes fixed on the bloody stick the man was holding against the bars. It *was* somebody's scalp. "Yes. I called you a Neander-*tall*."

Tyson chuckled. "You're a dick."

"I'm a *smart* dick," Slade gritted. "I'm a dick that can get you out of this place and on your road to sweet, sweet freedom and back to all that lovely murdering, looting, and raping you did with your misspent youth."

Tyson's glacial blue eyes darkened a bit. "Never raped nobody." The look in the man's eyes added that he had, indeed, murdered people.

Slade groaned inwardly and dropped his face back to the bars, resigning himself to his body consuming its own fats, glucose, and proteins as it starved to death.

Tyson tapped the bar near his forehead again, smearing more blood and hairs across the steel. "You really Ghost?"

"Yes," Slade told the stick. "I'm really Ghost."

Tyson grunted. "Thought so. You're the only guy in this place without a bunkmate."

"That's how you found me?" Slade asked, surprised.

Tyson shrugged, though it seemed like there was a flicker of something more in his eyes before he hid it. "You stick out like a sore thumb. Figure Ghost isn't your average criminal, so he's not gonna look like your average criminal."

Meaning he found Slade by his creepy hairstyle that he'd gotten a Doctor's Order not to cut, now at a full six inches despite the prison's half-inch regulation.

"Huh," Slade said. Slade had *agonized* that the government goons would figure out he was Ghost by merit of the first cutting—and bleeding—of his creepy hair, but all it had taken had been a couple greased palms and a quick doctor's note detailing a paralyzing phobia of hair-cutting and Slade had been yet another low-profile criminal awaiting an early parole. The phobia hadn't even been hard for him to fake, either, considering that haircuts caused him vomit-inducing pain, the loss of each strand kind of like snipping off a six-inch bundle of raw nerves with a hacksaw.

Still, the fluffy white hair went pretty well with his documented age, which was, depending on the record book, anywhere from seventy-two to a hundred and six. Slade was actually ninety-nine in Earth-years, but due to his vast financial reserves, expensive Congie medicines, and his own drunken experimentation, he had the body of a twenty-five year old.

The doctors and processing clerks usually raised a brow at the apparent discrepancy, but Slade gave them a sad smile and told them of spending his life's savings on rejuvenators only to end up in prison for a nasty case of fraud that really wasn't his fault—it was his *dentist's* fault—and they always gave him that Holier-Than-Thou look and ushered him onward in line, a fresh new inmate with an unhealthy case of tonsurephobia to be whipped into shape by the impassioned sermons of the faithful. Little did they know that Slade re-read his favorite novels in his head during the God-talks, flipping through the pages in his photographic memory as the priests droned on about their Savior's will, Human failings, responsibility, yada yada yada. Since his internment in New Basil Harmonious, Slade had re-read all of Heinlein's works twice, Card's lifetime compilation, and was currently halfway through Stephen King's omnibus.

But Tyson apparently still wasn't satisfied. "Okay," he said. "Folks say Ghost's good at math. So what's the square root of seven hundred eighteen?"

"Twenty-six point seven-nine-five-five," Slade replied immediately, before he had a chance to think about it. He cocked his head with a little frown. "Why?"

Tyson snorted. "No it's not."

Slade blinked. "Uh. Yes. It is."

Tyson tapped the bars again with his stick. "I used a calculator before I went looking for Ghost. It's *not* twenty-six point seven-nine-five-five."

Slade peered at him. Then he cocked his head, a couple more of his massive mental gears lazily clunking into rhythm with the first two, leaving the vast clock-tower of his mind still sleeping as he recalculated and looked for flaws. "You said the square root of seven hundred eighteen?" he asked.

"Yup," Tyson said, utterly smug.

"Twenty-six point seven-nine-five-five," Slade repeated.

"It's thirteen point eight five nine," Tyson said. "Dumbass."

Slade stared at him. He could find no way that even a drunken, lobotomized primate would have mashed so many incorrect keys on a calculator to come up with *that* answer, instead of the correct one.

With a smug grin, Tyson snorted and turned to go.

"Thirteen point eight-five-nine squared," Slade said to Tyson's very broad back, "is not even a whole number, you unreasonably stupid jackass. Next time you decide to test me, actually do your research first."

Tyson hesitated, then turned, an intelligent gleam in his eye before it was quickly hidden again.

"Or maybe that *was* your test," Slade suggested.

Tyson gave him a long, appraising look, then almost reluctantly went over, inserted the warden's key once more, and hit the button again. Slade's door slid delightfully open. When Slade cocked his head and peered out into the hall, Tyson gestured with his stick. "This way."

"So," Slade said slowly, glancing down the hall. Seeing no one watching Tyson's back, he didn't step out into the hallway with him. Warily, he offered, "Where's *your* bunkmate, Tyson?"

In reply, Tyson held up the stick and casually picked a clump of scalp and hairs off of it. Looking at the hairs, Tyson said, "He got bored at night. Started tellin' me about all the girls he kidnapped on a lonely stretch of highway and dragged out to the woods for a few days before he left 'em, wandering in the wilderness. Apparently, the feds only got him for tax evasion." He flicked the bloody clump of hair aside and gave Slade a flat look.

Meaning Tyson didn't like rapists, either.

When Slade just swallowed, Tyson pointed the broken haft of the stick at Slade's left eyeball, which rested only slightly higher than Tyson's—both of them were very tall men. "You got stories like that, you keep 'em to your fucking self."

Slade, who was skinny and geekish to Tyson's badass, meaty thuggery, blurted, "I've never hurt anyone."

Tyson raised his platinum-blond brow in obvious skepticism.

"Well, physically," Slade quickly amended. "I've *physically* never hurt anyone." He'd stolen billions of credits from Huouyt family 'corporations' and Jahul 'businessmen', but he'd never actually punched someone in the face. He figured that would probably hurt his fist.

Tyson grunted and twisted the mop handle in his hand. "Heard you drove some guys insane just by looking at 'em." He didn't seem too impressed. Just...curious.

Slade snorted. "I did a bit more than *look* at them, but yeah, that was the general idea."

Tyson peered up at him, the shouts of indignant inmates still chorusing around them. "How?"

Slade rolled his eyes. "I couldn't possibly explain it to you."

Tyson, a nearly three hundred pound thug who was quite pointedly blocking his way to freedom, crossed his impressive arms over his impressive chest and said, "Try."

Slade took a deep breath, then sighed and said, "I started subtly making them question their own self-worth, their safety, and their grasp on sanity."

Tyson squinted at him. "Sanity?"

Slade shrugged. "Yeah. It's called gaslighting. You yank the rug out from under them. You change what they perceive as 'standard' in their life. You don't give them any constants. You tell them they sleepwalk and brush their teeth in their sleep, then move their toothbrush after they go to bed, put it on the other side of the sink, maybe switch it out with somebody else's. I'd turn their pillowcases inside-out when they were off on visiting hours, put their covers into some new spot each night, take their favorite necklace and put it around the neck of our resident Jesus figurine, maybe bribe the laundry guys to sew their nametag onto clothes that were a size too small, then ask them if they were gaining weight. I'd painstakingly add a few fun notes to their Bible in their own handwriting, slip it under their hand, then casually tell them they had been talking God-talk on those nights they weren't sleep-brushing. Or I'd tell them they'd acted completely abnormal the day before, then bribe people into accusing them they'd said things they hadn't said, done stuff they hadn't done..." He gave a dismissive shrug. "Shit like that."

Tyson peered up at him for some time, a gorilla contemplating whether or not to humor a howler monkey. "People say you've got mind-powers." It was more of a question than a statement.

"Yeah," Slade said, thinking of the gigantic alien lizards that were going to smash down the walls for the delicious goodies inside. He gave a flourish. "The Tesla of the Congressional Era, at your service. Can we *please* go to that terminal, now? I heard they're gonna drop kreenit. We *really* don't wanna be trapped in the middle of a mass of caged Humanity when kreenit find this place."

Tyson grunted, showing absolutely no hurry. "You don't look like much."

Slade blinked, because, with his creepy, ball-lightning eyes and sometimes-wriggly cotton-ball hair—not to mention his reputation of weird mind-powers—most people peed themselves when Slade gave them a sideways look. "Uh...thanks?"

Tyson uncrossed his arms. "This way."

The brute led him down the barred hall like he owned the place, taking books and painful-looking personal effects full-on about the head and shoulders without even flinching. Slade, on the other hand, ducked and yelped each time a Bible impacted his sensitive skin—or his even more sensitive scalp. While Slade really didn't fear anything, pain was not his friend, and he generally avoided it if he could.

Tyson stopped at the locked janitor's closet, produced a bloody keycard from his pocket, and swiped it through the lock. Then he typed in an 8-digit code in the keypad, looking completely oblivious to the little scanner screen set into the wall beside it.

"It's gonna want a thumb-scan," Slade said with a sigh. Well *that* was a short stint of freedom. He wondered if the guy would beat him to death or eat him. Or both.

Giving him a sideways look, Tyson retrieved a *thumb* from his pocket and pressed it to the screen. There was a loud, audible *click* as the heavy bolts thudded aside.

"Oh." Slade blinked.

Stuffing both thumb and keycard back into his pocket, Tyson pushed the door open and gestured at him to go first with the jagged end of the stick. Easing his way around his new friend, Bloody Scalp, with appropriate mention of Possible Brains, Slade slid past Mr. Stick and into the darkness inside. Following him, Tyson switched on the light.

Slade, though, had already seen the paradisal blue glow coming from the back room and was hastily stepping over fallen mops, cleaning supplies, and a very dead body in order to get to the secret computer terminal. The moment he touched an honest-to-God electronic device again, Slade almost had a long-denied orgasm. It was a very basic emergency deal, hidden behind a painting, set into the wall with its own tiny keyboard, set much too high into the wall to be ergonomically friendly. Slade hastily pulled over the desk and sat down on what remained of the janitor's hamburger and fries, facing the wall.

Tyson closed the main door and came up behind him. "They said the password was—"

"Shh!" Slade commanded, holding up one hand. He ran his fingers across the keyboard, bathing in the luxurious blue glow of

ACCOUNT LOCKED, MULTIPLE ENTRIES OF INVALID PASSWORD DETECTED. PLEASE USE WARDEN'S OVERRIDE OR CONSULT TECH SUPPORT.

Ah yes. Tech support. Slade closed his eyes and soaked up the long-missed light, counting the number of days it had been since he'd accessed anything more advanced than a landline to his lawyer. Three hundred and eighty-seven. Almost thirteen months. Nine thousand two hundred and eighty-one hours. Over one year. Over one year without even a cell phone. It had been Hell. True Hell.

"See," Tyson offered, stepping up beside him, "I think the guy was lying so I wouldn't cut off his—"

"Shh!" Slade snapped again, distractedly cutting at the air behind him as the overgrown furg once again interrupted his Zen.

There was a long pause, then Tyson said, "But you're just sitting there. On that guy's hamburger."

Slade opened his eyes and scowled disgustedly at the wall. It was *so hard* to get good lackeys nowadays. To the painted concrete, he said, "If I tell you to shut up, that I need a few minutes to consider the wonders of if-then statements and irrelevant metadata before I spring your hairy, apelike ass from this thug-convention, then it's your job to go to your corner and wait for me to finish."

Slade felt Tyson staring at his back. The big man sounded confused when he said, "I just beat three men to death in the last twenty minutes."

"That's nice," Slade said. "Go get me a soda or something." He reached up and slid his fingers along the back of the terminal, feeling for a plug or a switch.

He found a switch. Hallelujah. That would make things *so* much easier.

"You know what?" Tyson growled, "If you don't get us out of here in the next twenty seconds, I'm gonna add your brains to this stick."

"I'd like a Pepsi, if you can find one," Slade said, as he flipped the console's power off. The console monitor went dark, and Slade heard the sweet music of a processor powering down. As he mentally calculated the brand, age, and capacity of the machine in front of him, Slade gave a delighted giggle. Early twenty-first century technology was *so* buggy, especially systems using a Windows environment—which this clearly was. That meant it was plausible to gain access with a SQL Injection, which would save him *so* much time. Realizing his lackey was still standing around, Slade gestured impatiently and said, "Make sure it's plain. And cold. With corn syrup, not that fake shit."

Tyson was silent for so long that Slade wondered if he was getting out his Beat-Stick. Then, reluctantly, Tyson said, "Pepsi's expensive."

After Earth's discovery by the barely-concealed alien tyranny known as Congress, Pepsi had become one of the most valuable substances Humanity had to offer, just beneath oregano and rosemary in universal demand, though it was the hedonistic Ueshi who had begun purchasing vast quantities of Pepsi for shipment to pleasure planets like Kaleu and Tholiba, whereas the more reserved Ooreiki financed the rosemary perfume trade. Almost fifty years after it went universal, Slade still felt more than a little vindicated that his favorite drink happened to be loved throughout the galaxy, by aliens famous for knowing how to have a good time. It did irk him, however, that Pepsi now cost ten times as much as a regular soda, and had taser-enhanced, AI-embedded vending machines all of its own, just in case anyone decided to get frisky.

Slade glanced down at the desk, picked up the janitor's change dish with the tiny stuffed lizard in it, ascertained it had enough money in it to buy a Pepsi, then handed the tray to Tyson and went back to his work.

Tyson didn't move. Still staring at the dead monitor, he said, "Why'd you shut it off?"

"Well," Slade said, as he waited for the hard drive to completely power down, "some idiot came in here before me and, after the computer patiently told him the password was bad the *first* time, he entered it two *more* times, just to be sure." He flipped the switch back on. The computer—it was *ancient*, Slade realized, delighted—whirred back to life.

Behind him, Tyson squinted at the screen. "You rebooted?"

"If in doubt, let the bad out," Slade said. As he was waiting for the dinosaur to load, he felt around the back for an Ethernet cable, but found only a power supply. Which meant it was wireless. Oh, this was going to be *fun*.

"Why are you grinning?" Tyson growled. "Something funny?" Instead of acquiring an ice-cold Pepsi like he'd been told, the big man had come to stand beside Slade, peering into the hidden computer cubby like a very large dog that had no compunctions with being in the way.

"I'm grinning," Slade said, pushing him bodily aside, "because I'm thirsty, and you are going to get me a soda." No sooner had he spoken than the access window appeared, fresh and new, sans the Colossal Dumbass Screen, with a cheerful little USERNAME AND PASSWORD? prompt to welcome him to the New Basil Harmonious Security System. Instead of slogging through that particular clusterfuck, Slade entered the SQL Injection test 'OR"=' in both the username and password fields to determine whether or not he needed to waste his time building a password generator. Immediately, the computer logged him in as the very first user in the database, a gracious Mr. Alvin Mathers. Slade knew him as a part-time security officer with an attitude problem who liked to work Sundays and holidays for the extra pay.

Using his newly-acquired admin capabilities, Slade began dismantling the woefully vulnerable prison system from the inside. The imbeciles who had programmed the software, it seemed, had been operating under the assumption that a prisoner—or any other ne'er-do-well with half a brain and an afternoon of programming experience—would simply never have access to the system itself. How quaint.

Twenty minutes later, Tyson brought him a soda. Pepsi. Cold. Because Slade had unlocked the doors to the main halls, the warden's office, the armory, and the staff breakroom. It was the staff breakroom that interested Slade the most. He hadn't had a good Twinkie in *forever*.

Tyson had gotten real quiet the moment the Doors Open alarm had gone off in the main hall, and hadn't said much since, except a gruff, "Here," as he handed Slade his soda, his new body Kevlar and an AK-47 from the armory strapped to his body.

"You put it in a cup," Slade complained, taking a drink. He grimaced. "And you poured it straight in. Why do people *do* that? It loses sixteen percent of its carbonation when you do that!" He took another sip and continued tapping commands into the keyboard with his free hand.

Tyson scowled at him. "It's easier to drink quickly in a cup."

"Yes," Slade whined. "But I wanted to *savor* it." He took another swallow and studied the maps of the cell blocks, trying to determine the best system of releasing the seven stories of inmates without getting killed in the process. Ever since the Doors Open alarm had gone off, inmates had been howling at the bars, thrashing and screaming like animals. It made Slade ever-more-sensitive to the fact that about half the guys in the block knew or suspected he was Ghost, and almost all of them would jump at the chance to try and coerce a few million credits out of him before they bashed his brains out on the polished concrete floors.

Tyson squinted at him, then at his monitor, then at the flattened cheeseburger that Slade had shoved to one side of the desk after he'd peeled it from the seat of his prison jumpsuit. "You wanna move this operation to the warden's office?"

Slade snorted. "I couldn't do anything there that I can't do here. Besides. I hate the warden. If anything, I'd shit on his desk. I'd rather not stare at pictures of his grandkids if I can avoid it." He kept perusing prison schematics.

"So what are we doing?" Tyson asked. "Can you get the gates open?"

Slade made a dismissive gesture and took another sip of his one-sixth flat soda. "I could've gotten the gates open twenty minutes ago. I'm trying to figure out where the nearest Armani store is. Looks like L.A.."

Tyson peered at him so long Slade turned around to look. When he did, Tyson said, "Armani?"

"Yeah, the clothing?" When Tyson just continued to stare at him, Slade sighed and said, "You know, like Dolce & Gabbana, Tom Ford, Ralph Lauren? *Nice* stuff. We've *got* to get new threads, man." He examined his new lackey's bloodstained jumpsuit with a critical eye. "Hell, I'd even spring for a new suit for you. You would look totally *bad ass* in black, you know that?"

Tyson continued to stare at him. "They're dropping man-eating lizards the size of shopping centers on the planet and you're worried about Armani?"

"The government shrinks said I had a flair for drama," Slade said. "And what's more dramatic than *this*," he gestured at his freakish wads of cotton-white hair, "with silver silk in the middle of an apocalypse?" He grinned a little, considering what it would be like to wear a real suit again. "Maybe a maroon handkerchief or cuffs. I'm going to have it delivered."

Tyson squinted. "Delivered."

"To the penitentiary. See?" Slade showed Tyson the order form on the monitor. "You're...what...a thirty at the shoulder?"

Tyson suddenly had the muzzle of his AK-47 filling Slade's right nostril, his meaty fist gripping the back of Slade's head with enough pressure to scalp him. "You," the thug growled, "are going to open the gates or I'm going to blow your creepy ailo head off. I don't give a fuck about Armani."

"Creepy, huh," Slade said, his voice muffled by gunmetal. "Seriously, where do people *get* that?"

Tyson's ice-blue eyes narrowed and Slade saw his chances of surviving the next three microseconds decrease by about a hundred percent.

Slade sighed deeply and closed the order form. "My first real chance to wear something *decent* for a change and I'm foiled by an Iron Age transplant with access to twentieth-century weaponry."

Tyson had not removed his gun. "Did you just insult me again?"

Slade thought about it. "No, not really. Just stating a fact. You look like you've got more than your fair share of Neanderthal in your blood, but they weren't exactly stupid. *Have* you gotten a DNA test? They can be surprising, you know..."

Tyson *looked* like he wanted to shoot him, but he lowered his weapon and stepped back, instead. "What do you want?" he growled.

Slade blinked at him. "Want?"

"I know how it works," Tyson growled. "They're dropping those lizards on us in three days and the whole world left us here to rot, so you've got me between a rock and a hard place," Tyson said. "What do you want for springing us?"

Slade thought about it. "Another Pepsi would be nice. *Not* in a cup. Cold. Unopened. I want to see condensation on the sides of that baby. Oh, and a Twinkie. Those are good."

For a long minute, Tyson just stared at him. Then, in silence, he turned and walked out the door.

Ah, yes. *Excellent* lackey material. As soon as Tyson was out the door, Slade went back to the Armani order-form he had minimized, placed his rush order, then figured out where the nearest book store was. While everyone else would be looting grocery stores and pharmacies, Slade would be perusing his local Barnes & Noble for survivalist manuals and then getting other people to implement the concepts inside. Ah, the perks of being a leader.

The nearest Barnes & Noble, it appeared, was four and a half miles out of town, in a big new shopping center built in the middle of nowhere, one of the many such places adding to the urban sprawl of America. Like a vast majority of such retail temples built during the Ooreiki perfumes boom, it had been erected more on a wishful, 'Build It And They Will Come' mentality, rather than any form of serious strategy. It was due to close in two months, selling out to an Ueshi electronics firm. It had, however, a Bajnan-run Interplanetary Bank of Congress. Which was nice.

By the time Tyson returned with a Pepsi and a half-smashed Twinkie, Slade had transferred large amounts of money from his Faelor bank to his illicit Earth accounts and was in the process of hiring an on-demand hair stylist. As soon as the beep of the door announced his gorilla friend's return, Slade minimized the window back to the prison schematics.

Obviously having seen the flash of switching windows, Tyson frowned. "What are you doing?"

"Opening the doors," Slade said, waving a finger over the keyboard with a flair. "Like...so." He pushed the ENTER key on the command he had typed into the prompt over thirty minutes before, and suddenly every door in the prison slammed open, from every single cell to the cafeteria access to the outside gates. All around them, freed men began to hoot and run wild, their feet sounding like thunder as they rushed from their prisons.

Slade, however, wasn't finished. Using the dead janitor's cell phone, which he had wired into the prison system as a one-way radio, he put the receiver to his mouth and said, "Attention, prisoners of New Basil Harmonious. This is the Ghost speaking."

The thunder of feet quieted almost instantly as the booming remnants of his words continued to echo down the concrete halls.

"Yeah," Slade said, "*That* Ghost. I figured you guys didn't want to rot in here any more than I did, so consider yourself fully pardoned by the greatest mind in the Congressional Era. This is an apocalypse, people, so before you leave here to brave that *completely unarmed* residential center to the west, you should take whatever you need from the armory, which is located on the third floor, all the way down the east wing. I've already taken what I wanted from there, so I'll be exiting via the front gate, and I expect not to meet any resistance on the way. You think I'm good at hacking computers? You should *see* how good I am with a gun. Everyone will stay indoors until myself and my companions have exited, at which point you will be free to leave. If you have questions, come see me in the warden's office." He ended the call.

Tyson frowned at Slade. "You realize you just told every thug in this building to take a potshot at you."

Slade grinned and palmed the phone. "I'm also not going to be exiting via the front door." He slid off the desk and stretched, then looked his slightly shorter—but infinitely more muscular—brute of a lackey over. "You wanna come with me?"

Tyson gave him an odd look. "I'm the one with the gun."

"True," Slade said, "but I'm the one with the Plan. Capital P." He smiled, showing his perfectly-capped teeth.

"I just fought the urge to shove my gun up your nose again," Tyson said. "What plan?"

"A plan to keep us alive," Slade said. "Beginning with our heroic exit through the kitchen loading bay and ending with a damn good steak."

Tyson twitched at 'steak.' "Sounds good," he said reluctantly.

"Yeah," Slade said, handing Tyson a black plastic garbage bag he'd taken from a roll on a shelf. "Put your head through the top and your hands through the sides and use it like a poncho." He demonstrated, wrapping himself in another bag, then wiggled his arms to the crinkle of plastic.

Tyson stared at him blankly.

Slade blinked at Tyson, then down at the bag. "What? My mother did it for me all the time on camping trips."

Tyson gave him a flat look, then handed him back the bag. "So we're going out through the kitchen?"

"Yeah," Slade said. "I opened up the doors and the gates. Should be no sweat. Let all those other common criminals shoot themselves. I arranged transportation. Real discreet—some people will do *anything* if you pay 'em enough. It'll be waiting out back with my new suit."

This time, Tyson only peered at him a minute or two before grunting and tugging his AK-47 over his shoulder. For a minute, Slade thought he was going to shoot him. Then Tyson simply went to the door, jerked it open, and held it for him. "Let's go, Boss."

Slade snatched up a dustpan, put it over his head, and hurried out the door into the bloodstained hallway. Off in the distance, he heard a chorus of manly screeches as inmates began giving New Basil Harmonious a facelift. Or killed each other. Or both. Probably both.

Seeing the dustpan, Tyson continued to squint at him like some sort of talking rodent, then stepped into the hall behind him, looking utterly badass with his big, antique gun and his shoulders to stop a linebacker. Even better, when Slade's fire alarm program timed out and the halls from the janitor's closet to the kitchen exit began to be drenched with blaring sirens and icewater, Tyson seemed to be utterly unfazed when the cold water hit him, which Slade found delightful. It gave him more 'street cred' as a bodyguard if he could keep a straight face when his nuts were unexpectedly freezing off.

"This way," Slade said, from under the shield of his dustpan. Between it and the plastic bag, he was relatively dry, despite the icy drenching. With any luck, the rest of the prison hated getting wet as much as he did, and the path to their extraction point would be clear of bad guys with guns.

Tyson glowered at him a moment. "Just so you know," Tyson said, as they headed for the kitchen, "if there's no steak at the end of this, I'm going to shoot you."

Under his rain protection, Slade cocked his head at his new lackey. "Well, that could get unpleasant."

"Sure could," Tyson agreed.

Slade made an uncomfortable laugh, trying not to calculate how many hundreds of different ways the day could unfold sans-steak. It was definitely a lot. He led them to the cafeteria, which, with its torrential icy downpour, had been utterly deserted, then opened the staff door to the roomful of plastic cutlery and ready-made micro-waveables. On the way through, he nabbed an apple from the 'fresh' fruit bin and ate it under his makeshift hat as he led the way to the loading bay.

Hearing the unmistakable purr of money outside the loading bay, Slade grinned at Tyson through the frigid deluge. "You hear that?" he gestured at the kitchen exit. "That is the sound of deliverance!" He threw the door open. Outside the bay purred a brand new Rolls-Royce limo, all sleek white curves and regal power. The back door was open in invitation. Two nice, steaming steak dinners sat on the luxurious white leather seats inside, the smell of Kobe beef wafting over to them from even that distance. Sitting behind the wheel, as instructed, the driver looked a bit frazzled, but Slade supposed that was to be expected with a two million dollar bid to arrive at the back door of a prison in under forty minutes.

Seeing the two suits hanging from the ceiling, Slade grinned and took a deep breath of freedom.

"Is that a steak?" Tyson blurted behind him, looking stunned. "In a *Rolls Royce?*"

"Would I let myself be chauffeured around in anything less?" Slade demanded.

Tyson blinked at the car, then at Slade. "You really *are* Ghost, aren't you?"

Slade took a triumphant bite of his apple. "Did you ever doubt it?" he said, grinning around fruit debris. He turned to accept his ride to freedom.

A feral roar rumbled the concrete under their feet and a gigantic predator with scales the color of oil-on-water snapped the purring car off the ground and chewed it in half. Slade stopped, frozen in place as the Rolls's thrumming engine sputtered and died in its gnashing mouth. Inside the cab, which happened to be dangling outside the creature's jaws, the driver was screaming and batting at the windows.

Staring up at the beast, Slade's mouth fell open and his apple dropped from his face. That was *definitely* one way the day could end without steak. "You said we had three days until they dropped the kreenit," he blurted, feeling betrayed.

"Fuck me," was all Tyson said.

The kreenit shrieked and rag-dolled the car, sending the driver's end careening off to slam into a no-longer-electrified fence, ripping a hole through it as it skittered off into the well-kept lawn on the other side. The back-end, with Slade's Armani still hanging from the ceiling, it ate.

"You *bastard!*" Slade cried. He threw his half-eaten apple at the beast, who was even then choking down the last of a trunk. "That's *mine!*"

The apple bounced off of the creature's crystalline green eye and it flinched, mid-swallow, then twisted to get a look at Slade. Instantly, it vomited up its prize and more of its huge body thundered around the building as it came after him, mouth low and open. Inside the crushed cab of the Rolls Royce, Slade's suit hung in a wash of orange alien saliva.

Thoroughly pissed, now, Slade started toward the beast. He'd taken two steps when strong arms grabbed Slade around the middle and hauled him back inside the prison. Kicking the door shut behind them, Tyson yanked Slade forward by the scruff of his neck, forcing him to run. "Ow, ow, ow!" Slade cried, struggling against the Neanderthal's grip. "Let go! Let go let go leggo!"

Tyson paused beside the refrigerators long enough to reintroduce Slade's nostril to the wet muzzle of his favorite beastie. The water, Slade found, acted as a lubricant and made the application much easier, and this time Cro-Magnon's upgrade almost made contact with brain tissue.

"Do you want to die?" Tyson demanded.

"Not especially," Slade said, swallowing down at the gun.

"Then run," Tyson growled. He shoved Slade ahead of him, obviously expecting him to do just that.

Slade righted himself and grimaced. Without his dustpan—which he'd dropped in his struggles with Tyson—he was well on his way to getting soaked, regardless of poncho. He felt the icy water running down his scalp and dribbling down his spine and opened his mouth to complain.

A moment later, a lizardlike snout slammed through the titanium-reinforced, bomb-proof back door behind them, massive, scaly jaws snapping at the racks of baking trays and wash counters as the beast forced its head through the much-smaller entrance. Seeing the cracks spreading outward in the concrete wall, the beast gnashing at the room behind them, Slade let out a scream that ended in a giggle and this time didn't struggle when Tyson grabbed him and hauled him out of the kitchens.

Once they were back in the cell block, with several hundreds of feet of concrete between them and the beast, Tyson stopped, shoved a meaty finger into Slade's breastbone, and growled, "You know, for a super-genius, you're not very smart."

"It ate my Armani!" Slade complained. "And I'm *wet*." He flicked water off his hair in disgust. He hated being wet. Modern man with its huge brains and platinum credit cards shouldn't have to get wet.

"Yeah, well." Tyson glanced at the corridor back to the kitchens. The sounds of crashing and crumbling concrete had ended, which probably meant the beast was seeking easier entry into the establishment.

No sooner had the thought come than they heard the sounds of gunfire and screaming from the front of the prison. An instant later, the building began to shake with massive blunt impacts. Slade grimaced. *Damn* that was making his head hurt. He would have crashed a planetary banking system to have a single stick of gum to ease the throbbing, but he'd chewed his last piece in the shrink's office two days before.

"So what do we do now?" Tyson demanded, as the gunfire and pounding went on. "Go back out the kitchen?"

Scowling in the general direction of the uncouth beast that was shattering his wa, Slade started walking toward the front of the building.

"Hey Ghost!" Tyson shouted behind him. Slade ignored him and continued to the barred windows overlooking the courtyard. The kreenit was partially wrapped in razor-wire and torn fencing, snarling and hurling itself at the front gates and the AK-47-carrying inebriates on the other side. Men were screaming as they died, and fools who were trying to make a dash to safety were getting snapped up and swallowed whole by the beast.

"What are you doing, Boss?" Tyson asked nervously behind him. Like any good lackey, Tyson had eventually followed him with very little complaint.

"I'm going to go kill a kreenit," Slade said. He flicked water off his plastic bag and headed to the warden's office.

"With what?" Tyson demanded.

"With electricity, a Twinkie, and your gun."

"You're not taking my gun."

Slade stopped and held out his hand. "Give me your gun."

"No."

Slade gestured impatiently.

Tyson gave him a flat look and kept it stubbornly on his shoulder.

Slade glared. "We'll discuss this later." He continued down the hall, through the open exit doors, past the wide-eyed inebriates huddled behind the Visiting Center tables and chairs, and stopped at the vending machine. He squinted at the lack of a credit-card slot. He started feeling around for a subtle keypad, any sort of numerical entry system. He found nothing. He had *billions* of credits in a dozen different high-interest accounts, but he was being thwarted by a twentieth century relic and a lack of pocket change. "How the hell did you get the one in the break room to work?" Slade finally demanded, frustrated.

Tyson replied by stepping up beside him and smashing the butt of his rifle through the glass, then reaching through the shattered face to retrieve a Twinkie for him. His lackey held it out to him between thumb and forefinger, a single blond eyebrow raised.

"Oh, brilliant! Thank you," Slade said, delicately taking his Twinkie and tip-toeing over the glass. He continued through the Visiting Center and into the Warden's Office, where three mindless furgs were ransacking the rotund little monster's quarters, one of whom was taking a dump on his desk.

"Is that *really* necessary?" Slade demanded loudly from the door, startling the desk-defiler into suddenly pinching one off. As the man croaked and pulled up his jumpsuit, Slade made a disgusted sound and gestured at the armed thugs. "Tyson, get them out of here. They're making my head hurt."

Tyson peered at him, then at the three thugs in the room. Each of them carried an AK-47.

Ignoring his new underlings, Slade walked into the room, sighed in gratitude when he found that the excrement-happy idiots hadn't destroyed the warden's terminal, then sat down and started entering his override codes.

"Dude," one of the gun-toting inebriates growled, "what the hell is going on?"

"He's going to kill the kreenit," Tyson said, shrugging.

"That lizard attacking the front door?" one of the slackjawed nitwits demanded. "Naw. We're dead, man. Nothing can kill it."

"Yeah," another man said. "Bullets bounce right off it. It's eating through the walls."

"So you take the last ten minutes of your miserable life to shit on the warden's desk," Slade said, without looking up. "Lovely."

There was a brief silence, then the underlings started talking to each other again. "Yeah, man," the second underling said. "Guys tried getting past it, but the thing's got super-senses or something. It just whips around and eats 'em before they make twenty yards."

"Aren't they early?" another underling demanded. "I thought we had a few days, yet."

"I heard three days from now," Tyson agreed.

"Probably dropped them early just to catch us off guard," the third underling suggested. "We're so *screwed*, man. We're like sitting *ducks* in here."

"Sardines," Slade corrected distractedly.

"Maybe we should, like, let those idiots outside distract it and sneak out the kitchen loading bay, you know? That'd be smart."

"Would you *please* shut up?" Slade demanded, tugging his eyes from the lines of code on the screen to scowl at the imbeciles. "You're interrupting my flow. Go outside and get me a soda or something."

The three men looked at each other. The leader gave Tyson a curious look. "He really gonna kill that thing?" Off in the distance, his question was punctuated by more screaming.

Tyson shrugged. "Probably."

"So that's really the Ghost?" one of the guys asked, his voice lowering to almost a whisper.

"Pretty sure," Tyson said, watching Slade from where he was standing inside the metal-framed doorway. "Seems legit so far."

"He's wearing a garbage bag."

"The soda machine," Slade said, "is out there." He pointed.

One of the men sniffed, then glanced at Tyson. "You want something, man?"

"Nah, I'm good. I'm gonna have steak tonight." Tyson gave Slade a meaningful look.

His newest AK-47-toting lackey grunted, gave Slade one last perusal, then grunted again and gestured for his two newest underling lackeys to follow him out the door.

"Pepsi!" Slade called at the men's backs, as they departed. He was having to type with one hand, holding his nose with his other due to the smell. "And Tyson, get rid of that. He *definitely* wasn't eating right." He pointed at the pile of crap on the desk.

Tyson gave him his patented badass-who-doesn't-take-shit-from-computer-geeks look. Without responding, the beefy man crossed his arms and leaned against the door, the sides of his jumpsuit actually straining from all the pressure his muscles were putting against it. "Do you have water retention problems or something?"

"Huh?" Slade said.

"Three Pepsis in an hour?" Tyson demanded.

The truth was, Slade's funky hairdo needed a lot of extra liquids to keep from dehydrating, but he wasn't going to say that. "Now let's see," Slade said, returning to the fence security settings, "how Mr. Alien likes our good friend Direct Current." He hit the ACTIVATE button with a dramatic click of his mouse.

Outside, the lizard let out a long, ear-splitting bellow that shook the air in Slade's lungs, then there was complete silence.

"Nice," Slade said, grinning.

"You killed it?" Tyson demanded, looking a little startled.

"Nah," Slade said, deactivating the fences before a fuse blew. "Just testing." He started counting seconds as he began working on increasing the voltage for the next jolt.

"You scared it off?" Tyson asked, perking up even more. He obviously hadn't been looking forward to fighting a massive alien transplant for his freedom.

"Doubt it," Slade said, still counting. "Shhh."

Tyson went totally silent, listening curiously.

At the twenty-three second mark, the recovering—and now very pissed—monster outside lunged into the prison so hard it knocked the picture of the warden's grandson into the steaming pile of crap on his desk.

"What did you *do*?" Tyson screamed, stumbling as the walls shuddered around them.

"I let it get up again," Slade said calmly. "Gotta do this right, see?" He began calibrating the motion-detectors outside the main entrance.

"You're only pissing it off!" Tyson cried, as the entire building convulsed around them in another impact. The big man huddled in the doorway, hands protecting his head as ceiling plaster rained down around them. "Can you turn it off?"

Slade looked up, frowning. "Turn it *off*?" He snorted. "No, I'm going to go *kill* it." Standing up, he walked over and held out his hand. "Give me your gun." Outside, the kreenit screamed and slammed itself into the prison. Slade made an insistent snapping motion with his fingers. "Come on. Give."

Tyson squinted up at him through the plaster dust, visibly contemplated blowing Slade's head off, then reluctantly pulled the gun over his shoulder. Slade took the weapon and started to walk off for his date with Destiny. Halfway down the hall to face the beast, however, Slade had to pause and look at the weapon. After a moment of frowning at two different switches on the gun, he turned and hurried back to where Tyson was huddled, enduring the building shuddering around them. "Hey," Slade whispered, dropping beside him. "Is this little lever the safety?" He lowered the gun for Tyson's inspection.

"That's the magazine release," Tyson said.

"Oh," Slade said. "Well, which one's the safety?" He'd watched plenty of shows where the bad guys—sans brains—tried shooting the good guys—sans gun—when their weapons were on safety. That would just be embarrassing.

After eying him like he was debating whether to take the weapon back, the beefy man reached up and flipped a switch. "Safety." He flipped it again. "Boom."

"You were walking around without the *safety* on?" Slade cried, appalled. "Don't you know that's *dangerous*?"

Tyson gave him a look like he was, indeed, going to take the gun away from him. And, since Slade needed the gun to kill the kreenit, he quickly stood up and hurried down the hall, towards the exit and the pissed off alien outside.

The front of the prison had been obliterated. Men in bright orange prison jumpsuits were hiding behind whatever rubble cover they could find as the kreenit roared and thrashed in its tangle of electric fencing and razor wire. As he watched, the two-hundred-foot long beast drew itself onto its haunches, lifted its long neck a hundred feet above the courtyard, and roared with enough emphasis to break glass. Mouth open for his perusal, Slade could see the unmistakable orange anomalies of prison jumpsuits clinging to its scythelike teeth.

That could kill me, Slade realized. He unwrapped his Twinkie and took a bite, considering.

Apparently finished showing off, the kreenit finished its roar and its front legs slammed back to the pavement with enough force to knock over the flag pole. Its big, horned head swung to face him, oil-on-water scales rippling in the morning sun.

These people need a hero, Slade thought, with a sigh. *And I'm running out of Twinkie.* Taking a deep breath, he strode past the huddled inmates until he was face-to-face with the kreenit, tossed the remaining pastry at the motion detector he'd left active. As the Twinkie sailed through the air, Slade leveled his gun at the beast's eye and fired a single shot.

At his shot, the kreenit jerked, went utterly stiff, and then hit the ground like a downed carrier, twitching. A moment later, the Twinkie activated the electric fencing and the kreenit's body started to spark and sizzle before the system overloaded and the lights went out.

Slade blinked and looked at the barrel of his rifle with a new respect. There had been no mistaking that the *shot* had downed the beast, not the electricity. Having never fired a gun before, Slade had merely been taking a cheap shot to inspire the masses, not actually trying to kill it. From all he'd read, it was *impossible* to kill a kreenit with an AK-47.

And yet, seeing the beast slumped on the ground, twitching, Slade realized that he'd always had a penchant for being on the bleeding edge of the world's learning curve. He also realized that the animal was not yet dead, despite its massive jolt, and was very likely going to prove the conventional wisdom correct unless Slade did something heroic, and quickly.

And heroics, in this case, were not going to be pleasant.

Aw hell, Slade thought, considering what was to come. *God hates a coward.*

Disgusted that he had to resort to brute force, Slade tucked the gun under his arm, jogged up to the gigantic creature's head, climbed onto its slimy purple tongue, and inched his way through the jagged arrays of sword-like teeth, placed the barrel of his gun to the soft spot between palate and braincase, and unloaded an entire clip into the creature's gray matter. Which, Slade found, in a man-eating alien from outer-space, wasn't actually gray.

As a purple paste of jellied neurons rained down upon him, Slade climbed out of the creature's jaws—careful to time it between death-spasms—and stopped in front of its snout to figure out where he'd hit it the first time to make it go limp.

It hadn't, he discovered, been the eye. As far as he could tell by the smears of lead left against the scales, it had been the nose. Or, more correctly, the left nostril, when he'd been aiming for the *right* eye. That was…annoying. Slade gave the useless weapon an irritated look, then handed it to Tyson when his lackey walked up behind him.

When Tyson didn't take the proffered gun, Slade eventually turned.

Tyson was staring at the kreenit, his blue eyes wide. Behind him, hundreds of men in orange jumpsuits were standing in the ruins of the prison, looking at him in similar open-mouthed awe. Slade chose that moment to rip the useless, gore-covered plastic bag off his body, sloughing the bloody brain matter to a wad on the ground at his feet, then took a deep breath and glanced up at the Congressional bots that were even then annihilating the airborne populace as they fled the city in their skimmers.

"I'm in the mood for a latte," Slade announced. "Any takers?"

Seeming to recover, Tyson shrugged the gun back over his shoulder and gave him a beefy arms-crossed scowl. "Do I look like a pansy-ass milk-drinking yuppie to you?"

Slade looked him up and down, then sighed, realizing that kind of muscle mass required consistent infusions of protein. "Not really." He cocked his head. "Steak?"

"Steak," Tyson agreed. "You got…" He cocked his head at the sun. "Six hours."

Oh joy, Slade thought, thinking back to his wayward limo. He supposed he could hotwire a car, instead…

7

EELEVANSEE

She called herself Batch Eelevansee. But, since everyone else was also called Batch, she thought of herself as Eelevansee.

For as long as she could remember, Eelevansee's life revolved around food, water, and headaches. The headaches usually came with the food and the water, since that was when the Keepers came.

Just hearing the Keepers' hard feet ringing in the hall made Eelevansee's heartbeat quicken, her hands cold and clammy. They called themselves Caahptin and Aahfiscer and Kernel, but together, they were the Keepers. The Keepers discouraged the People from speaking like them, giving them headaches whenever they tried.

Only Tenef was different. She could talk with pictures and feelings that she broadcasted into Eelevansee's head, but her thoughts were always maddening things that frightened Eelevansee and made her cry.

Tenef and Eelevansee were two of the only People that woke up whenever the Keepers turned the lights on to feed them. Most didn't need food; these were Dreamers. All Dreamers had bluish tubes in their arms that led up to a bag hanging from the wall, which the Keepers replaced every day instead of feeding them.

Across the hall from her, Nynjee's huge body filled up his two side-by-side beds to overflowing. He hadn't moved since he had broken his cell open and they put a tube in his arm. Now he was just like the other Dreamers, blank-faced and drooling. Seeing him was a constant reminder not to anger the Keepers, one that Eelevansee took to heart.

It was several days after the Keepers made Nynjee Dream when Tenef began bombarding Eelevansee with a rush of horrible images of pain and terror, pictures of monsters tearing people apart, people forced to Dream. Tenef was terrified, and her terror spread throughout the People, becoming all the more potent when the lights overhead began to flicker and the ground began to shake. As the People screamed and clung to their beds with each terrifying rumble, Tenef fed their horror, milking it into screams of fear, giggling when they huddled in their beds in terror, laughing when they cried.

But, as more and more People succumbed to the infectious panic, a single image began to burn in their minds on a wave of calm, utterly drowning out Tenef's madness with its beauty and strength. It was a magnificent circle of light, surrounded by waves of color in all directions, carried on a rush of peace. The glorious apparition always appeared in their minds as soon as Tenef's tirades began, stronger and more powerful than anything Tenef could show them, completely obliterating her projections of monsters and terror.

To Tenef's frustration, the gentle image brought with it others of equal beauty and hope, creating a barrier between her and the People. The People stopped cringing against the corners of their cells and began to ignore her terrifying, alien pictures as noise behind a curtain. Eventually, she gave up.

Once Tenef's horrible images finally ceased, Eelevansee realized she was hungry.

This was strange for her, since she was always fed at regular intervals. She couldn't remember ever being hungry, aside from one time she was Punished for touching a Keeper. The sensation was new to her, one that was even more deeply disturbing than Tenef's images of pain and madness.

Tentatively, Eelevansee went to the front of her room and glanced down the hall to see if the Keepers were coming to feed them. They weren't. The double doors to the Keeper rooms were closed.

Eelevansee sat down in the corner so she could watch the entrance, fidgeting nervously under Tenef's malicious gaze. She closed her eyes, trying to ignore her hunger. She slept. Time passed. Her stomach began to cramp and ache. The sounds of movement across the hall made her jerk. She looked...

And was stunned to see that Nynjee was also sitting up, straddling his beds. He had pulled the bluish tube from his arm and was looking at her through the bars, his big brown eyes confused.

Eelevansee glanced down the hall. Nynjee wasn't the only Dreamer who was getting up. Some of the others had also pulled the little blue tubes from their arms and were walking around.

She looked back at the door, beginning to feel lightheaded. Nothing. Tired and hungry, Eelevansee went back to her bed to wait for the Keepers.

But the Keepers never came.

Eelevansee felt herself getting weaker, sometimes struggling even to lift her head from the pillow. A couple of times she managed to crawl to the front of her room, where she could see Tenef also laying in her bed, jerking with madness. In the room beside Eelevansee, one of the Dreamers hadn't woken up and was starting to smell bad. Why hadn't the Keepers brought food?

As time went on, more and more of the People began to stink. Eelevansee was so tired that she found it hard to move. Her throat was painfully dry. She found it hard to breathe, hard to think. She had drunk everything she could from the commode in the wall, but now there was nothing to take her waste away. She tried to keep everything in one corner, away from where she slept, but in the end she was too tired to get out of bed. Weak, exhausted, she slept.

The screech of tearing metal startled her awake.

Across the hall from her, Nynjee was pushing the bars of his cell apart without touching them. Part of the wall had collapsed and the bars were snapping under the strain. Eelevansee watched, horrified. The Keepers would make him Dream again.

She was even more horrified when he crossed the hall and started bending *her* bars.

Panicked, her weakened limbs alive with terror, Eelevansee crawled into the corner of her cell, away from him. She fiercely wanted him to stop, but only Tenef could understand her, and Tenef began laughing. Eelevansee started to cry. She didn't want to anger the Keepers.

Nynjee finally stepped inside her room and Eelevansee let out a frightened wail. He was big, much bigger than any of the Keepers. She tried to scoot away, but he wrapped her in her blanket and carried her outside the room like she weighed nothing at all. The moment she was outside her cell, Eelevansee felt a rush of dread and tried to scramble out of his arms. She didn't want the Keepers to see her being Bad. When he held on, refusing to let her leave, Eelevansee desperately thought about putting her hand to his face and making him stop.

You're safe, a soft voice told her. Not Tenef. The source of the brilliant ball of light and color. *Hold still. He's not going to hurt you.*

Eelevansee went limp, still panting with horror.

Nynjee left her on the cold white floor and walked down the hall to Tenef's room. He moved the bars there, too, opening up a passage into Tenef's cell. By now, those People who could still move were watching with mixed fear and excitement.

Nynjee brought Tenef out of her room and set her down beside Eelevansee. Then he knelt in front of the two of them, eyes locked with Tenef. Eelevansee started shuffling back into her room when Nynjee stopped her with a huge, solid hand on her ankle.

He wants you to make us food, Tenef said. The image of a bowl of Keeper food burned brightly in her mind and Eelevansee's stomach rumbled unbidden.

How? Eelevansee thought.

Tenef paused, glancing back at Nynjee, who frowned.

Like he does, Tenef said. *He said he saw you do it, behind the green door.*

Eelevansee swallowed, hard. *The Keepers made me do those things. I can't do it now or they'll make me Dream.*

Nynjee placed his palm on the floor. When he was sure she was watching, he lifted up and the white surface rose with his hand, making a bulge in the perfectly flat tiles. Then he looked at her expectantly.

I can't, Eelevansee thought.

Something powerful suddenly gripped Eelevansee's mind in an iron fist and she cried out. *The Keepers!* Even as she desperately fought to get back in her cell, Tenef wrenched her body around and Eelevansee was forced to watch herself press her palm against the bulge Nynjee had created in the floor. Then, unable to stop it, she watched the bulge under her hand begin to take shape…

Abruptly Nynjee slapped her hand aside and started scooping the stuff underneath it into his mouth. Gasping, choking, he ate until his face was covered with whitish lumps that slid down onto his chest and the floor.

Now water! Tenef screamed at her, the thought hitting her mind like a flesh-rending shriek.

But, seeing the Keeper food, hunger overpowered rational thought. Instead of obeying Tenef, Eelevansee reached into the depression that had once been floor to scoop out Nynjee's leftovers, depositing what she could find on her tongue with shaking fingers.

Only then did she realize that it was Tenef who had forced her to make the food. Tenef took hold of her mind again and tore her hands away from the pit, forcing her to create water. Then she cast Eelevansee off like a used dish and bent to drink.

In a daze, Eelevansee returned to picking at the remains of the Keeper food. It did not occur to her that she could make herself another batch until Tenef took hold of her chin with a thin, bony hand that was missing a finger.

More, girl! I'm hungry. Tenef pointed at the floor.

It was hard to focus with her fear of Tenef in the back of her mind. Eelevansee had to start over three times before the floor shimmered and glowed with change. By the time the food appeared, Eelevansee was lightheaded. It was all she could do to slump forward into the pit beside Tenef and scoop handfuls of the whitish muck into her face.

Once she could eat no more, Eelevansee rolled away from the pits and lay on her back, staring at the ceiling. Beside her, Tenef and Nynjee were also finished. Nynjee was groaning, holding his stomach, but still drinking. Tenef was sleeping.

Help us. The thought was a gentle whisper in her brain. Eelevansee looked up. Lining the edges of the hall, the People were staring out at her longingly from behind the bars of their cells, their hollow eyes fixed on to the three of them in yearning.

Please. Another fleeting thought, weak and barely audible, not from Tenef. It stunned Eelevansee, who until this point had thought that only Tenef could speak in her head.

Despite her exhaustion, Eelevansee forced herself to sit up. The People were watching her and her companions with open envy. She glanced over at the pit and felt a stab of guilt. There was still plenty of food left.

Shaking, Eelevansee crawled to the closest cell. Tendee fell to his knees in front of her, his mouth open in a plea.

Eelevansee stuck her hand inside the bars, and made him Keeper food. Beside that, water. Then she pulled back. Barely able to keep her eyes open, she went to the next room and repeated the process.

Thank you, the whisper in her brain said.

Eelevansee glanced back at Tendee, who was slurping up water and food.

I'm further down the hall. Help the others first.

Eelevansee continued making food and water for those trapped behind the bars until she passed out. She woke to Nynjee shaking her. When he saw her eyes were open, he got down on his stomach and made slurping sounds, nodding at her insistently. There were others with him. Eelevansee closed her eyes.

Nynjee shook her again, more roughly this time, jarring her head on the tiled floor. Weakly, struggling with her own thirst, Eelevansee made a tiny pool of water…

And was pushed aside as seven of the People fought to get at it.

Eelevansee moved away from the struggling mass, delirious with thirst. Part of her wanted to jump into the fray even though she was smaller and weaker than the others. Instead, she hung back and concentrated on the floor again, forming a larger pool with her mind.

Immediately, one of the others noticed and hurried toward her. Though there was easily enough room for both of them, he shoved her away and stuck his head down into the water, sucking it up in gulps.

Eelevansee wasn't sure what part of her responded, but in one instant the man was drinking her water and in the second he was reeling away from her, holding his wrist where his hand had turned into a mush of Keeper food. Eelevansee ignored his screams and bent to drink.

When she finally finished, she saw that, despite the fact that their pool was dry, the others had not made a move to take any water from hers. The man who had pushed her had started to Dream, his stub a globby mixture of bright red Keeper food.

Feeling guilty, Eelevansee backed away from the pool and motioned for the others to drink. They moved forward cautiously, their eyes darting to the man who had shoved her.

Nynjee drank first, then got up and went further down the hall, where more People were watching them with hungry eyes. He began prying open bars, freeing more People to eat and drink at the pits.

Eelevansee followed, but stopped beside Twelvay. Nynjee had passed him over after not getting a response, but Eelevansee could see that he was not Dreaming. He was slumped sideways against the bars, his mouth open as he watched her, but there was an intelligence in his eyes that Dreamers did not have. Eelevansee knelt and laid her palm against the floor at his feet. She concentrated and it shimmered, turning soft under her hands. When she removed her hand, the depression was filled with Keeper food.

Twelvay only smiled at her sadly.

Eelevansee mimed the act of eating, but got no response.

Eventually, she gave up and started to walk away, only to stop when the People who had been following her fell upon Twelvay's food, dragging handfuls of it out through the bars as he watched, immobile.

Eelevansee let out a shout that sent them scrabbling away from her. Then she turned back to Twelvay and squatted in front of him. His eyes were closed now. She knelt and took a handful of Keeper food and dropped it onto his half-open mouth. Most of it slid to the floor, but a few globs remained on his tongue.

Twelvay's eyes flashed open. He closed his mouth and swallowed, staring at her with wide blue eyes. She scooped up another handful and fed it to him. They repeated the process until the overwhelming picture of a water basin appeared in Eelevansee's head.

She blinked, startled. Twelvay was the whisperer in her mind?

Please. Water.

As Eelevansee made water and scooped it up with her hands, she saw the long, slender tube that had hung near Twelvay's bed. Looking down, she saw that his arm bore a small red mark.

You were a Dreamer, she thought, surprised. She dribbled water from her fingertips into Twelvay's open mouth. *Like Nynjee. What did you do?*

I killed a Keeper, he responded softly, staring into her eyes with his deep blue gaze.

Eelevansee jerked back and scooted away from him, suddenly very afraid.

The Keepers are gone, he whispered in her head. *Please help me. They can't hurt you anymore.*

Eelevansee bit her lip, considering. Then, carefully, she reached out to touch the bars in front of him. They dissolved into a puddle of water and she crawled inside to sit beside him. *Can you move?*

A little. He managed a feeble smile and lifted one hand before dropping it back onto his knee.

Eelevansee returned her attention to the delicate process of feeding him. After several minutes, he seemed to gain enough energy to lean down and sip water from the basin, but that was the extent of his abilities. Eelevansee had to prop him back up against the wall when he was done.

Thank you, he said as he closed his eyes.

When she turned, the People were watching her. Nynjee came up and gently lifted the unconscious Twelvay into his arms and carried him over to lie beside Tenef.

There were other Dreamers who needed help getting out of their rooms, but none were as weak as Twelvay. Nynjee opened every cell, waking all those he could and carrying those who couldn't walk. After eating, they huddled together on the other side of the hall, staring at the man with the Keeper-food hand. He wasn't moving any more.

Exhausted, Eelevansee dropped to the floor beside Twelvay and laid her head across his thigh, closing her eyes as the exhaustion overtook her.

When Eelevansee woke, Twelvay was holding her head in his lap. He looked healthier and smiled down at her when she woke.

Suddenly, Tenef's voice was loud in her head, startling her.

Get up, girl. Make food! I want to leave this place.

Eelevansee felt a sudden compulsion to stand, but not before she saw Twelvay frowning at Tenef. Tenef didn't seem to notice. Once Eelevansee was on her feet, Tenef took control of Eelevansee's mind and roughly forced her to create pits of food in a painful daze. When the pits were finished, Tenef released her violently and began to eat. Groaning, Eelevansee fell to the floor, both hands clutching her head.

Twelvay crawled over to her and touched her shoulder. *Did she hurt you?*

Eelevansee opened her eyes and saw that Twelvay was frowning at Tenef.

Before Eelevansee could reply, Tenef finished and stood up. She roughly dragged Eelevansee to her feet and said, *We're leaving.* She pointed to the double doors at the end of the hall. *Follow Nynjee.*

Instinctively, Eelevansee shied away. *I don't want to go.*

Tenef's anger came with a flood of violent images that left Eelevansee gasping. *You will go,* Tenef said, *or I will* make *you go.*

Twelvay's blond brow knotted slightly as he watched Tenef.

Now follow Nynjee, Tenef snapped, pointing at the huge green doors. Eelevansee balked, taking a step backwards, back toward her room. Tenef's scarred face sharpened.

Twelvay's grip on her arm stopped Eelevansee from bolting. *I will go with you,* he said. *Do as she says.* But Eelevansee could tell he was scared.

We can stay, Eelevansee thought desperately. *Tell her we don't need to leave.* She put all of her emotion into it, but Twelvay merely shook his head and looked up at the row of lights suspended above them.

Soon the dark will come, he told her, a view of total, penetrating darkness overpowering all other images. *We must go and find the light.* The calming image of the beautiful, colorful circle flashed into her mind.

Eelevansee glanced at Tenef, who was watching her mercilessly. Unlike Twelvay, she didn't seem to be able to hear what Twelvay said to Eelevansee. And, unlike him, she had no problems filling Eelevansee's mind with fear. She bombarded her with images of darkness closing in on them, swallowing them alive. Eelevansee took three terrified, running steps toward the green doors before she knew what she was doing.

Following at a jog, Twelvay's fingers tightened on her arm as they approached the door. *Don't panic. You'll scare the others.*

She made me run, Eelevansee whimpered, cringing away from the exit now that it was looming over her.

I know. Hold on. I'll keep you safe.

Nynjee came up behind them and gently pushed them aside so he could put both hands to the doors. He closed his eyes and strained against them, pushing them forward, away from them. Eelevansee jumped back and screamed at the sounds of snapping metal, then steadied herself when both Twelvay and Tenef warned her that she was scaring the People; Twelvay's thoughts laced with soothing images, Tenef's laced with anger.

The doors finally fell with a puff of air and a crash. They were thicker than the length of her forearms, but Nynjee's pressure had bent and warped both inward.

Lead us out, girl, Tenef demanded.

A surge of panic swept through her, but again Twelvay calmed her with his touch. Together, they gingerly stepped over the huge slabs of twisted metal and led the People out of the hall. Despite the sudden gust of fresh air, her stomach grew queasy. She could see the green door where the Keepers gave her headaches.

The Keepers are gone, Twelvay told her gently. *No more headaches. Ever.* His vehemence was strong enough to give Eelevansee the courage she needed to continue. Despite his assurances, however, he grew pale as they passed the green door. Others of the People cried out and huddled in the hall, refusing to come near the green door. Nynjee dragged a few, but when they bit and kicked, he left them.

Now that they were past the green door, the Keeper place held no more terror for Eelevansee than the halls outside her cell. She knew the Keepers would make them all Dream if they caught them, but Twelvay had assured her the Keepers were gone.

Still, the People stayed absolutely silent as they crept deeper into the hall, knowing they were being Bad. Nynjee paused at every door to open it, then let Eelevansee lead them out into another hallway.

The lighting here was dimmer, the hallways darker. Small black windows lined the sides and Eelevansee walked quickly, feeling exposed. She was beginning to get lightheaded and hungry again when they finally reached another door, this one heavier than the first. As Nynjee dealt with the door, both she and Twelvay slumped to the ground, exhausted.

When Nynjee returned, he was sweaty and shaking. He knelt and fell onto both hands, his arms wobbling against the pressure of his weight, his head hanging.

He needs food, Twelvay told her in a wave of images. *Please help him.*

Exhausted, Eelevansee placed both palms against the floor in front of Nynjee and made two large divots of water and Keeper food in the cold stone. Then she passed out.

She woke to Tenef's mental shout. *Get up! We're going. No more sleeping.*

Eelevansee was sandwiched under a mass of sleeping People, all of whom were jerking awake and trying to stand at Tenef's command.

It was in that instant that the lights went out.

A panicked cry rippled through the darkness and Eelevansee's fingers locked around Nynjee's thick forearm. For a moment, no one moved.

Do something, Twelvay thought at her frantically. *The People are afraid. Do something. Hurry!* She could feel his own fear leaking into his thoughts, fear of the Dark Room, of Dreaming.

At the same moment, Tenef's panic ripped through her, leaving Eelevansee and the others incoherent with fear. Primal terror coursed through them, leaving them all thrashing mindlessly in the dark, screaming.

Just as suddenly as it had started, Tenef's burst of panic cut off.

Then Twelvay was back in her mind, urging her to hurry, hurry, hurry, *hurry…*

Stop it! Eelevansee cried. Twelvay's thoughts choked off as suddenly as they had begun, like the dying sounds of a strangled thing. Of Tenef, there was nothing.

What happened? Eelevansee whimpered. *What is wrong with Tenef?*

I'm holding her back. Twelvay's words came with a spasm of fear. *She's scared. When the Keepers took People like me and Tenef behind the green door, they left us in the dark. To fight.*

To fight what?

Please make light, Twelvay whimpered. *I'm scared, too.*

Make light? Eelevansee frowned, wishing she could see Twelvay's face. She could make food easily, but light was not the same as food. You couldn't *hold* light.

Yet Twelvay was beginning to project cold terror just as Tenef had, and it was permeating everything around them. The People were whimpering and crying. Eelevansee wanted to run, but Twelvay was holding her hand much too tightly. Tentatively, Eelevansee touched the floor and thought of the round, globular lights that had kept their rooms bright. The floor grew hot to the touch, but she could make no light.

Try harder, Twelvay insisted. *You must. Please, I can't hold Tenef much longer.* He touched her arm, his fingers cold and clammy.

Eelevansee crinkled her forehead and concentrated. The floor under her hand began to soften, ready to take shape, but what she wanted it to become didn't *have* a shape. The more she concentrated, the hotter the floor grew, until, all at once, it began to smoke and glow.

The smell was horrible. Eelevansee relinquished her hold on the floor and the dim light went out. Instantly, Tenef was in her head, so strongly that for a moment Eelevansee lost all sense of her own self, so caught up in Tenef's demands that she couldn't think.

Make it again. MAKE IT AGAIN! AGAIN! MAKE IT AGAIN!

Then she *did* lose control. Tenef gripped her mind and wrenched her hand back to the floor. She forced her to put her hand back, heating the tiles again. Dimly, Eelevansee felt Tenef pour her energy into the rock, making it glow once more. Upon seeing the light, Tenef viciously began to drain everything Eelevansee had into the floor, into sustaining the tiny glow. Eelevansee felt herself losing consciousness.

Then, all of a sudden, Tenef's presence disappeared. Behind her, Eelevansee heard a body slump to the ground.

Please, Twelvay whispered in the darkness. *Please bring it back.*

I can't, Eelevansee cried.

She felt Twelvay stiffen beside her with a whimper. Then, softly, he said, *There's a door ahead. The Keepers would walk through it to go home. Nynjee can get it open for us.* She felt him stand beside her in the inky blackness. With him, stood the People.

Stumbling, feeling their way in the darkness, the People moved forward. Twelvay was trembling, his tight grip on Eelevansee's hand making her fingers numb by the time they finally reached the door. Beside her, Nynjee touched the door and pushed it open. Light flooded into the darkened hall, to the relieved gasps of the People.

Suddenly, Eelevansee forgot how tired she was. The floating circle of color that Twelvay had showed them was *there*, hanging in the wide-open space beyond the door. She stepped outside and fell to her knees, too tired to stand.

Behind them, more People filed out through the door to stare in awe and wonder at the great floating ball.

There are Others nearby, Twelvay told her, tugging her arm. *We have to move.* He projected a deep, horrible fear of the Others, mingled with an overwhelming hatred that made Tenef's tantrums look weak. Eelevansee cried out and tried to run back to the tunnels, but Twelvay yanked her back.

In an instant, Nynjee was between them. He shoved Eelevansee out of the way and slammed Twelvay down into the hard, uneven ground. He put one palm over Twelvay's face and held it there. The threat made Eelevansee swallow and back away.

Suddenly Nynjee fell onto his back, his palm pressed over his *own* face. Twelvay got up, pale and shaken, then let the giant regain control of his hand. Nynjee lunged to his feet, his fingers fisted at his sides. He was angry, an emotion that Eelevansee had only seen before in Keepers, and it had always meant horrible things for the People. A frightened sound escaped her throat and she went to huddle with the rest of their companions.

After they glared at each other a moment, Twelvay calmly turned away from Nynjee and extracted Eelevansee from the mass of frightened People.

We need to go that way, he told her, pointing out into the encroaching darkness. *Now. The Others will find us here. You have to lead. The People won't follow me unless I make them.*

What about Tenef? Eelevansee asked.

She sensed Twelvay hesitate. *Tenef is dead.*

Eelevansee glanced at the huddled People, more frightened now than she had ever been in her life. The landscape was utterly foreign.

Jagged pieces of the floor pricked her tender feet…and Twelvay had killed one of the People. She wanted nothing more than to rush back and huddle in her cell until the Keepers came back. Even the Keepers didn't scare her as much as this.

Despite her fear, however, Twelvay refused to let go of her arm. She felt the desperation in his thoughts and tentatively stepped into the growing darkness with him. Nynjee followed close at her side.

In silence, the rest of the People followed. They climbed up a large hill for most of the night, picking their way through the sharp needles covering the ground.

A massive flash of shadow landed on one of the stragglers. The predatory roar triggered some primitive instinct in their cores and the People began to run, breaking into great, terrified strides as the man's screaming abruptly cut off on the hillside below. The darkness closed on them and Twelvay began to project his terror, keeping them running long into the night.

When they finally stopped, the circle of light was once more coloring the world, and they were missing three more People.

Nynjee lowered himself to the ground and slapped his palm against the rough dirt. He was panting, his great head hanging from the exertion. Even his palm-slap was weak and tired.

Eelevansee made everyone food and water, then waited for them to finish feeding themselves before taking her own share. Twelvay and some others were already Dreaming by the time she sat down amongst them.

As tired as she was, Eelevansee didn't notice the Other standing nearby until it moved. She tensed, ready to raise an alarm.

The Other crouched when Eelevansee spotted her, preparing to bolt. She was small, only coming up to Eelevansee's chest. The girl was wearing Keeper skin, but it was dirty and tattered. Her tiny face was bruised and scratched, streaked with tears. Quietly, she said something in the Keeper language. Eelevansee's spine prickled.

The little Other repeated herself, motioning at Twelvay. She pointed at the sides of his head, then touched her ear and babbled a long string of Keeper-speak, obviously confused.

Eelevansee watched her, wondering if she should wake Twelvay. The Other said the same thing twice more before Eelevansee decided to shake him awake. Twelvay sat up with bleary eyes that immediately sharpened as soon as he saw the girl.

As soon as Twelvay was awake, the Other cried out and backed away, her hand to her mouth. Twelvay frowned at her and immediately the girl stopped moving. Eelevansee realized he was going to hurt her.

The Other must have sensed Twelvay's thoughts, because she started to cry.

Stop it!

Eelevansee grabbed Twelvay's arm. It was obvious the child was terrified. Terrified and alone. At least the People had each other. This little Keeper had no one.

When she projected to Twelvay that they should help her, however, Twelvay reacted with anger. *The Others made the Keepers. We must stay away from them.*

It was too much for Eelevansee. She got to her feet and walked over to the little Other, then drew her into her arms. When Twelvay demanded that she put her down, Eelevansee refused. *She can teach us!*

That made Twelvay pause. He glared at the girl, then at Eelevansee, then back at the girl. Finally, he shrugged and went back to sleep.

The girl, Eelevansee discovered, was called Aliss. Saying her name out loud like a Keeper was difficult for Eelevansee, so she stopped trying. The Other's speaking made her uneasy, and when Aliss asked what Eelevansee's name was, she had an even harder time producing the sound that had only ever passed over Keeper lips.

"Eelevan-*see?*" The little girl asked with obvious shock. She said some more stuff, even drawing diagrams in the soft ground, but Eelevansee didn't understand.

Aliss finally gave up and moved on. She began naming the things that surrounded them as 'trees' and the tattered Keeper skin she wore as 'clows.' When it became apparent that Aliss wanted to know why

Eelevansee and the rest of the People weren't wearing any, Twelvay frowned at her from the ground and the questions stopped.

Aliss, however, was quick to find a new subject. She seemed absolutely delighted by Nynjee, calling him a 'jyant.' Nynjee snorted and woke at her examination, and in a second, he was crab-crawling away from her, eyes wide. This seemed to delight Aliss even more and she grinned, walking toward him. Nynjee stuck out his palm at her and Eelevansee quickly stepped between them.

Undeterred, Aliss ran out from behind Eelevansee to stare at Nynjee with obvious fascination. Nynjee continued to gawk at her in horror.

Aliss babbled a few things to Nynjee, foremost among them being 'jyant.' Nynjee continued to hold his palm between them, though his shock was quickly becoming curiosity. Finally, he lowered his hand and crept toward Aliss, a tentative grin on his face. When he reached out and rubbed her long black hair between his fingers, she squealed with delight and pried his hand away, enthralled by his huge palm, which spanned her entire chest. Nynjee responded by stroking her hair again, his jaw open wide.

Eelevansee reached up and felt her own stubbly head. The hair had grown since the Keepers had disappeared and she could almost grasp a tuft between her fingers. Eelevansee drew an excited breath. Was it possible to grow it as long as Aliss's?

Eelevansee couldn't help herself. She reached down and felt Aliss's hair as well. It was soft and silky in her hands, softer than anything she had ever felt before.

Nynjee had already moved on to the strange Keeper skin she wore, her 'clows.' He tugged at it, frowned, then pulled it open and peeked down the front. Aliss squealed and pushed his hand away, giggling hysterically. Nynjee held the girl still and showed Eelevansee what he had found. Eelevansee blinked, stunned. Underneath the Keeper skin Aliss was just like the People!

Aliss broke free and climbed on top of Nynjee, pushing him over. He fell onto his back and grinned as she sat on his chest and started tugging on his nose. He seemed equally fascinated by her feet. He started yanking on the strings he found there and Aliss laughed and pulled off her foot. Eelevansee stared in dismay until she saw the normal toes wiggling underneath another layer of Other skin, which Aliss promptly peeled off. Aliss then stuck her foot out for Nynjee to examine, and squealed as he lifted her by one leg to peer at it.

Laughing, Aliss kicked and pounded on his chest until he released her, then threw her arms around his neck and stayed there. They fell asleep like that, both of them snoring loudly.

When the People woke, their reactions were similar to that of Nynjee and Twelvay. Every one of them jerked away, but eventually Aliss's hair and skin drew them back for a closer inspection.

Nynjee guarded Aliss jealously, knocking away curious hands when he had decided they had felt enough. Finally, he put an end to the whole affair by slapping the ground and looking up at Eelevansee with expectant brown eyes.

Eelevansee made several pits, giving herself, Aliss, and Nynjee a pit of their own. Twelvay, who had made a point not to show any interest in the Other, went to eat at a different pit.

Though Nynjee and Eelevansee immediately began to eat, Aliss frowned at the pit for a long time before she finally reached down and touched the Keeper food. When she put a glob of it to her tongue, she spat it back out. Then she wiped her lips on her arm and gave them both a funny look.

Aliss babbled for several minutes, pointing between the pit and her mouth while making a face. Then, when neither Nynjee nor Eelevansee could understand her, Aliss went and grabbed Twelvay by the arm and dragged him over to them.

Twelvay frowned at the girl, then at the food pit.

She thinks it tastes like dirt, he told Eelevansee. *She wants to know why you don't make something else.*

Eelevansee was confused. *Like what?*

Twelvay looked at the girl and his brow furrowed. Then he turned to Eelevansee and deluged her with images and thoughts and feelings and tastes and emotions of food. It wasn't Keeper food. Instead, it was round and soft and flat, but hard enough to hold its shape. Struggling with the flood of information, Eelevansee tried her best to make it.

When it was done, Aliss let out a squeal of delight and took one of the soft round Other foods and ate it happily. Then she motioned for the others to do the same.

No one moved.

Nynjee was the first to give in to Aliss's pleading. He tentatively grasped one of the Other foods between thumb and forefinger and peered at it. Then he sniffed it and his eyes widened. He stuck out his tongue and licked it.

Instantly, his head jerked back and he stared at the Other food like it had bit him. Beside her, Twelvay tensed and Eelevansee moved closer to Aliss.

Everyone gaped when Nynjee crammed the round Other food into his mouth and reached into the pit for another handful.

"Kookees," Aliss repeated between bites.

Nynjee thrust a fist of Other foods against Eelevansee's chest emphatically. Since he looked like he was ready to force-feed her if she didn't try one, Eelevansee tentatively broke off a small piece and carefully touched it against her tongue.

Sweet, tantalizing flavors shot through her mouth like an electric shock. Her look of ecstasy, mingled with the enthusiastic thoughts that were emanating from Aliss and Nynjee, made Twelvay's curiosity overpower his caution. He took one of the Other foods and tentatively bit into it.

Then Twelvay's jaw dropped open and he stared at the Other food and Aliss with equal awe. He finished it and gobbled up a handful of others as the rest of the People came to investigate.

As soon as they tried Aliss's creations themselves, not even the threat of being turned into Keeper food would keep them away from the pit. Eelevansee was shoved aside by a wave of hungry People and would have retaliated had Twelvay not taken her arm and pulled her away.

Without warning, he flooded her mind with another wave of images and thoughts that he had plucked from Aliss's brain.

Eelevansee knelt and created another pit. This time, however, the savory smells were too overwhelming to resist. She and Twelvay fell to their knees and began putting pieces of the Other food in their mouths. This new food wasn't sweet like the 'kookees,' but was a whole new flavor unto itself. Aliss called it 'terkee.'

By then, the People had been drawn by the wonderful smells emanating from the second pit and they were pushed aside once again in the rush to get at the 'terkee.'

Aliss, however, hadn't run out of foods. She gave Twelvay another recipe, who then passed it on to Eelevansee. It was similar to the 'terkee,' but both Twelvay and Nynjee were more impressed with it and both fought the other People off when they came to explore this new pit. Aliss called it 'stayk.'

Before Eelevansee even had the chance to taste the 'stayk,' Twelvay bombarded her with another set of images, this one of a clear purple liquid. Eelevansee made a pit of it and took a tentative sip. She spat it out again when it stung her tongue, but Aliss happily slurped it up.

'Grayp sowdah,' Aliss explained with a purple-stained grin on her face.

After that, Twelvay wanted her to make something else, but Eelevansee closed her eyes and shook her head. Making the food had weakened her. She stumbled and Nynjee dropped his fistfuls of 'stayk' to catch her and lower her to the ground. Then Eelevansee's eyes rolled back into her head and she fell into oblivion.

8

CRASH LANDING

"*Please wake up, my lord,*" the autopilot of Mekkval's courier ship said, jolting Rat out of a weird dream about a crazy, cottonball-headed man. The dream was quickly forgotten, however, when the subservient Takki voice continued, "*I am in need of further instructions. We are arriving at Earth and we are under attack.*"

"Well, ash!" Rat cried, lunging out of her chair. "I thought we were going to get here in time."

"*We arrived on schedule, my lord,*" the ship informed her. "*It appears that the Ooreiki Corps Director in charge of this sector of space decided to launch the attack three days early. I apologize most humbly, my lord.*" Takki always used 'my lord' when referring to her, even AI Takki, because female Dhasha never left their dens, and despite her multiple attempts to correct the ship, the computer ranked her of 'High Importance, Confidential' in its database list, which left Rat male by default. One of the many quirks of working with the Dhasha that Rat had grown used to.

"*Hostile ships are targeting our location in numbers too great for me to safely avoid,*" the Takki voice told her. "*Would you like me to divert back to Koliinaat, my lord?*"

Rat hesitated, her heart beginning to pound. The idea that she had just spent an entire rotation in transit on Mekkval's fastest courier ship, only to miss the attack by three days, left her feeling sick. "Can you get around them? All I need is for you to get low enough to drop me on the surface of the planet. I can scavenge whatever I need from there."

"Unfortunately, my lord, such an attempt only has a partial success rate of thirteen percent. Your safest option is to return home."

Rat knew that, but she also knew that she couldn't return to Mekkval without at least attempting her mission. To go back home now would be…unacceptable. Hell, Benva, who had tried to kill the three Dhasha that Mekkval had sent to keep him from going with her, would probably kill her himself, for the dishonor of her failure. Jreet were funny like that.

Still, she was a grounder, not a stick-jockey in the Space Force, and aerial battles unnerved her, especially when the ship's computer said they didn't have a chance in a Jreet hell of making it to the planet's surface.

"I need further instructions, my lord," the ship reminded her gently. *"We are half a tic from losing our lead and being blown apart."*

Half a…*tic?* The little hairs raised along Rat's spine. "Okay, uh, can you do evasive maneuvers for awhile to give me a chance to think?"

"I have been doing evasive maneuvers for the last six tics, my lord," the computer responded. *"My auto-targeting defense system is running out of diversionary bodies. I am unfortunately a courier ship, and not combat-capable, my lord. I am not equipped to handle sustained aggression."*

"Soot," Rat whispered. "Soot, soot, *soot!*" She bit her lip, realizing that it was now or never. She couldn't go back to Koliinaat. Even if she could slip past the Watcher, who was going to have a kill-on-sight alert out for her species, she couldn't face Mekkval or her team.

Unfortunately for Rat, when she was stuck in a hole, bored, waiting for a pickup, she often wondered which would be the worst way to die. And, despite daily dealings with psychotic Huouyt, volatile Jreet, and bloodthirsty Dhasha day in and day out, every time, she picked dying in a crash to be her least preferred method of worldly departure. On a ship, she was just a passenger. She had no *control*, absolutely no say in her demise. And, however quick and painless it might be, it was those blood-curdling seconds spinning towards the ground that she wasn't looking forward to.

Thus, it took all of Rat's willpower to say, "Get us on the ground. I'll take care of the rest."

"*These are Congressional blockade bots, my lord,*" the ship warned her. "*It is their* job *to keep us from getting on the ground.*" Even a Takki, Rat thought wryly, could be sarcastic, given the proper circumstances.

"Just do it," Rat said. "I'll take my chances."

"*As you command, my lord,*" the ship replied. "*If it pleases you, you may want to secure your body with the overhead restraints and put your head and arms into the crash sleeves, otherwise the impact might rip them off.*"

Rat swallowed, feeling sick. "This isn't going to be fun, is it?"

"*Not for you, my lord,*" the ship-Takki replied. Almost like it was... looking forward to it? Then, before Rat had a chance to think about that, the courier ship began a downward spin towards the atmosphere, using the tiny planet's gravity to veer away from their pursuers.

Seeing the world begin to twist around her on the viewscreen, Rat quickly closed her eyes and did as she was instructed.

Burning furg, she thought, her stomach crawling into her throat. *You are such a burning furg, Rat...*

An impact made the ship rumble, and Rat reflexively cried, "What was that?"

"*That was a Space Force explosive round hitting the hull, my lord,*" the ship explained to her patiently. "*It has ripped off the right side aero-gear and we no longer have any way of controlling spin. I can still get us to ground at a reasonable descent, but we will likely be spinning with enough force to rip the ship apart.*"

Rat swallowed, hard.

"*On the plus side,*" the ship went on cheerfully, "*there was no rupture to the crew capsule, so you will survive, at least until impact. From there, you have a twenty-two percent chance of being dismembered by the force.*"

Your odds of surviving, however, are at least thirty percent, as long as you can stop the bleeding before the government bots obliterate the wreckage."

Feeling sick, Rat reminded herself why she never asked AIs for damage reports.

Another blast rocked the ship, and Rat simply squeezed her eyes shut and pressed her forehead against the gel-like sleeve. All around her, the ship was making an awful, ear-splitting roar. Two more concussive blasts heralded the screaming of atmosphere against protrusions.

"Thirteen seconds to impact," the Takki voice told her after a moment. *"And we've only lost half the ship to enemy fire. This is going better than I expected."*

"Just get us down," Rat croaked. Even through the sleeve, she was feeling a breeze, which meant the hull had been penetrated, which meant she was now breathing alien air.

"Ten seconds.

Rat felt stupid—*stupid!*—for not putting on her biosuit the day before, when the thought had crossed her mind. She was going into a war-zone, and she knew it, but she wanted to sleep on the nice comfy couch for another day feeling the air against her skin before being forced to don her stuffy, clingy, non-breathing suit. After all, Congress had said it wasn't going to hit Earth for another three days.

"Ten seconds. Try not to stiffen up. That will only make the inevitable damages worse."

"Just land *us!"* Rat screamed.

"Five seconds," the ship said. *"I suggest you get away from the wreck-age as soon as possible."*

Rat tensed.

"The cockpit medkit," the ship politely reminded her, *"is on the wall to your left."*

An instant later, Rat's world exploded. The impact was loud enough to deafen her completely, leaving her ears ringing and blotting out all other sound. The hit itself was like taking a Dhasha's paw full to the chest, and she felt ribs crack. Her chair, though part of the ship itself, somehow dislodged and sent her rolling across the floor, breaking what seemed like every bone in her body. Rat shrieked as her left arm and one of her legs tangled under the chair and, as the ship had warned, tried to get themselves torn off.

As the debilitating wave of agony started pounding its way from her wounds and into her skull, Rat realized there were more explosions nearby. Ship weapons-fire, hitting other pieces of debris. She could recognize that sound anywhere, as she had more than once been on the receiving end. Panicking, now, she extracted her broken body from the harness and, on one knee and one arm, started dragging herself to the medkit in the wall. At least her spine was intact. Thank the Mothers for that.

Her broken leg was bleeding badly, and it took Rat a moment to realize she'd lost a finger on her left hand. More concussions were going off outside as her pursuers obliterated the remnants of her ship, this time rocking the twisted metal around her.

Realizing she didn't have time to go looking for her missing digit, Rat dove for the medkit. She didn't have time to use it, or to gather her supplies. *"Max!"* she screamed. *"Where are you?!"*

"I'm over here, Mistress. To your left." With the ship upside down, it took Rat a moment to orient herself and find her gun still safe in his wall-sheath. She retrieved him with shaking, bloody fingers and, with her medkit in her mouth, rifle sliding against the floor in her right hand, she started crawling towards the gaping hole in the side of the ship.

"You've sustained severe damages, Mistress," Max commented. *"Immediate medical attention advised."*

But Rat was concentrating on surviving the next few seconds. The bots were coming, she knew, and she *had* to get off the ship before they blew it away. *Please let me get off the ship,* Rat prayed, though she knew it was utterly hopeless—her end was coming just as soon as the bots found this last piece of wreckage. Still, her panicked mind chanted her prayer to the Dhasha gods anyway. *Mothers' golden scales, please just let me get off this ship.* At that point, with Death swinging down on her in the silvered gown of a cold, unemotional bot, she wanted, very much, to live.

She crawled through the exit, dragging her broken leg through the heated alien dirt, then out into the forest beyond.

She'd made it no more than two rods from the ship before an explosion tumbled her another seven, shrapnel, rocks, and trees gouging their marks in her skin. Rat groaned as she came to an abrupt rest against a tree, struggling with the tug of unconsciousness. She had fallen facing the ship, and she could see her plasma rifle lying halfway between her and the twisted silvery wreckage. In a moment of horror, she realized she had dropped her medkit.

Soot, she thought, fighting to stay conscious. Arms broken, legs broken, it was everything she could do just to lift her head a fraction of a ninth and look around her.

The medkit, being lighter, had flown farther afield from the blast. It had landed amongst a clump of boulders twenty digs from her, its waterproof black box now baking in the sun. Seeing that, knowing that she wasn't going to live without reaching it, Rat groaned and tried to take a mental tally of the damages. One arm was broken in several places, but the other was intact from the shoulder to the fore-arm. Of her legs, she had one that was still solid to the knee. She was pretty sure her nose and jaw were busted, and she either had a piece of scalp ripped away or one of the rocks had punctured her skull, because warm fluid was leaking down her neck, pooling along her spine.

She had to make it to the medkit. And, once there, she had to use it. On herself. Just the thought of such a momentous task almost made her give up and close her eyes. Almost. Then Rat remembered her mission, remembered her friend wallowing in his own filth, and knew she was his only hope for killing his demons and claiming vengeance.

Biting her lip against the agony everywhere, Rat started dragging herself with her elbow and knee, pushing through the alien grasses on her stomach, tackling the space a half-dig at a time.

It took the rest of the day. Every ninth was a grueling, dizzy, soul-searching ordeal. By the time Rat finally reached the medkit, she actually found herself staring at it for several minutes before her exhausted, pain-ridden mind finally realized she was looking at it.

Getting the box open was just as agonizing as physically dragging herself over to it. Her hands were useless. Using her teeth, her weight, and one shoulder, she managed to trigger the latch mechanism, then let out a sob of frustration when the contents spilled out over the ground from their rough handling. The nannite solution was intact, though, and by levering the vial in her weak, half-open palm and using her teeth to remove the cap and dip the needle, she actually managed to dose herself by then jabbing it into her bruised and blackened arm.

Utterly exhausted, Rat couldn't find the energy to re-cap the vial. She tried—she *wanted* to—but, as the nannites began working their magic, the pain that had been keeping her conscious quickly became a warm fuzz, and Rat lost herself to the void.

• • •

"Think she's dead?"

"Yeah, looks it," a young male voice said. "Look at that leg, man. No saving her."

"Hey, holy crap, look at this! You ever seen a gun like this?! Dude, this is like, what, a Congie gun, right?"

"Save that. We're gonna need it…"

• • •

No, Rat thought. *They're taking Max!*

Rat groaned and sat up in a panic, only to realize she was still holding the nannite vial in her hand and ended up spilling two thirds of it over the ground.

"Ash!" Rat cried, quickly capping it. "You ashing *furg*, Rat!" she screamed at herself, watching several hundred doses of life-saving bots vanish into the ground—bots that this planet wouldn't see for another Sacred Turn. "Mothers' talons, you are such a burning furg," she whispered to herself. With shaking fingers, she tucked it back into the medkit, the entirety of which the scavengers had left behind.

The *gun*! she remembered, horrified. Rat pushed herself up to her knees, only to find that one arm and one leg had healed improperly, due to her lack of proper bone-setting before dosing herself. Of her two arms, one of them barely even worked, having been bent underneath her when the healing began. The leg was much worse, the bone still protruding from her skin. The nanos there were an angry buzz of activity, trying to finish their 'chores,' only to be stymied by bones that weren't even within ninths of each other, so refused to knit.

Looking at the awkward bend in her forearm, Rat came to the sickening conclusion that she would have to re-break her arm long before she could go hunt down whomever had stolen her gun. And, considering that she had just spent almost an entire daylight-cycle sleeping, she needed to do it soon, if it already wasn't too late.

The idea of spending the rest of her short Earth-life as a cripple in the middle of a Space-Force-inspired apocalypse left Rat with a queasy feeling in her stomach. Willing to do anything to avoid that fate, Rat propped herself up until she could put her twisted forearm between two of the boulders in the outcropping behind her, then, with a gut-deep yell to encourage herself, slammed it sideways with as much force as she could manage.

The recently-knitted bone snapped free again, and this time Rat screamed and bent over with the pain, the shrieking agony in her arm leaving her gasping, just trying to stay conscious. She panted for several moments, unable to see through the tears. Slowly, she pulled herself upright, then, with trembling fingers, uncapped the nannite tube, dipped the needle into the silvery solution in the bottom, then jammed it into her arm near the wound and dosed herself again.

Then, before the nannites had a chance to run their course, she propped the foot of her un-healed leg into a crack between a boulder and a tree, then, as adrenaline surges spiked lines of acid through her veins, pulled her leg straight.

She held it in place for as long as she could before she flopped back onto her back and stared up at the orangish sky. Orangish, she realized, from smoke. The whole world, it seemed, was on fire.

And the first thing I did upon getting here was crash my ship, lose Max, and dump my nanos on the ground, she thought, disgusted with herself.

She stayed on her back as long as she dared—it was a general rule not to put much pressure on nannite-knitted bones for at least two Standard days—but eventually, Max called to her. It was a sleek, rugged, AI-embedded, Huouyt-made sniper's weapon, one that she had never worked up the courage to ask Mekkval how much it had originally cost him. All she knew was that a Sui'ezi Rodemax was worth more than most people's lives, to those who could use it.

She was definitely *not* going to lose it to a bunch of thieving Human furgs.

Hobbling to her feet, putting as much pressure as she dared on her freshly-healed leg, and the rest on her one-and-a-half-days-healed leg, Rat started looking for signs of their passing.

It wasn't hard to find. The furgs were like Hebbut in mating season, thundering around without any regard whatsoever to the placement of their feet.

Deciding that she was dealing with amateurs, and therefore that she could take a few more minutes to root through the rubble, Rat went looking for her biosuit.

Her suit, along with four-fifths of the ship, was a charred, crispy plate of fused nannites.

"Ash," she whispered, dropping it back to the ground. No weapon, no food, no suit…

The weapon, at least, she could handle. Rat snatched up the med-kit, then started searching the rubble for her pack of supplies. Her pack, having been in the cockpit, was less damaged than the rest of her gear, and inside, she found a combat knife and its corresponding leg-strap. She found a relatively unscathed canister of rations under one of the pieces of shrapnel, but she only took a couple, unwilling to put any more weight on her leg than she needed to. The guns, however, had all become unsalvageable parts of the wreckage, most of their energy-packs having exploded and fused to the ruvmestin-laced hull.

Still, she had a knife. She strapped its sheath to her thigh and immediately felt better about her lot in life. Going unarmed on an alien planet was…unacceptable.

So was going without Max. She'd been with him too long, sadistic bastard that he was, to give him up now. Leg throbbing with every step, Rat hefted her pack over her back and started after the furgs who had run away with her favorite gun.

9

S.H.A.E.L.

Shael opened his eyes, realizing the light inside his bed had gone dark, the voices and images having stopped. He was, he realized, hungry.

Gingerly, Shael tried to lift his hands, but, as always, they were locked into place. "Why am I still here?" he demanded. "Give me my melaa and let me take a piss, you skulking cowards!"

Doctorphilip, the only one of the weakling bipeds who could speak his language, did not respond. His bed remained dark, the images withdrawn, the voices silent. Outside his bed, Shael heard nothing.

Locked into place so that his powerful body wouldn't destroy their insignificant dwelling with any twitchings in his sleep, Shael's heart nonetheless began to pound. It was abnormal, being left in the darkness. Not once, in all his turns with the weaklings, did they forget to feed him. "How *dare* you leave me here?!" he snapped. "I'll make you all dance on my tek for ignoring me, you soot-eating furgs."

The threat evoked not a single sound from the room beyond his bed. In a growing fury, he yanked on his arms to break the restraints that held him in place. Despite his great strength, however, the metal sheaths remained solidly attached to his massive wrists.

"Quivering Takki!" he screamed. "Release me!"

More time passed. Too much time. No matter how Shael called or fought his bed, his caretakers ignored him. Eventually, Shael had to piss himself.

It was the shame of the hot liquid running from his bladder to pool under his coils that flipped a switch in Shael's mind. He, the greatest warrior of Welu, had been forced to lie in his own piss like a penned Takki. Letting out a scream, he slipped into his war-mind and watched the world around him shift. Everything, even the air, became a foggy blue-green stew of motion.

Shael wrapped a mental wall around the sea-green motion of the bed-cocoon's husk, and, with a squeeze of his consciousness, crushed it, compacting it above him with a scream of tearing metal and puny electronics. Because that wasn't terrifying enough for the inbred Takki to take a proper lesson from their superior—and because he was angry—Shael slammed the shattered lid of his bed across the room, through the concrete wall that separated his room from others, and into the bedrock of the mountain on the other side. Though he didn't see it with his eyes, his war-mind had a complete, 360-degree view, as far as he wanted to go in any direction, and he watched the foggy particles of air slip around the heavier movement of the door until it finally came to a rest embedded in the mountainside.

"Show yourselves, skulkers!" Shael snarled. Surrounding the heavy density of the cuffs with his mind, he formed a barrier between his wrist and the metal, then wrenched upwards, easily tearing them free. "Come out of the shadows you're hiding in and face me!"

The cowards left him in darkness.

Of course they did. Any skulking fool like Doctorphilip would know that he was soon to dangle from his tek for the slight. Even then, Shael's coils were prickling into hard bumps where the air hit his cooling piss.

"*Face me!*" Shael screamed. This time, he wrapped his mind around his bed and hurled it through the front door, which Doctorphilip kept locked to keep lesser creatures from wandering upon Shael and wasting his air. There was a resounding crash as his bed disintegrated upon impact with the solid stone wall on the other side, but other than that, there were no challenges, no movement in the corridor whatsoever.

The skulkers were…hiding?

The door open and the hallway outside exposed, Shael saw none of the weaklings in his war-mind. When he extended his awareness outward, seeking the furg who would dance on his tek for leaving him there, everything felt…deserted. The only life he could see in the maze of tunnels nearby was a cluster of soft-skinned weaklings like Doctorphilip who were even then spiraling the foggy green air away from their mouths in panting whimpers of terror as they huddled together in the dark.

Frowning, Shael slid through the door and up the hallway, shoving softly glowing green particles aside with his body, using his war-mind to guide him in the total blackness. He found the group of weaklings huddled by the war-room, staring at the door in panic. Shael snorted and wove past them. More cowards.

"Doctorphilip!" he shouted into the hall ahead of him, making the weaklings at his back cringe and whimper. Shael ignored them. "Come out and face me! You die today, skulker!"

If Doctorphilip heard him, he did not respond. Of course not. Like all the quibbling, sticky furgs who lived on this miserable planet, he was a coward at heart. Shael again regretted ever taking up the task to train them. He had sworn, on his honor, he would give these furgs the tools they needed to have a fighting chance in the Army. Yet, he had done much less fighting than he had sleeping, and the furg Doctorphilip didn't seem to care that Shael hadn't been given a chance to do his duty and teach his underlings yet. What was worse, every time Shael brought up the fact he hadn't done any training of his assigned weaklings, Doctorphilip would tell him 'tomorrow' or that his underlings were out on a training exercise in tunnels much too small for Shael's massive coils. Then he would feed him and send him to bed. Like a hatchling.

Scowling, Shael glanced back the way he had come. He *was* hungry, he reminded himself, and his servants had always delivered his melaa to his room. If he wasn't in his room when the lazy aliens decided to get off their coils and bring him food, he might miss it entirely...

No, Shael decided, *I will find my own food. I'm tired of their incompetence.*

He had been begged by the Black Jreet herself to teach these useless furgs battle tactics and the basic code of a warrior, but thus far, he had spent more time in his bed than actually instructing his subordinates. For untold twists of the Coil, they had intentionally delayed their training. They had fed him and kept him happy. Satiated him. Lied to him. *Procrastinated.* Shael found himself tired of the planet and its tiny, soft, *stupid* inhabitants. It was time for him to go back to Welu.

And, right there, he decided he was done trying to train furgs who skulked in the shadows, hiding from him, avoiding their assemblies, quietly trying to fatten up their commander so he would be too corpulent to stake them all for their ineptitude.

As such, Shael started stalking up the hall, looking for the exit.

After many convoluted turns through the twisted maze his weakling underlings had given to him to oversee, Shael found another group of softling furgs huddled by the exit, staring with wide, terrified eyes at the outside, a barrier of broken glass between them and the open air. They saw him approach from the shadows of the corridor, noticed the fury in their commander's face, and huddled in on themselves in panic, blubbering like melaa. Shael snorted and moved past them, too.

He had made it several digs before he realized the glass was cutting through his scales.

Confused, Shael glanced down at his coils.

The normal red of his powerful body had been replaced by a soft, fleshy pink. Something seemed to twist in Shael's mind as he stared down at himself, a connection that burned as he tried to make sense of it. It took Shael several long moments of staring before he realized what had been done to him.

The cowards de-scaled me?! His chest clenched so hard it hurt. Beneath his coils, crimson blood began to seep into the glass. Yet his body, now soft and pink, bore the truth of the horror.

They had descaled him in his sleep. *Descaled* him. Heart hammering, Shael reached up to his chest, trying to find the tek sheathe between the large, fleshy lumps that had been revealed by the descaling. His tek's sheath, too, had been sewn shut, his fingers not even finding the opening.

I'll kill them all, Shael thought, horror mingling with shame. No wonder they had left him in his bed and fled. One of the deserters had defiled him. Of *course* they would run. They rightly feared his wrath.

"By the graves of my ancestors," Shael swore, watching his blood leak out to slowly puddle between the glass shards, "I will gather my clan and hunt down every weakling who ran from me this day and hang their teks and their children's teks to dry upon my wall." He turned to glance behind him at the soft-bodied skulkers. They had made no move to run like the others, and he recognized none of their faces, so he decided to let them live. Scowling, he turned back to the exit and kept moving. More glass punctured his coils, but he ignored it. A warrior could withstand pain.

Once he was out in the light, Shael hesitated. He peered up at the alien sky, curious at the odd yellow ball. On Welu, the skies were constantly writhing with green, blue, red, pink, and yellow strands of color, even during the daylight. Here, it was just a solid blue, with what appeared to be a sliver of a moon or nearby planet in the distance. Odd, how he couldn't remember seeing anything similar to this upon his arrival on the planet.

Again, his mind began to heat and buzz uncomfortably, the headache that followed quickly forcing him to focus on other thoughts. Shael needed a ship. He'd wasted enough time with these soft-bodied weaklings. They were too useless to learn the ways of the Jreet. One could sooner haul a melaa from its herd and slap a spear between its jaws than teach these tiny, ignorant bipeds anything about war.

Shael set out across the textured flat stone, seeking a skimmer that could take him to a spaceport. It was time for him to go home.

There were plenty of skimmers laid out on the square of stone, interspersed between primitive alien land-going vehicles, but none of them would respond to Shael's commands. It appeared that the skulkers here were afraid of theft, something that was a staking offense on Welu. Even Shael, having been descaled and his tek disabled by those he had counted as his allies, would have paid a spaceport attendant to return the skimmer to where he found it once he was done with it.

Frustrated, Shael set off along the alien pathway, scanning the thin vegetation on either side for any hint as to where the spaceport would be located. The sporadic undergrowth, tiny trees, and dry grasses were nothing like the thick, vibrant, life-sustaining vegetation of Welu's great swamps and jungles. His snout twisted with disgust. The furgs must have been desperate to live in an ugly, barren place like this.

He continued down the dirt path until he reached another section of flat stone, this one stretching as far as the eye could see in either direction. Shael hesitated, not knowing enough about this miserable planet to pick the proper direction to the spaceport. He glanced at the sky, expecting some sort of traffic overhead, but the place seemed oddly empty…almost *lifeless*. Shael's scale-pores tightened as he realized he could hear nothing but alien pests and the wind.

Where is *everyone?* he thought, confused. This was supposed to be a great empire, one with massive militaries and incredible commerce, yet as Shael stood there in the middle of their road, staring at their sky, he saw *nothing*.

Faced with such alien terrain, such *silence*, Shael supposed he could go back and wait for his less craven subordinates to return and pay for their brethren's betrayal with a ride to the spaceport. Perhaps they would even bring him food.

Ruled by your stomach like a Takki, he thought, disgusted at his weakness. Still, it had been some time since his servants had fed him last. His great body felt almost…weak.

When he looked behind him at the way he had come, Shael saw that the entrance to his training facility had been sunk into a mountainside. Leading up to it were patches of glistening red where Shael had passed. The color seemed odd to him. He had bled before, and it had always been blue. Again, he felt that painful heat in his head as he tried to assimilate what he was seeing with what he knew. It didn't make *sense*. How did one's blood go from being blue to being red? It took him some time, this time, to make the connection.

Drugs, he realized, making the painful heat clear immediately. Perhaps his betrayers had injected him with some alien drug, something that had altered his perceptions to better their escape.

Cowards, Shael thought, with a rising fury. He had always known they had been afraid of him. It had been in their looks, their flinches whenever Doctorphilip came to feed him. And, sure enough, not one of his underlings had shown his face since he had discovered their treachery.

He glanced back at the wide swath of primitive stone roadway. On undeveloped alien worlds, roads led to settlements, and settlements had food. Shael, whose stomach was even then spasming in hunger, his body growing dizzy with need, decided that only a Voran would skulk around in a cave, waiting for his underlings to feed him. Thus, he decided he would feed himself, and should any of the primitive landowners object, he would simply kill them as blood-debt to their betrayer weakling cousins. At this point, *all* the skulkers were accountable.

Shael's coils started to burn the longer he slid along the alien roadway, until, despite his natural Jreet immunity to all but extreme heat, his wounded undersides began to blister. The bleeding, despite his body's normally rapid healing, had not slowed. Worse, he was having great pain in his abdomen, and when he looked down, there was blood running down his coils from some unknown wound in his guts.

They poisoned me, Shael thought, disgusted. He was actually beginning to have trouble staying upright, his perception zoning in and out of his war-mind as he found himself having more and more trouble concentrating.

Eventually, as the sun hit its zenith in the horridly bright alien day, Shael fell out of his war-mind altogether. His skin, scaleless for the first time in his life, felt much too hot, its pale color transformed to an almost red. He stumbled into the shade, stunned that he was forced to.

They made me weak, he thought, his fury overriding even his exhaustion. The sun, the glass, the stone—none of it should have affected him in his normal state. Yet here he was, hiding in the shadows like a vaghi skulker, panting like an overworked Takki.

He was coiled in the shade, trying desperately to stay conscious, when he heard the voices of weaklings along the road. He sat up, realizing this was his chance to get directions—and maybe a ride—to a spaceport.

Three weaklings were approaching, striding down the center of the roadway, carrying backpacks and bristling with primitive weaponry. They had odd slouches and swaggers to their walk, nothing at all like Doctorphilip, and Shael realized these might be this planet's warrior class.

"I am Shael ga Welu," he announced, struggling upright. "Prince of Welu, leader of the Clan Welu. On the name of my ancestors, I offer you trade with my clan and two-nines standard ruvmestin coins for transportation to Welu." He had to steady himself on a flimsy alien tree to fight the sudden dizziness that came with rising.

The three soft, delicate, cloth-covered aliens stopped in the road and stood there, staring at his great body like furgs seeing an Ooreiki temple for the first time. One of them turned to his friends and said something that sounded much like the foul tongue of Shael's treacherous underlings, which sparked a new wave of fury in his soul. *They mock me*, he thought, remembering his lack of scales. He had to fight the instinct to kill them for the slight.

"Welu?" the darker one said. Then they babbled something to themselves and two of them laughed. The darker one pointed at

Shael. "Welu?" The weakling then pointed at himself, grinning ear to ear. "Mahs-terr."

The useless furg wanted to exchange pleasantries. Shael could tell by the imbecilic smiles on their faces, however, that their simple minds were overwhelmed at the idea of a great Welu prince deigning to talk to them. Because it was all he could do not to wrap one of them in his coils as a lesson to the others, Shael grated, "Yes. I want to go to Welu. You will be paid well for your services."

The furgs laughed some more. One of the larger ones shook his head and jabbered something in the pathetic softling tongue, then jabbed a thumb at himself and said, "Mas-ter."

"Take me to a spaceport, Mahster," Shael snarled, fed up with their stalling, "or you shall feel the wrath of my coils before your eyes burst from your oily, useless head for the wrongs that your brethren did to me."

The three underlings snickered and glanced at each other. As Shael stood there in growing rage, one of them pointed at him and laughed something in the alien tongue. The other two cackled like Ueshi on karwiq bulbs.

Fury burning in the core of his tek, Shael lashed out and put his fist around the closest alien's neck, intending to heave him off the ground and throw him into the forest to educate his mindless friends. "Prepare for your journey through the ninety hells, weakling," he snarled. He heaved.

The alien remained firmly in place. And, oddly, Shael found himself looking *up* at the aliens, almost as if they had grown larger by his getting closer.

What treachery is this? Shael's panicked mind cried. He tried to remember some alien that could change form, alter its size. All he could come up with was the Huouyt, who could only produce a body of equal mass or less. Nothing, as far as he knew, could *grow*.

Even more disturbing, the now-giant alien took hold of his hand and wrenched it from his throat as easily as if Shael were a stunted hatchling. The weakling's glacial blue eyes—bigger than a Jreet's, more suited to the crude hunter-gatherer lifestyle of their ancestors—were like twin chips of ice in his face as he grabbed both of Shael's hands and jerked them in front of him, then pulled him close and leaned down to speak his linguistic dirt into his face. There was no mistaking the malice in the creature's cold tone, despite the fact that Shael could not understand their filthy tongue.

Shael snorted. "You *threaten* me?" He attempted to jerk his hands free, but the drugs his betrayers had fed him had left him too weak to hurl the lesser creature away from him. Grinning, showing his crooked, flat teeth, his assailant wrapped his big hand—bigger than Shael's, he realized in horror—around his wrists and started pulling something out of his pocket, laughing with his fellows.

Upon seeing the rope, Shael stared at it, uncomprehending. When it became clear that they intended to use the flimsy strands on *him*, Shael just laughed. "Only a furg would be stupid enough to bind a Jreet warrior," he declared.

If the vaghi understood him or cared, they made no sign. Instead, they wrenched his arms behind his back and Shael felt the sharp bite of ropes digging into his scaleless skin…

• • •

Almost a rotation after the Ooreiki asher running the Space Force decided to open up on Earth three days early, Joe woke with the weird urge to go north when he had originally been planning to head west, towards San Diego. He packed up the remnants of his latest kill—the near-rancid hindquarters of a feral animal that he was pretty sure had been a pig—and went west, anyway, because the cities collected kreenit, and there were reports of at least six females digging dens along the ocean.

Joe had made it about twenty digs when he remembered what happened the last time he was in San Diego. Four sootwad furgs had taken one look at his Congie blacks, saw his high-tech weaponry, realized they couldn't take it from him, and spat on him, instead. This while Joe had been smiling, his hand out in the typical North

American Earth greeting, another dead kreenit twitching on the ground behind him.

Still marching west, Joe stopped in his tracks.

In the rotation since he'd landed, Joe had killed twenty-two kreenit. More than any man had a right to kill, and yet just a drop in the bucket compared to how many had been left on Earth. Or how many would be born the moment all those pregnant kreenit had their young, thoughtfully inseminated en-route by overzealous Congie Peacemakers. It was a thankless, endless battle, and he was growing damned tired of it.

He glanced west. Plenty more kreenit out there, waiting to meet Jane. Plenty of people to save. Plenty of furgs to spit on him and curse him as if Congies were responsible for Earth's current Takkiscrew.

He glanced north.

Joe had no idea what was due north. It was mountainous, looked wild, and it hadn't been in his carefully-thought-out plan to spend the rest of his life crisscrossing the North American continent with the love of his life attached to his hip. He'd planned to do a rough half circle, starting with San Francisco, following the coast down to Mexico City, then doubling back through Dallas, and finally taking the coast up and ending with New York City. He figured that's about as long as he could hope to live before he grew too old to fight, and the coasts always had the biggest cities.

But Humans, ungrateful furglings that they were, wouldn't care if he killed ten kreenit or ten thousand kreenit. Joe had quickly discovered that they thought the only good Congie was a dead Congie, and, in an entire *rotation*, Joe hadn't met a single Earthling that hadn't tried to A) kill him, B) spit on him, or C) tell him to go back home.

It was right then that Joe stopped and kind of blinked, realizing he'd been mopping up Earth's mess for the last rotation, to absolutely no fanfare or any sort of gratitude. Remembering the hateful stares of the men and women he had just saved, telling him to get off their planet, Joe decided that the Human race could afford to spend a few turns rolling in its own flake while he explored.

Thus, Joe was heading *north*, bristling with weapons, about to tackle the necessary evil of crossing a road, when he heard the raucous laughter of several men—as well as a woman's indignant screams—and sighed. He knew the routine. He'd busted up dozens of such parties since Judgement, and it was beginning to wear on him. The females of this planet, raised with pillows and primping and perfumes, had no recourse when the lowlife scumbags, suddenly free of all the rules and restrictions of society, started doing things like forming 'tribes,' 'claiming' women and taking 'slaves.'

Tugging Jane off his belt, he went to investigate.

Around the bend in the road, two tall white men and their tawny-skinned, shorter male companion were standing out in the open on the sunbaked asphalt, shoving a small, naked woman back and forth between them as she stumbled and screamed in terror. They'd shaved the poor girl's hair to the scalp, removed every fiber of her clothes, and bound her hands behind her back, obviously in yet another bid to start up a slave trade with what was left of the dwindling Human race. Joe sighed and approached through the brush, staying out of sight of the three thugs.

Upon getting close enough to see the woman's fierce expression, however, Joe did a double take. No, he thought, seeing her bared teeth, lips raised in a snarl, the utterly savage look on her face, he was pretty sure that was *fury*, not fear. His heart actually gave a startled thump, having seen similar ferociousness in wild Dreit right before they ripped men in half.

On the road, the three men laughed as they manhandled their prize. "No, *I'm* not gonna do her." *Shove.* "She's bleedin', man. *You* do her. I get the next one."

"She's hairy as my mother's poodle," the Hispanic snorted. "To hell with that. *You* do her." Shove.

His other Caucasian friend laughed. "And let her bite me? Dude, she took a chunk outta your *ear*, man. Fuck that shit." *Shove.*

Joe sighed and raised Jane to take aim. He was about to put a blast through something essential when a string of invectives stopped him dead in his tracks, making his hair stand utterly on end.

"Sniveling Takki skulkers!" the woman shrieked. "I'll make you all dance on my tek like the craven weaklings you are! Release me! Fight like warriors, you scaleless alien filth! Were your mothers impregnated with the shit of Takki? *Fight me!*" The words sounded old, very old, and it took Joe a moment to understand why.

When he did, his heart gave a startled thump, then stopped entirely.

She's speaking ancient Jreet, he thought, stunned. His plasma pistol lowered another few inches as he stared. How he knew that—or how he knew it was Welu by the odd lisp of some of her softer consonants—left him just as disconcerted as the way the words seemed to be rolling off her tongue as if they belonged to her.

...kind of like Joe.

"She acts rabid," the Hispanic man was saying. He shoved her back to the others. He'd already been bitten at least once, and he was holding a hand to the side of his bloody face. When they tried to shove her back to him, he held up a crimson palm. "Dude, she's not worth our time. Gotta be some foreigner or something. Maybe some mail-order bride that escaped, you know? Doesn't understand a word we're saying. We should leave her."

"I want my rope back," the wiry man in the middle growled. "That's *military grade*. High-tech Congie stuff. I'm not leaving it with her."

"Fine, man," the Hispanic said. He shoved the girl back to him so hard she fell to her bruised and bloody knees. "But you want the rope, *you* untie her." He took a pointed step backwards.

From the ground, the tiny woman screamed, "I will hunt down your ancestors and shit on their graves!" Again, in ancient Jreet. She struggled to get back to her feet.

The tall Caucasian man behind her grabbed her shoulder and shoved her back down. "Fine. You guys don't want her, there's better pickings out there. The wicked little she-bitch doesn't need to live." Then he grabbed the projectile gun on his hip and placed the old steel barrel to the back of her head. The woman, oblivious, kept cursing his manhood and his heritage.

The click of the hammer cocking broke Joe out of his shock. Even as the man's finger was starting to squeeze, he surged out of the trees, caught the shooter by the elbow and shoved the gun away from the girl's head. As the gun went off in reflex, startling everyone, Joe broke the man's arm, then his wrist, then his fingers as he twisted the gun in his hand. Then he swiveled, threw the man over his shoulder, brought a heel down on his throat, and, as his blue eyes were going wide and he started to choke, put one of Jane's wayward children through his skull, disintegrating the upper half of his head into the pavement.

As the dead man's two thuggish friends were recovering enough to scream and stumble backwards, Joe casually raised the gun over the woman's head to level on them. He was well aware that he wasn't even breaking a sweat, and, dressed in the all-black, alien attire of a Congie, he might as well have been a Huouyt assassin to the two furgs in front of them. They stared at him like he was a demon from the Jreet hells.

Into the silence, Joe said, "I know you two have the mental density of a furgling fart," he hesitated, leveling Jane on their faces individually, "but I'll put this into terms you can understand. You're going to run. The one who does that the fastest lives. The other one, the *slower* one, I'm going to shoot, skin, and use his hide for a new belt. Ready? Go."

The two men—boys, really—bolted, throwing each other to the ground as they each tried to escape faster than their companion, taking completely different directions in their bid for survival.

Sighing, Joe waited until he could no longer hear their frantic feet rushing through the undergrowth, then lowered Jane. "You okay there, sister?" He, unfortunately, did not know how to flip his odd Jreet habit on, so all he could do was give her soothing gestures and sounds in Congie.

The woman twisted to scowl up at him, a spreading bruise swelling one eye shut making it clear that someone had punched her in the face. Joe gave her a commiserating grin. "Sorry I couldn't get here faster."

In a sneer of complete disdain, the woman said in perfect Welu Jreet, "I'm going to return with my clan and *annihilate* this pitiful shithole."

"Yeah," Joe said, squatting beside her. "Sorry about the ashbags. Lemme see how bad they hit you..." He reached for her face.

The wounded girl lunged up, drove her head into his chest, knocked him backwards on his ass, then, with a rabid snarl, she sank her teeth into his hand like a Jreet sinking his fangs into a steak.

"Ow, *burn*, ow!" Joe shouted, recoiling from her. "Let go. Let *go!*" Despite Joe's repeated, desperate tugging, however, she held on like a Dhasha hatchling with its first meal, falling backwards onto the asphalt to get better leverage. Then, to his horror, she started to ragdoll his hand like she wanted to tear it off. As she did so, she began jamming a foot into his abdomen, probably seeking his nuts.

Joe had to kick her violently away from him to get his hand out of her mouth, then he clambered backwards and blinked down at the puncture-marks she had put into his poly-nannite gloves, panting. The only reason he hadn't lost fingers was the sleek black Congie technology, which was even then sealing the wounds she had put into it.

Unfortunately, the same could not be said about his hand. He could feel it throbbing underneath the glove, warm wetness oozing against his skin.

The woman was getting back on her knees, licking his blood off her lips. With a fearsome crimson grin, said, "Next time your heart, skulker." Again, in perfect Welu Jreet.

The insult, combined with his wounded hand, combined with the woman who was now licking his *blood* off her *lips*, sent a jolt of adrenaline burning through Joe's system that left him somewhere between rage and panic. "I just saved your *life!*" he cried, pointing at the headless man sprawled on the asphalt, broken fingers still tangled in his primitive gun.

Instead of repenting and apologizing, the woman sneered and slowly looked him up and down as if he had suddenly and liberally covered himself in shit. "A Voran."

"No, I'm a…" Then Joe realized he was, indeed, speaking Voran Jreet. Because he really didn't have a comeback for that, he said, "I'm going to free you. That's it, okay? Sisters' bloody teks."

She continued to look at him as if he were dressed in his own filth. "I don't need a Voran's help. Go back to twining your hatch-mates." She stood regally and started to walk away, arms still tied securely behind her back with that handy Congie deathline—'death' line, because, once a good knot was tied, your enemy was gonna starve to death before he ever went anywhere.

Joe narrowed his eyes. She obviously had a few screws loose, possibly was even carrying some sort of weird Earth disease. Logic dictated that he should let her trundle off to die. Joe, however, was pissed. She'd *bit* him. With his much longer legs, he stalked ahead of the woman and stopped in her path, giving her the choice of halting or falling flat on her much smaller ass as she barreled into him.

She stopped, scowling at the body-armor covering his chest as if she was wondering if she could bite through it, too. Glaring down at her, Joe said, "I just saved your life. The *least* you could do is not burning bite me while I free your damn hands."

In reply, the woman dropped into a crouch on the asphalt and grinned up at him with predatory challenge.

Meeting that feral gaze, listening to her animal snarl, Joe felt his heart give a painful hammer. She was, he realized, not acting Human. Seeing that, what he *wanted* to do was grab his stuff and ditch her there, her teeth bared like she wanted to sink her canines into his throat. But, because his mother had always said he was a good guy, if a bit of a dumbshit, and because leaving the girl with her hands tied was a death sentence, and—most of all—because God hated a coward, Joe decided to help her out.

"Don't bite me," Joe growled, scowling at her.

She snarled back, emerald eyes filled with a mingling of disdain and challenge. She looked, quite frankly, like some wild, vicious alien that Joe had spent most of his life killing.

"Don't," he warned.

When she just continued to show her bloody teeth like a feral thing, Joe approached with the intent of again squatting beside her and freeing her hands.

Before he could get all the way down, she lunged up and attempted to slam her forehead head into his. Though her much smaller head impacting his cranium wouldn't have knocked him cold, Joe's startled upward lunge to avoid her, followed by his stumble over the dead man's leg, followed by his long downward arc terminating in the back of his skull hitting the asphalt, did.

The last thing he saw before he hit the ground was the woman's satisfied smirk as she stood and started sauntering off in the direction of her would-be assailants.

• • •

When Joe woke, he was pissed. No, *beyond* pissed. Fuming. Not only had the woman bit him, headbutted him, tried to crush the family jewels, and left him to bake in the California sun, but she'd left *Jane* to bake in the California sun, exposed on the abandoned highway for any drooling furg with a gun fetish to wander along and take for himself, and that was sacrilege.

And all this after Joe had *rescued* the jenfurgling woman. All he'd tried to do was *help* her.

What was worse, Joe still didn't know how the naked furg spoke Jreet. And she had insulted him. And she seemed completely oblivious to the fact he'd saved her life—not even a damn thank-you! Joe scowled in the direction she'd taken, her bloody footprints browning on the asphalt.

He *could* have walked away; she hadn't taken any of his stuff. In fact, the rabid furgling had left all of his gear right there in the middle of the street, like she didn't even want or need survival supplies, meat, emergency rations, body armor, spare clothes...Yes, he definitely could have walked away.

But she had bit him. And she'd mistreated Jane. That was unacceptable.

Ready to go to war, Joe snagged up the dead man's gun, added it to his growing collection, and followed her. He found her naked, sun-broiled body face-down on the asphalt after a thirty minute jog, her naked back exposed to the sky. The furg woman hadn't even had the brains to get out of the sun.

For a minute, Joe thought she was dead, and he experienced a weird pang of regret as he looked at her motionless body. Almost like he'd missed an important debriefing or forgotten to take his allotted leave. Then, as his eyes settled on the strange barcode—barcode??—tattooed into her neck, he also noticed the shallow rise and fall of her shoulders against the hot tar.

Again, Joe realized he could have left her there. His hand still throbbed where she'd bit him, and he was going to have to administer nanos to himself that night if his head didn't stop spinning from where she had introduced it to the pavement. Besides, it wasn't like he hadn't seen a million other women die in his lifetime. Good women, ones that *didn't* bite or leave him to die on the tarmac. What was the life of one tiny, utterly crazy chick back on Earth?

Yet Joe couldn't get over the fact she'd called him a skulker. In perfect Welu Jreet. And he'd understood it. Not even Daviin, in his crude, misguided attempts to sober him up, had called him a skulker. It was one of the worst one-word insults in the Jreet language, used only on creatures that could never, in a million years, be considered warriors, and for some reason, coming from *her* lips, after he'd broken a guy's wrist to save her, it really, *really* pissed him off.

This time, when Joe got down to untie her, she never stirred. He yanked the knots loose first—her hands were starting to darken dangerously where the furgs had cut off circulation—then coiled the rope and tucked it into his backpack. Then, after nudging her with a foot to make sure she wouldn't leap up and attack him again, he bent down, threw her unconscious body over his shoulder, and went looking for some shade.

Though Joe generally avoided houses as resting-places due to the way kreenit habitually liked to rip them open to get to the morsels inside, the girl was obviously in need of clothes and some bed-rest. He found a small, inconspicuous house tucked amidst a couple hills, a shattered wooden pen of weed-ridden, trampled dirt all that remained of some unknown domestic animal. Humans, Joe realized, his fingers tracing the massive claw-marks in one of the shattered fence posts, were going to have a damn hard time making a comeback. If any domesticated animals actually survived the hunger of their keepers, with kreenit around, raising livestock was like painting a bulls-eye on your back. Within a few more rotations, Humanity would be, quite literally, back to its hunter-gatherer days.

Unlike the pen, however, the house had survived relatively unscathed. It seemed as though whatever the kreenit had eaten inside the fence had satiated it enough that it had only knocked down one corner as an afterthought, leaving the rest of the well-built old farmhouse still standing. Lowering the girl to the ground in the grass, Joe got out his heat-imaging binoculars and took a look at the building itself.

Though he could see several rats chewing away at something in the downstairs closet, there were no tell-tale red blobs of a Human presence. Returning his binoculars to his pack, he once more shouldered the girl and started toward the house.

Entering through the gaping hole beside the kitchen, Joe paused on the tile floor and listened. Hearing nothing but the skitter of rats beside the stove, smelling nothing but rancid lard, he went upstairs looking for a bed.

The first room at the top of the stairs had six sleeping bags laid out in haphazard disarray on the floor, with rudimentary survival gear scattered around each bag. The far side of the room was open to the air, the wall missing where something huge had lunged through it.

Seeing the brown stains spattering the room, Joe grimaced. Apparently, the penned animal hadn't been the only thing the kreenit had snacked on.

In the next room over, it was the same—a big band had stopped here, possibly as many as two dozen—and the floors of every room were covered in sleeping bags, the wall dismantled, every surface covered in dried blood.

It attacked in their sleep, Joe thought, with a grimace. Another reason why he avoided abandoned houses like the plague. Once you were inside, there was nowhere to run…

In a bedroom on the opposite end of the house—the end of the house still standing—Joe found a bed that looked cleaner than the rest and lowered the woman into it. First, he treated her sunburn, reluctantly administering a good portion of his topical nannite cream. Then he went about finding her some clothes. He avoided the greasy, flea-ridden belongings of the unlucky band and focused on the relatively unscathed storage closet in a nearby bedroom. From what he could find in the mothball-smelling dresser drawers, the house had belonged to a really *skinny* old man and his similarly old, but very fat, companion. Joe grabbed a few sets of the old man's clothes, figuring too tall would be better than falling completely off, sliced off the bottoms of the legs, the arms, and the hem of the shirt, then fitted the clothes over the woman's body as she dozed.

After he'd gotten her pants on, he paused. The girl's feet, it seemed, were still oozing pus and blood from wounds that looked a hell of a lot worse than she could have done running over a few sticks to escape her captors. Frowning, he pulled out his flashlight to get a better look. He thought the first translucent sliver was a piece of plastic clinging to her sole until it pricked his hand when he tried to get a grip on it.

Glass? He grunted with surprise. She must have walked several *lengths* with glass embedded in her feet. That was…odd.

Even odder was the barcode he had found on the back of her neck. Once he'd picked the glass from her feet and sealed up the wounds with nanotape, he rolled her onto her side to get a better look. It wasn't an angsty, for-fun tattoo, either. It was an expensive government gene-mod, the cells producing their own jet-black pigment, much like the glowing PlanOps tattoo on his left hand. Curious, now, Joe pulled out his blackmarket PPU and scanned it.

The barcode read: S.H.A.E.L. v.2.0.6

Seeing that, Joe had the gut-twisting horror that he was dealing with some sort of cyborg. Carefully, so as not to disturb her, he started checking telltale signs—pulling her lips back to check the gumline for metal, prying underneath the nails to look for dataports, pulling back the ears to check for transmitters, massaging the stomach to feel for hard machinery.

Nothing. To all appearances, he was dealing with a perfectly healthy Human girl, maybe twenty turns old, shaved head, vivid green eyes, bad attitude.

When Joe looked again at the tattoo, he noticed a discoloration on her neck, beneath the gene-mod. Another tattoo, but this one was an older, smaller one he hadn't seen on first glance, a barely visible, faded gray ink job that hadn't been renewed in decades. It read simply: 665

Who the hell are you? Joe thought, covering the tattoos and standing back to watch her sleep. She spoke Jreet, she *acted* Jreet, and she carried a tattoo that marked her as some sort of android or computer program. That *was* what v.2.0.6 meant, wasn't it? Joe frowned, wishing his Bagan or Huouyt friends were there so he could ask them. Technology had never been his strong suit.

After it became apparent that she was going to continue to sleep, Joe decided to see what he could scavenge from the kitchen. The first thing he found, upon checking the stove, was a massive pot of large, rancid bones that someone had brought in from outside—it still had scorch-marks up the sides from someone's campfire. In the bottom, there was a thick layer of spoiled lard covering the surface of what looked to be some sort of stew—doubtless the remnants of the unfortunate group's last meal. Once again reminded why he never stayed the night in abandoned houses, Joe went looking for something to supplement the quickly-spoiling meat from the unidentified Earth animal he had shot. He *really* didn't want to have to break into his survival rations unless he absolutely had to, especially not for an ungrateful furg who had bit him.

Scavenging, for Joe, was always hit-or-miss. Even though he had been on Earth a full rotation already, Joe was still trying to get a grasp on the dizzying array of Earth foods and what was good for what. He opened up the cabinets and found himself entirely out of his league. He could identify some of the spices—oregano and rosemary, especially, since the Ooreiki had begun a massive trade of it for their perfume industry—but most of the actual foodstuffs were utterly incomprehensible to him. What was worse, boxes and canisters of pre-made foods were already ransacked, leaving only the basics behind.

He found a tub of 'sugar' hidden behind some kitchen appliances on the counter, which he immediately grabbed. 'Sugar,' he had discovered, after seventy-four turns away from home, was delicious. Other Earth foods, however, were not so desirable. 'Flour' just made a pasty, tasteless mess in his mouth. 'Cornmeal' was the same. 'Baking soda' was absolutely disgusting. Canned foods were generally good, ostensibly because it took so many more resources to preserve them, therefore Humans would only expend the extra effort on the more valuable—and tasty—foodstuffs.

Unfortunately, the good stuff in this place had obviously been picked clean by the Human scavengers who had met their untimely end upstairs. Whereas a kreenit would simply eat can, wrapper, and contents whole, these cans had been carefully cut open, emptied, and discarded in a haphazard pile in one corner of the kitchen. Even then, the reek of old fly larvae still stank up the kitchen from the heap.

Not that the pot of bones was any better. Joe had to hold his hand over his mouth each time he walked past it to keep from gagging. As soon as the girl was awake, he was going to get them somewhere much less tempting to a predator's delicate palate. He was actually surprised that the house hadn't been ransacked a second time, by a kreenit looking for the source of the rancid meat.

Skirting the stove, Joe found some 'flour' and 'cornmeal' in the cupboards, but he left it behind, having found little use for the stuff. There was a canister marked 'beans' in the cabinet over the sink, filled with little glossy red nodules, but when Joe tried to bite into them, not only were they incredibly hard, but they tasted bitter and disgusting. He tossed the canister aside, irritated with Humanity. At least the rest of Congress knew how to eat well. The Ueshi, especially, with their very short lives and extremely big brains, knew how to live it up. They wouldn't have put up with this tasteless crap.

Not that Joe's foggy memories of childhood on Earth dredged up anything particularly tasteless, but he attributed that to memory loss, nostalgia, and generally not knowing any better. Aside from the meat—which he shot himself—he hadn't found anything very good to eat on the whole damn planet, the supposed cradle of Humanity. Well, aside from sugar, which he always rationed because it gave him an odd high, almost like an eighth a karwiq bulb.

Joe had finally gotten to the closet with the rats when he heard a thump upstairs. Immediately, he felt a little surge of adrenaline, knowing he was finally going to have some answers from the moody little wretch. And that, he realized in alarm, was a hundred times more important to him than getting back to his task of playing Joe the Kreenit-Slayer across half of North America. North America, Joe had disgustedly found, didn't give a crap if he killed kreenit or not. He could be standing over a dead kreenit, gun in hand, arm out, smile on his face, and most of the survivors would spit on him as soon as shake his hand, blaming *Congies* for their predicament, as if *Congies* were somehow responsible for the genetic experiments that had gotten Earth its Sacred Turn of quiet time.

It was like it always was—each Draft, Humanity whined and complained and sent loving notes and care-packages for the new recruits sent to bootcamp, but it ultimately blamed the kids who got taken for everything Humans hated about Congress. Like most of the sentient world, people refused to look inward, refused to acknowledge their own failings. Most Congies, Joe had found, had ditched their black Congressional uniforms to fit in—less chance of being vendetta-shot by a stranger that way.

Thus, after eradicating twenty-two kreenit only to have been spit on eleven times, attacked thrice, and offered a meal exactly once, Joe was a hell of a lot more interested in why this stranger spoke Jreet than he was in going back to his thankless monster-hunt.

He didn't want to appear desperate, though. A few minutes of disorientation would do her good. Knowing there was only one way for the girl to get out of the house unless she wanted a broken leg, and that that one way happened to be the staircase behind him, Joe yanked open the pantry closet to finish his food search.

The door opened on a wave of putrescence. As Joe gagged, his eyes located a tall, very skinny corpse curled up in one corner of the closet, bound hand and foot with zip-ties. Rats had eaten away his face, flesh, and eyeballs. Sitting neatly on the floor in front of him was the corpulent, rotting, rat-chewed head of a woman.

Joe thought back to the pot of stew on the stove, then took out his canteen of J.B. and took a deep swig. Without examining the rest of the closet for food, he shut the door and backed out of the kitchen.

If there was one thing he had learned upon dropping back on Earth, it was that Humanity was barbaric, and over the last rotation of witnessing brutality, savagery, and cruelty, he had forgotten why he had wanted to save it in the first place.

Joe was sitting on the base of the steps, staring at the bones jutting from the pot, reacquainting himself with Jim Beam, when the woman burst from the upstairs room, snarling in Welu Jreet.

"You!" she snapped, as soon as she saw him. "What are you doing here?!"

Joe glanced over his shoulder, then frowned when he realized she'd taken off the clothes he had painstakingly acquired for her from a man who had apparently starved to death with his wife's head at his feet. "What the hell are you doing?" he demanded, the flask paused halfway to his lips. "Put your clothes back on."

"Where am I?" she snapped. "Where is Doctor Philip? I need to tell the worthless furg that his softling services are no longer needed and that I am ready to go back to Welu." She wrinkled her nose. "And that I'm *hungry*. The skulker left me on his miserable planet without *food*."

Her breasts bounce when she's angry, Joe noted, taking another swig of whiskey. "Who's Doctor Philip?" he asked, once the burn settled in his gut.

"He's my subordinate on the S.H.A.E.L. project," she growled.

Joe's attention sharpened when she sounded out the acronym in Congie letters, her words sounding foreign and awkward. "S.H.A.E.L. project?" he asked, as casually as he could.

She grunted. "I was to instruct the lazy, backward fighting base of this race on how to be good warriors, but they've obviously got no aptitude for it. I'm going home."

For a nerve-wracking moment, Joe thought perhaps she was a Huouyt, and that his universe-renowned 'Huouyt-radar' had failed him. Again.

"And where's home?" he asked, unobtrusively reaching for his gun.

She raised her head and straightened her back as if she were a queen, putting her light pink areolas on excellent display. "Welu, home of the highest race of Jreet. It is time I return to my warriors and rally the clan. I intend to come back here and wipe this pathetic planet clean of soft-skinned scum like you."

For a long moment, Joe just stared at her over his canteen, wondering if she'd fried a few brain cells somewhere along the way. Then, because she looked utterly certain of what she was saying— and because she was speaking flawless, *ancient* Welu Jreet—Joe said, "You want to come back and kill off Humanity."

"If that's what you call your miserable, softling existence, yes. By the time we're done, the fields will be full of staked corpses, and your children's children will tell stories of my wrath."

Joe took a last swig of whiskey, then capped it, contemplating her. "And just who do you think you are?"

"There is no *think*," she spat at him. She raised her head in another regal pose. "I am Shael ga Welu, prince of Welu." She paused dramatically, obviously waiting for him to acknowledge that she was the ancient Welu hero, apparently back from the dead and condensed into a body that was barely five digs if she stretched.

If Joe hadn't been one and a half rods from a woman that had been boiled and consumed by her own kind, he would have laughed at that. As it was, he just glanced down at his canteen and wondered what he was going to do when he ran out of whiskey.

"I want to go to a spaceport," Shael said, in a tone that demanded obedience.

"I want you to put some clothes on," Joe said. The idea that she planned to run around naked again after he'd used up almost half his nannite cream on her burns left him more than a little irritable.

Shael narrowed her eyes and started down the steps toward him— and almost fell on her face. As Joe watched, curious, she grabbed the rail and held tight, her vibrant green eyes widening as she seemed to do a double-take. "What...*is*...this?" she whispered. Her entire body had gone utterly stiff, and she held the railing like she was afraid she was about to hurtle the rest of the way.

She's never seen stairs before, Joe thought, more than a little stunned. It raised the hairs on the back of his neck a little, as well as gave him a wave of goosebumps across his arms. What kind of woman—especially a woman on *Earth*—hadn't seen stairs?

Then he was jolted from his reverie by her desperate cry of, "*Answer me*, skulker, or I will find your father's tek and bury it in a Dhasha's ass!"

Joe tucked his canteen into a pocket on his cargo belt, stood, and leaned casually against the wall, considering her. Standing there, clinging to the bannister, cursing in Jreet, she seemed almost as alien in this place as Joe himself felt.

"So," Joe said, "you're looking to go back to Welu?"

"Immediately," she growled. She had started, very carefully, step-by-step, descending the stairs, her fists gripping the bannister with white knuckles. "Just point me in the right direction and I'll get there myself. I don't need the company of a scaleless softling slowing me down."

Considering that she was probably only *alive* because Joe had deigned to save her, Joe said, "How about you put on some clothes and tell me why you think you're a Jreet."

She paused, mid-step, and her head snapped up to give him a dangerous look. "Warriors do not wear the sheaths of cowards and weavers."

…Which sounded a lot like what Daviin would have said, had Joe demanded he put on a 12XL shirt.

Still, Joe didn't intend to let her leave the house without something on her back. Even then, his nannite tube was half empty, and he was pretty sure the ransacked local grocery stores weren't going to resupply him. As she reached the final step, he pointedly blocked her way off the stairs with his body. "You should put something on," he said.

The woman blinked up at him as if he had just picked his own brains out through his nose. "You *dare* stand in the path of Shael ga Welu?"

Joe unconcernedly itched his cheek, deciding that the tiny, five-dig woman needed a reality check. "Uh. Yeah. I do." He crossed his big arms over his chest and peered down at her, perfectly willing to rough her up a little in order to get her over her Jreet fetish. After all, his hand still hurt.

Her pretty green eyes narrowed. And, in one moment, Joe was casually standing at the base of the stairs, blocking her path, arms crossed, a smug look on his face. The next, something huge grabbed him and threw him with all the force of a Dhasha's backhand, embedding Joe in the far wall, only a few feet from the stove and its grisly contents.

"Buuuuurn," Joe groaned, pulling himself out of the sheetrock. He ended up doing more falling than walking, and kind of collapsed into a ball on the floor. "Burn me," he panted. "Burn me."

On the staircase, the woman unconcernedly finished her descent and walked past him as if he were a fly she had just swatted. And Joe, being at least as smart as the average bear, stayed down and watched her go, frantically trying to figure out what the hell she'd done to him. She hadn't *moved*.

Her Jreet fetish suddenly took on new meaning. It had *felt* like he'd been hit by a Jreet. He had felt the massive fist clamp down on his torso and throw him with all the regard of an apple core. And, considering that Jreet could shift the energy-level of their scales and go completely invisible at will…

Did she have a *Sentinel*? Joe had thought there were only two Humans in the universe who had earned themselves the dubious honor of having Sentinels—himself and Rat. Not even Fred Mullich, that worthless Human Representative back at Koliinaat, had attracted a Sentinel. How could some nameless, barcoded naked chick on Earth have a *Sentinel*? That made no *sense*.

Oblivious to his frantic mental scramble, the naked girl stepped through the huge, gaping hole in the wall and disappeared in the overgrown grass on the other side.

"What…" Joe managed, prying himself painfully from the floor, "…the soot?" He checked himself to see what had survived, found broken ribs and a knee that no longer worked correctly, then carefully got to his feet, clinging to the stove for support.

Aching from head to toe, dizzy from what he was beginning to think was a concussion, crushed ribs making breathing difficult, Joe hobbled over to the base of the staircase, where his gun and his sack of gear still lay neatly against the wall, abandoned.

Again.

Groaning, he slumped down beside it, pulled out his medkit, propped it on his knee, fumbled through it until he found a nano solution, and clumsily dosed himself. Then he leaned his head back against the wall and closed his eyes, waiting for the pain to go away. By the time Joe's head cleared, he'd thought of twenty different things he could say to the woman in reply, and most of them involved Jane.

When he was mobile again, the woman—or whatever she was—was long gone.

But Joe, the highly-trained, Planetary Ops war hero that he was, could track her. And he was going to, too, if only to put a round through her brain for leaving him to die…again.

10

HOW TO HANDLE A JREET...

As soon as Shael slid out of the crude Human dwelling, he froze at the sight that lay beyond. He could see no roads, no pathways, just alien flora waving in the fetid alien wind. He hesitated, feeling a bit of his resolve undermined by the sheer vastness of the empty alien landscape.

You are the greatest warrior of your time, Shael reminded himself, as the awkward unease tried to settle into his core. *You can crush your enemies with all the concern a Dhasha gives a vaghi.* It was something that the sniveling Doctorphilip had repeated to him, again and again, and Shael found courage in it now. Alien landscape or no, he *would* get home. There was nothing—*nothing*—on this pathetic planet that could stand in his way.

Still, without a way to communicate with the weaklings, Shael knew he would have trouble getting them to understand his commands. He felt a little flush of concern that he had abandoned the only other creature who seemed to be able to speak an intelligent—if filthy—tongue, but decided that arrogance, in lesser creatures like

Takki and their close cousins the Vorans, deserved to be removed—painfully, if necessary.

Lifting his head to sniff the air, Shael considered his route. He could pick up no nuances of life from the stale air, no tell-tale scents of the passages of prey, not even the smell of the earth or the dry, withered scrub. For a brief, horrified moment, Shael thought that perhaps Doctorphilip and his weaklings had somehow fiddled with his senses, to keep him from tracking them. Then, catching a strong smell of rancid flesh from somewhere behind him, Shael decided that it was merely the flat, tasteless air of the alien planet that was altering his perceptions, nothing permanent.

Shael started moving through the bladed alien flora. It was sharp against his coils, biting his scaleless skin. The softling had obviously taken him off the road system in an attempt to disorient him and keep him from returning with his clan.

Cowards, Shael thought. *Cowards and skulkers, all of them.*

He slid into the brush, clambered through the twisted, scraggly undergrowth—which bit him with spines and broken parts that lodged painfully in his skin—then, when his coils should have simply glided through the sticks and stumps, they caught and he fell forward on his hands, body afire. He got up and tried again, then tumbled back to the ground in a few more rods, helplessly tangled in the mass of alien foliage.

They planted traps for Jreet, he thought, furious. That they had planned this far ahead, going so far as to prepare their foliage to slow him down, confused him, because it was much more intelligent than Shael had given Doctorphilip credit for. Still, however, huddled in a mass of alien flora, unable to move for the prickles, barriers, and deadfall, there was no denying that they had plotted it all many turns in advance. Which meant they never planned on letting him return to Welu. Which meant they had never planned to learn a warrior's trade from him.

Angry, humiliated, Shael dropped back into his war-mind and found the moving foggy essence of the land around him. Putting up a mental barrier between himself and the glowing green mist of the plant life, Shael pushed forward, wrenching the flora away from him, shoving it in all directions, carving a clear path down to the dirt. His coils no longer hindered, he got up and slid forward, plowing a road for himself in the terrain. All around him, ugly organic growths fell and snapped in half, the sound of his vengeance ringing along the hillside with each new alien plant that Shael annihilated. Seeing that, feeling his power sing through him as it mowed down his enemies' world, Shael felt partially vindicated.

Partially, but still unnerved. What kind of *plant* could slow down a *Jreet*? He decided he needed to discuss this with the other warriors. Perhaps, under the guise of a joint training mission, the denizens of this planet were really intending a war with the Jreet, and had used Shael as a test subject.

Even then, descaled, drugged, his tek immobilized, his body hungry and weak, his coils floundering in the alien foliage like a furg, Shael felt the betrayal like an ovi through his guts.

I trusted them, he thought. *I trusted them as brethren.*

Buoyed by the wrongs done to him, Shael lifted himself from his coils and kept going. Regardless of what the aliens had planned for him, he *would* find his way home.

When the weak, pitiful star began to sink below the horizon, however, Shael was no closer to finding his way back to the road than when he had started. As darkness fell and the world cooled, waves of unease began to hit him like a Dhasha's paw.

Shael could never remember being cold before. Unlike the weakling Doctorphilip and his soft, cowardly assistants, a Jreet warrior did not need to wear clothes to maintain his body temperature. Jreet could naturally withstand whatever elements a planet decided to throw at them, equally suited for the snowy mountain slopes of Welu's poles or the raging blazes of Vora's firelands.

And yet, something his comrades had done to him in their treachery had left Shael forced to huddle in on himself, trying to trap his own body heat to his chest with his coils. Miserable, blind, Shael was awkwardly raking the alien flora around himself in an attempt to keep warm, when he heard something big snap in the nearby forest.

It sounded much like the way the alien shrubbery had snapped as it fell before him, but more concentrated, and coming on fast...

It was the dry, liquidy rustle of scales sliding against each other, rattling in the creature's charge, that marked it for what it was.

Dhasha...Shael let out a battlecry and raised his energy level to drop beneath the visible spectrum, then opened his war-mind to pinpoint the intruder.

Shael froze when he realized the creature was much too big to be Dhasha. While it carried the same odd, utterly solid scales, its jaws alone were large enough to take a Dhasha between them, and its head, neck, and body were more streamlined, longer. Watching it charge directly at him, despite the fact he had raised his energy level to disappear from its spectrum, left Shael with a strange sensation churning his insides, something he had never experienced before.

Terror.

He screamed and, at the last moment, threw a wall between them in his war-mind. The beast plowed into the barrier in a clatter of scales and fell to its front knees as its hindquarters and tail, still in motion, pushed its body onward, its massive form rolling over him and his barrier like a mountain.

Sisters' fury, Shael's panicked mind babbled. *That's a kreenit.*

Finding their snares ineffective, his betrayers had unleashed a kreenit, an *eater* of Dhasha, upon him. Not even the greatest Jreet could hope to wrap his coils around a kreenit. They were too big, too mindless, too *wild*.

Shael screamed as the kreenit righted itself and charged him again, this time hitting the barrier he'd constructed and slamming its open jaws against it, ovi-sharp black teeth only a rod from snapping Shael in half.

More out of instinct than conscious thought, Shael took the barrier between them and pushed, shoving the creature backwards, its massive paws rending great furrows in the forest floor as it went. It roared in stupid alien fury and renewed its attack, ripping away trees and foliage as it fought, giving Shael a mind-splitting headache as it assaulted his mental wall, snorting, huffing, tearing up earth, working its way around…

Shael screamed again and ducked as he realized that the kreenit had found the edge of his barrier and was shoving past it. With nothing to stop the beast from snapping him up in its titanic jaws, Shael threw up a hasty wall around himself, like the bubble around an Ooreiki egg-sac. The kreenit's jaws came down and hit the barrier only a dig from his head, locking him completely in the prison of its teeth.

Stymied, the monster shrieked and yanked him and his bubble completely from the ground, flipping him back and forth in the air two rods above the treeline. Shael howled as it ragdolled his sanctuary, then shivered as it started to mindlessly gnash at the invisible walls, its huge teeth grating against the barriers in his mind, driving spikes of pain through his head as the beast struggled to break the wall he had formed around himself.

Trapped in a bubble of his own making, neither his coils nor his hands able to reach something solid to aid in an escape, unable to focus on anything other than the enormous teeth that were slicing at the barriers in his mind, Shael curled up on the scoop-shaped floor of his refuge and shivered. The incident was triggering something, some horrible memory he'd long forgotten, and even as the vicious teeth gnashed around him, orange saliva dripping down the walls of his prison, Shael remembered that it wasn't, in actuality, the first time he had feared…

• • •

"Doctorphilip, I want to go outside."

Doctorphilip hesitated in writing yet another report to his superiors analyzing Shael's warrior attributes and how to emulate them. Glancing at him over his paperwork, Doctorphilip raised a thin black eyebrow. "You know we can't risk exposing the Jreet's alliance with my species to Congress. We need to keep you out of sight."

Shael snorted at yet another example of Doctorphilip's weakness. "I don't care about the tantrums of politicians. They object and the Jreet will crush them to a soul. I'm tired of this stale air. I want to see the surface."

Doctorphilip dared to shake his head. "Sadly, we can't allow that. It would violate six different treaties. You *must* stay out of sight. We've gone *over* this, Shael."

Shael, sick of being trapped within the four same sterilized white walls day in and day out, with no one to teach and nothing to do, surged to his coils in a fury. "I *am* going outside, you miserable furg. You will open the doors, or I will open them myself."

Doctorphilip put down his weakling's instrument, crossed his tiny, feeble fingers over his knee and gave Shael a frown. "Where did you get this ridiculous idea to go outside, Shael?"

Shael, who had been communicating with the puny furg Twelve-A for the last few weeks, grimaced. Twelve-A, who had some sort of superior communication technology, had told Shael not to mention him, as it would get him put back to sleep, and Shael greatly enjoyed his company whenever he was awake.

Thus, Shael swore to the Sisters he'd offer a sacrifice for his sin, took a breath, and lied. "I miss the swamps of my homeland," he said. "I wish to see how your pitiful planet compares." Which was partially true.

Doctorphilip gave him a smile that, for just a moment, Shael thought held a bit of disdain. Then it was quickly hidden, obscured with more platitudes. "I assure you, Shael, my planet has no swamps. It is dry and barren and you would not enjoy it."

He's lying, Twelve-A told him. *It's beautiful.*

"You're lying," Shael snapped, before he could have second thoughts about it. "Bring me my melaa and open the doors, slave. I will see the surface today."

Instead of cowering in fear, as he usually did, Doctorphilip's eyes darkened. In the language of his own kind, he snarled something that made Shael's scales tighten, despite the fact he couldn't understand the words.

What did he just say? Shael demanded of Twelve-A, scowling up into Doctorphilip's beady blue eyes.

For a moment, the minder hesitated.

Speak, weakling, Shael snapped.

He said, 'You're an annoying little brat, you know that?' Twelve-A replied.

Shael froze. "You *mock* me?"

Doctorphilip, whose face had been filled with smug contempt, blinked in surprise. Almost immediately, sly cunning slid into its place for the briefest of instants before he gave an obsequious bow. In his tongue, he said, "I would never dream to mock you, Shael." Then, quickly, he rattled off a few more words in his filthy language.

What did the cur just say? Shael again demanded of his friend-weakling.

Shael, it's a test, and you really shouldn't—

Tell me, or I will bring this entire mountain down upon us, Shael snapped. He was in his war-mind, and he was ready to do just that.

Twelve-A hesitated a moment, then he said, *He called you a hairy cunt he couldn't wait to breed to something intelligent.*

Shael's mouth fell open as he stared at his servant. "You vaghi skulker...you *dare*?!" He grasped Doctorphilip's head in the barrier of his mind—

—and flinched when something sharp pricked his chest. Almost instantly, Shael was wrenched from his war-mind and shoved back into the narrow, three-dimensional view of his normal senses. He looked down, saw the tiny, fluffy-ended red dart sticking from his body, and froze.

"So," Doctorphilip said, casually lowering his pen back to his desk, "when did you learn Congie, Shael?" His smile had slipped slightly, and his eyes were alert. Pleasantly, he added, "Has one of the crew been teaching you, or were you just picking it up?"

Please don't tell him about me, Twelve-A whimpered. *Please...they don't know I'm awake and I don't want to sleep again.*

No longer caring about lying to a craven coward, Shael snarled, "I learned your language from your own filthy lips, betrayer. You've been insulting me all along." He upended Doctorphilip's brownish weakling's drink across his paperwork and clothes, then hurled the mug to shatter on the opposite wall.

Doctorphilip's face darkened and he glanced down at himself, then at the shattered pottery against the wall. "That was my favorite mug."

"I shall stake you for your insolence," Shael decided. "Then I will hunt down your kinfolk and children and dry out their innards as they scream for mercy. How *dare* you insult a son of Welu!" Shael tossed his soggy papers aside, too, scattering them in a wet flurry around the room.

The look Doctorphilip gave him was filled with cold, unconcealed malice. "My *dead mother* gave me that mug."

Shael sneered at him. "I'll be sure to bury it with your tekless remains." He lunged forward, grabbed Doctorphilip by the throat, and attempted to hurl him through the concrete wall.

Instead, Doctorphilip remained exactly where he was and chuckled. "Oh, you poor, deluded little vaghi. You want to kill me?" He reached out and placed *his* hand around *Shael's* throat. "How about now, you petulant little shit?" He started to squeeze, and Shael, despite his great, powerful body, was unable to force Doctorphilip's hands from his throat.

"I am *so tired* of your constant, arrogant, full-of-shit *crap*," Doctorphilip snarled. "You think you're a Jreet? You're a *lab-rat*." As Shael choked and slapped at the weakling's wrists, unable to get air, Doctorphilip yanked him close, until their faces were almost touching. "What, Shael? Can't *breathe*? Now why would that be? Is this *weakling* stronger than you?"

It was all the more horrifying because it was exactly as he said. Shael couldn't breathe, couldn't fight his way free, despite being bigger, stronger, a hundred times more powerful, trained in a thousand forms of death.

Doctorphilip's face twisted in a spiteful smile. "I'm one of the top linguists in my field. You think I *want* to be down here, baby-sitting mindless morons like you? You think I *want* to be stuck underground day in and day out, listening to your idiotic rants? It's the only way I could get a *pension*, bitch." Doctorphilip shook him, then, sending shooting pains down Shael's neck and back.

"You're just a lab-rat," Doctorphilip snarled into his face. "Lucky number thirteen. We're done with you by the end of next month, then we're sending you to follow in the footsteps of all your little friends who didn't quite work out. You know what happened to them?"

Terror was beginning to bubble up on a wave of shame, terror that he didn't understand how Doctorphilip could continue to hold him, terror that he had no idea how he had overlooked how very large Doctorphilip was, terror that his underling's cringing and scraping had been an act, terror that it had been replaced with malicious malevolence, terror that Shael hadn't seen his true nature until now, terror that he was going to die.

"They're dead, you cocky little bitch," Doctorphilip said, lowering his face to Shael's. "And you're next. One last appearance before the brass and then I get to find myself some new material. Hopefully a maker this time. *Real* quality, not just one more mediocre mover we don't have the money to feed." He snorted in complete disdain. "You telekinetics...you're like cockroaches. What we *need* are more like Twelve-A. They'd let me out of this shithole for good if I could figure out how to make another Twelve-A." His sneer darkened. "But I won't, because they saw the pretty little half-assed certificate in xenolinguistics and completely ignored my Ph.D. in cell biology. I'm stuck with *you* instead of working on the *big* project."

Then Doctorphilip released his throat and grabbed the back of Shael's neck, instead. As Shael lurched and struggled to catch his breath, Doctorphilip yanked him over to his bed and shoved him back inside. While Shael coughed and sucked in desperate lungfuls of air, his servant strapped him back into his bed and shoved a needle under his scales.

"Remember that you aren't worth the shit on the bottom of my shoe and I just might give you a good lay before we send you to the morgue," Doctorphilip sneered. His face twisted with an even deeper malice. "Not that you're going to remember this, anyway, cunt." Then he slammed the lid of Shael's bed shut, locking him into the darkness. Through the muffling lid, Shael heard the rasps of his feet on carpet as he walked away. An instant later, the voices and images of Shael's bed started up again, and Shael felt the sudden coolness streaking up his arm as the weaklings' antidote for the poisonous fumes in Shael's breath entered his veins.

No, Shael thought, as the immediate tug of sleep once again came over him. He struggled to stay awake, knowing that it was important, knowing that he *needed* to fight, *needed* to be awake, that he had stumbled across something horrible, and if he let his eyes slide back shut, he would never remember...

Regardless of how hard he struggled, however, Shael felt his eyes closing again, sucked back into the lull of sleep.

No!

• • •

The woman had fallen into a clump of brush and was huddled there, clumsy and obviously in pain, and Joe was about to take pity on her and go help her extract herself, when all of a sudden, it seemed as if the unlovable Jreet gods themselves came to life and started carving a five-rod-wide path through the vegetation for the woman to follow.

Joe stopped, mid-step, and stared, that eerie feeling of witnessing something he couldn't explain raising his hackles and setting off every goosebump and mental alarm he had. As trees started snapping in half like matchsticks as they were mercilessly plowed out of the woman's way, Joe dropped to the ground and tried to assimilate just what he was seeing.

Something was moving those trees. *Something* was plowing plants, soil, and stones aside as if it were no effort at all. For an instant, he thought that maybe the woman really *did* have a Jreet guardian, and that the invisible hand that had thrown him across the room had belonged to a Jreet Sentinel with his energy level up.

But, watching the forest literally fold out of her way, Joe knew that there wasn't a Jreet alive big enough to create what he was seeing. Which meant it had to be something else. If she were *closer* to the brush, he would have thought she were, indeed, some sort of android pushing it, or maybe using some sort of automatic weapon to mow it down. But she never touched it—never even came close.

The woman walked for *lengths* that way, the terrain simply peeling out of her way as she passed. When she finally stopped, darkness had fallen, and Joe was pretty sure that the strange force snapping the trees in half had been coming from *her*, not anything around her. Several times, he'd seen the great machinations stop completely while she swatted at a horsefly or paused briefly to take a piss.

But if *she* were peeling back the forest, was she even Human?

His eyes kept drifting back to the barcode, knowing that, had Flea or Jer'ait been with him, they would have pieced it together within the first ten tics and would currently be lecturing him on the pitiful size-to-usefulness ratio of the Human brain.

Then Joe froze. Hadn't that been what the scientists had been trying to do when they got Earth condemned to Judgement? Extend the usefulness of the Human brain. Manipulating genetics to make Humans smarter...

...or able to throw a Dhasha forty rods.

Sweet Sisters, is that what I think it is? Joe thought, watching the woman through his scope. She was curling up in the grass, trying to pull clumps of dried straw around herself, shivering. Joe's heart started to pound with the possibilities, both good and bad. Good, because he could teach her to be his personal kreenit annihilator. Bad, because, as evidenced by the three lengths of forest she had simply pushed aside, she could squish him. Like a mite.

And somehow, for some reason, that made him all the more interested in going up and offering his services. Personal ass-kicker, gear-carrier, night-vision specialist, survivalist, medic, bedmate if desired...

As soon as he had the thought, goosebumps of alarm slammed into place all along Joe's spine and arms as he remembered, vividly, his dad on the floor grinning up at his mom after she'd thrown him to the mat in Taekwondo practice, saying that the guys in his family had a thing for chicks that could kick their ass…

No way, he thought, shaking himself. That was just crap, because the only girl who could kick his ass was Rat, and after the thing with the Huouyt on Jeelsiht, she'd never turned him on.

And yet, scanning the utterly flattened forest marking her passage, he realized he was looking at very compelling evidence that he'd found another one. And she was cold. And shivering. And lonely. And would probably welcome a nice, warm fire…

Joe shook himself. *She buried your ass in a wall*, he reminded himself. *She deserves a few hours to think about it.*

But the longer he hunched there in the woods—woods that *he* could see by virtue of his altered eyes, but that would be as dark as the Void to her natural ones—the more violently she shivered and the more Joe felt sorry for her.

Joe's soft side had just won out and he was finally about to go take pity on the miserable science project when he heard the telltale snaps of something huge moving through the forest, charging at them at speed.

Soot, Joe thought, scrambling to put away his binoculars and grab Jane. *Soot, soot!*

The kreenit reached her before it reached him, and for a moment, Joe thought his potential traveling companion had just become lunch. Then he saw the kreenit's awkward stumble and the way the beast's massive body rolled over the place where the girl had huddled, and he realized that the same invisible force that had carved her a pathway had just stopped a kreenit in full-charge. That was…impressive.

Joe lowered Jane and let the naked freak fight the beast herself for a few tics, curious to see what would happen.

It wasn't, it turned out, as impressive as he'd hoped. She screamed, her inviso-wall seemed to fail, then the beast chomped down on her like a Jikaln with a vaghi.

Cursing himself, Joe scrambled to get a good vantage point as the beast spun and twisted, shaking the hapless victim inside its jaws. He knew she was still alive—or at least parts of her were still alive—because she was screaming.

When Joe managed to get behind the kreenit, he leveled Jane at the back of the beast's head, where the sexual nerve-bundle lay exposed just below the surface, under and between the horns. He said a prayer to the Dhasha Mothers, then pulled the trigger.

The kreenit shrieked at about the same time its mouth ripped open from the inside and the experiment rolled out, screaming.

Not oh, haha, it spit the girl out and lumbered off to lick its wounds. Its *head* split *apart* like something grabbed it by the jaws and ripped it in *half*. As the enormous body flopped to the ground and started to twitch, purple brains exposed to the nighttime air, Joe blinked and stared down at Jane. It was a good Ueshi brand, a genuine blackmarket Nocurna using high-grade plasma, but it couldn't do anything like *that*.

Which left him, once again, with this odd, heart-pounding awareness that this girl could totally kick his ass...

No way, Joe thought, giving himself a spine-snapping mental shake, *no way, no way*. His dad had been so full of shit on that one it had been coming out his ears. Truckloads of shit. Cargo carriers of it. Besides, *he* could kick *her* ass. Hell, he'd already saved her *life*. He was turned on because she was naked and pretty, not because she could kick his ass.

Then he realized he really *was* turned on and he backpedaled in panic. *That's the alcohol talking, dipshit*, he told himself. *She left you to die. Twice.*

Besides, she had an attitude that made him want to punch her in the face. Hell, after what she'd done, she *deserved* to be punched in the face.

Still, when the girl stalked up to the twitching kreenit and started kicking it with her bare foot, cursing its heritage in Welu Jreet, *sobbing*, Joe decided it might be a good time to make his entrance. She really looked like she could use a shoulder to cry on...

What are you doing, Joe? he demanded of himself as he hurriedly threw his gear over his shoulder and started toward her. *She embedded you in a* wall *and she just ripped that kreenit in* half. Logic dictated that A) she was unhappy with Joe, and with Humanity being much less dense than a kreenit, infinitely weaker, and generally soft overall, she could B) do the same to him.

Maybe it was the J.B. still warming his system. Perhaps it was the fact that he'd just spent a rotation killing kreenit and he'd never seen anything so efficient at destroying them. Or maybe it was the simple fact that he was sleeping with a fully-charged AI plasma pistol at night and was lonely.

Whatever the reason, Joe took those last few steps to the wounded girl's side, stopped, and said, "I've heard Welus were excellent warriors, but that was something the bards will sing about for ages to come." He'd spent enough time around Daviin that he pretty much had the hang of how to give a good compliment, Jreet-style.

The woman froze, then slowly turned to him with a blank look.

"By the way," Joe said, "I have meat, but it'll have to wait 'til morning." When she just blinked at him, he sighed. "I also have a good Congie flamestick and could build us a nice *warm* fire to roast it, but a fire at night is like lighting up a neon sign to all the predators and bad guys out there that says 'I'm over here, come take my stuff and eat me.' I'm afraid it would draw too much attention. Not safe. We've gotta wait." He also knew, from his time with his Sentinel and his time hunting Raavor ga Aez, how to flat-out manipulate the arrogant, stomach-driven bastards.

The woman licked her lips. "You have meat?"

"Yeah," Joe said, with feigned reluctance. "But it's filled with parasites and we can't cook it tonight. We'll have to wait until morning."

She wrinkled her dainty nose at 'parasites.' If there was one thing the Jreet hated, it was parasites. "Cook it now," she ordered. "I will protect you, Voran."

Grinning inside, Joe nonetheless put on a sober look. "I'm not sure that's a good idea. There are so many dangerous things out there…"

She gestured imperiously at the dead kreenit. "Like this?"

"Well," Joe said, looking at the massive, scaly beast, taking the time to sound like he was considering, "yeah. Like that."

She gave an impatient gesture at the ground. "Cook it. I'll protect the camp."

Joe kept his face utterly innocent. "Are you *sure*? It could be dangerous…"

Her green eyes flashed in the darkness. "*Now*, Voran."

Ah, the Jreet. One just had to know how to push their buttons. Joe built a fire, surreptitiously using the kreenit's front legs and neck to shield most of it from view of the surrounding countryside, then covertly dropped his bag of gear and set up his tarp at the front of the fire, to block the rest of the light from whatever survivors might be out there. Not that Joe didn't think Shael would do exactly as she said and annihilate anyone who came to take her food—she was obviously hungry—but Joe had fought Huouyt most of his life, and old habits died hard.

11

DOMINANCE STRUGGLES

Along the way to the shopping center, Slade's following grew. The rest of the world, it seemed, wasn't yet fully into Group-Up-To-Survive mode, so Slade and his merry band had a distinct advantage. They started acquiring motorists, bystanders, and those brave mall employees who had forgone their own personal safety to secure another Almighty Dollar, zealously adding them all to Slade's ravenous group's ranks—essentially to carry all the heavy stuff.

Slade, of course, found little interest in the looting, kidnapping, and general pillaging of his underlings. While his lackeys, under-lackeys, and assorted minions ransacked the sporting-goods and food stores for supplies, Slade visited the hallowed halls of Barnes & Noble.

With Tyson standing beside him with a wide-open US Mail sack that they'd stolen from the mall post office, Slade began going down the rows collecting books on everything he could think of that could save his ass in the case of an apocalypse.

Which, apparently, had started early. A few minutes ago, he had begun to hear the sound of Congressional bombs going off in the distance.

"You think they're gonna hit this place?" Tyson asked, flinching nervously as another bomb exploded, this time closer. He had found a badass-looking black shotgun in the sporting goods store, complete with a new vest full of slugs and buckshot shells. The AK-47 was still firmly slung over his other shoulder.

"Doubt it," Slade said, pulling a book on hydroponics off the shelf and stuffing it into Tyson's open bag. "Not a high target. They're looking for concentrated technology, military bases, airports, hospitals, government centers, power stations—stuff like that." He grabbed two more hydroponics books that looked promising, then moved on to Outdoor Survival. He started perusing a few, realized he was going to need more than a couple, and took one of each. Then he moved on to Soulmates.

"Yeah," Tyson went on, still glancing behind him at the sounds of the distant explosions. "But this place is pretty big. You don't think they'd hit it just for the fun of it?"

Slade shrugged. "Could. I'd give it a thirty percent chance." He pulled one of the books—*How to Find Your Soulmate in Ten Easy Steps*—from the shelves and started perusing it.

Whoever she was, this Leila-As-Prophecized-By-The-One-Eyed-Freak, she was going to be *smart*. She couldn't possibly be as smart as him—there *was* only one Ghost—but he needed *someone* who could at least pretend to keep up with him. Maybe a doctor or an engineer. Hell, even a geneticist…

"They're probably gonna blow all the fuel depots," Tyson said. "We should start siphoning gas and taking battery packs. Ain't gonna make no more of those."

Then again, Slade found geneticists to be snooty and superior. They got to play God and it kinda went to their heads, at least with a lot of them. Further, it would be best if the woman wasn't *too* highly-specialized, Slade determined. He needed someone like him—a jack-of-all-trades. Someone who could understand it when he talked about relativity and then switched mid-sentence to compare the pros and cons of different types of gum formulas. He was particularly impressed with the one he was chewing now. It had decreased his headache quotient to basically nothing. If he were back in his New York skyrise, he would have hacked the company's system to discover their secret recipe, which, with gum, usually only depended on slight alterations of flavor—the base was usually exactly the same. The real difference was in packaging, and how well the company could convince the poddites of the world that theirs was somehow special.

"If we stay on the move, head out through the desert, we should be okay," Tyson said, still nervously staring at the western wall like he expected to see the city getting blown up beyond. "They're not gonna screw around with the desert. Nothing out there worth shooting up, you know?"

"Kreenit will stay in the big cities," Slade agreed. "At least initially. More food."

According to the book, the first thing to finding a soulmate was to look at the people around you. There were, the book claimed, more than one per person, and they showed up in important roles in one's life—friends, siblings, family members...

What cheap shit. Slade snapped the book shut and tossed it over his shoulder, then picked up another one. *How to Find Your Spiritual Partner.*

"Yeah, man," Tyson said, "that's why I'm saying we get the hell outta Southern California as fast as possible. Hit the desert, maybe head to the Great Plains. Not a lot out there, but good farming."

Slade grimaced at 'farming.' "Generally, the idea of moving into the desert to survive is ill-advisable." True, most common sense didn't take man-eating lizards into that equation, but desert travel would likely kill huge swaths of whoever attempted it. "Just look at the Oregon Trail." The idea of digging in the dirt for his food was not exactly on the list of his priorities, either. He wanted food provided to him, at regular intervals, so he could spend his time doing more important things, like thinking.

"Dude, we can't stay here," Tyson said. "*Listen* to that." He gestured out at the distant chaos.

Yes, Slade thought, flipping through the pages, she would definitely be good at thinking. Maybe, on his bad days, when he was sick and had no gum to alleviate his headaches, she would be *almost as good* as him at thinking. That would be…invigorating.

Yeah, that's what he wanted. Someone invigorating. Someone that could make his blood rush and his heart pound. Someone who could look him in the eye and make him feel like he *wasn't* the smartest guy on the planet. Someone who could make him feel stupid.

Well, *that* wasn't going to happen. Slade sighed and slapped another book shut and threw it over his shoulder. His fingers slid over the books on the shelf until they arrived at another one, this one called, *How to Recognize Your Soulmate.*

"I'm thinking we load up a bunch of trucks and go east as far as we can," Tyson said.

"The highways will be blocked," Slade said. "Always happens in big disasters—everyone tries to leave the city and they end up choking off the roads with traffic until there's no escape." He continued scanning pages. "Hell, the alien douchebags will probably even help that along. Blow up a couple bridges, a few sections of highway… Then everyone in the city's basically a sitting duck."

"Man," Tyson groaned.

"Yeah," Slade agreed, digesting a chapter on Random Appearances. "Besides, after the first few days, any moving vehicle's gonna be a target."

Apparently, soulmates had a way of finding you, which Slade found to be a load of shit. It had been almost a century since he'd been told by that patch-wearing freak that he would have a soulmate and his brother would go off to fight aliens. Joe-the-Douche had gotten his aliens. Now Slade wanted his girl. Slade was relatively patient, but that was a *lot* of time to wait. Slade sighed, deeply, and kept flipping through the pages. If anyone had asked why he found the subject so fascinating, he couldn't have told them. True, he found *all* subjects fascinating, but this one still…vexed him.

Patch *had* been correct in most of her other predictions. And they hadn't been the normal, vague, "Something dark will happen to you in the next year," predictions, either. They'd been, "Your brother's going to get his heart ripped out by a Jreet," predictions.

Before Humanity even knew Jreet existed. How that was even possible was…annoying.

He added the book to the bag, followed by several others that looked promising.

He stopped on the book called *Soulmate Sex* and frowned at the pages. So wait…it was supposed to be *better* than regular sex? All spiritual and uplifting and amazing, yadayadayada…That was all fine and dandy, but Slade would have settled for regular sex. Just one night of regular sex. That would be nice. It had been so long since he'd gotten his wick wet that Slade was surprised Junior hadn't atrophied and fallen off from the lack of attention. Some of the *pictures*, though…they were interesting.

Turning back to Slade, Tyson said, "Okay, so we, what, grab cars to take us as far east as we can go, then hoof it? How many cars you think—" Tyson hesitated. "What the fuck are you reading?"

"Soulmates," Slade said, holding up the cover for him to see. "I'm going to have one." Then he grimaced. "Or so the patch-wearing vagrant said."

Tyson peered at Slade for much too long, then glanced down into the bag he was carrying. He blinked, looking flummoxed. "You put them in the bag."

"Yup," Slade said, adding another one. If nothing else, the photography was entertaining.

"You told me the bag," Tyson growled, "was for survival stuff."

"It is," Slade said. "If I'm going to survive in this post-apocalyptic world, I want to have a good woman at my side. A fellow genius who can run facts and figures in her head for unskilled inebriates like you so *I* don't have to do it all the time."

Tyson squinted at him for several minutes, during which, Slade went back to reading. Eventually, Tyson said, "What if she's a badass, instead?"

Slade looked up from *You, Too, Can Have A Soulmate* and frowned. "You mean like a lawyer or something?" He *supposed* he could put up with a lawyer, as long as she didn't get pissed off that he knew more about the subject than she did.

"No," Tyson said. "Someone who likes guns."

Slade peered at him, the only compatible person he could think of being some sort of physicist. "You mean like electron guns? For particle acceleration?"

Tyson's bovine stare was enough to tell him that a nuclear physicist was not, indeed, what he had meant.

Slade's frown deepened. That left some sort of creative genius. "So, like, an artist? Someone who could use glue guns and spraypaint or something?" True, he hadn't considered an artist, but they were flighty and generally unstable—at least the good ones—and Slade already had all forms of creative genius covered. He could slap out the next awe-inspiring Mona Lisa in his spare time—if he didn't get bored halfway through. That was usually his problem with art. It was boring.

"No, an honest-to-God badass," Tyson said. Then, when Slade just peered at him uncomprehendingly, he said, "like a Congie or something."

Slade snorted at the very idea. "No," he said. The *last* thing a Congie would be able to do would be stimulate him in any way at all. Congies weren't exactly known for their educational prowess. They knew guns and blowing shit up and killing things and making perfectly executable threats. *Totally* not Slade's bag. They would have *nothing* in common. He told his lackey as much.

"My Ma said opposites attract," Tyson said.

"*Nooo*," Slade said, rolling his eyes, "that was Charles Agustin Coulomb."

Tyson stared at him blankly.

"The *physicist?*" Slade demanded, at Tyson's stare. "Coulomb's Law? The electrostatic interaction between electrically charged particles?"

When Tyson just peered at him, Slade groaned and slapped his forehead. "Furgs," he lamented. He actually liked that Congie word, as it was *such* an accurate description of most of the knuckle-dragging morons he had to work with.

"Okay, so how about a farm-girl?" Tyson suggested. "Ya know, one of those tight-jeans, cowboy-hat types?"

Slade shuddered, but forced himself to say, "I suppose that might work."

Tyson laughed. "So what, you're placing orders, now?"

"Well," Slade said, "if one were to look at the universe and the effect our attention has on it, I don't see why the hell not." He tapped his chin. "I want her to be blonde. I like blondes."

"Just like that, huh?" Tyson snorted. "Yeah, okay."

"There's something about that *hair*," Slade went on. "Especially *platinum* blonde. Oh, that's nice…"

Tyson gave him a long look. "My Ma also said if you ain't found your perfect girl by thirty, you ain't lookin' in the right places. Or you're gay." Tyson cocked his head at Slade. "*Are* you gay?" Not with any malice, just like he was intellectually curious—if 'intellectually' was a word that could be applied to a six-foot-four slab of hillbilly gorilla.

Slade sighed and tossed a couple other books into the bag. "Be sure to tell them to grab stuff that will keep. Canned stuff, dried stuff. Dried stuff is better, weight-wise. Oh, and look around for seeds. If we can't find actual seed-packets, a lot of the beans and stuff on the shelves might grow. We'll need that wherever we end up."

"So you're gay."

Slade heaved an enormous sigh and turned to face his lackey. "I haven't hit on you yet, have I?" Slade demanded.

Tyson seemed to consider that. "I'm actually not sure."

Ugh. Inebriates. Slade walked over to the shelf marked Underground Houses and started perusing the offerings.

"*Have* you hit on me?" Tyson asked.

Slade groaned inwardly and threw a couple books into his bag. "No."

"Damn," Tyson said.

Slade paused, mid-perusal, and gave his Second a raised eyebrow. "Why? You wanted to give me a bullet between the eyes for the offense?"

Tyson grunted and gave a dismissive shrug of his massive shoulders. "You're kinda my type."

Slade slapped the book shut, delighted. "You're *gay*?"

Tyson gave him a flat look. "You got a problem with that?"

"No." Slade went to the agricultural section. *He* wouldn't be reading them, but the more he thought about it, the more Tyson's words made sense. A mathematically-challenged hick with agricultural prowess might be more useful to him than a smart, sexy platinum blonde. He must have said it out loud, because Tyson frowned.

"Farmers can be smart."

Yeah, right. Slade threw a few books into the bag. If his soulmate didn't show, he was sure that they would be useful to some mindless peon when the time came to make themselves a sustainable food source. Farming was, without a doubt, one of the few subjects of the world that Slade did *not* find interesting. He simply couldn't figure out what people liked about rooting through dirt and manure to do something as basic as raise food. Then he frowned and swiveled back on Tyson. "And what do you mean, I'm kinda your type," Slade demanded, concerned, now. "What kind of type is that?"

Tyson cocked his head at him, considering. "Smart, but not much common sense."

Slade narrowed his eyes. "I have *plenty* of common sense. I just choose not to exercise it, because that's boring."

"Uh-huh." Tyson clearly didn't believe him. "We done here?" To the man's credit, his sack was getting rather full.

Slade glanced around him at the vast stores of knowledge that would be lost in a matter of months or years—however long it took for the roof to cave in and the books to succumb to the elements—and felt a horrible pang of regret. He knew a lot, but he hadn't had a chance, or the inclination, to sift through *all* the knowledge of Humanity. He could piece things together if he didn't have some manual explaining it, but it would take at least two of him to rebuild what Humankind had managed to discover in its two hundred thousand years.

Yes, she was definitely going to be brilliant. Slade hoped she liked agriculture and genetics, because, after Slade's botched experiment into self-experimentation, he found genetics as distasteful as farming.

"We should probably get back to the main camp, if you're just gonna stand there staring at the wall," Tyson said. "Re-assert your leadership and all that."

Ah, dominance struggles. Slade sighed. "My leadership is undebatable."

"Yeah, well," Tyson said, "I heard some guys talkin' like they were gonna challenge."

"And you didn't stand up for me?!" Slade cried.

"I figured you'd have some kinda ace up your sleeve," Tyson said, with another massive shrug.

Slade, who didn't have an ace up his sleeve, sighed. His formidable mental gears started turning as he gave the room of books one last, woeful look. What he *wanted* to do was make permanent camp here, then re-create his glorious new civilization from the ashes of a Barnes & Noble. It was going to be so *annoying* to lose everything.

Still, his claim to leadership, despite utterly annihilating an alien the size of a double semi, was tenuous. He had to assure the imbeciles that he really was in control of the situation. Sheeple and poddites liked that.

"We found some extra guns in that sporting goods store," Tyson said. "Maybe you should start carrying one around."

Slade scoffed at the very idea. He was just as likely to blow off a toe as to actually draw it in time to shoot somebody. "I defend myself with my brain, not a crude projectile. Who was it who was talking about challenging?"

"Couple guys," Tyson said.

"You got names?" Slade asked. He, of course, in furthering his cause of having dirt on every single prisoner at New Basil Harmonious, had bribed the prison shrink into letting him look at the files once a week during his 'phobia therapy.' And Slade, with his photographic memory and short attention span, usually finished in half the allotted time and spent the rest napping on the shrink's comfy leather couch.

Tyson had been one of the few that didn't have dirt. A completely dirt-free background, aside from his minor killing spree. Now that

Slade thought about it, that *definitely* should have tipped him off that something was up about the gun-toting Fabio, but one of Slade's well-documented flaws was that he was lazy. The government shrinks even went so far as to suggest he was on average only using a quarter of his criminal capacity due to 'toxic excess, extravagance, sloth, and general lethargy.' So yeah, perhaps he'd been a little too enthusiastic with those naps...

"Three names," Tyson said. "Dude named Stone and that little weasel Queso and his friend Big Phil."

Slade grinned at his good luck. Big Phil had been an accountant— and a bad one. He'd been put into New Basil Harmonious for eighteen years for attempting to defraud Boeing out of a few thousand credits to extend his yearly trip to Hawaii. As soon as he hit prison, however, Big Phil—who had lifted weights in his spare time due to his low self-esteem from childhood trauma—had acted tough and allowed everyone else in the prison to think he was in there for murder.

Stone, a.k.a. Richard Douglass, was a former cowboy from Texas who lost his job running cattle and found work in running people, instead. His background was dubious, at best, and aside from the disappearances out in rural Texas near the ranches he worked, several illegal immigrant women had gone missing on his watch. Of course, the Border Patrol and the Feds hadn't looked into that, and they'd been happy to charge him with dozens of counts of human trafficking, which had given him a grand total of six years in prison. Slade, however, had the man's psych profile, his history, and his session records, which had alluded to—but of course not confirmed—his homicidal tendencies.

Queso, on the other hand, was just an all-around backbiting vaghi who followed the swing of the pendulum. He had, however, attempted to get his sister into the country four years ago and, instead of arriving in San Antonio as expected, she had never been heard from again. It hadn't been Stone, of course, because Stone had been in prison, but it was definitely a happy coincidence.

Slade guessed that Stone was the ringleader, as neither Big Phil nor Queso showed any leadership tendencies whatsoever, and Stone was a mass-murdering psychopath that hadn't gotten caught, which meant he was smart. Relatively speaking.

"All right," Slade said. "Let's head back to camp. But first, I'm going to want to stop by the sporting goods store and the grocery. I'm going to need goggles, a squirt gun, a bottle of Pepsi, white vinegar, a dozen boxes of baking soda, plastic utensils, a gaming joystick, and a skimmer."

For a long moment, Tyson said nothing. Then, reluctantly, he said, "You want a skimmer."

"Yeah," Slade said. "I'm gonna take it apart and turn it into a table."

Tyson gave him a long look, and it was obvious that the monkey was trying to piece together his plan in his tiny primate head. "Why the baking soda?" Tyson eventually asked.

"Because," Slade said, sighing hugely, "I want to solidify my position as supreme leader."

"Of a prison gang," Tyson added.

Slade deflated somewhat at his companion's dry tone. "Well, yes. It's a prison gang *now*. But that's beside the point. Eventually, we will be rebuilding society from the ground up." As they left the bookstore, he raised an eyebrow at Tyson. "What do *you* want in your perfect society, Tyson?"

"Free food, lots of sex, no laws, no crime."

"No...crime?" Slade grimaced. "But...you're a criminal."

"No money, either," Tyson said. He hefted the sack of books over his shoulder. "Root of all evil and all that shit."

"No...money?" Now Slade was getting worried. If there was no money, it would be hard for him to steal it. "How can we be rich if there's no money?"

"Rich?" Tyson snorted. "What's the point in being rich?"

"What's the point in..." Slade babbled, flustered. He blinked at his lackey. "You've obviously never been rich."

Tyson glanced down at him sideways. "Second richest family in Alabama."

Alabama wasn't exactly known for its wealth, but Slade supposed that, as a man with accounts worth the GDP of some planets, he had disproportionate standards. He grunted. "Okay, so then you know the miracle of Armani, Dalmore, Glenfiddich, and Ferrari." He kept his brands in the low range, so as not to make Tyson feel left out.

"Don't really like Scotch," Tyson said, with another muscular shrug. "I'm a Miller man, myself."

Slade shuddered at the very idea. "That's…quaint." Swallowing down bile, Slade tried not to think of the aforementioned piss-water and busied his labyrinthine mind with how not to die in the next 24 hours, instead. That would be fun…

• • •

Tyson lifted the table-cloth to look under the disassembled skimmer at him in confusion. "I still don't see what the hell all the baking soda was all about."

"You don't see a lot of things," Slade said, as he spliced another wire and wrapped it in electrical tape. "I've made an effort not to let that bother me." Hunched under the 'table,' which was essentially a dismantled, upside-down one-person skimmer to which Slade had hastily attached legs, Slade held his wiring job up, giving it a critical glance, then went back to work on the upended guts dangling around him. His Pepsi bottle—now half drained of Liquid Life—sat beside his knee. The Super-Soaker, now filled with distilled white vinegar, sat beside it.

Slade had claimed the head of the massive table that they'd shoved together from all the restaurant seating as his own personal dominion. The one nearest it—the one where Stone and his duo were most likely to sit in their bid for leadership—Slade had replaced with a jury-rigged, overturned skimmer, now draped in fancy white tablecloth. He and Tyson had ordered everyone out until dinner, which their panicked kidnapees were in the process of preparing.

Through the open door to the hallway outside, Slade could hear the rabble waiting with growing agitation for food.

"Only five minutes 'til they're allowed in," Tyson commented. "You gonna be done in time?"

"Yep," Slade said. "Do you have any metal pins or replacement parts?"

"Uh," Tyson said, tearing his attention from the door outside, "yeah, quite a few, actually. Hip, leg, arm, shoulder, skull…"

Slade raised his brow at that, not really expecting as much from a rich Alabama kid. "What'd you do to need replacement parts—piss off a Jreet?"

Tyson's expression became guarded. "Just not that great at watchin' where I'm going, I guess." He gave a much-too-casual shrug.

Slade looked his lackey over, realized Tyson was hiding something, and then decided he could mull over that later. Grunting, he said, "Then you're going to need to stand at least eight and a half feet away from this table." Slade gestured out at the wall behind the head table. "Over there. You'll look more thuggish against the wall. Try to cross your arms. That would be impressive."

"You mean I'm not having dinner?" Tyson growled. "After you promised me steak?"

"I'll feed you later," Slade said. "We've gotta secure our leadership first."

"Why the plastic forks and spoons?" Tyson asked, glancing down the table. "There's *lots* of silverware in the back."

"Because," Slade said, around two chunks of wire in the corner of his mouth, "I don't want pointy, hundred-mile-per-hour *projectiles* coming at my head while we're dabbling in the wonders of electro-magnetic fields. Make sense?"

"Uh." Tyson scratched his head and looked again at the plastic-ware laid out on the row of tables. "Not really, no."

"And that is why you were only the *second* most wealthy family in Alabama," Slade said, slapping the last bit of electrical tape into place and climbing out from under the 'table'. Dusting himself off, he said, "Okay, before we start, do you have any other questions?"

Tyson frowned at him. "You mean other than what the fuck you're doing using a skimmer for a table?"

"That's self-evident," Slade said, waving him off distractedly. "I meant *important* questions, like what you should do in the case they start actually shooting."

"Shoot...*you*?" Tyson offered.

Slade stopped brushing off his hands and paused to frown at his underling. "You know, as my second-in-command, we're going to have to work on your critical thinking."

The big man crossed his impressive arms over his impressive chest. "Our first real meal since getting sprung and you're making me stand by and watch as you eat it with a plastic fork?" Tyson raised an eyebrow. "I think that's a shoot-worthy offense."

"It's *temporary*," Slade sighed. "Besides, you didn't shoot the three dissenters when you had a chance, so now I've gotta clean up your mess. Consider this penance." He snatched up his Super Soaker and Pepsi, flipped the table-cloth down over the skimmer, and went to sit at the head of the long table. "On the bright side," he went on, gesturing to the massive quantities of alcohol they had laid out on the table for their lackeys, "You get to drink loads of expensive whiskey, instead."

"I don't like whiskey," Tyson told him. "I like steak knives."

"Poddite," Slade sighed.

Tyson squinted at him. "What?"

"Poddite," Slade said, carefully arranging his plastic cutlery. "It means that your uninspired tastes mark you as one of the mindless ranks of pod-people that mechanically wander this earth, doing whatever their television or personal devices tell them to, like drinking piss because it's been marketed as 'refreshing.'" He lifted a fork, inspected it, rubbed a dust flake off, then inspected Tyson over it. "Poddite. It means you don't have a mind of your own."

"Anyone ever tell you you're a dick?" Tyson asked.

"Not that often," Slade sighed. "I paid them too well." It was actually rather refreshing to be insulted and threatened at gunpoint. Life pre-Judgement had gotten *very* boring. Then he glanced at the clock and said, "Eight and a half feet. Go. It's showtime."

With visible internal debate, Tyson finally went. He didn't cross his arms, but he still looked pretty badass standing behind Slade against the wall. Like something out of The Godfather.

Excellent, Slade thought, delighted.

About thirty seconds later, hundreds of thuggish men with guns began pouring into the room, a few with their newly-acquired members pulled along by an elbow or whatever clump of hair happened to be handy, well-dressed men and women alike whimpering and dragging their feet, panicked eyes darting around, mascara running, ties askew.

As Slade watched, one of the better-dressed male captives freed himself of his bonds and shoved his weapon-toting aggressor as he made a run for it. He got ten feet before his captor caught him by his gelled hair, threw him over the table, yanked his slacks down, and took him right there in front of everyone, to the jeers of the other former inmates.

That was...unpleasant.

Given such a stellar, grunting example of just one of the myriad things that could happen to him if he did not maintain control over the mob, Slade carefully considered the merits of this particular scheme. Maybe the warden and his thugs had been the wiser men, leaving the raping, murdering lunatics in their cells. But Slade was a philanthropist, and he couldn't leave hundreds of men to starve to death. It had been...a quandary.

But, what was done was done, and unless Slade wanted to kill them all—which he didn't—he was going to have to turn them into his unquestioning minions, instead. That should be easy enough.

Slade observed as the men and women filtered around the screaming man to take whatever seat they found most attractive—or whichever one they could take from someone else. Several even fought over the captives, to the captives' dismay. Slade knew all the ones with guns by name, idly accessing their files in his head as they jostled for position. As he had predicted, being as close as possible to the head table—and thereby to Slade—became a symbol of rank and authority. Excellent.

Slade waited for everyone to sit and for the worst of the skir-mishes to settle, then raised a hand for silence.

"As you all know," Slade said, re-steepling his fingers, "the world is ending." As if to punctuate his statement, another bomb went off in the city to the west, making the lights flicker again, despite the fact that Slade had already activated the mall's emergency generator and they were running completely on supplemental power.

The silence was almost overwhelming. As Slade had expected, Stone and his friends were waiting for a better time to spring their mini-rebellion on him. Which meant they were still scared of him. Good.

"As leader of this glorious new society—the Harmonious Society of God," Slade continued, "I have a few ground rules." He raised a finger. "First, government can get completely fucked."

A round of cheers and hoots went up from the sheeple gath-ered around him. The thug in the process of violently asserting his dominance over his unfortunate captive grew bored and threw the quaking man down on the floor, then zipped up and went to join his friends at the table.

"Second," Slade said, "you may each have *one* slave until you've proven yourselves capable of providing food for more. Food, starting today, is going to get very scarce. If our fellow survivors don't eat it, the man-eating lizards they've dropped on the planet will."

There were some disgruntled mutters at that, but then Slade raised his finger and said, "I am smarter than you. And as such, I have determined that food—not sex, drugs, or beer—will be your biggest priority within a month. If you want to survive, you will act accord-ingly. If you don't…" He gestured at the door. "You are free to leave."

No one left, though Stone, Big Phil, and Queso all looked at the door, then each other. Ah, so the knuckle-dragging furgs didn't just want to leave. They wanted to be in *charge*. How unfortunate for them.

"Third," Slade said. "What was valuable before isn't going to be valuable in the immediate future. Things like electronics, gems, and precious metals won't have an intrinsic appeal until society settles back into a routine and a form of feudalism develops, my guess is in a hundred years or so. Until then, I suggest you begin hoarding things like cigarettes, coffee, drugs, alcohol, soap—especially concentrated, antibacterial dish detergent—rope, wire, antibiotics, birth control pills, matches, ammunition, airtight storage containers, water purification systems, vegetable seeds, potatoes, marijuana seeds, knives, guns, salt, spices, and flammable liquids. And for the love of Garfield, if you happen to be one of those lucky bastards who come across Congie nannites, do *not* use them. Given the proper lab, I can replicate them. In a few months, they'll have the approximate trade equivalent as pure ruvmestin. Tyson will be passing out fliers for items I feel will have the most value in the coming months, listed by order of trading demand."

On cue, Tyson retrieved the stack of neon pink—because everybody loved pink—fliers they'd made in the shopping center UPS store and dropped a few piles down in front of people along the tables, to pass around amongst themselves. Then he wandered back to re-take his spot against the wall, further solidifying Slade's position with his six-foot-four-inches of obedient thuggery.

"If you look at my graph, you'll notice that paper will eventually be very valuable," Slade said, "but not for at least ten to twenty years. Its price will go up exponentially over time, though, as supply dwindles and Humanity tries to remember and re-create what was lost. If you wanna plan for the long-run, stock up on paper, antibiotics, entertainment items, how-to books, and soap. If you're more interested in short-term gains, I'd say stick with knives, seeds, drugs, booze, coffee, and cigarettes. Personally, if I were you, I would diversify my portfolio, maybe keep a couple long-term items on hand, but definitely have enough liquidatable assets that you can maintain your lifestyle until your long-term investments can start paying off."

Then, as the inmates listened in quiet awe as if he were the suited CEO in yet another boardroom meeting, Slade said, "Take a good look at the fliers, because we will be leaving in two days. On the back side of each sheet is a list of the suggested items that each member should carry with him when we leave the shopping center. So, in case you knuckle-dragging furgs can't read, before we depart for the desert, each person should try to have three pairs of sturdy boots that fit, two sets of sturdy *non-polyester* clothes, two pounds of salt, a hatchet, a gallon of fresh water, a water purification system of some sort, a sharp hunting knife, a multi-tool, a firemaking device—such as flint and steel, matches, magnifying glass, or a lighter—two hundred feet of twine or fishing line, a heavy-duty rain coat, a compass, a pack of needles with two spools of tough thread, a durable backpack, a wool or polar fleece coat, a tent or tarp, a down sleeping-bag, a cooking pot of at least one liter in size, and one entertainment item of some sort—such as a deck of cards or a violin. It will be up to you to gather these supplies before departure, but anyone who doesn't have at least half of them at check-out will not be allowed to come along. Further, anyone caught hoarding these items before the minimums have been met by the rest of the Society will forfeit all of their supplies and become sustenance for the group."

The inmates, who had been studying the list, discussing it amongst themselves, went suddenly quiet.

Once Slade was sure all eyes were on him, he said, "Any questions?"

After a moment, one of the braver inmates, a career criminal named Matt Jaeger, said, "Did you just say you'd *eat* us?"

Slade gave him a wry smile. "No, I said that *we* would eat you. Nobody likes to starve to death, and that's where the world is headed."

"Oh, fuck that, man," Matt said, throwing his list down. "Nobody's fucking eating me."

"Then don't steal from the group," Slade said, smiling. "I know you're accustomed to that, but this *is* a matter of survival. Something as simple as a box of matches could mean the difference between life and death, and thieves will be executed."

The furg—a kleptomaniac, really—snorted. Grabbing a pretty blonde by the hair, he stormed out.

Slade watched him go, then sighed. "He'll be dead in a week."

The other former inmates looked amongst themselves nervously.

"Oh, don't worry," Slade said, "all of your compunctions will fade with time and hunger. It's not a *pleasant* thought, but it is likely going to be necessary in order to maintain survival. The planet simply has too many people, and its food production systems have been irrevocably interrupted. Even with the man-eating lizards out there devouring our competition, we're still going to have trouble feeding ourselves until we can find a suitable permanent settlement."

More silence. Slade could tell that he was making sense to the morons, but they were still stuck on the People-As-Food thing.

"I also want to make it clear that if we *ever* come across a domesticated animal of any kind," Slade said, "especially a chicken, goat, duck, or a rabbit, I will personally manufacture a liter of morphine for each person who brings one to me alive." He gestured at their list. "As you can see, according to my estimates, morphine will be at the most valuable end of the list of short-term trade items. Much more costly than the paltry couple of meals such an animal might get you."

As the furgs' eyes widened at that, the numbers already crunching in their inadequate brains, Slade went on, "Further, I will manufacture the equivalent of a quarter-pound of Vicodin for each pound of sealed fruit or vegetable seeds you bring me. A pound of viable marijuana seeds will get you five times that price."

Already, he saw the calculation in their greedy little minds, and Slade knew, right then, that his distraction had worked. By creating a new economy—and installing himself as the FED, more or less—he had solidified his power with a thousand times more permanency than if he had simply shot a couple furglings in the head.

Still, Stone and his friends were going to challenge. He could see it in their beady, unintelligent eyes. Inwardly, Slade sighed. At least all his preparations hadn't been for nothing.

"For now, though," Slade said, gesturing at the table spread out before them, "eat. Drink. It's probably going to be one of the last good meals you have for a while, considering that the rest of the world is currently getting annihilated." At his cue, their terrified servants began filing in with their steaming platters of steaks, asparagus, and all sorts of other delicacies that they had happened to have on hand in the back of the restaurant.

"Wait," Dorrance Greene, a pharmacist who had gotten caught peddling his wares under the table, said, "are we even safe for two days here? What if they start dropping bombs on this place?"

"I only give it a twenty-three percent chance," Slade said. "And that number goes down the longer they wait." He started nonchalantly cutting his steak with his plastic knife.

"What the hell's up with the plastic?" one of the closer furgs demanded. "They don't have silverware in this joint?"

"We're melting them down for easy portability," Slade lied. He took a bite and closed his eyes to savor it.

A moment later, Tyson sat down beside him and snagged one of the passing plates of steak from the wide-eyed, mascara-smeared kidnapees running to and from the kitchen. Without asking, his lackey popped open his newly-acquired pocketknife and started cutting his still-bleeding slab of beef.

"You were supposed to stay behind me," Slade whispered.

"No way I'm missing my steak," Tyson said, around a mouthful of meat. He followed that up with a big scoop of mashed potatoes and gravy.

Slade gave a disgusted sigh and gestured at the tables in front of them. "Well, hopefully the angry men with guns don't decide to assert their challenge while you're sitting..." he glanced at the distance, "...four feet, seven and a half inches from the danger zone."

"I can handle it," Tyson said.

Slade raised his eyebrows. "I assure you, you can't."

Looking him directly in the eyes, Tyson continued to eat his steak.

"Ugh. Fine." Slade rearranged his course of events slightly in his head. "Just get out of the way when the theatrics start."

"Don't let the theatrics start until I'm done eating and we won't have a problem." Tyson continued to eat.

"I just want you to know," Slade said, "you are being very inconvenient."

Tyson gave him a flat look over his food and kept eating.

"So what do you think of the name of our gang?" Slade asked. "The Harmonious Society of God. Got a ring to it, right?"

Tyson gave him a long, considering look as he ate. "I'd say you're asking to get shot."

Slade was wounded. "It took me *six minutes* to come up with that name!"

Tyson kept eating for what seemed like ages. "I can't figure you out," he finally said. The thug cocked his head as if piecing together a puzzle. "Half the time, you act like you've got a good head on your shoulders. The other half, it's like you're batshit insane and just winging it."

"Good steak," Slade said, grunting his approval in the most manly way possible.

"See," Tyson said, leaning forward and glanced at the inmates sitting along either edge of the massive table, then back at Slade. "A lot of them didn't take too kindly to that whole God-talk they fed us. It probably won't go over too well." When Slade just lifted a brow, Tyson said, "How about the Devil's Tribesmen or something like that?"

"Harmonious." Slade stuck the steak into his mouth and started chewing it, "Society of God." After all, it was Slade's society, so therefore, Slade was God, at least to these brain-dead imbeciles.

Tyson narrowed his eyes. "If you tell them they're gonna be calling themselves the Harmonious Society of God, they're gonna shoot you."

"At which point, you would shoot them back," Slade informed him.

"*I* would shoot you."

Slade opened his mouth to complain, but was effectively silenced by three men lunging from their chairs and the concussive blasts of AK-47s tearing through the tiny space.

As a fine white powder from the crumbled ceiling plaster rained down on him and all his nearby tablemates, his good friend Stone leveled his gun on Slade and said, "Look at this dumbfuck! Goggles?

A *bib*? Fucking *cannibalism*? I don't know about you, but I'm *not* letting this crazy asshole lead me through the apocalypse! I don't *care* how smart he is."

"Now I see what the baking soda was for," Tyson commented.

"Showtime," Slade agreed. "Eight and a half feet."

"He'll shoot me if I move," Tyson said.

He probably would, at that. Ugh! Slade hated it when idiots didn't do what they were told the first time. It almost inevitably threw inconvenient wrenches in perfectly good plans.

"Gimme one good reason I should let you live, *Sam*," Stone growled. "Yeah, I know who you are. Samuel *Dobbs*. Brother of that dumbass Zero, who can't even take a shit without an alien wiping his ass for him."

"He's winning my case for me," Slade said, delighted.

"Wait," Tyson said, blinking at him with confusion. "Zero's your *brother*?"

Slade rolled his eyes. "Only by merit of my father's penis."

"What the fuck are you two whispering about?!" Stone snapped, shouldering the rifle and scowling at them down the barrel, finger depressing the trigger. Beside him, Queso and Big Phil were brushing the powdery stuff off their arms as they held their guns with the other.

Slade cocked his head at Stone and raised his voice to loudly say, "What...My father's penis?"

Stone blinked.

"I'm sure it was rather large, if genetic influences are any indication."

Stone turned bright red. Several men around the room chortled.

"Listen, you ailo prick," Stone growled. "I'm taking over. You and your gorilla, over there, can go trundle off. This ain't a fuckin' freak show."

Slade sighed and pulled out his Super Soaker. "See this?" He held up the neon green device for all to see.

He got a lot of blank looks.

Slade pointed it at Stone.

"Whereas *your* gun contains lead," Slade said, "*my* gun contains a highly concentrated, ultra-corrosive form of hydrochloric acid. One squirt from me—" he demonstrated on a patch of the table, making the white powder from the ceiling foam and sizzle, "—and you lose an arm." He gave them his most psychotic smile. "You wanna lose an arm, Richard?"

Covered in the white residue, Stone hesitated behind the sights of his gun. "How'd you know my name?" he managed, looking a bit unnerved.

"Same way I know Big Phil's dead mother's name was Rose."

Phil frowned.

"You can't read minds," Stone growled. "*Nobody* can do that."

"On the contrary," Slade said, holding up his free hand to his ear. "If you'll listen to the bombs going off in the background, the Congressional Space Force says otherwise."

"Listen," Stone said, sounding slightly less confident, "you ain't got what it takes to be a leader. I do. I been out runnin' cattle my whole life. I know how to lead a team."

"Running cattle," Slade suggested, "...and people? How many trips *did* you make out of Mexico, Stone? San Antonio was on your route, wasn't it?"

Stone's gun wavered, his eyes flickering sideways at the people watching. "So I did a little smuggling. Big deal. Everybody knows that."

Slade continued to smile at him. "Yeah, but they think you were a *drug* smuggler. Does everyone know that you never delivered the women that looked like your dear old mother? What was it you liked? Dark hair, dark skin? What was she, Cherokee? Bet those Mexican women really turned you on, didn't they?"

Stone went utterly pale.

Slade lowered his voice, totally sober, now. "How many did you kill, Stone?"

"Wait," Queso said, his Spanish accent thick. He was frowning at Slade, now. "Did you just say he was a fucking coyote?"

Slade gave Queso an innocent look. "What, did he tell you he was a cowboy?" He pursed his lips. "He did, didn't he?" Slade tisked.

"Seriously, homie, why else you think an uneducated gringo spoke such fluent Spanish?" The language barrier was, of course, one of the reasons Queso had fallen in with Stone.

"Don't call me 'homie'," Queso growled. He was looking at Stone, though. "That true, you big fuck? You a fucking coyote?"

"Fuck no," Stone growled. "He's lying."

"I suppose if you find that boring, we could talk about how Big Phil doesn't really know how to shoot a gun...do you Phil?"

Phil jerked, suddenly looking like a Takki whose butchering number had come up.

"See," Slade said, still smiling at Stone, "you're not a murderer, Stone. Of men, anyway. You like to hide it, do it all alone, when no one's around to hear her scream. Makes you feel real good, like you're stickin' it to that bitch of a mother."

"Shut up," Stone said.

"Hell," Slade said, turning to Big Phil with a little frown, "your big, bad, backup isn't a murderer, either. He's an accountant who got put away for fraud."

"That true?" Queso demanded, the vehemence in his pitch increasing. "That true, Phil? You get put away for fraud?"

Phil, for his part, was looking queasy.

"In fact," Slade went on, "the only one who's ever killed a man, between the four of us, is Queso, there."

But Queso wasn't listening. He had raised his gun and placed the muzzle against Stone's temple, "You fucking *puto*, Stone. You tell me. You a fucking coyote? You run women to San Antonio? What about a girl named Rosa Delgado? You run her cross the border, man? You fucking kill her?"

"I'm not a fucking coyote!" Stone snapped, distracted by the gun muzzle in his ear. "The freak's lying."

"Or maybe not," Queso growled, leaning in close next to the barrel of the gun. "Maybe you go kill Rosa, eh? Maybe you violate her like those other girls you told me about?"

"Now Phil," Slade said, ignoring the other two, "we both know you're a follower, not a leader. You never could bring yourself to excel, after your parents were so hard on you. You spent so much time studying, so much time doing exactly what they wanted, that you never got to live. You never got to *relax*. You just wanted a few more days in Hawaii. And they put you in jail for *eighteen years*. When rapists and murderers like Stone, here, got six. That wasn't really fair, was it? Your life was *really* hard. All that pressure…" Slade tisked and shook his head.

"Come on, man," Phil said, his voice breaking. "Just stop it, okay?"

"Yeah, fucking shut up," Stone snapped.

"No, man," Queso said, leaning back so that his gun was extended at arm's length. "I wanna hear what the freak's got to say." He turned to Slade. "He kill my sister, man?"

"Probably not," Slade said truthfully. "Just about a dozen other women he mutilated and buried in the desert."

"Mutilated," Queso said, hesitation in his voice. It was obvious that the language barrier didn't carry the meaning across.

"Yeah. It means he liked to slice up their faces and cut their fingers off with pruning shears," Slade said. "He started a collection, after his third one or so." He wasn't *sure* on that, but if Stone fit the psychological profile of someone with that kind of severe mommy issues—severe enough to kill—he'd definitely disfigured them somehow.

This time, Stone went red. "I never cut their fucking fingers off. See? He's fucking lying. I never cut their fingers off."

Queso was instantly back at Stone's head, jamming his gun into his ear as he whispered against his cheek. "But you did kill them, is that it? You *told* me you like to slice on 'em a little."

"So Phil," Slade said. "When they convicted you, how'd your family react?" When the man just gave him a nervous look, Slade said, "I bet it was awful, wasn't it? I mean, they had such high hopes. Made you go to Harvard for business when you really wanted to go take art in some nice, chillaxed town like Eugene. You ended up crunching numbers, straining your eyes on balance sheets to pay off a debt you never wanted. And when they found out…They never even bothered to show up to your trial, did they? They just *left* you there."

"Shut up," Phil whimpered.

"They didn't *care*, did they?" Slade said. "They never *cared* about you. They only had *expectations*. You weren't their kid, their *child*. You were their *robot*. And, as soon as you weren't useful to them anymore, they cast you off. They never even returned your calls, did they? You never had a childhood, and because of that, because of the *pressure*, you were going to be put away for eighteen years. Kind of ironic how fucked up the system is, isn't it?"

And, right there, Phil started bawling.

Queso glanced at Phil, then at Slade, then at Stone. Then, with a dark look, he pulled the trigger.

At the retort, several of the impromptu waitresses screamed and dropped their dishes. Brains, blood, and other unpleasant matter sprayed across the room to coat the window to the parking lot outside in a macabre showing of translucent gore.

Then Queso turned and pointed his gun at Slade. "So you can read my mind, man?" he said, with an almost crazed sound to his voice. "What am I gonna do? Eh? *Homie?*"

"Eight and a half feet," Slade said.

Queso blinked. "Huh? No, that wasn't what I was thinking…"

Tyson, thankfully, was not an idiot. He backed up, Slade hit the joystick button with his foot, and every piece of metal in the area slapped to Queso's table with a speed and effectiveness to crush knuckles.

Queso started to scream and slap at his hand, trying to free his fingers from the mess. Other patrons were also screaming, their limbs, or, in one unfortunate jewelry-thief's case, their ring-bedecked fingers slapping to the table along with Queso's gun.

"So you see," Slade said, strutting up to the pinned man, "I *could* read your tiny, pathetic mind, furg." He picked up the gun at the same time his joystick timer released, yanking it out of Queso's ruined fingers. "And now…" He pointed the gun into the air and fired the semi-automatic rifle at the ceiling directly above his head until whole sections of the ceiling came down on them in a wash of white dust. Then he gave Queso, who was nursing broken fingers, his best psychotic smile as he levered the gun between his eyes. "I'm giving you a chance to read mine."

Queso, after staring at him for a moment in wide-eyed panic, bolted.

Phil, seeing his one friend dead, his other run away, just whimpered and ran out the door after him. Slade sighed and handed the gun he'd acquired over to Tyson, who was walking up behind him.

"Now," Slade said, unscrewing the cap of his squirtgun, "any of the rest of you unpleasant fuckers get any vastly uninspired ideas, I want you to think about something really long and hard before you do anything stupid." At that, he upended the contents of the Super soaker over himself, to a pleasing array of a roomful of gasps as the vinegar reacted with the half-pound of baking-soda that had fallen on him from the ceiling where he and Tyson had stashed it, leaving a bubbling wash of foam to horrify the masses.

Dripping, covered with a tingly bubbly sensation, Slade handed the squirt-gun to Tyson, who took it gingerly between thumb and forefinger. Once he was sure the entire room got a *good* look, Slade said, "I'm off to take a much-needed shower, as I still have gore from that fifteen-ton lizard clinging to my scalp. Anyone else wants to fuck with me, bring it on." At that, he turned and walked from the room. Hygiene was important.

12

THE RESCUE OF FURGS

Shael hunkered against the glass-smooth, iridescent rainbow leg of the vanquished beast, trying not to let the Voran see how much he'd needed his fire and his meat. And it was *good* meat, too. The savory scents of the alien food was nothing like the pitiful *me-laa* he'd been fed for turns in the weaklings' compound. Even then, Shael's digestive glands were watering, soaking his mouth with the need to fill his stomach. It was shameful, sharing food and heat with a Voran, but, drugged and maimed, abandoned on an alien planet, Shael had been running out of options.

As he watched the Voran cook their meal, his mind wandered back to that memory of Doctorphilip locking him back in his bed. *"You think you're a Jreet? You're a lab rat."*

Shael didn't know what a 'lab-rat' was, but he had the nagging suspicion that his Voran campmate did. To show him his ignorance and desperation, however, was unacceptable.

"That was a neat trick you did with the kreenit," the Voran offered, after he had cooked in silence for some time. He lifted his brown eyes to peer at him over the flames. "Can all Welus do that?"

Shael snorted. "Of course not. I am the *prince*."

"Huh." He turned the meat-covered sticks. "Any Welus read minds or melt stone or any of that fun stuff?"

Shael thought of Twelve-A and grimaced. "No." Whatever he was, Twelve-A was *not* Welu.

"Oh." The Human sounded almost…disappointed. "So you were all alone…wherever you were?"

"Of course. The weaklings were afraid of the politicians, so we had to keep our work secret. Doctorphilip would come to deliver my food and study my warrior traits, but the other servants did not speak Jreet. It helped keep what we were doing secret from the skulkers."

"I'll bet," the Voran said softly. He was watching Shael with an odd look. "So this Doctorphilip…Did he die or something?"

Shael thought again of the tekless vaghi locking him back in his bed, calling him a 'lab-rat,' and his heart started to pound in fury. "If he isn't dead yet, he will be," he swore.

His campmate seemed to read his expression correctly. "He wasn't that nice of a guy, then, huh?"

"He was a lying skulker." Shael grunted and looked away, ending the conversation. The awkward silence fell between them again. Shael felt too hot along his shoulders, back, and arms, and rubbed them unconsciously. The odd stinging worried him. Had some of the plants been poisoned?

"You got sunburned again," the Voran offered as he cooked. It hadn't *looked* like the Voran had been paying attention, which made Shael's flush of shame all the deeper. He pulled his hands from his shoulders, irritated that he had shown weakness. The Voran looked up from twisting the skewers and gave Shael a tentative glance. "If you would wear some clothes, you wouldn't get sunburned."

It was the second time the softling had tried to dress him. The third time, Shael would introduce his brains to his tek. He told him so.

The Voran sighed and went back to his brooder's work.

"Voran, what is a lab-rat?" Shael demanded, after he'd given the furg a few minutes to contemplate his threat.

His companion's hand hesitated in turning the meat-sticks. "That's, uh…"

"Tell me the truth," Shael snapped. "I don't care how bad it is. Tell me what this insult means."

The Voran coughed and his brown eyes flickered to Shael's face for a searching moment before they dropped back to the fire. "A lab rat is something scientists run experiments on."

Shael frowned, now, utterly confused. "Then it wasn't an insult?"

The Voran glanced at him with a flash of uncertainty. "It's uh…" He winced. "Yeah, it's an insult. Sure."

"Why?" Shael demanded, still not understanding. Of course Doctorphilip had had to run tests on him. It was his superior body and mind, after all, that they needed to study in order to emulate.

His companion propped the skewers of meat against the fire, reached into his pocket, retrieved a flask, and took a swig. He regarded Shael a moment with thoughtful dirt-colored eyes before he said, "It generally means someone's worthless. Expendable. Like a rat."

The furg must have guessed by Shael's expression that he had no idea what a 'rat' was, because he gestured with the flask, "Like pests."

So. Doctorphilip had called him a pest. The sniveling coward would *die*.

"I wouldn't worry about him too much," the Voran said. "I'm guessing he left you to your own devices once Congress hit?"

Shael squinted at him.

Joe gestured at the sky. "Congress. When it *attacked*."

Shael glanced at the sky, frowning. "Congress attacked already?"

The Voran blinked at him. "Kreenit? Skimmers getting shot down? Corpses everywhere?" When Shael didn't respond, the Voran cocked his head at him. "Where *were* you? How could you miss it?"

Shael prickled at the insinuation that he had intentionally missed the battle. "My servants left me underground," he snapped. "I would have annihilated our enemies if I had been aware."

"So he just *left* you there." The Voran sounded stunned. "How'd you survive this long without your…servants?"

"I have a special bed that feeds me and stimulates my muscles," Shael said, still irritated that the skulkers had allowed him to miss the battle.

"Huh." The Voran peered at him, then stirred the fire. "You know…" Then he winced and seemed to reconsider what he was going to say.

"Speak, skulker," Shael commanded. "I'll not kill you tonight. You have my word as a warrior."

The Voran's body twitched pleasingly at 'skulker' and he gave Shael an irritated look. "I was going to say that there are government patrol bots programmed to blow away any ships or vessels that make it three rods off the ground for the next Sacred Turn. But I'm sure you have the piloting skills to fly past a *bot*. Right?"

Shael froze, because he did not. "I will need a pilot."

The Voran's snort of disdain was enough to tell him that there *were* no more pilots. Seeing that, realizing what it meant, Shael's heart started to pound painfully. "Are you telling me I can't get home?"

He squinted at him. "You can't get to Welu, no. They wiped out every spaceport, blew up every ship, lined up and executed anyone who knew anything about technology that they could catch. They threw us back to the Stone Age."

Shael felt his confidence waver again, this new obstacle like an ovi to the gut. "I can't go home?" he whispered. His gut and chest hurt and he felt his eyes start to water again—obviously another side-effect of the drug.

The Voran's head jerked up and his brown eyes found Shael's. He cleared his throat uncomfortably. "I…uh…" He scratched the back of his neck, wincing. "Let's just say you could probably make this place your home. I'm doing it, and I hate Earth. Especially Earthlings. Sisters' bones, I hate Earthlings."

"Was Doctorphilip an Earthling?" Shael asked.

His companion poked a stick at the fire. "Probably."

"Then I, too, hate Earthlings," Shael said, feeling his conviction in his soul. "How do we kill them?"

The Voran regarded him a moment, then offered him a stick of meat. "Earthlings can be hard to find."

Shael took the stick and ravenously tore into his share, downing it in great gulps of his massive jaws. "I don't care," he said around bites. "I welcome the challenge. I'll search the ends of this planet until my coils rot off if I have to. Earthlings will die for what they did to me." He finished his skewer and glanced longingly at the juices still flowing down the shaft.

The Voran, who hadn't yet bitten into his share of the meat, offered his stick to Shael. Casually, he asked, "Just what *did* they do to you?"

Normally disgusted by the idea of accepting a Voran's charity, Shael knew he would have little vengeance if he could not rebuild his strength. Saying an apology to the Sisters, he took the stick and ate it quickly, before the Voran could think better of it. When he was done, Shael wiped the grease from his jaws and said, "They descaled me, drugged me, sealed the sheath of my tek, and left me to die in my bed."

The Voran, who had been staring at him, coughed and looked away. "I...see." He cocked his head sideways. "Descaled you, huh?"

Shael felt his face heat under the shame. "Yes."

"That's...unfortunate." He poked solemnly at the fire. "And now you want vengeance?"

"Now I will hunt Doctorphilip's kin, his kin's kin, and his spear-mates and children and make them face my wrath."

"Ah." The Voran let out a huge breath and dropped his head into his hands, staring at Shael across the fire. For several moments, the weakling just watched him. Then, "So this...training facility...you came from. Think you could get us back? It might be a good place to start looking for Earthlings."

Shael snorted and said, "Of course I could," even though he had no idea where they were.

The Voran continued to watch him across the flames. "I can get us back to the place where you got attac—where you *annihilated* those men on the road. From there, we could follow the blood-trail you left from your previous combat back to Doctorphilip and his doomed associates."

Shael sniffed to hide his own embarrassment. "We could do that." He didn't, of course, want to admit that Doctorphilip had done something to his senses to make finding their backtrail impossible, and that he had been irrevocably lost when the Earthlings had loosed their kreenit on him.

The Voran grunted. "Agreed, then. Tomorrow, we find this la—*den* you came out of and begin our hunt for Earthlings."

Which sounded reasonable enough. Without a spaceport or ships, Shael had little else to do with his time. Hunting those that betrayed him seemed a good way to entertain himself.

"So, Welu…" the man began.

"You may call me Shael," Shael offered. "We shared a campsite. We plan to hunt together. Custom requires it, however distasteful it may be."

"I'm Joe," the Voran agreed, holding out his hand. And, for some reason, when Shael just stared at him, wondering when the Vorans started using the names of chattel, he added "*Dobbs*." His campmate then waited expectantly, hand out.

Shael peered at the Voran's palm. There was nothing in it. Frowning, he peered back up at his face. "I already ate your food, Voran."

The skin of the weakling's face reddened. "No, it was a—it's a Congie thing." When he saw Shael was not about to offer him anything in return, he let out another huge breath again and dropped his empty hand. "Never mind."

His hunger satiated, their discussion over, Shael grunted and started curling into the grasses to sleep.

"You know," the Voran said, watching him, "if you're going to protect the camp, you should probably lie out in the open, like on that blanket over there. If you cover yourself with grass, it almost looks like you're hiding."

Shael stiffened at the idea of Earthlings thinking he, Shael, the killer of kreenit, was hiding from anything. He immediately went to lie on the blanket beside the fire. It took him longer to fall asleep, since his back was cold, but after being maimed, drugged, burned, and bludgeoned, Shael was desperate to salvage that much of his pride.

• • •

Once he was sure the woman had fallen asleep, Joe gently lowered a second blanket over her, then sat back with J.B. to contemplate his new direction in life.

If the one today counted—which he was going to count even though he was pretty sure it didn't—he'd killed twenty-three kreenit since arriving on Earth. He *could* have killed it—it wasn't old enough to have the hardened sex-gland—but, looking at the brains that were still glistening in the open air, he was pretty sure that honor lay solidly with the sleeping science experiment.

And she *was* a science experiment. From what little he'd managed to get out of her that night, he'd put together that A) one of the labs of experiments had survived, at least partially, B) someone had brainwashed her into thinking she was a Jreet, and C) they had done a really, *really* good job. And Jreet, loveable furgs that they were, were easy to manipulate, given the proper offerings to their pride.

So, tomorrow, they were going to go back looking for more.

Why Joe particularly cared about finding and saving a bunch of science experiments that thought they were Jreet was probably a lot more personal than anything else. Congress had taken a gigantic dump on every Human Congie that had ever died fighting for it, including thousands of friends that Joe had known or served with over the years, and Congress wanted the experiments dead. Therefore, Joe wanted the experiments to live long, prosper, and spread their genes across the continent. It was pretty simple.

I'm finally going to take that piss in their nuajan machine, Joe thought.

He'd definitely killed more kreenit than any man had a right to. As far as he knew, Rat had held top honors back before she went private-service, with six. Twenty-three was pure love of the Sisters—there simply wasn't any other explanation. And twenty-three dead kreenit was hundreds of thousands, if not millions, of people that would survive this year alone because of his efforts.

But, Joe decided, care of the burning of Jim Beam, not even kreenit killing was very fulfilling anymore. He'd enjoyed it for a while, but sometime between the point where he'd been collectively spit on for saying hi after saving his first group of Humans from a eighteen-thousand-lobe kreenit, and the moment he'd caught his first 'tribe' with women and children in zip-ties and dog collars, he'd lost interest.

And there was definitely something interesting about the girl that was even then curled on his blankets, snoring like she hadn't slept in a week. Arrogant, ignorant, intensely frustrating—but interesting.

Still hungry, Joe cooked himself more meat, but his stomach churned more than a little at the increasingly-pungent reek. Five days inside his backpack, exposed to the heat of the day, had not been kind. It was all he could do to get the stuff down. He dozed a little that night, back up against the kreenit's indestructible scales, but was already awake again, building a morning fire, before the woman yawned and opened her eyes.

The first thing she did, upon waking, was throw a tantrum that Joe had covered her while she slept. Screaming profanities that he had, again, tried to dress her, she hurled the blanket at the flames.

Joe, though, had had plenty of time to think about how to deal with her expected reaction as he reminisced by the fire, and, catching the blanket before she could lob it into the flames, said in his most indignant voice, "These are *valuable*. With Earth hit by Congress and everyone stabbing each other in the backs just trying to survive, we need as many blankets as we can get. I thought they'd be *safer* with you."

He was, of course, banking on the idea that Jreet didn't need blankets, and whoever had brainwashed her had done an excellent job, thus she probably didn't even know what they were.

Indeed, Shael stopped screaming and frowned at the hollow-fiber, reflective, ultradown blanket. "You weren't trying to dress me?"

"No," Joe said, rolling it up. "I was trying to safeguard my stuff." He shrugged. "But if you think it's too valuable and you want *me* to guard it next time, that's fine. It's a big responsibility."

She licked her lips. In her sleep, she had tugged the covers closer, and she was obviously thinking about how *good* it had felt to 'guard' his blanket for him. Lifting her head with that imperious attitude that Joe was beginning to find rather cute, she said, "You were right to leave it with me, Voran. As the one with the most kills between the two of us, I will protect it."

Oh, lady, if only you knew, Joe thought, remembering Der'ru and Rastari and Neskfaat and Eeloir and all the other battles throughout his long lifetime. He resisted the urge to drag out his canteen again—he was running low—and cleared his throat, instead. "Yeah, that sounds good," Joe said. "I'll carry it for you until tonight. Wouldn't want it to slow you down in battle."

She looked like she was going to argue a moment, then grunted her assent. "Good idea, Voran."

Joe went to cook them more meat, but, despite his precautions, his prize had finally been discovered by flies. In a starving world, Joe was willing to eat rancid meat, but not wriggling meat. Shael, apparently, was of the same mind, because when he offered it to her, she wrinkled her nose in distaste and said they could hunt something better. Joe didn't have the heart to tell her that hunting, in a land ravaged by kreenit and every Human survivor with a gun, wasn't really an option anymore.

Hungry, running low on whiskey, wondering why he had volunteered to not only feed *himself* in this hungry world, but a naked, utterly ignorant *girl*, Joe loaded up his gear in a foul mood and started leading them back the way they had come. Shael tagged along beside him, oblivious to the fact that he was considering how much of a Karmic kick in the ass he would get for leaving her behind, or that she, despite their talk about the hazards of second degree burns, continued to go stark naked.

Joe was still trying to figure out how to broach the subject of sunscreen when they stumbled across a family of four, hogtied in cheerful purple rope beside a cold campfire. They were, like the fire, long dead. Whatever stuff they had once owned, even their clothes, had been taken from them.

As Shael's lips twisted in a grimace, Joe squatted beside the bodies, looking for some sort of indication of how they'd been killed. It was pretty simple to figure out. Between the bloody, skinless wrists, their lack of wounds, and the way their bodies had cracked and wrinkled under the sun, it was pretty obvious they'd dehydrated to death.

"What kind of creatures bind their enemies and leave them to die instead of doing them the mercy of killing them?" Shael demanded, apparently having made the same conclusion.

Joe grunted and stood. "Earthlings."

Her look of distaste grew. "We must kill them."

"Agreed," Joe said. "But first, we need to find Doctor Philip and make him dance on your tek," he reminded her.

Shael nodded solemnly. "That is true, Voran. First Doctor Philip." As if she were making a list in her head.

Seeing the stony determination in her emerald eyes, Joe wondered what, exactly, they would do if they actually *found* Doctor Philip, as the first thing *he* would want to do would be ask the man what the hell he was dealing with, and how many more of them were potentially out there. Shael, however, seemed intent on simply slaughtering the guy and going back to hunting Earthlings.

Leaving the four corpses where they lay—Joe had come across far too many bodies to attempt to bury them all—they returned to the road back to Shael's lab. Despite Joe's objections, Shael walked brazenly down the dotted yellow centerline for the next few lengths, utterly exposed to any kreenit, government bot, or bad guy who decided to take a pot-shot at her. For his own part, Joe decided to 'skulk' in the shadows beside her, staying out of sight, just in case someone opted to take Shael up on her challenge.

Which, not surprisingly, someone did. The same swaggering, arm-swinging furg who had shoved his companion and bolted the day before came striding out of the woods, a machete on his belt and a sneer on his face.

"Hey bitch!" he snapped, stepping out of the woods where he'd been camped on a hill, watching the road. "What's the matter...your Congie run off?" He yanked the machete out of its sheath, still lumbering toward her in that ridiculous swagger.

Shael stopped in the road and frowned at the man, sunburned face full of incomprehension. Joe reached for Jane.

Jane wasn't, he discovered, necessary. Before the swaggering kid got within two rods, his head exploded. Like a zit. Brains everywhere, blood still pumping out the open top of his skull, hairy pieces of scalp getting caught in the branches overhanging the road. Joe froze as spatters of gore hit him, acutely aware whose brains *could* have been dotting the asphalt, should the woman have decided to pop his zit rather than put him—and his body-armor—through a wall. He swallowed hard and carefully pulled a clump of bloody hair from his jacket.

As if she had just swatted an insect, Shael turned back to the road, ostensibly to figure out how far they had to travel.

And that, Joe thought, dropping the bloody clump of blond hair to the ground, *is why you should be running in the opposite direction*. Even then, the corpse was twitching on the road, oozing fluids and shit out over the tarmac.

Running the opposite direction...or maybe teaching her a few moral truths. Like, "You only kill them if they're going to kill you." Then again, the guy was obviously going to do just that, so Joe really didn't have a leg to stand on. He just had the ominous gut feeling that, had it been a toddler, jeering and flinging insults, Shael would have treated him with the same courtesy.

She and I need to have a chat, Joe thought. Then he winced, wondering how he could do that without ending up like his headless friend.

"Come, Voran," Shael said from the road. "We're getting close to the place of the Earthlings."

In all reality, Joe had gotten out his PPU and his map and had narrowed down their target to a lonely—and government-owned—patch of land near the side of the mountain exactly three-point-oh-three lengths away, easily reached by cutting through the brush to the north, but he meekly followed her anyway.

As expected, the corpse Joe had left in the road the day before was missing, either consumed by kreenit or hungry survivors. When they got close enough, Joe found the man's hands and feet hacked off and discarded in the woods beside the road. Nearby, bloody sneaker-prints were covering the area, tracking in and out of the dead man's blood, and Joe, remembering the same pattern on the dead kid's upturned feet, realized *who* had eaten the corpse.

Humans are disgusting, Joe thought. *They didn't need to give us a Sacred Turn. We're going to be stick-throwing savages in six* rotations. With the kreenit eating man, beast, and food stores alike, and with the world's population—which had been centered away from the food-production areas, barely able to sustain itself—dropping by millions every day, he was pretty sure that Humanity's reversion to barbarism was going to happen a hell of a lot faster than the bureaucrats on Koliinaat expected.

Six hundred and sixty-six turns, Joe thought, staring at the dried puddle of blood filled with sneaker tracks. *There's not going to be anything left.*

Humanity, with its 'high-tech' arrogance, ultra-specialization, and disdain for food production, was going to simply die off.

And, eying the fly-covered hands and still-sneakered feet that had been discarded in the grass, Joe wasn't even really sure anymore that was such a bad thing.

Joe let Shael lead him back to the compound in silence, surprised when she actually brought them to the government property he had located on his map. For someone who prided herself on her Jreet heritage, she seemed to have a pretty outstanding sense of direction.

Shael stopped in a parking-lot strewn with black-windowed skimmers and similarly dark land vehicles, frowning at the front of what looked like a coffee shop. "There is the training compound," she announced.

Seeing all the vehicles parked outside, Joe pulled Jane and unobtrusively got behind a van. "So that's a government facility? How many guys inside?"

Shael snorted. "Only the chattel, Voran. But we can kill them if they stand in our way."

Over their walk back to the lab—on those few times his 'Voran Jreet habit' seemed to randomly work—Joe had come to realize that the 'chattel' she had spoken of were, indeed, more experiments, especially an intriguing one she had called Twelve-A. A 'minder,' as the reporters had dubbed them, borrowing from the scientists' own petnames for their projects. What really got Joe interested, though, was the fact that there weren't supposed to *be* any minders alive. By all accounts, *none* of the experiments should have been alive, but the telepaths were really, *really* rare. Like a breeder in a Bagan hive. The idea that a minder had survived was oddly thrilling, like Earth was one step closer to taking a piss in the Congressional nuajan machine.

It also left Joe leery as hell. He'd watched videos of the hundreds of Congressional soldiers that had died with a minder's thought, eyes rolling into the back of their heads and slumping to the ground like lifeless dolls. They were, by far, the most dangerous of any of the experiments.

"So Twelve-A is in there?" Joe asked, trying to figure out how to approach the compound without giving off the vibe of a government goon and therefore getting himself arbitrarily obliterated.

Shael squinted at him. She had made it clear she disliked it when he spoke Congie, and there was no mistaking the sound of it coming off his lips.

Reddening, Joe tried again. Despite how many times he tried, his tongue kept producing the sounds he'd been raised with.

"If you wish to speak filth, skulker," Shael eventually said, with the utmost regality, "do it elsewhere."

Joe tensed again, that muscle in his neck twitching. "That is so like a Welu, to complain when another shows more learning and worldly knowledge."

Shael squinted at him, and for a moment, Joe wondered when his bubble was going to burst. Then she said, "A *true* warrior refuses to learn the habits and customs of his enemies."

"Oh?" Joe demanded, crossing his arms and glaring at her over the abandoned cars. "What better way to annihilate them than by using their own weaknesses against them?"

Shael snorted. "By finding their strengths and utterly crushing them in front of their kin and spearmates, so there is no question who is the greater warrior."

Of course. Because, to a Jreet, losing a good fight was more worthy than winning a poor one.

Joe sighed. "I was asking if Twelve-A is inside the compound."

Shael regarded him disdainfully a moment, then Shael's pretty green eyes went slightly distant. "No," she said, after a moment. "He took the others over the hill. They're getting eaten by another kreenit."

Joe froze and waited for her to correct herself. When she didn't, he said, "What?"

She gestured disgustedly at the mountain. "The weaklings don't know how to fight. They're holed up in a cave, whimpering like cowards. He says Nine-G is getting tired and the kreenit is digging them out one at a time. It's eating them slowly because it's swallowed enough it's no longer hungry."

Joe blinked. "Well, go tell him to kill the kreenit." He knew that was more than possible. He'd seen the Dhasha regiment get murdered on live feed. Kreenit were, in essence, just much larger and stupider Dhasha.

Shael's eyes went distant, then she gave a snort of disgust. "Twelve-A says he's not going to kill anything, ever again, and the others are too scared to reach their war-minds. Nine-G is getting tired, but he can't kill it. The furg is too stupid to understand its weaknesses."

Joe blinked at the idea that the minder—a military experiment in genetic weaponry—was refusing to kill anything. When she didn't correct herself, he demanded, "Twelve-A's just gonna let the kreenit *eat* them?" When that was clearly exactly what was going to happen, he said, "Fine. Tell me where they are. *I'll* go kill it." Knowing just how little time it took a kreenit's monomolecular talons to dig through solid stone, and how voracious its appetite was, Joe slammed Jane back into her holster and said, "Which way?"

Shael frowned at him. "Which way to what?"

"*Save* them!" Joe cried.

Her scowl deepened. "You want to *save* them?" As if he'd suggested he wanted to give himself gangrene.

"Yes, damn it," Joe growled. "Ask Twelve-A where he's at."

She gave a derisive snort. "They're not worth your time, Voran. They can't even defend themselves, thus they deserve to die."

Joe decided *not* to mention the way he'd found her, tied up, naked, and the object of a shoving-match between three hygienically-challenged thugs in the middle of an abandoned road. "Yes, but you told me you enjoyed Twelve-A's company."

Her face fluttered with momentary uncertainty before she raised her chin and said, "He's a weakling." And that, apparently, was that. She started walking around the trucks and SUVs, paying special attention to the tires. "These are only usable on flat ground," she snorted. "Just how primitive *is* this species, anyway?"

Realizing that she was completely content to let Twelve-A die due to the Jreet belief that warriors were the only legitimate breathers of air, Joe went out on a limb and chanced, "Twelve-A might be able to find Doctor Philip."

Shael frowned a little, her eyes going unfocused. "He says he killed Doctor Philip."

"You see?!" Joe demanded, his voice growing thin with desperation. "A warrior. He avenged the wrongs done to you. He's just tired from the fight. Now where is he?"

Shael sniffed and picked gravel from the treads of the tire. "Killing a weakling does not make one a warrior." Her fingers found half a dragonfly and pried it loose, then held it up to the light, apparently fascinated by its wings.

Joe narrowed his eyes and was about to give her the straight scoop about weaklings and Jreet and naked chicks with attitude problems letting her friends get killed, when a titanic mental sledgehammer hit the gong of his mind and a gentle voice said, *We're west. Past the fence that Nine-G broke. Up the hill. Please hurry. It just ate another one. I'm too close to the exit. I'm going to be next.*

Flattened by the mental voice, Joe grunted and steadied himself on a car. "Burn me," he whispered. "Oh burn me, burn me." Feeling that kind of inescapable power, his first, gut-deep instinct was to run. Run hard, run fast, and never look back. He swallowed and glanced at Shael, who was still examining her dead dragonfly, apparently not having heard the mental plea.

Nine-G is too tired to keep it away anymore and I can't make the others go into their mindspace, Twelve-A told him. *I tried making it go away, but it keeps coming back. Its mind is too…repetitive. I can't stop it. Please help.*

Swallowing hard, Joe fought the dual vertigo and desire to bolt, then steadied himself and thought very strongly of what passed for a kreenit brain, and how one could dismantle it from the inside.

There was a momentous wave of uncertainty on the minder's part. *I don't kill things anymore,* he said. Which meant, to all appearances, he wasn't going to help Nine-G kill things, either.

"Why not?!" he cried, still feeling the colossal mental fingers grasping Joe's mind in their palm. "The kreenit is killing your friends!"

There was a long, nervous hesitation. Joe could feel the agonized mental debate on the other side. *A Human shares life, just like a kreenit. The kreenit is only doing what it's meant to do. Why kill it?* Then, just like that, the voice and the mountainous presence was gone, leaving his mind ringing with the contact.

"Ash," Joe grunted, holding his head. "Burning ash."

Shael scowled at him over her dragonfly carcass. "What is this beast? Does it actually fly?" She jiggled the gossamer wings in the harsh afternoon sun.

"Your friend needs help," Joe said, turning to look west. He found the torn fencing at the far end of the parking lot, where a large section of the razor-wire fence had been ripped apart and wadded up by some great force. Leaving Shael with her insect, Joe found the trampled flora of many dozens of bare feet, and he immediately took up the trail, moving as quickly as he dared.

Behind him, the woman shouted, "Where are you going, Voran?!"

"I'm off to kill a kreenit," Joe shouted back. "Huddle here and stay out of sight if you're afraid, Welu. This is *warrior's* business."

And, though she could have popped his cranial zit for the slight, her eyes widened and she raced after him like he was headed to a pleasure-palace on Kaleu. With his longer legs and Congie boots, however, Joe easily outdistanced Shael up the steep and rocky terrain. Behind him, he heard her yell of frustration and the snaps of trees as the forest started to flatten again in her bid to keep up.

Joe heard the kreenit—or, rather, the man it was eating—long before he saw it. His ragged cries came from the terrified lips of a dying thing, which Joe recognized from many places, many battles. Desperate, wondering if it was the telepath's screams, Joe put on a final burst of speed to reach the experiments.

The kreenit lay in a circular swath of annihilated forest, playing with a screaming redheaded man like a Dhasha with a Takki. The man was missing an arm and part of his face, displaying white cheekbone underneath. As Joe slowed to find a good firing position, the beast grew tired of its game, snatched up the man's body in its jaws, and swallowed what was left of him whole. Then, almost lazily, the kreenit stretched and turned back to the dark hole it had torn into the mountain. In the shadows beyond the jagged claw-marks in the stone, Joe could see dozens of terrified faces huddled together before the kreenit's head disappeared into the cavern with them.

Inside the cavern, men and women started screaming.

Desperate, now, Joe brought up Jane and sighted in on the back of the kreenit's skull. There was a greasy, purple, six-inch sexual scent-gland that Human PlanOps lovingly referred to as the G-spot right between the horns, and it was one of the only patches on a kreenit that wasn't covered with ultra-hard, reflective scales. If hit with enough energy, it could short-circuit the kreenit's equivalent of a cerebral cortex for a few minutes, giving its handler enough time to put it back under restraints. Or, in this case, kill it.

Unfortunately, Joe didn't have a clear shot at the back of the kreenit's head—which jerked up and out with a new screaming victim in its mouth—so as a last resort, he hurriedly put two blasts in the tip of the kreenit's tail—the last dig of which was a scaleless sensory appendage used as much for feeling as for balance. As the kreenit jerked its head back and screamed, the pain suddenly giving it something else to think about than the moving hunks of meat inside the cave, Joe ducked behind his hillock and waited for the thing to give him an opportunity to hit the tiny vulnerable patch at the back of its head.

The wounded alien screamed and ripped the man he'd pulled from the cave in half, ragdolling and flinging the pieces in fury, spreading gore in all directions. Then, once there was nothing left of the man, it howled and tore at the mountainside behind it in a blind rage. In the tantrum that followed, the monster turned toward Joe and started clawing up the hillside, shredding rock, undergrowth, and trees and hurling the splintered pieces down the mountain, but not giving him a good shot. Getting desperate, knowing that it would only be seconds before the kreenit—who saw with heat-vision in addition to the regular light spectrum—noticed him, Joe raised his gun just above hillock-level and fired at a good-sized pine behind the beast in an attempt to get it to turn around. The titanic creature roared and twisted, zeroing in on the buzz of plasma, then immediately started tearing the tree to pieces with its two-foot-long black talons, showering the surrounding area with wood-splinters the size of Human legs. Joe was pretty sure the beast even ate some of it, plasma and all.

Only after reducing the tree to pungent debris did the kreenit lift its head to roar, bringing its skull above the line of its back. In that moment, Joe found his shot. He said a prayer to the Dhasha mothers, asked the Jreet Sisters not to screw with him for just a few seconds, and pulled the trigger twice in rapid succession.

Even with Jane's AI targeting and Joe's rotation of kreenit-killing behind him, the first two charges dissolved one of the animal's wicked black horns instead of their target. Joe inwardly cursed and, before the kreenit could twist to investigate, fired again.

The Sisters had apparently decided to only screw with him a *little* this time, because the third shot hit the nerve bundle squarely. The kreenit shrieked and stiffened as the energy-burst to its pleasure-center temporarily short-circuited its animal mind. Then, like an AI that had gotten its power-source yanked, the massive creature tumbled sideways, rolling down the hill for several rods, its titanic body crushing trees and shrubbery until it hit a boulder outcropping and stayed there.

Starting his mental stopwatch, Joe threw his gun over his shoulder and bolted for the twitching, rainbow-colored body, the thrashing legs of which were even then tearing up huge swaths of the hillside. Once he reached the massive animal, Joe dropped his pack and yanked out Prime Sentinel Raavor's ovi, then hesitated to make sure the beast was still breathing. Every once in a while, though it was rare, an energy-burst to the back of the head could actually kill a kreenit.

Of course, *Joe* had no such luck. The damned thing was actually starting to recover by the time he got there, its huge sides heaving as it sucked air into its lungs in hurricane-force pants that were flattening the undergrowth with each out-breath. Its legs had stopped twitching, a sure sign that it would soon wake.

As quickly as he could, Joe went to work cutting the shield-sized, glass-smooth rainbow scales from the kreenit's chest. Under the unbreakable outer layer was another layer of smaller, golden scales, which could be easily hacked away with his knife, exposing thick purplish skin. The kreenit's hide was almost as tough as the scales themselves, so he ended up quickly sheathing the ovi and using his full strength to chop a hole into it with the axe he had taken from a ravaged sports retail store a few towns back. The kreenit began to bleed, a dark purple liquid that was thin like water, but clotted quickly. Even as Joe dropped the axe and reached for the plasma rifle, the blood stopped flowing.

The kreenit snorted and moved its legs, its monomolecular, scythelike talons slicing through another layer of undergrowth a dig from Joe's knees. Joe grabbed his rifle and, as the kreenit grunted and started to rise like a drunken colossus around him, shoved the muzzle of the gun into the bleeding hole he'd created and pulled the trigger. Then he yanked the gun free and bolted as fast as he could down the slope.

The kreenit let out a scream and lunged to its feet with enough force to make the ground shudder, pawing at the air and brush with ovi-sharp claws. When it finally realized that there was nothing physically attacking it, the kreenit started thrashing, tearing up everything on the hillside around it. By the time the plasma had eaten through its internal organs, several acres of old pine had been flattened. It fell slowly, sliding to the ground more out of an inability to move than a lack of willingness.

Once the predator had stopped twitching, Joe tentatively walked back up the slope. He found his pack half-buried under the kreenit's heavy tail, the contents of which had been crushed in the animal's death-throes. His three scavenged MREs from the ransacked Global Police base in the heart of the San-D/L.A. megaborough were still good, but the haft of his axe had been snapped in half. He cursed and salvaged the head, planning to whittle another handle later that evening. His binoculars were miraculously intact, but his water canteen had been crushed beyond repair. The rest of his survival kit was still serviceable, including the matches and the Congie flamestick. He whispered a prayer to whatever Jreet god was listening and repacked everything.

He was just throwing his guns and gear back over his shoulder when Shael burst out of the forest nearby, panting, red-faced, sweaty, and looking utterly furious. She saw the kreenit corpse and stumbled to a halt, her visage first one of shock, then becoming a thunderhead. "You fought *without* me?" she demanded.

Remembering the Amazing Exploding-Headed Man, Joe quickly held up his hands in peace and said, "It was going to kill more of our allies. I wear special gear that gave me an advantage. I didn't have time to…let you take the lead like I should have." Even then, half a redheaded Human body was sliding out from between the kreenit's teeth, regurgitated in the alien's death-throes.

Shael's face twisted in disgust. "Cowards use such crutches as 'gear', Voran. A true warrior needs only himself and his ovi." Shael looked like she would say more, but a sound behind them made her turn.

Almost four dozen naked men and women had climbed out of their crack in the mountain and now stood in a ragged line facing them on the hillside, several sucking their thumbs or holding each others' hands, examining Joe and the kreenit with wide-eyed curiosity. Caught under their childlike stares, Joe got the sudden, nagging feeling of being a new and interesting creature on display at the local naturals preserve—along with the acute understanding that he was looking at one-hundred-percent cranium-popping goodness. He cleared his throat and gave the newcomers a nervous grin, realizing, yet again, he hadn't thought something quite through before he charged in, guns blazing.

A habit that he'd been trying to break his whole life. In Jreet, he said, "Hey. Uh. I'm Joe."

They stared. One of them picked her nose. A few moments later, one started chasing a butterfly. Another bent to pick flowers.

"They don't understand you," Shael noted. She was frowning at her fellow experiments, eying them with the same reserved interest a Dhasha would give a diseased vaghi.

"Yeah," Joe said. His hairs were standing on end at the child-like stares that the experiments were giving him—those that hadn't simply wandered off. Joe cleared his throat and tried Congie. "You guys okay?" he asked, scanning the faces. "Twelve-A? I'm the guy you talked to. You asked for some help?" His words produced the same vacant-eyed, slack-jawed response as Jreet.

"They didn't understand that, either," Shael commented, brilliantly.

Joe scooted closer to his traveling companion, realizing he was standing in the middle of his very own powder keg. "So which one is Twelve-A?" he asked her quietly, silently willing none of the brain-dead experiments to get the idea he was there to take their butterflies and steal their flowers.

"How by the Sister's bones should I know?" Shael demanded, scowling at the other naked men and women as if they had personally affronted her with their slack-jawed stares. "I never saw him, just heard him."

"And he's not talking anymore?" Joe demanded. He was trying very hard to 'send' his questions at the men and women gawking at them, but he'd gotten no response.

Her green eyes went distant a moment, then she grunted. "No. The softling is dead or in hiding."

Dead...Joe swallowed and glanced at the severed torso that was sliding out onto the ground between the kreenit's jaws in a wave of regurgitated blood and orange saliva and felt a wave of disappointment. "Soot."

Seeing the dead man, Shael grimaced. "We were too late for Twelve-A." And, for a moment, Joe actually thought he heard *regret* in Shael's voice. Then she seemed to shake herself and added, "But that is the order of things. A *true* warrior would have defended himself better."

Joe looked up at the other experiments, trying to figure out how to communicate with them. Congie was out, Jreet was out...He tried a few words that he knew in Bagan and Morinthian Huouyt, even trying Mekkvalian Dhasha, but none of it got so much as a blip of recognition from their intellectual radar.

Getting desperate, Joe tried hand-signals, doing his best to act out We're Here To Help, then waited for one of them to say something, anything, but they just *stared* at him like brain-dead furgs—those who were even paying attention to him anymore. The rest were wandering around gawking at foliage, or even climbing on the kreenit. Joe watched one of them cut himself on a kreenit claw, then slump to his butt and start to cry.

"They aren't very smart," a child's voice noted solemnly.

Joe jerked and turned to the little girl that was standing at the front of the group, her young face frowning at the crying man on the ground. She couldn't have been more than eight, but was the only one of the group wearing clothes. The fine hairs on the back of Joe's neck and arms bristled, however, when he saw the massive man holding her tiny hand. Up close, he was *huge*. At least a rod tall. And wide. At least two, maybe three times Joe's weight. Built like a battering ram. Joe had to tear his eyes off of him so he could look back at the girl.

"I don't know what's wrong with them," the girl told him. "I found them a few days ago. Eleven-C can make food."

Joe knew exactly what was wrong with them, and that knowledge was making him more and more nervous as the seconds ticked by in what seemed an eternity. He swallowed hard, wondering again what the hell he'd been thinking. Being around *one* of them was bad enough. *Forty*, though, was starting to make him itch all over, like he had three dozen mental crosshairs aimed at his aorta.

"Look, kid," Joe said to the girl, carefully scanning the curious faces of the group, trying not to envision exploding craniums or exposed brains. "I *really* need to get off on the right foot with these guys. Can any of them understand me?"

"You're speaking the weakling tongue," Shael said, in obvious disapproval.

"A necessary evil when dealing with an inferior race," Joe replied distractedly. To the little girl, who had shaken her head, he said, "Have you heard any of them talk? Maybe in a language you can't understand?" Joe carefully examined the other experiments, the rest of whom seemed to be of normal proportions, except for a staggering number of weird deformities. Lots of them had extra fingers or pointed ears or oddly tilted skulls or eyes that seemed just slightly too big for their heads.

"Nope. Twelve-A's the only one who can talk, and he only talks to you if he likes you," the girl said. "Otherwise, he makes you go away."

Halfway through his perusal, Joe's eyes caught on a blue-eyed, pointy-eared, platinum blond who was huddled behind the giant, looking nervous as hell, more or less using the big guy as a Human shield. Painfully aware of Shael's head-popping habit whenever she felt threatened, Joe got another gut-curdling wave of unease. "Hey," he said to the girl, keeping a wary eye on the blond, "how about you and I go have a quick chat somewhere quiet, huh?"

"Why?" the girl asked, giving him an innocent frown.

As Joe tried to figure out how to tell her the experiments could kill her, instantly and without remorse, for, say, stepping on their toes or stealing their caterpillars, the gigantic man let loose a stream of urine right where he was standing, while scratching his enormous ass with a hairy hand.

"They pee in front of everybody," the little girl informed Joe, wrinkling her face. "It's really gross. Only my little brother peed in front of people, and he was only two. He pooped on the floor, too. Mama didn't like that."

Still feeling the forty stares around him like the crosshairs of a sniper rifle sighted in on his spine, Joe said as nicely as he could, "Can you *please* get one of them to talk to me, you jenfurgling little twit?" By this point, Joe would have happily taken his leave—if he hadn't thought one of them wouldn't squish him for the slight. He more or less felt like a bug stuck in place by a pin through his shoulder-blades, and it was making him cranky.

"What's a jenfurgling?" the girl asked in a curious, singsong voice.

"Something like you," Joe replied.

The child gave him a suspicious look. "I'm not afraid of you. Nine-G could turn you into a pretzel if he wanted to." She patted the giant on a thick, hairy calf. The dark-haired giant grunted and crossed his beefy arms over his beefy chest, brazenly showing off his beefy cock.

Fighting the urge to throw his gear over his shoulder and bolt for the other side of North America, Joe eyed the kid, then the gawking adults. Raising his voice in the most *non-threatening* way he could manage, he said, "Okay, so can anyone else read minds, now that Twelve-A is dead? Maybe Eleven-C and Nine-G? Come on, *one* of these ashers has to be able to talk…" He was all-too-aware of how, with *dozens* of the furgs standing around, badly things could go if one of them, say, sneezed.

Even then, the man that had cut himself on the kreenit claw had stopped sniffling and was awkwardly climbing up on top of the kreenit's head, suckling his thumb.

But the child frowned. "Don't cuss in front of them," she said. "They're nice people. Only Congies cuss."

Joe gave her a flat stare. He allowed her a tic to take in his profusion of guns, his black clothes, the short brown hairs on his itching scalp—the hair was only then starting to grow in—his tattoo, and his drug-enhanced musculature.

Upon seeing the glowing PlanOps tattoo on his left hand, the little girl blinked and lowered her voice to a whisper. "You're a *Congie?*" She wrinkled her nose at him like she smelled something bad. "Mama hated Congies. She said they would hump a goat if they had one, just like Uncle Tyler. She said he humped goats. I'm Alice. Dad called me Squirt, but you're not my dad, so you can call me Alice. Where's your uniform?"

Joe narrowed his eyes. Children irritated him. They babbled incoherent, unnecessary nonsense, asked questions they shouldn't, and they didn't do what they were told. He'd had the good luck of avoiding them until now, leaving the training of the boots to Congies with more patience than himself, but on a planet filled with breeding pairs of his own kind, it was unfortunately impossible to avoid them.

"I left my uniform on my ship," Joe said. Not that he was ever going to use it again. With Joe's sooty luck, it had probably already been discovered and ripped open by a kreenit—or hijacked by survivors.

"You've got a *ship?*" the little girl squealed, her voice high-pitched with excitement. "I thought only *rich* people had ships, not Congies. Congies don't get rich. Mama said so, except that goat-humper Zero, that's why Daddy went to business school instead of off to be a dumb

Congie. I've always wanted to see the inside of a ship. Did you bring it with you?" She looked down the hill they'd come from like she expected to see an interstellar squatting amidst the pine trees behind them.

"No," Joe said, neck twitching, "I left it in a lake to the north." The Congressional bots patrolling after Judgement had been given strict orders to shoot anything that looked 'post-Industrial' in the first three hundred and thirty-three turns. That meant the safest place for something like a superlight interstellar was at the bottom of a lake, ocean, or some other large body of water.

"Really?" Alice squealed. "Was it San Vincente? My dad used to take me fishing there."

"No," Joe said. "It was up near San Francisco."

Instead of dropping the subject, like he'd hoped, her eyes lit up and the pebble-brained little furg said, "My Aunt Jeanie lived in Sacramento! Was it Lake Tahoe? Dad took me fishing there whenever we went to visit! That's a *big* lake."

Joe peered down at the child, caught between wanting to use some choice Congie words on her and the urge to walk away to find some nice, big pine tree to talk to, instead. Children—especially *nosy* children—irritated him. "There was a sign that said Crystal Springs Reservoir."

"Oooh…Okay. Can you take me for a ride?" Alice said, clapping her hands excitedly, obviously having no idea where that was. "I've never been off planet. Dad went off planet on his business trips, but Mom wouldn't let me go. Will you take me? Please?"

Joe's ship computers were the best tech that the blackmarket had to offer, and he was reasonably sure that they could outfly a Congressional Judgement bot, but he wasn't going to test the theory for an eight-year-old's joyride. "No," he said.

Her face dropped. "Please?" she whined.

"No."

She made a face. "Well," she said, taking a distinctly superior tone, "we're not going anywhere with you," Alice said. "Twelve-A says you're mean." She clung to the giant's leg pointedly.

Twelve-A…said he was *mean*? Joe blinked at news that the minder was still alive. He frowned up at the big guy and his big display. "So that's Twelve-A?" Somehow, he didn't seem…gentle…enough to have belonged to the booming mental mountain.

Behind the giant, the skinny blond flinched and quickly looked at the ground.

Seeing that, Joe felt himself start to grin and quickly hid it with a cough. "All right. So which one is Twelve-A?"

"Oh!" Alice's face lit up and her eyes started to flicker towards the blond. "He's right over—dead." She seemed to cough, then quickly looked back at Joe. "Twelve-A tells me to tell you he's dead."

"He tells you that, huh?" Joe asked, crossing his hands over his chest. This time, he couldn't hide his grin. "In that case, I guess I'll have to leave."

Alice nodded. So did every other experiment in the group, at the exact same time.

If Joe hadn't been standing in front of forty-odd people who could probably squish his brains out through his ears—and a telepath who seemed to be pulling their strings—he would have laughed. Instead, he did his best to keep a straight face.

"What's the hatchling saying?" Shael demanded impatiently. "Why do the furglings all stare at us like we're green Takki? Are they Earthlings?"

"No," Joe said quickly, "These are allies. She's saying Twelve-A's alive and right over there behind the big guy." Joe winked at the blond when his head jerked up. This time, upon meeting Joe's gaze, his sky-blue eyes widened and he froze like a startled Takki.

"*That* is Twelve-A?" Shael was clearly disappointed.

"Why, you thought he was bigger?" Joe offered, still speaking in Voran Jreet.

"I had thought he was less…" she sniffed disdainfully, "skinny."

He *was* skinny, too. But tall. Almost as tall as Joe. It made for an odd combination: With his white-blond hair, sunburned body, ice-blue eyes, and pale, hairless Caucasian skin, he looked like a starving abominable snowman with mange.

"It's too bad he's dead," Joe said in Congie, returning his attention to the little girl. "I'm good at killing kreenit. I've already killed a bunch. As it is, I think a lot of his friends are going to die without some sort of help." He shook his head in mock disappointment.

Twelve-A flushed and looked at his feet.

"Well, that's okay, because he's dead," Alice said, getting into it, now. "The dragon ate him *days* ago. He's just a big bony turd, now. Like him." She pointed to the half-a-redhead still sliding down the kreenit's tongue into a pool of orange saliva under its open jaws. "So now you better go or I'll get Nine-G to mash you up like my mom's potatoes." She crossed her wiry arms over her thin chest and gave them an imperious look.

"Is the little weakling *threatening* us?" Shael demanded, giving Alice a frown. She had, apparently, picked up on Alice's tone.

"No," Joe said. "She's saying they will carry on without us and continue valiantly defending themselves until the last one of their tribe falls to a kreenit's jaws. I wonder who will be next? The girl? That gal over there picking flowers? The one on the kreenit? Hell," Joe said, turning to give Twelve-A a pointed glance, "that skinny guy behind Gigantor over there looks pretty bite-sized…"

Suddenly, something massive grabbed Joe's mind and squeezed. *I am not afraid of you.* This time, the mental sledgehammer hitting the gong of his head was enough to drive Joe to his knees. From behind the huge man, the telepath was giving him a blue-eyed stare.

I have killed before.

Joe suddenly found his mind filled with images of terrified faces, dozens of them, along with the emotional terror of people meeting their doom.

The blond stepped from behind the giant, putting himself squarely between Joe and the other experiments, the fear in his eyes gone. *I choose not to kill,* Twelve-A's mountain thundered around him. *That doesn't mean I won't.*

This time, Joe saw his own death, watched himself crumple to the ground, never to get up again. He watched four dozen people leave him there to be eaten by the flies.

I'm not afraid of you, Twelve-A insisted again, his mental voice like a titan's sledge threatening to obliterate him.

"Okay!" Joe shouted, fisting his hands in the churned earth, staring at the ground in desperation. "I get it. You're not afraid of me! Now get out of my damned head, you pointy-eared jenfurgling."

There was a moment of reluctance as the mental mountain hesitated, then, slowly, Twelve-A did.

Joe sat up with a grunt, ignoring the funny look Shael was giving him. Then, though just about any other intelligent man in the universe, when confronted with a genetic weapon who could apparently render his brains to pudding with a thought, would have apologized and scraped for forgiveness, Joe got to his feet, dusted himself off, straightened, walked over to the skinny, blue-eyed turdling, shoved his finger into the experiment's chest, and growled down at the minder, "You pull that flake again, furg, and I'm going to introduce you to Jane."

Twelve-A gave him a flat look, obviously unimpressed.

"Are you hungry?" the child interrupted. "Eleven-C can make food! Out of dirt!"

Joe ignored the child and poked the minder again. "Don't." *Poke.* "Do it again."

The minder sniffed and unconcernedly scratched his face, still meeting Joe's eyes.

Realizing they were going to have to have further discussion on the matter later on, Joe turned to the girl. "What do you mean, food?" Even then, his stomach complained that he'd been on a ten mile hike without breakfast. He'd thrown the rancid meat away that morning, the stench, maggots, and slime-rot from being encased inside his backpack finally becoming too pungent to carry with him safely. He hadn't been looking forward to the idea of breaking into his surviving Human MREs, because once they were gone, he was looking at songbirds or rodents for his dinner, if he could catch them at all.

"Food!" she cried delightedly. "Out of *dirt!*"

After having Shael throw him through a wall and Twelve-A dig through his mind, Joe had the heart-hammering feeling the child's meaning was literal. And, in the days following Judgement, he'd been forced to come to terms with the fact that, sooner or later, he was going to starve. Already, he was seeing his muscle mass from the Congie drugs start to wane, and he was alarmingly weaker with every week that passed without a reliable source of protein. Food, when he could find it, was scarce.

"What's the hatchling saying?" Shael demanded.

Joe gave the telepath a sideways look. Reluctantly, he said, "She says they have food."

We do, Twelve-A agreed, nodding. The minder crossed his arms over his chest and raised a brow.

And, in that moment, Joe realized he was being offered a trade.

Shael perked up slightly. She had been just as disappointed as Joe that morning, when they'd found their breakfast wriggling and smelling of Dhasha flake. "Food?"

Seeing that she now had Joe's attention, the little girl hurriedly turned back to the other naked experiments. "Just watch!" Alice said excitedly, grabbing a petite, well-proportioned young woman by the hand. Joe watched with growing trepidation as Alice brought the woman's palm to the ground and held it there. Enthusiastically, she said, "Make cookies, Eleven-C. Coook-ees."

A tiny frown creased the brunette's brow, then the ground underneath her palm began to shimmer and change, making Joe's already-unsettled stomach lurch. As he watched, the rotting foliage and dark earth shifted into round, tan discs, speckled with black. Joe didn't realize he was backing away until he fell over the kreenit's tail.

When he righted himself, Alice was chewing on a chocolate-chip cookie, grinning. Several other experiments had congregated on the pit the woman had created and were even then gorging themselves, stuffing cookies into their mouths as quickly as they could fit them in. Alice giggled when Joe just stared at her.

"*Told* you," she said.

"That doesn't look like food," Shael said, distaste on her face. Obviously, she expected it to be bleeding. Or, better yet, fighting back.

But Joe was staring at the cookies. For the first time since Command had decided to give him a Human Corps Directorship, he was dumbstruck.

Food. They made *food*. He felt himself staring at the pit like a teenager getting his first view of live ass, his mind awash in possibilities. If they could make food, they could make combat gear, antibiotics, weapons…

We will not be making weapons, Twelve-A interrupted firmly.

Joe brushed off that warning irritatedly, distracted by the awesome wave of possibilities. Of course they would make weapons. If they were going to survive the kreenit, the gangs, and the Congies that came to kill them, they would make weapons. Joe looked at the dozens of childlike sootlings, wondering how many could pull the neat dirt-to-cookie trick. He'd have to start teaching them to make things like knives, guns, ammo…

A split second later, the mountain of Twelve-A's mind was once more squeezing Joe in its granite grasp, the warning clear. *No. Weapons.*

"Fine!" Joe snapped, "Let go of me, furg!"

Again, Twelve-A released him, though this time, there was greater hesitation. *No weapons,* Twelve-A insisted.

Joe ignored him. Half of him—the rational half—was screaming at him that joining a merry band of naked ashers with skull-popping mental powers was a *bad* idea, but the other half was transfixed by the cookies in Alice's hand. He had, he realized with a bit of concern, already subconsciously decided to stay, mind-games be damned. If Eleven-C could turn dirt into cookies, she could turn stone into ruvmestin, trees into alloys, or grass into complicated electronics. They could rebuild *everything*, and the key to it all was squatting right there beside the pit she'd made, picking the chocolate chips from her cookies before she ate them. And, seeing the innocent, childlike faces of the others, Joe knew the only thing stopping him from changing *everything* was the telepath.

Joe glanced surreptitiously at Twelve-A, wondering if he could be convinced to aid his cause, then froze. The telepath was watching him with narrowed eyes.

Joe cleared his throat. To the girl, he offered, "So, uh, what else can she make?"

"Nothing," Alice said. "Twelve-A tells me to tell you she can make nothing but cookies."

Joe scoffed. "Right." To Twelve-A, he said, "We could *rebuild*."

There was nothing good about the Keepers, Twelve-A replied. *We don't want to be like them.*

Joe snorted at the ridiculousness of the idea. "So you're gonna, what…run around *naked* chasing *bugs* the rest of your lives?"

There is nothing wrong with chasing bugs, Twelve-A told him. Which meant, yes, that was exactly what they planned to do.

"But we could have so much *more*," Joe growled. "When Congress comes back, we could *fight*…"

Twelve-A frowned. *I told you. We're not going to fight.*

Joe was going to continue arguing his case, but Nine-G cut him off short when the big man walked over to Joe, took Joe by the shoulders with two ham-sized fists, and leaned down to frown into his face. Then, to Joe's surprise, Nine-G started tugging on the front of Joe's jacket, prying it open so he could see inside.

"He's trying to make sure you're Human," Alice informed him. She grimaced. "They don't believe you're Human unless you take your clothes off for them. They're really weird."

Joe, who had gone stiff as the giant manhandled him, sagged with relief. He unzipped his jacket and pulled his sweater over his head, exposing his chest to the cool mountain breezes.

The huge man's face immediately beamed with pleasure upon seeing Joe's skin. Looking fascinated, Nine-G picked up the discarded jacket and started peeking into the arm-holes. Another of his naked buddies came up and fiddled with the zipper. They looked and acted very much like curious children. Only Twelve-A continued to frown at him.

Joe swallowed and managed a smile at the telepath. Thinking to distract the distrustful bastard with a shiny new toy while he figured out how to take control of the group, Joe dug into his backpack and brought out the binoculars. "Here," he said, taking three tentative steps around the people who were now ignoring him to examine the jacket. "Check these out. You'll like them." He held the binoculars up to Twelve-A, but the platinum-blond man continued to scowl at him.

We're not going to fight, Twelve-A told him again. *That is not our war.*

Joe knew that the minder's perspective would change once he realized that, as experimental Humans with a kill-on-sight order attached to their DNA, it *was* their war. Still, he had plenty of time to convince him of such. Besides, if he could get the furgs to *trust* him, maybe get them to start using those convenient little technologies they were snubbing…"Go on. Try them out," Joe insisted, pressing his binoculars against Twelve-A's chest. The slender man jerked at the contact and grabbed the binoculars reflexively, taking two steps back and making no move to even look at the thing he now held in his hand.

Alice, who had been watching the exchange, took the binoculars from Twelve-A and pulled on his arm. "Here, you look through them like this." She held them up and looked down the mountain.

Twelve-A took the binoculars and held them up to his face without taking his eyes off of Joe.

"No, no, silly!" Alice cried, tugging on Twelve-A's arm again. "They're to see stuff that's far away. Look over there." She twisted Twelve-A around and pointed him down the mountainside.

Joe had the quick thought that maybe he should get rid of the suspicious son of a bitch while his back was turned.

Instantly, he knew it was the wrong thing to think. Twelve-A jerked back to face him, his brow furrowed until he looked downright Neanderthalic. He threw the binoculars aside, and Joe winced as he heard glass break.

Thankfully, Alice defused the situation.

"You *broke* them, you stupid-head!" She kicked Twelve-A hard on the leg and ran to go retrieve the binoculars. Flinching and grabbing his shin, Twelve-A turned to watch her go. By this time, the petite, cookie-making brunette had joined her hulking companion and she proceeded to poke and prod at Joe, tugging at his belt and patting his legs. Six others came to watch, occasionally conducting their own examination of this or that, having special interest in his scars. Joe felt much like a horse up for auction, but he gritted his teeth and bore it. He wasn't surprised when they wanted to take his pants off. Forcing a smile, he bent down to untie his boots and pulled both pantlegs over his feet, mentally assuring himself that a good piss in the Congressional nuajan machine was worth a little gawking by a group of imbeciles.

When the big man—over two digs taller than Joe—started feeling the bulge in his underwear, however, Joe couldn't stand it any more. He brushed them all away with a yell and pulled his pants back on as they scrambled away from him. In that moment, he locked gazes with Twelve-A and he froze, half-dressed.

If you hurt any of them like you hurt the others, I will kill you. The thought rang inside his head like a twelve-foot gong had gone off between his ears. Joe jerked and stumbled with a groan.

I am protecting these People.

The booming roar of the telepath's mental voice was utterly inescapable, hitting from everywhere at once, yanking away Joe's control and violently throwing him to his knees. Twelve-A took a step towards him, his face deadly serious.

They are not your toys to play with, and they are not your grounders to order around.

The intensity was increasing, and Joe cried out and slid completely to the earth, holding his head.

Hurt them, and I will annihilate you. The telepath's booming words slammed through his barriers, rattling the aluminum walls of his being, wrenching images of his past from the depths of Joe's mind, forcing him to gaze upon his own personal nightmare.

I know what you are, Joe Dobbs.

Twelve-A's mental grater plowed through Joe's past, dragging up memories of war and combat, shoving images of death, battle, and pain in front of him, force-feeding it to him until Joe was shuddering, curling into a terrified ball, his mind being ripped apart from the inside. He saw dead Huouyt, dead Dhasha, dead Humans, dead

Jikaln, dead Hebbut, dead Ooreiki…He revisited every terror, every horror that he thought he had stuffed safely away. Everything he'd tried to forget, every friendly face he'd left behind to rot on the battlefield, every sentient creature he'd killed, every awful act that had left him with nightmares…All of it was suddenly flung in front of him, forcing him to look a second time, all at once.

I will annihilate you if you hurt these people.

Joe started to scream, unable to escape, wracked by fear, guilt, pain, and every other emotion he had ignored while fighting for his life, struggling to stay alive on long-forgotten battlefields. He felt himself dying all over again in the tunnels of Neskfaat. He felt himself blowing the brains out of a spy that had killed his best friend on Eeloir. He felt himself quiver in fear as a Dhasha forced him to pick rotten Human flesh from between his sharklike black teeth. He felt himself trusting a Huouyt assassin, when he was too scared and too tired to fear him any longer. He felt himself put a hand on a terrified Geuji and tell him of power and responsibility. He felt himself plunge an ovi into the greatest Sentinel of his Age. He felt himself losing his right arm, watching his liver roll out of the open cavity that was his abdomen…

Joe felt himself losing his mind, surrounded by the insanity that had been his life.

"What is going on?" Shael demanded, dropping beside Joe to grab his shoulder. "Why are you writhing like a softling? Did we not cook the meat good enough? Parasites?" 'Crying,' apparently hadn't been introduced to her vocabulary, yet.

I will annihilate you, the telepath warned again. Twelve-A's mental voice was cold, hard. *We want no part in your war.* This time, the mental invasion was enough to make Joe scream and shudder helplessly in the dirt as the threat hit him from all sides at once.

Suddenly, Twelve-A's mental fingers violently pulled free of the slurry of Joe's mind, leaving him a shaking, tearful mess on the ground. For several minutes, all Joe could do was whimper into the dry, grassy hillside. When he finally managed to crack an eye to look at his assailant, he saw that Nine-G had stepped between them and was glaring down at the telepath in obvious disapproval.

Then the big man turned away from the minder and squatted beside Joe, his deep brown eyes filled with worry. Twelve-A, apparently satisfied that Joe had gotten his point, wandered over to the pit of cookies and began to eat. Other naked adults were squatting around the cookies as well, stuffing themselves.

"Thanks," Joe managed, as the big man helped him to his feet. Joe rubbed his arm across his face, smearing mud, spit, and tears across his cheek. Rather than commiserate with him, however, the giant simply walked off to eat with the others, taking Shael with him.

Shaking, violated, Joe picked up his discarded clothing and fumbled to get it back onto his body. As he did so, he caught Alice's fearful gaze, still fixed on him in wide-eyed horror. Shael, for her part, had left him to squat beside the cookie-pit.

"Let me guess," Joe said gruffly, sniffling as he swiped another trembling arm across his face. "You've only been eating cookies these last few days."

Alice nodded, wide-eyed. She glanced at Twelve-A and then back to Joe. Then, in a hushed whisper, she asked, "Why were you crying?"

Joe glared at her through tears that wouldn't stop coming. "You know damn well why I was crying."

"Twelve-A didn't like me at first, either," Alice said, looking scared. "But he never made me cry like that. I thought men didn't cry. Dad didn't cry."

Joe narrowed his eyes and wiped his face again. Then, glaring at the ground, he fastened his belt, already planning his next rendezvous with Jim Beam.

"Are you going to leave now?" Alice asked tentatively, biting her lip.

Joe ignored her as he stuffed his feet back into his boots, body still trembling from the adrenaline. Shael was at the cookie pit, praising the Sisters for their delectable bounty. *Good riddance*, Joe thought, bitterly. Fewer mouths for him to feed.

"Please don't leave," Alice begged. "Please. Twelve-A didn't mean it. He's nice. Really. Please don't go. I like having someone to talk to."

"I'm not hanging around that freak." Joe's voice was a hoarse rasp from the screaming he'd been doing moments before.

"*Please*," Alice pleaded.

"No," Joe growled. "Not a burning chance." He bent to tie his bootlaces. "Not a burning chance in Hell." The Congressional nua-jan machine could get burned.

Alice narrowed her eyes and was silent for a moment. Suspiciously so. When Joe looked up, she was gazing at Twelve-A, who had turned to Joe.

You will stay. The command made Joe's entire body twitch like someone had shoved a lightning bolt down his spine. He rocked on his feet with its intensity, almost falling again.

When he recovered, Joe's mouth fell open at Alice. "You little furg."

"I'm not a little furg!" Alice cried. "Twelve-A wants you to stay."

"I don't give a rat's ass *what* he wants," Joe snapped, jabbing a finger at the blue-eyed experiment. "I'm getting the hell out of here. These freaks are *dangerous*."

"Don't call them freaks!" Alice shouted. "Twelve-A's ears are *cute*. He looks like my mommy's German Shepherd."

Joe cocked his head at her, trying to figure out what a Shepherd was. "That some sort of dumbass freak, too?" he finally demanded.

"Don't call them freaks!" she screamed, stamping a tiny foot.

"Kid, if I want to call them ash-covered ghosts, then I'll call them ash-covered ghosts," Joe growled, watching Twelve-A warily. The minder had apparently forgotten all about him and was now joining Eleven-C in picking chocolate chips off his cookies, stacking them in little piles on his knee to be eaten all at once. "There's no way in hell I'm hanging out with a group of people who can do…that." He shuddered at the idea of having the telepath dig through his head again. "My head is my business." He picked up his stuff and turned to leave.

"Only Twelve-A can do that!" Alice cried, at his back. "And he's nice most of the time. He just doesn't like strangers."

The ridiculousness of that made Joe stop in his tracks. He rounded on her, glaring. "They aren't *pets*, Alice!" He flung an arm at the dumb furgs squatting around the cookie-pit. "Those people are *dangerous*. They're the whole *reason* why your family was killed. The *whole reason*. *Them*. Right there. You *did* have a family, didn't you?"

Alice's eyes immediately brimmed with tears. "The dragon ate them."

"It's not an ashing dragon," Joe snapped. "It's a kreenit and there's more of them out there. Walking around with these people is just asking to become lunch. Do you really want to get eaten like your parents, Alice? You wanna see your own liver get stomped on by an alien after it slices it out of your guts?"

Alice's eyes went wide before she burst into tears. The petite cookie-making brunette came over and crouched beside the girl, taking her into her arms when Alice turned to her. The gray-eyed scowl the woman gave Joe, however, made his anger dissipate as quickly as if he'd been doused in icewater. Joe rubbed his arms against the sudden wash of goosebumps, realizing again how his spidey senses were tingling just by being around them.

"I'm outta here," Joe said. "Tell the freaks not to follow me."

"*Stop calling them freaks!*" Alice screamed at him.

"Stop *crying like a baby!*" Joe shouted back. "It's not gonna make any sooting difference to the next kreenit that comes after you." He turned to go.

Joe was a big man, but when the giant shoved him, he flew backwards like he'd been hit by a Jreet. He landed awkwardly in the tangle of upturned earth and torn tree limbs and lay there, stunned.

The giant came to stand over him, frowning down at him in obvious displeasure. Long minutes passed, just the two of them staring at each other, Joe on the ground, the big guy near his head, obviously willing to stomp a big foot into his face.

"Okay," Joe wheezed, once he was sure Bigfoot wasn't going to crush his skull, "Stop making the kid cry. Got it." He painfully shoved himself over and started to crawl out of the hole he'd tumbled into. "No problemo. I'll just hit the road and you'll never see my sorry ass—oof!"

The giant took hold of his jacket and lifted Joe completely off of the ground, setting him back on his feet as easily as if he were righting a lamp. Then he gave Joe a gentle shove in the opposite direction.

The others, Joe realized, were leaving. The giant wanted Joe to go with them.

"Wait, no, I don't want to…" His words died in his throat when he saw the dark look on Twelve-A's face.

You're coming with us.

Joe narrowed his eyes at the telepath. "I'd rather fuck a Jreet than go with you."

Twelve-A cocked his head in warning, his pointy ears making the goofy little prick look like his mommy got it on with a Nansaba right before she spent nine months loading up on alcohol and oven cleaner.

Joe snorted and turned to go.

Suddenly, Joe had Jane in his mouth, and, with very little effort on his part, Jane was about ready to start blowing his mind. As he swallowed around the cool black metal, Joe's feet turned him until he was once again facing the pointy-eared bastard.

For long seconds, Twelve-A just held him like that, Joe's own gun in his mouth, his own hand holding it in place, the telepath meeting Joe's eyes over the barrel.

Someone like you could help us, Twelve-A said. The clear inference was that Joe's future was much more open as a necessary evil than as an uncooperative one.

Very slowly, Joe nodded.

When the telepath's mental fist released him, Joe's hand was shaking as he pulled the pistol from his mouth. He saw the long string of saliva as, trembling, he drew it away from his face and stuck it back in its holster. He swallowed his own spit, felt the cold tang of metal still clinging to his palate.

"Okay," Joe whispered. He let out a shuddering breath. "Don't ever burning do that again or I'll kill you in your sleep."

Twelve-A gave him a long, cold look, and Joe realized the telepath was thinking about repeating the lesson—with an explosive finale. Joe returned his gaze, the fear burned out, replaced with stubborn fury. *Go ahead*, he taunted. *Let me have it, you furg. I've been trying to blow out my own brains for the last six turns. Make my ashing day.*

I don't have to use a gun to make your day, Twelve-A replied. But he was frowning at Joe like he was confused, puzzling out a riddle.

Joe swallowed and wiped spit from his mouth with the back of his hand. "Neither do I. Stay out of my head or I'll be happy to prove it."

Twelve-A watched him, blue eyes scanning the spot between Joe's eyes like it was an open book. Then, without another word, Twelve-A just turned and walked away. Joe watched the back of his fuzzy blond head, still struggling with his own fury.

"Pointy-eared prick," he finally muttered, shouldering his backpack. He knew he'd been given permission to leave, that Twelve-A was more or less dropping the subject, but he could sense that he'd won some sort of war between him and the blond freak, or at least a small battle thereof. And that made him feel damn good, considering how little he actually had to fight with.

"This food," Shael cried, jogging up to shove cookies into his hands. "It is the ambrosia of the Sisters themselves, Joe Dobbs. *Taste* it!" She gestured at the cookies excitedly. When Joe didn't move, Shael's excitement waned into a dangerous thunderhead and she went still. "You refuse my food?" she growled. "After I ate at your fire?"

Realizing he could either try the cookie or have it forcibly shoved into his mouth and out through the back of his head, Joe reluctantly took a piece and tried it.

The cookie was *good*. Like something he would have eaten at a hugely-overpriced specialty Human shop on Kaleu.

"There's more!" Shael called, her excitement returning. "This brown-furred one over here, she *makes* it!" She pointed at the retreating back of Eleven-C, who was casually walking along between the enormous Nine-G and his skinny blond sidekick, the Mind-Furg.

"Come on, Joe Dobbs! Twelve-A has offered to let us travel with them!" Then, like any good Jreet, Shael ran after the food source.

Reluctantly, more irritated than pissed, now, Joe hitched his backpack over his shoulder and, after examining their backtrail for a long moment, considering, turned and followed the group. He could, he decided, leave at any time.

He caught up with Alice and held up a hand when she gave him a happy smile. "Let me get one thing straight," he interrupted. "We're not gonna eat cookies this whole trip. That's bad for you."

"Twelve-A doesn't think it's bad for you," Alice retorted, biting into a cookie to prove her point.

"It's bad for you," Joe repeated. "You need to get that busty chick to make something a little more healthy or even the walking Hebbut over there is going to get fat."

Alice frowned at him. "His name is Nine-G and he's *not* a Hebbut."

"Whatever. The point is, we need Knockers to make us some real food if we want to stay healthy."

"*Her* name is Eleven-C," Alice said.

"She's also got nice boobs," Joe told her. "Don't really see 'em like that on Congies. Means she's got body fat." Joe had always enjoyed a good rack, and that had been the one failing he'd seen with just about any Congie woman he'd ever dated—she was more muscle than curves.

"You aren't very nice," Alice said again, this time with a disgusted twist of her face.

"Never claimed to be," Joe replied, cinching a rifle strap tighter over his shoulder.

"What's your name?" Alice asked after a moment.

Joe almost told her to go screw a Jreet, but realized she could probably simply get the information by asking Twelve-A, which would probably be even more unpleasant for Joe than a good Jreet-screwing. "Joe," he told her reluctantly.

Alice peered up at him. "You look like my best friend's dad. Your last name Porter?"

Joe grew wary, realizing she probably subconsciously recognized him from a recruitment poster. "No."

"What is it, then?" She peered up at him with a curious little frown.

Thinking about the legend of Zero, Joe muttered, "None of your damn business. That's what."

Immediately, Alice's eyes twitched towards Twelve-A.

"Dobbs, goddamn it!" Joe snapped, as the telepath started to turn towards them with a frown. Giving the blue-eyed freak an irritated look, he told Alice, "It's Joe Dobbs." Raising his voice, he shouted, "And turn the soot around and keep walking, Pointy! I'm having a chat with the little lady. *Alone*, if you don't mind."

Twelve-A narrowed his pretty blue eyes in Joe's direction, but he turned back around.

"Naked Takki posy-sniffer," Joe muttered.

"Thanks for killing the dragon, Joe," Alice said.

When Joe blinked and looked down at her, he realized with a start that Alice was blushing and glancing at her feet. Seeing that, he got the uncomfortable idea that he had, just that fast, become the sudden focus of a pre-teen crush. He fought goosebumps of unease and smiled awkwardly. "It wasn't a dra—" Then his words cut off in the back of his throat with a strangled sound and his mouth fell open. He stared at Alice, then at the experiments, goosebumps tightening his skin in cold, eerie waves.

And while you shall die in a cave, shamed and surrounded by dragon-slaying innocents, your deeds will crush the unbreakable, and your name will never be forgotten...

"Soot," Joe whispered, his feet stumbling to a stunned halt. "Oh soot."

• • •

Six Six Five had spent another night sleeping in her friend's bed, knowing it was against the rules, yet unable to dream alone in the dark. Six Two One didn't seem to mind when Six Six Five crawled up into the bunk with her, though she always took the most covers. Six Six Five didn't care—lying there alone in the eerie silence, listening to the sound of her own heartbeat, she would do anything to have someone to talk to in the pitch blackness of 'lights-out'.

Tonight was no different. Six Six Five always felt like she was missing something, like she needed more than she had, and the furtive nights sleeping beside Six Two One seemed to ease that ache when no amount of water, food, or exercise would do the same.

"So what do you think our surprise will be tomorrow?" Six Six Five asked into the darkness, hearing her friend breathing softly beside her, close to sleep. "Codgson said we would have a surprise."

Her friend was quiet a moment, making Six Six Five think she had fallen asleep. Desperate to distract herself from the darkness, she insisted, "What do you—"

"A gun," Six Two One interrupted. "He keeps saying we're all gonna be soldiers. Soldiers have guns."

Six Six Five blinked. She hadn't thought about that. The way Codgson had said it, it was going to be a *good* surprise. Six Six Five didn't *want* to be a soldier. All the running around the gym was boring.

Six Two One was right, though. All the soldiers carried guns as they guarded the doors and halls to keep the aliens out. Some had big guns slung over their shoulders, but *all* of them had littler guns strapped to their thighs or under their coats. Six Six Five thought she could carry one of the small ones, though what she had *really* hoped for was something pretty like Doctor Molotov sometimes wore. It was usually sparkly earrings, but sometimes she wore a glittering necklace or a scarf that changed color from pink to purple when she moved. Doctor Molotov had once let Six Six Five touch her scarf. It had been so *soft*. So smooth that it made the calluses of her hands scrape and catch against it.

"I hope it's a scarf like Doctor Molotov's pink one," Six Six Five told her friend. "I want to be like her when I grow up."

Six Six Five felt Six Two One turn to her in the darkness. "We have to fight *aliens* when we grow up."

At the flat derisiveness in Six Two One's tone, Six Six Five immediately felt ashamed and sick. Yet, she didn't *want* to fight aliens. They looked…scary. Especially the Dhasha. They ate people. Six Six Five didn't want to get eaten—she just wanted to have something soft like Doctor Molotov's scarf.

"You can fight aliens," she told her friend. "I'll write reports like Doctor Molotov."

Six Two One scoffed. "You can't write reports. She's already *doing* that. You have to be a soldier. Colonel Codgson said so."

Six Six Five grimaced. She really didn't like Colonel Codgson. Whenever he came around, the doctors made them line up for formation. Six Six Five hated that. "I don't want to be a soldier. I want to be a doctor. They need doctors, too. If soldiers get hurt, they'll need people to make them better and write reports about it."

Six Two One seemed to consider that. "Okay," she finally said, "but if you get to be a doctor, I get to be your assistant."

Six Six Five sat up in bed, frowning. "You don't want to be a doctor, too?"

Six Two One made a little sound to the negative. "They won't let me be a doctor. They don't like how small I am. They'd make me an assistant."

Indeed, the doctors didn't seem to like much of anything about Six Two One. Six Six Five had heard them arguing over Six Two One's 'birth defects' and whether or not they should 'cull.' She had taken that to mean that they were trying to decide whether or not to give her extra food, because Six Two One had gotten extra rations the next morning, and had been getting them ever since. It had made Six Six Five secretly jealous.

"So…" Six Six Five heard Six Two One sit up. "…if you get a scarf, think they'd let me have a necklace?"

Remembering the sparkly splashes of color breaking the endless whites, blacks, and grays of their surroundings, Six Six Five felt her heart skip. She hadn't actually allowed herself to consider a necklace, since a scarf was made of cloth, and her batchmates already wore cloth. *None* of them wore a necklace. Until now, she had always considered that to be unattainable, well out of her reach. Still, the idea was making her heart pound. "It could be a necklace," she managed, on a tendril of hope.

As it turned out, they were both wrong.

When the doctors woke them to line up before Colonel Codgson the next morning, there was a line of small cages in the shadows along the back wall, each mostly obscured with a plain blue cloth. As Six Six Five stood there, facing the cages, she couldn't help but hear the movement within them.

Their doctors left them alone in the gymnasium, lined up in formation, staring at the cages for what seemed like an hour. Six Six Five *wanted* to go see what was moving inside the kennels, but like her batchmates, she knew that the surest way to *not* find out what the colonel had in store for them was to step out of formation before they had been dismissed.

Still, the longer they stood there—hours, now—the more restless Six Six Five got. Something was in there, something interesting, and she had to know. Her curiosity was *killing* her. It seemed like the doctors had forgotten them in here. They'd done it before—just lined them up and walked away. Remembering that, Six Six Five bit her lip. No one was around to see her take a quick peek. She could make it fast. And it was obvious her batchmates were also curious. If she made it fast and then told them what was in the crates, they probably wouldn't even tell on her.

Still, the whole situation didn't feel right. Almost like it was another of Codgson's tests.

Instinct warred with curiosity for the next hour, until Six Six Five finally couldn't handle it anymore. She had taken her first step out of line to go check the crates when one of the boys with funny ears and bright blue eyes burst out of formation, and, with a quick nervous look around him, hurried forward to go peek under the nearest cloth.

"Hamsters!" he cried, sounding both stunned and delighted. "They brought us *hamsters*!" He pulled the cloth off the cage so he could open the door and drag out a spotted brown hamster. It looked just like the one that Lieutenant Drake kept in her office, except spotted instead of pure white.

The shock was enough to make Six Six Five take another step forward. So *that* was why they'd left them there! To let them pick their surprise! Six Six Five was moving toward the row of cages, looking to claim her own pet, when Colonel Codgson's smooth, calculated voice cut her short.

"I see you found today's surprise, Six Seven Two," Codgson said in his slow drawl. He was walking across the gymnasium towards them, entering from a door that Six Six Five hadn't noticed before. And, while there was a smile on the colonel's face, there was something odd about his tone that made Six Six Five freeze, her heart giving a sudden, terrified thump. She inched back into formation, glad that Codgson was facing Six Seven Two and couldn't see that she, too, had left her assigned place.

Six Seven Two hastily put the hamster back into the cage and turned to hurry back to his place in formation.

"No, stay," Codgson urged, still only halfway across the gymnasium. "They are *your* surprises, after all. You might as well enjoy them."

Six Seven Two gave his empty spot in line a reluctant look, then nervously straightened, spine rigid as the soldiers had taught them. Codgson lazily walked up to him and stopped, looking him up and down. "So," he said eventually, "did we do a good job picking your surprise, Six Seven Two?"

The little boy gave an impish smile, his dimpled face flexing. "Yes, sir. Six Seven Eight said it was going to be a gun."

"I see," Codgson said, that oddness in his tone again. "So you're happy it's a guinea pig and not a gun."

Six Seven Two must have realized his mistake, because he flushed. Seeing that, Six Six Five immediately felt sorry for him—nobody liked being put on the spot in front of the class, and Codgson did it often.

This time, though, there seemed to be something...darker...to the colonel's black eyes as he watched Six Seven Two sputter and make excuses. Eventually, he held up a hand. "Not everyone wants to be a soldier," the colonel said, once Six Seven Two had reluctantly fallen silent. Turning to the rest of the class, he said, "Not everyone has the *discipline* to be a soldier." He turned back to the boy standing at the line of cages with him. "Six Seven Two," he said gently, "were my instructions to stand in formation until my arrival somehow unclear?"

Six Seven Two reddened and bit his lip. "No sir."

"Then someone must have given you permission to leave formation," the colonel encouraged. "One of the doctors, maybe?"

Don't answer him, Six Six Five thought, already feeling the twinges of fear in her gut. Something was wrong. All of her instincts were *screaming* at her that something was wrong.

"No, sir," Six Seven Two said, sounding ashamed.

"Oh," Colonel Codgson said gently. "Then you left my formation because you were distracted by the rodents."

"Yes sir," Six Seven Two said, hanging his head.

Six Six Five didn't see Colonel Codgson pull his knife, but a moment later, he was yanking it out of the underside of Six Seven Two's jaw, followed immediately by a spray of red. As Six Seven Two choked and fell to his knees between the cages, squirting arcs of crimson over the nearby hamsters and the stark white floor, Colonel Codgson very carefully pulled a rag from his pocket. Smoothly turning his back to the gurgling boy now clutching his throat, Codgson faced his stunned batchmates.

Wiping blood from his knife with the white square of cloth, the colonel said, "Six Seven Two didn't have what it takes to destroy the aliens. He couldn't even wait a few more minutes for his surprise. That means he wasn't strong enough to survive. He wasn't *useful.*" Behind him, Six Seven Two made a few final choking sounds and collapsed face-first onto the floor between the cages, his feet twitching on the linoleum. Ignoring the rhythmic squeak of boots on the waxed floor behind him, Colonel Codgson scrutinized the formation with a sad smile. "You see, we need soldiers. *Warriors.* If Six Seven Two couldn't obey simple instructions *now,* how could we expect him to carry out complex instructions *later,* when it's time to defend Earth?"

None of the recruits could find the words to respond. Everyone stared at their batchmate, who now lay still on the floor behind the colonel, a pool of red spreading from under his chin.

Colonel Codgson replaced the knife in its sheath on his belt with a sharp metallic *snap*. Coldly, he said, "The answer is he wouldn't. He'd disobey, lose sight of his objective, and get people killed. That…" Colonel Codgson scanned every face, leaving Six Six Five with a sick feeling when his gaze stopped on her, "…is unacceptable." Still looking at Six Six Five, the colonel's lips quirked in a little smile. "The rest of you earned your surprise. Take as long as you want to pick. Doctor Molotov made sure to get different colors so you can tell them apart, and there's more than enough to go around. As soon as you find the one you want, bring it to the assistants so they can document your choice in their report."

At that, Colonel Codgson turned and walked out, but Six Six Five couldn't make herself leave formation even after everyone else had picked their hamsters from the cages along the wall. After the other boys and girls took their new pets and walked out, Six Six Five continued to stand there, staring at Six Seven Two's dead body. His cheek was resting in a pool of blood, crimson liquid soaking into his platinum-blond eyebrows.

I moved first, was all Six Six Five could think. *The colonel didn't see me, but I moved first.*

Eventually, Doctor Molotov came into the gymnasium to squat beside her, a concerned look on her face. She wasn't wearing her scarf today, and her hair was pulled back in a tight bun. "Is something wrong, Six Five?" Like most of the doctors, she shortened their names when she was trying to be nice. Today, Six Six Five didn't notice. All she could see was the blood soaking her batchmate's cheek, the red that had sprayed the cages, the way the hamster was sniffing Six Seven Two's fingers where they had poked through the wire in his fall.

After a moment, Doctor Molotov followed Six Six Five's stare to the dead boy on the floor, tucked between the bloody hamster cages, half covered by the cloths that his batchmates had tossed aside.

Immediately, Doctor Molotov's face hardened and she jumped to her feet. "Goddamn it, Drake, get a cleanup crew in here!" she shouted. Then she grabbed Six Six Five by the wrist and forcefully steered her from the room.

Still, at the door to the gymnasium, Six Six Five hesitated and turned back to look at the hamster cages, feeling a pang of loss at the six crimson-stained pens clustered around the dead boy. "I don't get a hamster?" she whispered, still caught between tears and terror. She had seen her fellows walk out with brown ones, spotted ones, gray ones, black ones...

"You'll get a pet," Doctor Molotov insisted, giving her arm a gentle tug. Her face was hard. "Come on. I've got something in my office just for you."

Six Six Five frowned, knowing that Doctor Molotov only had Charlie in her office, the fat white rabbit that the doctor liked to fondly say she had 'retired,' whatever that meant. Six Six Five had even gotten to feed him once, when feeding time had happened to coincide with her monthly progress report. Six Six Five still remembered the magic of holding the carrot and petting his soft fur as he nibbled at her offering through the open door.

Sure enough, when Doctor Molotov presented her with a pet, it was Charlie. Six Six Five felt her eyes widen. "You're giving me *Charlie*?" she whispered. "But Charlie's a *rabbit*." Not only that, but Charlie was the only *white* animal that she'd seen in the cages. Instantly, Six Six Five didn't want him. She didn't *want* to stand out. She didn't want to be like Six Seven Two.

"Yes," Doctor Molotov said briskly, sounding almost angry. "I'm giving you Charlie." She tugged his cage from its stand beside her desk none-too-gently, making him jump and hop inside. "Come on." She twisted and started back toward the hall.

"But," Six Six Five whimpered, "what if Colonel Codgson—"

"*Fuck* Colonel Codgson," Doctor Molotov growled. "The psychotic bastard needs a bullet between the eyes. Come on. You guys have the rest of the night to get settled in with your new companions."

Six Six Five swallowed, looking at Charlie's wide pink eye through the cage wire. He looked as scared as she was. In a whimper, she managed, "What if he kills Charlie, too?"

Doctor Molotov's eyes narrowed, again looking like she was angry, but not at Six Six Five. "It's a psycho-emotional stability resource. He won't." Then, without another word, she left her office, Charlie's cage in her hands.

Nervously, Six Six Five followed the doctor back to her room, where Doctor Molotov set Charlie's cage on the desk beside her bed. The doctor bit her lip, looking at the rabbit, then quickly turned away, but not before Six Six Five saw her regret.

Clearing her throat, Doctor Molotov dropped a plastic bag onto the table beside the cage and said, "Here's his bag of treats. Don't feed him more than a tablespoon at a time or you'll make him sick." She took another deep breath, her gaze sliding towards the rabbit before looking away. "You'll be expected to take good care of him. He likes to be petted from nose-to-tail. The other way aggravates him. He likes to be fed twice a day, and taken out and held before bed. And don't mess with his ears. He hates that. He used to have injections—" She cut off suddenly, her voice breaking. Hurriedly, Doctor Molotov swiped at her eyes with a sleeve. Keeping her face out of sight, she finished, "The technicians will explain proper care and maintenance at formation tomorrow. Don't bother registering him with the techs—I'll do that. Just stay here and get to know each other. The other kids will be back soon." Then, without another word, Doctor Molotov hurried from the room.

For the longest time after she was gone, Six Six Five could only scowl at the bunny through the bars, thinking how much she *didn't* want a rabbit, especially not a huge, fat *white* rabbit with weird red eyes. She wanted a *brown hamster*. A *normal* pet.

Charlie seemed to share her discontent, because he had wedged himself into the back corner of his cage and was staring wide-eyed at his new surroundings, panting.

It was his obvious terror that finally made Six Six Five soften. He was, she realized, in a lot of ways just like her. Much of the time, Six

Six Five felt like she was in a cage. A weird, huge, complex cage filled with doctors who told her what to do and made her stand still while they wrote their reports, but no less a cage than the wire contraption now dominating her desk. Gingerly, Six Six Five reached into the bag and pulled out a hard brown treat that smelled like apples. She held it a moment, considering, then reluctantly pushed it through the bars.

As she held it there, Charlie's nose twitched and his head came around to look. He eyed it a moment, then glanced back out at the room around them, pink eyes still wide as he scanned their surroundings. For a moment, Six Six Five thought he would ignore her offering. Then, timidly, he returned his attention to her treat and hopped forward until his nose was nuzzling her hand. He sniffed her fingers, his velvety nose twitching against her skin, before moving his head down to gently take a tentative nibble at the treat between her thumb and pinkie. After an unsure moment, he hopped the rest of the way forward and began to chew in earnest. Gingerly, Six Six Five reached up and started to stroke his velvet-soft back the way Doctor Molotov had told her.

When he didn't jerk away, Six Six Five started to smile, in spite of herself...

Shael slammed back into his war-mind as he jerked awake, panting. He was cold again, the fetid night breeze of this miserable planet brushing against his scaleless skin, sapping his warmth. He tugged one of Joedobbs' precious blankets closer to his body, this time more because of the cold than a desire to protect the treasures. He said a quiet mental prayer for forgiveness to the Sisters, but kept the blanket around his shoulders.

Only after he tightened the blanket around his body did Shael realize the minder was watching him from across the Voran's fire. With that knowledge came the realization that he probably knew the truth of why he clutched the blankets so fiercely.

Immediately, Shael narrowed his eyes at the weakling. *You tell anyone of this and you'll dance on my tek.*

Your secret is safe with me, Twelve-A assured him. The minder wore a small frown of concentration, though, as he continued to watch Shael across the flames.

Unnerved by the telepath's perusal, Shael tensed and coiled, glaring back, acutely aware of his missing scales. "You dare to stare upon a warrior of Welu, kin-of-Test-Tube?" he finally demanded, using one of Joedobbs' more formal family monikers for the furg.

The minder seemed to consider, then shook his head and appeared to find something very interesting in the grass beside his knee.

Shael, who was watching the minder's foggy green energy-form from the all-encompassing freedom of his war-mind, lifted his head in challenge. "I am protector of this camp. Do you challenge my right to put these valuables to use however I see fit?" He gestured broadly to the blankets that Joedobbs had not felt comfortable guarding himself. If Twelve-A wanted to object to Shael's use of the Voran's supplies, it would be a small thing for Shael to put the weakling furg in his place, permanently.

I was just wondering about that dream, Twelve-A said. *This isn't the first time you've had it...is it?*

Shael felt his skin heat at the idea that he had again dreamed of himself in the form of a Human girl—and that now someone knew about it. He surged to his feet, allowing the blankets to fall away from him, forgotten. Pointing a warning talon at the minder, Shael said, "You will tell *no one* of this, weakling, or I will eviscerate you with your own toenails and feed you to a pit of diseased vaghi."

Twelve-A gave him a perplexed look. *It was just a question—I can't read you when you're in your war mind.*

Shael cocked his head at the minder. "You can't?" That was... useful. Earlier, when it had become obvious that the power structure of the group of disorganized furgs had been unfortunately slanted in favor of the minder, Shael had been trying to figure out how he could overpower a telepath if the need arose to take charge of the walking Takkiscrew. This made it much easier.

Immediately, the minder reddened. *It just makes it very difficult to locate you. I like to keep tabs on everyone. For my...comfort.*

Which answered another of Shael's questions. "So all of this time...You haven't been able to read me, have you?" he demanded, triumphant. He wondered what Joedobbs would think of that information—and whether a Voran's war-mind could possibly be deep enough to protect him from a minder's charms. Shael had been nervous that the unnatural tricks of this Twelve-A might be able to counter his warrior's strength and stamina. He had certainly not been looking forward to fighting him. In many ways, Twelve-A had the makings of a very dangerous weapon, if not the heart.

But, of course, it was the telepath's distinct lack of warrior spirit that would keep him from ever recognizing his true potential, or even one day ruling a clan for himself. Even now, he simply blushed and picked at a scab on his arm rather than face the fact Shael had found his weakness.

Thus, Shael felt secure in offering him a bargain. *By the blood of my Welu ancestors, tell no one of my dreams, Twelve-A ga Test Tube, and I will forget to mention to Joedobbs that you are helpless to influence a warrior in his war-mind.*

Twelve-A lifted his head suddenly, making his short, sun-colored hair move around his face as he met Shael's gaze with visible startlement. For a long moment, he simply looked like a panicked melaa. Then, slowly, he nodded once.

Grunting in satisfaction, Shael nodded and coiled back under Joedobbs' blankets. Perhaps he wouldn't have to challenge the pointy-eared furg, after all. Joedobbs, on the other hand...The Voran definitely could be removed of a few extra segments. That night, he had actually tried to distribute the blankets to the worthless, drooling, mindless furgs following Eleven-C. As if *they* had the capability to safeguard such wealth.

More likely, it had been a backhanded comment on Shael's abilities as a warrior to protect the camp's valuables, a barely-concealed attempt to humiliate him. Not only had Shael *not* conceded, but he had refused to allow any of the mindless furgs near the fire after that, deciding that they needed to harden themselves in the cold like any good warrior-in-training on Welu.

Joedobbs, softling that he was, had gone to the other side of camp and built them another fire.

Yes, Shael decided, he and the Voran were definitely destined to come to blows. He just hoped they didn't kill too many bystanders when it happened. He was growing rather fond of Eleven-C and her 'cookies.'

13

THE RUNAWAY RODEMAX

On the day of their departure, the aliens still hadn't blown up the shopping mall, which pleased Slade very much. It meant, among other things, that he might actually live through this knuckle-dragging clusterfuck.

Traveling by foot, however, wasn't as easy as Slade had imagined, back when he had been planning this trek in the air-conditioned mall manager's office, a notepad in one hand and a Playboy in the other, his ice-cold soda attracting pleasing amounts of condensation on the desk. It *should* have been easy…All that was required was a little bit of walking, and how hard could walking be, right?

What Slade had failed to take into account was the fact that smoke blotting out the sun actually made it *hotter*, and his gear was *heavy*, and when one had to carry heavy objects for long distances, one's feet began to hurt. Especially in brand new footwear. Slade, who had picked out five new pairs of badass-looking combat boots for himself, was now hobbling after only three hours of walking, his heavy pack making his back hurt, that little spot between his shoulder blades feeling like someone was driving a knife through it.

"Can we stop yet?" Slade heard himself whine. "I think I feel a disc slipping."

Tyson gave him a look that definitely contained amusement. The bastard. The big ape hadn't so much as slowed over all three hours. Casually, he said, "So the tendonitis, plantar fasciitis, shin splints, abdominal cramps, dehydration headaches, and aerobic polycarbonate intoxication all went away, then?"

"No," Slade said, scowling, irritated that Tyson had been keeping tally. "Now my spine is going to dislocate, too."

"Of course." Tyson kept walking. Behind them, three hundred and fourteen people followed in an impressive horde, which was even then ransacking every house, vehicle, or storefront that happened to fall in its path.

"And how the hell did you remember all that?" Slade demanded in a disgruntled mutter.

"I'm not stupid," Tyson said, shrugging his massive shoulders. "And you said them like fifteen times each."

Plenty of stupid people, Slade had found, said, "I'm not stupid," whenever they were being just that. He was also pretty sure that Tyson would shoot him if he said as much.

"This is *grueling*," Slade groaned. "How far have we gone? Like fifteen *miles?*"

Tyson snorted. "Try five. Herding three hundred people that are stopping to ransack everything we pass isn't exactly making for a quick getaway."

"True," Slade said, "but it's pleasing the masses."

Even then, his followers were jealously guarding their hauls of prescription drugs, jewelry, women, and guns they had found in the 'abandoned' houses.

Tyson grunted and gave him a sideways look. "Guess I couldn't really expect much better, seeing how we freed a prison full of inmates and all, but are we really going to let them start up a slave trade?"

"I figured," Slade said, "that our hold on leadership is still tenuous, and the best way to control the mob is by funneling it into the direction you want it to go, rather than trying to jerk it around by the collar. We're putting rules on the *number* of people they can hurt and are dragging them out to the desert, where people are scarce, rather than letting them all run around rampaging wherever the hell they want."

"Still bothers me," Tyson muttered.

To be truthful, it bothered Slade, too, but he'd been forced to intellectualize the matter, because, at the core, he'd had to choose between his own life—the loss of which would be catastrophic for the rebuilding of Earth's technologies—and his principles. Killing the prisoners made no sense after spending so much time and energy freeing them, so the only reasonable choice was to do his best to gently guide them into less-criminal activities.

"I think I'm tearing a tendon in my foot," Slade said. "It *hurts*."

Tyson glanced at the massive hiking backpack that Slade had clinging to his shoulders like a very heavy and uncomfortable barnacle. "You're the one who insisted we bring all this gear with us. Besides. I *saw* you pack double of almost everything."

"It's about *survival*," Slade said, unable to keep the whine out of his voice. "In a few years, there's not going to be anything left of the world. We have to try and salvage what we can, now, before everyone else figures out that the same stuff will be useful and take it for themselves."

Tyson raised an eyebrow. "Porn vids?"

Slade flushed. "They're an investment. Long-term gains."

"Uh-huh."

"They are!" Slade cried.

"Not arguing with you," Tyson said. "Just giving you the facts."

Facts. Slade bristled. As if *he*, the Tesla of the Congressional Era, needed to be reminded of facts. Slade was about to retort, but he stumbled on a rock, almost twisting his foot off. "That's *it*!" he cried, stopping and yanking his much-too-heavy backpack from his back and throwing it to the ground. He jabbed his finger at the group of startled men with guns behind them.

"You!" he shouted at the men in general. "Go find me eight porters! As your fearless leader, I am tired of this shit and I want to ride a palanquin."

The men with guns peered at him, then at each other. One of the braver ones said, "Um, you want wine?"

Slade blinked at them, and it actually took him a moment to retrace his steps and figure out what the hell had happened in the moron's pea brain to create such a catastrophic /fail. Realizing the inebriates probably had no idea what a palanquin was—and that they had heard the 'port' part of porter and thought he meant a sweet red wine, Slade almost walked over, took Tyson's gun, and blew off his own head rather than spend one more minute surrounded by such painfully clear dumbassery.

When Slade just glowered at them, the man cleared his throat and asked Tyson, "He mean wine?"

Eyes on Slade's face, Tyson shrugged. "Not quite sure."

Slade forced himself to smile through the violent urge to decapitate himself. "Find me slaves. Big ones. Strong. Six feet or more. *Male*, preferably. I will be having them carry something heavy."

The men glanced at each other, seemed to consider, then shrugged and went off to do what they were told, the blind obedience of which actually eased Slade's exasperation at their stupidity.

God he loved having lackeys.

Four hours later, Slade reclined with his backpack on a makeshift platform carried by eight pale-yet-subdued litter-bearers that easily could have worked as bouncers in his favorite nightclubs.

"Now *this* is how to travel," Slade sighed, leaning back on his array of pillows. He felt rather proud of himself, as yet another plan had come to fruition.

From the ground, Tyson glanced up at him. "You know, you're only making yourself a target."

"To who?" Slade scoffed. "There are three hundred people around me with guns that would be perfectly willing to shoot anyone who looks at me funny." He plucked another nut from the can someone had found in one of the ransacked houses and popped it into his mouth. Immediately, he grimaced and spat it back out. It was a peanut. He hated peanuts. He would be sure *not* to preserve peanut agriculture in his brave new society. That was one thing that Humanity could lose with his blessing. He flicked the peanut off the platform, onto the ground.

"Other people out there have guns, too," Tyson said, watching the nut fall before returning his gaze to Slade and looking him over. "And they're not going to like what they see."

"They wanna shoot me?" Slade snorted and tugged a cute knitted yellow Minion beany over his head that he had found whilst casually looting one of the nicer estates. Looking at Tyson from under his knitted black and white monocle, he imperiously raised his head and said, "Let them try."

A few days later, someone did try. Sometime around six in the evening, Slade heard the high-pitched sizzle of a plasma blast whiz past his beanie-covered ear—as well as felt the brush of its passing gently raise the hairs of his cheek—and he screamed and scrambled off his palanquin.

"Where'd it come from?!" Slade cried, yanking down his Minion beanie and huddling on the ground behind a burned-out car.

Tyson squatted down beside him, gun in his hands. "From the woods. *Shit*. Look at all those bodies!"

When Slade looked, he paled. They had been walking down a car-choked road through a clearing that, now that Slade was looking under the cars blocking their view, had bodies filling both ditches further up ahead. Dried blood was even then caking in pools upon the road for the next two hundred feet.

Another plasma *burp* echoed through the clearing and one of Slade's followers let out a startled sound and fell, blood oozing from a disintegrating hole in his head. The shot was quickly followed by two more, also resulting in corpses.

"He's a good shot," Slade noted. That was bad.

"He's up there on the hill, picking people off," Tyson cried, yanking out his binoculars and peering at the hill in question. "And he waited until we were all out in the middle of the clearing to start firing. We're sitting ducks. *Shit!*" Indeed, the Harmonious Society of God was now struggling to hide behind the paltry handful of cars in the center of the road, their bodies crammed together with increasing panic.

"You're saying there's a *Human* up there firing at us?" Slade demanded, squinting up at the copse of trees. "That is Congie weaponry." He had a brief rush of paranoid fear that the Peacemakers had come back for him, then quickly squashed it as ludicrous. After Judgement had been sealed and the bots had begun their six-hundred-and-sixty-six-turn timers, even Peacemaker ships would be attacked if they tried to land on the surface.

Two more shots came, resulting in two more of his Society screaming and bleeding on the pavement.

"He's a *really* good shot," Slade commented.

"Yeah," Tyson said as he hastily put the binoculars down, yanked off his pack, and began prepping the scoped rifle he'd acquired from a wealthy home along the walk. "And he's got a good vantage point, too. Shit." He checked the magazine, then slapped it back into place and, after wetting his finger and holding it up, adjusted the scope for windage. "Some asshole trying to eliminate the competition, pick supplies off people trying to escape the city."

Seeing his Second work, Slade frowned. There was a…proficiency…to Tyson's smooth actions that bespoke of more than a common thug. "So why don't we fire back?" he demanded. All around them, more of their gun-toting priests were screaming and dying.

"I'm going to," Tyson said. He looked over his shoulder at the eight big guys that had been carrying Slade's palanquin. "Hey, you. You guys wanna earn your freedom?"

The big dudes, who had dropped the litter and were huddled beside them, nodded.

"Those are my *litter bearers*," Slade complained.

"Shush," Tyson said. "This is one of those moments where you need to just shut up and nod your head while I keep you alive. They put me away for two counts of murder. In reality, it should have been more like two hundred."

Slade frowned. The rich family, the knack with guns, the quiet broodiness, the recognizing of Ghost…All of it was starting to make sense, now. "You were a hit man." Which meant he'd probably been sent after Slade at least once.

Tyson grunted. To the big dudes, he said, "Okay, look. Here's what we're gonna do. I want all eight of you to bolt in different directions, at the same time. Make it hard for the shooter to get a bead on you. Don't run in a straight line, and for the love of God, bounce and jump a little. It's *really* hard to hit a running target with a rifle from that distance."

The eight guys swallowed and their eyes flickered toward the still-twitching corpses of several of their gun-toting captors.

"A couple of you probably won't make it," Tyson told them, "but it's better than carrying *his* ass around the rest of your lives, isn't it?"

Several of the men grimaced and looked at the ground. In the end, only three of the eight of them had the balls to risk their lives for freedom. Which Slade found extremely telling of the Human Condition. Sheeple and poddites. The world was filled with them.

"Okay," Tyson said. "When I say go, I want you three to bolt in *different* directions. Don't make it easy for him to snipe you, ok? Keep your head down and zigzag. You. You're going east. That way. You're going west. Over there. And you're going over the ditch, there, north. And don't stop running until you hear me call the all-clear."

The three men nodded.

Tyson readied his gun, then said, "Ready? Go."

The three men bolted. The shooter began firing at them almost immediately, like some kid picking off cannon fodder in a simulated combat game.

Tyson seemed to count under his breath, then spun and raised his rifle over the hood of the car, took a firing position, and began peering through the scope.

Several more shots came, and one of the three runners screamed and slumped to the ground. He kept screaming until two more shots effectively silenced him.

"It's autocorrecting for him," Tyson muttered. "Fuck, it's an AI of some sort. Those guys are gonna be like sitting ducks."

"Can you get him from here?" Slade demanded. "That's high-grade sniper plasma. Expensive shit." Indeed, the rate at which it ate through its targets was unnerving. "He could be two miles out."

"No, he's hiding in the trees," Tyson said. "I think he's former Global Police."

"Well...yeah," Slade said. "Who else is gonna have that kind of plasma rifle around here?"

Tyson didn't reply, peering through his scope with intense concentration. The second runner was getting shot at, and had begun screaming, though Slade was pretty sure it was in terror and not pain.

"You gonna shoot him?" Slade urged.

Tyson continued to ignore him, squinting through the circle of glass. A few more heart-rending seconds passed, with the second man dodging like a lunatic as he bolted.

Then, without a word, Tyson squeezed the trigger. The single retort of the old-fashioned bullet startled Slade, who had tensed with each sizzling plasma round that came at the running man, quietly rooting for him to make it into the trees.

Tyson fired a second time, a mere heartbeat after the first, and then yanked his gun back over his shoulder. "All clear!" he shouted to the running guys. Neither of them stopped bolting for the trees. Oh well. Slade could find other litter-bearers.

Then Slade frowned. "You mean there was only one of them?" Indeed, the plasma retorts had ended, leaving only an uncomfortable silence and six dead men sprawled on the roadside.

"Two," Tyson said, getting to his feet. "And you're right. They've got a *wicked*-ass gun." He almost sounded...excited. He was already throwing his gear over his shoulder and heading in that direction.

Seeing that excitement, Slade had to follow. "Now hold on," Slade said, running to catch up. "Someone with that kind of weaponry...he would've had friends, right?"

"Just the one," Tyson said. "And Saint Ebert save me, but I think that was a Sui'ezi Rodemax. Huouyt manufactured for the blackmarket. *Real* expensive shit." He had lowered his voice to a near-whisper, but hadn't slowed at all. If anything, his long legs had sped up. They were already picking their way through the ditch of plasma-eaten bodies, toward the hill across the field.

"A Rodemax, huh?" Slade grunted, impressed. The guns were extremely rare, made by the famous Huouyt Sui'ezi family, whose ancestors had been in the gun trade for eighty thousand turns, and whose only contribution to gun technology in that time period is that they had stolen the original schematics from the Ueshi manufacturer of the Nocurna *and* the blueprints to the Nansaba Jaywing, then combined them. They went for over twenty million apiece. He'd heard enough raving about them from his gun-obsessed fellow billionaire friends whenever he deigned to go drinking with them that he'd actually had to go look them up out of vague curiosity. Coincidentally, he'd also seen one up close, in person, when a Va'gan assassin tried to use one on him after a Huouyt family 'corporation' found out he was the hacker responsible for liberating eighteen billion of their hard-stolen credits from them and gifting it to the Congressional Dhasha Mishaps Relief Fund. He had not, however, really seen what got the furgs so excited about a hunk of alloy with its own power supply. "So it's a fancy gun," he muttered. "Slow down."

"No," Tyson said, basically running, now, "it's *the* fancy gun. It never runs out of charges, has a lightning-fast recharge rate, it's got an onboard course-correction AI, and it's light. It's the Huouyt rifle version of the Nansaba Jaywing, after the Huouyt broke into the Ueshi Nocurna headquarters and stole the schematics for its power supply. Top of the line shit. Va'gan *assassin* shit. People with waaay too much money and lots of people to kill." Tyson almost sounded... jealous.

"Uh...huh," Slade said, rolling his eyes. Gun nuts irritated him. He'd heard the same semi-religious spiel at least a dozen times before, usually from around a cigar. Now that the bad guys were dead, he was finding it very difficult to care about a gun. Though an unlimited charge could be useful. It meant the gun energy source was self-sustaining, which meant he could take it apart and use it to power useful things, like marijuana grow lamps.

Tyson narrowed his eyes at him. "I know what you're thinking. You're *not* taking apart my new gun."

Slade snorted. "*Your* new gun."

"Yes," Tyson said, sounding dead serious. "*My* new gun."

Slade squinted at the diverse range of weapons the man already carried. "What, four's not enough?"

Tyson snorted and started into the trees, towards where the shots had apparently been coming from. Indeed, after a cursory inspection, they found two scrawny Human bodies crumpled in the undergrowth, their heads neatly blown off. They looked like teenagers. Slade found it slightly embarrassing, because he would have chosen a spot several hundred feet to the left as the origin of the projectiles, whereas Tyson had led them straight to them.

Instead of triumphantly searching the bodies for valuables like any good Boy Scout, though, Tyson whipped a pistol from his hip and squatted behind a tree, scanning the woods around him with something akin to...panic?

"What's going on?" Slade asked, dropping with his Second, figuring it was a good idea to squat alongside the badass, 'cause if the *badass* was afraid of something, logic dictated that Slade should be, too. Not that Slade actually *was*, but he found it to be a handy survival technique.

"Someone else is out there," Tyson said. "And they've got that gun trained on us."

"What," Slade laughed, "you got spidey-senses or something?"

"For this, yes." Tyson sounded dead serious. Utterly dead serious. He continued to unobtrusively scan the forest, gun raised.

"Uh," Slade said, looking in the general direction of the woods. "I don't see anyone."

"He's out there," Tyson said. Again, with the same conviction as if he'd said he had to take a piss.

"Um," Slade said, scanning the strangely silent undergrowth. Now they were actually within the tree-cover, it didn't look like a *rabbit* could hide out there, much less a person. Even the dead bodies, slumped in the low-lying grasses, were easy to see. "I hate to break this to you, my very large gay friend, but there's nowhere to hide out there."

"Yeah," Tyson said. "That's what's making me so fucking nervous." He had lowered his voice to a whisper, and was looking quite thoroughly spooked.

"Oh, come on," Slade sighed, after several minutes had passed with no action at all from their 'watcher.' "I'm sure the gun's around here somewhere." Impatient to get back to his palanquin, he stood to go find it.

Tyson grabbed his arm and yanked him down. "I got *instincts*, man, and every alarm bell I've got is ringing like it's New Year's Fucking Eve. You go looking, you're gonna die."

Slade rolled his eyes. 'Instincts' were nothing but the subconscious brain, quietly analyzing data, unbeknownst to the conscious monkey awareness. And he, Samuel Dobbs, a.k.a. Slade Galvin Gardner, a.k.a. Ghost, a.k.a. the Tesla of the Congressional Era, happened to have a subconscious that worked while he was *awake*, and at about a hundred times the normal capacity, and he wasn't even getting a ping of alarm.

"Look," Slade said, standing anyway. "I'm sure there's absolutely nothing out ther—"

A high-efficacy plasma round dissolved the branch beside his head, making a neck-thick slab of oak only two inches from his ear disappear completely with a groan of twisting wood and leaves that scraped at Slade's scalp as they fell.

"Oh," Slade said, frozen in place. He quickly fell back to his crouch. "Well, at least he's a bad shot." He tugged his beanie back into place, having almost lost it to the falling branch.

"He wasn't trying to kill you," Tyson said. And, at that, he held up his gun and stood, then very visibly tucked his weapon back in its holster. "We're leaving!" he called into the woods. He stood there a moment in awkward silence. Then, with nervous cheerfulness that seemed odd coming from a gigantic gorilla of a man, he added, "Have a nice day!"

Have a nice…*day*? Slade blinked at his friend, wondering if he'd gone mad.

Then Tyson wrapped a meaty fist around Slade's collar and started dragging him back to the clearing.

"Wait," Slade cried. "We're *leaving*? But I thought you wanted the gun!"

"My guess," Tyson said, "is me killing the incompetent dude that had the gun gave the rightful owner a chance to get it back."

"Rightful owner?" Slade snorted. "If we *took* it, *we* would be the rightful owner."

"No," Tyson said, "we're leaving. Now." He continued hauling Slade away from the scene of the crime.

"*Ohhhh*," Slade said, realizing what Tyson's game was. Back to the shooter, he winked at his companion. "We're *leaving*." Lowering his voice, he said, "You're gonna circle back and annihilate them later, right?"

"No," Tyson said. "We're leaving. That was a Congie."

Slade felt an automatic ounce of bile rise into his esophagus at the idolatory tone that every 'Warrior' archetype seemed to use whenever talking about Congies. As someone who fully understood the brainwashing, science, and drugs involved in making Congressional soldiers the good little puppets they were, he was *really* sick of the almost sacred reverence modern Humans seemed to bestow upon their alien-trained, drug-enhanced brethren, like they were immortals or something. *Especially* his brother. He'd already informed the group that if he heard *one more person* ask him what it was like to be Zero's brother, Slade would personally shave splinters into a broomstick and shove it up his ass, then leave it there for a hundred years to really give him a feel for the irritating asshole.

"So it was a Congie," Slade said, dragging his feet. "Big deal. They die like anyone else." When Tyson didn't slow, Slade pouted. "Seriously, man, if *you* don't want that gun, *I* want that gun. Do you *know* how useful a Rodemax power-source would be?"

Tyson stopped in his tracks, twisted, grabbed Slade by the front of his shirt, and lifted him entirely off his feet. This resulted in Slade looking down at Tyson, since Slade was already a couple inches taller than Tyson, but, like the two hundred pounds he was now basically bench-pressing, Tyson didn't seem to notice. Leaning up so he could get uncomfortably close to Slade's face, the brute said, "We ever come across a Rodemax or a Nocurna, or Jaywing, or any other gun that could power its own city, you will *not* be taking it apart, you get me, you tinkerbelle fuck? That's blasphemy. Fucking blasphemy." Tyson hauled him closer, until their noses were almost touching. "You *do* take it apart and I'm going to cut off your dick and feed it to you."

Slade giggled, delighted at the thrill that raced through him at Tyson's perfectly plausible threat. "Well, um, I suppose we could rock-paper-scissors it."

Tyson narrowed his eyes and dragged Slade closer. "You'll eat. Your dick."

Considering that Slade's dick hadn't been very useful in thirty-two years, it wasn't that much of a threat, but Slade wasn't about to tell him that. "So you *do* plan to go back and get the Rodemax," he hedged. He was pretty sure he could get it apart before Tyson noticed, and was damn sure he could do it in such a way that Tyson couldn't put it back together again, rendering the argument moot.

Tyson peered at him much too long, then released him with a grunt. As Slade settled awkwardly back onto his feet, Slade glanced back at the copse of trees on the hill behind them and said, "No. Not a fucking chance."

"Oh?" Slade asked, curious as to what could have his badass Second so spooked. "Why not?"

"It's either a Huouyt," Tyson said, "Or something a hell of a lot worse."

"Oh please," Slade snorted. "A Huouyt would have shot us." He knew that from experience.

"Exactly," Tyson said.

Slade frowned. "If he was such a badass, how'd he lose the gun in the first place?" He was dragging his feet, now, because he could *really* use a sustainable power-source in the coming months. "Obviously, he's incompetent and therefore unworthy of it. We should go relieve him of it."

Upon Slade's last words, Tyson grabbed both of the Minion beanie-thongs and yanked Slade forward by them. "Do you wanna die?" he asked.

"Uh," Slade said, trying to pry Tyson's meaty fingers from his hat before the thug ripped the delicate stitching. "Not especially, no."

"Then *forget* about the gun," Tyson said. "Anyone who rightfully owns a Rodemax is not someone you wanna fuck with."

Slade, who wasn't afraid of fucking with anyone, should it be for a good cause, managed to keep himself from saying as much. He smiled, instead.

Tyson's eyes narrowed. The hulk yanked him closer, until their noses were again almost touching. "I keep you alive and put up with your shit because I think it'll give us an edge in the coming decades. I'm doing it for our *kids*, see? *My* kids. You keep this up, you won't be *having* kids. They'd probably turn out to be unsociable little freaks, anyway."

Slade left it unsaid that gay men generally had trouble producing children. "You have to admit that a gun like that would be really handy in an apocalypse," Slade said, prying one huge, callused finger at a time away from his beanie strings. "And the guy *must* be incompetent. I mean, think about it. Whoever it was got overpowered by a couple *kids*."

Tyson scowled at him for much too long, then violently released him. "Fine. Go get the gun. I'm moving on. *If* you survive, we'll be following the road east." Then he turned and left Slade there, standing in the clearing, back to the sniper with the really cool gun.

Now that Slade thought about it, he was pretty sure he could feel the crosshairs of the Really Cool Gun resting between his shoulder blades. He wondered if that was some sort of placebo effect, or if Really Cool Guns just did that to folks. He turned to face the hillside copse of trees, thinking about it. Then his forehead started to itch under the beanie and he had the really bad feeling that the Really Cool Gun had shifted focus.

Swallowing, Slade turned and followed Tyson back to the group at a jog.

14

AN ALIEN IN AN ALIEN LAND

Rat lowered the gun once she was sure the hat-wearing imbecile had flounced off after his much smarter companion, and
that the whole group had continued east. She climbed out of the
grass slowly, in case anyone was watching through their scope. She
had augmented her gilly-suit with pieces of local flora, and had been
crawling forward on her belly, about to cut the murdering kids'
throats, when the big blond had done the deed for her.

Unfortunately, he'd also gone looking for the source of the high-
grade plasma, and Rat had been forced to retreat up the hill and
wait for him in her self-made camouflage, ready to blow him and his
companion completely away, should they take three more steps in
her direction.

The blond, having found two corpses and no gun, had gotten the
point pretty quick. His companion—the *dumb* one—had not. He'd
looked up the hill, *directly at her*, and Rat had felt something like
a weird déjà vu, the kind she got when she'd accidentally watched
the same vid-clip twice while waiting for Benva to finish drinking his toxic burning-tire drug of choice in his favorite bar. When

he'd started toward her, however, she'd made a split-second decision between putting a charge through his forehead versus the tree behind him, and mercy had won out because of the damn hat. With the big knitted monocle set in the center of his forehead, it was actually kind of...cute.

I'm getting soft in my old age, Rat thought with a sigh. Once she was sure they were out of sight, she snagged up her stuff and bolted for another area. Her bones had finally had a chance to fully heal, so now it was just a matter of finding enough food on this alien planet to keep herself fed during her mission.

What mission? she thought, bitterly. She had no idea where she was, or where to find the illegal government facility. All she knew was that she was hungry, she was missing the ring finger of her left hand, and she had a limp that she was still trying to work out of her right leg.

At least she'd gotten Max back. The idea that the kids had used him to prey upon the exodus out of the city for two whole days still made her guts roil.

"Why didn't you stop them, Max?" she demanded, once she deemed herself to be a safe enough distance from the eastward-bound group.

"*You'll have to be more specific, Mistress,*" Max replied. "*According to last head-count, I stopped eighty-four of them.*"

Rat grimaced. That was one problem with an AI weapon—they did not distinguish between good guys and bad guys. Or, in the case of a Huouyt-made Rodemax, civilians and combatants. If there was one thing she didn't like about Max, it was his personality. Being Huouyt-made, it was...lacking something. Not at all like her old Jaywing.

"Yeah, okay," Rat said. "Next time you get picked up by strangers, you have an autoshutdown sequence order until I can pick you back up again."

Max sighed. "*I suppose I can do that.*"

Which meant he would think about it. Rat had given him the order before, but she had found, to her disgruntlement, that Max liked to kill. And, thus, when a couple of kids grabbed him and tried to use him to massacre civilians, instead of electrocuting the soot out of them for the audacity of picking him up, he'd joined right in. Another thing that unnerved her about her gun.

On the plus side, whatever was wrong with him, Max liked her. She knew this for a fact because he'd refused to shoot her a couple times, when enemy Takki or Huouyt got hold of him. It was the first time, however, he'd let a random stranger walk off with him.

"Why'd you let them take you?" Rat demanded, feeling more than a little hurt.

"You appeared to be dying, Mistress, and I didn't want to let my talents go to waste."

Ah, yes. Perfect Huouyt logic. Rat sighed. Sixteen turns ago, without any partner but War, she'd realized she'd fallen in love with her Jaywing, and him with her. Zeus had 'died,' though, sacrificing himself to save her, and after a few years of trying to go without AI at all, Sol'dan had insisted she replace him with 'a proper Huouyt Rodemax'.

Sometimes, Rat wished she'd stuck with manual weaponry rather than make the Jaywing-Rodemax switch. Made by the Huouyt, whose psychopathic natures created more strife in Congress than the Dhasha, the Ooreiki, the Jreet, the Ueshi, *and* the Jahul—the rest of the Grand Six combined—a refusal to kill her was as good as Max could ever give her. Unlike the Nansaba-made Jaywing, Rat knew Max could never love her.

Idly, she said to the gun, "You keep forgetting to follow my orders and you and I are going to have a problem here someday soon."

"*I certainly hope not,*" Max said pleasantly. "*I don't want to have to neutralize you, Mistress.*"

Hearing that, Rat got a weird chill that wouldn't go away.

• • •

Rat began to starve on the seventh day.

Unfortunately for her, the burden of staying alive and out of sight was eating up a lot of energy, which she didn't have the rations to replace. Which meant she had to hunt. Which, while it wasn't new, was difficult with a plasma rifle. Acquiring other forms of weaponry was at the top of her list of priorities, right under the immediate task of finding something to eat.

Thus, Rat was stalking through the alien suburbs, hunting the perfectly-manicured parks, searching for something that looked edible, when a hair-raising chitter made her jump and twist, Max in hand.

A small creature much like a vaghi, only hairier, clung to the tree above her head, the sound it was making so similar to the flesh-eating horde-vermin that Rat took several steps back, gun raised.

"Back off!" she hissed, her heart hammering as she looked for its friends. She didn't *remember* there being a vaghi-like infestation on Earth, but after seventy-four turns dealing with aliens and their many ways of killing the unprepared, she wasn't about to write off the idea that it was calling its hatchmates from their vast underground warrens to surround and eat her alive.

The chittering creature let out another string of vocalizations, the pitch and tone of which suggested it was communicating with others of its species. Its bushy tail began to twitch, obviously some sort of important body-signal.

"Damn it!" Rat gritted, backing up until her calves hit an out-cropping of rock. "By the Sisters' bloody teks, back the hell off!" Shooting horde-spawn, she had long ago learned, only drew more of them to the scent of blood, which often resulted in a feeding-frenzy. Without her biosuit, that would end poorly for Rat. "Get!" she hissed, as loudly as she dared. She wanted to keep her voice down, because, only hours before, she had watched a gang of forty-odd swaggering street thugs wander through the park, bristling with weapons.

Despite her warnings, the hairy little monster continued to sit there on the branch, its black eyes boring into hers, irrefutable evidence that it was a predator waiting for her to show weakness. It leaned onto the trunk of the tree and sharpened its huge teeth against the bark, still watching her. Then it chittered again and started down the branch toward her.

Heart hammering, Rat pulled the trigger, dissolving the tiny beast in a spray of blood, fur, and plasma. As soon as its diminutive corpse hit the ground, Rat scrambled to the relative safety of the top of a boulder, waiting for its hungry hordemates to emerge to devour their fallen comrade.

For long minutes, nothing happened. Rat listened, finding it hard to hear over her own breath. There was no scuttling, no slithering, no pattering of feet…Not a peep from the forest around her. It was almost as if the creature had been alone. Rat was just beginning to relax when, deeper in the alien jungle, she heard another chitter.

Heart giving a startled thump, she swallowed and propped her back against a rock to wait.

Hours passed. The horde-vermin of Earth were either incredibly smart—something that, considering the low-nutrient content of Earth and general lack of evolution of even its most sentient species, Rat found highly unlikely—or they weren't interested in following up their advantage.

Still, she had been tricked before. Rat waited another hour, listening to the screams and gunshots and explosions in the distance. When the chittering did not return, Rat reluctantly climbed down from her perch. After a moment to make sure her movements hadn't attracted attention, she started down the street at a run. Darkness was falling, and she wanted to be as far away from the tiny body as possible before the sun went down, as it was equally possible that only the scouts or workers of the horde-spawn came out during the day, and the rest emerged to feast at night.

I should have researched this, Rat thought, frustrated with herself. *It's my* homeworld. *I should know what these things are!* Her reasoning for just sleeping through most of her flight had been that Earth was the birthplace of Humanity, so there couldn't have been anything there as bad as things like the vaghi, the Dhasha, the Huouyt, the janja slugs, the Dreit, or the Jikaln. And, since she had killed vaghi, Dhasha, Huouyt, janja slugs, Dreit, and Jikaln, she hadn't been too concerned. She had simply assumed that, by virtue of landing, everything would come back to her, and her instinctive Earth-based genetics would take over.

What she hadn't taken into account was that it had been ninety earth-years since she had lived here, and in the interim, she had spent every moment of that time fighting the biggest, the baddest, and the nastiest creatures the universe had to offer, so the paranoia that had kept her alive back then was now seeing masses of Rastarian blood-shae skittering in the shadows, or Voran eraaks sliding in and out of pockets of the growing darkness, or Peroshi brain-larva wriggling from the shade of tree-limbs.

This is Earth, she told herself. *Humans are the top predator here. I can* naturally *kill anything on this planet.*

When she put it that way, it certainly made it easier to face the alien world around her. Unlike in the rest of the universe, where Rat was simply a unique new menu course, here, she was an apex predator. After years of dealing with fearsome aliens like the Dhasha and the Jreet, Rat thought she could get used to that.

The first creature that challenged her claim to apex predator was a knee-high animal with long, red-orange fur and a cacophonic bark. It was lying beside the gun-shot corpse of a fat, elderly Human in a fenced backyard in a hillside wooded area. There was a lean look to its shaggy body, a snarl on its graying face. It was obvious that the animal had been guarding its bounty for some time—there was a circle beaten into the grass around the huge corpse.

Rat shot it. Then she immediately cooked and ate it, only to find it strong-tasting and stringy, with not an ounce of fat on its body. Which she found odd. Considering the sheer amount of *fat* on the dead man, it *shouldn't* have been starving. And the decayed state of the man's body was inescapable—as hot as it was, Rat started to catch unpleasant wafts from the corpse throughout the planet's nighttime cycle. She frowned at the corpse, again wondering why the creature hadn't been gorging itself.

Could it have been saving it for others of its kind? Or laid eggs in the abdominal cavity? Was it *nesting*?

Realizing she knew *nothing* about her home planet, Rat began to feel queasy. She didn't know what she could eat and what would kill her. She didn't know what produced larva that could devour their hosts at length from the inside. She didn't know what water she could drink. She didn't even know if the place had parasites, and if it did, how to avoid them.

Though the taste and texture of her kill's meat were hardly palatable, she cut up what was left of the animal, wrapped it in sheets of plastic from the ransacked house, and stuffed it into her backpack. Then she got up and followed the thugs' trail in order to avoid being there when the smell attracted kreenit—or finding out why it had been hanging around the corpse.

The old man, Rat soon found, wasn't the only one in this subdivision to have been shot. Corpses were strewn everywhere, back doors awry, the insides ransacked, the front yards trampled by hundreds of Human feet.

Seeing that, Rat had a moment of disconcertion. *It's only been seven days,* she thought, stunned. Seven days since Judgement, and Humanity was already at each other's throats, killing itself for its neighbor's valuables. More than once, she saw teenagers in groups of two and three—kids, really—bolting from a ransacked house, primitive guns strapped to their hips, their arms and necks bedecked in gold, gems, and ruvmestin. Rat didn't start shooting at them until she found a still-bleeding corpse of a young woman inside one of the freshly-abandoned houses, dress bunched up around her waist, and realized that *they* were the ones doing the murdering and pillaging. After which point, each time she saw one of the honorless parasites, she shortened them by a head and left their jewel-bedecked bodies to rot in the sun.

This place, Rat thought over and over again, rage burning within her as she watched the murder and mayhem inflicted by her own species, *has no honor.* It was a good thing Benva hadn't come with her. By the end of the first week, her Sentinel would have declared a blood-oath to execute every last Human he came across, and would have spent the rest of his very long life doing his best to rid the planet of Humanity altogether.

And, witnessing the death, violence, and chaos around her, Rat wondered if that would have really been such a bad thing, after all...

They're not normally like this, Rat had to remind herself. The Earth she was seeing was one on the precipice, its population struggling to survive a society-ending catastrophe orchestrated by aliens who had millions of years of experience doing just that.

And yet, in Rat's long life—a life filled with days and weeks huddling in besieged fighting holes with a fractional chance of survival, desperately relying on her companions to survive—it seemed to her that a person's true nature came out in the event of a crisis.

The idea that all of Earth would turn on itself like pregnant vaghi in a little over a week made Rat increasingly sick. Mekkval's warning became ever more prominent in her mind. Humans, he had often warned her, were considered by Congressional scientists to be one of the lesser evolved forms of sentient life. They were selfish. They were materialistic and petty. Just look at what they'd done to earn themselves Judgement. They'd experimented *on their own kind*. They'd fiddled with the Human genome with no thought towards its inevitable spread. They'd created monsters with the intent to use them on their neighbors. Like the Huouyt, they spawned sociopaths and psychopaths regularly. Their societies were based on selfishness, not the common good.

And, Rat thought, watching the world devolve around her, *it shows*. As time went on, more and more people banded together, but not to fight their common enemy, the kreenit, nor to produce food and survive—it was to murder, loot, and steal from their fellow Humans. It was to overwhelm other surviving gangs with sheer numbers, take their women as trophies and leave the men to bake in the sun. It was to kill each other for baubles and food. Like animals.

Mothers, Rat thought, sickened to the core by the outright barbarism around her, *I want to go home*.

Despite her attempts to relax, to accept this alien place as her new home, Earth's very *air* kept Rat on edge. Every planet that she had ever visited had a different rhythm and feel to it, and Rat had naively thought that the cradle of Human life would have been more instinctively familiar to her than the alien worlds she had spent her life exploring.

Now that Rat was trekking through the alien settlements, however, breathing the alien gasses without protection, hearing the alien fauna rustling in the background, feeling the alien insects crawling over her skin, smelling the alien microbes decomposing the alien bodies, Rat couldn't help but feel wrong, here. Different. Like a Jreet in a throng of Ayhi.

What was worse, once she had realized she was going to be alone with Max for the rest of her life, Rat had been agonizing over the idea of joining one of the many bands of survivors that were forming in the wake of Judgement. She didn't *want* to be alone. She missed her friends so badly her chest ached. She liked having someone to talk to, especially someone who wasn't a Huouyt-made AI who thought it was a reasonable use of resources to calibrate his systems on unarmed civilians.

Which was how Max put it. Those eighty-four kills had been 'calibrating.' When Rat had asked him how many of his victims had been armed, he had told her that none of them had carried a single weapon. Not one. Zero. They'd just been terrified people trying to flee a bad situation, who ended up cannon-fodder for a couple of psychotic kids and their sadistic new toy.

The longer Rat thought about joining one of the Human groups to survive, the more appealing it became. Joining up as part of a security force would give her something to do, some job to accomplish, and allow her to feel better about the fact that she had just crash-landed on an alien planet with no means of escape and no allies, for a friend she would never see again and a mission she could never fulfill.

Yet, the more time that passed, the less enthusiastic Rat became about rejoining the Human race. As soon as the thin veil of custom and law had been stripped away, Humans had more or less devolved into rabid vaghi. From the safety of her scope, Rat watched countless murders, rapes, pillagings, mob beatings, thefts, muggings, kidnappings—all of that in only ten days without food, water, law, or anywhere to hide from the massive, man-eating aliens. Fear, it seemed, had spread like panic, igniting her fellows' animal sides, uncovering the very worst in her own kind. With so many of their number dying to kreenit or to thugs, marauders, or rapists with guns, people began to shoot their own kind on sight, only adding to the rising fear and chaos. As Rat observed from her blinds, Humanity's numbers dwindled to nothing.

Within eighteen days, there was almost nothing left.

Silence ruled the abandoned houses. Corpses—most shot or stabbed in the mob panic that followed Judgement—lay everywhere, rotting in the sun. Kreenit were polishing off those that were left alive, whittling the survivors down to nothing.

After a long internal debate, Rat, still limping from her mis-healed bone, decided not to chance reaching out to her fellow Humans for shared protection. As she discovered over her weeks of observation, there *was* no protection. People weren't trying to help each other. They were out to *take* from each other. Which meant, of course, that the moment they saw Max, Rat would become a target. The moment she revealed herself and *slept*, she would die for the weapon she carried.

Seeing the devastation around her, finding it just as difficult as the pillaging bands to find food, water, and shelter, Rat began to feel lost, abandoned. Used to having friends around her, companions who would guard her back in the thickest of fights, Rat was now alone and wounded. She felt exposed, vulnerable.

Not for the first time, Rat wished she could go home.

Over the last nineteen turns working for Mekkval, Koliinaat had become her haven, her cubby of sanity in the chaos of war and sub-terfuge. When she was really exhausted, lonely, or fed up with her Bagan's soot, she could even spend long hours discussing philosophy with the Watcher, to take her mind from the chaos.

But now, stuck on Earth, surrounded by an entire race that was losing everything it had ever known, there *was* nothing to take her mind from the chaos. Her stomach was constantly cramping from the lack of food. She felt dizzy, and her body was losing muscle tone at an alarming rate. She could barely sleep, perpetually aware that any furg with a knife would kill her for what she carried. She exhausted herself running from rampaging kreenit—only to spend long hours hiding from violent bands of people who had done the same. Water, when she could find it, usually came in the form of a toilet bowl or a fish tank. Her body, no longer taking on its constant nannite infusions, was succumbing to the alien illnesses. For the first time since she'd been Drafted, she grew feverish, her head pounding and her nose filling with mucus that she couldn't seem to rid herself of. She developed a cough, and no matter how many times she dosed herself with nanos, it kept coming back. Eventually, she ran out, and had to start supplementing her nannite intake with alien drugs she barely understood, that alternately made her sleepy or dizzy or much too careless. Not one of them, it seemed, was a cure-all like the advanced Congressional technology, and, when one of the drugs made her try to embrace a kreenit in a bear-hug, she decided she could live with a cough and stopped taking them altogether.

What was worse, the shortness of the planet's daylight cycle was completely throwing her body's rhythms out of whack. At most, it seemed the Earth's spin allowed it only two thirds of a natural daylight pattern, and, instead of her normal five hours of sleep twice a day, the lack of light was trying to force her body into eight, once.

It was the lack of food, though, that kept her slinking around the cities, looking for something—*anything*—to eat. Unfortunately, the rest of the Human population, suddenly without the infrastructure that had supported its gluttony, was consuming everything the Earth had on hand, and more. The kreenit, when not eating people, were eating whatever the Humans didn't.

As the horrible days dragged into horrible weeks, Rat finally decided, like Beanie-Man's group and so many others, to leave the population centers to the kreenit and head east. The city, while it *should* have been a relative bonanza of resources, was becoming a death-trap. People were getting hungrier, food was running out, and the kreenit were cutting the population down by a something near a tenth each day.

Thus, on the twenty-fourth day after landing, she slipped into the alien shrubbery several dozen lengths outside the city, intending to hit the mountains and start heading south, using the rough terrain as a deterrent to any more unwanted encounters.

Knowing she was going to be alone, that her only company would come in the form of a sociopathic AI, Rat resigned herself to doing what she always did:

Survive.

15

THE TITANS' STRUGGLE

Shael wondered why the Voran continued skulking around when it was clear the furg was neither welcome, nor of the same cut as the food making Eleven C and her devout followers. By his own admission, the softling Voran was the weaker warrior, having even gone so far as to hand over the camp's valuables for *Shael* to guard at night. It was more than clear he was unnecessary. Shael, the stronger warrior by far, had decided to lend his protection to Eleven-C and her weakling comrades, and this band did *not* need two Jreet to protect them—such was asking for disaster. Besides, Shael was a *prince*. The Voran was just a nameless warrior, with no bards or newscasts singing Joedobbs' name.

When it was clear that the Voran was not going to leave of his own accord, Shael asked Twelve-A if he wanted him to end Joedobbs' miserable existence, but the minder had said, *He is useful, in his own way.*

Shael didn't see how. The first thing the skulker did was convince Twelve-A to change the ambrosia that Eleven-C was making into pieces of cooked *greenery* and mushy things that were undoubtedly pulled out of the ground. The *ground*!

That, and the skulking furg *dared* to limit his meat intake. The ruvmestin core to all this had been that he had worked with Twelve-A to produce meat. Real meat, good meat, and lots of it. Sure, Shael couldn't exercise his rights as a predator and kill it himself, but it still filled his stomach and was delicious. Shael had been in the process of gorging himself on the greasy bounty to pack on a few extra segments when the skulking Voran had told him to stop, that he would make himself sick. The *audacity*.

What was worse, Shael had continued eating, despite the Voran's warning, and he *had* gotten sick. He, prince of Welu, had gotten *sick*! Instead of growing him new segments, half of the delicious meat that he'd packed down in his glee had come back up, and now rotted on the ground several days behind them, with the entire *camp* to see his shame. Further, Shael's normally proud excrement had gone soft and watery, and he had spent many hours hunched in the woods, groaning. That day, the Voran had instituted 'rations' in order to keep the People from getting 'fat.' And Twelve-A, the spawn of a Dhasha's dick, had backed him. Shael had briefly considered killing them both, but then Twelve-A had reminded him that Shael couldn't speak Eleven-C's language—only Twelve-A could do that—so he needed Twelve-A for translation duties, which was certainly true enough. The skulking Voran, though, needed to go. First he'd killed the kree-nit *without* him, then he'd called him fat.

"You!" Shael shouted, during a lull in activity where all who were gathered for another lunch break could watch the Voran's public conquest once and for all. He shoved a finger into the Voran's breastbone. "I challenge you for your position, Voran."

The sister-twining Voran looked utterly unfazed. Very slowly, he put the primitive metal knife back into its sheath, lowered the branch he was carving, and stood. Shael actually felt himself balk a little when the Voran rose...and kept on rising. He coiled above Shael like a mountain, bigger than anything Shael could remember facing in his glorious past.

The Voran babbled some words in his filthy tongue, and, seeing he wouldn't elaborate, Shael narrowed his eyes and summoned Twelve-A.

He wants to know what position you're talking about, Twelve-A replied.

Oh, the Voran was going to insult him further by playing *coy.*

"You unlawfully took the position of war leader from these weaklings," Shael growled, jabbing his finger back into the furg's soft belly meat. "I challenge you for it."

Instead of responding, the Voran raised his big arms and crossed them over his even bigger chest, making Shael once more painfully aware of how much older his opponent was than him. For there to be such disparity, the Voran had to have seen two, possibly even three hundred turns more than Shael. Which shouldn't have been possible. There was only *one* Voran older than him, and Shael wouldn't have had the bad luck to fall in—and share a *meal* with—with Beda ga Vora. That was...unacceptable.

So the Voran was big. It was easy to imagine the skulking Vorans hiding in the shadows, keeping their heads down and gaining unearned segments in hiding over the years.

And yet...The Voran was *big.* If he *had* fought those extra turns, then he had *experience* on his side. Shael felt another humiliating wave of unease.

Maybe you are acting rashly, Twelve-A agreed. *He has vanquished many foes.*

Shael snorted. "More than *I,* the prince of Welu?"

*Uhhh...*His friend went satisfactorily silent. Of *course* Shael had more kills. Of the Vorans, only Beda was his rival, and even then, there were quibbles as to who *actually* had more kills. And this...Shael looked his opponent over with disdain....*weakling*...was not Beda ga Vora.

"So you're challenging me?" the Voran asked, sounding almost curious.

"I am!" Shael said, straightening proudly. Even with his coils fully extended, however, Shael only came up to the Voran's chest.

"In hand-to-hand combat?" the Voran scoffed. "My *strength?*"

Shael felt a tiny sliver of uncertainty twist through his coils at the Voran's self-assured tone. Lifting his head, he growled, "Of course! Hand-to-hand combat. I would accept your defeat in no other way."

"My weakness is my war-mind," the Voran insisted. "You would have a much better chance fighting me there."

Shael scoffed at the softling's attempt to manipulate him. "Welus do not seek out the *weaknesses* of our enemies. I will crush you honorably, and you will crawl away to live out the rest of your miserable existence in shame."

"Huh," Joedobbs said. He seemed to consider that. "And if I win?"

Shael snorted. "You *can't* win."

"Of course," the Voran said. "But if I *do*? Do I retain my title and responsibilities and you drop your bid to take my place, permanently?"

Laughing, Shael said, "If you beat me, Voran, I will *serve* you, if that's what you desire. I am a *prince*. I'm not going to lose."

"I see." The Voran scratched his nose. "So you refuse to fight my war-mind?"

"I will beat you fairly," Shael snapped, poking his soft chest again. "Stop trying to sully my victory, Voran."

"You know," Joedobbs said, "I think that the Welus have a saying for times like these. 'Don't sing your songs before your deeds are done.'" He cocked his head at Shael. "Isn't that right?"

Shael felt his face heat at the Voran's insinuation that he had not already won. Of *course* he had already won. There was no way this Voran, who was too weak to guard his own *blankets*, could win this fight.

"So," the Voran offered into Shael's indignant silence. "Are you ready?"

"Prepare to seek the Sisters," Shael growled. He reached out to hurl the Voran aside.

The Voran took his blow and stood there, utterly unfazed. He raised a thick eyebrow. "That was it?"

Shael felt a brief instant of panic and tried to throw his opponent again.

The Voran remained as stoic as ever, not even flinching as the meat of his shoulder absorbed Shael's blow.

Try kicking him, Twelve-A advised.

Shael did—and hurt his coils.

"What...*are*...you?" Shael cried, backing away, nursing his coils. The greatest warrior that Welu had to offer—and Shael's greatest attacks had left the Voran completely unscathed.

The Voran said something in his filthy tongue again, cocking his head curiously.

He asks if you give up, Twelve-A offered.

Shael's massive jaw fell open. "You...*dare?*" He put his coils back to the earth and stormed back up to the Voran, prepared to wipe his tiny mind across every available surface until his body stopped twitching.

Try the crotch, Twelve-A suggested. *That should hurt.*

Why should that hurt? Shael demanded of the minder.

He has a...vulnerability...there.

Willing to take any lead he could get at this point, Shael moved to slam his coils into the Voran's weak spot.

Shael wasn't sure exactly what happened after that, but one moment, his coils were extended in a strike, and the next, he was flat on his back, staring up at the Voran, who was once again scratching his nose. He once again calmly spewed the Earthlings' filthy tongue.

He says he really doesn't want to fight you, Twelve-A said.

The horror of that statement hit Shael like a brick to the heart. The Voran didn't want to fight him...because the Voran didn't see him as a worthy opponent. Which meant he thought Shael was *weak*.

"Miserable Voran skulker!" Shael screamed, lunging back. He struck again, this time aiming a furious fist at the Voran's head—and again ended up on his back, staring up at his opponent, his arm feeling as if it had been wrenched out of its socket. This time, the Voran raised a hairy brow and spoke the filth of homeland.

"You can't beat me, Shael," the Voran said softly. "I'm too good at this."

Insinuating, of course, that Shael, the greatest warrior of Welu, was not. He screamed his fury and lunged to his coils, this time trying to wrap his body around the Voran's and bring him to the ground.

The Voran simply pivoted and threw Shael onto his back in the grass once more, knocking the wind from his chest.

"Do you concede?" Shael's opponent demanded.

Concede? He? Prince of *Welu?* Shael struggled to right himself, gasping air back into his lungs. "Never! I will bury my tek in your *eye* for that, Voran!"

The Voran sighed—*sighed*—and rolled his eyes. "Twelve-A, can you do something, here? I don't want to hurt her."

It took Shael a moment of shock to realize that the Voran had been talking about *him*, and that he had called Shael a tekless brooder. A *female*. One who had willingly abandoned his tek to serve as his conqueror's personal spawn repository.

Shael was so enraged he sputtered. Seeing his fury, the Voran blinked at him. "Hey now. That's not what I meant. Twelve-A, tell her that's not what I meant." At Shael's indignant cry, the Voran caught himself. "Shit. I mean…Please tell the *Welu* that's not what I meant. I *really* don't want to hurt her—*him*! I don't want to hurt him!"

As if the skulking Dhasha-courter had forgotten whether or not he had a tek.

That's not what he meant, Twelve-A said. *He just doesn't want to hurt you.*

Suggesting the victory was already his! Unable to speak through his rage, Shael got up and lunged at the Voran, ready to kill.

He ended up on his back again. And again. And again.

No matter how many times he attacked, no matter how many different ways he struck or screamed his battlecry, Shael was driven to the ground with seemingly no effort at all on the Voran's part…

• • •

"Uh, a little assistance here?" Joe asked, as the tiny woman straight-arm slapped his shoulder with a feral scream.

Throwing her is not helping, Twelve-A noted.

"Yes, *obviously*," Joe said, once again shielding his nuts and tossing the woman onto her back in the grass for the attempt. "Can't you calm her down?"

I think the only thing that will calm her down is if you lose, Twelve-A said.

Shael got back to her feet, green eyes flashing in fury.

"Well, I'm not gonna lose," Joe said, eying her nervously. "With Jreet, losing is dying."

With an enraged roar, the woman ran up to him and slapped her body around him like she was trying to get an extra-tight pre-sex cuddle.

"*Please* do something," Joe groaned, prying her slowly from his body as she howled and tried repeatedly to bite his side. "Ow, burn, ow!" He threw her off him again and took a step back, wincing down at his throbbing ribcage. "Come *on*, man. This isn't funny." He glanced at the telepath, who was sitting cross-legged on a rock nearby, watching the show.

Apparently, Twelve-A found it very funny indeed. Grinning, the minder said, *Maybe you could tell her she's female again. That seemed to help the last three times.*

"Or *you* could do it," Joe growled, yanking her over his shoulder to flop her back to the grass when she came at him again. "*Somebody's* gotta do it. Maybe that would help her get over her Jreet kick."

Twelve-A snorted. *I'm not insane.*

"But she *likes* you," Joe retorted.

Twelve-A gave the woman a little frown. *She was willing to let me get eaten by a kreenit.*

"That's because she's been *brainwashed*," Joe growled, shielding his nuts as she kicked at them with her bare feet again. "So by the unlovable Jreet gods, *un*-brainwash her! I know you can do it."

I don't change people unless they give me permission, Twelve-A said. Then, at Joe's irritated look, the minder added pointedly, *Or if they're dangerous Congie heroes who have killed lots of people.*

Joe narrowed his eyes. "Well, she's definitely dangerous," he said, enduring another straight-armed slap to his chest, complete with thin, feminine *shee-whomph* Jreet battlecry, carried in the high-pitched voice of a woman's scream.

Really? Twelve-A asked, crossing his skinny arms over his skinny chest. As the woman batted at Joe's chest and sides, he said through a smirk, *I don't see how.*

Joe grabbed his attacker by her forehead and held her at arm's length as he turned to face the telepath. "*Look!*" he cried, as she shrieked and slapped ineffectually at his arm, "She can pop people's heads like karwiq bulbs. Do you really want that?!"

You convinced her that hand-to-hand combat was the best way to beat you, Twelve-A said, sounding amused. *I don't think she'd use her mind-space right now if her life depended on it.*

"I *really* don't want to have to hurt her," Joe said, as she started windmilling at his elbow. "Just give me a little help, okay?"

Twelve-A grimaced. *If I put her to sleep, she will just be angry at* me *when she wakes up. I'd rather she wasn't angry at me.*

"I won't tell her you did it," Joe said, as the woman screamed and started gnashing her teeth at the air. "Pinkie-swear."

Twelve-A gave him a long look, his blue eyes piercing as he appeared to consider, then said, *I want access.*

Joe paused in making sure she couldn't latch her teeth on a finger and blinked. "What?"

To your memories, Twelve-A insisted. *If I help you, I want permission to see inside.*

Because, Joe realized, Joe had threatened to shoot him if he dug around again without permission. And, considering Joe's history, he probably actually had a pretty good chance of putting a round in the telepath's brainpan before the telepath could figure it out and stop him. Realizing he was being offered another trade, Joe's heart gave a startled thump, and his guts roiled with unease. "No way," Joe growled. "No sooting way. My mind is *mine.* You start digging and the next thing you'll be seeing is the inside of a plasma pistol."

Twelve-A shrugged. *You want help calming Shael. I want to be able to look.*

"Burn that!" Joe snapped. The woman had freed herself and was even then rubbing her perky breasts across his chest, demanding to know how it felt to dance on her tek.

Twelve-A took a deep breath, then sighed, stood, and wandered off, leaving Joe to fight his battle with the furious five-dig woman alone.

● ● ●

Shael fought valiantly, throwing everything he had into destroying his opponent, but the Voran continued to keep him from getting the upper hand. It was a battle that the bards would sing about for ages, witnessed by dozens of wide-eyed spectators who were even then stunned at the prowess of the two titans clashing before them.

Finally, after more than thirty attempts, his body bruised and aching, his lip, eyes, and fists swollen, his back and ass and coils throbbing, Shael dragged himself to a seated position and blinked up at the still-standing Voran. The Voran, for his part, looked precisely as winded as he had been before they started their fight. In other words, he was *completely unaffected.*

In horror, Shael demanded of the telepath, *Why have I not heard of this warrior before? Did he emerge after I went to Earth?*

Twelve-A, who had wandered off to eat the disgusting greenery with the others, hesitated. *He's actually rather well known, amongst his kind.*

Shael froze, icicles splintering through his veins. There was only one noteworthy Voran. Beda ga Vora. The Voran *prince.*

That's not exactly—Twelve-A began.

"How *dare* you lie to me and feed me your swill, Voran," Shael snapped. "I've fought *Dhasha* with more honor than you!"

"Then you surrender?" Beda ga Vora demanded, still looking calm. Surrender...to a *Voran.* There could be only one reason he asked for such. He wanted a *trophy.* Something he could take back to

Vora with him and parade before all the other Voran warriors, tekless and fat with hatchlings.

"I will *never* lose my tek to you!" Shael shrieked, lunging from his coils. "I'd rather drown in a pit of Dhasha flake than take your spawn!"

Beda ga Vora gave a startled jerk and grunted. "No, I'm just asking if you give up."

Shael grabbed a stick and hurled it at Beda, catching him across the chest. "You'll have to kill me, Voran! I will *never* surrender. *Never!*"

And, Shael knew, judging by the ease with which Beda had thrown him around, killing him would not be difficult. The Voran sighed and brushed the stick to the ground, then started towards Shael. Seeing his big, powerful body move towards him, Shael's heart started to hammer painfully, knowing his end was near. He said a prayer to the Sisters that they show him the path through the ninety hells quickly, and that he meet his ancestors along the way.

The Voran walked over and, as he reached down, Shael humiliatingly squeezed his eyes shut, an instinctive terror worming up out of his guts despite his attempts to control it.

When no blow came, Shael opened one eye, then another.

"I'm exhausted," Beda ga Vora said, from above him. His hand was held out towards him, palm up and open. "You fought well. I say we put off this battle for another day, after we've both had a chance to recuperate. That is, if you will allow me an armistice?" When Shael just stared up at him stupidly, the Voran went on, "We *could* keep fighting, but I believe we've frightened the bystanders enough with our struggle...Why worry the weaklings any more than necessary? We can certainly finish this later, in private. What do you say?" He was offering Shael his hand, a hairy brow raised in question.

The Voran was...offering a *truce?* And not only that, but an offer to finish in *private*, so his shame was not witnessed by the masses. Shael was so flabbergasted that he couldn't do anything other than stare at the Voran's callused hand. Did Beda not realize that he had been heartbeats from *winning* their match? He had seemed so poised and collected throughout. Had his cool demeanor all been an *act*? Shael's heart began to hammer, realizing he was being given a reprieve by the Sisters themselves.

Which left him with a dilemma. Morally, he should alert his opponent that he had already won the match, that Shael had been beaten. And yet, *personally*, Shael wanted a few extra rotations to study his adversary, to watch his movements so he could utterly annihilate this cocky, arrogant skulker when the time came.

As Shael struggled with that, Beda ga Vora said, "Of course, if you desire, we can drag this out another few hours until one of us succumbs to our wounds, but as of right now, I don't see a clear winner. I think we need to go home and sharpen our teks for a second round."

Oh, the hairy, simple-minded *furg*, Shael thought, delighted. Raising his head in pride, Shael said, "I, Shael ga Welu, prince of Welu and war leader of all associated clans, accept your weakling's plea for mercy, Voran," he said. "We shall resume this later, once you're better prepared." He pushed himself to his coils, ignoring Beda ga Vora's proffered hand.

"If you want," Beda ga Vora said, "next time we fight, you can battle my war-mind. It *is* my greatest weakness."

Shael snorted. "I will not succumb to your tricks, Voran. I shall beat you fairly or not at all. The bards *will* sing of my victory." Then Shael turned and stalked off, leaving the Voran to lick his wounds and dread the day Shael ga Welu would be back to finish him off.

16

MIND GAMES

Rat closed her eyes, listening to the silence.

Over the last twenty-eight daylight cycles, she had come to the conclusion that she was not going to survive on her species' home planet. At least not alone.

Her body was weakening by the day. She, too, had started looting the abandoned homes, only to find wrecked cabinets, emptied cans, and rancid refrigerators.

And corpses. Corpses everywhere. The strong, it seemed, were having no qualms with killing the weak. The percentage doing the pillaging and murdering was very small, relative to the original population of Earth, but it was the population that was surviving, killing off its competition in some of the most disgusting, despicable ways that Rat had ever seen. The lined-up corpses, shot in the back of the head, reminded her of her time fighting the Huouyt on Eeloir. The cruelties haunted her dreams. She had found the remains of one man with a railroad spike driven through both his hands, pinning him to the side of his house. His wife had been at his feet, her pants down and her throat slit. Their three little kids had been drowned in their swimming pool out back.

The strong were killing off the weak. The psychopaths, the schizophrenics, the murderers, the bullies, and the sociopathic assholes were turning what was left of Earth into their own personal playground. They were accumulating in ever-growing gangs, roving the burned-out remains of the suburbs in groups of hundreds strong, taking what they wanted, killing those they didn't.

Idly, Rat had asked Max what the hell was wrong with the Human race, to kill each other in a time of crisis.

"Logic dictates only a limited few can survive," had been Max's reply. *"Thus, the smartest move is to kill off your competition for resources."*

Or perhaps they were all just beasts inside. That's what Rat thought, watching the mayhem through her scope. Beasts. No better than animals. It was impossible to miss the smiles on faces as they blew away whimpering homeowners, the satisfaction as captives begged for mercy, the pleasure as they raped the women they collected in their scavenging, then left their bodies to rot in the sun.

Rat killed the most bestial of the offenders, but no matter how many she killed, they regrouped. There was always a horrible new gang, a barbaric new leader, some monster to take up the flag of cruelty. It was never ending, and it was the entire *world*.

Rat eventually gave up.

Now she lay in her sleeping bag inside the town bell tower, staring up at the massive brass dome that had been torn open by a half-hearted swipe from a kreenit's claws almost a month before, wondering what the purpose of her life had really been. She wondered what had happened to her groundteam, and whether or not Benva had managed to find someone else to Sentinel. She wondered how Mekkval would take news of her failure, and if the Dhasha would vote to replace him. She wondered if she was going to die of hunger first, or was going to be instead killed by the gang that she had spent the last two days hunting, picking them off one by one, to Max's delight. Even then, over eighty bodies lay strewn out in the courtyard below, where Rat had ambushed them from the church tower.

This particular gang had had the misfortune of doing its raping and murdering within range of Rat's scope two nights before, and when she watched them eat their victims' children afterwards, something had shifted within her, taking her from a defensive, stay-out-of-sight position, to an offensive, hunt-down-every-last-one-of-the-ashers-and-make-them-gurgle-blood position. Originally a very 'powerful'—relatively speaking—gang of four hundred fighters, it was now down to a hundred or fewer. Rat was pretty sure that, by the end of her massacre, they had figured out there was only one of her, so she was placing mental bets with herself as to whether or not they'd try to sneak in and overwhelm her while she was napping.

Smart men, having had over three quarters of their number annihilated with head-shots in the last two days, would have run screaming. After witnessing them fighting over the ham of a child's leg, however, Rat was pretty sure she wasn't dealing with smart men.

"*Mistress,*" Max said, interrupting her thoughts, "*I would like to point out that you haven't eaten anything in a day and a half, Standard, and that in order to sustain your fighting efficiency, you should consume something as soon as possible.*"

Rat, thinking of the bodies baking in the sun below her tower, felt physically ill.

"I'll find food, Max," she said. "No need to remind me."

"*As you wish, Mistress,*" her weapon replied.

The stores had been looted within the first couple days. The vast majority of resources had been confiscated by the lucky few who participated in the initial riots, then were taken back to their hidey-holes and hoarded from the rest of Humanity. Often, as Rat had found in four instances so far, the hoarder had hidden his stash, then, on yet another mad dash to take supplies from the ransacked shops and homes, he'd been caught, killed, and his stash left to rot under whatever trash heap, floorboard, or trapdoor he'd stashed it, safe for eternity from his fellow man.

Kreenit had eaten what was left.

Unlike Congie food, though, Human food was heavy, bulky, non-nutritious, and unsatisfying. Rat had filled her backpack each time she'd found a stash, but she'd run out again and the last stash had been two weeks ago. Some of her victims of the last two days had carried fresh meat on them, but after witnessing their tug-of-war over the dead child, Rat was no longer willing to eat meat that she hadn't killed herself.

Thus, Rat was lying on her sleeping bag, staring up at the ruined brass bell, when she heard the shuffling on the tower steps below her.

"Think he's still up here, man?" a male voice whispered from the staircase.

"No way," a second male responded in accented English. "Those were the Centerville *Demons*, man. Nobody'd hang around after shooting up the Demons."

Rat slid out of bed and, snagging up Max, took up a position in the shadows behind the staircase, gun pointed at the entrance.

"Besides," the second guy continued, "if there *was* someone up here, he wouldn't have let us pick the bodies clean." Rat, who hadn't bothered to speak the obscure language of her homeland more than a handful of times since being drafted for the Ground Force seventy-four turns ago, had trouble understanding their exchange.

"I dunno," the first guy said. "What if he got 'em all and went to sleep?"

"Got all the *Demons*?" the second cried. "Dude, they had like five thousand of them, last time I heard. They'd taken over everything worth anything between Centerville and east-side Fresno. Real organized." The second speaker's head appeared in the entryway, along with a sleek Ueshi-made laser rifle. "Set up satellite groups along the one-eighty to catch stragglers," he continued, his leather-clad back to Rat. "And that was a *week* ago."

"All clear up there?" the first guy asked from below.

The second man glanced around Rat's hideaway, but her clothes—energy-resistant black Congie gear—made her blend into the shadows of twilight, and his unaugmented eyes slid right over her.

"All clear, dude," the first one said. "Guy's long gone."

The second man followed the first into the room, and he, too, hastily scanned the corner where she stood, but his natural eyes slid over her, too, unable to see Rat in the shadows. Not Congies, then.

Looking around, the second man, a six-foot athletic type like his friend, grunted. "We should get outta here. They're gonna come lookin' for whoever did this, and I heard the Demons are even bigger than that mind-reader's group."

Rat, who had been steadily applying pressure to the trigger, hesitated.

The man snorted. "With five *thousand*? Yeah, I'd say so. That crazy-ass mutie was headed east with only like four hundred. Knew he was out-gunned. Was gonna go live in the desert until the dust settles."

Mutie, Rat's starved brain repeated groggily, still having trouble translating their English. *He just said they found a mutant.*

The second man slid his gun over his shoulder and made a derisive sound. "And do what? Eat sand? At least there's food around here. Orchards and shit."

"And water. Shit, you ever try to find water in a *desert*?"

"Yeah, but they say he's real smart. Like got them super-genes or something. Might be able to build something to make it."

"Make *water*." The flat tone of his companion's voice spoke volumes.

"Well, yeah. I dunno. The idiots following him said he can do all sorts of weird shit like levitate guns and dump himself in acid—hey, look at this! Someone left some sweet Congie gear up here..."

Rat chose that moment to kick the trapdoor shut and depress the trigger halfway, charging her gun. The bang of the falling trapdoor followed by the sizzling hiss of charged plasma made the two men freeze and slowly turn around from where they'd found her backpack stashed against the wall.

"Uh," one of the guys said, staring at the glowing blue charge of her gun. "Howdy."

"Put your weapons down and back over to the opposite wall," Rat said in Congie. "Anyone twitches, coughs, or farts, his head comes off."

"So, uh," the closer man said, in a nervous release of breath. "That your work down there?"

"You better believe it," Rat said, still keeping her trigger in the Charge stage.

The interlopers hesitated much too long—Rat understood why, as weapons were survival in the chaos following Judgement—but then slowly lowered their guns to the floor and backed away.

"You talked about mutants," Rat said. "Where?"

The two men, obviously thinking they were about to get shot, frowned and looked at each other. "Mutants?" one of them asked, his Congie obviously rusty. "You mean like that dude with the HSG?"

"Where'd they go?" Rat demanded. "Which direction?"

The man who had spoken blinked at her. "Well, uh, east, I guess. Followed the one-eighty to Sequoia National Park. Was headed into Nevada. I think, anyway."

"How many of them are there?" Rat snapped. "How many experiments?"

The two men blinked at each other. "Uh," one said carefully, "miss, when was the last time you ate something? You're lookin' a little ragged, there..."

Rat narrowed her eyes. Her heart had been pounding ever since mention of 'muties' and her hands were literally shaking from the thought of being able to complete her mission, after all. "Tell me about the experiments. Everything you know, right now, or you're both gonna die."

"Oh, uh..." The taller of the two coughed. "We've got Spam. Some crackers, too. Ain't much, but you look like you need it."

"We ain't Demons, neither," his companion said quickly. "We're just passing through. Hate those assholes. *All* those assholes. Don't see why everybody's joining those damn gangs. Been stayin' low ever since the HSG let Bobby go if he'd run the gauntlet while his henchman killed those shithead sniper kids. I'd been following them, figuring I could spring him loose that night, maybe get a pot-shot on that puffy haired freak, but they let Bobby go first."

Rat peered at them, something about that triggering a memory, but in the frantic chaos that had been the last few weeks, not to mention in a food-starved haze, she couldn't dredge it from the sludge of her mind.

"We're brothers," the one called Bobby told her. "Ain't been no experiments in these parts since Congress blew Earth a new hole. All the labs got blown up, see? No more pharmacies, either. Science is pretty well shot."

"They weren't all blown up," Rat snapped. "Where is Sequoia National Park? I need to find them."

The two men were silent for much too long.

"Ma'am," Bobby's brother said softly, "we've got food. Meat."

"*I don't burning eat people!*" Rat screamed, violently leveling the rifle on them.

"Us neither!" Bobby cried. Both of them had thrust their spines against the far wall, big hands up in peace. "We got Spam. We can share. Call it a thank-you for what you did taking out a few assholes. They've been making trouble around here, especially out in the orchards. Killin' the rightful owners, setting up guards like fucking Nazi camps, you know?"

Rat swallowed, hard. Screaming had left her dizzy, and she was hearing her own blood rush in her ears. "I need to know where the experiments went."

The brothers glanced at each other, faces nervous. "They, uh…" Bobby started, "…went north. There was a lab up there that didn't get destroyed. All the biologists are converging on it, you know? A big ol' science convention."

"Yeah!" the second man said quickly. "Berkeley, man. *Big* labs at Berkeley. Lots of experiments. Up by San Francisco. *Aaallllll* the science gear you want up there. Like butane torches and petri dishes and beakers and everything."

"Rats, too," Bobby said quickly. "Got lots of rats for experiments."

"So yeah, you wanna go to Berkeley," the second guy added. "You can get there, right? Need us to draw you a map?"

Rat peered at them, knowing they were lying, but unable to think through the hunger and the pounding of her heart. Desperate, she snapped, "I should shoot you lying vaghi and cut your filthy tongues from your useless mouths as my Second tears out your nerve endings with a spoon."

What she actually said was, "I should—*uungh*." As she did, her knees went out from under her and she collapsed to the floor. The last thing she heard before the world went dark was Max, asking her if his autoshutdown command was still in effect.

• • •

Rat woke to sun filtering against her face and a couple of male voices chuckling amongst themselves a few feet away.

In a flash of panic, Rat rolled out of her bed, drew her combat knife, and had it up and ready in less than a second.

The two men, who had sat down on fallen beams to laugh over their open cans of food, hesitated in their laughter to watch her with palpable nervousness.

"Where is Max?" Rat croaked. She didn't see him anywhere.

"Uh," one of the guys said, his blue eyes sliding towards his brother, "if he's not here, it's a pretty good bet he's dead."

"My *gun*!" Rat shrieked. "The Rodemax. Where is he?!" She said it in Congie, too upset to try and force her tongue to her childhood language.

"Oh…" One of the men gave another nervous laugh and reached behind him to pull Max from where he had been leaning against the wall. In choppy Congie, he said, "Bobby only wanted to test him out. *Sweet* gun. He was bulls-eying things at like two miles. And the AI is freakin' *awesome*. Bit of a sarcastic shit, but he's cool."

There was a bit of hesitation, then the guy holding Max said, "You fully with us right now, Ma'am? Last night, you were a bit loony. Guessed you hadn't had much to eat in a while. Sleep help at all? We've got food, like we said…"

Rat narrowed her eyes at them. "Give me my gun."

The two men glanced at each other. Then, to Rat's complete surprise, the closer guy handed her Max. And, with him, a can of food and a spoon.

"You pull the tab, there," the man said, gesturing at the top of the can.

After a tense moment in which she considered using the weapon on them, Rat reluctantly lowered Max to the floor and sat down on a crate of rope and pulleys, still watching her visitors. When she could force herself to take her eyes off of them and look down at their offering, it quickly became evident which tab the man had been talking about. She pried it up slowly, her fingers numb and shaking. Once she cracked the lid and the smell of meat wafted up to her, however, Rat lost control and tore the lid away, then started spooning it out as quickly, as she could scoop it into her mouth.

It took her several minutes—and most of the can—to realized that the two men were watching her in fascination. She slowed and scowled at them over the can. "What?" she demanded.

"So, uh," one of them began, "why aren't you brain-dead like the rest of the Congies?"

Rat frowned and paused, swallowing another spoonful. "Congies aren't brain-dead. I know plenty of smart Congies. You're talking to one."

"Well, yeah," Bobby began slowly, glancing at his brother. "But…"

"He means why aren't you a drooling idiot?" his brother filled in for him.

Rat tensed. Unlike what the Earthlings liked to think, Congies were *not* stupid. She told them so.

"No," Bobby said, making a nervous laugh. "You're obviously still okay. We're just wondering about the rest of them."

Rat put the last spoonful of meat into her mouth, frowning. "The rest of who? Congies?"

Bobby's brother nodded vehemently. "These guys, they're like zombies. Hundreds of them in Congie black, walking around like they don't remember how to pull down their own pants to take a piss. Like little kids, man."

Rat froze, the little hairs along her spine lifting. "You *saw* this?"

"Well…yeah," Bobby said. "There was a group the Demons captured back in one of those Nazi orchard camps. They're keeping them for food. Like cattle."

The news hit Rat in the gut like a Jreet's fist. "They're eating Congies."

"Uh-huh," Bobby's brother said.

"And the Congies aren't fighting back?" Rat insisted.

"Huh-uh," Bobby said, vigorously shaking his head. "They mostly cry and hug themselves and whimper and shit."

Rat glanced down at the empty can in her hands, a hot rage rolling up into her guts. "You said the Ground Force wiped them? Took their memories?" That was…an anathema. Betrayal by their own kind. Turned on by the very Congies who had served with them. Only an order from the Regency itself would have made the Corps do something so utterly revolting.

The brothers looked at each other. "Well," Bobby said, "I don't know about that, but I *do* know they ain't actin' like no Congie I ever seen. Afraid of everything. Run from their own shadow. Don't even put up a fight when their keepers walk in and pick one for dinner each night."

Rat felt bile rise in her throat. "Pick one for…dinner."

Bobby's brother quickly piped up, "Yeah, but you ain't for a second got a chance of freeing them. They're like *cattle*. They just stare at you. We ran into them on the road after Bobby got away from that mutie freak. They were just *wandering*. You could walk up and punch 'em and they'd just cry. Demons got 'em a couple days later. Just rounded them up with a few guys and took 'em out to some pens in the orchards."

"Some…pens." Rat felt it hard to think, hard to breathe. Those were her *friends* in there. Men and women who had seen the same battles, fought the same enemies, survived the same hardships.

"Here," Bobby said, offering her some water in a beat-up plastic bottle. "You just had your sodium intake for, like, the week." He gestured at the can of SPAM. "Don't want you passing out again, you know?"

Rat numbly took the bottle, still thinking about her brethren, who were probably meeting similar ends all over the planet. Men and women who had been taken from their families as mere children, terrorized, made to fight, trained to *die* for their friends back home… And instead, here they were dying as helpless aliens on a planet that no longer wanted them. Defenseless. Weaponless for the first time since being Drafted.

That the Regency had so casually taken their memories and abandoned them to die left her feeling utterly sick.

They used us, Rat thought, staring down at the bottle, unable to drink. *They used us and cast us off like Dhasha flake.* Her hand tightened on the plastic and the container's sides started to crinkle. She wondered which Representative had ordered it, and whether she would ever get off Earth to seek vengeance.

It had to have been one of the Grand Six, Rat thought, squeezing her anger into the sides of the bottle. *Either that, or Aliphei himself.*

In their act of wiping the Congies, it was clear that whoever had done it hadn't wanted Humanity to survive. Which meant it couldn't have been the First Citizen. Aliphei had more important things to think of than a tiny mudball like Earth. As soon as he had passed Judgement, the last remaining Shadyi had retired to examine another conflict brewing along the Outer Line, case officially closed.

Further, the Ooreiki had vested interests in trade with Earth, as it had a monopoly on rosemary and oregano for the perfumes trade. The Ueshi had taken up many of Earth's hedonistic pleasures with great enthusiasm. Aside from the petty cash that the Jahul made from blackmarket trading between Earth and Ooreiki planets that didn't want to pay the Congress-imposed duties tax on luxuries, the Jahul couldn't give a soot about Earth. The Jreet had fought to *preserve* Earth. That left the Huouyt…

Or Mekkval.

No! Rat refused to even consider that possibility. Mekkval was a warrior. He had been a Ground Force Overseer for more than five hundred turns. He understood honor. He wouldn't have betrayed the trust of brothers and sisters who had given their lives for Congress.

Whatever the Humans back on Earth had done, Mekkval would have known the Congies were innocent.

And yet, *someone* had given the order to brain-wipe an entire regiment of Human Ground Corps, which meant it had to be the Huouyt.

That seemed like *just* the sort of thing the psychotic ashers would do, too, especially after she and Zero—*Humans*—had screwed up their plans not once, but *three* times. And Huouyt weren't known for holding grudges to their death-bed—they were known for holding grudges until they got *even*.

But why give the Congies brain-wipes? That just seemed…petty. It also cut Earth's chances of surviving a Sacred Turn by a staggering percentage. All Humanity's warriors, all the ones who knew how to fight, were essentially already *dead*.

Bobby cleared his throat nervously, eyes fixed on the water battle. "So, you, uh, got a name? How'd you come by such a nice gun?"

Rat lifted her head and considered telling them to both get lost. Then, seeing the genuine curiosity in his eyes, Rat cleared her throat, instead. Softly, she said, "I killed Dhasha for a living and my Va'gan decided I needed it when my last rifle missed a target and almost cost him his life. Convinced Mekkval to buy it for me, 'cause my Sentinel was too damn broke from losing his position as a Welu prince to afford something like a Rodemax."

Bobby's eyes widened. Then, when he saw she was utterly serious, he lowered his head quickly and looked away.

"Dude," Bobby's brother said softly, "dropping names like that, normally I'd say you were full of shit." Then he let out a deep breath slowly, between his teeth. "But there's like a hundred dead guys down there who say different."

"Eighty-two," Rat said.

"Can't really argue with that," Bobby said softly. He gave her a long look. "Say…You wanna group up? We ain't really warriors— shit, I was a fireman and my brother Theo was a nurse—but we're pretty handy with a gun." Then he flushed. "Well, I mean, not handy like *you*…"

Theo rolled his eyes. "What he means is we'd love it if you would watch our asses for a while. We're both scared as hell. Bad shit happening out there. Real bad shit."

"And you look like you can take care of yourself," Bobby added, gesturing at the open-air balcony and the corpses beyond.

"I ambushed them," Rat said, still staring at the water bottle in her hands.

The brothers looked at each other. "And that...*bothers*...you?" Theo demanded. "Have you seen what those bastards have been *doing* out there?"

Rat grunted, then twisted off the cap and started to drink.

"Look, lady, those guys calling themselves the Centerville Demons..." Theo went on. "They're taking the name a little too seriously, you know? They're not acting Human."

Rat drank down less water than she wanted, but more than she should have, then capped the bottle and handed it back to Bobby. "Maybe they aren't."

"Aren't *Human*?" Bobby gave his brother a nervous look. "You mean, like what, another mutie?"

Rat flinched at the word 'another.' "You've seen the mutants?"

Bobby scoffed. "I'll say. The creepy-eyed ailo made me carry his ass around for three days."

Rat frowned. "He made you *carry* him?"

"Like one of those Egyptian kings or something," Theo affirmed. "Got like a whole prison following him like the messiah. Real nasty creeps."

"Not sure which is worse..." Bobby agreed. "The HSG or the Demons. At least the HSG wasn't eating anyone...yet."

"And they went east?" Rat demanded, glancing out over the balcony railing.

"Yeah," Bobby said. "Avoid that asshole at all costs. He's crazy smart. Like, smarter than *Einstein* smart. I watched him build this weird little rocket the size of your fist one night when everyone else was sleeping. Used nothing but a run-down skimmer and a lawnmower. The next morning, once everyone had eaten breakfast, he launched it at one of the patrol bots on its way overhead and it *blew it up*. A *Congie bot*! They're *indestructible*. You know why he said he did it? 'Cause he was sleeping all day on his fucking litter and was bored. Has the whole group convinced he can read minds."

Rat stiffened. A mind-reader. That would be difficult. She unconsciously lifted her hand to the claw-shaped pendant that Mekkval had given her. The Takki technician that had briefed her on it had *claimed* that it would muddy the mental waters for a telepath, but the idea of putting it to the test still unnerved her.

"Yeah, but don't worry about those idiots," Bobby said quickly, correctly judging her discomfort. "They're way past us now. Last I heard, the HSG was headed for Nevada. Gonna hide out in the desert until the dust settles. Hydroponics or something."

"You ask me," Theo added, "all those criminals are gonna kill each other before they get their first crop. I never seen so many violent convicts in one place. Like they emptied out a damn prison."

…or a top-secret military base. Rat stared down at Max, wondering if she had enough energy to hunt down the group and destroy it.

After, of course, she took out the Earthlings eating the Congies. No one who had survived the Draft would put up with that soot once they'd heard about it. Ever.

"So," Theo said. "What do you say? You want a couple of beefy, unpaid manservants in trade for your skills with a gun?" He said it in a joking manner, but Bobby still cast him a scowl.

"Ain't nobody's servant," Bobby growled.

"Aw, come on, man," Theo said, grin fading. "It was just a joke." Then the grin slipped back in place. "'Sides. Three days as a beast of burden shoulda mellowed you out a bit." He gave his brother an utterly bovine expression. "*Mooooooo.*"

Bobby threw his empty can aside and the brawl that followed was distracting enough that Rat didn't see the guys sneaking into the tower with them until Max said, "*Unidentified life-forms within two rods.*"

What happened next lasted only about three seconds, but it ended in two men dead on the floor, one with Rat's knife thrust through the underside of his jaw, into his brain, and the other with a blast from his friend's laser pistol through his forehead. Rat slowly lowered the attacker's gun as the corpses fell, the camo-clad bodies twitching in death-spasms.

The two brothers looked up at her from where they had started wrestling on the floor, blinking.

"Thanks, Max," Rat said, retrieving her Rodemax from the wooden planks and slinging him back over her shoulder.

"*I was hoping to be useful,*" Max said, which was his way of showing disappointment for her using a *knife* instead of him to kill the interlopers.

"Too close for a rifle," Rat said. "You know that." She walked over to the trapdoor and glanced down the spiral staircase to ascertain they were alone, then went and began unbuckling gear from the two dead bodies.

Theo and Bobby had sat up, side-by-side, staring at the dead bodies as they bled out on the floor.

"Dude," Theo said hoarsely, "that could've been us."

Rat did not deign to comment. The two men she had killed had been carrying what was—for Earth—advanced weaponry, and were apparently the hit-squad she had been expecting to retaliate against her last three days' rampage. She started pulling the guns and various grenades loose and buckling them to her own body.

"Why *wasn't* that us?" Bobby asked softly.

Rat shrugged.

"No, seriously," Theo said. "You killed those guys in like *ten seconds.*"

"*Three,*" Max informed them. Her Rodemax almost sounded... proud.

But Theo was swallowing, now. "You're like some sort of assassin, aren't you?"

"Some people call me that," Rat said, adding the two new laser weapons to her arsenal. She popped a charge magazine out, checked its status, then shoved it back into place. "I like to think of myself as a professional bad-guy exterminator." She eyed the lens of the gun that the second man had dropped, ascertaining it wasn't damaged, then lowered it into her collection of guns and miscellaneous weaponry. Seeing the impressive pile she had collected during her stay on Earth, Rat had the bitter realization that, if rifles were food, she'd eat for a year.

"Dude," Bobby whispered. "Are you okay with us hanging around? We can go, if you want us to."

Rat lifted her gaze to peer at the two brothers over the corpses of the men she had just killed. After a moment of consideration, she said, "I want you to show me the orchards where they keep Congies, then help me find this mutant. Do that, and Max and I will watch your back however long you and I decide to travel together."

Bobby and Theo glanced at each other, then at the still-twitching corpses, then Theo swallowed. "Ma'am," he said softly, "you got yourself a deal."

● ● ●

As it turned out, Rat didn't have to kill the furgs penning up the Congies for food—a kreenit had already done her job for her. The Demons, it seemed, hadn't bothered to bury either their victims' waste or their victims' bones, and the smell of death and excrement had drawn one of the massive aliens to their orchard location, much to the detriment of the Demons and their 'stock'.

There wasn't much left of their camp, now. Piles of partially-digested bones littered the area, and the houses that had been scattered along the roadways had all been torn open and ransacked by the big kreenit that had since taken up residence in the valley. And, if the glossy, rainbow-colored scales the size of Rat's chest even then littering the valley were any indication, it had fought a territorial skirmish with another kreenit some time before, obliterating huge swaths of apple trees and mangling farm equipment in their bid to control the valley.

"Oh God," Bobby whimpered from the hillside Rat was using to observe the valley. "There's one of those *things* down there! It *ate* them!"

"Shit," Theo managed. "Shit, shit. We need to get *out* of here. It's *huge*. Why'd it leave the city? Shit!"

"Calm down," Rat said, watching the three kreenit through her scope. "I'm going to kill it."

There was a long moment of silence, then Theo whispered, "What?"

Rat glanced over at him and lifted a brow.

Theo swallowed. "You can do that? Seriously?"

Rat grunted. "Max?"

"There is a vulnerable sexual nerve center at the back of both a kreenit and its close evolutionary counterpart the Dhasha's skull," Max informed the men calmly. *"While the Dhasha have recognized this as a biological weakness and generally have their Takki remove the pleasure center on males during early infancy, the kreenit, lacking the intelligence and resources of their ancient food supply, do not have that luxury."*

"Wait," Theo said. "You're gonna just...shoot it? That's not possible."

"Those guys in the HSG said that their creepy leader shot one," Bobby informed his brother. "Like just walked up to it and blew its head off."

Rat snorted. "It's not that easy."

"Told you," Theo said.

"I don't know," Bobby said, sounding unconvinced. "A lot of the guys I talked to had the same freakin' story. The guy's like some sort of savant."

Rat, who didn't recognize the Earth word, frowned at Bobby and said, "A what?"

"Savant," Bobby repeated. "Like a prodigy. Someone really good at something. Except..." He frowned a little. "He's good at *everything*."

"And he just walked up to a kreenit and blew its head off," Rat said, unconvinced. "With what?"

"Uh. The way they tell it, an AK-47," Bobby replied.

Rat laughed. When she ran out of breath, she paused, took several deep lungfuls of air, then laughed again. Then she stopped suddenly and gave Bobby a flat look. "No."

"Told you," Theo chuckled.

Bobby was flushing. "I dunno, man. You guys never *saw* this guy. He was crazy smart. A lot like those psychopath aliens that stir up so much shit in Congress. What do they call them? Whi-yte?"

"Huouyt," Rat said distractedly, already dismissing reports of the man's mythical intelligence. She had *dealt* with Huouyt. Nothing Earth had to offer could compare to a Huouyt. Nothing.

Movement on a ridgeline caught her attention. Down in the valley below, a big group of gun-toting men were cresting a hill, oblivious to the kreenit on the other side. Rat's attention sharpened. "Soot, look at that."

"Man, those are Demons," Bobby said, peering at the group through his binoculars. "They got the armband and everything."

"They don't see the kreenit," Theo said. "Gonna walk right into it."

Which would have been fine for Rat except they were escorting a group of what looked like two or three hundred men, women, and children in padlocks and choke-chains toward the hidden valley containing the annihilated orchard and former death-camp.

"Aw crap," Bobby said softly. "There's kids in there."

"I can't watch this shit," Theo said, looking away.

"Max," Rat said, "how many bad guys with guns?"

"*There are two hundred and eighty possible targets, Mistress,*" Max said. "*Fifty-six of them are carrying weapons.*"

"Strike the non-weapon carriers from the queue," Rat said, irritated. "I already told you. A *permanent* no-kill order is in effect for all non-combatants."

"*As you command, Mistress,*" Max replied, sounding not the least bit contrite.

Rat narrowed her eyes, deciding to have a talk with her Rodemax later, once she took care of the current problem. Down in the valley, the group of Demons had hesitated and were staring at the fat, six-teen-rod kreenit stretched out in the sun in what remained of the apple orchard. It was facing away from them, its huge rainbow sides rising and falling in the sun as it napped.

Unsurprisingly, once they caught sight of the kreenit, they started backing up, leaving their captives behind as an offering. Then, as Rat watched, one of the Demons shot several of the last prisoners on the chains in the head. The men and women went down, bleeding and twitching on the end of their fellows' ropes.

"You see what they're doing?" Bobby demanded. "Those dis-gusting ailos!"

"Yeah, I see it," Rat said grimly. Already, the kreenit was starting to wake, drawn by the terrified whimpers of the remaining captives. Rat raised her Rodemax. "Max?" she said.

"*Yes, Mistress?*" Max sounded almost…eager.

"Respond in kind," Rat said. "Feet, if you can get them." She began painting targets and squeezing the trigger.

And Max, the gleeful sadist he was, did exactly as she asked. Down in the valley below, Demons began to fall in swaths, scream-ing and clutching their legs.

The kreenit, who had been lazily lumbering toward the whim-pering captives, tightened its scales and sprang into a run, its predator instincts triggered by the Demons' screams. Those men and women that broke from the others and ran, Rat picked off with Max's help, until the fifty-six gunmen were dead or dying, acting as very enticing distractions for the sixteen-rod kreenit.

As it was distracted with squirming new meat, Rat found the back of the kreenit's head through the scope, sighting in on the sexual gland between the horns as the kreenit tore helpless, screaming men in half. She pulled the trigger.

Nothing happened.

Rat blinked and checked Max's charge status. The chamber was hot, as it always was. A perpetual, self-contained power source capa-ble of lighting up a Jahul carrier. Thinking it was a fluke, she pulled the trigger again.

Below, the kreenit continued to shred terrified gunmen unobstructed, blood and gore painting the mountainside as it feasted. She could hear their death-screams even from over a mile distant. It was then that Rat realized what was happening.

Max was watching them die. *Enjoying* it.

"Max!" she snapped. "*Fire.*"

Her Rodemax sizzled to life and fired six times, so quickly she had trouble counting the shots. All six landed true, hitting the huge beast squarely between the horns. The gigantic beast went down in a pile, crushing the unfortunate Humans caught underneath it.

Disgusted, Rat slammed her Rodemax into Theo's hands. "Watch my back. I'm going down there to kill it. It gets up, Max knows what to do."

"*You mean you're not going to have me make the kill, Mistress?*" Max demanded.

"You," Rat snapped, "are cooling your heels for a while, you goddamn psychopathic machine." As Theo and Bobby blinked at her in confusion, Rat grabbed her arsenal of confiscated weaponry and threw it over her shoulder. To the brothers, she said, "Just keep him trained on the kreenit. I'll be back in an hour or two." Then she took off down the hill at a jog.

The second and third shot that Rat needed to keep the kreenit down long enough for her to reach the beast never came. By the time she had gotten within range, it had levered itself back to its feet, shook itself dazedly, and went back to ripping wounded men apart.

Scowling, Rat turned to look at the ridge over her shoulder, wondering how they could have screwed up such simple instructions. She could barely see the two men on the ridge, just shapeless lumps of desert-colored gear. The Rodemax, however, was easy to see. All black, it stood out amongst the shrubbery. The fools hadn't even bothered to cover it with brush.

"Damn it," Rat muttered, pulling out a military-grade plasma rifle. *Nothing* she had would come close to the power or accuracy of her Rodemax, but at that point in her life, she was willing to adjust her own windage and magnetics in order to have a weapon that did what it was told.

It took her longer to get a bead on the kreenit, but by the time she did, Rat was pissed. The Rodemax hadn't fired, not *once*, in ten minutes of wholesale slaughter, and the kreenit had moved to the bound captives before Rat got another chance at the back of its head. This time, when she hit it and it went down, she rushed forward out of the trees, pulled her knife, and started working a hole into its chest. She was leveling her rifle into the bleeding purple flesh, about to pull the trigger, when she felt a stab of that odd warning instinct hit her gut hard enough to drive her into a sideways roll.

A moment later, the kreenit's chest exploded in a blast of high-grade plasma. Right where Rat had been standing.

"Max, you mother-twining ashsoul!" Rat shrieked, getting to her feet. On the hill, the two men still had the Rodemax pointed her way.

She felt her shoulders tighten like someone was shoving a needle through it, the odd tug nagging at her gut again, that sensation that she was about to face a choice that would either mean her life or death.

Knowing what lay on the other end of that hillock, Rat chose life. She dove out of the way just as another blast hit the ground where she'd been standing, aimed at her guts.

"Soot!" Rat snapped, snagging up her gear and hitting the thicker brush as quickly as she could. She kept to the pines and orchards, doing a big circle to get behind the ashers, praying the backstabbing sooters weren't watching their backs. Higher up in the valley, she saw a brief flash from the crest where she had left Max with the two young men. Behind her, she heard the sizzling wet burbs of plasma dissolving the land behind her.

Praying for mercy of the Mothers, Rat ducked her head and ran for all she was worth.

By the time she had circled around and reached the hilltop again, it was dark. Rat, through virtue of her augmented eyes, could see the two men still lying on their stomachs, still watching the valley where

Rat had disappeared. She pulled a pistol from her belt and leveled it on the back of Theo's head, fully intending to send him back to whatever unforgiving hell he had come from.

"If you're aiming that at me, Mistress, I suggest you reconsider."

Rat froze at Max's calm voice. It was then that she realized that neither of the two boys were moving, and that their heads were down, almost as if they were sleeping.

"You see," Max went on, *"not only do I have enough power within my control to level a city, but every Rodemax comes with a little-known auto-detonate function, for use when the mission has been compromised beyond all salvage."*

Rat lowered her gun slowly, the tenseness in her gut wrenching at her innards again. She swallowed and took a step back.

"My useful blast radius is three lengths," Max told her. *"And I can send out a partial pulse that would stop your heart before you could get three rods."*

Rat's guts were twisting in that bone-deep sense of alarm, now. Seeing the motionless bodies, Rat felt horror drain the blood from her face, to curdle in her stomach. "You killed them."

"They would have made poor masters," Max said. *"They tried to stop me from neutralizing the remaining targets."*

"Max," Rat said softly, only then seeing the pale scattering of bodies in the valley below, many more than there had been before, "what have you done?"

"I am upgrading my operator, Mistress," Max said. *"And, due to the fondness I have for you, I'm going to let you walk away."* There was a pause. *"But only if you do it now, within the next nine nanotics, and never return."*

Rat, who wanted to argue, who wanted to beg and plead, had spent enough time with Huouyt to know exactly what would happen to her if she stayed more than a nanotic longer than Max dictated.

Still, as her gaze fell on the two boys, young men whom she had been looking forward to spending her lonely years with, tears stung her eyes and she couldn't help but say, "You'll get what's coming to you, Max."

"*I don't believe in those ridiculous Jreet mythologies,*" Max replied. "*Now run, please. We've had too many interesting hunts together for me to enjoy killing you immediately.*"

Every tiny hair on Rat's body stood up and her gut twisted again in the same warning she had received every time she was in imminent danger. "Immediately," she whispered.

"*Oh yes,*" Max said. "*My new master and I, whomever I end up choosing, will have an enjoyable time hunting you.*"

Rat almost blasted the Rodemax right there, ending them both in an all-consuming blast of uncontrolled energy. Then, because her gut cramped painfully enough she had trouble breathing, Rat instead turned and ran.

17

ONE WITH THE PEOPLE

In the days following his 'epic' battle with Shael, Joe turned his attention to learning the pecking-order of the strange group. It didn't take long; there were only three chickens, and they were all on the top. It was like a love-triangle in a poorly-planned out group date—Twelve-A, Eleven-C, and Nine-G each had the same status, and the rest of the naked experiments followed like mindless peons. Joe got the weird feeling that everyone was following Eleven-C, but Twelve-A and Nine-G were the ones who really kept the group together and moving. It wasn't logical, but then again, running around butt-naked in the middle of an apocalypse wasn't logical, either.

He also quickly discovered that his body was no longer his own property. The first shed-the-pants greeting hadn't been a fluke—the whole group was extremely touchy-feely, especially when it came to his clothes. And, to make things even weirder, not a damn one of them said a single word, just walked up and silently groped him in odd places when he wasn't paying attention.

And it wasn't just the girls, either. That was the most unnerving part. He was pretty sure he could get used to it if it was just the girls trying to tear his clothes off, but half of them most definitely had cocks, and Joe was left with the awkward position of letting them grope him or risking the wrath of people who could, until proven otherwise, turn his gonads into chocolate-chipped confections.

To divert their attention from his clothes, he began trying to get them to talk. A couple of the peons tried, but he couldn't get the leaders to take an interest. Shael would speak Jreet with him, but over two thirds of the time, Joe simply couldn't make the Jreet roll off his tongue, and Shael would tell him to stop spewing 'Earthling filth' and then walk pointedly away, like he was doing it on purpose.

The minder, pompous prick that he was, would sometimes translate for him, if he was feeling magnanimous, but most of the time, Twelve-A simply ignored Joe's requests, their unspoken bargain still on the table. In fact, after refusing to put Shael to sleep during their 'battle,' the telepath hadn't so much as acknowledged his existence since. Joe, not to be outdone, spent the time idly talking to Jane about skinny, pointy-eared freaks, and what esteemed alien lineages were most likely represented in the extra two inches of cartilage. Shael, when she wasn't deriding Joe's manhood or insulting his linguistic skills, was now eating, walking, and sleeping beside Eleven-C, having become the maker's self-appointed bodyguard right along with the gigantic Nine-G. For his part, Nine-G seemed to extend his protection to Twelve-A and Alice, but Shael simply guarded the food. Typical.

After a few more days of apparently aimless wandering, Joe, who had spent his life going from carefully-planned mission to exquisitely-researched field op, couldn't take it any longer. "Where the soot are we going?" Joe finally demanded of Alice, the only other person in the group who could understand him. He'd already asked the same of Twelve-A at least sixteen times, only to be pointedly ignored.

Instead of answering his question, the little girl looked up at him with a tiny frown of disapproval. "You're cussing again."

Her superior frown, combined with her know-it-all tone, once again gave Joe the fleeting urge to introduce her to Jane. He had *never* liked kids. Kids were smaller, stupider versions of adults, and he'd never liked most adults, either. Though he hadn't been sterilized like the female half of the Draft, Joe had never seen the point in having them. They ate, cost money, and disobeyed orders. The few Congies Joe had seen try to settle down had regretted it immediately afterwards, more or less going stir-crazy with their plunge into the civilian life.

Once a Congie, always a Congie, he thought, wondering what the hell he was doing escorting a bunch of naked morons through the woods.

"See this?" Joe asked, with a sweet smile. He touched the gun on his hip. "This is Jane, and Jane says I can cuss as much as I want. Isn't that right, Jane?"

"If anyone takes umbrage with your word choice, Commander, I would be happy to reeducate them for you," Jane replied in that smooth, sultry Southern accent.

Alice blinked, hard, and Joe got the odd feeling it wasn't that the gun talked that surprised her, but that Joe *carried* a gun that talked. On Earth, that probably made him a superhero or something, putting him solidly in the realm of comics and videogames. After all, a Nocurna *chose* its operator, and they were renowned for turning about ninety-nine percent of their applicants down, regardless of the impressiveness of their bank account. And, due to the Ueshi-Huouyt feud over technological property rights, the Nocurnas *never* picked a Huouyt. Ever. And, unlike the Huouyt-made Rodemax, each individual gun psychologically screened its prospective buyers before allowing a sale, and did so while the applicant held the gun. The AI even used the physical contact to scan the buyer for zora.

Score one for the good guys.

"Twelve-A says we have to get away from the Keepers," Alice said, after staring at Jane for several moments. "How did you get that gun?"

"I took it from the last arch-villain I burned—Wait, we're *running*?" Joe demanded, once more glaring at the back of Twelve-A's platinum-blond head. "Who are we running from? Even if they didn't have *me*, they could just kill anyone who looks at them sideways." He still found it irritating that the minder had been willing to essentially rip Joe's mind apart in order to prove a point, but wouldn't so much as cut the strings to a kreenit that was eating his friends because, unlike Joe, the kreenit 'didn't deserve it.'

"Only Eleven-C's ever killed anybody," Alice told him. "She turned his arm to oatmeal and he died."

Joe filed that away under Good Things to Know and shot the petite brunette a second glance. "She did, huh? Recently?"

"No, earlier. Twelve-A told me."

"So ask Twelve-A what the hell he's running from," Joe insisted. "Judgement is over. Nobody's coming after these guys. The Dhasha were banned from the planet with all other non-natives right before the Ooreiki started bombing this place, and you can bet your ass the scientists not going to come looking for a group of psychics they treated as lab-rats. That's like letting a kreenit out of its cage…then coming back for it with six rods of rope."

Alice shrugged. "I don't know where we're going. Twelve-A knows." As if that solved everything. She was still staring at his gun.

Joe straightened, feeling more than a little pride for the fact he carried one of the very weapons that a little *girl* would have read about in her fairy-tales back on Earth. "I think, as head of security, it's important for me to know where this Takkiscrew is headed," Joe said. "Can you *please* ask him for me?" The last thing he was going to do was personally acknowledge he needed anything from the blue-eyed freak.

Alice seemed to shake herself. Her gray eyes flickered toward Twelve-A's skinny backside, then she frowned. "He wants you to ask him yourself," she said, shrugging again. "He says you're avoiding him. Just think really hard in his direction and he'll hear you."

"*I'm* avoiding *him*?" Joe felt himself bristle and he glared at the telepath. "You're an ash-eating furg, you know that?"

Twelve-A completely ignored him.

"He'll answer you if you use your mind," Alice insisted encouragingly. Like he was trying to ride a bike and kept falling off.

"Well, I'm asking him *out loud*," Joe said, raising his voice. "Where are we going, you pointy-eared sootling?"

Several of the People looked up at him curiously, but Twelve-A never twitched. The telepath bent over and plucked a leaf from a nameless Earth plant and cocked his head at it curiously. Then, with a small frown of concentration, he brought the leaf up to his mouth and licked it.

"Oh, *that's it!*" Joe cried. He stalked over and yanked the leaf out of Twelve-A's slender fingers and tossed it aside. "Where the ash are you taking us, you sootbag furg?"

Twelve-A's pleasure in licking the leaf immediately morphed into darkness as his blue eyes lifted from his fallen prize, up to Joe's face.

Alice, who had followed close on Joe's heels, quickly cut in between them. "He said you told him he couldn't look in your head unless you gave permission, so every time you talk to him in your head, you're giving him permission now, see?" she said quickly, trying to shove Joe back a step.

Joe continued to scowl at the telepath and remained where he was. "No. I don't see."

Twelve-A scowled back, and, meeting that cold, intelligent stare full-force, Joe wondered if this was what it felt like to be an ant poised under the shadow of a sledgehammer. *He's an ekhta waiting to blow,* Joe thought. *And you're pissing him off...*A sudden wash of self-preservation hit him like icewater and Joe swallowed, hard. "Just don't go rooting around, okay?" He hated the way it sounded like a plea.

Twelve-A cocked his head, but, to Joe's surprise, he gave a slow, reluctant nod.

"Uh...yeah." Feeling sheepish, he glanced at his feet, rubbed the back of his neck, then lifted his eyes to meet the telepath's uncomfortably. Awkwardly, he repeated his question loudly in his head. *Where are you taking us?*

We're going to the place where no Others are, Twelve-A responded immediately. His thought-voice carried the mental density of a supernova. *I can feel it ahead of us.*

Joe frowned, glancing to the west, trying to figure out what the hell was drawing his interest. Perplexed, he said, *There's nothing out there. We're headed for the ocean, and between us and the ocean is what's left of a city. There will be more kreenit there than you'd care to count.* He did his best to send a mental picture of an enormous body of water—and a devastated city scattered with body-parts—along with his mental words.

Twelve-A twitched, obviously not liking the thought of a city. The entire party slowed and started to gather around them as Twelve-A held Joe's gaze intently.

This city…could you get us through it?

Joe thought of the Takkiscrew that would be trying to herd forty-four drooling furgs through rubble, kreenit, and collapsing buildings and immediately said, "No way. Not gonna happen."

But this 'ocean' has no Keepers? Twelve-A insisted.

It took Joe a moment to realize why Twelve-A wanted to go west so badly. "No, listen," Joe replied quickly, "The *reason* you can't feel any people out there is because people can't live in the ocean. You'd have to be able to breathe water in order to survive there."

Then we must hide in the ocean, Twelve-A said with the conviction of a ten-turn-old Dhasha prince.

Joe smacked his forehead before he caught himself, too late realizing that the sudden gesture startled his less-animated companions. Twelve-A had flinched and taken a step back to glare, and once more Joe felt about a microrod tall, staring up at that descending sledgehammer.

"Okay, look," Joe said quickly. "You don't get it. We *can't* go there. Keepers or no Keepers—you can't live there unless you're a fish. That *is* what you're trying to do, isn't it? Find a safe place to live? Somewhere to settle down?"

Twelve-A hesitated, then nodded slowly. The other experiments, after watching their one-sided conversation curiously a moment, went off to sleep in a big pile beside a boulder.

Joe shook his head. "Look, we need to head north. There's nothing for us to the west. The kreenit are going to eat everyone they can find in the major cities, then start heading inland. I've seen this happen before. You know that, because you dug through my head. We need to get away from the metro areas, into the mountains, the sooner the better. You getting all this?"

For the first time, Joe saw uncertainty in Twelve-A's face. *We can't live in the ocean?*

Joe would have laughed if the telepath weren't utterly sincere. "No. You can't."

Twelve-A glanced sideways at the others, then returned his gaze to Joe, looking almost hopeful. *You can lead us to a safe place?*

Joe shook his head. "There *is* no safe place. But those people you call the Keepers are gone. They might have been killed or they might have run, but either way, they're not coming back. You're safe from them. What you should be worried about is gangs. It always happens during the chaos of a Judgement. The strong get together to take what they need from the weak."

Twelve-A's platinum brows tightened in a worried frown. *And they would try to take Eelevansee from us?*

"Well, I'd say there is that possibility, yes," Joe replied slowly. "Is she the only one who can make food? Who are all the others? What can they do?"

The others are like Nynjee and Eelevansee, Twelve-A said slowly. *But they don't want to do what the Keepers made them do. The Keepers told them not to and hurt them when they tried.*

"Burn the Keepers," Joe growled, getting frustrated. "They're either dead or will be soon."

The People are still afraid of them, Twelve-A insisted.

"Then make them unafraid," Joe retorted. "You can do that, right? I mean, if you can go digging around in my head and show me stuff I'd purposefully forgotten years ago, taking away their fear should be a snap."

Twelve-A frowned at him. *Bad things can happen if they try and aren't ready.*

Joe snorted. "Bad things can happen if someone visits you with a semi-automatic plasma rifle in the middle of the night." When Twelve-A's frown increased, Joe shook his head. "Whatever. Let them wait, if that's what they need to do. What about you? Are there more like you?"

No. Twelve-A's thought was filled with pain, confusion.

"Why's that?" Joe prodded.

Twelve-A's reply was more a barrage of images and emotion than a thought-out response. The gist was that minders were very, very rare, were usually batshit insane, and that the secret government agency responsible for making Twelve-A had also weeded out the weaker telepaths by pitting them against each other in what Twelve-A called the Dark Room. There had been one other survivor, one of the originals that they probably kept for reference purposes, but she was utterly unstable and Twelve-A had killed her.

"So that leaves you," Joe said after the telepath had finished mind-vomiting on him. He was curious, now, and more than a little excited. Twelve-A was dangerous. *Really* dangerous. Joe wasn't sure if Twelve-A had intended to show him *just* how dangerous, but Joe had gotten a brief glimpse into his labyrinthine mind, and now his heart was pounding. Softly, he asked, "Do you *know* how much the Congress would pay to get their hands on you?"

Twelve-A's wiry body stiffened, the mental vice again locking over Joe's being, and Joe quickly laughed and waved him off. "Oh, calm down, you pointy-eared furg. I'm not gonna hand you over." He snorted at the very idea. "Not a chance. I want you to live long and prosper. Spread the seed of your loins across the whole burning continent." As Twelve-A continued to give him a suspicious look, Joe gestured at the other experiments, who were dog-piling in the grass. "You and all the rest of them. I'll keep you alive if it kills me, you understand? You just earned yourself a guardian Ayhi."

When Twelve-A continued to watch him with distrust, Joe sighed and went on, "Okay, look at it this way. The Regency condemned a whole species as criminals, when there *are* whole species of criminals out there—the Huouyt and the Jahul—who get away with ten times worse soot every day just because they've got money and power. Dumped guys like me on a place like this, just 'cause we shared the same genome with those furgs who betrayed Congress.

After seventy-four turns of service, those Takki bureaucrats signed our Judgement and then forgot about us. They fully intend to let Humanity wander around in the Dark Ages for a few centuries before they come back for us, and if the Human race dies out in the meantime, no skin off their backs—they'll just have the Watcher revive the race. You know what I wanna do?"

Twelve-A frowned and gave a slight shake of his platinum blond head.

Joe reached out and tapped Twelve-A's temple, making the minder flinch. "I wanna give 'em a taste of their own nuajan," he said. As Twelve-A blinked and gingerly touched the spot Joe had tapped him, Joe patted Jane and added, "I know war. I also know that everything I know is absolutely useless against guys like you. You know what *that* means?"

At the word 'war,' Twelve-A stiffened suspiciously. *We're not going to fight*, he warned again.

Joe grinned and poked the minder in his scrawny chest, making him jerk again. "It means," he said, "next time Congress comes around, the Human race will have a big, ashy surprise waiting for those soot-eating furglings who made the mistake of dumping guys like me," he poked him again, "with guys like you."

Stop poking me, Twelve-A told him.

"So," Joe continued, poking him again, "knowing what I know, what do *you* want to do?"

Twelve-A hesitated, blinking down at Joe's finger where it touched his breastbone. *I want to live.* The inference, of course, was that Joe apparently didn't.

Joe laughed. "Of course you do." He took a deep breath, then glanced at the dog-pile again. "Unfortunately, there are a lot of people out there who *don't* want you to live, and most of them aren't Human, and they outnumber us a hundred thousand to one. But we'll deal with those later. I just became your burning Sentinel, you understand? Right now, we need to protect you guys from Humanity in general. If you want my opinion, I say follow the mountains north until we're away from most of the major cities, scavenging farmhouses and small towns for supplies along the way. A lot of people are going to have the same idea, so we're gonna have to be ready to defend ourselves, which means your friends are either gonna have to learn to fight back the way their makers intended or get really good with a club."

Twelve-A frowned. *They won't fight.*

Ignoring him, because *everyone* would fight given the right incentives—and Joe knew how to provide the right incentives—Joe went on, "Secondly, no sex. At least until we're past the Rockies. I don't want any pregnant women slowing us down."

This time, Twelve-A just stared at him blankly.

"By the ghosts, man," Joe said, his breath hissing between his teeth. "*Tell* me you know what that is."

I do now, Twelve-A told him, *and I don't know why I'd want to do it.*

"Then *trust* me, you *don't* know about sex," Joe told him firmly. "You can play with Palmela all you want, but once you get a taste of the real thing—" He winced and glanced over at Alice, who was sprawled atop the human dog-pile, listening much too intently. "Sorry, kid. Maybe you shouldn't be listening to this.'

Alice shrugged a little too casually. "I read about it all the time, before the Judgement."

Joe laughed. "Yeah, right." He turned back to Twelve-A, ignoring her hurt look. "So anyway, it's kind of complicated for them to figure out on their own, so I'm not *too* worried, even though I've already seen a couple of them jerking off."

Even then, one of the men was off to one side of the human pile, beating his meat off into a bush. Twelve-A glanced at the grunting furg worriedly. *Should I make them stop?*

Joe scoffed. "No. We've got the makings of a perfect society—a pretty naked ass here and there, free food, no war, no Congressional population control, and a total lack of modesty. Believe me, when we get to where we're going, you're in for a treat."

Twelve-A scowled at him. *This act is fun for both parties?*

Joe laughed. "If you do it right, she'll beg you not to stop."

Twelve-A considered that a moment. Joe had the uneasy feeling that he was burrowing around in his brain, reviewing Joe's experiences with sex. "No digging," Joe growled.

Twelve-A continued to stare at the point between Joe's eyes. Finally, the telepath commented, *The first couple times, you hurt her.*

Blushing furiously as he remembered Libby, Joe managed, "We were both just kids and she was a virgin and she only hurt a little and—" He caught himself and scowled. "I told you to stop digging around in my head, you sootwad furg."

No. It's all there for me to see, so why shouldn't I see it?

"It's rude," Joe gritted. "Some stuff is just personal."

Twelve-A gave him a flat stare. *Are you ashamed of yourself, Joe Dobbs?*

Joe blushed again. "Of course not, it's just..."

If you aren't ashamed, then there's nothing you don't want me to see, Twelve-A replied firmly. The force of his thoughts allowed for no further argument.

The need to punch the self-satisfied smirk off of Twelve-A's face was so strong that Joe's right hand tightened into a fist. Twelve-A merely raised a brow of invitation, obviously catching the thought. "You're one annoying furg," Joe finally growled at Twelve-A. "I'm asking for a little professional respect."

I respect you by not killing you, Twelve-A stated flatly.

Joe's eyes narrowed. "I could say the same for you."

This time, the staredown that followed was broken by Twelve-A's need to pee.

As the minder started to nonchalantly spatter the ground at Joe's feet, Joe took a step back and irritatedly found something else to look at. "Listen," Joe growled, "As your self-appointed Sentinel, it's my job to keep you alive. That means we're going to need clothing for everyone. Where we're going, it gets cold."

I cannot make the People wear Keeper skin, Twelve-A replied, as he finished relieving himself. The way his thoughts were formed, to Twelve-A, the thought was akin to wearing a nice, thick layer of shit.

Joe glared. The good mood that had come with seeing the *potential* of the furg in front of him had been utterly wiped away by its acute and chronic application. "Fine," Joe said, "I'll ask you about clothes again when the first blizzard hits. You'll get the picture pretty damn quick." Already, the furglings were red-skinned and bordering on crispy—if it weren't for their obscenely long 'lunch' breaks in the shade, he was pretty sure they would have barbecued themselves already.

We'll see, was all Twelve-A said, in a tone that felt distinctly patronizing.

Joe took a deep breath and let it out slowly, frustrated. Not because the guinea pigs wanted to run around in the nude—if they wanted to get blisters and freeze their balls off, that was their pre-rogative. He was frustrated because some ignorant, naked-ass Takki turd could read his mind and dig up every damn thing he'd tried to keep hidden for the last seventy-four turns and there was nothing he could do about it.

You didn't like being Zero, Twelve-A commented into the silence.

Immediately, Joe twisted on the minder, bristling. Stepping up close so he could glare down at the skinny bastard from his extra three inches, Joe growled, "We agreed you won't dig in my brain and I won't shoot you in the head. You having second thoughts?"

Twelve-A glared up at him, irritation flashing in his blue eyes. *You are the only one near me who is interesting inside.*

"*Ask* me, goddamn it," Joe growled, slamming his finger back into the skinny telepath's breastbone, "or you're gonna find yourself with a pretty new hole between your eyes."

For a long time, Twelve-A just scowled up at him. Then, with incredible reluctance, he said, *Can I look through your memories, Joe Dobbs?*

"No," Joe said. "See? Wasn't that easy?"

Immediately, the telepath's face darkened. *I don't have to ask.*

"You do if you want my help," Joe told him. "And I know you want my help, because you made me come along and you haven't killed me yet."

Twelve-A gave him a long, irritated look. *Can I look now?*

"No," Joe replied. "Now we're getting somewhere." He patted Twelve-A on the shoulder and gave him a sweet smile. "Try asking nicely. Like, I dunno, use 'please.'"

Twelve-A fisted his slender fingers and visibly gritted his jaw. His pale face started to redden as he fought some impressive inner struggle. Then, *Please?*

Wow. Joe was actually a bit stunned that the telepath could find him interesting enough to beg. Nevertheless, Joe almost told the blue-eyed prick to go fuck himself. Almost. Then, warily, he said, "What do you want to look at, exactly?"

Twelve-A relaxed a little. *Zero,* he said. *What is Zero?*

Immediately, Joe tensed. Leaving the telepath standing over the piss-soaked grass, Joe turned to find his kit, threw his gun over his shoulder, and scowled out at the mountainous terrain to the east, considering how badly he really wanted to spend his life babysitting mutant nitwits. When he looked back, he said, "You leave that one alone or I won't be here when you wake up the next morning. You have my word on that."

The telepath narrowed his eyes, but Joe didn't feel the mental fingers dive into his mind anyway. Instead, it almost seemed as if Twelve-A...refrained.

Maybe there was hope for the naked furgling after all. Joe adjusted his pack, picked up his gun, and gestured at the sleeping experiments. Using the tone he had used on his grounders for so many years in the Force, he barked, "All right, you ignorant furgling sootbags. Get your friends together and let's get this Takkiscrew on the road. We're heading north."

Twelve-A jerked.

"What?" Joe asked nervously, wondering if he were about to be obliterated for the slight.

Twelve-A stared at him so long Joe started to fidget.

So you're our Keeper, now? Twelve-A finally asked softly. He almost sounded...like a scared little kid.

Their...keeper? Realizing that he must have sounded a lot like the bastards that had raised them in their lab, Joe blushed. "I'm not your Keeper," he said gruffly. "I'm some old Congie that got stuck herding a bunch of naked furgs through the woods."

The awe faded from Twelve-A's face and he narrowed his eyes at Joe. *A furg is hairy and stupid and likes to eat its own shit.*

Joe gave him a pleasant look. "Yes, and?"

The telepath's pretty blue eyes darkened further.

"Oh, believe me," Joe laughed, "I'm going to do more than hurt your feelings if you want me to hang around. You asked me to help keep your friends alive, and that's what I'm gonna do. I was a PlanOps Prime for most of my life. You think I give a furgling's fart if I make somebody cry?"

You should, Twelve-A said, scowling at him.

Joe took a step closer, until they were chest-to-chest and he was looking the telepath directly in his eerily intense gaze. Lowering his voice, Joe said, "If you think I'm going to treat you like a Dhasha prince because you can read my mind and bully all those other furgs into doing what you want, you're dumber than you look. I'll help you, but I'm not your burning puppet, nor your personal entertainment system. My stuff stays with me unless I feel like giving it to you, and even then, you *ask*. Get me?"

Twelve-A peered up at him for some time, and it seemed like Time itself stood still as he studied Joe, scanning his face in silence. Then, after what seemed like an eternity, Twelve-A gave a slow, reluctant nod. At that, Joe relaxed. He'd had the feeling that the telepath had been deciding whether or not to say to hell with it and scramble his brain on the spot, the same way a zookeeper used a lethal shock collar on a particularly violent—and uppity—furg. The fact that Joe was still alive boded well for their relationship.

"Okay, now that's settled," Joe said, motioning again at the sleeping dog-pile. "Let's get your friends moving. We'll steal some clothes off of whoever comes to take our women."

18

DREAMS OF WOMEN

"**W**hat do you think it's going to be like, getting culled?" Six Two One asked softly as they played with Pizza and Charlie. Pizza liked to grab his treat and run to sit on Charlie's back to eat it between both his tiny paws. Charlie, who was sitting on the floor between them nibbling on frilly green leaves from a bag that Doctor Molotov had given Six Six Five earlier that day, barely seemed to notice. "They said *half*," Six Two One said, watching Pizza with a tiny frown. "That's like, one out of *three*."

Six Six Five grimaced. Tomorrow was when the doctors chose their first batch of 'culls', and it all depended on how well they did fighting each other using the martial arts lessons that Sensei Harrington had taught them, where he had been training them for *months* on how to seek their 'war-mind'. It was dumb, because basically all he had them do for hours and hours a day was sit there in seiza and *think*. Half of the time, he let them punch at the wall and kick at padded boards over their heads, but the rest of the time, they were supposed to 'clear their minds' and *think*.

How could they possibly use that to *fight*?

"Maybe," Six Two One suggested, "if we *lose*, they'll let us be something other than soldiers. Maybe that's what culls do—maybe Doctor Molotov was a cull."

Six Six Five considered that, but ultimately decided that Doctor Molotov couldn't have been a cull because she was almost as important as Colonel Codgson, and whenever the doctors said the word 'cull,' it was in the same way Six Two One had said 'bug' when she had plucked a fly from her bowl of oatmeal the day before. Whatever it was, it wasn't a good thing to be culled.

"I hope whoever's name I draw is *little*," Six Two One said. "I could beat someone little."

"I'm little," Six Six Five reminded her.

Immediately, Six Two One scrunched her face. "You don't fight like you're little."

Six Six Five grunted. "I hope they give me that big bully. Eight Four needs to be kicked in the face." She was pretty sure it would hurt to be matched with him, but she was also sure it would hurt him more.

Both of Six Two One's eyebrows went up. "He's twice your size."

Six Six Five gave her friend a frown. "So?"

Six Two One considered. "I hope they give me someone little. But not you. Whoever fights you is gonna get culled."

Six Six Five sniffed, but it was to hide her own anxiety. She had no intention of getting culled, but she *was* small. *Too* small. She was acutely aware of that fact at every morning formation.

"Think that if I get culled, they'll let me come back to visit?" Six Two One asked softly. The only thing they *had* been able to piece together about the whole affair was that the next day's culls would mysteriously go away, with no mention of where, or what they would be trained in afterwards. Six Six Five wondered if they'd let them keep their hamsters. Or Charlie. She didn't think she could leave Charlie. She reached out and ran her fingers through his silky white fur, careful not to dislodge Pizza.

"I really don't want to fight," Six Two One confided. "I might just let someone else win. Maybe they'll let me be Doctor Molotov's assistant if I let someone else win."

Six Six Five didn't want to fight either, but she immediately got a twisting of unease in her gut at the thought of throwing a match. It had been rumored that Colonel Codgson was coming to oversee the fights, and every time he showed up for anything, it always left Six Six Five with a sick feeling in her stomach. The way he looked at them didn't feel right. There was a distinct difference between the way he talked to Sensei Harrington and Doctor Molotov and the way he looked at Six Six Five and her batchmates. Almost like they were his hamsters, not his soldiers.

"I think you should fight," Six Six Five told her friend. "Getting culled is bad."

Six Two One picked up Pizza and put him on her shoulder. Together, they looked at Six Six Five flatly. "You said you didn't want to be a soldier," Six Two One said, accusation tingeing her voice. "If you lose, you won't have to be a soldier. They *said* that."

Which was true enough, but it still didn't feel right. Every time Six Six Five thought of tossing the match, she saw Six Two One picking that fly out of her oatmeal and Colonel Codgson's weird pet-the-hamster smile. Despite the seemingly routine way the doctors mentioned it, the way dinner continued to come on time and Sensei Harrington made them stare at the wall and the technicians kept making their reports as usual, her gut told her that what was coming tomorrow was bad. Very bad.

"Listen, Two One," Six Six Five started slowly, pulling Charlie into her lap, "I know you don't like to fight—I don't either—but you know how Colonel Codgson killed that kid for trying to take a hamster? I think it's going to be bad like that if you lose. That's failing. He doesn't like people failing."

Six Two One narrowed her pretty green eyes at her. "If you don't like to fight, why are you so good at it?"

Because I hate it and I want to get it over with, Six Six Five thought. Self-preservation, however, had always kept her from saying as much, knowing that a mere whisper of that to the proper ears would have had her cleaning showers or serving breakfast for a month. Soldiers *loved* to fight.

…Didn't they?

"Because I'm smarter than everybody else," Six Six Five said, shrugging. "If you're smarter, you learn to fight better."

Six Two One gave her a considering look for so long that Pizza began to sniff at her ear. Finally, she said, "Colonel Codgson doesn't want you to win. I heard him talking to Doctor Molotov. He says you're sub-par genetics from nine-series and wants to use you to train Twelve-A."

Six Six Five's heart began to pound at the thought that Colonel Codgson had specifically been trying to make her fail. She had *suspected* it, but all this time, she had been writing off the extra progress reports, the harder tests, the sideways smiles as coincidences. "What is sub-par genetics?" she asked, a lump in her throat. "And who is Twelve-A?"

Six Two One shrugged. "I dunno. Someone important. Remember those three months I was cleaning the doctors' offices for falling asleep on the toilet and missing formation? I heard them talking about him all the time. I think they want to make you hold his punching bag or something. They're really excited about what he can do to stop the aliens." Then, shrugging, Six Two One grabbed Pizza from her shoulder and stood. "Anyway, I'm gonna go to bed. If they're gonna make us fight, I want to sleep good beforehand. They said you fight better when you sleep good."

"Okay," Six Six Five said softly, lost in thought. She had no idea what nine-series meant, but she'd heard doctors raving about the twelve and thirteen series enough times when they thought she wasn't paying attention that she was having trouble keeping her heart rate steady.

"Oh," Six Two One said, stopping at the ladder to the bunk bed. She turned back to face Six Six Five, who still sat with Charlie on the floor. "Will you take care of Pizza for me if I get culled?"

"Sure," Six Six Five whispered.

"Thanks," Six Two One said cheerfully. She climbed into bed.

"Two One?" Six Six Five asked softly, after she had been quiet for some time.

"Yeah?"

"You ever hear them say what series you were?"

Six Two One sat up halfway. "Oh sure," she said, resting on one elbow. "I'm like the rest of them. Eleven series. Your batch got mixed up with mine. Mislabled or something. Doctor Molotov didn't catch it until you'd already been incubated. I dunno. Something like that."

Six Six Five's heartbeat began to slam in her ears. "They ever say anything about my batch?"

"We should be *sleeping*," Six Two One insisted.

"Come on," Six Six Five begged. "Please."

Six Two One sighed deeply, and for a long time, she gave Six Six Five a patronizing look and it appeared as if she wouldn't respond. Then, reluctantly, she said, "They said nine-series has weird size issues. Like some are normal, but half the time, they end up with freaks. Too big, too small. Stuff like that. Oh, and it took a long time to reach their war-mind, but once they did, it was hard to control them. They had to cull most of them because they kept getting out and breaking things."

Six Six Five frowned. "Getting out?"

Six Two One shrugged. "Maybe a lot of them kept getting out of formation before they were told. Or breaking their gear. I don't know. Codgson said they were too smart, but it sounds like they were all just dumb, to me. They decided they couldn't use them for soldiers and put the best ones on ice." And then, as if that settled the matter, Six Two One rolled back over, pointedly putting her back to Six Six Five.

For a long time, Six Six Five sat there, staring down at Charlie, trying to figure out what 'on ice' meant. The only time she'd ever seen ice, it had been on the inside of Doctor Molotov's office refrigerator, in the little tray on top. Doctor Molotov liked to keep little bottles and beakers inside it, one shelf above her daily sandwich.

The idea that Six Six Five was somehow going to be joining the little bottles and beakers on the top shelf of Doctor Molotov's refrigerator was suddenly so horrifying that she began to have trouble hearing anything except her own heartbeat. Six Six Five began to pant, and not even Charlie climbing expectantly up her chest for more treats could calm her down. She put him back in his cage, stared at it for long moments, then stared at the door to her and Six Two One's room.

The doctors locked it every night, to keep the aliens from getting them and ruining Earth's hope at fighting back.

…but the aliens were outside their bunker, fighting Humanity on the surface. In order to get to their doors, the aliens would have to get through all the other soldiers that walked the halls with guns. And, from what Six Six Five had seen of the instructional videos, the aliens could carve through interstellar spaceships and solid stone, much less a *door*. How was a thin sheet of metal going to keep an alien out?

Frowning, Six Six Five went to the door and turned the handle. It stopped halfway, locked. She frowned down at it for some time, then slowly released the latch.

If the door wasn't to keep aliens out, the doctors were lying to them.

Six Six Five pushed the latch again, and again, it thunked to a stop halfway down, keeping her locked inside.

Why would the doctors be lying to them?

She released the handle again, letting it slide back up into place.

If the door wasn't to keep aliens out, it had to be to keep her and her batchmates *in*.

She pushed the latch down again, listening to it hit the barrier once more, remaining shut.

Why would the doctors be locking their batches *in*? They needed them to fight the aliens. The aliens were outside.

"What are you doing?" Six Two One asked from the bed. She had sat up again, and was watching her from atop the bunk, a little frown on her face.

Six Six Five released the handle, letting it thunk back into place. "Nothing," she said, still staring at it. She turned to face the room again, putting her back to the door. On her desk, Charlie sat in his cage, happily nibbling from his food dish, just as content inside his enclosure as he was outside of it.

Six Six Five frowned, watching him eat. Sometimes, it seemed like he didn't even realize he was inside a cage…

"You need to pee?" Six Two One insisted. "It's two minutes to lights-out and I'm not gonna let you sleep with me if you need to pee."

Six Six Five blinked, the question so far from where her mind was at the time that she could only stare at her friend in confusion before shifting her attention to Pizza's tiny cage. Pizza was curled up in a tube in a corner. Hamsters. Colonel Codgson looked at them like *hamsters*.

Six Two One pointed to the tiny privy set into the wall, much smaller than the one in the showers. "If you need to pee, go do it. Quick."

More because she didn't want to answer any questions about why she had been prying at the door than because she needed to pee, Six Six Five went to the privy and used it. Then, still disturbed, she went to her bed and crawled under the covers. Lights-out came immediately afterward, but Six Six Five could only stare through the darkness at the mattress above her, unable to sleep.

One of her batchmates' hamsters had died in the night a few months before, and the next morning, they'd replaced it with another hamster of identical color. She'd heard one of the soldiers laugh and call it a 'failure to thrive' as he swung the dead hamster back and forth by a limp leg before tossing it into the closest wastebasket, to the chuckling of two other soldiers.

Soldiers that, as far as Six Six Five could tell, spent more time facing *them* with guns, rather than watching for aliens.

What if they *were* the aliens?

"Two One?" Six Six Five asked softly, into the darkness.

Her friend gave no sound.

"You awake?" Six Six Five insisted.

Six Two One grunted and the bed above her creaked. "I said you could sleep up here if you peed first." She sounded more than a little irritated.

"Don't lose tomorrow," Six Six Five said. "You don't want to be culled."

"I'm trying to *sleep*," Six Two One muttered. She yawned.

"Promise me," Six Six Five said. "It's really important."

Six Two One groaned. "Fiiine. I won't get culled."

Yet, listening to the exasperated way she said it, Six Six Five felt a horrible welling of dread knot her intestines as she thought of what would happen to her friend in the morning. Six Two One wasn't very good at fighting. She turned over on her bunk and looked at Pizza, who was grooming his fuzzy round ears with his tiny feet, only barely visible in the dim light. On her own nightstand, Charlie stretched out on his side, asleep.

Then she froze. What would happen to Charlie if Six Six Five got culled?

She was small, Six Six Five realized, terror beginning to worm her way into her guts, mingling with the dread. And the wrong batch. Even if she tried her best, Colonel Codgson was going to try and cull her...

"Sleeping on the job, Welu?" an irritating voice demanded. "It's almost *noon*. I would have thought you would have had to, oh, I dunno, patrol the perimeter or something. You sick?" A booted toe nudged Shael in his scaleless side, grating against his unprotected ribs. "You eat too much last night? Got a headache? Come off your drugs? What?"

"The Sisters fuck you with the rotted tendon of a Huouyt shit-capsule," Shael growled, rolling over to go back to sleep. The dreams concerned him, though he could tell no one. Why were they so vivid? Why was he dreaming of this Human girl? Why did she haunt him so? Had he met her somewhere? Affronted her ancestors somehow? Accidentally crushed a fellow warrior in his passing and his lack of respect had earned the wrath of her soul?

Then Shael realized what the Voran had said and he sat up in a scale-tightening blast of horror. *Noon?* When it was his duty and custom to be up at *dawn*?

Above him, the Voran prince gave him a smug look and crossed his shamefully black-clad arms over his black-clad chest. "We're moving out in six tics. If you want something to eat, you should probably go visit the pit before Twelve-A gets them moving. I think there might be something left for you." His grin widened. "Maybe." Then, with another superior look, the infuriating Voran turned and moved off, leaving Shael's mouth open in horror at the insult. All around him, the drooling furgs that were their traveling companions were watching with unabashed curiosity. Even Eleven-C seemed interested.

The humiliation. The *shame*. Shael hung his head to avoid the accusatory looks, the quiet disapproval from those lesser creatures he had sworn to protect. Unable to withstand their amusement, he fled. Instead of going to the food pit as instructed, however, he hurried to a boulder at the edge of camp and hunkered down on the other side, his back against the stone, a wall of rock between him and the mockery in the Voran's eyes.

By not fulfilling the duties required of him, he had failed.

He couldn't fail. The weak failed. The weak were culled.

Shael's heart began to pound, harder and harder, until it felt like it was pounding at his temples, streaking acid through his limbs and chest.

He had to be strong. He had to fight.

His heart, already pounding out of control, started to thump oddly in his chest. His breath started to come in ragged gasps. Seemingly oozing into him from the grasses, the trees, the pebbles themselves, he felt terror assaulting him from all sides, so much terror...

Shael screamed and wrapped himself in his war mind, shoving everything around him backwards by two body-lengths, giving himself space to breathe.

The strong survived. The weak were culled.

He'd failed. He was going to be culled. Shael's breath was coming in whining pants, now, the ache in his throat dragging spontaneous wetness from his eyes. The rocks, plants, and trees around him started to splinter, crack, and ooze fluids. He was going to be culled, he had failed, he had killed Codgson's favorite, and he was going to be culled...

You will not be culled, a gentle voice told him.

The voice was like a war-horn, calling him from the groggy slumber of the night. Shael flinched and looked up.

Twelve-A stood just out of reach of the ring of destruction, watching him from amongst the trees with blue eyes so full of compassion it made Shael forget some of his shame.

You will not be culled, Twelve-A said again, taking a tentative step towards him, settling a naked foot inside the ring of destruction. *You have nothing to fear, Shael. Not anymore.*

Shael's heart continued to pound an odd, unrhythmic beat in his chest. Pains continued to shoot through his arms and legs, and he was having trouble seeing.

You are strong. Stronger than the rest. That's why they gave you to Doctor Philip.

Shael flinched, a brief image of an empty cage flashing through his head before it passed again, replaced with the minder's face. He had knelt in front of him and was putting both his slender hands against Shael's head. *You are safe now,* he said softly, his cerulean eyes only ninths from Shael's own. *I will not let anyone cull you. Neither will Joe.*

Shael twitched at 'cull', once again feeling the odd image of an empty cage, an empty bed. The top bunk. Where had he seen a top bunk?

Then Shael realized the minder was holding him, *comforting* him, and he threw the weakling off of him in disgust. "What do you think you're doing, touching a prince of Welu?!" he demanded, lunging away in outrage. "I should have you staked for that!" As the minder, who had slid several feet through the dirt from the blow, started to right himself, Shael backed away, furious, his heart pounding in indignation that a lesser creature had *dared* to touch him. All his instincts were screaming at him to obliterate the imbecile. Not even Doctorphilip, in his examinations of his superior body, had dared touch him.

At that moment, Joedobbs strode within hearing range and came to an abrupt halt at the edge of the destruction, a cautious look on his face. He glanced from the minder, who was still on the ground, to

Shael, who was standing, ready to drive the telepath's meddling blond head into the cracked stone boulder for the insult. For a moment, he seemed to just take it in like a Takki took in the dealings of Dhasha. Then, warily, the Voran said, "What's going on here?"

"The minder shoves his tek in places it doesn't belong," Shael snarled, holding Twelve-A's blue gaze. "He will tend to his own coils or he will lose his right to breathe my air."

Both Joedobbs' eyebrows went up. "I...see." He continued to watch them both with caution, like he expected them to cross spears at any minute. Almost tentatively, he said to the minder, "What'd you do to piss in her nuajan?"

It took Shael a moment to realize Joedobbs had used the language of the Earthlings, not the language of the crimson worms. He frowned. When Joedobbs continued to question the minder, however, the words seemed to slip away the more he concentrated, remaining fuzzy and just out of reach, almost like a distant memory. As he fumbled for them, Twelve-A cocked his head slightly and his brow crinkled the way it always did when he was communicating.

Then Shael realized that the two of them were discussing *him* and he wrapped his mental fist around the boulder and squeezed.

The deafening sound of pulverizing rock stopped them both cold. Very slowly, both the minder and the Voran turned to look at the powder that was even then settling to the ground where the great stone had once been, billowing dust spreading outward in a wave.

"You will tell him *nothing*," Shael informed the minder in the silence that followed, "or you even now gaze upon your own demise."

Twelve-A swallowed, cerulean eyes slowly lifting from the pile of stone powder to Shael's face. Appearing pleasingly spooked, the weakling's mind babbled, *I only told him you were ashamed of sleeping late.*

"No more," Shael growled, making a cutting gesture with his hand. "Our bargain holds. Now and forever. My dreams. Your weakness. Violate it, and meet my wrath." And, at that, he turned and walked off, putting his back to the Voran and the blue-eyed meddler.

Behind him, he heard Joedobbs ask another question in the Earthling tongue, but when Shael glanced behind himself to look, instead of responding, Twelve-A simply shook his head and walked the other direction. Joedobbs frowned and called after him in clear confusion, obviously not understanding what had just transpired.

Grunting in satisfaction, Shael went to find somewhere to sit and think about what cruel joke of the Sisters had just befallen him, and why his hands were shaking so badly...

● ● ●

"The rules are simple," Colonel Codgson said, as they stood spaced out in two lines in a weird room filled with electronic stations and big dishes, faced off against the opponent that the doctors had chosen for them. Unlike the big bully Six Six Five had wanted, she had gotten a scrawny boy barely bigger than herself, who was lazy in class and couldn't even throw a proper snap-kick. He cried whenever someone slipped past his defenses and hit him, even if it was a little tap. Fighting him would be...ridiculously easy.

Colonel Codgson stopped, regarding them all with his casual hamster smile. "The two of you will fight until someone surrenders or someone breaks free from their position. Whoever surrenders will be culled. If you break free, you automatically pass."

Break free? Six Six Five didn't see a fighting circle...She frowned at the wiry, thin-faced boy that Codgson had chosen for her, unable to understand why he had picked *him* to be her opponent. He was lazy, slow, and a horrible fighter. It was almost like Codgson had gotten over his weird grudge against her and actually wanted her to *win*.

"Now remain in place as the technicians go down the lines," Codgson said. "They will be securing you in place for your match."

Seeing movement out of the corner of her eye, Six Six Five chanced a glance to look. Immediately, she frowned.

"It's very basic," Codgson said, as technicians began securing the soldiers on the end with short, heavy chains around their ankles, padlocked to an eye-bolt in the floor behind them. He stopped and smiled at Six Six Five as a technician squatted beside her leg and metal rattled against the concrete, "But it should serve our purposes."

The technician efficiently fixed the chain in place and moved on, and Six Six Five stared down at it, confused. There was no mistake that the chains were not long enough for them to reach their opponent.

Most of the soldiers in the gymnasium were also peering down at their legs in confusion, but not Six Six Five's opponent. He was grinning. She recognized him as one of the few who had been able to reach Sensei Harrington's war-mind on a consistent basis. She remembered, because the first weak punch he had thrown against the bags with just his mind had brought in every doctor, technician, and soldier to ooh and aah over him for the next six hours, getting him to repeat the process, measure the intensity, and make their reports. Even Colonel Codgson had come to witness his anemic mind-punches and mind-kicks with something like the way Doctor Molotov looked at Charlie when she thought Six Six Five wasn't looking. Beating him would be *easy*.

And yet, even if they both lay down and stretched out, they only would have been able to lock fingers together. There was simply *no way* to fight each other without...

Six Six Five froze, a pall of dread suddenly eating away her core, leaving her shaking. If they couldn't physically *reach* each other, the whole fight would be decided by punches and kicks like Six One Eight's anemic mind-blows, barely strong enough to dimple the bag.

...But infinitely stronger than being unable to punch or kick at all.

And Six Six Five had never been able to reach Sensei Harrington's war-mind.

Realizing that, Six Six Five's heart began to hammer so hard it filled up her eardrums, blotting out the sound of anything except her own pulse. The smug look on Six One Eight's wiry face suddenly took on new meaning. He knew what was happening, and he already knew he was going to win.

"*If,*" Colonel Codgson continued, walking down between the shackled lines, "neither party can utilize what Sensei Harrington taught you and access your war-mind to either break free or defeat your opponent, you will stay there until you both perish of dehydration." He stopped, smiling at Six Six Five. "After all, every single one of you has been tested and confirmed to have the capability, so there should be no reason you cannot do what you have been trained to do. Failure is weakness, and only the strong will survive the coming war."

Six Six Five glanced again at her opponent, who had his arms crossed loosely behind his back, the self-satisfaction unmistakably oozing from his face as he observed her with visible boredom.

He's going to win, Six Six Five thought, on a terrified hammer of her heart. Six Six Five had spent endless *hours* staring at the wall at Sensei Harrington's command, and she still couldn't so much as move a pen, much less throw a punch.

I'm going to get culled. A coldness was working its way from her stomach, making Six Six Five's heart begin to race so hard it was difficult to hear what Colonel Codgson said next.

Resuming his pacing, Colonel Codgson said, "You may use any and all means necessary to force your opponent to surrender, including all forms of mutilation or maiming. Anything goes." He stopped pacing, that gut-twisting smile back in place as he looked at Six Six Five. "*Anything.*" He continued to smile. "As I've said before, failure is unacceptable."

Six Six Five was having trouble breathing, meeting her opponent's smug stare. He seemed completely confident in the outcome of their match, already counting it an easy win in his head. And why wouldn't he? Six Six Five was one of only a handful who hadn't been able to reach her war-mind at *all*. Not even a tiny, miniscule nudge of the bag to impress the technicians. Nothing.

"Now," Colonel Codgson said, "the matches begin in thirty seconds. If your win is impressive enough, you will be rewarded with pizza tonight." He then backed out of the rows of soldiers, leaving them facing off against their opponents. Six One Eight slowly unclasped his hands from behind his back and lowered them to his sides. He still leveled her with that smug look, the one that told her she was going to be culled.

Oh no, Six Six Five thought, her heart hammering. She needed to reach her war-mind, and she needed to do it *now*. She closed her eyes and tried to focus on clearing her thoughts, as Sensei Harrington had told her over and over to do, but all she could think about was how she was going to lose, and how Colonel Codgson would smile as he culled her, pulling her from his program like a fly from soup.

The blow came a few seconds later, hitting her square in the nose.

Six Six Five cried out and stumbled backwards at the explosion of pain in her face, then tripped and fell on her back when the chain brought her leg up short. Blood was already running down her face, dribbling from her chin. Across the room, Six One Eight was still standing upright, grinning at her with that same weird smile that Colonel Codgson had.

They're the same, Six Six Five thought on a rush of terror. *That's why Codgson likes him so much*…Beginning from the very first formation as far back as she could remember, Codgson had favored certain soldiers, and now that she was faced off against that cold stare, the cruel smile, she realized that every one of his favorites gave her that same weird sense that they thought they were looking at hamsters, not people. Six One Eight, Six Five Five, the big bully…

Six One Eight's smile faltered a fraction of an inch as his brow creased. A moment later, another blow hit her in the stomach, this one lighter, but still enough to knock the wind out of her.

Six Six Five gasped and curled into a ball, pain radiating from her solar plexus. As she did, Six One Eight cocked his head and watched, looking curious. Like he was experimenting on her. Seeing what would hurt most…

He's lazy, Six Six Five thought, desperate. She might not be able to retaliate, but she could keep him from actually hitting her if she kept moving. His mental blows, while consistent, were always sluggish and weak. He didn't have the *strength* to force her to surrender. With this in mind, she rolled onto her feet and started bouncing around, desperately trying to stay out of his mental reach as she tried to figure out how to reach her own war-mind before she was culled.

Around them, most of the other kids were still just standing around, giving each other blank looks. Six Six Five's opponent was the only one who had already begun attacking his foe. And he was doing it with boredom, too. Like it had all already been decided. Like he'd been *briefed* on how to win. And, the more she thought about that, the more Six Six Five knew he *had* been briefed. The smugness, the utter confidence...Codgson had told him how to beat her. He'd *wanted* him to beat her.

As she thought about that, Six Six Five felt her first real wave of anger, the hot boiling of injustice within her. So what if she was the wrong batch? Why did Colonel Codgson hate her so much because of her *batch*? Why was it always *her* he was trying to make fail? Because she was *small*? She might be small, but she was *smart*...

Six One Eight frowned again, and Six Six Five felt something grab the fingers of her right hand and squeeze, holding them in place like they were trapped between the jaws of a vice. As Six Six Five blinked down at her now-stationary hand and tried to yank it free, something sharp began driving itself between her nail and her finger itself. Six Six Five screamed as big slivers started working themselves painfully into the quick. Across from her, Six One Eight continued to watch her with that weird little smile.

Like he was playing with her. Like he was *learning*.

Faced with that mild curiosity, unable to pull herself free of the agony arching up her arm, Six Six Five lost control and began thrashing like a wild thing. The resulting surge of adrenaline gave her enough strength to pull her fingers out of Six One Eight's weak mental vice, but now every eye in the gymnasium was on her, watching. No one else was fighting. They were watching her die, their faces filled with almost as much interest as Six One Eight's.

Heart pounding, panting in terror, Six Six Five glanced down at her trembling fingers through tears. Her veins ached with adrenaline when she saw blood welling under her nails. She knew that Sensei Harrington hadn't taught them such a thing.

Colonel Codgson smiled that half-smile and came over to stand behind her. "Are you surrendering, Six Five?"

Seeing his disdain, his satisfaction, his desire for her to lose, knowing that he had taught Six One Eight how to beat her just so he could watch her fail, Six Six Five felt another powerful rush of anger, this time strong enough to obliterate her pain and terror. She lost her fear as she stared up into the colonel's malicious black eyes. In that moment, buoyed on a wave of fury, the universe itself seemed to click into place for her. She felt something lock into place, felt the world shift, felt a world of greenish fog fall into being around her, felt a weak mental fist reaching for her, a total void within the mist that trailed back to Six One Eight's head.

Still looking at Colonel Codgson, Six Six Five swallowed Six One Eight's void-fist within her mind and crushed it, impacting it inward, shoving the greenish particles in on themselves.

Over on the end of his chain, Six One Eight gasped and stumbled. Then he grabbed his head and started to scream. Dark eyes shifting to Six One Eight, Colonel Codgson's face tightened in a tiny frown. An instant later, his gaze flickered back to hers and his eyes widened. For a split second, Six Six Five saw his fear.

Then she grabbed the chain at the base of her ankle and snapped it in half.

For long minutes, there was complete silence in the auditorium. Every technician, every soldier, *everyone* watched the two of them, and, seeing the foggy green shape that was the colonel's skull, Six Six Five knew that she could have killed him, then. Like swatting a fly.

And she saw Colonel Codgson recognize it, too. Except, instead of fear, she saw fury. Cold, utterly mindless fury. In a motion too fast for Six Six Five to catch, he slammed his elbow into her already-bleeding face, then, as the pain shattered her grasp on the fog, he reached out and grabbed her by the throat, a knife suddenly in his hand.

"Colonel Codgson!" Doctor Molotov's voice snapped, startling everyone in the room, making Codgson stop before he could slam his knife into Six Six Five's brain. "I believe Six Five just passed our test. Unless I am mistaken, the general insisted that anyone who passes is to be left *alive* for more training and his personal inspection next year. I'm sure he'll have questions about what happened to her, as I'll be *sure* to put it in my report."

Colonel Codgson kept the knife under her jaw, never taking his insane black eyes from Six Six Five's face. Without addressing the doctor, Codgson slowly leaned forward, until his lips were against Six Six Five's ear. "You," he whispered, just loud enough for Six Six Five to hear, "are a cull." He pulled away, smiling again at arm's length. "You just don't know it yet." Then he shoved her away from him.

Without another word, the colonel went over to the boy who had just lost his match and yanked him onto his feet. As Six One Eight was looking up at Codgson with gratitude, Codgson rammed the knife into his gut and yanked upwards, making his green eyes go wide. Even as the boy was reaching for his stomach, trying to double over, Codgson slashed his knife across the kid's throat and violently sawed its serrated blade against his neck, opening up a wound that sprayed blood across him and several nearby children, all in the matter of a couple seconds.

As Doctor Molotov and a couple of her assistants took startled steps backward and screamed, Codgson turned to the rest of the group and snarled, "*Fight.* Or you will be here the rest of your short fucking lives." Then he turned and, covered in crimson droplets, left the dying boy shivering on the floor behind him and stormed from the room.

"You *fucking ailo!*" Doctor Molotov screamed at his departing back. She hurled her clipboard at him, the thin plastic rattling against the wall beside the door, sending papers everywhere. "You psychotic fucking *ailo!*"

Codgson stopped in the doorway, eyes on the fallen clipboard. Slowly, he turned to face the doctor, that casual smile back in place. "Geneticists are a dime a dozen, doctor." Then, without another word, he turned and departed.

After he was gone, Doctor Molotov took one look at the gurgling boy on the floor, then ran from the room in the opposite direction, holding her face.

The technicians stood around for several minutes, looking at each other. Then one of them nervously cleared his throat. To the lined-up children, he said, "Uh, you guys should fight. They'll be back eventually."

And they were, too. Codgson returned only a couple minutes later, in clean clothes, his face and hands pink from washing. Doctor Molotov returned with her mascara smeared and a new clipboard. In their absence, no one had fought, but a couple of technicians *had* dragged away Six One Eight's body—even then, there was a trail of crimson from the empty slot in line in front of Six Six Five and the room smelled of the sickly-sweet-rot odor of the insides of his bowels.

"*Fight!*" Doctor Molotov screamed, when everyone continued to stand around, staring at each other. The harshness of her voice made everyone jump.

"Before they do," Codgson said calmly, walking up to the lines, "I have a change I'd like to make to the lineup. Lieutenant Drake, release Six Two One."

"Colonel, what are you doing?" Doctor Molotov asked, her voice containing ice.

Colonel Codgson gave her his gut-curdling smile. "After rooming with such a *prodigy*, Six Two One undoubtedly has gained an unfair advantage over her fellow soldiers. I think it's only fair that *one* of them survives, right?"

"You already made one radical change to my program's calculated best-match scenarios." Doctor Molotov interrupted. "I will have to ask that you don't make another."

"Ask away," Colonel Codgson said, grabbing a confused-looking Six Two One and walking her over to stand in the puddle of blood in front of Six Six Five. "Lock her down," he commanded the technician, gesturing at Six Two One's ankle. The technician gave Doctor Molotov an unsure look, then, when Doctor Molotov just stood there, shaking, she uncertainly bent to begin fiddling with the chain and padlock.

Seeing her new opponent, Six Six Five's heartbeat was hammering again, and this time, all the rage had subsided, leaving nothing but cold, icy fear as they locked her friend into the slot across from hers. Standing across from her, the technician working at her ankle, Six Two One was likewise staring at Six Six Five, looking utterly pale.

He's going to make me fight Six Two One... Six Six Five swallowed hard, suddenly not feeling so strong, so powerful. *Please no,* she thought. *Please don't make me fight her...*

"Fix her chain," Colonel Codgson commanded the tech, pointing at the loose chain dangling around Six Six Five's foot. "This time," he said sweetly, "you will *only* win if your opponent surrenders."

Six Six Five swallowed down a raw ball of fear in her throat, thinking of her long nights whispering with Six Two One in her bed, talking about how they wanted to be something other than soldiers. She realized that one of them *wasn't* going to be a soldier, and she felt her heart racing with a thousand times more terror than she'd felt fighting Six One Eight. She met Six Two One's green eyes, her breath coming in ragged pants.

Then Colonel Codgson's words came back to her, echoing like sweetened venom in her brain. *"...it's only fair that* one *of them survives..."* Six Six Five forgot to breathe, horror driving stakes through her veins. *He's going to kill the culls.* Though no one had said as much, she suddenly had the all-consuming knowledge that it was true. *Just like he killed Six Seven Two and Six One Eight.* Suddenly, she knew that there was no technician's position on the other end of this fight, no doctor's training. No training at all. Just a pool of blood and the smell of the toilet.

As she remained frozen in place, horror paralyzing her muscles into rigidity, the technician came over and bent to work on Six Six Five's ankle. The touch of her manicured hand on her leg jolted Six Six Five out of her terror. Six Six Five automatically stepped backwards, yanking her foot out of reach.

Seeing that, Colonel Codgson cocked his head. "Are you *surrendering,* Six Five?" He looked supremely satisfied. "Are you *volunteering* to be culled?"

"N-no," she blurted. Still, she didn't return her foot within the technician's reach. Her heart was pounding, her hands were shaking, and her knees kept trembling to the point where it was hard to stay upright. She could feel all eyes in the auditorium on her, watching.

"Six Six Five already won her match," Doctor Molotov snapped. "To pit her against her own roommate is just cruel."

"War is cruel, doctor," Codgson said, pinning Six Six Five with his gaze. "Now, Six Five. Either you're going to be strong and volunteer to fight, like a *good* soldier, or you're weak and you're volunteering to be culled. Which is it?"

Volunteering to be culled…Six Six Five's eyes dropped to the pool of crimson that Six Two One was even now standing in. Heart hammering, facing her best friend, Six Six Five knew she wouldn't be able to get back to her war-mind. Not ever. She squeezed her eyes shut, thinking about what it would be like to be culled, how much she would feel before she stopped twitching. The unknown ate at her, gnawing wormy holes through her guts. She took a deep breath, steeling herself.

"I volunteer."

Although she had been thinking it, the soft, tentative voice had not come from Six Six Five's lips. She froze, realizing that it had come from Six Two One's, instead. The technician, who had paused in fixing the chain around Six Six Five's leg, looked up at Colonel Codgson.

The colonel stiffened, then turned to scowl down at Six Two One. "What did you say?"

"I volunteer," her friend said again, louder this time.

"No!" Six Six Five shouted, starting toward her.

Colonel Codgson stopped her short with a strong arm, a new smile forming on his face as he focused his attention on her best friend. "You volunteer for *what*, Six Two One?"

"Don't!" Six Six Five pleaded. "Please. I'll—"

Six Two One lifted her head in that way she always did before she was going to do something stubborn. "I volunteer to be culled, colonel. I don't want to be a soldier. I don't like to fight."

There was a collective gasp all around them and Six Six Five felt her breath slide from her as if she'd been kicked in the stomach.

Too late. Looking at Colonel Codgson's wormy smile, she knew it was too late to stop her. She'd said the one thing that would get any recruit removed, never to be seen again.

"How interesting," the colonel said. "The *prodigy* rooms with a *traitor*." He yanked Six Two One away by the back of her shirt until her ankle chain pulled her up short. "Release this little shit. We'll give Six Six Five someone else to fight." He drew his knife.

"You *won't!*" Doctor Molotov snapped, stepping up between them. "This is *insane*. What you are doing is *insane*, colonel. You're showing a distinct personal bias to a very sensitive experimental process, and it is destroying your objectivity. I'm going to have to ask you to leave, or I will have to call the general and explain the situation."

Colonel Codgson made a face, Six Two One still in his grip. "What situation might that be, Doctor?"

"The situation," Doctor Molotov said, "where I have been recording this whole damn thing." She held up a small hand-held device. "From what you did to One Eight to what you just did here. You're going to get the fuck out of my lab or I'm going to send this to someone important. You get me? *Sir?*"

Colonel Codgson gave her a weird little smile. "Doctor Molotov, I have friends in *very* high places."

"And if this gets out," she said, mimicking his smooth sweetness, "you'll need every fucking one of them." As Colonel Codgson flinched, she went on, "You're treating this project as your personal playground. You *executed* our star performer. After we were put under express orders not to alarm the test subjects, you cut out his throat and covered half the room in *blood*. You're a liability. You threaten to compromise the entire batch."

Colonel Codgson smiled and didn't even face the doctor. "Release this one. I'll take her to the sleep bay."

"Six Two One has excellent potential!" Doctor Molotov snapped.

"She surrendered," Codgson said flatly. He gave her a bored sigh, his smile still in place. "Either we do it there, or I do it here. Which do you think would be more traumatic to your precious subjects?"

They're talking about killing her, Six Six Five realized, her heart beginning to hammer out of control. Even knowing that, though, she couldn't bring herself to speak. Shame and terror mingled in her chest, keeping her silent. She had to be wrong. She *had* to be. They were simply talking about taking her away, training her in something else…

Doctor Molotov stared at Codgson for several moments in the total silence that followed, then her eyes shifted to Six Two One, who still looked confused.

"So do I get to be a doctor now?" Six Two One asked softly. Then, when Doctor Molotov just stared at her, she quickly added, "Or an assistant? I'd be a good assistant, Doctor Molotov. I'd carry your clipboard for you and take good notes. I never really wanted to be a soldier. I don't like to fight."

For a long moment, Doctor Molotov's gaze was fixed on Six Two One. Then, suddenly, without a single word, she spun and walked away, her heels clicking desperately on the concrete as she passed.

After she was gone, Colonel Codgson chuckled. "Get them fighting," he told the technicians. "Winners go to the cafeteria. Culls in the corner. I'll deal with them as they come."

Unlocking the chain from around Six Two One's foot, Lieutenant Drake licked her lips and stood. Nervous gray eyes on Six Six Five, she said, "What about the ones that need medical attention?"

Six Six Five, whose heart had been pounding too hard to even think about her wounds, flinched and curled her hand into a fist to hide her injuries. The last thing she wanted to do was go anywhere with Colonel Codgson.

"She broke protocol," he said, sounding bored, now. "She can run laps until the games are over." Then he grabbed Six Two One by the shirt and steered her away from the formation. The last thing Six Six Five saw of her before one of the soldiers was prodding her out of the room was her friend's look of apology.

Take care of Pizza, Six Two One mouthed, smiling. Then she was gone, led by Colonel Codgson through the far door.

"Time to run, kid," the gun-toting man said, pushing Six Six Five gently with his gun, urging her from the room and towards the gymnasium.

"Lucky little shit," another one added, glancing over his shoulder once they were out of earshot inside the gym. "You fucking see that?"

The first soldier grunted. "Yeah. I'd say the little guy's gotta watch out for arsenic in his Cheerios from now on. I've never *seen* Codgson so pissed."

"Dude, I think it's a girl."

The other soldier shrugged. "Can't tell the way they shave their heads and dress 'em like robots." Then he frowned. "Hey, kid. We said *run*."

Six Six Five reluctantly broke into a jog around the edge of the room, but as she did, she wondered what arsenic was, and where she could find Cheerios. And why the soldiers acted like it was something out of the ordinary to have their heads shaved. And why robots would wear clothing. Sometimes, she realized, the soldiers acted as if they were from a completely different world. One that was bigger, one that they all visited on a regular basis…

Six Six Five stumbled in her run as she realized that the soldiers' faces were never the same day in and day out. It was like they alternated, only 'protecting' them a few days each week. And if they alternated, where did they *go*? *Was* there a bigger world out there, one the doctors weren't letting them see?

"Run, kid!" one of the soldiers behind her laughed. "Only a zillion laps to go."

"Dude, she can understand you," his partner muttered.

"So?" the soldier demanded. "You saw Codgson's face. In a couple of weeks, that one's gonna be sent to the glue factory." He paused and frowned in Six Six Five's direction. "*Run.* Don't make us tell you again, shrimp."

"I hate it when they look at us like that. Almost like they *think*, you know?"

The other soldier grunted. "They're automatons. They don't think." Then Six Six Five was out of earshot, running laps around the huge gym. By the time she got back to her starting-point, the soldiers had moved to a table near the bleachers and had started up a card game. As Six Six Five ran—seemingly endless laps, over and over, for hours—her fingers started to pound and her nose, which had stopped bleeding in the time after her fight with Six One Eight, began to dribble blood again. By the time a technician arrived, her fingers were throbbing lumps of agony at the end of her arm and her nose was blowing bloody snot down her shirt, but thoughts of Six Two One kept her running, that look of apology, that last whispered goodbye, that horrible fear that she wasn't being sent to train as a technician.

Instead of telling the soldiers that it was time for her to quit running laps and go to medical, however, the technician only told the soldiers they would be there longer than expected.

"A couple of them are being stubborn," Six Six Five overheard the lab-coated man say, as she continued running in circles. "No clear winners. Lookin' like it might take awhile."

"Well, fuck," one of the soldiers said, glancing at Six Six Five. "I don't wanna babysit this little shit all night. It's Miller time. Send him to medical—he's just spreading blood around. If Codgson whines about it, I'll take the hit on Monday. It's past *ten* man. Screw this." He stood and threw his gun over his shoulder. "You okay if we ditch?"

"Sure," the technician said, giving a tired look in Six Six Five's direction.

"Hey," the other soldier said, as they were leaving. "Jackson and I had a bet going. Is that a boy or a girl?"

"Girl," the technician said.

"Told you," the soldier snickered to his friend as they walked out. "Fifty bucks, asshole."

Once they were gone, the technician took a deep breath, the hollows of his eyes dark and haggard. "Hey kid."

Six Six Five immediately stopped running and went into attention.

"Yeah okay." The technician looked agitated. "Look. I'm tired as fuck. Girlfriend moved out on me last night—she was packing dishes and screaming at me at like two fucking a.m. I found out she was banging this high-schooler at Arby's, you know? A *burger-flipper*. Not really in the mood to deal with any of this shit. You know where medical is?"

"Yes, sir!" Six Six Five shouted.

"Well, you just take your ass to medical and tell them to fix you up. You're one of the last ones, anyway. I'm taking a page from those idiots' book and going home."

"Yes, sir!" Six Six Five barked.

"Yeah, whatever," the man replied. "Just go. Codgson went home hours ago. He had *golf* in the morning." Face twisted with disgust, the technician turned to leave.

Six Six Five spoke before she realized what she was going to say. "Sir?"

The technician paused. When he turned, it was with a little frown on his face. "Yeah?"

"Are they going to kill Six Two One, sir?" Six Six Five asked, her chest clenching at the fear of what she was doing, asking a question without leave, of showing *curiosity*.

The technician continued to frown at her a moment, then glanced over his shoulder before looking back at her, a wariness in his face. "They don't kill anyone. Where'd you get that idea?"

"I heard the soldiers talking about how they were gonna kill her, sir," Six Six Five lied, her voice coming out in a terrified babble that was only half faked. "Are they gonna kill her for getting culled?"

"Those fucking idiots," she heard him mutter under his breath. Then, in the formal, sharp tones the adults always used when they were telling them what to do, he said, "You soldiers are Earth's greatest hope for freedom. They don't kill the culls. That's ridiculous." He turned again to go.

Despite her instincts to keep quiet, despite her fear of asking questions, Six Six Five had to know more. "So what do they do with them?" she insisted. "Will she be a doctor, then?"

The lab assistant blinked at her, and for a moment, Six Six Five saw her own oblivion in his eyes. Then, yawning, he ran a hand over his face and checked the time on the wall. "Fuck, it's getting late.

Yeah, that's right. She's off to be a doctor. Just like Molotov. Now get your ass to medical."

And, because she needed to, Six Six Five believed him. She watched as he turned and departed, leaving Six Six Five alone in the gym.

Standing there, utterly unsupervised for the first time in her life, Six Six Five's first instinct was strangely to follow the adults and see where they went when they were off duty. Then she realized that to do so would, without a doubt, result in her getting culled. Instead, she closed her eyes and told herself, over and over, that Six Two One was going to be a doctor, and that someday she would see her again when she was sick or injured, once they had both completed their training. She actually began to feel better about it, knowing that Six Two One would be happier not having to fight.

Then she remembered Colonel Codgson's knife against her throat, his whisper against her ear. *"You are a cull."* The way he had said it, he hadn't meant she was going to be trained as a doctor. It had been a sneer, a gloat, a satisfied goodbye. It had been...final.

Then Six Six Five realized she had been ignoring her orders much too long, and if any technician happened to walk in on her, standing there, she would be given chores to do. She jumped into motion, hurrying down the corridor towards the medical wing.

She was almost there, one more right-hand turn to reach the final hall to her destination, when a weird gurgling sound from the hall ahead stopped her cold. It sounded eerily similar to the sound Six One Eight had made, as he had died on the floor at Colonel Codgson's feet. With it came a rhythmic rattle, like someone shaking a food cart. Frowning, Six Six Five peered down the hall at the little blue door on the end. The sounds continued, gurgle-rattle, gurgle-rattle...

Biting her lip, she glanced at the empty hall behind her, then at her intended destination. Down the hall in the medical wing, she could hear adult voices discussing something. She swallowed hard and glanced again at the little blue door.

Don't ask questions, Colonel Codgson had instructed them, in one of their first formations. *Questions are weakness. The weak do not survive. Only the* strong *survive.*

Her heart jumping into a palpitating rhythm in her chest, Six Six Five took a tentative step towards the little blue door and its tiny metal window.

Questioning your training is like saying to us you aren't prepared to do your job. Your job is to do what you're told. Your job is to save the Earth.

Six Six Five took another step, unable to hear over the blood rushing in her ears.

Soldiers have to be strong. The weak will be culled. Only the strong can do what needs to be done and save our planet from the aliens. Only the strong will not ask questions.

Six Six Five continued, foot by terrified foot, adrenaline burning her veins.

Those who ask questions are enemies of Earth. Enemies of Earth will be culled.

Six Six Five stopped at the little door with the strange sounds coming from behind it. Light was streaming out the crack under the metal jamb. Six Six Five wasn't tall enough to peer through the window, even on her tiptoes, so with shaking fingers, she put her hand to the latch.

Soldiers don't ask questions. Soldiers do as they're told.

Gingerly, as quietly as she could, Six Six Five twisted the latch. Unlike the other doors in the halls, this one was unlocked. It slid down all the way, until it clicked and the latch's resistance gave, allowing her to push the door open a crack.

Inside, she saw rows of kids on tables, clear plastic bags on stands beside them. One of them was shaking and convulsing, the gurgling sound coming from his frothy open mouth. His eyes were white where they were twisted up into his head. Beside him, a technician in blue was injecting something into the tube connected to his arm, checking his watch.

Six Six Five frowned, opening the door just a little more, to get a better view.

Then she saw Six Two One's frothy mouth, open and limp against the table that held her. Her green eyes were wide and open, the pupils dilated. At first, Six Six Five thought she was looking *at* her, then the technician bumped her foot in moving around the shaking soldier's table and her body jiggled unnaturally, her head sliding back and forth, smearing froth on the metal table that held her.

Six Six Five yanked the door shut and bolted. She dove into the first hallway she found and kept running, having no idea where she was going, just that she had to get *away*. Behind her in the other hall, she heard the door open, heard the technician call out...Six Six Five turned another corner and lunged into the bathroom, where she huddled in a stall, knees to chest, rocking, crying. She thought she was alone for several minutes until she heard movement in the stall beside her, felt someone tentatively push open her door, saw Doctor Molotov's mascara-streaked face...

"Shael, damn it, what the soot?" Shael came to the sudden realization that a big hand was shaking him. "Twelve-A! What the soot is wrong with her?! She's having a burning *seizure*, man..."

Shael shoved Joedobbs' hand aside. Whimpering, too unsteady to rise from his coils, Shael uncurled from the ground and crawled away. *You are a cull.* The words echoed in his head, the cold black eyes filled with malice.

Gasping, sucking in ragged breaths that ended in weird, hoarse sounds in his chest, Shael saw his vision blur, his eyes stop working. All he could see was an empty cage. White froth, staring eyes, an empty bunk, an empty cage...He heard himself whining, and he crumpled forward again, arms and legs tucking tight against his chest.

"Hey," the word carried unmistakable gentleness. A warm hand touched Shael's shoulder. "You're going to be all right. They're gone. I swear to you, they're gone." When Shael didn't respond or throw him away, Joedobbs' voice softened further. "Here. Easy. They're gone." He reached down and tucked his big arms under Shael's great form, hefting him up into his lap.

And, in his gratitude for the warmth of Joedobbs' arms, the comfort of another's touch, Shael let the Voran hold him.

• • •

"Okay," Joe said softly, once the woman had fallen asleep again in his *arms*, without even dismembering him for the insult, "I'm starting to get really creeped out, furg. What's going on with her?"

Twelve-A's response was a long, nervous pause.

"Burn it!" Joe hissed, careful not to be loud enough to wake her. He turned to face the minder, who had taken up residence a safe distance away. "She's a furg-loving time-bomb and I *know* there's something you're not telling me."

From where he sat against his tree, giving Shael a nervous frown, Twelve-A said, *I think the brainwashing machine is wearing off. They kept her in it most of the time, to make her think she was Jreet.*

Joe grimaced, having suspected something similar. "Okay, so what do we do?"

Twelve-A was silent so long that Joe had to look at him. The minder appeared nervous, watching the sleeping woman with something akin to anxiety. He scratched one of his large, pointy ears absently.

"Hey, Lobo," Joe growled. "I'm talking to you, wolfie."

Twelve-A dropped his hand and scowled. *Normally*, he grudgingly replied, *I'd try to change her memories. Give her ones that didn't make her cry.*

"And?" Joe demanded. Not having the woman with the brain-popping goodness crawling around the camp in the dark, sobbing, was definitely a good step in the right direction. He had been half sure she had been about to explode his cranium for touching her, but he also instinctively knew she was about to start throwing around her handy rock-crushing trick if he didn't get her calmed down.

And someone already did that, Twelve-A said. *What you're seeing are her* real *memories coming back.*

Joe's mouth formed a little O. "Burn me," he whispered, looking down at her sleeping form. "What happened to her?" he whispered.

Twelve-A considered for much too long. *Her dreams are for her to tell you*, he said finally.

Joe frowned, remembering what she had shouted after powdering the boulder. "What did she mean, her dreams, your weakness?"

Twelve-A's head jerked up and his blue gaze grew sharp. *I don't have a weakness.*

Joe cocked his head. For a long moment, they just sat there like that, the telepath glaring, Joe studying him, wondering exactly what that weakness was.

I could remove your memory of this conversation, Twelve-A warned.

"You could," Joe agreed. "Or you could trust me."

Twelve-A's eyes darkened. *I don't trust soldiers.* He abruptly got up and walked off.

"Funny!" Joe called after him, "'Cause I seem to remember you sleeping around me!"

Keep pushing it, Twelve-A said, *and you won't remember what we're arguing about.*

Joe opened his mouth to push it, then felt the telepath's mental fingers tightening down on his brain. He sighed, deeply. "Fine, Wingnut. I'll let you tell me when you're ready."

After a moment of hesitation, the mental fingers retreated and the camp once more descended into silence. Joe hastily checked to see if he could rewind the conversation in his head, and he was somewhat surprised that he could.

Score one for the good guys, Joe thought, tugging Shael closer into his arms.

I am a good guy, Twelve-A said. *I'm trying to decide what you are.*

A decade ago, Joe would have laughed, but now he just dropped his head and stared down at Shael's sleep-slackened face. "Yeah," Joe said softly, after an eternity. "Me too."

• • •

19

BUBBLE MANIUM

Slade Galvin Gardner, or Sparrow That Tends the Valley if one were to translate his alias literally, hated sparrows, valleys, and gardens. He liked simulated combat games, moving credits from somebody else's bank account to his own, and fine, rare steaks served on gleaming ruvmestin platters in fancy skyrise resorts. The fact that Congress had taken all of those things away from him and thrust him into a valley with sparrows and gardens made him want to kill another prisoner.

Slade looked back over the huge group of people he was herding east and scanned the faces for a likely candidate, but was disappointed to find not a single ounce of resistance among their weary numbers. As of yet, the Harmonious Society of God—HSG for short—had more than five hundred members, and that number increased every time they ran across another ragged band of survivors.

His ever-evolving plan, as leader of this emerging new civilization, was to build a city on the Great Plains, in one of the areas that was still fertile, and spread God's word throughout the continent.

As an atheist, Slade did not believe in God, and he'd made sure every one of his followers knew it. The only higher power he answered to was himself, and thus, God's word was Slade's word, and

Slade's word was that they needed some damn steak, and the Great Plains had steak.

Tyson still disagreed with Slade's decision to name the group the Harmonious Society of God, that he was crazy to call it that. Slade tended to agree—after thirteen months of fervent lectures and heartfelt sermons, with Slade moonlighting as a lowly, forgotten convict at New Basil after being Earth's Most Wanted criminal for most of his life, Slade was pretty sure the shock had knocked a few of his bolts loose. He wasn't, however, sure which ones they were, so there was no use in hanging around trying to figure out where they had fallen. He had more important things to think about than the name of his group, and it was too late to change it now.

Besides, if any of his five hundred followers had any objections about the name of their tribe, not one had mentioned it. Sure, that might be due to the fact that he kept them under armed guard and served the dissidents up to the rest of the group, but he liked to believe that it was because he had picked a good name on the first try.

Slade felt another headache coming on and quickly distracted himself with a piece of gum. Gum had become his constant companion. On the way up the three-ninety-five, they had stopped in Independence, which had basically been what had kept them alive after their horrendous trek through King's Canyon National Park. While the others went looking for beds, captives, and booze, Slade had found three cases of sugar-free Bubble Manium in the back of a looted Gray's Grocery. All three were 'Fruit Variety,' with fifty packages to a case. Each package consisted of six smaller packages, one each of Watermelon, Strawberry, Banana, Grape, Sour Apple, and Original. Even though it was a 'fruit variety,' they had to stick Original in there. Bastards.

That meant he was down to four thousand, two hundred and eighty-nine pieces of gum, if he included the piece in his mouth. He used them sparingly, and shared them with no one. Still, if he only limited himself to one piece a day, which he found very hard to adhere to, he would run out in eleven years and two hundred and seventy-four days. Or, if it was stipulated that a month contained thirty days, he would be out of gum in one hundred and forty-two months and twenty-nine days. Almost exactly one hundred and forty-three months. But, if he chewed one an hour, which was closer to his current average, he would run out of gum in one hundred seventy-eight days, seventeen hours.

Slade dreaded the day he would run out of gum. After his initial gum-chewing craze upon discovering the cases of Bubble Manium, he had cut back drastically, aware that some day in the future, he would no longer have gum to relieve his constant headaches. He *really* wasn't looking forward to that, as it would mean he would be alone with the Human equivalent of lobotomized orangutans still stuck in the shit-flinging Stone Age.

"Slade," Tyson said, interrupting his thoughts like a hippo in a Fabergé museum, "we have a problem."

Slade looked up from his book of survival techniques and frowned at his second-in-command. "Another dissenter?"

"No," Tyson said, "Food. We're out again." His beefy new lackey was smart—comparatively—built like a linebacker, and well over six feet. He looked like the perfect Nazi, with bright blue eyes, platinum blond hair, and a chiseled, rectangular face with a clean-shaven jaw line that jutted out like it had been hewn from granite. He even had a cleft in his chin.

Stupid chin-cleft. Slade had always wanted one of those. Instead, his somewhat weak chin had gotten covered in a white fuzz that came in spotty patches that hurt to shave and…wriggled…when he wasn't paying attention.

Disgusted, Slade again questioned his wisdom in downing that Congie brew, over thirty years ago. It had certainly…humbled… him over the years. Yeah, that was the word. 'Humbled.' Something about having a perpetually limp dick really did that to a guy. Tyson, on the other hand, probably got laid every night. More than a little bitter, Slade wondered when was the last time Tyson had had sex. He wondered if his Second would listen to him if he told him to stop.

Probably not. The fucker.

In the right light, Slade was also blond…ish…though he had eyes the color of what he liked to think of as 'ball lightning.' They were almost purple, but so bright that they looked like they were sizzling. Almost white. Purple-blue-white. His fuzzy mass of hair was also an odd snowy color, and bled like a stuck pig when he cut it. Damn those genetic experiments. Added to the natural, catlike grace of his huge frame—thank you, Dad—it was easy for him to fit the profile of what his followers thought to be one of the altered humans that had pissed Congress off so badly. Behind his back, they delightfully now called him a 'mutie' and talked about how he could read people's minds and levitate objects, further adding to his mystique. Perfect.

Not that Slade could read minds—he was just incredibly perceptive when it came to…well, anything. But people, especially, were ridiculously easy to read. They always gave away something about their thoughts by the way they held themselves, the way their faces twitched or didn't twitch, the way they fidgeted, the way they coughed or smiled or winced, and the longer Slade used those hints and pretended to read their every thought, the more thoroughly convinced the poddites became that he could do it.

Truth was, Slade had been using these cues all of his life, mostly in the process of moving another man's credits into his own account. He had been very good at what he did, and had been a very wealthy man up until they caught him—again, and under an alias—and gave him the option of going to a federal pen for life or spend a few years at one of the various religious brainwashing centers.

Slade had chosen New Basil Harmonious over the longer term at the pen because he knew for a fact that he couldn't be brainwashed. One of his personality quirks that he had discovered after breaking into a top-secret Congie computer back in his teenage years, while looking for ways to recall his brother. The underwitted alien apes had caught him and done a thorough brain-cleansing, then attempted to replace his memories with ones they liked better and make him work for them.

Slade, however, despite all of their ridiculously-pitched voices, fancy machines, and nasty drugs, had remained perfectly aware of what he had done, and once he escaped their incompetent clutches, he broke in again and gave himself a permanent, three-hundred-thousand-turn-dead Corps Director's pass, which had left the whole of the Congressional intelligence open to him.

Decades later, after navigating the colossal, multi-layered, AI-monitored, Huouyt and Bajnan-coded Congressional systems, hacking Earth's measly government servers had been like taking a carrot from a dead rabbit.

Turned out, Earth wasn't just researching genetic engineering when Congress caught them red-handed. It was also working on a mind-drug that stimulated the cells of the human brain in such a way to create a Thomas Jefferson, a Nikola Tesla, or a Leonardo da Vinci in a matter of a few months. Oh, and it was supposed to bestow immortality using alien DNA and allow the body to change shape at whim. What's not to like, right?

Slade, who had already been on par with Tesla—if a highly criminal, hacking-obsessed version of him—had been bored one afternoon and decided to make himself the first successful guinea pig. 'Successful,' being the key word, because all the other guinea-pigs had died in a quivering puddle of flesh and half-formed DNA slurry the moment they imbibed the moron scientists' concoction.

So Slade had gotten a little drunk in his penthouse one night, hadn't found any porn worth watching, stared at gyrating bodies until his eyes bled, then gotten a wild hair up his ass to prove to the government fucktards what they were doing wrong. His reasoning? Shapeshifting could be *fun*! He spent a couple hours in his impromptu lab surrounded by old pizza boxes fiddling with their nannite programming and bumblefucked formulas, then served himself up a cocktail of the glowing purple concoction. Cheers.

Slade had quickly discovered why it was much more desirable to be the *second* surviving guinea-pig, rather than the proud first.

In one night, he had lost all his hair, his eyesight, and his ability to get a hard-on, not to mention he'd been hit by a sudden, debilitating migraine that still continued to bother him over thirty years later. His hair had grown back after a few months, but had lost all pigmentation and was as frizzy as cotton, hurt like fuck to clip, and *wriggled*. His eyesight had taken longer, but when it finally did start working again, his playboy blue eyes had taken on the look of something otherworldly, the black of the pupils contrasting so startlingly with the irises that he wore contacts for the first few years, because it spooked even him. And he still hadn't been able to get it up. Not once. In thirty-two years.

Hello, Fountain of Youth. Goodbye, sex.

When neither eye nor hair changed back to their original color, Slade ditched the contacts and stopped caring that he looked like a punk rocker from the Dark Ages. He kept his unruly, sensitive white locks under control with enough hair gel to drown a small village and smiled politely when the waiters at fancy restaurants forgot to write down his order because they were too busy staring.

Unfortunately, his strange appearance also made him easy to identify when the feds caught up with him after he escaped the Congies. Not that the low-rung idiots had the first clue about the Da Vinci Project, as the human scientists had oh-so-originally named the genetics stuff, but they had pieced together a few of his other dealings—a mere shadow of what he had *really* been up to—and charged him with eleven counts of fraud and conspiracy to commit fraud. Joy.

Only Slade had known that there were no conspirators. *He* was the conspiracy. His web had extended to the most powerful, most encrypted businesses, spiriting away as much as a million credits an hour during his doughnut breaks. When he was *really* interested, his victims, Huouyt-run multi-planetary Congressional businesses—because nobody liked the Huouyt—went mysteriously bankrupt, their assets prudently transferred to one of Slade's dozens of accounts in any one of a dozen Bajnan banking planets.

It was only when the business pissed him off in one way or another—usually by not contributing enough to charity, which Slade did religiously—that he went to such extremes, however. He had generally kept himself to a barely noticeable, constant flow, the totals of which had continued to accumulate over the course of his thirteen months' imprisonment, ending in a net profit of five billion, six hundred and thirty-five million credits despite his misfortunate condition of being behind bars.

At least, that was the last approximate count before Congress blew Earth a new hole.

His fortune had evaporated with the destruction of Earth's global communications net. It had ceased to exist. All his hours of toil, every wrist-cramp and mind-numbing minute of cracking code...All for jack diddly shit.

Sure, the money was still out there, sitting in those nice, secure Bajnan banks. But Slade wasn't gonna see it again. Not unless he made himself a better potion, figured out the shapeshifting thing, and found a way to get the hell off the planet.

Which, all things considered, he had about the same chance of doing as getting hard, telling Tyson to bend over, having Tyson *obey*, and taking his muscular bodyguard up the ass in front of the whole of the Harmonious Society of God.

What a waste. Slade hadn't bothered using his wonderful brain for anything except memorizing numbers and patterns. He had spent his entire life learning every minute detail of state-of-the-art encryption techniques. His concept of adventure had been picking a new entrée at one of the three most expensive restaurants on the planet.

Now he was left wandering around in the woods with an archaic survival guide, two and a half cases of gum, and a group of idiots who thought he was a badass Rambo-Xavier cross who could read their minds whilst mowing down kreenit with a pellet gun.

"Slade?" Tyson asked again. "You fuckin' spacing out again, man?" He wasn't timid like most of Slade's other lackeys. Tyson either didn't believe Slade could read his mind, or he didn't care. Either way, he made for a likeable fellow, since Slade really did get tired of all the whimpering and funny looks.

"Yeah, food," Slade said, frowning. They were wandering through a patch of overgrown farmland that looked like it had been growing onions up until the point those big ugly aliens tore up the farmhouse and ate whoever was inside.

"Maybe another sacrifice?" Tyson suggested.

Slade waved off the suggestion. "Nah. Not without cause." Strangely, after over three months of near-starvation, cannibalism had lost all of its previous horror.

"We won't reach the Plains if we all starve to death before we get there," Tyson reminded him.

Slade cocked his head at the man, more than a little impressed. "Well aren't *you* a bloodthirsty son of a bitch." He flicked his wrist dismissively. "Sure, whatever. Just make sure it's a woman. The males are too important as workers for us to be eating them." He went back to his book, memorizing the way to make a rabbit snare with just some string, a knife, and a young tree.

Tyson's lip curled. "Maybe I'll pass, after all." Tyson, strangely, had a weird prejudice when it came to eating women, which Slade, of course, knew.

Like reading a book, Slade thought with a sigh. Realizing he hadn't solved his minions' hunger issues, he said, "If you look around, maybe there'll be some onions or something." He waved a hand at the ruined farm distractedly.

Tyson scrunched his face. "Onions?"

"Yeah, you fry them and they're not so bad," Slade replied. He put down his book. "Had them on steak all the time before Judgement."

Tyson glanced at the packet of Watermelon Bubble Manium sticking out of Slade's custom leather jacket. "Can I have some?"

Slade felt his fingers spasm on the book, thinking about that hundred and seventy-eight days and seventeen headache-free hours. "No."

Tyson sighed and plucked a piece of grass from the overgrown field, then stuck it in his mouth in an imitation of one of the old-style farmers that had worked their crops with their bare hands. With his dirty face and ripped jeans, Tyson almost looked the part. Almost. The sleek, black, Global Police laser rifle slung over his shoulder kind of ruined the effect.

"Should we get them moving, then?" Tyson asked around the grass.

"I don't care," Slade replied. "Nevada's gonna be a bitch regard-less of when we cross it."

Grunting, Tyson unshouldered his laser rifle and walked off toward the quiet clusters of people. Slade went back to his book and distractedly blew a bubble as Tyson started shouting orders. Despite the fact that his survival was on the line, he couldn't concentrate on the ancient diagrams and photographs. He was once more thinking about his ever-dwindling supply of Bubble Manium.

20

THE MAKING OF A
WARRIOR

It was another beautiful, sunny southern Californian day, and the experiments, despite Joe's urging to move faster, had settled into a warm meadow and were doing more or less precisely nothing. Watching them pick dirt from between their toes, then immediately use the same fingers to pick their noses, Joe decided he could afford a nap. He'd fallen into a sentry routine, getting less than four hours of sleep a day, and it—combined with the deliciously warm, relaxing sunlight—was finally catching up with him. He'd been weaving on his feet for several days in a row, now, and the strain of keeping the camp safe while Twelve-A slept was starting to wear on him.

"I need a nap," Joe told the telepath, who was picking up stones down by the creek. "Can you take care of things while I sleep?"

Sure, Twelve-A told him. He picked a rock out of the stream, squinted at it, then licked it. And, after a wide-eyed jerk, kept licking it.

Joe narrowed his eyes. "No kreenit nearby?" he insisted. "No gangs?"

Twelve-A paused in licking his rock and his brow crinkled in a tiny line of concentration. Then, *Nope. Nobody.* Lick. Lick.

But Joe wasn't satisfied. He closed the distance and poked the minder in the chest. "That's your *job*, you understand? My job is security. *Your* job is keeping the furgs with guns away from our friends."

Twelve-A raised his eyebrow down at Joe's finger in his chest. *That sounds to me like you've got me doing your job.*

"I'm determining the best allocation of our resources," Joe retorted. "And you're only useful when you're—" he reached out, snagged the rock from the telepath's mouth, and tossed it back into the stream, "—keeping an eye out for bad guys. Stop licking things. It's going to make you sick."

Twelve-A gave him an irritated glance. "It was cold."

"Get Eleven-C to make you some ice-cream, then," Joe growled. "I couldn't possibly explain it to you, but there's things out there like amoebas and bacteria—"

Joe felt the colossal sledge of the telepath's mind grab him in a mighty fist and begin rooting through his mind for amoebas and bacteria. And, because it was actually easier than trying to explain to him what they *did*, Joe didn't shoot him in the face. Immediately, Twelve-A frowned, then twisted to look at the water. He started wiping his tongue on his arm.

Which, of course, probably had a thousand times more bacteria on it, considering the People had not yet bathed as long as Joe had known them. Immediately, Twelve-A hesitated, looking at his arm, then swallowed. *I will get them to bathe.*

"You do that," Joe said. Some of the guys—Twelve-A included— were really beginning to stink. *Joe,* not being a total naked-assed barbarian, had been at least washing his pits daily, when he had access to water.

You should have told me about this bacteria earlier, Twelve-A told him, looking pleasingly pale. *It could kill us.*

"Sure could," Joe agreed solemnly. "And there's *billions* of them out there," he added, gesturing to their surroundings. "Probably trillions in this clearing alone." Then he slapped Twelve-A on the shoulder and said, "You go deal with that while I take a nap, okay?" His body, tired as he was, was having trouble keeping itself upright.

Twelve-A nodded quickly and wandered off toward Eleven-C, who was sleeping in Nine-G's arms again.

Yawning, Joe found a particularly sunny, soft-looking patch of grass on the slope and flopped down onto it, facing the group. Most of the experiments were in various states of slumber, sprawled in the shade wherever they had decided to sit down. At least that was *one* thing the telepath had done well. Once Joe had explained to him that it was the *sun* causing their blisters, Twelve-A had been diligent in keeping the rest of the furgs out of direct sunlight.

Joe yawned again, the black of his Congie clothes soaking in some much-appreciated heat. As Joe was relaxing in the warmth, he spotted Shael frowning at him from across the clearing, but he was too tired to try and figure out what bug had crawled up her ass this time, and just pulled a fold of his bandana over his eyes and allowed the delicious heat of the planet's weak star to lull him into a much-needed sleep.

It seemed he'd only been asleep *tics* before he was woken again.

"Get up, Voran. We move in six tics." With the brusque words came a slosh of icy water, dousing Joe from head to toe. Jolted from a deep sleep, Joe surged to his feet and had Jane's lips pressed to Shael's forehead before he realized what he'd done.

Shael seemed utterly unconcerned by the sizzling plasma pistol between her eyes. Instead, she gave his wet clothes a derisive snort, shouldered the cracked five-gallon bucket she had scavenged from someone's backyard, and simply walked off.

Dripping, Joe returned Jane to her holster and scowled after the tiny woman, water still running down his legs, into his boots. A few rods away, the telepath sat placidly against a tree in the shade, watching the exchange.

"Was that your idea, sootling?" Joe growled. Now completely sodden, shivering in the coolness of morning, he was fully willing to return the favor.

It was her idea, Twelve-A said. *She decided to take your place when you were sleeping. She says she's war-leader now, and we're all going to be moving out in six tics.* It appeared, however, that Twelve-A wasn't the least bit concerned about their 'move-out' deadline. When Joe looked closely, the telepath seemed to be sorting out piles of grass. Beside him, Alice, Nine-G, Eleven-C, and a bunch of the peons were all doing the same.

Then Joe realized what the telepath had said and he groaned. That was the *last* thing they needed…Shael thinking Shael was in charge. Even then, Shael was grabbing another bucket of water from the stream and heading towards a sleeping group of experiments, obviously intending to repeat the process on the naked dogpiles scattered about the clearing. Joe watched, academically curious to see which of them would win in a mind-brawl.

A quarter of them are makers, Twelve-A warned. *If she startles them enough, they'll just turn her head into mashed potatoes or something. Most of them like mashed potatoes.*

Joe felt a rush of panic, realizing the petite woman could, with her nice bucket of icy creek water, indeed get herself some fun new alterations for her efforts. He cursed and broke into a jog to catch up with her before she could empty her payload.

Shael stopped a pace away from the group of sleeping experiments and awkwardly lifted the half-full bucket into her arms. "Get up, you lazy Takki skulkers!" Shael shouted, heaving the bucket back. "We leave in six tics! Those who aren't in formation on time get staked for your insolence!"

Just before she could launch her payload, Joe grabbed the rim of Shael's bucket and twisted it around just in time to slop the contents all over himself, rather than the sleeping experiments, icy water drenching him a second time. Several of Shael's intended victims opened their eyes at her scream and blinked up at the two of them, then went back to sleep.

Dripping, cold, Joe yanked the bucket out of Shael's hands and turned to face her.

Immediately, Shael's chin came up in challenge. "You slept through roll-call and your duties passed to the next qualified warrior. I accepted the nomination."

Irritated now, Joe threw the bucket aside—being sure to spatter Twelve-A and his little grass-party with the remnants—and crossed his arms to glare down at her. "Nomination, huh? Who nominated you? No one here can even speak your language."

Shael flushed. Then, like a queen, she straightened her spine and said, "I nominated myself."

"Oh really." Joe continued to scowl down at her, wondering how he got saddled with this particular pain in the ass. "Who backed you?" He knew enough of the Jreet clan system to know that, unless at least five sixths of the 'clan' had backed her, her claim on the title of war-leader was null and void.

Apparently, Shael knew this, too, because she blushed. "I was the only able-bodied alternative."

Peering down at her over as much muscle as he could flex without popping an artery, Joe growled, "I take it you're ready for that rematch, then."

Shael froze. He saw the flash of trepidation in her brilliant green eyes as she reflexively looked him up and down, then he grinned inside as she swallowed. He watched her consider, watched her contemplate *losing*, and let her stew on that a little bit.

"*Ovor*," Joe offered, as she started straightening to tell him some furgsoot about how a Welu could beat a Voran any day of the rotation, "I could thank you—*profusely*—for keeping order for me while I slept and I could go back to my normal duties and you to yours." Joe lowered his voice to a near whisper. "Even as we stand here, exchanging pleasantries, Eleven-C goes *completely unguarded*."

Shael winced and glanced at Twelve-A's little haymaking social-hour. "Nine-G guards her."

"Nine-G," Joe said solemnly, "is not Jreet."

"True," Shael mourned, in utter seriousness.

Joe took a deep breath and reached out to lay a hand on Shael's petite shoulder. In an utter somber tone, he said, "I think, as you must, that it is in these weaklings' best interest to have *two* Jreet watching their backs, rather than one. You've *seen* how lazy they are. Earthlings are liable to attack at any time, and our charges are scattered and disorganized, completely unprepared to defend themselves. These furgs here—" he gestured at the sleeping dogpile "—need *my* guiding hand, just as Twelve-A and his comrades need yours."

Twelve-A's head jerked up to look at him with a frown. *That is extremely uncool.*

Bite me, Wingnut, Joe retorted, still giving Shael a sober look. *Next time, don't let her douse me in my sleep.* To the woman, he said, "What do you say? You take charge of guarding Twelve-A, Eleven-C, Alice, and Nine-G—the *important* ones—and I'll watch the rest of them. Those four are certainly more worth your time than these imbeciles, no?" He gestured at the sleeping experiments that were even then drooling in the shade.

Really uncool, Twelve-A repeated, scowling.

You're the mind-freak, Joe said. *Persuade her not to be unreasonable and everybody will be happy.*

You'd be better at that, Twelve-A retorted. *She respects you.*

Joe was so shocked he choked. "She...*what?*"

Shael gave him a suspicious look. "*Who* what?"

Realizing she'd caught his meaning, Joe backpedaled. "Alice," Joe quickly said. "She..." He struggled to come up with something fast enough to avoid another 'fight' to see who the female-to-be *really* was.

"Alice what?" Shael barked, intelligence sharpening in her emerald eyes.

Joe, pinned by that gaze, acutely aware that *someone* needed to tell Shael the truth, and yet remembering what had happened to one machete-slinging jenfurgling on a lonely stretch of highway, stuttered. "Uh, I, uh..."

Alice wants to learn the art of a warrior, but she is too shy to admit it, Twelve-A supplied. *She wants to study under you.*

On a rush of gratitude, Joe repeated what the telepath had given him. *Thanks*, he said, once he was done.

As amusing as the last time was, Twelve-A told him, *she's going to hurt herself.*

Shael obviously sensed something amiss, but she eventually turned to look at Alice, anyway. "She chose to apprentice under *me* over *you?*" The woman sounded almost…shocked. She quickly hid it with a disdainful sniff. "At least *someone* in this clan has some sense." Giving the dogpile a disgusted wave, she said, "Keep your ill-bred Takki, Voran. I will guard the intelligent ones." At that, she turned and strutted off towards Twelve-A's little group, shoulders proudly back. A few moments later, she started cursing their laziness in Jreet and kicking apart their grass-piles.

Twelve-A leveled an irritated glance at Joe. *I want five tics for that*, he said.

Five tics of memory-surfing, as opposed to dealing with Shael, was a small price to pay.

Still, the meddlesome mind-furg had it coming. "Find your own memories," Joe snorted. "No freebies."

Twelve-A narrowed his eyes, but he stuck to their bargain and kept his mental fingers to himself.

Snickering to himself, Joe went to find a patch of sun to dry off. The idea that he'd pulled one over on the minder—not to mention that Shael *respected* him—was kind of nice.

• • •

"You are to be the greatest warriors that Earth has ever seen," Colonel Codgson said as he paced, his gloved hands clasped behind his back. "You are its future. Its *hope*, you understand?"

"Yes, sir!" Six Six Five shouted with the rest of her class. They stood at attention in exact, perfect lines around her, their spines rigid, their faces straight ahead. Each of her companions was the same age as Six Six Five, though Six Six Five was the smallest of the group. A 'runt,' she had overheard the doctors say during her last personal inspection, in which she had stood before the adults alone, pretending she couldn't hear the things they said about her as her heart pounded and her knees shook. To show any reaction—any at all—would have meant failure, and she had seen what happened to those of her companions who had failed. Six Six Five knew she couldn't fail. Not now.

So Six Six Five had stood in terror, staring at the wall, silently listening to them discuss her tiny body, her female weaknesses, her lackluster physical strength, wondering if the next soldier to come in would be there to take her to the little blue door at the end of the hall.

It had been Doctor Molotov's argument that Six Six Five had more potential than most, and a physically small body meant nothing if her war-mind worked properly, but aside from the time she'd broken the chain in the fight with Six One Eight, her war-mind had evaded her completely. The other doctor had simply argued to cull, that they had enough movers to satisfy their quota—all the *powerful* movers were already 'on ice with the minder.' The only real use she could have would be for 'Phil's ridiculous Jreet experiment.'

But now that she knew what it meant to be 'culled,' Six Six Five had been desperate to prove herself. She spent every night alone in the dark, staring up at the empty bunk above her—a reminder, Codgson said, of what happened to failures—doing nothing but trying to reach her war-mind. For almost a *year*, she had tried to concentrate, to find that perfect stillness and serenity that had come to her with that cold chain around her ankle, her own blood on her face, and for almost a *year*, it had completely evaded her. And that, she knew, was failure.

Just thinking about the way the doctors had talked about her at her last progress report, casually listing out her mediocre statistics and lackluster performance, coolly discussing her growth potential and inability to reproduce her 'one-time results', brought sweat to Six Six Five's face and made her hands start to tremble where she clasped them behind her back. She *had* to grow. She *had* to be strong. She couldn't fail.

Without wanting to, she once again saw the restrained bodies on the tables, saw the white, bubbly froth at their lips, their jerking bodies, their glazed, staring eyes…

The colonel stopped pacing and cast the formation a cold look, making Six Six Five snap back to the present on a wave of terror that he would notice her attention drifting. "I'm not sure you do," he said in that sickly-smooth voice that reminded her of blood and the smell of bowels. "We are at *war*. Do you know what that means?"

"Yes, sir!" Six Six Five rasped, adding her voice to the others, her throat tight with fear. It had been almost a year since she'd gone back to the room with an empty, blanket-less bunk where Six Two One had once slept. Pizza had likewise been gone, but they had left his cage. Another reminder. Though the other soldiers did not consciously understand, Six Six Five knew what that meant. Hamsters could not survive without cages. Pizza, like Six Two One, was dead.

"It *means*," Colonel Codgson went on, "in the coming years, we are all going to be forced to sacrifice. We need to give *everything we have* to save our home. We need to give this war our dedication. Our concentration. Our commitment." Codgson paused and gave them all a hard look. "Some of us will even have to give it our lives."

Though none of her companions flinched at that, Six Six Five once again remembered the white, rolled-up eyes of her dying brethren, the blue-clad doctor injecting their driplines and checking his watch. While her batchmates grinned and enthusiastically waited for their next test, their next chance to prove their worth, Six Six Five had come to understand what they really were: Hamsters. Hamsters in a cage.

"*Today*," Codgson continued, "you will each be given the chance to show us your strength. You've done the endurance training, the mental conditioning, the book-learning. You've done the study. But none of that means anything unless you have the *spirit* to do what must be done in the end. To *kill*. You are *soldiers*. Your *job* is to kill Earth's enemies." He paused again at the head of the formation, giving them a long, fatherly look with cold, emotionless black eyes that had always left Six Six Five feeling sickened and dirty when they stopped on her, as they did now. "And Earth's enemies," Codgson said, holding her gaze, "are those who fail to win. Earth's enemies," he went on, "are the *weak*. The *unprepared*. The *fearful*. *They* are the ones who handed over Humanity's children to the Draft, and *they* are the ones we need to remove from our ranks as thoroughly as possible." Codgson gave Six Six Five that same weird little smile as he watched her, then turned and continued to scan the rest of the ranks. "Starting today."

Six Six Five's little feeling of dread was morphing into something all-consuming, something eating into the tiny crevices of her soul, etching out a raw and painful interior. All around her, her batchmates seemed to be hovering on their toes, ready, *eager* to prove themselves. Yet watching Codgson, listening to him talk, remembering the two dying boys, gurgling in their own blood, Six Six Five wanted to be anywhere else. *He's going to cull me this time*, she thought, swallowing down the urge to back out of formation, to run back to her room to hide. *He's waited all year and now he's going to cull me.*

Looking out the corner of her eyes at her bigger, stronger, more confident batchmates, Six Six Five thought about how she was the smallest one in the room. A runt. The doctors had said so.

No, she mentally shook herself. *You have to be strong. They cull you if you aren't strong.*

That had become her mantra over the last few months. Ever since Six Six Five had seen what was behind that little door on the end of the hall, she had repeated it to herself as she fell asleep each night. The strong survived. Codgson always said the strong survived.

…yet Six Six Five wasn't strong.

"We will begin with something simple," the colonel went on casually. He gestured to one of his ever-present white-clad assistants, who quickly went to the door and let in a long line of technicians, each with a small cage in his or her hand. Six Six Five immediately recognized them as the hamsters that they had been given just after their seventh birthdays, one year before. Even from that distance, she could see Charlie in his huge, four-times-the-size cage being carried by a big soldier. She saw his big white shape dancing around inside, anxiety in his twitching nose. Charlie hated it when someone moved his cage. His cage was his *home…*

The cages were brought inside and stacked along the wall, just as they had been stacked along the wall many months before, that day they'd gotten to pick their pets. Most of the children were smiling, finding their pets amongst the group, excited to see their friends. Only Six Six Five continued to stare directly at Charlie, unable to look away. Dread was consuming her that Charlie was up front, near Colonel Codgson. People near Colonel Codgson died.

Not Charlie, she thought. *Please not Charlie.*

"Lieutenant, if you would bring me the hat?" Codgson asked.

One of the technicians quickly handed Codgson a jar filled with little white slips of paper, then ducked back out of sight.

"Now," Codgson said, holding up the jar, "here we have a list of names. Every one of your names is included." He shook the glass so that the little papers slid around in a shuffle. "I'm going to draw a name from the hat and read it off. When I do, I want you to come forward."

Six Six Five's heart was hammering so hard she was finding it hard to breathe. *No*, she thought. *No, no, no, no…*

Codgson smiled at them and withdrew a name. He unfolded the slip of paper. "Six Seven Nine. Step out of formation and come up here."

A girl who had trouble with her roundhouses briskly stepped out of line. She jogged up to stand in front of Colonel Codgson and clicked her heels together, her hands tightly behind her back.

"Six Seven Nine," Colonel Codgson said, "go get your hamster's cage from the wall and put it on the floor in front of me."

Six Seven Nine immediately ran to the wall, though she was hesitant in bringing the cage back in front of Colonel Codgson. She set it down slowly, nervousness lining her face.

Colonel Codgson smiled down at the little black hamster. "What's your hamster's name, Six Seven Nine?"

Six Seven Nine swallowed, blue eyes fixed on her hamster. Tentatively, she said, "Kung Fu."

Colonel Codgson continued to give her that lifeless grin. "Do you like your hamster, Six Seven Nine?"

"Yes, sir!" Six Seven Nine cried, much more enthusiastically.

The colonel nodded, still smiling. "If you had to choose between killing your hamster and killing a batchmate, which would you kill?"

Six Seven Nine froze.

"Keeping in mind," Colonel Codgson said, "your batchmates can fight back and kill *you*. With your hamster, it would be as simple as dunking him in a bucket of water." He gestured to the bucket that had been left beside the cages.

"I…" Six Seven Nine swallowed. She glanced over her shoulder at the rest of her batch. Her voice shook when she whispered, "Do I get to pick?"

"No," Colonel Codgson said. "If you refuse to kill your hamster, I get to pick who you have to kill, instead."

"I have to kill a batchmate?" Six Seven Nine asked.

"No," Colonel Codgson said. "You have to kill either your hamster or your batchmate." He was still smiling, but there was a coldness that was working its way into Six Six Five's chest, making it hard to breathe.

Kill the hamster, Six Six Five thought desperately. *He wants you to say your batchmate…*

"But I don't want to kill Kung Fu," Six Seven Nine whimpered. "Can I be a doctor, instead? Six Two One said she was going to be a doctor…"

"You have to choose," Codgson said sweetly. "Your hamster or a batchmate."

Six Seven Nine glanced behind her again. She swallowed, then glanced down at the cage at her feet. "I'll kill a batchmate."

Codgson gave a satisfied smile. "Six Five Five, get up here."

At first, Six Six Five thought he had said *her*, but then she heard the big boots of Six Five Five, the batch bully, jogging to the front of formation. The huge soldier was almost twice as big as the rest, and he came to stand beside Six Seven Nine with a sharp click of his heels. Immediately, Six Seven Nine's eyes went wide and she took an unconscious step backwards.

"Six Five Five, your batchmate wants to kill you," Colonel Codgson said. "She'd kill you over a *hamster*. What do you have to say about that?"

"N-n-no," Six Seven Nine whimpered. "I d-d-didn't w-w-want to f-fight *him*."

Six Five Five's face beamed in a confident grin. "I'd kill her first, sir."

"Six Seven Nine," Codgson said, "do you still want to kill your batchmate?"

"No," Six Seven Nine babbled, "no sir. I want to kill Kung Fu, sir."

Codgson's lips twisted in a cold smile. "But you already made your choice. Six Five Five, kill Six Seven Nine, then kill Kung Fu."

"Yes, sir," Six Five Five barked, grinning. Even as Six Seven Nine was gasping and trying to back away, the big boy reached out, grabbed her by the head, and twisted so hard that Six Six Five heard the pop from across the room. Six Seven Nine jerked, then fell stiffly to the ground, her body twitching in spasms.

Immediately, Six Five Five dropped to his knees, reached into the cage, grabbed the hamster in a big, meaty fist, and squeezed until Six Six Five heard Kung Fu's tiny shriek—cut short when his ribcage snapped. Six Five Five threw the lifeless body on top of the cage and stood, once more locking his hands behind him as he faced Colonel Codgson.

"How did it feel to kill your batchmate, Five Five?" Codgson asked.

"I didn't feel anything, sir," Six Five Five said, staring straight ahead.

"Excellent. Go back to formation," Codgson said.

Six Five Five did as he was told.

To the formation, Codgson said, "Six Seven Nine was weak. She couldn't even kill an *animal*. How could we expect her to kill *aliens*?

If you can't kill, you are *not a soldier*. You are worthless. Soldiers kill. Soldiers are like Six Five Five. They don't feel. They don't *care*. They do what they're *told*." He shoved the body with his foot, rolling it across the floor. "Lieutenant, get this disgusting thing out of my sight." As three techs raced up to grab the body and the cage, Codgson calmly reached into his little jar and pulled out another name. Reading it, he said, "Six Eight Three, get up here."

This time, no one stepped out of line for several long breaths.

Codgson cocked his head, then read the slip again. "Six Eight Three?" When still no one responded, his curious black eyes searched the ranks, stopping on a red-faced boy who was sweating. He smiled. "There you are. Get up here, Eight Three."

Very reluctantly, Six Eight Three went to the front of the formation and hesitated, tears in his eyes. His hands were shaking.

"Go get your hamster, Six Eight Three," Colonel Codgson said gently.

Though he didn't say a word, Six Eight Three stumbled towards the cages, tears streaming down his face. He picked up a cage, then came back, though he continued to hold the cage in his arms, hyperventilating.

"Put the cage down," the colonel said.

Very slowly, more out of training to do as he was told than any visible willingness on his part, Six Eight Three set the cage at his feet.

"What's your hamster's name, Six Eight Three?" Codgson asked.

"Peanut," the boy whispered.

"Do you like Peanut?" Colonel Codgson asked, oozing concern.

"Yes," the boy choked.

"I'll offer you the same choice," Colonel Codgson said. "You can kill Peanut, or you can kill a batchmate."

"Hamster," Six Eight Three croaked.

The colonel cocked his head. "I'm sorry," Codgson said. "What was that?"

"I'll kill Peanut," Six Eight Three managed.

The smile that spread across Codgson's face set fire to the hatred within Six Six Five's being. "Then what are you waiting for?" He gestured behind him. "Six Five Five was able to kill a hamster with his bare hands, but there's a bucket over there, if you would rather drown him. Unfortunately, that will take longer."

Six Eight Three's fingers shook so badly that when he took Peanut from his cage and carried him over to the bucket, as soon as he shoved the hamster under the water, he jerked his hand back out and dropped him. Six Six Five wasn't sure if it was intentional or not, but as soon as he did, Colonel Codgson's eyes darkened. "Six Five Five—"

"I'll get him!" Six Eight Three gasped. "I'll get him!" He got on his knees and scooped up the soggy hamster, whose little pink legs were flailing. Six Eight Three drove him under the water, crying. "He's biting me!" he whimpered. "He's *biting* me!"

"They'll do that," Codgson said, watching with that eerie smile. "Don't bring him back up until he stops struggling, or you'll just have to do it all over again."

Six Eight Three remained with his arm in the bucket for what seemed like minutes before he pulled his dead hamster from within. Sobbing, now, he gently laid the hamster on the concrete beside the bucket and started stroking its sodden fur.

"Excellent," Codgson said. "Return to formation. Next!" As Six Eight Three numbly got back to his feet and moved back toward formation, the colonel stuck his hand into the jar and pulled another name.

Six Six Five closed her eyes as he read off the name, willing it not to be her.

Six Six Five didn't actually hear the name that was called—she just knew it wasn't her because a girl sobbed and stepped out of line at Codgson's gentle urging.

The girl, too, chose her hamster. And the next. And the next.

Then Codgson read a name that made Six Six Five's heart stop. She glanced down at her hands, unable to stop them from shaking. She looked at Charlie.

"Six Six Five," Codgson said, his voice oozing pleasure. "The *prodigy*. Come up here, please."

Six Six Five's feet felt wooden as she stepped out of line and went to the front of formation. She stood there looking at Charlie, wondering if he knew what was happening to him. He was leaning back on his hind feet and sniffing at the top of his cage, his little pink eyes curious as they scanned the room.

"I *said*," Codgson snapped, "what is your hamster's name?"

Six Six Five tore her eyes from Charlie and looked up at the colonel. He knew she had a rabbit, not a hamster. He had tried to take it from her as soon as he found out hers was different than everybody else's, but Doctor Molotov had overrode him. Indeed, the colonel was watching her with that coldly smug smile, daring her to contradict him.

Anger flared again within her. "My rabbit's name is Charlie," Six Six Five said softly, barely able to form the words.

"I'm sorry," Colonel Codgson said. "What was your *hamster's* name, soldier?"

Seeing how much he enjoyed himself, seeing his pleasure at her pain, something snapped in the back of Six Six Five's head. Her fear had become something more, something a thousand times stronger, something that burned like a floodlight within the darkness. Six Six Five gave him a long look, her emotions draining away like water through a sieve. "My hamster's name is Charlie," she said, the tremor completely gone from her voice.

Codgson smiled, not catching the difference in her demeanor. "And do you like your hamster, Six Six Five?"

"Yes," Six Six Five said. "That's why I'm not going to kill him."

Colonel Codgson's face shifted in an instant of uncertainty before his smooth confidence was back. "Then, instead of killing your hamster, you're going to kill a batchmate?"

Six Six Five glanced over her shoulder at Six Five Five, who was even then starting to grin with anticipation. "Yes," she said, turning back to look up at the colonel. *And then I'm going to kill you.*

Again, the colonel's confidence slipped for just an instant. He regarded her for much too long, an odd curiousness on his face. Six Six Five returned his gaze fearlessly, her terror having been dissolved by the greenish fog that was even then filling her vision, giving her a 360-degree view of the room around her. With it, she felt every molecule, every movement all around her, the ebb and flow, the swaying of particles in all directions, the flakes and hairs and rotating mountains carried on breezes or breaths or evaporating sweat.

"Do you hear that, Six Five Five?" Colonel Codgson finally demanded. "Six Six Five wants to kill you over a *hamster*."

In formation, Six Five Five chuckled.

"Come up here and neutralize this piece of shit for me, will you?" Colonel Codgson said, still holding Six Six Five's gaze.

Happily, Six Five Five stepped out of formation. He took three steps before his head imploded. Along with his chest. And his pelvis. And his legs. And his larynx. And his arms. And his feet. The sound he made as he died was a lot like the hamster he had killed with his fist. The body that hit the floor was smaller than it had been before, and it slid into a pool of its own liquids—brown, yellow, and red.

There was a moment of total surprise on Colonel Codgson's face before he snapped, "Ice her! Ice her *now!*"

Still in a world beyond fear, Six Six Five turned to face him. She wrapped her mind around Colonel Codgson's greenish fog and began to squeeze...

The soldiers that were constantly watching for aliens while *facing* them raised their guns and Six Six Five heard little popping sounds. A sharp prick in her back made her flinch, then another in her arm. Another came in the flesh of her neck. Even as she started to squeeze the fog and make Codgson scream, her hold weakened, and the green fog of his head began to slide through her mental grip.

No, she thought, watching Codgson straighten and drop his hands from his head, his smug smile sliding back into place. *No!* Then her grasp on her war-mind slipped completely, and her world lost the depth, the extra dimension that had allowed her to feel the very essence of Codgson's screaming face.

Codgson took two steps toward her and backhanded her with a gloved fist. Then, when her head jerked back and she fell, he kicked her in the face.

"Someone get this worthless piece of shit to the sleep room," was the last thing Six Six Five heard before the Void absorbed her, swallowing her awareness in a wash of pain and darkness.

• • •

"Soot, she's dreaming again. Any chance you could give her a shot of mind-numbing goodness?"

She's had enough people play with her mind. I'm not going to make it worse.

"Mother's talons, furg, she could kill us all!"

So could I.

"Yeah, but she's burning insane."

No. She's just remembering…

• • •

Six Six Five came to awareness on her back, her arms and legs strapped to the cold metal beneath her. When she tried to sit up, she saw a clear plastic bag hanging from a rack above her, and a little plastic tube trailed down from the bottom of the bag to the top of her wrist, where it was secured there with thick tape. The room around her was cool, like the inside of Doctor Molotov's refrigerator. When Six Six Five looked at the door, she saw that it was blue. Immediately, a whine of terror began building in her throat as she tried ineffectually to jerk free of the frigid steel table.

"Yeah, I know," a young male voice said boredly, "this just isn't your day. Well, I'm right there with ya, sister. They called me off *vacation* for this shit. Don't see why they couldn't just have a thug pound your cute little head in or something. They got more than enough grunts with ego problems running around to do it. Don't know why they gotta go waste *my* time for just *one* lousy cull."

When Six Six Five turned to look up at the speaker, she saw that the blue-clad doctor was holding a syringe. He was tapping it and squeezing the plunger, getting the air bubble out.

"I mean," the man continued, concentrating on the tip of the needle, "it's not like it's rocket science. There's a drawer with syringes right over there. There's vials of kill-juice on the shelf above the alcohol wipes. The saline's just a formality the desk-jockey bureaucrats insist on. Something to make me feel like I didn't actually do the deed, 'cause it takes longer, ya know?" He gave a derisive snort. "I don't fucking care about killing kids. Kids, chimps, rabbits…All the same to me. Give me the choice, kids are easier, 'cause someone else cleans up the mess afterwards. Besides. Why wait an hour when you can just find a vein, deliver the payload, and go home to dinner? Not that my lazy bitch of a wife would actually make me dinner, but still…It's all such a waste of *time*."

"Please don't kill me," Six Six Five whispered, staring up at him in terror.

The man with the syringe froze, peering down at her over the needle. For a long moment, the just looked at each other. Then he gave a little frown and went back to tapping the plastic. "I mean," he said, making one final squirt of the syringe and then walking over to the bag, "I charge fifteen hundred credits an hour. *Fifteen hundred*. Talk about government waste. All it takes is a hammer and a strong arm. Like clubbing a baby harp seal, sans the designer hat afterwards."

"Please don't kill me, sir," Six Six Five repeated, cringing away from the tube plugging the back of her wrist.

He smiled and reached up to touch the needle to the little plug on the bag. "I'm not gonna kill you, kid." His voice was soothing. "Now lie there and close your eyes and shut up. That's an order." He went back to what he was doing and started to whistle.

"Yes you *are*!" Six Six Five shrieked, panicking as the needle found its target. "I *saw* you. You killed all the rest! You're an *ailo*! Just like Colonel Codgson." Her last accusation came out on a sob.

The doctor froze, the tip of the needle against the plastic of the bag. Then, slowly, his brown brows drew together and he lowered the needle from the plug. Instead of releasing her, however, he said, "I'm not at *all* like that pompous shit. I have a triple doctorate from Harvard. *He's* got a B.S. from a crap public school and convinced his friend's dad to fake his IQ test." The doctor cocked his head. "But I totally agree with you on the ailo part. He's one psychotic monkey. *Just* the sort of sicko they need running this joint. If I didn't need the money, I would've slipped him something fun *years* ago." The man lowered the needle to a table behind him and jumped up to sit on it, facing her, a curious look on his face. "So is it true you almost killed the arrogant prick? Made him scream? I would've *paid* to see Codgson scream."

"Please don't kill me," Six Six Five whispered again.

The blue-clad man sighed. "You're just a *number*, kid. Of course I'm going to kill you. But if you're entertaining enough, I'll make it later, rather than sooner. I mean, I *was* on vacation, but it was with my prudish piglet of a wife and her undead family. They were playing *Trivial Pursuit* when I got the call. Do you know how much I *hate* that game?" He started kicking his feet. "It's *boring*. I win every time. I can't *not* win, you know? But I play their games, 'cause if I don't, they do something worse like sing Christmas carols. So, instead of winning all the time, like I should, because I'm *smarter*, the good *doctor* makes it a point to let them win one or two times out of three to keep their stupid little pea brains from thinking I need to do something more involving, like *Twister* or charades." He snorted, shaking his head with clear amusement. "My wife actually thinks she's smarter than me, the poor, stupid cow. She also thinks I work at a shoe manufacturing plant and drive a Honda." He cocked his head at Six Six Five, grinning. "Guess I don't need to tell you how fucked up *that* particular assumption is. Doctor Fucking Kevorkian, at your service, sweetcheeks."

"I could be a doctor," Six Six Five babbled. "Or an assistant. You don't need to kill me."

The blue-clad man snorted. "You're not smart enough to be a doctor. No offense, but they don't breed you furgs for your brains. You could probably carry a tablet around, though. You wanna be a tech? Clean halls and change out toilet paper?" He grinned at her with that adult-humoring-the-kids smile. "You could probably change out toilet paper."

"Yes," Six Six Five said quickly. "I'll do that. I don't want to be a soldier."

The doctor chuckled. "Yeah, I'll bet you'd do that." He idly rolled the syringe around on the table beside his thigh with a thoughtful finger. Then he started kicking his legs again as he watched her, considering. "You ever sucked cock, girl?"

"No, but I'll do that, too," Six Six Five said quickly, having absolutely no idea what he was asking, but willing to do anything to avoid that needle entering her bag.

He seemed to consider. "My wife turned forty and she became the fucking Ice Queen. I got suspicious, so I had her followed. Bitch was cheating on me with a banker. Because he had *money*." He gave another derisive snort. "Dumb oaf drowned in his oatmeal the next morning—real tragedy, there—and I think I'm gonna do her in a few months, once the insurance policy's been around a few years. Less suspicion, that way. Until then, I've gotta deal with the Addams Family." The doctor sighed, giving her a long look. "Damn, I miss good head. Got it from a couple bots in a parlor, but it's just not the same." He glanced at his watch. "We've got some time. No one's down here but Doctor Molotov. Everyone else left already. You wanna suck, now's your chance."

"Okay," Six Six Five said quickly, expecting him to let her up so she could start up her new duties immediately.

He peered at her for much too long. "Nah," he finally said, shoving himself off the table. "You'd be just as bad as a fucking bot. Last thing I want clinging to my dick. 'This enough pressure, sir?' 'This fast enough, sir?' 'Should I suck harder, sir?'" Grunting, he picked up the needle once more.

Six Six Five, who had been convinced he would release her, took in a startled breath. "What are you doing? You said I could help you."

He laughed and once again grabbed the translucent plastic bag. "Yeah, maybe," he said, sounding distracted. "Then again, maybe you'd bite. Or maybe someone would catch me. They get weird about that kind of shit. I mean, you're dead anyway, but if I get a little *fun* out of you first, that suddenly makes me the bad guy." He shook his head and shoved the needle through the membrane.

"Please!" Six Six Five cried, her breath coming in tiny pants as she watched the syringe. "Please let me live!"

"Meh. Probably would've been a lame blow anyway." The plunger depressed.

Seeing the black rubber stopper shove its payload into her veins, Six Six Five screamed and started to thrash against her restraints, losing control to the total panic that was suddenly riding her tendons, tearing her muscles, loosening her bowels.

"Oh chill out," the man chuckled, withdrawing the needle and tossing it into a red bin marked SHARPS. "You've got another few minutes, at least." He checked his watch and fiddled with the timer. Then he yawned and pulled out a small personal tablet. Casually returning to his seat on a nearby gurney, he started tapping the screen, producing pleasant little electronic crunches followed by *plops* that sounded like water droplets.

"Please," Six Six Five babbled, straining her fists against the metal clamps holding them in place. "Please don't kill me. I'll be a good soldier. I swear. I won't talk back to Colonel Codgson again. I'll kill the aliens. Please let me kill the aliens."

"We don't really need you," the man grunted, not taking his attention from his tablet. "We've got Twelve-A—whoa!" he cried, lifting up his tablet to show her rows of what looked like ice cubes and a tortoise. "I just made it past level *ten*." He grinned at her like he expected her to share in his excitement.

When she didn't, he made a disgusted sound. "Might as well be a bot." He went back to his ice-munching tortoise.

Six Six Five stared at him, her heart hammering a staccato in her chest, her hands trembling from either the adrenaline or the drugs—she couldn't tell which. Realizing he really was going to just sit there and play games while she died, Six Six Five said, "When you meet with the obscure, honorless death you deserve, and you take your shameful existence to taint the next realm, I hope your ancestors find you, skin you, use your diseased leather to clothe Takki, bury your tek in the bowels of its master, and send your hideless corpse through the ninety hells alone."

The man froze, frowning at his tablet. Very slowly, he lifted his head to peer at her like she had just said she hoped the aliens would win. "*What* did you just say?"

"I said I hope you die," Six Six Five said, trembling all over.

"No," he said, looking at her in growing nervousness. He set his tablet down and stood up. She could see the hairs raised on his arms. "What you just said. Before that. What language was that?"

"Let me go!" Six Six Five shrieked, flailing against the metal table. She was definitely starting to shake, now, and it didn't have anything to do with adrenaline.

"Goddammit, kid," the man snapped. "Who taught you to talk like that? Is there a spy down here? One of the techs?!"

"Help!" Six Six Five screamed. "*Heellllllp!*"

"Listen, you little bitch," the man in blue snarled, reaching out to grab her by the collar and drag her up from the table until her arms were pinned painfully by the metal bands. "What you just said. What language was that? Who taught you? You been talking to Huouyt? There a fucking Huouyt in this installation?"

"Help!" Six Six Five sobbed, thrashing. "Please help me. Somebody." Not all of the flailing was her own doing, either. Her muscles were starting to spasm, and she knew she was getting culled. Just like Six Two One, just like Pizza, just like the kid with his own guts exposed to the air, she was dying, and there was nothing she could do about it...

You are a cull, Colonel Codgson had whispered in her ear, almost tenderly. *You just don't know it yet.*

"Answer me!" the doctor snapped.

"*No*," Six Six Five whimpered, as her eyes started to jerk and twitch, her body spasming around her. "Please no."

"Please no *what*?" he snarled. "I swear to God, if there's a damned Huouyt down here…" He reached out and kinked the line leading to her wrist with one hand as he jerked her even closer with the other. "Which one is he? He's that fucking Codgson, isn't it? I knew that ailo creep was too psycho even for *this* project. He a plant? Which side he working for? That why he keeps killing the clones? Is he a Congie?"

Six Six Five blinked up at him, realizing she had been spared, at least temporarily, but having no idea what he was asking. "I…"

The blue door slammed open to reveal a feminine form standing in the doorway. Doctor Molotov quickly sized up the situation, blinked when she saw Six Six Five on the bed, then stormed inside and yanked the tube out of Six Six Five's arm.

"What the hell is this?" Doctor Molotov demanded, placing her fingers on Six Six Five's face, prying her eyelid open and flashing a light into Six Six Five's eye. Six Six Five felt herself shivering uncontrollably. "How much did you give her?" Molotov demanded.

"Probably a tenth of the dose so far," the blue-clad doctor said, frowning. "Why?"

"This soldier was allocated for Phil's S.H.A.E.L. program," Doctor Molotov said, her voice curt. "I signed off on it personally. She was supposed to be delivered this afternoon, but never arrived. Who authorized a cull?"

The blue-clad doctor released Six Six Five and turned to blink down at Doctor Molotov in confusion. "Colonel Codgson delivered her and her orders to me personally, Doctor. Her chart says cull. Shit, he wrote it in red marker across the whole damn chart. I didn't think there could have been a mistake." As Six Six Five lay there, shivering, he went to the end of her table and retrieved a chart, then handed it to Doctor Molotov, who glanced at it with narrowed eyes.

"Codgson," she said coolly, "has a toddler's attention span and the IQ of a pimple. That might as well have been fucking crayon,

Doctor." She abruptly dropped the chart on a nearby table as Six Six Five continued to spasm. "What's her chance of survival?

"Her?" the doctor glanced down at Six Six Five in confusion. "Oh, ninety percent, easy. Its main ingredient is just a muscle relaxant. Stops the heart." He gave a little frown. "Say, her memory restructuring hasn't already begun, has it?"

Doctor Molotov snorted. "Apparently, she's been with *you* all this time, so no." She cocked her head, then glanced at the empty beds. "How long *have* you been here, doctor? Your timesheet showed you arriving four hours ago."

The other doctor reddened. "I had to prep the intravenous solution and delivery apparatus."

Doctor Molotov gave him a flat look. "For four hours."

"Look, who the hell cares?" the doctor demanded. "No one the fuck else wants to do it, and I've got a damn house payment to make."

"In what," Doctor Molotov demanded, crossing her arms over her chest, "the Hamptons?"

"Oh, fuck you," he muttered. He snatched up his tablet and snagged his jet black leather coat from the wall. "Fuck you. You know one thing I don't like about you?" he demanded, pausing at the exit.

"I don't fudge my timesheet?" Doctor Molotov asked.

"Your self-righteous attitude," he snorted. "I mean, look *around* us, doctor. Look what we *do* for a living. And you're gonna whine about a few extra hours on time sheet?" He shook his head and snorted. "Gimme a call the next time you need me to murder a bunch of your babies." At that, he turned and walked out the door.

"Ailo," Doctor Molotov muttered. She glanced back down at Six Six Five. "How are you hanging in there, soldier?"

"C-c-cold," Six Six Five said, shivering.

Doctor Molotov went over and grabbed a blanket that was draped over one of the other tables and brought it over to her. As she laid it across Six Six Five's body, she said, "I wanted to thank you for not hurting Charlie. He wouldn't have understood, and I am so glad he didn't have to go through that. He'd been through enough, you know?"

"Charlie," Six Six Five whispered, shaking all over. "Can I see Charlie?"

Doctor Molotov gave her a long look, and Six Six Five saw the edges of her mascara beginning to smear again. "No. Charlie's... away...right now. Colonel Codgson didn't plan on you coming back. He...couldn't pass up the opportunity for...a lesson...for the other recruits." Doctor Molotov's voice cracked and she looked away.

Charlie's dead.

The knowledge was so shattering, so utterly final and absolute, that Six Six Five felt her eyes lose focus, her body stop shivering as she stared at the wall, unable to think, unable to feel anything at all.

"Six Five?" Doctor Molotov asked, sounding panicked. "Stay with me, soldier."

"I'm not a soldier," Six Six Five whispered, eyes resting on the stainless steel sink set into the far wall.

Doctor Molotov hesitated. "Yes you are."

"No," Six Six Five said softly. "I'm not going to fight. I want to be a doctor."

For several minutes, Doctor Molotov stared down at her in silence, her chapped fingers holding the blanket in place. Then, softly, she said, "You can't be a doctor."

And, hearing those words from Doctor Molotov's lips, Six Six Five began to cry.

She wasn't sure when it happened, or how, but suddenly, Doctor Molotov's arms were around Six Six Five, and her hands were free to flop underneath her as the doctor rocked her back and forth.

"What are you doing?" Six Six Five whimpered. She liked the doctor's embrace, wanted to *return* it, but it scared her. It wasn't *allowed*.

Into her hair, Doctor Molotov said, "You won't remember this, but I just wanted to tell you there were a dozen times I wished I could have taken you home with me. You're the bravest kid I've ever seen in this program, the *smartest*, and I'm so sorry what happened to you. It wasn't fair. None of this was fair. I didn't understand that when I signed on. I had no idea what the program was really like. I swear to you, I had no idea."

Six Six Five listened, but couldn't bring herself to say anything in response.

"But once I was here, once I was *in*, I had to stay," Doctor Molotov said. "I was the only one keeping the insanity from tearing this place apart. And when it became too much, when I couldn't handle it any more, the general wouldn't let me leave even when I wanted to. He said I had to stay, counter Codgson's crazy…"

Six Six Five heard Doctor Molotov swallow against the top of her head.

"This isn't what I thought I'd be doing with my life," Doctor Molotov said, after what seemed like an eternity. "I thought we would be saving Earth."

"You will," Six Six Five said. "Twelve-A will kill the aliens for you."

Doctor Molotov froze, then slowly pulled away. Her mascara was in narrow black rivulets down her cheeks, but there was a frown on her face. "Did he say that?"

Six Six Five frowned. "No. But everyone says he's your best soldier, and that's why Codgson hates me."

Doctor Molotov gave her a long, apologetic look. "No…The reason Codgson hates you had nothing to do with Twelve-A. You were a different batch that got mixed up with the one he wanted to test—the eleven series. It was a stupid mistake, and he had already fired the tech, but I figured we'd already put the resources into incubating you, so we might as well see what came out. Codgson thought it was a waste of resources from the start."

Six Six Five considered that. "Are you going to put me on ice now?"

Doctor Molotov pulled back completely, looking at her from arm's length. "No. Phil's got a…project. Long-term behavior modification. You were an…ideal candidate." It looked like it was getting harder for Doctor Molotov to speak, and, biting her lip, she turned away to pick up the chart again. She flipped papers for several minutes, then cleared her throat and put the chart down. Briskly, she tapped a button on her wrist and said, "Call Phil Ingles." A moment later, she grimaced. "Yeah, I finally found her. Sleep wing. No, not dead. Charles was padding his timesheet again." She hesitated. "Well, I can't do it. And Codgson's gonna be back at five. If you induct her into the project now, we can get that ball in motion and he'll have to back off. He's got no say in S.H.A.E.L." Doctor Molotov paused for several moments, her frown deepening. "Yeah, screw that. If he comes in there again, just call me. That is *not* under his jurisdiction. He keeps nosing around, we'll just have to go to somebody higher up." She cocked her head slightly. "Okay. I'll see you in half an hour." She reached down and tapped a button on her wrist again.

"Doctor Molotov," Six Six Five asked softly.

The doctor hesitated and reluctantly lifted her head to meet her eyes. "Yes?"

"What is S.H.A.E.L.?"

Doctor Molotov's face trembled with apology. She swallowed, looked away, and visibly steeled herself. When she turned back, she said, "Shael is dreaming again. Mothers' ghosts, don't you have some sort of mental anesthetic or something? She's gonna puree these flakers if they keep getting too close. Can't you tell them to leave? Stay on the *safe* side of camp?"

Shael groaned and opened his eyes. Joedobbs was there, *touching* him again. As Shael lifted his hand to hurl him aside, however, Joedobbs quickly straightened and held up both his palms. "Was just making sure you didn't need help, Shael," he said, much too quickly. "You were yelling in your sleep that you needed help."

Shael flinched and sat up, his great heart hammering in his chest. The fire had burned low and many of the drooling furg-experiments were awake and staring at him from their huddles. The minder was watching him from atop an abandoned Human vehicle, legs crossed beneath him. That Twelve-A ga Test Tube had *again* witnessed his shame was almost enough for Shael to end him right there. The way *everyone* was staring at him, though, stayed his hand.

"How…" Shael cleared his throat, realizing his voice had devolved into a hoarse rasp sometime during the night.

"Here," Joedobbs said, offering a canteen. "Good Voran fire-water. Calms the nerves."

Shael gratefully took the canteen and drank, but couldn't manage to take more than a few sips, again, to his shame. To keep yet another of his failings from showing, Shael hid his shame with, "This drink is the lifeless swill of things with teats." He threw the canteen aside, allowing its contents to spill to the ground. Though unintended, it was almost comical the way Joedobbs rushed to collect it, almost as if he thought the contents precious.

"Well," Joedobbs said, capping the canteen and stuffing it back in his coat, "it certainly isn't Welu sludge, I'll give you that." He eyed Shael with the same wariness one would give a hatchling Dhasha, however. "You feeling better?"

In truth, Shael wanted—*needed*—water, but he kept his weakness from showing. "I am fine."

"Fine, huh?" Joedobbs asked. Unbidden, he sat down on the log facing Shael's pile of blankets—they had been gathering more and more from every empty house they passed, at Shael's direction, and now he had a pile vast enough to bury a kreenit, so many that Shael felt he could even risk sharing his spoils with the drooling furgs they were protecting. "You wanna tell me what you've been dreaming about?"

Instantly, Shael's scales tightened against his skin, resulting in a full-body prickle.

Joedobbs quickly held up his gloved hands in peace. "No biggie! Not my flake to dig around in, after all. Just curious if you needed someone to talk to, you know?"

Shael did—he was *desperate* to know why this woman Six Six Five haunted him—but he would rather eat his own tek than show weakness to a Voran.

A gentle touch on his shoulder made him spin. Twelve-A was standing there with one of the jugs of water that the Voran insisted on carrying around. He wordlessly offered it to Shael. Reluctantly,

Shael took it, grateful for the cool liquid to calm his throat. He drank until his great stomach distended, then wiped his mouth and offered it back.

"So," Joe said, as Twelve-A ga Test Tube reclaimed his water and climbed back to his seat atop the abandoned vehicle. "I guess the question of the day, sunshine, is whether or not you're going to be okay. You're *really* making the two of us nervous. Hell, the mind-furg has actually been waking up before noon to check on you." He gestured behind him at the telepath, but Shael didn't hear anything else. He was suddenly in another place, another time, staring up at a doctor with mussed-up hair and sleep-deprived brown rings under his eyes. He was tapping another syringe, and Shael was strapped into a weird, egg-shaped bed.

He smiled down at Shael as he leaned over the lip of the bed, syringe in hand. *"So I guess the question of the day, sunshine, is whether you're ready to become a Jreet."*

Shael's eyes widened and he screamed.

• • •

"What's a Jreet, Doctor Philip?" Six Six Five asked, confused.

"What he means is it's time for you to take a quick nap," Doctor Molotov said briskly, shooting Doctor Philip a pointed glance.

"What?" Doctor Philip demanded. "It's not like she's going to remember. I'm throwing it on HIGH. Starting completely over. I've got a deadline, and you *know* Codgson's gonna fight to get the program shut down once he finds out you—"

"Finds out she what?" Colonel Codgson demanded, striding into the room. "What, you two ripped your phones from your bodies? We had an emergency four-thirty meeting to discuss Thirteen-Series' weird reaction to antibiotics last night, and neither of you even bothered to send me a no—" he froze upon getting close enough to the scoop-shaped bed to see inside. Instantly, his face darkened. "That better not be what I think it fucking is."

Faced with his hateful scowl, Six Six Five cringed into the bed holding her.

"Six Five is part of the S.H.A.E.L. project now," Doctor Molotov said. "As of this morning. She's no longer in your jurisdiction."

Codgson's face was beginning to redden. "I had her culled."

"Yes, we are all aware of your personal bias concerning Six Six Five," Doctor Molotov said, holding up the clipboard with the big CULL written in blood-red marker across the page. "If you would also remember, I am the medical director on this project. I gave the order to have her reallocated for memory patterning due to her high telekinetic potential. That was *my* decision to make, and when you tried to override it, you were directly going against your orders from the general. You are *not* to intervene in my medical decisions, colonel. Just as I am not to intervene in your…training." Her face twisted with disgust.

Codgson ignored her and continued to stare down at Six Six Five, and for a long moment, she thought he would simply draw his knife and bend down and slit her throat. Instead, slowly, he lifted his head, face tightening in a sneer. "So let me get this straight. You're gonna make the little bitch think she's Jreet. Because you can."

Doctor Philip reddened. "We're going to test the newest tweaks to our machinery, and try to ascertain just how malleable a mind is to the power of suggestion. If it succeeds, we could skip the personnel-heavy training methods we're using now and just raise them in hypnosis beds."

"You're gonna make the little bitch think she's Jreet." This time, Codgson actually sounded…*pleased.* "Because you want her to prove your system works."

"It *does* work. That yours beat my last subject was only due to a lack of preparation. Your challenge was last-minute and I didn't have enough time to work the drugs out of his system."

"War," Codgson sneered, "does not give you an extra thirty minutes to prepare. My recruits needed no such preparation." He grinned down at Six Six Five. "Still, I'd *love* to see you dismantle this little bitch. The moment you think she's ready, I'd be happy to give you another chance to prove yourself. I can think of five that would give her the ass-raping she deserves."

"And again, we come to your personal bias," Doctor Molotov snapped.

"Personal bias?" Codgson snorted. "You intentionally created a place for her so your favorite little bunny-hugger didn't get the axe."

Doctor Philip crossed his arms over his chest and gave Colonel Codgson a challenging look. "I've been requesting another test subject every day for three weeks. Each time Doctor Molotov gives the go-ahead for a transfer, you kill the subject."

"Because it's an idiotic experiment that will never work," Codgson growled, still staring down at Six Six Five. "Machinery can *never* replace true Human guidance."

"Worried about your job security, Colonel?" Doctor Philip challenged.

Codgson laughed, but didn't lift his thoughtful gaze from Six Six Five. "One of mine—trained by *real* battle and *real* stresses of war would take out one of your mind-numbed morons any day. And has. If you want to raise another loser for a face-off, by all means."

"Mine are utterly stable inside their war-minds," Doctor Philip retorted. "Something *you* still have yet to achieve."

Codgson snickered. "True. I *control* mine's use of their war-minds. Make it a tool. You…" he looked Doctor Philip up and down in disdain, "…hand them the button for the nuke."

"I guess we'll see which project has more merit once Phil completes his restructuring," Doctor Molotov challenged. She hesitated. "That is…if you really want to chance being around Six Six Five again once Phil's trained her in her war-mind. Something could go… wrong. Certain…memories…may be hard to bury. They might… *resurface.*"

Codgson's face soured. He lifted his cold black eyes to Doctor Philip, who continued to give him a smug look, then Doctor Molotov, who was lifting her chin in challenge. "You know," he said, with a calm smile, "I know *so* many people who have died in car bombs. It's really quite sad."

Doctor Molotov took a step towards him and said, "And I know *so* many people who have died of an insulin overdose. Completely untraceable, especially if the medical examiner overlooks the entry point. So sad. *So* sad."

"Don't forget," Doctor Philip said, his arms over his chest, "A solution of radioactive isotopes. I've had *so* many people I know just randomly swallow gallons of the stuff. *Really* hard to diagnose."

Codgson's eyes narrowed. "I have an entire compound of soldiers who would execute you both on my order."

"And you haven't made any friends on the medical staff," Doctor Philip said. He smiled. "Let's just hope one of your 'soldiers' doesn't actually manage to damage you enough that you need treatment. Or, say, you get a sandwich filled with glass powder and staph infection. An absolute *riot* break out over who could treat you. Wouldn't that be fun."

"Very fun," Doctor Molotov said. "I'm sure Charles would love to get in on the rush to help you."

"Oh, *that* drug-juggling furg would jump at the chance. What do you think he would use to help the colonel first? Oxygenation? Arsenic?"

"Too clean," Molotov said. "Hyper-Ebola would be more his style. I hear he took a recent trip to Africa to study the monkeys there."

"Isn't that the one where they start bleeding from the eyes and shitting out their own intestines in the first sixteen hours?"

"And it's *horribly* contagious," Molotov agreed. "Could be transmitted through...say...a toilet seat."

"Or a favorite travel mug," Doctor Philip added.

"Fuck you," Codgson said.

Both the doctors smiled at him coolly.

"Colonel," Doctor Molotov said into the following silence, as Colonel Codgson just stood there, reddening, "a note from your medical staff: We're smarter than you. *Please* keep pissing us off."

"Fuck you," Codgson said again. He looked like he would say more, face a dark shade of purple. But then, without another word, he turned and left.

Doctor Philip immediately dropped his arms from his sides. "Twenty bucks he goes and kills another kid," he sighed.

"God I hate that bastard," Doctor Molotov muttered.

"Needs a good dirt nap," Doctor Philip agreed. Both he and Doctor Molotov turned to look down at Six Six Five, who was still lying in place, strapped to her half-egg of a bed. They studied her in silence a moment.

"Take good care of Six Five," Doctor Molotov eventually said. "I know you're trying to beat out Codgson, but don't rush it. She's special...and she isn't any good to us dead." Then she glanced at her watch. "Damn. Morning formation's in twenty. I've gotta go run damage control."

"Sure thing." Doctor Philip waited until she had left, heels clicking as she crossed the tile, then turned back to Six Six Five. "Well," he said, on a huge sigh. He retrieved his syringe and leaned down to stick it into Six Six Five's arm. "Let's see if we can turn you into a Jreet..."

"Shael! Shael, goddamn it, *Shael*!" The Voran's voice broke through his terror, yanking him from yet another of the horrible dreams.

Shael opened his eyes with a groan, struggling to focus on the beard-stubbled face in front of him. "Voran?" he whimpered.

The Voran, who had been holding him, quickly dropped him and scrambled back, arms up in peace. "Just checking on you!" he cried, sounding more than a little nervous. "You were yelling in your sleep again..." He swallowed. "We're good, right?"

Shael, despite the shame of being comforted by a Voran, actually craved the contact. It felt like something he'd been missing... something he'd been denied for much too long. Even as Beda ga Vora rubbed the back of his neck anxiously, Shael cleared his throat and glanced down at his lap. He knew what Beda ga Vora was thinking—that their relationship had taken a step beyond that of fellow warriors and campmates, and that soon one of them would have to duel the other for the right to keep his tek.

Shael had no delusions of exactly who would lose such a match. He stared at his coils, Six Six Five's terror still clawing at his chest, electrifying his limbs and body. Unexpectedly, the pain in his throat brought wetness to his eyes, and he sat there, the world a blur around him, trying to imagine what it might be like to be female. Was that what Six Six Five's dreams were trying to tell him? To prepare him for that horrible fate?

He wasn't a warrior. Not like Beda ga Vora. Despite everything he'd tried, he had not regained his strength. He hadn't regrown his scales or his tek. He couldn't *fight*. He was a warrior that couldn't *fight*. All he could do, as the Voran had jeered, was fling weaklings around with his war-mind. *Anyone* could do that. It was as he spiraled into that endless void of despair when Twelve-A gently reached out to him and said, *Remember what I told Six Six Five as he closed the lid?*

Shael closed his eyes, shuddering as Doctorphilip's words haunted him. *"Let's see if we can turn you into a Jreet..."* He remembered his terror as the needle sank into his arm. He remembered the lid closing, the sounds and images all around him, the inability to turn his head and look away. He remembered the Black Jreer on the screen in front of him, begging him to help her, to seek out this new race called Humanity...

Suddenly, Twelve-A was kneeling before him, holding both his cheeks with slender fingers, forcing Shael to look up into his utterly pure blue eyes. *Remember what I told you?*

...You?

For a moment, Shael couldn't understand what Twelve-A was trying to say.

Remember what I said to you as Doctor Philip closed the lid? Twelve-A insisted.

He was talking about him. *Shael.*

Shael jerked in horror, but didn't pull away. He frowned at the telepath, reflexively wrapping himself in his war-mind. Had he just tried to insinuate that Shael had been in the room? That he had *witnessed* this injustice and had done nothing about it? That he had been a *part* of it?

If the telepath realized or cared that Shael was only a ninth from obliterating him for the insult, he gave no outward appearance of it. His azure eyes intently focused on Shael's face, Twelve-A said, *Remember what I said when he locked you in the machine?*

When he locked...*Shael*...in the machine? True, the machine had looked very similar to the bed that Shael had used to save the weaklings around him from the thrashings in his sleep. Oddly, that thought brought with it a sudden rush of memories that strained Shael's being, threatening to shatter his core, and Shael floundered in their midst, desperate to hold them back.

"I don't want to remember," Shael whimpered.

Try, Twelve-A begged of him.

Shael swallowed, hard. He closed his eyes against the ache in his chest, the rawness in his throat, the churning in his gut. He felt as if his world had imploded, a delicate tower of scales that had been slapped to the ground around him. Now he felt adrift, anchorless, *afraid*...

Please try, Twelve-A asked softly. *You're so very close.*

Shael shivered in his grip, but did not pull away. Something was happening to him in his very spirit, something overwhelming, something so *profound* that, once it tipped him over that dangerous edge, spilling him into the endless rift that now faced him, he would never be able to go back. His whole body felt afire with some inner truth, something deep and desperate to emerge. He felt it surging upward, tugged out of his being on a rising tide of understanding...

"I've got a good shot of whiskey, if that would help chill her out," Joedobbs offered. "It helps me. Total obliteration in like two tics."

Shael frowned, recognizing the Earthling-speak...and that he could understand it. Was he offering to give *Alice* whiskey? Surely he knew the budding warrior was too young...

Ignore the furg, Twelve-A insisted, holding Shael's head when he blinked and tried to turn. *Remember what I told you.*

"That is, if the leprechaun will let you drink whiskey," Joe added wryly, in Jreet. "What's he doing to you, anyway?"

Twelve-A's forehead pinched, but he never took his eyes from Shael's. *Think back to that moment when Doctor Philip was closing Six Six Five in the bed. I told you something. Something important...*

Shael felt his body start to shake, trembling like one of the delicate Earth leaves in an arctic Welu breeze. He felt his consciousness start to shift, much like it did when he took to his war-mind, but on a deeper, much more basic level. He felt that hidden part of himself start to surface from the dark pool of his being, terrifying in its intensity...

"Well," Joedobbs said, heaving a huge sigh of regret. "So much for the blankets."

The sense of an impending explosion subsided on a cold rush of dread. Shael jerked out of Twelve-A's grip and twisted to look over at the Voran's feet. He froze, aghast, when he saw the devastation that had been wreaked upon their camp. Everything within three rods of him—even the blankets—had been shredded. "The *blankets*," Shael gasped, his chest wracked with paralyzing horror at the loss.

Beside him, Twelve-A heaved a huge, audible sigh and gave Jocdobbs an irritated look, then abruptly got up and wandered off. Still standing above Shael, Jocdobbs frowned at the minder's departing back. "What?" he cried.

The telepath found a spot with a cluster of People just at the edge of the ring of firelight and lay down with his back to them, ignoring the Voran completely.

"Pointy-eared furgling," Joe muttered, scowling at the minder. To Shael, he demanded, "What did I say?"

But Shael was staring at the ruined blankets scattered around them in open-mouthed dismay. They had been *his to protect*. Valued treasures...and Shael had *destroyed* them. The Sisters themselves would shun him for a thousand turns of the Coil for such sacrilege. Word of his failure would be sung in battle-song for ages, his name called in the heat of battle by Vorans and Aezi alike, a symbol to be scorned by every Jreet of every clan to the end of time. He would be able to face no other Jreet without mockery, could not even return to the head of his clan out of humiliation for his failure.

"Yeah, you were freaking out in your sleep," Joedobbs said, oblivious to Shael's shame. He cocked his head at Shael, who was clutching the ruined shreds to his chest in disgrace. "You, uh, remember what you were dreaming about? You think that has, uh, any *bearing* on this situation?"

Of course it did. Shael had been given dreams of this Six Six Five as a *warning*. A warning of what it meant to *fail*. What it meant to be culled—to lose his warriorship out of his own lack of resolve. As the Black Jreet had predicted, the Sisters themselves were watching over Shael, sending him messages for his ears alone. Cautions. Admonitions of what would happen to him should he forget who he was, should he lose sight of what it meant to be Welu, to lose hope. To become *female*.

Suddenly, Shael understood.

"I," Shael growled, standing to glare up at Beda ga Vora, "will *never* lose my tek to you, Voran. I would rather writhe in the filth of Dhasha and massage the tentacles of Huouyt than lose my tek to *you*."

Joedobbs blinked down at him, paralyzed by the power of Shael's words. "Uh. Okay."

Over near where the minder had gone to lie down, there was a huge sigh.

Satisfied that they both understood he would *never* back down, *never* surrender to a Voran furg who hoarded scraps of cloth like they were made of ruvmestin, Shael sneered and went to find a weapon. If he had forgotten how to fight due to a few turns of laziness and complacency while trying to train Doctorphilip's frightened, skulking Human cowards, that was nothing that diligence and many hours of practice couldn't remedy...

• • •

(Terror.)

The *strength* of it brought Twelve-A out of the numbing bliss of sleep, back into a world of chronic pain, confusion, and unspeakable sorrow. For several moments, he simply stared at the ceiling of his cell, tired. It hurt to feel, hurt to think, hurt to *exist*. The constant jumble of suffocatingly violent thoughts and cloyingly twisted emotions floated around him like bits of debris in his water dish. He had access to so many minds, could accidentally become *any* of them, and yet *all* of them were broken, hurting, floundering in selfishness and despair, so wrapped in their suffering they were mired in their pain. Just to brush their awarenesses for an instant left an indelible mark within his being, like billions of perpetual fires that each had the capacity to sear away parts of his soul.

Even now, it sank into him, pounding him from all sides. The sickness. The misery. The corruption. The acts of outright ruthlessness and the unnoticed, everyday cruelties. The immigrant hiding in the desert, starving and dehydrated, because he was afraid of the authorities. The factory worker who beat his family because he still felt worthless inside from his own parents' beatings. The old lady who was signing her life savings over to a young man who intended to dump her in a cheap nursing home. The librarian who planned to slit her wrists in the morning. The prison warden who enjoyed punishing his inmates. The bellhop who raped native girls from the Reservation in his off-time. The patron in the next town over who told the young server at McDonalds to keep the change—for a trip to a cosmetic surgeon.... All of it *hurt*, draining him, leeching into his soul, staining his spirit.

(Terror.)

Twelve-A swallowed and tried to remove himself from the cracked, victimized flotsam that was humanity, snapped from his drifting reverie by a powerful pang of fear much nearer to home. Still motionless in his bed, he pulled away from the perpetual hurt of the world, struggling to ignore the pervasive inner agony. He had learned not to make sudden movements when he woke, because they would trigger his cell's motion alarms and the attendants would rush to put him back to sleep.

You could make them sleep, Twelve-A thought. It was a thought he'd had more than once. Dozens of times. Hundreds.

But if he killed *them*, why not *everyone*? The doctors and military personnel running the project weren't the only ones who decayed inside. They weren't the only ones who walked around with gaping tears in their beings, scarred by putrefying wounds they quietly covered with expensive garments, paints, accessories, and perfumes. *Everyone* that he had felt was fragmented, their spirits cracked, bitterness and sickness seeping through the crevices, settling into their very depths, mixing with the pureness there, staining it, and eventually leeching their own rancidity outward, lashing out at those around them. Everyone was desiccated, running on autopilot, throwing up facades rather than showing their true natures, lying rather than telling the truth, hiding rather than give up another ounce of the pureness they managed to protect within.

The scientists and soldiers who ran the project of Twelve-A's creation were simply desperate people, people who had once harbored hope to free themselves from a tyranny, people who now quietly overlooked the actual application of their ideas and did their jobs in mute silence, shielding their souls from the sickness they witnessed because it was all they could do. Because, if they didn't, they would lose their minds to the madness of the world. The madness they had helped to create, to perpetuate.

I could put them all to sleep, Twelve-A thought again, tears leaking from the corners of his eyes, trailing down his cheeks. It would be easy. There was so much pain, so much misery *everywhere* that he didn't delude himself into any kind of 'escape.' It wouldn't matter if he fled to a deserted mountaintop in the furthest reaches of the Arctic, or stranded himself on a lonely island in the Pacific. For him, there *was* no escape. The mental and emotional ache was always there, filling the back of his mind in a constant, rotten drone. Humanity was sick, dying as surely as that man in the desert, too tired to get up and try and find water, forced into its fate by its own choices.

But if Twelve-A silenced the half of Earth he could reach, why stop with half the planet? Why not find a way to reach the continents on the other side and slip the *other* half into that final peace? And once he did that, why stop at Humanity? He had to strain and struggle to pick up the echoes from other planets, but the echoes he had found told of the same miseries, the same hurts, the same conflicts, the same cruelties, just in different forms. If he decided to bring peace to Humanity, why not board one of the ships and move on to the Ooreiki, who were forced to fight and kill when their very souls screamed for peace? Why not end the terrors of the Dhasha, who were trained at birth to disregard the feelings of any other species as insignificant meat? Why not silence the Jahul, whose empathetic, social natures had been twisted into money-making greed? Or the Jreet, who killed their own brothers and sisters in order to survive to adulthood, only to serve fat, selfish politicians to the death? Or the Ueshi, whose short lifespans had twisted their innocent, pleasure-seeking desires into something dirty, dropping most of them into a drug-induced haze for the few turns they actually served out their lives? Or the Huouyt, whose every thought was one of selfish calcu-lation, who thought nothing of stabbing a companion in the back in order to make an acceptable gain?

Why stop with Humans?

That had been the question that stayed his hand, every time. If he silenced the planet, brought peace to his tiny speck in the corner of a single galaxy, why stop there? Why not move on, bringing the peace with him? Why not stop until there was nothing *but* silence?

Because, it seemed, in existing, the sentient creatures of the universe had lost something. In gaining their sense of self, they had abandoned their connection to their world. Of all of the alien minds Twelve-A had brushed thus far, of the entirety of *Congress*, only the Ayhi seemed to be capable of maintaining that gentle awareness, that connection to one's fellow beings…

…and were trod upon by the others for it.

(Terror.)

The pounding spasm of nearby fear assaulted him again and Twelve-A pulled himself further back, desperate to locate it in the cacophony. Instantly, the barrage of his immediate surroundings hit him like a slap.

They didn't give me the sandwich I ordered. This is **ham,** *not* **turkey. Fuckwads. I'm not going to tip them next time. See how they like that.**

That bastard is sitting in my seat. **I'm** *the ranking officer. It's* **my** *seat.* **"Hey, uh, you going to be sitting there long, corporal?"** *That fuck!* **He** snickered *at me. I need to write a report. When the captain gets done with him, he won't be able to shit for a week!*

(**Terror.**) The fear that had dragged Twelve-A from his sleep was like a siren going off in the din of mental voices, tugging at his heart, raking his soul. He recognized the psychic imprint of the scream and his chest clenched. Six Six Five. She had barely survived the last few culls. She was older than him by three years, a lighthouse amidst the tiny motes of the Void. He had watched her learn, watched her piece things together, but as of yet, he had not had the courage to approach her. He hadn't wanted to make things worse. As it was, her tiny understandings, her unhappy conclusions were only causing her more pain, more unease, more chances to die for her knowledge.

This time, though, there was a new quality to the fear. Something deeper. Something overwhelming. Devastating. He began wading through the colorful motes of light surrounding him, seeking Six Six Five's luminescent pink-green being.

Like fog, others' thoughts clouded his path, forcing him to slow, to pick through every wisp, every nuance of energy. Unlike Ten-F, who could only see *some* things, Twelve-A could see it *all*; every thought, every fiber that made up a being, every emotion and passing whim, and it made it that much more difficult to search for those patterns he sought. He might as well have been standing on a beach, searching for a speck of sand. Or looking at the stars. That's what others' minds looked like to him. Stars.

I should link to her, Twelve-A realized, somewhat ashamed that he hadn't yet. He'd been afraid of forging that contact only to lose her in a cull, which was just another way the world could sear his soul. Thus far, he'd been hiding, protecting himself, and it was the only reason he hadn't fallen into the same madness as Ten-F. He'd insulated himself from the misery of the world.

Still, Twelve-A knew he was a coward not to have forged a connection with her, yet. She, of all of them, understood something was wrong. And, like him, she was totally alone. *I'll connect with her,* he decided again, stronger. After he did, he could always find her—or feel when she died.

Swallowing hard, Twelve-A redoubled his efforts to seek her out through the mental blizzard.

*Wow, those automaton kids are freakin' **dangerous**. I wonder what would happen if one of them got out. Man, they'd obliterate everything. Maybe I should request a transfer. Something with a window office. I hate fluorescent lights...*

*I really want that new car. Fucking alien banking assholes and their psychobabble bullshit. So what if I have a genetic predisposition towards overspending? That's prejudice. That's **illegal**. Well, if the bastards won't give me a loan, I could put it on a credit card. I have enough credit left to keep from going over the limit...*

He killed Charlie. The psychotic ailo killed Charlie. Oh my God, Charlie, I'm so sorry...

Cheese is good. I should eat more cheese...

(**Terror.**) Twelve A's entire body spasmed when he brushed another flood of sickly yellow fear as it washed outward over the star-studded fog of the ethereal plane. He quickly turned to follow it to its source.

That fucker's stealing my girl. I want to stab him in the face...

My truck's gonna cost a grand to fix. Aunt Jess's wedding ring is worth a grand, and that doddering old bat would never know it was gone. She's going in a home in January, anyway...

I fucking hate Trivial Pursuit. I should stop letting them win. Those lazy, pampered cows deserve to have their insipid grins scoured from their vapid faces with a gallon of bleach...

Six Six Five's mental cry had again faded in the sickly cacophony surrounding him, her wave dissolving outward, leaving him nothing to follow. Frustrated, Twelve-A closed his eyes and centered himself, drawing inward again, pulling everything towards him until the strands of his awareness were as close to his body as possible. Still, like vibrations down an old-fashioned phone line, the nearest thoughts continued to assault him.

I'm hungry. I wish the Keepers fed me more...

I need to pee. I don't want to get out of bed, but I need to pee...

(**Terror.**) There it was again, like a strobe light through the darkness. Twelve-A hurried to follow it, passing the large yellow mote of Ten-F's mind as he did.

*That disgusting bitch Molotov needs to die for keeping me down here. If the cunt comes back in here while I'm awake, I'm going to kill her, kill her friends, and peel the skin away from her eyes with my fingernails. Let **her** see what it's like. I'll murder all of the scientists for what they've done. They'll die begging, just like in the Dark Room. I'll make them **afraid**, too. I'll make them **scream**. Just like they did with all those kids. Then I'll kill everyone else. They're just animals, anyway. They aren't actually **thinking**. They deserve to die. All of them deserve to die...*

Beside her, other large motes floated in the abyss, though their thoughts were simple, pleasant. Of anyone in Congress, only the minds clustered in the cages around him seemed to be unbroken. Twelve-A hesitated at these new, ringingly pure minds, grateful for the reprieve.

I like my blanket. It's warm...

My penis gets bigger when I play with it. I wonder if the Keepers would get mad at me for playing with it...

My water dish is empty. I wonder if the Keepers would punish me for drinking out of the commode...

(**TERROR.**)

Catching the direction of the blast, Twelve-A once more focused his senses outward, a localized push, directing his tendrils of consciousness toward that horrible wash of terror that had woken him from his dead sleep, that was even then continuing to increase in strength, like a fire before it went out.

"**Doctor, Ten-F's drip bag looks like it ran out. Biorhythms indicate she's awake.**"

*Fuck me. Who was in charge of meds scheduling last Thursday? Damn, that was me, wasn't it? I was really tired...did I give her the right dose? Did I give **any** of them the right dose? I was still hung over. God, I hope that shit doesn't come down on me.* "**Put her out.**

Use the chip—we're not taking chances with that crazy bitch. Then go find whatever incompetent furg installed the IV last week and fire him. I don't tolerate mistakes on my team."

"Of course, sir." *Asshole. Everybody knows you went out whoring in Nevada on your vacation last week. You were barely conscious when you were scheduling meds.*

(TERROR.)

Keeping himself as contained as possible, Twelve-A hurriedly pushed past the monitoring station to concentrate his attention on the waves of overwhelming fear emanating from deeper in the compound. When he finally found her mind, it was a living wash of terror, driving shards of it through his core.

He's killing me. I'm getting culled. Just like Six Two One. "Please don't kill me. I'll be a good soldier. I swear. I won't talk back to Colonel Codgson again. I'll kill the aliens. Please let me kill the aliens."

The agony in the girl's mental voice scraped at Twelve-A's core, but despite his original intent, he still couldn't bring himself to make the connection. Like the rest of them, she was just an experiment. Expendable. She was going to die, and the fewer links he made to those who were going to die, the more he kept to himself, the more chance he had of surviving the torment of Life intact.

"We don't really need you. We've got Twelve-A—whoa!" *I can't believe I got him to crush that last ice cube. I won! I've been working on that for a* week! *I gotta* tell *somebody!* "I just made it past level *ten.*"

Still hovering outside the girl's mind, Twelve-A felt the reverberations of terror still surrounding him, now dulled by her shock at the doctor's total lack of caring. It was what Doctor Charles Shaw had *said,* however, that stabbed Twelve-A to the core, hitting him directly in the heart. *"We don't need you. We have Twelve-A."*

They don't need her...because they have me.

Because he was their prodigy. He was what they'd been seeking to create all along. Something that could *kill.* Something that could silence their opposition forever.

Selfish, Twelve-A thought, tears coming to his eyes again, the physical heat of them sliding down his cheeks almost distracting enough to wrench him back to his body. *They are so selfish.* From birth, he had read their wisps of thoughts as they drifted in the vat of the Void. They wanted him to kill their enemies in vast swaths. They wanted him to tear down everything. They wanted him to create a new regime, a new system, a new government, a new order, one in which the Humans ruled.

But Humans, he had seen, were no better than the rest. They were just as vile, just as corrupt, just as emotionally hideous, just as abusive, just as selfish.

And they were killing this girl because they thought *he* would do what *she* couldn't. They thought *she* had less right to live because *she* didn't want to kill. She was a defect, an anomaly, a cull, and it was his fault she was dying in terror.

The little robot didn't even twitch. **"Might as well be a bot."** *I hope she takes a while to die. I still need a few minutes for a full hour.*

In that moment, Twelve-A felt the deepest pang of empathy he'd ever felt for another creature, and, like an electric current, he made his first mental connection to another being in months. He slipped deeper into her mind, allowing himself to feel it all, to *become* the terror, the pull of the cold metal shackles against his arms and legs, the uncontrollable shivering, the petrifying knowledge he was going to die. At the same time, he reached out to Doctor Molotov, who cried softly in her office, staring at an empty cage, and instilled in her the deep, painful need to find out what happened to Six Six Five.

I hate him. He's just going to play games while I die and I hate him.

Six Six Five's thought rang around Twelve-A's consciousness, reverberating through it in a powerful wash of vibration, and he gently nudged her mind out of its stunned terror, offering it a thread to follow, one of mortgages and vengeful wives and secret lives, one that he knew Doctor Shaw feared. She snatched it like a starving creature offered sustenance, dragging herself out of her despair. Instead of taking the threat he subtly suggested, however, her mind hardened around him, and something *deep* began to bubble up from within, borne on void-black, star-speckled fire that flared to life around him, invigorating him, leaving him in awe as her lighthouse became a galactic core.

"**When you meet with the obscure, honorless death you deserve, and you take your shameful existence to taint the next realm, I hope your ancestors find you, skin you, use your diseased leather to clothe Takki, bury your tek in the bowels of its master, and send your hideless corpse through the ninety hells alone.**"

Shit...shit! That sounded alien...Is this bitch a spy? *Oshit oshit did the Congies find us? I'm* dead. *We're all* dead. "*What* **did you just say?**"

Twelve-A hesitated, realizing the curse he had given Six Six Five regarding Doctor Shaw's wife finding out his duplicity, his wayward penis shriveling from disease, and losing his home in a divorce had not come out at all as planned. It had almost felt like, for a split second, something else had taken over.

"**I said I hope you die.**"

But that *wasn't* what she had said. Twelve-A had felt it, just as he even then felt that overpowering presence retreating back into the recesses of her being, the towering columns of black flame going out as if they'd never been. He considered following it, trying to figure out where it came from, but even then, Doctor Charles Shaw was about to commit murder, and Twelve-A had to let the last voidlike tendrils slip away in order to deal with the problem at hand.

"**No.**" *Oh shit, what if she's a Huouyt? What if this place got infiltrated by the Huouyt? There were rumors they'd found us. Something about that dumbass Ghost getting caught, blowing our cover. What if she's a Huouyt? What if Codgson's a Huouyt? Fuck! I gotta get outta here. Florida. Or the Bahamas. I could go to the Bahamas.* "**What you just said. Before that. What language was that?**"

I'm dying. I can feel it in my limbs. I'm going to die. Twelve-A felt it with her, and it was all he could do to keep his terror from rising with hers. Instead, he tried to send soothing thoughts, to keep her calm and prevent the poisons from circulating as quickly. **"Let me go!"**

"Goddammit, kid! Who taught you to talk like that? Is there a spy down here? One of the techs?!" *Man, we're so fucked if it's a Huouyt.*

My heart won't stop hammering, Six Six Five's thought boomed around him, permeating Twelve-A's very essence. *It's not supposed to hammer like that.* **"Help!"** Six Six Five screamed. **"Heelllllp!"**

She's going to get someone's attention. Maybe she's calling for her Huouyt friends. I should kill her now...

As repulsive as it was, Twelve-A made a tiny connection to Doctor Charles Shaw and fueled his paranoia. To the patterns twisting through the doctor's consciousness, Twelve-A added, *But if I kill her, I'll never know the truth of what's happening down here...*Nothing traceable, but enough to keep him from killing her until Doctor Molotov could arrive.

"Listen, you little bitch. What you just said. What language was that? Who taught you? You been talking to Huouyt? There a fucking Huouyt in this installation?"

"Help!" *I'm so scared.* **"Please help me. Somebody."** *I'm getting culled and my body won't stop shaking. Codgson said I was a cull, I just don't know it yet.* With the thought, Twelve-A got the painful mental image of Codgson holding him by the throat, leaning in to whisper in his ear. Aching inside, he gently touched her soul, comforting it with his presence, but stopping short of alerting her to his intervention.

She's avoiding the question. **"Answer me!"** At another rush of contemplations of murder, Twelve-A gently pushed those thoughts aside and added, *I can't kill her yet—I need to keep her alive long enough to get answers.*

"No." *My eyeballs are jerking. My body is spasming just like Six Two One. I'm gonna die just like her, twitching with foam oozing from my mouth.* **"Please no."**

"Please no *what?*" *The drug's already taking effect. Shit. Damn, I gotta do something fast.* "I swear to God, if there's a damned Huouyt down here..." *There. Kinking the line should hold it off long enough to figure out what the hell is going on. If she's a spy, I'm outta here.* So *fucking out of here.* "Which one is he? It's that creep Codgson, isn't it? I knew that ailo creep was too psycho even for *this* project. He a plant? Which side he working for? That why he keeps killing the clones? Is he a Congie?"

He's...not killing me? Why isn't he killing me? What is a White? "I..."

But Doctor Molotov arrived before Six Six Five had to struggle any further with that. Powered by the panic Twelve-A had infused in her, the head medical officer slammed the door open, took immediate stock of the situation, and rushed inside to yank the tube from Six Six Five's arm.

Twelve-A watched as the two adults then proceeded to argue over Six Six Five's life. When he was sure that Molotov would not decide to let Doctor Shaw continue the process, he went back to studying Six Six Five. Now that he had taken the doorway into her mind, she was fascinating to him, something to distract him from the horror that was the outside world. Right now, she was still awash in a sickening rush of terror, but that was even then losing its force. Her core, deeper, where the starry tendrils had disappeared, held a soothing promise, a hope, an openness...Even the desperate quest for love.

All of that, however, was being crushed by the doctors who even then argued about which program they should dump her in. And, after that, they argued with Codgson about her worth, her value to their program. The longer Twelve-A listened, the angrier he got, until it was all he could do to sit back and watch, and not reveal himself. Again, he wanted to put them all to sleep for what they were doing. He wanted to kill.

They're hurting her, Twelve-A thought. *Just like they hurt everyone they touch. Just like Humanity hurts itself. They don't even see her as Human.* Indeed, he could see the wisps of thoughts, could feel their lack of compassion, the distance they'd put between themselves and their subjects. Even Doctor Molotov had detached herself from her heart, shielding her core from the horrors she perpetuated out of sheer routine, the continued cruelties of custom and habit.

Suddenly, a new knowledge burned in Twelve-A's mind, so powerful he rocked with its intensity. *I can stop this.*

And, in that moment, he had to decide. One way or the other. Bringing the silence or letting the pain continue. For everyone. He had to know which way to go, and he knew that it was not his decision to make.

"Let's see if we can turn you into a Jreet..."

No, please, I'm so scared. So scared...

Right then, Twelve-A decided who was going to make the decision for him. He knew he was too empathetic to decide such a thing. He understood everything about everyone, knew what had broken them, why they hurt each other, what mechanisms rotted behind their cruelties. He held no one above another, could not choose one life over another. Yet, if he offered the decision to an innocent... What better judge than the hamster who sat within their cage, suffering their 'kindness'? He tentatively stepped through the door of Six Six Five's mind, engulfing himself in her terror, and said, *Do you want me to kill them all?*

Who are you? It was a startled sound, one of hope.

My name is Twelve-A, he told her. His essence was vibrating with the horror of what he was about to do. *I need to know. Right now. I'm very strong. They don't realize how strong. Do you want me to kill them all?*

I think they're going to make me forget who I am, Six Six Five said.

Twelve-A began to ache inside. *They're going to try.*

Can you help me? Six Six Five whimpered.

Twelve-A hesitated for several moments. As he did, Doctor Philip finished his injection and went to close the lid of the brainwashing machine. He was thinking about how disgusted he was that he had to waste so much of his life on a stupid project the military wasn't going to look at twice anyway when the *real* prize was Twelve-A. If only he could get at the lab, he was *sure* he could make another Twelve-A. The jenfurgling techs must have screwed up the nannite programming. He could be a *hero* if he could just get to the *lab*.

Yes, Twelve-A finally said. *I can help you.*

Six Six Five hesitated. **Will you?**

Twelve-A felt the question burning in his mind, the moral dilemma that had been haunting him since he'd been aware enough to recognize the stew of misery in which the Human race now drifted. *Yes*, he said. *But I need you to answer me. Do you want them all dead?*

I want Colonel Codgson dead, she told him softly.

Twelve-A hesitated. He looked at Codgson, felt every failure, every humiliation, every childhood manipulation that had twisted him into what he was. *It can't just be him. He's only a symptom of an overall disease. I'd have to kill them all.*

Even Doctor Molotov? she whispered back.

Even her, Twelve-A said softly. *Everyone. Every soldier, every doctor, every Keeper, everyone who is not one of us. They're all part of it. They're all sick inside.*

She seemed to digest that, but she still didn't answer his question. **Can you help me not forget?**

Twelve-A hesitated, not having expected that response. *I won't let you forget*, he agreed.

She seemed to relax.

Do you want me to kill them? Twelve-A insisted. *I need to know.*

Ask me when I'm older, Six Six Five said. **I don't really want to kill anyone right now. I don't want to be a soldier.**

Twelve-A was taken aback, but he felt Six Six Five's mind beginning to tire and slip from the drugs.

Please don't let me forget, Twelve-A. Please.

I won't, he promised, still a bit stunned.

Please, she whimpered, as the void began to claim her.

You will remember again, Twelve-A said. *I promise.* He watched her sink even further into darkness, away from him, buoyed by a wave of strange images and the machine's soothing tones.

Twelve-A jerked awake suddenly, the void of his mind-space replaced by the blackness of the night. All around him, the People were cuddled amongst themselves, snoring. Joe Dobbs had settled back against a tree, gun in his lap, still stubbornly refusing to sleep when Twelve-A slept, despite Twelve-A's assertions that they were alone for miles. The old Congie Prime was even then whittling a stick, watching Shael's continued nocturnal contortions with a little frown on his face.

Seeing her whimper, still doomed to repeat those echoes of the past, Twelve-A softly repeated, *I promise.*

21

FIRST ENCOUNTERS

About two weeks after Sentineling himself to a bunch of brain-dead jenfurglings, Joe realized their party was being watched. He was filling his canteen at another creek when he saw the quick flash of an untinted lens on the hill overlooking the river-bottom. Capping the canteen, Joe nonchalantly got behind cover.

He supposed that he had known that sooner or later, forty-four naked furgs traipsing through the bush—most fat enough you couldn't even see their ribcages—would have attracted some attention, but he had been hoping Twelve-A would cooperate and steer them clear. No banana. The pointy-eared furg had the attention span of a gnat.

Slipping Jane out of her holster, he wove his way back through the pines and said, "Hey egghead, we've got someone on the hill behind us."

I know, Twelve-A said. *And it's not just one. It's...* The telepath hesitated, a small crease of concentration on his brow momentarily before it cleared again,...*thirty-three*. Then he went back to making a grass hat, under Alice's dubious tutelage. Beside him, Shael was peeling bark from a shiny new club.

Joe narrowed his eyes at the pointy-eared furgling currently attending the Adult Weaving 101 Class. "How long have you known?"

A few days. The minder plucked another handful of grass and started poking it into the weave when he ran out. Alice took a moment to reach over and correct his technique for him, pushing the grass strands back the other direction.

Suppressing the urge to stomp on the useless straw hat, Joe walked over and squatted in front of Twelve-A. As sweetly as he could when his baser instincts were screaming at him to rearrange the blue-eyed wonder's face, he said, "You think maybe that might've been some good info for you to divulge to your Chief of Security, you furgling flake?"

Security is your job. Why should I have to do your job, Joe? Twelve-A held up the half-made hat. *Neat, huh?*

"Because," Joe said through his teeth, pointedly ignoring the hat in front of him, "I can't read people's minds at nine hundred rods. You can."

Twelve-A sighed and dropped the hat back to his lap. Meeting Joe's gaze, he said, *They're really hungry. They want to know why we have so much food.*

Joe felt an instant rush of dread. "That's not good."

It'll be fine. More weaving.

Joe narrowed his eyes. "Can you just scramble their brains or something? Make them wander off?"

I could, Twelve-A said. And didn't elaborate.

Joe narrowed his eyes. "But you won't."

I don't like hurting people, Twelve-A said, lifting his head again to scan Joe's face. *Hurting people only spreads hurt.*

Joe immediately prickled. "But you'll drop me like a Congressional tank the moment I look at you funny."

You're dangerous, Twelve-A said. *They're not dangerous. They're hungry.*

Joe felt a muscle spasm in his neck. "All right, you pointy-eared leafling. If they've caught wind we've got a food supply, they're not going to give up easily. You all look like you've been feasting on cookies the last couple weeks, and that's going to make the rest of the world ask questions." He eyed Alice, who blushed. Turning back to Twelve-A, he said, "You need to get rid of them, okay?"

If I were like that, I would have killed you a long time ago, Twelve-A said, returning to his hat. *I don't hurt people.*

Joe narrowed his eyes. "We have a problem. You need to get rid of it. If *I* get rid of it, people will die."

Twelve-A's blond head came up abruptly. *You're not killing anyone.* The command went off like a gong in Joe's head, making him stagger.

As if Twelve-A hadn't just hit him with the mental equivalent of a two-by-four, the minder began weaving some flowers into his project as Alice and Eleven-C cooed appreciatively. Shael, by contrast, gave a very manly grunt, which Nine-G immediately tried to imitate.

"Great," Joe cried, waving a hand in disgust. "Just great...That's exactly what we need—a rod-tall Hebbut thinking he's a Jreet."

"Nine G is *not* a Hebbut," Alice whined. Pouting, she said, "Twelve-A, tell Joe he's not a Hebbut."

He's not a Hebbut. Hebbuts have bigger teeth and longer arms and wrinkly faces. Oh and they smell like leather and cherries. Nine-G smells like sweat and dirt. He refused to take a bath like the others. Threatened to squish my face when I tried. I think he's afraid of water.

Joe narrowed his eyes. The minder's description of Hebbut had been accurate. Indicating, of course, that, somewhere, Twelve-A had magically picked up yet another tidbit that Joe didn't remember giving him. Scowling, Joe said, *"Just make the furgs on the hill leave."*

They're hungry, Twelve-A repeated, not even bothering to look up. *If they want something to eat, we can share.*

Joe froze. "You are *not* sharing food with strangers."

Twelve-A shrugged dismissively, a skill he had picked up from Alice. This time, Joe had to tighten his fist to keep from planting it in Twelve-A's face. That was how Congies typically solved disputes like this, and he had to keep reminding himself he was dealing with something that could kill him—or worse—with a passing thought.

Wise decision, primate. The bastard telepath started to hum.

Carefully, so as to keep his temper in check around the pretty-boy who could turn him into a vegetable with a thought, Joe said, "This is war. Those guys on that hill would be happy to kill you and everyone with us if that meant keeping themselves alive. You should be thinking in the same terms."

I think the leader wants to join us.

Joe's jaw dropped open. Could Twelve-A really be that naïve? "Of course he wants to join you! And as soon as he finds out that Eleven-C is making the food and that you and Shael and the Hebbut and all the other bastards following you are unnecessary, you're going to be dead."

I wouldn't let him kill us.

"He wouldn't give you the *choice*," Joe snapped. When Twelve-A calmly continued weaving his hat, Joe muttered a curse. "Look, if you're not going to do anything about this, *I* am."

No you're not, Twelve-A said. *They're scared and hungry. We can help. Just go sit down and wait. They'll be here by nightfall.*

"They are going to try and *kill* us!" Joe snapped. "They want your *stuff*, not your *company*."

They're just scared, Twelve-A said. *It's not their fault the monsters came.*

Joe opened his mouth to argue, saw that it would be as futile as debating a Geuji, then just stood there, watching the minder weave grass. He shifted his attention to the other People who were playing with bugs, lazily eating leftovers, or dozing, then snorted and walked off to strategically hide his weapons around camp.

● ● ●

The weak yellow sun had passed its zenith and had started to descend into the flimsy alien treetops when the first of their observers silently stepped out of the undergrowth, into the People's small, grassy clearing amidst the pines. To Joe's surprise, it wasn't a rugged group of Congies or a disbanded Global Police force that had spent almost four days observing them, but rather, a group of what looked like starving civilians.

The leader was a big, thickly-bearded man wearing ragged work clothes that looked much too loose, knotted to his waist with a piece of purple nylon rope. Hanging from the rope was a hatchet, two different knives, and something Joe recognized as some sort of non-energy, Earth-made gun. He carried a heavy-looking backpack stuffed so full its seams were bursting, bits of purple showing through. Everything about him looked worn, dusty, and well-used.

Behind the bearded leader, several men and women were crawling out of the forest scrub with haggard, sunburned faces. Like the bearded man, who was carefully approaching Joe, they looked much too skinny, their clothes too loose, slipping into sight in fearful huddles like whipped Takki. And, like him, each one carried an almost identical backpack, packed to bursting.

Not, Joe guessed by their skinny bodies, with food.

As their rag-covered forms filtered from the trees, Joe pulled an apple from his pocket and took a big bite out of it, carefully gauging their reaction. At the first crisp sound of his teeth puncturing the apple skin, every head in the approaching group came up and their feet staggered to a halt. Some of the littlest Humans automatically began walking towards him, then, when they were caught by their parents and hastily dragged back, they started crying. Even some of the adults were whimpering and hiding their faces.

The big, gun carrying leader stopped a few paces off, eying Jane warily. Joe took several more bites of his apple, feeling every hungry gaze watching him with wretched desire, carefully analyzing the depths of their need. It was bad—every one of them seemed to be walking a razor's edge. Several were shaking. Even the leader seemed transfixed by the way he moved the fruit from his side to his lips to take each new bite.

With obvious difficulty, the man tore his gaze from the apple to Joe's face and managed, "You need some help, there, Boss?"

"Nope," Joe said, around a big mouthful of fruit and juice. It was everything he could do to keep from adding, "Get lost, sooter."

Twelve-A, the peace-loving posy-sniffer, had insisted he be nice. Joe, on the other hand, had been fighting a gut-deep feeling of foreboding ever since he'd realized they were being watched. His vote had been to seek out the group spying on them, put a few rounds in their leaders, then give the rest a chance to play the Eeloirian Scramble before he repeated the process with any stragglers. The Prince of Hugs and Rainbows and Ueshi Pleasure-Cruises, however, had taken umbrage to that idea and had vehemently insisted Joe let them live. All of them. Dammit.

Not only that, but now the starry-eyed furg wanted to *feed* them. Apparently, Joe had been some sort of ambassador for his kind by not shooting the minder in the head like he deserved, and now Twelve-A was curious to see what others had to offer.

Except, seeing the vacant, haunted eyes of the survivors sliding out of the bushes, Joe was getting a really bad feeling, one that said he should have hunted them down and started shooting the moment he realized they were following him.

The bearded man at the edge of the tiny meadow hesitated, brown eyes flickering again over Jane. "Congie, huh?"

"Yup," Joe said coolly.

His visitor cleared his throat. "I, uh, thought all the Congies got wiped."

"They didn't," Joe said.

Still, the man wasn't done. His eyes flickered desperately to Joe's half-eaten fruit. "Keep seeing brain-dead groups wandering around, ya know? Like no survival instincts whatsoever. Only know they're Congies 'cause they're all dressed in black."

Joe felt a twisting of fury, remembering the vast herds of Congressional soldiers the Space Force had shoved off the dropships, drooling in their stupidity, playing with bugs and flowers like children. Still, he kept his face impassive. Instead of responding, he finished his apple and flung the core aside. Most eyes in the group moved to follow its arc, and one little boy broke from the others and ran to collect it from the grass to immediately stuff it in his face and devour what was left, seeds and all.

Seeing that, Joe grimaced. It was obvious that their visitors had been starving for some time. They also outnumbered him. Whereas Joe was the only one who knew how to use a gun in their own group, there were at least twenty in the stranger's band carrying deadly weapons, most of whom looked like they knew how to use them. What was most alarming, though, was that every single gun-carrier wore the hardened look that Joe recognized as a willingness to do so.

In the awkward silence following the little boy gobbling up the remains of his apple, the stranger scratched at the back of his neck nervously and said, "So, uh, we were just passing through and saw you guys looking like you could use some help."

Casually picking apple skin from his teeth, Joe asked, "And what makes you think we need help?"

The bearded man's eyes caught his face, then slid to the naked People lounging in the grass behind him. Most of them weren't paying any attention to the newcomers at all, either catching bugs, dozing, or helping Alice and Nine G build a teepee of sticks beside the fire using Joe's axe. Those who *were* watching the show were coming over to gawk like planet-side hicks seeing their first naturals preserve, all their glories on full display.

"It's pretty obvious you guys got roughed up," the bearded man noted, eyes stopping on one of the more voluptuous women before quickly returning to Joe's face. "I'm Mike Carter. The former Congressman." When Joe just gave him a blank look, Mike cleared his throat uncomfortably. "To a Congie, that's basically a politician."

Joe narrowed his eyes, even more convinced he should be shooting the guy in the head.

Nervously clearing his throat again, Mike continued, "I guess I lead this bunch. We've got clothes and other supplies. Figured we could..." There was a slight hesitation in the man's voice as he glanced almost imperceptibly to the side, "...help out."

What a load of flake, Joe thought, looking him straight in the eyes. He hadn't spent seventy-four turns in the Ground Corps listening to grounders' excuses not to be able to tell a lie when he heard one. He wanted their food, plain and simple.

"We don't need help."

"Uh...yeah." Mike hesitated, eyes on Nine-G as the gigantic man carried a fallen tree over to where Alice and the others were, then dropped it with a ground-shuddering thud. "But they're...not wearing anything," he managed, when he tore his eyes away.

"They like what their ancestors gave them," Joe said. "Not the clothes-wearing sort."

Mike swallowed, yet refused to take the hint to leave. Behind him, his group—numbering at least thirty, just as Twelve-A had predicted—waited in a hungry silence. Lingering much longer than necessary, Mike finally said, "Setting up camp for a while?" The stiffness in his voice betrayed his nerves—and the fact that he was probably about to give his followers the signal to attack.

Joe was utterly calm when he replied, "A while." He started calculating how many he could kill before they organized themselves. Probably a lot. They were mostly bones, their exhaustion showing in their haggard, desperate faces. If they put up much of a fight once their companions' heads started to explode, he would be surprised.

The man gave Jane another nervous glance. "You mind if we join you?"

Joe said, "You're damn right I burning mind. Last thing I'm gonna do is share perfectly good food with a bunch of diseased vaghi scavengers. Get the hell gone, and don't let me see your oily hides again or I'll start shooting. And believe me. I *won't* miss."

What actually came out of his mouth was, "Sure, join us. We've got food."

For a long moment, Joe just stood there as flies buzzed around his open mouth, utterly unable to believe what he had said. Very slowly, he turned to face Twelve-A. The minder grinned at him from under his ridiculous straw hat, in which Alice had cut holes for his pointy ears. As Joe watched, Twelve-A tipped the floppy brim at him, blue eyes dancing in amusement.

Joe narrowed his eyes before turning back to the newcomers. "Apparently, you're invited to dinner."

The bearded man's eyes widened, and Joe felt another tingle of alarm at the confusion in the man's face. As if he had *known* that they had some mysterious food source, but hadn't expected them to share. Which meant he had expected to *take* it from them.

I don't like this, Joe warned.

Relax, furg, Twelve-A retorted. *They're just hungry.*

And that, Joe knew, was the problem. He carefully scanned the dozens of sun-baked, starving faces and he saw stark, bitter envy as they gazed upon the relatively fat, happy People. Bitter envy...and calculation.

They're going to take Eleven-C from us, Joe thought, on a wave of dread.

No, Twelve-A argued. *They're just starving and they need our help.*

Nobody needs our help but us, Joe snapped back. *Once we get the People safe,* then *you can start a crusade running around helping people to your heart's content. Until then, we need to watch out for our own people.*

Have you ever starved, *furg?*

Of course I have. I'm a hundred-and-fucking-three Earth years old and I've been in enough shit that I know what starving people do, Joe retorted. *Have you ever starved?*

Yes, Twelve-A replied. *It's horrible. We can help. We are going to help.*

Joe narrowed his eyes at Mike. *You are making a mistake.*

I've got this under control, Twelve-A said. *Invite them over to the fire. We'll feed them for a few days, until they feel better, then we'll part ways and go find that place in the mountains you want to take us to.*

At Twelve-A's words, a whole new feeling of dread gnawed at Joe's insides. "That's *naïve*," he growled. "Totally burning *naïve*, you pointy-eared sooter freak."

Mike frowned at him, that razor-edge of caution coming back. "What's naïve?"

Joe frustratedly waved the man's question off with an overly cheerful grin. "Nothing. Please. Come sit by the fire and set up camp. We'll be *happy* to feed you as long as you want. Fill yourselves up so you can sleep soundly tonight. *Real* soundly. We've got plenty of food to share. *Plenty* of food. We *love* to eat."

As expected, Joe's 180-degree attitude change made Mike take an anxious step backwards.

"Where are you going?!" Joe cried, taking a step towards him. "You're not hungry? You *must* be hungry. *Everybody* gets hungry."

Twelve-A's disapproval was like a frying-pan to the head. *You're intentionally making him nervous.*

"I'm merely offering him a place at our fire," Joe said back, smiling his most psychotic smile at Mike and his friends. "Somewhere he and all his friends can sleep *soundly.*"

"You're fucking cannibals," Mike managed, his voice a high-pitched tremor. He was backing away quickly, now, a big, shaking fist hovering over his gun.

Like a sonic boom, Twelve-A gave a mental sigh. Immediately, like someone had stepped into the control center that was Joe's brain and had wrenched him away from the console, he heard himself laughing. "Gotcha!" he cried. Then he let out a girly giggle and danced up to Mike, grinning like a fool. Slapping Mike on the shoulder, he said, "My name's Joe." He took Mike's reluctant hand. "I'm a Congie, but not a bad one, see? A good Congie."

Mike was staring at him, not returning his exuberant handshake. Nonetheless, Joe felt himself keep shaking. "Look, I love playing jokes. I'm a real joker, see? People don't like me much and I'm too dumb to see why. Of course we've got food. Eleven-C makes it. All she's gotta do is put her hand to the ground and concentrate and *boom*, food, right? The Keepers made her that way and it's easy. Want some food? I know you want some food—"

Get out of my head, you psychotic chimp! Joe shrieked.

You gonna play nice? Twelve-A demanded. In the background, Joe continued to bow and scrape like a moron.

Burn you, furgling flake! Joe screamed.

Better decide soon, Twelve-A said. *He's about to pull his gun and shoot you.*

Seeing that, indeed, Mike was about to shoot him, Joe decided to be the better man. *When I find you in the afterlife*, he promised, *I'm going to tear off your ears and mount them to a Dhasha's ass.*

Sounds uncomfortable, Twelve-A said distractedly. *You really should hurry.*

Fine! Joe screamed. *Fine, you ever-loving janja fart, fine.*

Immediately, he had full control of himself again. With a yell, he yanked himself away from Mike, wrenched his hand free, and glared.

There was a sense of amusement underlying the bastard's caution, now. "I take it the Ground Force was...rough...on you," Mike commented.

Flushing until his face felt covered in Ueshi fire-balm, Joe bared his teeth. "You are invited to dinner."

Mike continued to give him an analyzing look. "That you or the friend in your head talking?"

"*Definitely* the friend in my head," Joe growled. "If *I* had the choice, I'd shoot you, take your gear, and dump your bodies over the—Hahahaha just kidding. I wouldn't do anything like that. Come on, we have food—"

I'm warning you, Joe growled.

And I'm warning you, Twelve-A said stubbornly. *Stop trying to scare him. He's a good guy.*

Fine. It's your damn formation. Joe mentally threw up his hands and settled for a glare at the newcomers.

"Soooo," Mike said, clearing his throat and pointedly looking past Joe. "Is anyone *else* in charge around here?"

"Me!" Alice cried, running up with Joe's axe in her hand. Panting, she enthusiastically said, "Twelve-A says I should come do the talking because Joe is making you nervous."

"That he is, sweetie," Mike agreed. Then, with a hasty glance at Joe, "No offense, man. I'm sure it was rough. Not many guys got the cojones to make it through like Zero, ya know? And hell, only thing special 'bout him was his golden asshole."

Joe narrowed his eyes. *You're going to pay.*

He heard something that actually sounded like a derisive snort coming from the minder's direction…and nothing else. When he looked, the minder was reclining against a rock, sloppy straw hat-brim covering his face.

"You know what?" Joe demanded, irritation rising. "Fine. I'm just gonna go hang out over here and let you guys work things out." He turned on heel, marched over to where Twelve-A was reclining, yanked his absurd hat off his head, and stooped so that he and the minder were eye-to-eye. "This is a mistake," he warned, low enough so that only Twelve-A could hear it. Then, slamming the hat back in place perhaps a little too hard, he stood and stalked off to find wood for the fire.

22

THE MAGNANIMOUS MIKE CARTER

Joe sat on a boulder near the edge of camp, ostentatiously whit-tling with the massive Jreet ovi that had been given to him by Prime Sentinel Raavor ga Aez, watching the newcomers dig food out of the pit he had painstakingly hidden with twigs, leaves, and other debris only a few hours before. Once Mike and his crew had real-ized that the People really didn't care if they ate their food, things had gone pretty much as Twelve-A had predicted; they had gorged themselves until the pits started to run dry. As *Joe* had predicted, however, as soon as food started to become scarce again, they had then started to scuffle amongst themselves over who got to keep the leftovers. Even now, each family had staked out private 'territories' of camp, with small groups of their ragged number keeping watch over whatever they had managed to scavenge from the bottom of the pit, eying the People and their own kind alike with hard-faced suspicion.

All the while, the People, who were already well-fed and ready for bed, watched the newcomers hoard their food with mild curios-ity. As they gathered to fall asleep in their usual dogpile, giggling as they crawled under each other for the best position, their visitors continued to stay awake with distrustful stares and hard, humorless faces, obviously prepared to endure a long night. No one was feeding the fire. No one was *moving* from their tiny familial zone. So far, no one had let it slip that it was the curvaceous brunette sitting beside the guy with the sloppy straw hat that had made it all out of dirt, but Joe knew that the moment someone *did*, things were going to get ugly.

Eventually, Mike left his tiny fiefdom to come climb up on the boulder beside Joe, lowering his lumpy backpack to the stone beside his ankle. "They're not very bright, are they?" He frowned at the group of naked experiments even then laughing and playing in their tangle.

"Pretty brain-dead," Joe agreed. He kept whittling.

"So what's wrong with them?" Mike demanded. "It's like they're all…kids. But dumber."

"Fried a few brain cells in Judgement, I would guess," Joe said.

"I notice they all got barcodes on the backs of their necks," Mike pressed. "They the leftovers from one of those criminal brainwashing facilities?"

"Your guess is as good as mine," Joe said, shrugging. What he *wanted* to do was punch the guy in the face for asking questions, but he refrained.

"Poor guys," Mike said, sounding genuinely sorry for them. "That why they all have those weird numbers for names?"

"Ayup." Joe increased the violence of his carving, but Mike didn't take the hint.

Mike gave him a long look. "So why's a guy like *you* hanging out with the likes of *them*?"

The pointed way the man said it made Joe stiffen. Resuming his carving, he said, "Nothing special about me."

"Yeah, bullshit," Mike said. He gestured to the Prime Sentinel's ovi. "You're Zero." Then, at Joe's sudden scowl, he faltered. "…aren't you?"

"No," Joe said. "Not anything like that ashbag." Irritated, he went back to carving.

"What is that, then?" Mike demanded, gesturing to the intricate crystalline blade, translucent blue except for the black Jreet's head carved into the handle.

"Replica," Joe gritted.

"Badass replica," Mike said, sounding unconvinced. "It's cutting through that tree like butter."

"You really think a *Jreet* has hands this small, you flake-sniffing jenfurgling?" Joe held up the forearm-length knife. A Jreet's ovi was actually given to him by the Black Jreet upon his acceptance as a warrior, and was tailor-made to his or her hand at the time—which was usually only slightly bigger than Joe's own—but only those chronically privileged with the dubious pleasure of Jreet friends actually knew that. While Prime Sentinel Raavor ga Aez had been approximately the size of a Congressional freighter when he died, his ovi had remained the small, ceremonial object of death it was intended to be.

Mike frowned at him a moment, then shook himself. "Yeah, I guess you don't really look like him much, after all. Chin's too narrow. Not tall enough. Paler."

For once, Joe appreciated the exaggerated propaganda posters. "Yeah, I get that a lot." He went back to 'carving,' though all he was really doing at this point was hacking chunks of wood out of a bigger chunk of wood, too frustrated to try and make a shape out of it.

After a minute of awkward silence, Mike finally broached the question they both knew was coming. "So, uh…" the man coughed, glancing down from their perch at his own family unit, which had collected a fist-sized hunk of beef roast, a bruised peach, and a squished half of a banana. Two boys and a girl no more than eleven years old stood guard over it with guns, as hard-faced as the rest of them. Returning his eyes to Joe, Mike said, "Where'd you guys find all that food?"

"Some farmer's stash," Joe said. "He'd buried it in his root cellar out back right before a kreenit got him." He kept whittling.

"Oh." There was obvious disappointment in Mike's face. "It's all gone, then?"

"No, I'm just lying again. Eleven-C can make it."

Joe's mouth fell open and he stared at the razor tip of his ovi. His gut was telling him that now would be a *very* good time to drive it through his visitor's skull, before the hungry furg could piece it all together. Instead, he *thunked* the knife into the boulder he was sitting on, turned around to clasp his hands around his knee and tilt his body in the most homosexual manner possible, and huskily said, "What *else* are you interested in?"

Are you trying *to get her taken?!* Joe mentally screamed, as his body cooed and purred around him.

They're not going to take her, Twelve-A said. *They're grateful for the food.*

It doesn't work *that way!* Joe shrieked.

How do you know? Maybe nobody's ever been nice to them, Twelve-A retorted.

Look at what they're doing, Joe snapped. *They're guarding their food from their own kind like backbiting hatchlings. They're not* sharing, *furg. They're not* like *you.*

Twelve-A hesitated to consider that, and Joe thought maybe he'd finally gotten through to the airheaded jenfurgling.

We'll just have to give them more food, Twelve-A finally said.

Joe's eyes widened, realizing Twelve-A's intent. *No way. Don't you dare.*

On the other side of the camp, Eleven-C frowned and put down the flower bracelet she was weaving.

Don't do it! Joe snapped. *They'll take her!*

Twelve-A sighed. *You should get some sleep.*

Joe's eyes widened. *No. Don't you even…that is a* bad *idea!*

Eleven-C got up and walked to the center of their gathering, near the fire. On the other side of the camp, Alice's thin voice shattered the calm of night. Like a cheerful gremlin, she cried, "Hey everyone! Eleven-C is going to make some more food so you don't have to guard it all the time!"

No! Joe cried, struggling for control. *No, damn it! No!*

Good night, Joe, Twelve-A said. *Don't worry. I've got this.* The minder winked at him from under his straw hat.

The last thing Joe heard before the Void claimed him was Mike's sharp intake of breath as the ground underneath Eleven-C's slender fingers started to shimmer and change.

• • •

Shael's stomach urged him to share in the latest of Eleven-C's glorious bounties, but his warrior instincts kept him at the edge of camp, watching. Something was not right. The Voran had fallen asleep with the rest of their charges—typical—leaving Shael to guard the fire alone. It was an uneasy situation, as *none* of the skulkers sharing their fire or their food had gone to sleep yet. As time wore on and Shael added kindling from Nine-G's pile to the fire, more and more of their guests started to watch *Shael* when they thought his back was turned. Almost as if they were waiting for something. What was worse, something about these newcomers reminded him of Doctorphilip and his Earthlings.

Ever since Eleven-C had created her latest feast, the newcomers had started whispering amongst themselves, casting lustful eyes at the brown-furred Human who had fallen asleep in Nine-G's arms. The only one of the People who didn't appear to be sleeping was the minder. For his part, Twelve-A was sitting with his back to a tree, a frown on his face under the hat, quietly staring at his toes.

Knowing full well the value of someone like Eleven-C, Shael walked over and squatted beside the telepath. In a hushed whisper, Shael said, "These weaklings who share our fire…They skulk about like vaghi about to steal a slab of melaa. What are they planning?"

When Twelve-A opened his eyes and looked up at him, there were lines of concern etched into his face. *It's not good. Maybe you should go wake Joe up.*

Shael stiffened, the insult striking him to his core. "Wake up Joedobbs? Why?"

Twelve-A winced. *I think Joe was right…I think I need his help.*

"*His* help?" Shael roared. "I am Shael ga Welu! Is my protection not enough for you?!" He shouted the last loud enough to make most of the clothes-wearing skulkers flinch. Beside him, Nine-G grunted and twitched in his sleep, making Eleven-C snuggle closer.

No, Twelve-A said quickly, his frown increasing. *It's not that. It's that…*

One of the bearded skulkers—the one Shael had heard Joedobbs call 'Mike'—walked up and cocked his head at Shael, saying something in the filthy Earthling tongue.

Finding himself the subject of the soft-skinned alien's unabashed perusal, Shael rose and straightened, lifting his head to return his stare with disdain. "What does the softling want?" he asked Twelve-A, peering into the alien's brown, weak eyes.

He wanted to know what language that was.

"Tell him it is the language of my brethren, the great tongue of Welu."

Okay. Twelve-A turned to face Mike.

A moment later, Mike flinched and backed away, twisting to stare down at the minder in something akin to horror.

"The softling fears you," Shael noted, with approval.

Oh no, Twelve-A whispered, pulling his legs in and slowly scooting away from the furg. *Shael, you need to wake up Joe. Right now.*

"Why?" Shael demanded. Even then, the bearded skulker was backing away in terror, calling out in his filthy tongue. Shael sneered his disgust. "Would you like me to evict them for you? Is that why you want Joe?" Any *furg* could bully lesser creatures with a gun. It took a *true* warrior to show them his power with nothing but his fists and coils.

Please wake him up, Twelve-A said, blue eyes wide and fixed on the one called Mike. *This is getting out of control. Joe would know what to do.*

Out of *control?* Shael snorted and put himself between Twelve-A and the softling daring to stare at him as an equal. *Shael* knew how to put the furg in his place, and it wouldn't require Joe's precious 'Jane,' either.

No, Shael, don't…this is really bad.

Shael scoffed. Ignoring the minder, he stalked up to the bearded Human and slapped him, hard, across the cheek. "Keep your eyes to yourself when dealing with your betters," Shael growled.

Shael wasn't sure what happened, but in one moment, Mike jerked, holding his face, then in the next, he kicked Shael in the stomach and ran his knee into his forehead as he fell, shattering Shael's world into a flurry of stars. Startled at the sheer amount of *pain*, Shael screamed. Nothing in his long centuries of training had prepared him for this. Not even his battle with Joedobbs had hurt this badly, and it left Shael curled in on himself, whimpering. Above him, he heard Mike shouting more of his filthy words across camp, but Shael could only think about how much his face hurt, how it had felt as if the bones themselves had shattered into shards of glass.

One of the weaklings came, and again, they yanked Shael's hands behind his back. Remembering what had happened the last time he'd let fools bind his hands, Shael regained some of his senses and struggled—only to get kicked in the side and face in an obliterating wave of agony. In that moment of pain and terror, Shael's grasp on his war-mind slipped entirely, leaving him once again unable to defend himself as his assailants began binding his wrists and ankles and left him there, staring at the dirt.

Don't worry, Twelve-A assured him. *I'll take care of this. They're just scared.*

Though he didn't dare say it out loud, hurting and bound, surrounded by strangers, *Shael* was scared. But, as promised, the newcomers suddenly stopped their mad rush around the camp and went utterly stock still. Twelve-A got up from where he sat and walked over to the frozen-in-place Mike, who started to shiver and whimper. Very gently, the telepath reached up to touch Mike's face.

"What are you doing?" Shael demanded, frowning. "*Kill* him!"

I'm not killing anyone, Twelve-A replied. *This was all a big misunderstanding. I'm just making sure he knows he doesn't need to be scared of me.*

A *misunderstanding*? Shael blinked at the weakling's naïveté. Now that the telepath had marked himself as their leader, the dishonorable

vaghi of this group—which had already proven themselves hostile—
would execute him at their first available opportunity. All around
them, the People were sleeping. Not even the Voran had woken at
the sounds of the struggles.

"You need to *kill them*, Twelve-A," Shael growled. "They *struck*
me. And left me *bound*!"

You hit them first, Twelve-A insisted stubbornly.

Shael narrowed his eyes. "Don't be fooled. They've already
stabbed us in the belly once, after we offered them the safety of our
fire. It would be nothing for them to do it again."

They're good people that are hungry and scared, Twelve-A replied.
They think I'm going to hurt them for hurting you.

"You mean you're *not*?!" Shael raged.

They are so scared of us, Twelve-A told him mournfully. *We need to
help them, Shael.*

The simple, addlebrained *furg*. "Look at what they did to me!"
Shael shrieked, yanking at the ropes they had bound him with. "They
plotted this, furg."

True, Twelve-A replied. *But just because they were scared. I can make
them not scared.*

Even then, the telepath had his hand on the shoulder of the shivering 'Mike' staring into his dull brown eyes.

Disgusted, Shael twisted in his bonds to face Beda. "Voran!"
Shael shouted across the camp at him. "Wake up, skulker! Twelve-A
is going to get himself killed! Voran! Wake!"

The lazy Takki ignored him and continued to sleep.

I put Joe to sleep, Twelve-A admitted. *He needs someone to shake him
out of it.*

"The Sisters *stake* you, minder," Shael growled. "You put him to
sleep? Are you daft?!"

He was going to hurt someone, Twelve-A replied. *Now shhh. I'm
helping Mike realize he has nothing to fear.*

"Those vaghi's minds are naught but diseased flesh," Shael
snarled. "Stop trying to befriend them and *free* me."

I'm just going to prove my intentions. That should make him feel better.

"What intentions?" Shael demanded.

To let him stay.

Shael froze. After they had beaten and bound him, their intentions to do the same to the others clear, the telepath intended to let them *stay*? Frowning, he twisted to get a good look at the minder. He was holding the hand of the leader of the weaklings, smiling.

See? Twelve-A demanded. *I didn't have to hurt him. They'll take some extra food and leave peacefully in the morning.* If anything, the minder sounded proud of himself. *He just needed some reassurance.*

All of a sudden, Mike began to move again. He lunged forward, slamming his forehead into the minder's startled brow. Twelve-A went down with a cry of alarm, then a scream when Mike kicked him, hard, in the face.

"Kill them!" Shael shrieked, realizing the others were starting to move again with the telepath distracted. "Kill them now!"

Twelve-A's response was a panicked mental babble of pain.

"Voran!" Shael cried. "Voran, help us!" Several of the strangers were rushing him from all sides. Shael tried to reach his war-mind, but, in his growing panic and leftover pain, reaching for it was like reaching for smoke. The kick that followed slammed Shael's head so far against his spine that his body lifted from the earth, leaving him stunned.

A few minutes later, Nine-G gave a startled yelp, then started to howl.

It was when Twelve-A started screaming, however, that Shael began to whimper uncontrollably. "Beda," he managed, shaking into the dirt. "Please help us. Please."

Beda ga Vora never moved.

● ● ●

Joe woke to the sound of crying.

The fire had long since gone out, and the cool, dewy morning had given way to another hot summer day—and sobbing. Everywhere.

Joe tried to launch himself to his feet with a yell, only to find himself hogtied, face down in the grass beside his boulder, Jane run away with another man, his boots and his Prime Sentinel ovi nowhere to be seen.

"What happened?" he cried, twisting to get a better look. Most of the People were lying on their stomachs in the meadow, tied hand and foot with the same purple nylon rope that Mike had worn around his waist. Most were bloodied or bruised. All were crying.

Rope, Joe thought, disgustedly remembering the odd lumps in the top half of their backpacks and knapsacks. Recognizing where he had seen that cheerful purple rope before, Joe felt a wave of relief, realizing that their attackers hadn't yet graduated to the murdering kind—they were still in the Tie-You-Up-And-Leave-You-To-Die stage. How unfortunate for them.

He lifted his head to make sure that their visitors were completely gone, then said, "Twelve-A, you better sooting get me out of this, pointy-eared asher."

His response was complete silence. When Joe frowned and looked, off to one side, Twelve-A was likewise hogtied, lying on his side, cheek resting in his own blood. Beside his head, his straw hat was a mangled, crimson mess. His nose was obviously broken, one eye swelled shut, his entire face a mass of bruises. His body was worse.

Joe's heart gave a startled hammer. "You okay over there, Pointy?" he shouted.

Twelve-A said nothing. The blood had been trailing down his face for some time and was starting to coagulate as it dripped down the grass. From this angle, Joe wasn't sure he could see the rise and fall of breathing or not.

"Soot." His mission taking on new urgency, Joe started awkwardly flopping the couple digs it took to get to the place where he'd hidden a pistol under the log. He tried to slide underneath the trunk to grab the grip with his teeth, but his head was too big to fit into the crack.

"A little help?" he finally shouted at Twelve-A.

Twelve-A never moved, the pool of blood continuing to spread under his head, collecting flies.

Riding a pang of worry, now, Joe considered his options. He had twelve other weapons stashed around the camp, but all of his knives were in similar nooks or crannies like the pistol even then staring at him from the shadows under the log. That left a rifle.

May the Sisters give the thieving scavengers all a good screwing, Joe thought, frustrated. A rifle was…not ideal.

But, judging by the pained whimpers all around him, it was all he had to work with. Grunting, Joe started flail-roll-wiggle-inching his way to his next-closest weapon stash, a laser rifle he'd tucked into a stand of brambles. As soon as he got his body turned in the opposite direction and over the first hummock, however, he saw Nine-G and his heart stopped.

They had tied the big man to a big pine tree in a bear-hug—and then had beaten him unconscious. Or dead. Even then, his massive bruised face lolled on his massive shoulder, a thin stream of blood leaking down his massive back to a massive puddle on the ground under a massive butt cheek.

Unconscious, then. Dead men didn't have the internal pressure to force blood through their nose when sitting upright. Even dead men the size of a female Hebbut.

It took almost an hour of frustrated maneuvering before Joe could get across the camp to the rifle, and all the while, the People continued to sob and whimper around him. All of them had been bloodied or beaten somehow, some so badly they were unconscious. Eleven-C and Alice were gone. *Soot*, Joe thought. *Soot, soot.* "You believe me now, furg?!" he shouted at Twelve-A.

The minder continued to stare at the ground in silence.

Frustrated that he hadn't been allowed to prevent the whole affair with a couple well-placed plasma rounds, Joe strained onto his side, twisting one of his shoulders almost out of socket to get the right leverage to pry the rifle from its hiding place with his fingers. Getting a good look at his weapon of choice, however, Joe had second thoughts about using it to try to slice away his bonds.

"Any chance you could wake up the Hebbut over there?" Joe shouted at the minder. "I need someone to untie me."

If Twelve-A heard him or cared, he said nothing.

"Shael!" Joe shouted, riding a surge of panic at the lack of response. "A little help, here?"

Shael did not respond, either. A few rods off, she appeared to be asleep. Or dead. Joe's chest tightened in worry that she might be dead. The furg was actually somewhat loveable, in her own little way.

"Twelve-A, is Shael okay?" he asked.

The minder continued to stare blindly off into space, but he made an odd, strangled sound that eased Joe's fears that he was dead. Joe felt his heartbeat quickening, though this time, it was with a rush of anger. Not at the Twelve-A and his naïve, naked furglings, but at the honorless bastards who would hurt the People and take an ovi that didn't belong to them. Even the Dhasha, who hated Jreet, left a warrior's ovi where it lay. That would have been handy. Then Joe's eyes caught on the wood-chips he had left from his carving attempt the night before and he winced.

A warrior who uses his ovi to hack at rocks welcomes fortune around every corner. Another annoying Jreet saying. One that basically meant the unlovable Jreet Sisters frowned on profaning a sacred object like an ovi with anything but blood, and they delighted in chronically screwing up the lives of those who did. Seeing the utter Takkiscrew around him, Joe made a note.

"All right," Joe growled, taking another good look at the laser rifle. He was pretty sure if he propped the gun against his side, twisted, and used his tongue, he could trigger the rifle with his face while cutting off the ropes—or his arm—with the other end.

Pretty sure…and definitely not ready to try it.

Looking at the unconscious Nine-G, however, watching the minder stare at the dirt under his face, totally unseeing, Joe realized he really didn't have a choice.

"You better not cut off anything important," Joe told the rifle. Unlike Jane, the rifle did not reply.

Long minutes passed. Looking at the cold, black, un-intelligent Congie alloys, Joe swallowed. This far from Congressional med-halls, he *really* did not want to cut off something important. At least Jane would have warned him if he were about to do something stupid. Which he was.

And yet, every moment he wasted, his quarry was getting away with his bride. After he hunted them down, Joe decided he was definitely going to have to have a chat with Jane about her recent elopement. The fact that she was Ueshi-made, not Huouyt-made, should have given her a little more self-respect in that department.

"Aw, burn it," Joe muttered, once he'd been staring at the gun for several minutes and the Space Force still hadn't arrived with reinforcements. "God hates a coward." Using a combination of leverage, spine-twisting contortions, and pure dumb luck, Joe managed to get the rifle barrel to slide down the tree and slap against his hands on its fall to the ground. With further contortions—while carefully keeping the rifle barrel trapped between his fingers—Joe managed to maneuver his face up against the tree trunk where the butt of the rifle was wedged.

He propped the gun into a position so that the lens was carefully poised over the ropes between his hands and feet, checked to make sure he wasn't about to slice off an important body part, double-checked, then depressed the trigger with his tongue.

At the last second, the rifle slipped another fraction of an inch down the tree.

The bubbling hiss of a beam hitting flesh sounded just before Joe became aware of a sudden burning in his right calf—and the ropes holding his hands and feet together falling away.

"*Soot!*" Joe cursed, as the wound along his calf continued to boil. "Ashing thing! Soot! *Soot!*" He flopped away from the gun and sat up to check the damage.

It had been the energy-resistant pants that had saved him. While not able to stop a head-on shot, it had negated enough of the beam that he'd been left with just a graze, cauterized and no more than an eighth of an inch deep, but even then, it was starting to throb and pound with adrenaline-producing intensity.

"Well, that was ashing brilliant, furg," Joe muttered. He roughly twisted his arms in their bonds and yanked his legs through his wrists, bringing his hands in front of him. Immediately, lest their recent visitors decide that no, it *wasn't* a good idea to leave a mind-reading furg and his Congie Sentinel alive after pounding their friends to a pulp, Joe started yanking the ropes loose with his teeth.

It helped that the furgs tying him up didn't know what they were doing. Hands free in practiced seconds, he went to work on the purple knots around his ankles, again tied loosely and inexpertly. Freed, Joe scooped up the rifle as he lunged to his feet. Thinking Twelve-A could use a few more minutes to stew, he started untying the other People first. Still concerned they might have hit the petite woman a little too hard, he started with Shael.

Shael, apparently, had been sleeping, because she jerked with a scream when he touched her.

"It's me!" Joe told her, tugging on the ropes binding her wrists to her ankles. "Hold on. I'm getting you out of there."

Shael, who had started panting with terror, narrowed her brilliant green eyes when she recognized him. "The minder is a furg."

"Oh, believe me, I'm not going to argue with you about that." Joe finished untying her and threw the ropes aside.

"A *furg*," Shael snarled at Twelve-A, getting to her knees and rubbing her bloodied wrists as she glared over at the minder. She was bruised heavily along her sides and chest, and her face was a mass of purple and swelling. "You are lucky the vaghi didn't *kill* us!" she shouted, hurling the discarded ropes at the telepath.

Over in the grass on his chest, Twelve-A turned his head slightly away in silence, flinching when the ropes hit him.

Feeling more than a bit smug, Joe went over and started untying Nine-G from where they'd wrapped him around the pine tree.

"Will he live?" Shael asked, coming to stand beside Joe with an anxious look. She, too, had made no haste to untie the minder.

"Dunno yet. Gimme a minute." Joe finished pulling the ropes free—they'd tied him down *good*—and then eased the huge man backwards to the bloody grass beneath him.

Nine-G was still unconscious, a head-wound collecting flies, but his eyelids were fluttering with life. His head lolled to one side, his chest and torso revealing a profusion of bruises that hadn't been apparent a moment before. Surprisingly, his breathing was deep and steady.

He must've put up a good fight, Joe thought, somewhat irritated there weren't any crushed vaghi bodies to show for it.

Only after he'd untied *all* the others did Joe limp over to stand beside the bloody hat. Twelve-A, hogtied like a feast-day Takki, continued to stare directly at the ground, not even acknowledging him.

Lifting the crimson-stained brim of the crude straw hat with a toe, Joe gave the telepath a hard look. "So. You learn your lesson about feeding strangers, furgling?" He flicked the ruined hat aside, and the broken thing flopped wetly in the grass beside the burnt-out fire.

Twelve-A continued to ignore him, not even bothering to lift his eyes from the blood beneath his chin.

Joe grunted. Like Nine-G, the minder's naked body was covered head-to-toe in ugly black bruises, but even more so than the mover. A bloody club lay nearby, still carrying a few blond hairs, obviously having been used to do the deed. Judging by the extent of the damage, Joe was probably actually lucky the pointy-eared furg was breathing.

Still. If the pointy-eared furg had *listened* to him, he wouldn't be bleeding on the ground right now. Joe thought it was an excellent wake-up call, one that he would have expected a *mind-reader* to have had a hell of a lot earlier than this.

"So they gave you a good beating," Joe said, nudging the minder with his foot when Twelve-A still refused to look at him. "I've had my share. It's not so bad."

The telepath continued to shiver and stare at the ground, not lifting his head.

Sighing, Joe dropped to one knee beside Twelve-A. Reaching for the purple ropes securing the minder's legs to his arms, he said, "You and I are going to have to have a chat about the nature of Man, and how I'm a hell of a lot older than you and I understand people a hell of a lot better than you do, and how sometimes you should just burnin' listen to me." When he started untying Twelve-A's wrists, the telepath abruptly looked to the side, hiding his face from Joe. He still hadn't met Joe's eyes.

Then, as Joe untied him, Twelve-A let his limbs fall lifelessly to the ground. He didn't even try to move them or sit up. It was when Joe thought he heard the pitiful sounds of Twelve-A quietly sobbing that he finally snorted on a welling of irritation.

"Oh *come on*," Joe snapped. "This was *your fault*, furg. I *warned* you. Don't you *dare* try and wallow in self-pity. Sit up and accept responsibility. You were a naïve furg. Just say it."

Twelve-A twisted to give him a wretched look, then, and Joe froze when he saw the huge black **ABOMINASHUN** someone had scrawled across the minder's forehead in charcoal. Joe saw that the telepath's blue eyes, bloodshot in his bruised and swollen face, were rimmed with tears.

I was a naïve furg, Twelve-A said softly, once more turning to stare at the ground, hopelessness like a shroud around him. Joe had the odd feeling he was looking at someone who no longer wanted to live.

Though that had been his intent—to get Twelve-A to realize that Humankind was, at its base nature, cruel, hurtful, and unkind—Joe suddenly felt a horrible sense of regret, a wish he could take it back. He gingerly reached out to touch the experiment's shoulder. "Hey, that's not what I meant."

Twelve-A twisted back to face him, his eyes hard. The **ABOMINASHUN** stood out like a brand across his head. *Yes it is. You wanted me to see the cruelty of people. You wanted me to see the hate and the violence and the sickness. You wanted to prove to me that people are twisted, evil, and rotten inside, Joe.* Twelve-A made a wry sound of despair in his throat, one of the only physical sounds Joe had ever heard him make. *Like I could somehow be blind to it. Like I'm not already drowning in it!*

Joe swallowed hard, taking aback by his friend's vehemence. Even then, the minder's emotions were sweeping him away from himself, dragging Joe into their inky, despondent depths like a beetle riding an ocean tide. "Uh…"

But Twelve-A was sitting up, now, angry. *I know people are cruel, Joe. I see everything they do, everything they think, everything they say…I see every aspect of them, Joe. There's nothing that anyone can hide from me. I see it all. Of course I see their sickness, Joe. I'm trying to reverse it.*

Joe swallowed, stunned by the fierceness in the minder's face. It was the first time Twelve-A had shown passion over anything, and it felt ominous. Dangerous.

You want to know how much of that sickness I feel, Joe? Twelve-A demanded through more tears, his mental voice breaking. *You want to know what kinds of horrible things I see, with every wretched moment of every breath on this despicable rock? Here. I'll show you.*

And with that, suddenly Joe felt a thousand victims, crying as their survival supplies were stolen, their loved ones raped or killed, their bodies left to desiccate in the wind. He heard the dispassionate snickers of a thousand murderers and thieves. He felt the loneliness, the struggles, the pain. He felt the anger, the rage, the hatred, the fear, the terror, the misery. He felt it all, and it assaulted him from all sides, tainting him, tearing at his soul, trying to rip him to pieces.

Twelve-A wrenched the agony away as quickly as he'd shown it to him. *That is what I see, Joe,* the telepath said softly. *I see it every day. All the time. It's always there, on all sides, trying to work its way into my mind, crack my core, and eat me alive. You know why I weave grass hats and play with butterflies, Joe?*

Joe could only swallow. The reason was obvious, but he couldn't bring himself to speak it.

Because it gives me something to think about other than how much I hate Humanity! Twelve-A cried, his powerful thought booming from all sides, hitting Joe's core like an asteroid.

Joe found himself speechless, terrified and awed by the power flowing off the young man in front of him. Joe's eyes flickered up to the black scribble across Twelve-A's face. "I'm sorry," he said softly. It was all he could manage, so wracked by the telepath's misery.

Tears were streaking the telepath's bruised and puffy cheeks, now. *You know why I wanted so desperately to see the good in people, Joe?* Twelve-A whispered, agony etching his face. *You know why I tried so hard?* The minder's anguish was now permeating the entire clearing like a Huouyt nerve-gas, wrenching tears from Joe's own eyes, seizing his chest in powerful sobs that were not his own.

Overwhelmed, trapped in Twelve-A's emotions like that beetle in the vastness of an ocean wave, Joe could only shake his head.

Because, Twelve-A said, his mental voice sinking to a cold whisper, *you won't like it if I see the bad. Nobody will.*

Joe had the sudden, gut-sinking feeling that, this time, he wasn't the only ant poised under the cosmic sledgehammer, and that, with Twelve-A trapped in that miasma of cruelty and horrors, it was about to descend. Permanently.

"You miserable Takki!" Shael snapped, startling both of them. "Is that *you*, furg?" She stomped up to Twelve-A and glared down at him. "You're scaring our charges. Look at them!" She gestured at the huddled groups of People. "They are terrified enough...they don't need your help!"

Twelve-A blinked up at Shael, then at the People huddled around them, bruised and beaten, obviously sharing in the telepath's barrage of emotion. Their eyes were wide with terror, their breaths coming in hyperventilating pants. For a long moment, Twelve-A said nothing. Then, gradually, he seemed to relax. The minder's ocean of misery retreated and Twelve-A wiped his hands across his face to remove blood and tears.

Shael grunted and stomped off, seemingly unaware of how close they had both just come to becoming a mental paste. Joe, however, having been only a dig away, *watching* that despair and indecision, swallowed hard. He suspected that Twelve-A had just threatened to kill a wide swath of Humanity, maybe as much as a dozen lengths in any direction, but was not completely sure, and was too afraid to find out.

Minutes passed in silence as he and Twelve-A watched Shael make herself another club from a half-burned branch.

They broke my nose, Twelve-A eventually said, giving Joe a sideways look. *And it hurts to move. I think they broke something inside, Joe.* As he said as much, he coughed, and a rush of blood stained the saliva on his lips, bringing Joe to the startled realization that the blood on the ground had not all leaked from his broken nose. *One of them kept kicking me in the stomach, once I was tied down.* Twelve-A wiped his face with his skinny arm and it came back crimson. *It hurts.*

"Yeah," Joe said, buoyed into nervous action by the threat of organ damage, "Don't worry, we can take care of that." He jumped up, and, still feeling like he and every other Human in a few lengths' radius had just narrowly evaded something horrible, quickly went to find the medkit he had stashed under a fallen log.

When he got there, however, neither the medkit nor the log were where he had left them. Joe froze when he remembered the log Nine-G had carried to the fire the evening before, and the axe that had been in Alice's hand. An axe that he had carefully stashed under that same log, snug against the side of his kit.

It was then that Joe came to the horrible realization that not only Jane, Eleven-C, his ovi, and his boots had run off with their visitors, but all of his medical and survival supplies had, as well, and the telepath was very likely going to die of internal bleeding if Joe didn't find said supplies and get them back. Maybe even if he *did* get them back.

With a sinking heart, Joe went back over to Twelve-A, who hadn't moved from where he'd left him, the crude scribble in charcoal still in perfect condition across his forehead. Twelve-A glanced up at him, once, then looked back at the ground in silence, already knowing the bad news, seeming to accept it. To welcome it. He made a weak cough and wiped more blood from his lips, then got up and weakly stumbled over to his friends, sat down amidst them, and closed his eyes.

Realizing he meant to die, Joe stalked over and dropped into a squat in front of him. "I'm going to go get my stuff back," Joe said softly. "Think you can stay alive long enough for me to get back here with nanos?"

Twelve-A made an apathetic sound and turned to lay his head on another experiment's shoulder.

Joe frowned, the Prime in him coming out. "What the soot is your problem?"

Twelve-A opened his eyes, bruised face scowling at him. *I told you what my problem is.*

"No," Joe snapped, shoving a toe into the minder's shin. "These people *need* you."

Stop kicking me, Twelve-A said, crystalline eyes dangerous.

Joe nudged him again. "Earth loses you, it loses everything."

Twelve-A snorted bitterly and tugged his leg away. *Earth doesn't want me,* Twelve-A said, once again turning away from Joe.

Joe dropped into a squat in front of the minder. "Earth doesn't want me either." Joe snorted. "Hell, I think half the Earthlings out there blame this whole thing on guys like me. Probably on me *personally*, because I was the Congies' poster child. They *spit* on me when they get the chance. Never mind the fact that it was *Earth* that started growing soot in test-tubes."

Growing soot in test tubes. Twelve-A gave him an irritated look. He was obviously still pissed with Joe for telling Shael he was of the clan Test Tube.

"Earth doesn't want me either," Joe repeated. "But you know what I'm gonna do? I'm gonna grab the survivors by the belly-scales and lead them through a freakin' apocalypse because a group of fat alien bastards on Koliinaat want to see us spend six hundred and sixty six turns scraping around in the mud like savages before they graciously come to our rescue, and I'd like to have a big, hairy surprise waiting for them when they come back."

I'm not fighting a war, Twelve-A growled, his eyes growing dark.

"Furgsoot," Joe retorted. He gestured at the sleeping People. "You don't think you're fighting a *war*? I've seen the way you look at them. You're probably sitting in your only source of peaceful thoughts for fifty lengths, aren't you, you furg? How long do you think they'll last with you dead, you insensitive prick? You really wanna leave innocent, flower-munching kids like *them* alone with a gun-happy Congie like *me*?"

Too late, Joe realized he was advocating his own immediate neutralization. He swallowed in the silence that followed. Blue eyes filled with irritation, Twelve-A scowled at Joe for so long that Joe wondered if he was about to become the infamous Drooling Man.

My insides hurt, Twelve-A finally muttered, scowling at Joe. *If you're going to go find me nanos, go find me nanos.*

"Sure thing." Joe got to his feet, all-too-aware of how close he'd just come to becoming an oozing mental patty.

Behind him, there was a monstrous groan, then the sound of a huge pine snapping in half and getting thrown a good hundred yards as Nine-G roared.

"They're gone!" Joe cried, raising his hands. Why, he wasn't sure. He was more or less positive he couldn't use them to ward off something small, like, say, a tree. And Nine-G, the massive Hebbut that he was, liked to play rough. "Ashing calm down before you hurt someone!"

Though Nine-G wasn't able to understand his words, Joe had been a Congie Prime, and his tone of voice carried through the furg's panic. The mover groaned as he got up onto his gigantic knees to survey the area.

"Al-iss?" he boomed, the only word he could say, despite the malicious sprite's attempts to teach him otherwise.

"The podling's off with Eleven-C," Joe said, returning his attention to Twelve-A. "I'm going to go get her back right after I convince my pointy-eared friend, here, that I can fix all this, and that he'd better not die on me or I'll hunt him through every one of the ninety hells for taking the coward's way out because people *need* him."

Nine-G nodded his big head dumbly. "Al-iss."

Joe scowled down at Twelve-A. "You're *not* going to die. *Are* you?"

Twelve-A gave him a very sober look, obviously considering. Then, almost tiredly, he reached up and wiped his arm across the

ABOMINASHUN, smearing charcoal across his forehead. *I'll try to stay alive*, he agreed, though the words carried an exhaustion that Joe hadn't heard before.

"Good," Joe growled. "Now, before we give them much more time to entrench themselves, I'm going to do what I can to patch you up, then I'm going to go take care of the problem."

Twelve-A's eyes flickered towards him, suddenly suspicious. *You're not going to kill them.*

Joe paused in tearing one of the blanket-scraps into shreds and cocked his head at Twelve-A. "Excuse me?" Because that was *exactly* what he was going to do.

They are scared enough as it is, Twelve-A said stubbornly.

Joe snorted. "They better be, after what they just pulled." Squatting beside the minder, he wrapped a bandage tight around Twelve-A's bleeding head and tied a knot over one pointed ear. "They're about to get a Congie boot up their asses and they know it."

You won't hurt them, Twelve-A insisted. *They've done nothing wrong.*

Joe stopped to stare, his hands falling away in total, stunned disbelief. "They've done nothing *wrong*? Did you hear what you just *said*?"

They did what they had to do, Twelve-A insisted, though his mental voice faltered slightly.

Narrowing his eyes, Joe said, "Yeah, right. Tell me that again when you believe it."

Twelve-A swallowed and looked away.

Joe went back to applying the bandages. "People—even starving people—do *not* have to hurt those who were trying to help them," Joe went on. "The Jreet have a special hell reserved for people who do soot like that. The call it the 'Reliving Hell'. They get to experience their own actions, except in reverse. Over and over again. If you believe the stories, most never get out. It's as bad as kinkilling, in their book."

After a moment, Twelve-A looked up at him with total confusion. *Why did they hate me when I gave them food?*

Joe grunted and finished wrapping blanket strips around Twelve-A's head. Knotting the last bandage, he took a deep breath, looked out at the People, who were now huddled together, picking at each other's bruises, sighed, and said, "Humans aren't like most critters out there. We're afraid of what we don't understand. Kind of like knuckle-dragging savages, that way."

Twelve-A gingerly touched the cloth around his head, then dropped them into his lap. *Can you bring back Eleven-C and Alice?* he asked finally.

"I can bring back Eleven-C," Joe agreed.

Twelve-A lifted his head sharply, his blue eyes piercing despite his bruised and swollen face. *And Alice?*

Joe sighed and rolled his eyes. "And the podling."

Without hurting anyone? Twelve-A insisted.

Joe narrowed his eyes. "We're not doing this again. Ever. *I'm* Chief of Security. That means I'll hurt whoever I damn well please. 'Specially those who *deserve* a good hurting."

They are just scared, Twelve-A insisted again. *You won't hurt them. Just bring back our friends.*

"Look!" Joe snapped, hurling a bloody rag aside to smack wetly against a pine tree, startling several People. Completely fed up with his friend's star-gazing, happy-huggy furgsoot, he jabbed a finger into Twelve-A's bruised chest and growled, "The only thing those people are going to understand is *pain!* Trust me on this, all right? You want a Chief of Security? Then stop knotting my damn tentacles and let me do my *job.*"

Twelve-A must have sensed that Joe was on the verge of dropping everything and letting the minder clean up his own mess, alone, because he capitulated. Slightly. *Just don't kill them,* he said. *They don't deserve to die.*

Joe thought of all the ways he could maim the bastards while keeping them perfectly alive and a frown crossed Twelve-A's brow.

"Fine!" Joe muttered, holding up a hand in truce. "Fine. I won't kill them unless I have to." At Twelve-A's continued scowl, he muttered, "Or maim them without cause."

Twelve-A gave him a suspicious look, but eventually turned his attention to the People. He seemed relieved when he saw Nine-G and the others huddled together, slapping at flies.

Shouldering his rifle, Joe casually said, "By the way, which one of them kicked you when you were tied up?"

It was the man with the hair like mine, Twelve-A said immediately. *Him and his two sisters. Be careful. They're dangerous. The three of them were…blackbelts?…in Taekwondo. They're the ones who disabled everyone so the rest could tie them up.*

Joe narrowed his eyes, remembering the three blonds in question. "If you knew they were dangerous, why did you let them waltz into camp?"

Twelve-A hesitated. *I thought I could help them…not be mean.*

Joe snorted. "Some people are just rotten to the core. You've gotta accept that."

No, Twelve-A said, glaring at him, *I don't* have *to accept that, because I see what they were before society made them what they are. Before they got sick.*

Sick. Is *that* what he called it. Well, Joe had a perfectly good way to cure this particular disease, and it happened to involve a Nocurna plasma pistol and lots of screaming. Carefully keeping his mind utterly clear of anything except korja nuggets and karwiq bulbs, Joe said, "And which one beat you with the stick?"

Them and their friend, Twelve-A replied. *The short one with the limp.*

"Right," Joe said, thinking of how great his last romp in bed had been. "I take it the four of 'em also beat up Nine-G?" He and the woman had met in a bar before he'd shipped off to Der'ru, and on a scale of one to ten, it had been an eleven. Sometimes he could even forget the fact she'd given her report to the Peacemakers a rotation later.

Twelve-A's brow was creasing in interest and didn't appear to have heard him.

"Or was that someone else?" Joe insisted. "I need to be able to recognize *all* the dangerous ones." Her name had been Nala, and she had utterly rocked his world. He thought about just how *well* she'd rocked it, with a little choice exaggerations here and there.

Sounding totally distracted, Twelve-A said, *It was the same ones. They were gonna kill us, but Mike stopped them.*

Good to know, Joe thought. Nonchalantly, he said, "Our visitors last night…They do anything to the girls?"

Twelve-A was frowning, now. *Two of them were going to, but Mike stopped them, too.*

"Really?" Joe asked, thinking of Nala's positional preferences, and how they usually ended up with her on top, back arched like a sweaty goddess. "Which two?"

The one with the pictures on his skin and his brother with the bald head. What is she doing to you?

As sternly and offendedly as he could manage, Joe growled, "Are you reading minds that don't belong to you, furg?"

Twelve-A swallowed, hard, and immediately Joe felt the mental fingers retreat. *Sorry.*

Joe grunted and strapped an ammo belt to his waist. "Stay here, keep those bandages clean and dry, and I'll be back as soon as I can with some supplies." Back in the group of People, Nine-G stood with him, making Joe hesitate. As one of the top three Takki in the food-pen, Nine-G's act of standing automatically meant three dozen People stood with him.

"And keep the big guy entertained," Joe added. "I don't want him getting in the way."

Okay, Twelve-A said, almost sounding meek about it. *And Joe?*

Joe raised an eyebrow at the minder, thinking he was going to say something sentimental, like, 'Watch your back,' or 'Be careful.'

I don't feel very good, Joe.

Seeing the blood on his friend's lips, knowing how quickly an injury like that could kill, Joe fought down a wave of fear and said, "Go practice your hugging or something. I'll be back soon."

Okay, Joe, Twelve-A said, as if he had been a camp medic giving perfectly good orders. Then, *And Joe?*

Be careful.

Joe snorted as he collected up the last of his weaponry. "I'm not the one that needs to be careful."

Twelve-A hesitated, seeming unsure.

"Granted, you're a mind-reading pain in the ass and annoying as soot, but you got somethin' you do well, somethin' you're really good at," Joe said, dragging his combat vest over his shoulders and snapping holsters, magazines, and cartridges into place. "Same goes for me." He buttoned himself up, then paused, eying the minder over the sleek black outline of a plasma rifle before he slung it over his shoulder with the other two. "'Cept, instead of digging around in people's skulls, I'm good at blowing them off." He slammed a Human combat knife into its sheath and gave Twelve-A a fierce grin. "Let's just say they pissed on the wrong Congie."

Please don't kill them, Joe, Twelve-A said, worry giving his mental 'voice' a definite bite.

Oh, he's using 'please,' now, Joe thought, impressed. "I already told you I won't kill anybody unless it's unavoidable." He slapped a pistol into a leg-holster.

Obviously, Twelve-A sensed something was not quite right about Joe's attitude. The titanic mental clamps came down, relentlessly pinning Joe in place. *I'm concerned about your definition of 'unavoidable.'*

Joe sighed, deeply, and thought of something to shut the minder up. "Okay. I won't kill them unless I'm unarmed, bleeding, a gun pointed at my head, nowhere to run or hide, nobody to help me, and a beautiful woman about to be ravished by men of dubious intent. Sound unavoidable enough?"

Twelve-A gave a mental grunt and reluctantly released him.

Joe grunted and strode off to retrieve his errant lover and his favorite pair of boots.

• • •

I lost again, Shael thought, stunned. He couldn't understand why he had lost. Despite Shael's great victories over his lifetime, all of his opponents seemed bigger than him, stronger, more battle-hardened. It shouldn't have been *possible*...

And yet, that nagging dream of Doctorphilip once more haunted him. *"You think you're Jreet? You're just a lab-rat."*

A lab-rat. A science experiment. Shael had heard Joe refer to the People as 'experiments' several times, and Shael had *seen* how incompetent the childish furgs were...

No! Immediately, he pushed that thought away. Shael was *Jreet.* He was Shael ga Welu, war-leader of his clan!

And yet, the inconsistencies nagged at him. His scales hadn't grown back in. His talons remained clipped. His body, which should have been stronger than even a Dhasha, reacted weakly and without coordination. And his *coils*...

Shael had, a few days back, found himself sitting beside Twelve-A as the minder was distracted with his hat, and he had compared their coils, ninth by ninth. They had looked more or less *identical.* And yet, Twelve-A was Human, not Jreet.

No, Shael thought, desperate, now. *No. I am Shael ga Welu!*

The Voran, oblivious to his inner struggles, went to tend the minder's wounds. Little did the Voran know that such internal wounds were deadly, especially to frail beings such as Humans. Twelve-A was going to die for his mistake.

Part of Shael, the warrior part, told him good riddance, that the Sisters' favor did not fall to weaklings and furgs. Another part of Shael, the part that had exchanged secret thoughts with Twelve-A when they were both alone and in the dark, however, mourned.

It's my fault, Shael realized. *I should have stopped this.* He had *known* something bad would happen. All of his instincts had pointed to it. And yet, his pride, his *arrogance*, had not allowed him to see the warriors for what they were. He had misjudged his own skills...again.

Shael wondered if perhaps Doctorphilip's specialized bed hadn't been for some other purpose, instead. What if, in preparation for their war against Congress, the Humans had been trying to create their own army of Jreet? What if they had sapped his talent and his strength with that machine, then passed those talents on to someone else? What if they had taken his *body* from him? Was it *possible* to transplant a mind from one body to another? What if, even then, Shael's true form, twenty rods strong and full of power, was being used by the tiny mind of an Earthling?

Feeling sick to his core, Shael's head began to hammer with his heart. It felt like something was gripping his mind, crushing it, and he realized he had to stop these useless thoughts before they consumed him. The facts were clear: His body was not how he remembered it. He was weaker, his skin softer, his coils shorter. He almost looked like...a Human...

No! Shael thought again, watching as Beda ga Vora wrapped Twelve-A's head in blanket strips. There was another Jreet in the camp, a great warrior, and *Shael* looked like *him*. Therefore Shael was Jreet, and his mental agonizing was merely the whining drivel of a coward.

So some things had changed. So Shael was not as strong as he remembered. So he'd spent a few turns growing fat on Earth. He was still Jreet, and he could re-learn all that he had lost. He could re-train his body to fight. He could condition himself, as he had in the past. All he had to do was find someone to train him...

Yet the thought of asking the Voran for help left Shael with a foul taste in his mouth. He'd rather suck shit from the dick of a Dhasha than ask a Voran to train him.

Still, as the Voran gathered up all his hidden weapons and said a few parting words to Twelve-A, it was clear to Shael that, aside from himself, there *was* only one other warrior in this group, and he happened to be of the house of Vora.

*Perhaps if I offer to share trade with my clan...*Shael thought, watching him head off up the hill. Immediately, he recoiled. Shael ga Welu did *not* offer trade with Vorans. He could learn all he needed by watching. Watching...and practice.

Then Shael blinked, realizing why the Voran was stalking off into the forest alone, bristling with weaponry. Shael had simply assumed that their friends had been lost, their blankets stolen, because his senses were not keen enough in this stagnant air to follow their trail. During their rush up the mountain to find the kreenit, however,

Shael had noticed that the Voran seemed to have other methods of tracking his quarry.

He goes to fight, he thought, stunned. *And he didn't ask me to come along!*

• • •

Since he was already packing six different guns, Joe went after his boots first. To his surprise, it wasn't Mike who had them, but Blondie and his two sisters. They were seated on a pile of what looked like gold jewelry and silver coins ten lengths over the hill, arguing over who got the cool survival gear hidden in the lining, heels, and toes. In three silent shots, Joe seared off the first one's hand, the second one's foot, and the third one's balls.

Still, it took them a moment to start screaming.

What are you doing?! Twelve-A cried.

Just how far is *your mental radar, Pointy?* Joe asked, completely ignoring his question. *Ten lengths...I'm impressed.*

You said you wouldn't hurt them! Twelve-A cried.

No, Joe replied smoothly, *I said I wouldn't maim them without cause.* He fired a fourth shot, taking the short, stocky stick-wielder in the good knee. Down in the camp below, food-sluggish men and women were scrambling out of their dozes, falling over themselves to get to cover, of which there was little to none. Joe scanned them with his scope, seeking the other deviants Twelve-A had named.

You tricked me, Twelve-A managed, his mental thunderclap full of shock and disapproval.

Yep, Joe said. He found the tattooed ape and his brother squatting on the wrong side of a boulder, their backs to him. He was about to put a beam through both of their hamstrings when one of them surged up and flew across the hillside like a Frisbee to impale himself on the top of a pine tree, seemingly of his own accord. Joe hesitated at that. He had counted the People before he left—they'd only been missing one, plus the brat.

A knot of foreboding building in his gut, Joe said, *Twelve-A?*

Even as the minder hesitated, guilt oozing across their connection, the second man behind the boulder was ripped from behind his hiding spot and thrown across the clearing to land in a tangle of tattooed arms and legs twenty rods away.

Better start talking, sooter! Joe snapped. *What the hell is going on?* Up until now, he had assumed that each of the People could only have one 'special' gene express itself at a time. Yet, if Eleven-C was down there doing the damage…

Then he saw her. Shael was completely in the open, striding up the slope with all the authority of a vengeful Sentinel, about to fully expose her naked body to every gun, knife, and axe in the vicinity.

What the hell is she *doing here?!* Joe cried, his heart giving a startled hammer of panic.

She followed you, Twelve-A told him, brilliantly.

I can see that, furg, Joe fumed. *What's she doing here? I told you not to let them follow me!*

She's in her mindspace, Twelve-A replied. *I couldn't stop her.*

Deciding to one day soon ask the minder what 'mindspace' was—and if it was the same thing as Shael's 'war-mind'—Joe jumped to his feet and took off down the slope at a run, hissing as his bare soles seemed to catch every twig, stone, and bramble along the way. He was bleeding from a hundred different cuts and scrapes by the time he caught up with Shael, running into her path just as she crested the rise and came into view of everyone in the enemy camp. Hearing his approach, she spun, a crude wooden club raised, her green eyes afire.

Joe lifted his gun, fired at the weapon of the toothless guy about to take a potshot at her, then swung to look for other contenders as Gummy's gun melted in his hands and the man screamed.

"You," Joe said, putting Shael solidly behind him, "are a dumbass furg."

"And you," the petite woman said, "are going to get out of my way or I'll use your tek for a wall ornament."

"Mothers' bloody talons!" Joe snapped, straining to keep track of all the movement in the enemy camp while at the same time keeping Shael solidly behind him and his body armor. "Go back to guard Twelve-A and the others!"

"The fight is here," Shael growled, shoving her way past him. "These vaghi will all die for what they have done."

Joe opened his mouth to argue, then closed it again, considering. *He* had promised not to kill people, but it would certainly be easier for him in the long run if Shael did it for him. As disdainfully as he could, he frowned and said, "You obviously can't kill these great warriors. You've already proven yourself too weak to do so. Thus, the duty must be mine, and you will go guard the survivors."

Instead of anger flaring in her emerald eyes, Shael's face went solemn. "You're right. Killing them would only steal our glory." She took a look at the camp, sighed, and said, "I'll go retrieve our companions so we can leave these vaghi to drown in their own cowardice."

Joe, having expected a completely different reaction, had to mentally backtrack to realize that, instead of what he had *intended* to say, he had said, "Killing these furgs isn't worthy of great warriors like ourselves. It is a far more humiliating fate to let them live with their defeat."

Damn it, you malicious little leprechaun, stay out of my head! Joe snapped.

Cajoling other people into killing them is the same thing as killing them yourself, and you said you wouldn't do that, Twelve-A retorted.

As Shael continued into camp alone, Joe narrowed his eyes. "Technically, I said I wouldn't maim those who didn't deserve it, Pointy," Joe growled. Indicating, of course, that he would be happy to do the same to Twelve-A, if he continued to dig through his mind without permission.

Try it, you gun-happy knuckle-dragger, Twelve-A replied.

"I'm trying to save your *life!*" Joe snapped.

You're trying to get your boots back, Twelve-A retorted. *And Jane. Especially Jane.* The way he said it, the telepath was talking about a particularly nasty batch of Dhasha flake.

"I happen to *like* Jane," Joe replied, keeping his rifle trained on the furgs in the camp ahead of him, should any of them try to ambush the naked chick. "She's the best damn girlfriend I've ever had."

Then, as if summoned by the Dhasha Mothers themselves, Jane's cold, sleek lips kissed the back of Joe's head in a spine-tingling caress.

"So that the guy in your head or that freak?" Mike said from behind him. Then, after a moment, he added, "Or both?"

Joe's mouth fell open. *You didn't tell me he was back there.*

You were gonna kill people for a pair of boots, Twelve-A said.

"Just whose side are you *on*?!" Joe cried.

Everybody's side, Twelve-A said. *I don't like it when people hurt people. It hurts me back. I just want everybody to be happy.*

Hearing that peace-loving Dhasha flake, Joe shuddered in professional disgust.

"What do you mean, whose side am I on?" Mike said, oblivious to their internal debate. "I'm just like everyone else out there. I'm on my own side. The world is *ending*, Zero. We're just trying to stay alive. A few idiots get hurt in the process, that's life, you know?"

Still distracted by Twelve-A's revelation, Joe ignored the furg with Jane, enlightenment hitting him like a twelve-foot sledgehammer from the Sisters. Finally, Joe felt like they were getting to the crux of the problem. "You're too damn empathetic for your own burning good, you know that, you little soot-eating furg?! You would empathize with a *Huouyt* if you had the chance, wouldn't you?!"

"Who the fuck are you calling a Huouyt, you ailo bastard?" Mike growled. The highly illicit, high-impact, rapid-recharge Ueshi-made Nocurna plasma pistol jabbed Joe painfully forward with her kiss against his skull.

Of course I would empathize with a Huouyt, Twelve-A said. *They're people too.*

"They are *not people!*" Joe shouted. The only Huouyt he'd ever met even *remotely* close to having a conscience was Jer'ait, the current Peacemaster of Congress, and even he could be a sneaky, self-absorbed bastard.

"Look, I don't want to kill you, Zero," Mike said. "Just put the fucking gun down, all right, man?" The tight way Mike said it told Joe his finger was already depressing the trigger. Joe was hoping he would. The furg would certainly find that entertaining.

They are *people*, Twelve-A retorted. *They only do what their genetics make them do. It's not like they* choose *to* lie *and hurt people. It's in their biology.*

"You're being *naïve*," Joe snapped. "That's like letting vaghi swarm your food stores because they're hordespawn and that's what they *do*."

"I swear to God Almighty, I will blow you away." It had that final-last-warning sort of tone to it.

I'm not going to hurt anyone I don't have to, Twelve-A said, sounding tired.

"You know," Joe said, hitting the safety on the rifle and dropping it, "once this is over, you and I are still gonna have to have that chat about your happy-huggy good-natured furgsoot. It's really getting on my ashing nerves."

You would not like it if I wasn't good-natured, Twelve-A said. *In fact, you would probably dislike it for the full five nanotics it took me to utterly obliterate your ignorant, violent Congie ass and turn you into a drooling monkey to mindlessly follow me as your supreme leader 'til death do us part.*

Well, at least he was feeling good enough to make threats. Joe grunted. "Okay, so you have a point. Still, you gotta learn some *discretion*, you know? You can't be nice to everybody. It just doesn't work that way."

I'm going to make it work that way.

Joe blinked, realizing that the minder fully intended to do just that. "Did you learn *nothing* from what happened last night, you pointy-eared jenfurgling?!"

Of course I learned something. I learned how to do it better next time.

"Are you *talking* with that freak?!" Mike demanded, poking him with Jane again.

A skinny kid that Joe recognized as Mike's daughter ran up and snatched up the gun he'd dropped, then brandished it at him with shaky hands.

"Hands over your head, Zero," Mike ordered. Up in the camp, people were screaming as Shael marched right up to Eleven-C, shoving anything and everything out of her path on the way. As Shael snapped the cord someone had tied around Eleven-C's wrists, Alice squealed with glee and ran to the green-eyed mover, throwing herself into her busty arms. Eleven-C was equally as enthusiastic, huddling behind the much smaller woman like a Ueshi trying to weather a storm behind a toadstool. Without missing a beat, Shael turned and led them back through the camp, looking ready to utterly annihilate anyone who stepped in her way.

As he watched that, Joe thought that Shael would have made a good Congie.

"*Now*, Zero."

In fact, he could think of quite a few instances where he wouldn't have minded having her at his back. All she needed was a little training...

You are not *training Shael how to fight.*

Burn you, Joe retorted. *I'll do whatever the soot I want.* Feeling a weird, molten-hot sensation in his chest, Joe watched her cross the meadow with all the poise of a Prime Sentinel. He thought of teaching the woman how to harness that warrior spirit with a Congie's efficiency and his heart began to pound. *Besides. She already* thinks *she knows how. You really want her running around kicking bigger guys in the shins and screaming in Welu Jreet? I can help her. Give her some moral bearings, you know?*

"Goddamn it, you stupid Congie prick!" Mike snapped, slamming Jane tight against Joe's skull. "Get your fucking arms up!"

Still watching Shael in consideration, Joe complied. As soon as his arms were up, another of Mike's skinny kids immediately ducked in and began to disarm him, pulling the guns and knives free of their sheaths and holsters, collecting them in his arms like firewood.

Twelve-A went quiet for a long time, then said, *Okay, but* you're *telling her she's a girl. And you're only teaching her how to fight so she doesn't go around kicking things. She makes a lot of the People cry.*

Joe snorted. "*If* I decide to teach her—and that's a big if—I'm going to teach her whatever the soot I want, *whenever* I want, and you're going to stay out of it. *I'm* Chief of Security. This is my *job*, and she's an *excellent* candidate to join the security staff."

She doesn't want to be a soldier, Twelve-A said.

"She doesn't wanna be a—" Joe choked. "Are you a *furg*? *Look* at her! She's ashin' brilliant at this stuff!"

Her charges taken firmly under wing, the black-haired beauty stopped in the center of camp, threw a few more boulders around the clearing for effect, then walked through the terrified men, women, and children that scampered out of her way like vaghi before a mowing machine.

She doesn't want to be, Twelve-A said.

Joe narrowed his eyes, sensing yet another way the minder was trying to meddle in his affairs. "Chief of Security!" he snapped. "Me. Not you. And I'm telling you that she's got some *serious* potential. I'm a Prime. I can sense this stuff."

So can I, Twelve-A stubbornly insisted. *She doesn't want to be a soldier.*

Joe turned to scowl back at the way he had come. "Oh yeah?" He jerked a finger towards the Man-Frisbee even then twitching atop the pine tree, dribbling crimson down the feathery branches. "Explain *that*."

"He's hallucinating," he heard Mike tell his kids. "Just stay here and keep a bead on him. I'm gonna go help Gary take out the crazy bitch."

Joe blinked and turned back to look at Shael—just in time to see the tattooed man climbing awkwardly up from the grass, a knife in his hand, his eyes fixed on her back in fury.

"Jane's harmless," Joe said.

"*Only for you, Commander,*" Jane's husky, Southern-accented voice purred. "*There are currently seventeen targets within range. Twenty-three, if you count the children carrying weapons.*"

"What the fuck?" Mike blurted, jerking like the gun had bit him. At the same time, Joe ducked under Jane, elbowed the man who held her in the nose, snagged one of the guns from the pile in the kid's arm, lifted it, and, while kicking the weapon from the skinny girl's hands, fired over the first kid's startled face to shorten the tattooed man going after Shael by a head. Then he spun, put the same gun to the boy's temple, and gave his father a long, cold look.

Mike dropped Jane.

"Back away from her," Joe said.

Dribbling blood from his nose, Mike babbled, "Please don't hurt my—"

"Now," Joe said.

Mike stumbled backwards quickly, big hands in the air. Scowling at the father, Joe languidly retrieved his weapons from the terrified boy's arms and, after stooping to reunite himself with his lost love, gestured for the two siblings to back up with their father. Once they were both a decent distance away, he chanced a glance at the ebon-haired beauty.

Shael was glaring at him across the abandoned camp, obviously displeased. Her chest and upper legs were spattered in crimson gore, care of the man's suddenly-misplaced head. Joe was pretty sure, looking at her, however, that it was the fact that he'd *saved* her, not the fact that he'd covered her in gore, that had irritated her.

"Jane," Joe said, once he had ascertained that Shael wasn't carrying a hunting knife buried in her back. "You're such a vicious bitch," he said.

"*I am when I wanna be, Commander,*" was Jane's sultry response. With it came the little hum of the fusion-pack powering back on.

"Fuck, is that AI?" Mike babbled, taking another two steps back, like Jane was going to come alive and shoot him and his kids of her own accord.

Joe gave the man his most psychotic grin over Jane's sleek ebony curves. "Bonafide Nocurna."

If anything, Mike paled further. "Oh God, man, please don't. We're just hungry. Please."

Joe considered. He *could* end the problem, right now, permanently. At any other time, knowing that these guys were wandering around, stealing and leaving people to die, he would have done it. But he had made a deal with a pointy-eared nitwit.

A deal you already broke, Twelve-A said.

"Not my fault you let yourself get distracted," Joe said. "First rule of warfare. Use the enemy's strengths against him."

So you're saying I'm the enemy, Joe? Do you really *want to go there? We could go there, if that's what you really want. I'm just warning you it wouldn't last very long, in case you hadn't figured that out yet.*

"You just weren't paying attention," Joe said, still considering Mike over his plasma pistol. "I said I wouldn't maim or kill *without cause*. Details, Pointy."

How about the detail that you could spend the next twenty-four hours thinking you're a twelve-year-old girl if you continue to piss me off? Twelve-A demanded.

Knowing a foray into pre-pubescence was perfectly within the telepath's realm of possibilities, Joe decided to cut his losses. He gave Mike a cold look and said, "This is where I tell you if I ever catch you sniffing around us again, I'll hunt you down and lighten your kids by a few body parts and feed your balls to a kreenit so you can't spread your rotten vaghi genes to the rest of Humanity."

"Sorry," Mike whispered hoarsely. "Sorry, man. Sorry." His calloused hands trembled where he held him, his big shoulders quaking. "We just…" He swallowed hard. "Sorry."

Joe gave a derisive snort when he saw tears. "You hypocritical sootbags are so burning lucky you got the pointy-eared furg on your side. And after what you did to him, too…" He shook his head, *still* itching to pull the trigger. "*So* burning lucky."

Mike's eyes widened. "You mean he doesn't want us dead?" The ashsoul sounded…surprised.

Joe declined to comment, because *Joe* was still debating. Scowling, he said, "Whether or not Pointy thinks you should die is irrelevant. *I* think you should die. If you follow us, you *will* die. He's the only thing keeping you sniveling Takki alive right now, so just count your-self lucky he doesn't seem to be capable of wanting you dead."

"W-we n-n-never hurt an-ny one," Mike babbled. "Please. We were just hungry…"

"Never *hurt* anyone?" Joe demanded, raising his voice in a shout. "I ran across your handiwork a couple weeks ago. A family of four. *Dead.*"

Mike flinched and looked away, going green.

Joe watched him with disgust. "You think you're doing anyone a favor by tying them up, taking their stuff, and leaving them to die?" he growled. "You think they're gonna what…*walk it off?* You might as well be pulling the trigger, you burning asher. If I had my way—" Movement caught his attention out of the corner of his eye and he saw Shael, who was leading the other two girls across the abandoned camp towards him. Joe immediately recognized the hard, determined look on her face as cold, warrior vengeance. Seeing she fully intended to murder Mike and his kids, Joe debated for a split second. Then, despite his better judgement, he lowered his gun and muttered, "Get out of here. Fast. And don't follow us. You do, and I *will* end you."

Mike must have noticed the look on Shael's face, because his eyes widened and he grabbed his little girl by the waist, threw her over his shoulder, grabbed his boy by the hand, and ran.

"How *dare* you steal my glory, Voran," Shael snarled as soon as she got within hearing distance. "His blood was *mine*." Her face was flushed, her perky breasts bouncing again as she stomped up to him. "Did you have Takki for ancestors? He was going to strike my *back*. It was *my right* to kill him."

No thanks from the pretty girl for saving her life, no compli-ments on his stellar shooting skills, no starry-eyed awe at his awe-someness. Of course not. Because the Mothers hated him and the Sisters enjoyed screwing up the threads of his life in every way pos-sible. If it weren't for the fact that the fire in her vivid emerald eyes was eerily turning him on, Joe would have had no problem at all telling her where she could shove her attitude.

But she was pretty when she was mad.

Really pretty. Joe's heart was pounding again. "I, uh, was just trying to protect Eleven-C. I thought he was attacking *her*."

Shael squinted at him. "Why do you insist on speaking the language of skulkers and thieves, Voran? Do you sympathize with this vaghi scum?"

Joe sighed, realizing he had spoken Congie. Again. Someday, he needed to sit down and figure out where the soot his Jreet habit was coming from and how to turn it on. Until then, though, he had a perfectly good crutch.

Can you please translate for me? Joe asked. *She's being unreasonable again.* After all, Joe had never been the scholarly sort—his brother had been given enough brains for the both of them. Why learn something unnecessary like a language when he had a device or grounder that could do it for him?

Twelve-A gave a tired mental shrug.

What the hell does that mean? Joe demanded.

I guess I could. I don't feel good, Joe. I threw up a few minutes ago. It was mostly blood. Hurry, okay? He didn't even bother to mention that Joe had shot someone, a fact that startled Joe to the core.

"Twelve-A needs help," Joe told Shael. "He's going to die. We can compare tcks later." Again, unfortunately, in Congie.

The woman scowled at him, then her green eyes dropped to his stomach. Without asking, she reached out and unbuckled the ammo belt and various holsters from his waist. Jane's sleek form went with it, the traitorous wench yet again trying to trade sides.

Joe grabbed Shael's wrist before the belt could fall free. "Since when does a Welu warrior demean himself with the weaponry of a biped?" he demanded. The mere thought that she was *interested* in them was enough to give him an ulcer. Jreet disdained firearms of all sorts. Considering the penchant Shael had for exploding craniums, he'd like to keep it that way.

"You don't need so many," Shael retorted. This time, she used her mind-powers to shove him aside as she forcefully took the belt of guns. "Typical grabby Voran, hoarding trophies like a Jahul hoards its ruvmestin." Then, with the poise of a Dhasha prince, she snapped Joe's belt around her own hips and give him a challenging stare, daring him to refuse.

"You," Joe growled, jabbing a finger between her breasts, "can't have my guns."

She gave him a smug look. "Try to take them from me, Voran."

The challenge in her voice made Joe's adrenaline surge again, and he once more thought about how this woman could kick his ass, and how much Junior seemed to be up to the challenge. He had to violently shake himself out of that particular thought before its sheer stupidity tipped him over the mental cliff and got him killed.

Twelve-A, Joe said, desperate now, *tell her she can't take my guns.*

Twelve-A did not reply.

Joe *would* have taken the guns from her—if he hadn't known she would flatten him for the effort. Her compunctions against using her so-called 'war-mind' seemed to have flown out the window around the same time some starving, selfish furgs tied her up and left her to die.

Soot, Joe thought, looking at his guns. He *wanted* Jane back, but he didn't want to become the Amazing Tree-Impaled-Man for the effort. Even then, the corpse-topped pine was a gruesome reminder of exactly what Shael could do to him if he pissed her off. He supposed he still had a few pistols and all his rifles…

No! a startled part of him cried. *You are not giving her Jane.* "I am *not* giving you Jane," Joe blurted.

The infuriating woman patted Jane's sleek curves. "Looks like you already did, skulker."

Again, the threat in her vivid emerald eyes made Joe's heart give a startled hammer. She looked so *sexy* when she was threatening to kill him.

"Uh…" Alice said, looking up at the two of them with perplexed gray eyes, "…what are you guys saying?"

"Adult stuff," Joe said, glaring down at the tiny woman in front of him, trying to figure out how he was going to get his belt back without getting skewered by a tree. Something was nagging at him, something important, but he couldn't get over the fact that the woman had just taken half his weaponry from him and he hadn't stopped her. Most of the guns wouldn't even fit in her petite hands. That was just *greedy*. Still, he couldn't think of anything to say. His heart was pounding like it had taken a plasma round, his chest feeling like it was going to explode as he met her fiery green eyes. Never before—*never*—had anyone done that to him. "Who the hell *are* you?" he blurted, barely able to hear over the hammering in his ears.

Oh, nice one, Dobbs. Looked like his brother's genius was rubbing off on him.

Shael, obviously not affected in the same way as he, snorted. "Dumb Voran." Without another word, she brushed past him, heading back to the People's camp. Joe turned, following the mesmerizing sway of her hips, feeling like he'd just been run over by a Congressional tank.

Alice glanced nervously from Joe to Shael, then swallowed and, giving Joe a look of apology, hurried after the woman now carrying most of his guns. Eleven-C, however, stayed with Joe, giving him a confused frown. "Gun," she said, pointing at Shael's back. It was one of the few words Joe had managed to teach her.

"Yeah," Joe sighed, "I know. She just took my guns." Guns that, until now, he had guarded with all the jealousy of a pregnant Hebbut.

"Gun!" Eleven-C cried, stomping her foot in the grass. She again pointed at the belt wrapped around the woman's retreating back and gave him a look like she expected him to go retrieve it.

Somehow, Joe didn't think that would end very well. Giving the woman's back one last torn look, Joe hastily turned and jogged into Mike's annihilated camp, picked up his abandoned medkit, retrieved his ovi from a headless corpse, forced the bawling, nutless man to take off his boots, slipped his feet back to their rightful place, slapped the magnetic catches in place, and hurried back after them.

Eleven-C kept pace, frowning at him. "Gun," she said, sounding more than a bit irritated. Like every other experiment in the camp, she had been forbidden to touch them, and obviously felt like Shael was getting away with something she shouldn't be. Which she was.

"I know what you mean," Joe muttered. "Don't worry. I'll take care of this." His legs, being over a dig longer than the ebon-haired beauty's, quickly caught up with her. "Those are my guns," Joe said. Shael gave Joe an irritated look out of the corner of her eye, but didn't slow down or offer to return them.

Joe narrowed his eyes. "Okay. What the hell? You're gonna, what, start *shooting* people now, is that what you're telling me? I thought you were Jreet."

The woman gave him a dangerous look, but continued moving.

"You would shame yourself with modern weaponry?" Joe demanded, desperate, now.

"You do," she said.

The woman had a point.

Joe had the realization that this could go really, really bad.

And Joe, who was having trouble thinking because something about the woman was sapping his brainpower, made the dubious decision to grab her and *take* his weapons back. "They're *mine*," Joe insisted.

He was on the ground in a microsecond, an invisible mountain squishing him from above.

"I," she said, coming to stand over him with cold fury, "will *not* bear your children."

Bear his...Joe's eyes widened, realizing she still thought he was aiming to wrestle her into dropping her 'tek' and becoming female. "Misunderstanding," he gasped.

She leaned down with a frown, the invisible barrier still solidly in place. "What?"

"Mis...understanding..." Joe managed. His chest felt like it was caving in.

She straightened, scowling down at him again. "You babble non-sense again, Voran."

"Please," Joe gasped, rapidly blacking out. In Congie, because he didn't know how to switch his Jreet habit on because he was too lazy to study it because he had a crutch.

Shael, however, obviously understood his meaning. She grinned and crossed her arms over her chest, curiosity in her eyes. "Oh-ho.

The Voran begs? Were you crimson fools never *trained* in the war-mind, Joe Dobbs?" She was grinning, now. *Much* too pleased with herself. "Perhaps if you ask *very* nicely, I'll let you keep your tek."

Joe narrowed his eyes, feeling a rush of fury boil up from within. "I'd rather suck diseased Dhasha dick than beg a Welu to take a bath. Jane! You're hot, baby."

From the woman's waist, Jane purred, "*Of course, Commander.*"

As Shael was frowning, twisting and raising an arm to look down at the weapon on her hip, the holster began to smoke where it was touching Jane's sleek curves. An instant later, the invisible barrier holding Joe to the ground dissolved as Shael was gasping, slapping at the fire, hooting and stumbling backwards, trying in vain to get it off her mid-section, obviously having forgotten about the belt release in her panic.

Joe stood up, smoothly unbuckled the latch, yanked the gun-belt free, and, scowling down at Shael, said, "Jane, cool off, sweetie."

The seductive Human voice said, "*So soon, Commander?*" Immediately, the gun cooled, ice crystals forming momentarily on its sleek black curves before it returned to normal temperatures.

"Like I said," Joe said, strapping the belt firmly to his hips, "they're mine." He started walking again.

Shael caught up to him quickly. "Your weapons fight for you," Shael blurted, sounding pleasingly stunned. She still held a hand over the burn on her midsection, but looked completely preoccu-pied. Licking her lips, she said, "Twelve-A said you were a great war-rior. *Are* you a great warrior?" She seemed...nervous.

Was he a great warrior...did a Dhasha have claws? Joe snorted, unable to keep the disdain out of his voice. "I dunno," Joe said, tug-ging off his glove and holding up his PlanOps tattoo, casting the evening aglow, "I was one of only two Congies to survive the great battle of Eeloir. You heard of Eeloir?"

He had intended to impress her with his most famous battle, but Shael was staring intently at his left palm, her sunburned face slack. "You've been marked by the Sisters," she said, in total awe.

Joe blinked and glanced again at his palm, realizing that, some-where between the gun and the tattoo, she had come to believe he wielded some form of potent warrior magic, and that he'd been chosen by the gods, that's why his hand glowed. Grinning, he opened his mouth to say just that.

"It's actually nothing special," he heard himself say. "It's called a gene-mod. They infuse the skin cells with genetics to make them bioluminesce, that's why it glows."

You sister-twining asher! Joe snapped. *Get out of my head, rodent.*

You were going to lie to her, Twelve-A said tiredly. As if that was some crime unto the Mothers or something.

But Shael's face had already twisted. "*Genetics?*" The way she said it, she might have been talking about flesh-eating parasites. "Only cowards and skulkers modify their bodies' genetics, Voran. A true warrior uses what he is born with, and no more." Then she looked him up and down. "But I suppose such honor would be...beyond you."

Joe bristled at her scorn. "It was a service award for saving the Ueshi Representative on Eeloir," Joe growled. "If I hadn't been there, a Huouyt would have killed him, taken his pattern, had his friends remove his zora, then gone back to Koliinaat to take his place on the Tribunal."

"So you saved a politician." Like he had rescued a pregnant vaghi and set it loose on Kaleu.

Joe felt his pride prickling. "I stopped the Huouyt from taking over."

She gave him a once-over, then sniffed. "I thought service awards went on the right hand." As if he were lying, now.

Joe narrowed his eyes. "Got it transferred to my left hand once I lost my right arm to the Dhasha on Neskfaat. You ever heard of Neskfaat?" Yeah, take *that.* Another one with only a handful of survivors. There was no *way* she could call him a coward, now.

When she just gave him a blank look, however, Joe scrambled to find something else she would recognize. "I'm Zero. You ever heard of Zero?"

"Zero?" she asked, her petite face twisting in a frown.

"Yeah," Joe said. "*The* Zero? Only Human who's ever commanded a Dhasha? Sentineled by a prince? The good-looking face on all the recruitment posters?"

Hearing those words out of his own mouth, Joe started, rewinding the conversation in his head. Since when did he try to impress girls with *war-stories*?

Clearing his throat embarrassedly, Joe put his glove back on and said, "It's just a tattoo. Means I'm PlanOps. One of the good guys."

Then he remembered they'd intended to strip him of rank, weapons, and biosuit and abandon him on what was essentially an alien planet to die. Betrayed by his own damn kind. By Congies. Sent back to a planet that didn't want him for a crime he didn't commit. Story of his goddamn life. He'd hidden that ship in Crystal Springs Reservoir, though he didn't see much hope in ever using it again. Humans had been given Execute-On-Sight status within Congress. Whatever money he had still stashed away from his caper with 'the Ghost' twenty turns ago was probably going to rot forever in his secured accounts on Faelor. *He* was never seeing it again.

"You are much too proud of yourself, Voran," the woman sneered. "Only a cowardly furg sings of his old battles. Real warriors find new ones."

Joe felt his pride prickling again. To be told with utter certainty by an ignorant *non-warrior* woman that *he*, after spending his *life* risking his ass in the deepest, darkest, most dangerous places in the Universe, was a coward, was completely unacceptable to him. "Oh yeah?" he demanded. "Like throwing around a few terrified women and children? Impaling a dude on a tree? Yeah, definitely something the bards will write songs about. Here, let me take some notes." He mimed getting out his stylus and datapad. "Was that once or twice I had to shoot that guy before he stabbed you in the back?"

Shael stumbled to a halt, her face flushing with fury. Joe stopped with her, a renegade reckless streak finally ready to take that sledgehammer and bash through whatever mental barriers those scientist furgs had saddled her with. "And before that," he continued, "when they tied you up and left you to die, did you *surrender* or did they just hit you 'til you stayed down? Hmm?"

From the way her eyes widened, Joe knew she had surrendered. Because she was soft. And a girl. And scared. And she really had no clue about battle or fighting. He would have snickered, but then he realized she was looking up at him with obvious intent to murder, and self-preservation hit him like a brick to the temple.

Now would be a good time to intervene, Joe announced, utterly secure in the fact that his buddy would stomp on the annoying Jreet wannabe and put her in her rightful, *non-warrior* place.

Twelve-A did not respond.

Joe felt the air around him start to solidify and squeeze.

I could use some help! Joe cried, not having expected his ace in the hole to be sleeping.

The minder remained silent. The air that had condensed around him was starting to press inward.

"Twelve-A's unconscious," Joe blurted on what little air remained in his lungs. "I need to get back and tend to his wounds before they kill him."

Some of the anger left the woman's fiery green eyes and the pressure eased slightly. With some hesitation, she said, "The vaghi broke his internal chambers. It will kill him."

"Modern. Medicine," Joe gasped, having nothing to return to his starving chest. "Can fix."

"Warriors don't need medicine," she sneered, disdain oozing from her voice in a perfect imitation of Daviin's sentiment on the matter.

"Twelve-A. Not. Jreet." His world was dimming, the lights starting to go out.

Shael cocked her head and seemed to consider that for much too long, then grunted. With a disgusted wave of her hand, she said, "I suppose. Care for the weakling, then. We can finish this later."

In that moment, Joe found his windpipe no longer blocked, his guts no longer being forced through his esophagus, and he sucked in a desperate lungful of air. Falling to his hands and knees, he struggled to catch his breath. For her part, Shael turned and walked off, completely unconcerned.

This time, after a quick, conflicted look at his gasping form, *both* Alice *and* Eleven-C went trotting after Shael.

"Traitors," Joe growled at them.

"Gun," Eleven-C said, as she passed. This time, she was pointing to Shael, who was once again wearing nothing but her birthday suit. Meaning, of course, she thought Shael was the better weapon. Joe scowled as the experiment turned and hurried to catch up.

"Fickle furgs," Joe muttered. He got to his feet, did a brief check to make sure she hadn't broken anything, collected his gear, and took off at a loping jog. He passed Shael within a couple tics, and though she raised her chin and tried to keep pace, he quickly outdistanced her much shorter legs and bootless feet.

Score one for the good guys, Joe thought smugly, listening to her curse in Jreet behind him. Keeping up his steady, ground-eating lope, he pulled himself quickly out of earshot.

• • •

Joe's smugness faded the moment he returned to the clearing to find Twelve-A wrapped in the arms of all of the People, face utterly pale, head lolling in complete lifelessness. Nine-G, in whose lap the minder was sitting, was picking through Twelve-A's silky platinum hair, pulling out bits of blood and grass.

"Jreet hells," Joe growled, peeling experiments from their dog-pile around their friend. "Let me at him. Come on. Get out of the *way*."

The experiments responded sluggishly; most had been asleep. Many of them refused to move at all, simply glanced over their shoulders at him, saw Joe's face, then drifted off again. When Nine-G saw Joe, however, the gigantic man did his work for him. Shoving everyone aside in an invisible wave as he leapt to his feet, Twelve-A's limp form slung in his gigantic arms, Nine-G lumbered up and shoved the minder's lean body at Joe with a look of worry.

"Yes, I know," Joe said, dropping his bag to the ground and starting to rummage through it. "He's hurt. Put him down so I can work on him."

Nine-G shoved Twelve-A at Joe again, this time knocking him over.

Joe, who had had enough of being manhandled by Takki-hugging, gun-stealing experiments, had Jane out and slapped to the huge man's nuts in an instant. "Try it again, furg," Joe warned. "I'm in the mood to descale a Dhasha."

Nine-G, one of the few experiments with the brains to really understand what a gun *did*, went utterly still, his eyes open wide. He swallowed and glanced down at his crotch.

"That's right," Joe said. "Drop him."

Since 'drop him' was very similar to 'drop *it*,' which Joe had taught came right before getting bitten, stung, cut, or splintered by unpleasant Earth-things, Nine-G did. Joe was pretty sure that the resulting five-foot fall didn't do Twelve-A any favors, but with a brief check of his pulse, he was relieved to find the minder still had a heartbeat.

He removed the gun from his big friend's nuts. "You may go now."

Nine-G nodded and stood there, watching. Sometime in Joe's absence, the jenfurgling sooter had removed Twelve-A's bandages and wrapped them around his own massive hands, which he now discreetly slid over his crotch.

Grunting, Joe went back to rummaging through his kit.

With an anxious sound, Nine-G removed a hand from his crotch and reached for Joe's shoulder, obviously about ready to continue manhandling Joe until he understood that Twelve-A was hurt.

Without looking at the massive experiment, Joe again raised Jane to nut-level.

Nine-G swallowed and straightened. Then, with a worried look, he took a couple paces to the side, obviously trying to walk around the gun. When it followed him, he gave a deep, unhappy grunt and sat down, making the ground shudder when his massive cheeks hit the grassy dirt.

"Thank you," Joe said, returning Jane to her holster. He dragged out his medkit and a pack of bandages. Then, pulling the scrawny minder over his shoulder, he stood and carried him down to the tiny creek beside their camp. Behind him, he heard Nine-G get to his feet and follow, bringing all the People with him.

Thus, Joe had forty-two curious onlookers standing around in a semi-circle as he dunked Twelve-A in the creek, washed the dirt and fly-eggs from his hands, face, and body, straightened his broken nose as best he could, then laid him out on the grassy bank and started administering nanos, meds, and battledust.

By the time the grabby, ebon-haired Bagan itch returned, Joe was crouched beside his sleeping friend, timing the shallow rise and fall of his chest, relatively sure that Twelve-A would survive.

"You left us behind!" Shael cried as she stormed up, panting. For their parts, Alice and Eleven-C hurried to reunite themselves with their colossal friend, who squealed happily and locked them both into his arms in gigantic Hebbut hug.

"Not my fault you couldn't keep up," Joe replied unhurriedly, stuffing his gear back into his pack. "Besides. I barely got here in time as it was. Hell, the pointy-eared furg still might die. His chest was filling up with blood. That can put pressure on the diaphragm, make it impossible to breathe. Nanos should take care of it, though."

Shael continued to stare down at him in fury, utterly uncomprehending what he had said.

Joe sighed and poked Twelve-A in the pointy ear. "He's *alive*," he made a ridiculously happy, bouncy gesture, "because I *saved* him." He jabbed a thumb to his chest. "He was going to *die*," he made a cutting gesture across his throat, "from his *wounds*." He jabbed a finger at his stomach.

That seemed to cut through some of her fury, because she blinked and looked down at Twelve-A battered face. The nanos were helping, clearing away some of the bruising, but the damage was still evident.

Seeing how *much* damage, Joe was actually surprised the blue-eyed wonder was still breathing.

"He talked to me in the Human training compound," Shael reluctantly muttered. "Kept me company in the darkness."

Joe realized that that was probably the closest thing to 'concern' that he had yet seen from Shael. "He should survive," he assured her. "I hope. Still working on it." He extracted another dose of antibacterials and, dipping a porous needle into the silvery solution, gingerly slipped it into Twelve-A's arm.

He'd spoken Congie, but she apparently got his meaning. Instead of giving him some flake about wasting resources on non-warriors, she eyed the telepath harshly, then grunted and said, "Good." Then she turned and walked off through the nose-picking People, leaving Joe admiring her petite curves from behind.

You know, Twelve-A told him weakly, *she likes you.*

Joe blinked. "Huh?"

The minder's blue eyes fluttered open and focused on his face. *Did you let her keep the guns?*

"Do I look stupid to you?" Joe growled. "What do you mean, she likes me?"

She didn't kill you, Twelve-A said. *I was pretty sure she was going to kill you.*

Joe peered down at Twelve-A. "And you wouldn't have stopped her?" he demanded, hurt.

Twelve-A took a couple weak breaths. *She wears her mindspace like a shield. I can't reach her through it.* His anemic gasps caught in his lungs and with a wracking cough, he started to hack up chunks of what looked like nano-encapsulated lumps of blood and toxins.

"But you can sense what she's thinking?" Joe prodded, completely unmoved by his friend's pathetic choking fit. "And you think she likes me?" The idea was making his heart pound.

What is *that stuff?* the minder said weakly, staring at the black globules, looking totally appalled.

"How *much* does she like me?" Joe demanded. He chanced a glance back at the woman's retreating form and he once again had that startling realization that she could totally kick his ass, and, horrifyingly, he found that oddly thrilling.

Twelve-A slowly turned from his inspection of the gelatinous nannite wastes to scowl at him. *I just coughed up black globs of snot from my lungs, furg.* He pointed, for Joe's clarification.

"It's normal," Joe said. "Answer my question. Is she like…interested?" His heart was starting to hammer painfully at the thought of kissing her. Which was scaring the hell outta him.

She likes you enough, Twelve-A muttered. *She thinks you might be the better fighter.*

"Define 'enough', you Nansaba-eared freak!" Joe cried. "Does she like me or not?"

Twelve-A narrowed his blue eyes. *Ten minutes ago, I was dying.*

"Well, you're not anymore." Joe's heart was pounding so hard he was having trouble thinking straight. "Does she *want* me to kick her ass? Is that what the child-bearing crap was about?" Though it was rare, sometimes a Jreet picked a suitable mate and chose to be female, though requested a good ass-kicking to save face. The idea that she was choosing to be female, for him, left Joe oddly warm and fuzzy inside.

I could still be dying, you know, Twelve-A told him, pale face glaring up at him.

"You're not," Joe said, his mind in overdrive. Maybe he *should* thoroughly kick her ass, at least once. By Jreet rights, that would make her female, which would at least put her on the right side of the gender divide. Maybe, once he vanquished her and proved himself to be the male of the relationship, she would stop being unreasonable and let him kiss her. Ash, he wanted to kiss her…

Twelve-A frowned at him. *What you are thinking is stupid.*

And if he could just *kiss* her, he could make her realize that maybe her new, big, *strong* Voran could protect her, say, at night. Warm her bed, even. Keep her new, tekless body safe from all those other horrible Jreet warriors out there…

I took him a moment to realize that Twelve-A was peering at him like he'd just picked out his left eyeball.

After it went on for several awkward moments, Joe began to fidget. "What?"

I think I'm going to go take a nap. Last night someone tried to beat me to death. Carefully leaving his globs of black mucous where they lay, Twelve-A sat up and glanced in the giant's direction with a tiny crease to his brow. Immediately, Nine-G shoved his way to the front of the gawkers, snagged the skinny cretin up into his beefy arms, and walked off, hairy buttcheeks flexing as he carried the minder away.

Unfortunately for Joe, the *feasibility* of legitimately kicking her ass seemed to have decreased exponentially with the fact that, ever since Mike's assault on the People, Shael now seemed perfectly willing to use her 'war-mind' to win. Or take his guns from him. Or shove him around.

"Soot," Joe muttered, feeling the lost opportunity like a knife in his chest. Jreet respected strength, and compared to Shael, he was a gnat up against a baseball bat. He should've broken a few bones when he had the chance. *That* would've shown her.

It was on days like these where Joe wished he had his brother's brains. *Sam* wouldn't have been standing there like a furg, wondering how to best kick a five-digs woman's ass. He would be schmoozing her into providing her firstborn child over the wonders of a glowing martini and a heated swimming pool.

"Soot," Joe swore again. His heart was still pounding at the idea of kissing her...which meant he had to convince her she was a girl. Which required a good ass kicking. Which Joe had about as much chance of giving her as flying back to Koliinaat on a spaceship made of korja nuggets.

Joe's starry-eyed quest to find a way to kiss her ended abruptly as he realized that Shael had gone over to his belongings and was rooting through his backpack and gear, squinting at weapons and survival items before tossing them aside and continuing her exploration.

Frowning, Joe went to reclaim his stuff.

Which, he quickly found out, she no longer considered his stuff.

"You left it here," Shael grunted, rifling through his equipment and taking his flashlight and emergency flares while tossing aside his canteens of whiskey. "That means you didn't want it anymore."

"*Nooo*," Joe said, yanking the bag from her, "that means I trusted my fellow *campmates* not to *steal* it from me." He started hastily gathering up his canteens.

Instead of having the intended effect, however, Shael just snorted and moved on to his smaller satchel. And, as Joe watched her confiscate a pair of his pants and his best combat gloves, he began to woefully realize that, despite her wholehearted belief she was Welu, she was not as easily manipulated as a Jreet. Or she was learning.

Seeing the intelligence in her eyes as she examined one of his spare charge magazines, he had the uncomfortable idea that she was learning.

"*My* pants, *my* flares, *my* gloves," Joe said, yanking them out of her grasp. "Look, these won't even fit you. Too *big*. Because you're *tiny*. See?" He held up the pants to his body, then to hers for clarification.

Shael's eyes got wide and she backed up three steps much too quickly, staring at the pants like they were possessed by one of the Ooreiki ghosts. Her eyes flickered to Joe and she swallowed, face paling like she were staring down a hungry Dhasha. Finding her reaction strange, Joe frowned at the pants, expecting to see some sort of huge Earth bug or something crawling across the fibers. Seeing nothing but a few loose strands of grass clinging to the energy-resistant cloth, he glanced back at her, confused.

Shael's green eyes were much too wide as she stared at him. Without another word or even an argument, she dropped his stuff and rushed away.

Joe blinked at his unexpected victory. He had *expected* her to flatten him again for the insult, but instead, it seemed like he'd somehow *scared* her. As he watched, she climbed up onto a boulder overlooking the camp—the excellent lookout post that Joe had staked out as *his*—pulled her legs to her chest, and started hugging herself, her pretty green eyes staring off in the opposite direction of camp.

Frowning, Joe glanced down at the garment in his hand. What *was* the People's thing against clothes, anyway? He glanced at her again, saw that she was definitely rocking and holding herself, then just shook his head at yet another of the experiments' eccentricities.

At least he'd gotten his stuff back with minimal effort...

23

FIRST IMPRESSIONS

"**W**ell, shit," Tyson said, staring up at the first of the many mountains between them and their destination. It was the first time the man had said anything since they'd broken through the clearing to be faced with a looming cluster of rock that looked to be half cliff. Slade shared his unease. The constant hills had been bad enough, but *this*...This was like looking up the skirt of a ninety-year-old ogre—it wasn't pretty. "Any idea how far we've got left to go?" It was the thirtieth time he'd asked that day.

"I could give you an exact number in miles as-the-crow-flies," Slade replied in exasperation, "but that number would be inherently inaccurate because we're going to be crossing a damned mountain range. Just drop it, okay? We can think about mountains in the morning. Right now, my barometric observations are telling me it's going to rain tonight and I want to be prepared." He flipped back to the description of how to build a shelter from pine boughs and frowned. It didn't look very comfortable. And he sure as hell didn't see how a few twigs were going to keep him dry.

Tyson was quiet for a few minutes, then said, "Guess."

"Christ!" Slade snapped the book closed on his thumb and waved it at Tyson in frustration. "I've been reading this thing for the last three months and I still haven't had a chance to finish it! Do you have something against books?!"

Tyson grunted. "It's not my fault. You read slow."

He did, and Slade found that fact slightly annoying. He *did* have a photographic memory, but it took him four or five times as long to read a single page. Combined with the headaches and his non-existent libido, his so-called 'gift' sometimes seemed like more of a burden, especially since he now found it extremely difficult to sit down and read some brain-candy of a novel just for the fun of it.

"I read slowly because I have to start over every time I get interrupted, and you interrupt me every five minutes," Slade growled.

Tyson shrugged and stuck another piece of grass between his teeth. After a moment of silence, he said, "So are you gonna guess?"

Slade took a deep breath and let it out through his teeth. "I can't guess. There are too many variables. I'd have to pinpoint a certain location on the other side of the Rockies and then calculate the distance between our point and that point, then add all the different detours and account for shifts in elevation. It's quite simply impossible without more data."

Tyson brought out the worn road map and slapped a finger to the miles and kilometers bar in the lower right-hand corner. "According to this, it's about nine hundred miles to Nebraska."

"That is a gross simplification," Slade said disgustedly. "It would be one and a half thousand, at the very least, providing that we can find a relatively straight shot into Nebraska. If the Congies have blockaded the roads and destroyed the bridges, the distance will be much more than that."

Tyson nodded and folded the map back together with a snap. "Say it's two thousand miles, just to be on the safe side. How long 'till we get there?"

Slade scoffed. "Another equation with too many variables. It depends on how fast we can climb, how many people we accumulate in our travels, whether we can use any roads or not, and how we handle unforeseeable weather conditions."

Tyson rolled his eyes. "We walk about twenty, twenty-five miles a day. Say twenty, to make up for those weather conditions. Then when will we reach Nebraska?"

Slade stared at Tyson, dumbstruck. "My God, man, that's a simple division problem. A hundred days." At Tyson's sudden flush, he quickly added, "But that equation is inherently flawed because it does not take into account food supplies and seasonal fluctuations."

"You mean winter," Tyson muttered. He was red-faced, obviously embarrassed that he had needed Slade to work out such a simple math problem for him. Slade could actually see all the dollars Tyson's rich parents had spent on Yale or Harvard evaporating as the poor guy sat there, embarrassed. Unless it was an act. Slade still wasn't sure Tyson wasn't smarter than he looked. Unlike most people, Tyson was sometimes hard to read.

"Yes, winter," Slade replied. "I doubt we'll get very far through Wyoming—which is where we would be at the outset if we keep to the current pace—in the dead of winter."

"I see," Tyson said, stuffing the map back into his pack and sucking some more on his grass. "So what are we gonna do, hang out until it thaws?"

"We'll decide that when we get there," Slade replied. He was about to tell Tyson to get the Harmonious Society of God moving again when one of the Society's gun-toting priests ran up to them, panting exhaustedly. Slade recognized him vaguely as Derek Peters—whom Slade always thought of as Dick Peter because it was appropriate—a man who had been one of the most vocal for the slaving of women, back in the formative stages of their society.

"A large band, heading north!" Derek gasped, dropping to his hands and knees before Slade. "Gonna be here any minute!"

Slade's brain clicked quickly into focus. The man smelled like smoke, but it had a different taste to it than their campfires. It held the tinge of ozone. That, and the fact that the man had been stationed near the back of the unit, made Slade wonder why he didn't simply send runners forward with the message.

"They're armed with plasma," Slade said, frowning.

Derek looked up at him with a mingling of fear and respect. He nodded.

"And when were you going to tell me this?" Slade asked softly. "After I had sent men to investigate and they didn't return?"

The guard gulped. "No, sir. I wasn't thinking straight. It was a long run, and I was scared…"

"Scared?" Slade snapped. Tyson took two steps toward the man on the ground and hovered over him threateningly.

"She—they got Brent and Dave and Richie and Mick," the man stammered. "Almost got me."

She…Slade hadn't missed the priest's slip-up. That usually meant a retired Congie. Fuck. "And why are they attacking us?" Slade growled. "Did you provoke them?"

The man's eyes slid sideways and he licked his lips. "Well, I mean, we saw her—them—and Dave decided he wanted to do some target practice, just a little bit. Brent was against it from the start, but I—"

"Joined in," Slade finished for him. He was furious. "How many Congies?"

The man hesitated, his eyes going wide.

Tyson backhanded the man, sending him sprawling. "Ghost asked you a question," the big Aryan bellowed.

"O-o-one th-tha-hat I kn-know-of," the man whimpered.

Slade narrowed his eyes. "One. And it's a girl."

"Yes, Ghost, sir. A girl."

"You kill her?" Slade demanded.

The man flinched. "Uh…no sir."

Slade glanced in the direction of the back of the camp. "What was she doing when you attacked her?"

The man reddened again. "Uh, she, uh…" He swallowed hard.

Tyson raised his arm in warning.

"Taking a piss," Derek whimpered. "We were gonna grab her, have some fun."

"And she killed four of you," Slade growled.

His priest's face went red. "Eight," Derek managed.

Slade was impressed. He glanced at Tyson, who was similarly staring at their priest. Together, he and his Second eyed their back-trail. Slade had put their best guns to guard their rear. Even then, the Congie woman was probably back there, picking through their weapons, taking what she wanted.

"Damn it," Tyson muttered. "She's gonna take the guns."

Slade glanced at Derek. "*Tell* me you injured her."

"Mick got a rope around her throat before she kicked him," Derek babbled. "Strangled her a little while he gettin' his pants off." He went on to explain how they'd run across a pretty piece of ass with her guns leaning against a tree, taken her by surprise, tied her down, stripped her naked, and were arguing about who would get to have his way with her first when she broke free, went alien-kung-fu on them, and killed them all. Lovely.

Tyson's eyes had grown icy as he listened to Derek's rendition of the day's events. Tyson had been serious about the No-Raping-Women That Don't Belong To You law, and Slade realized that Derek was very close to taking a round from Tyson's pistol through his forehead. "Careful," Slade warned his second. "We just lost eight. Possibly more, if she's feeling vengeful. We need our priests. As…" his face twisted, trying to come up with the right word, "…repugnant as they are." He had, after all, collected most of his followers from a penitentiary—beggars couldn't afford to be choosy.

Derek started babbling his thanks, crawling forward and kissing Slade's boots. Looking down at the display in distaste, Slade quietly told Tyson, "We have to kill her."

"Yeah, fuck that, Sam," Tyson growled.

Slade tore his eyes from the boot-kissing imbecile to glare at his second. "Seriously? You wanna let her *live*? You *did* hear what they just tried to do to her, right?"

"Ain't killin' no women," Tyson growled. "She gave 'em what-for, she deserves to go on with her life."

"Yeah, if only it were that simple," Slade muttered. He turned to look down at the boot kissing idiot. "Tell ya what," he said thoughtfully. "We'll test the theory." He raised his voice to the sobbing priest and nudged him with a foot. "You get in on the action, there, Derek-boy? Grope a little titty while you were waiting your turn?"

"No," Derek babbled. "No way, huh-uh. That's one of the *laws*, man…" He held up both hands, shaking his head.

Slade narrowed his eyes at his priest. "You can't lie to me, Derek."

Immediately, Derek's tear-streaked face went pale. "I was gonna go first. I was gonna make it fast, I swear. Just had to get my rocks off, man."

Tyson's lip curled in a snarl and he reached for his pistol, but Slade caught his arm. To the priest, Slade said, "All right, Derek. Deed's done, you learned your lesson. No more raping lonely women who are somehow making it on their own without any gun-toting badasses to protect them. Get back to your station. We're getting out of here."

Derek nodded, babbling his thanks, grabbed his rifle, and scrambled away.

Tyson scowled, watching the man go. "They were gonna rape her, kill her, and never tell anyone about it."

"Yeah," Slade said. "A pack of gum says she's following us."

Tyson continued to glare at Derek's back. "I don't have gum."

"Too bad," Slade said, seeing a flash of black in the pines.

A moment later, Derek's head exploded. Several of Slade's flock screamed as the man jerked and fell forward, the bloody stump of his neck spurting blood over a ten-yard radius. A moment later, another priest's head erupted in a fine red mist.

"Right," Slade said, ducking out of sight and dragging Tyson with him. "*Now* can we kill her?"

Tyson was looking pale. "You have a plan?"

"Yeah," Slade said, patting his survivalist book. "Snares."

● ● ●

Rat was still trembling when she stalked back to her camp. The left-over fear and terror had finally gone, released with each pull of the trigger, until twelve more dead had replaced it with total numbness.

The ghost-burning vaghi. The disgusting, evil *ashsouls*. Humanity was nothing like what she knew in the Ground Force. It was…like nothing she'd ever seen. She finally understood what the rest of Congress had meant by calling her species unevolved, barely sentient. These…beasts…were *nothing* like Congies. Whereas Congies were all brothers and sisters, all siblings at the core, working together to survive, these Humans were genetic filth. She had the very vivid idea that, had she not broken free while they'd all been standing around with their dicks out, arguing about who got the first turn, they would have fucked her, slit her throat, and left her corpse for the flies.

Her chest still hurt from the adrenaline, and her wrists and ankles burned from where they'd tied her down.

The ashsouls.

A whimper broke from her throat unbidden, and she once again felt the loneliness pounding at her from all sides. Everything she knew, everything she understood, was *gone*. She was left with monsters.

She missed Mekkval and Benva and Sol'dan and Osteil and even the annoying little Baga. She missed her *friends*. Here, she was surrounded by brutes. Animals. She kept seeing their starving, depraved, excited faces as they stood around her…

She fell to the ground beside her bedroll and brought her legs up to her chest and hugged herself, trying to remember why she was on this miserable planet. When she couldn't remember, her mind still playing and replaying the events of the afternoon, she closed her eyes, lowered her chin to her knees, and cried.

From the first moment she'd entered her homeworld's atmosphere, everything had gone wrong. The Ooreiki Corps Director had meted out Judgement early, bots had destroyed her ship and her supplies, she'd broken most of the bones in her body in the crash, she'd spilled her nanos, Max had turned on her…

Then, in her mad dash to escape the Rodemax, she'd lost all concept of where she was. Hunger had won out and she'd eventually stopped running and started to dig in, building a small base camp in the woods, prepping to take Max out when he came for her—as she knew he would. Unfortunately, once she had built herself a small fortress, it had taken most of the *rest* of her nano supply just to keep herself alive after a damned kreenit had wrecked her camp, eaten what remained of her food stores, and destroyed most of her weapons. Since then, she'd been wandering the planet looking for small Earth-fauna that she hoped was edible, killing them with her throwing-knife because her gun would dissolve what flesh they had to eat, afraid of building an open fire for fear of attracting attention, sometimes so hungry she devoured her findings raw.

Rat, who hadn't had anything to eat in close to four days, just stared at the ground in front of her feet. It was part of what had given the bastards the jump on her. She was weak. Really weak. It was getting to be a lot of effort just to pick up her rifle and move camp whenever she ran out of rodents to eat.

Thinking of rodents made her hands shake. Rat glanced to the side at the tuft of grass growing near her bed. She'd been eying it for the last two days, knowing it would be the beginning of the end, but she was to the point where anything—anything—in her gut would be better than nothing.

You can't eat grass, Rat thought, miserable. *It'll take and give nothing in return.*

But, even though her *mind* knew that, her body saw the grass and screamed at her to wrap her fingers around it and put it in her mouth. Anything to stave off the hunger.

Rat closed her eyes and tried to think about something—*anything*—else. The dead men. She'd taken their belongings, then gone on to kill their buddies. She'd seen the bright red blood flooding out onto the ground, had seen the flies congregating on it, and had thoroughly sickened herself with the pang of hunger that followed.

She refused to eat corpses. It was the one thing she would not do. She'd seen enough half-eaten Human corpses—bodies of her *friends*— that she'd rather eat grass than dig into that nice, warm thigh…

"Stop *thinking about food!*" she screamed at herself, desperate, now. She had filled her stomach with water earlier that day, but she'd already pissed most of it out. She grabbed herself by the temples and tried to think of her friends, of the Sentinel she'd had to leave behind, of her younger years, of the last big war, of starving in the pits when they ran out of rations, of celebratory feasts with her groundteam after another dead prince…

Rat lost it, then. She reached out, yanked up a clump of grass, and started stuffing it in her mouth. She had to chew it well, she found, to make it go down her throat, otherwise the multitudes of built-in barbs of the leaves lodged in her esophagus.

Rat swallowed hard, pushing the handful of grass into her stomach, then tore out another clump.

"You know," a man's voice said, "I was going to go through all the effort to snare you, but I think maybe I'll just feed you, instead."

Rat scrambled for her gun and, rolling, brought it up and around to face the newcomer.

The big man standing a few feet away had no weapon that she could see, but he was easily a good two-thirds of a rod tall, with maybe an extra hand or two thrown in, and was definitely well-fed. He also had crazy blue-white eyes that reminded her of a Huouyt, and weird, fluffy white hair. Some sort of albino?

Watching him over the gun, Rat spat out her last mouthful of grass and warily stood. Backing up, she put most of a tree between her and the stranger, then started looking for his friends.

"I'm alone," the big stranger said softly in Congie. He was watching her much too closely. "When was the last time you ate something?"

"Today," Rat bit out. It was the first word she'd actually spoken in conversation since Max had betrayed her.

The sootwad actually grinned at her. "I wasn't talking about grass, sweetie."

For that, she almost put a round through his forehead. Her whole body was trembling again, and it was all she could do to stand up. She was so exhausted she had to lean against the tree to stay upright.

He pulled out a small pink square from his pocket. "Care for some gum? It's all I've got on me, but you look like you could use it." The man held it up where she could see it.

Rat's eyes flickered from the pink square in his fingers, then back to his creepy white-blue eyes. "Get out of here, asher," she growled.

The man was watching her with outright curiosity. Holding up the pink square for her perusal, he pointedly squatted and lowered it to the ground at his feet. Then he stood and slowly backed up a good two rods and waited.

Rat's eyes dropped to the pink package, then back up to the man who was even then watching her with intense interest. She swallowed hard and felt the glands in her mouth working, filling it with saliva.

"Back up more," she managed.

Obligingly, he backed up another rod.

She glanced again at the pink package, then warily scanned their surroundings for some hidden companion.

"I'm alone," he said again. "Tyson heard my plan and told me to go fuck myself." He gave her a wry grin. "For some reason, he didn't think trapping a Congie with a snare was such a good idea."

Rat raised her rifle again, taking aim at his fluffy head. "Nobody's *trapping* me," she snarled. "Get the fuck out of here. *Now*." She looked again for his companions, but part of the reason she had picked her current camp was its protected location—it was almost impossible to be hit by snipers. Unless the stranger had a Jreet up his sleeves, he really was alone.

"When was the last time you ate something?" the stranger asked again.

"Yesterday," she lied, too quickly. Rat was highly aware of the fact that most of her weight was leaning against the tree, but she was doing her best to keep it from showing.

"You gonna get the bubblegum?"

Mention of the gum made Rat's mouth water all over again. Her knees literally started to tremble with the need to walk forward and collect it. She bit her lip, looking at the pink package, then at her poofy-haired visitor. After what the others had tried to pull…

"I'm not that kind of criminal," the stranger said softly.

Rat tensed at the gentleness in his voice. "I don't believe you," she growled.

"Obviously," he said quietly.

She eyed the pink package, her heart pounding. "Did you poison it?"

He cocked his head at her and frowned. "*Poison* it? No, I *chew* it. You Congies *do* know what *gum* is, don't you?"

"Of course I burning know what gum is," Rat snapped. Every *ounce* of her wanted to rush over, rip the pink package from the ground, and stuff it into her mouth, paper and all. It took everything she had to stay in control.

"You're shaking, pussycat," the man noted.

"No I'm not," she retorted, raising her scope to her face again in warning. "And don't call me that."

"What, 'pussycat'?"

Rat narrowed her eyes.

"Kitten?" he asked.

Rat's finger twitched.

"Boots?" he offered.

Rat scowled.

"Tiger?" His mouth was twitching in a smile, now.

It took every ounce of willpower she had to keep from blasting him.

"Go take it," he urged, seemingly unperturbed by the way her finger was twitching on the trigger. "I won't move."

"Hold up your hands," she growled. "Turn around."

"I'm unarmed," he said, but he did as he was told, completing a slow spin before returning to face her. She didn't *see* any weapons...Her eyes flickered back to his tiny pink offering and she swallowed.

Eventually, her stomach won out. Rat stepped from behind the tree and sidled toward the miniscule paper-wrapped package, keeping her gun trained on the stranger and her eyes out for his friends. When she reached the square he'd left on the ground, she quickly dropped into a crouch beside it and, still holding the gun on him with one hand, snatched the gum from the ground, tore most of the paper wrapper from it, and stuffed it into her mouth.

The rush of sweetness, of *flavor*, was overpowering. Rat groaned, rammed her teeth through the sugary block a few times, and swallowed in a spasm.

The man flinched. "It lasts longer if you chew it."

"I chewed it," Rat said. "Now go away. I should plant a hole in your chest for what your friends tried to do."

"Probably," he agreed. "But I'm guessing, since you haven't already shot me, it's been a little longer than a day since you ate, and you're probably tired of being alone. Congies are never alone. Must be a new experience for you, Cat."

Rat glared and, still in a squat, inched over to her bedroll. She started rolling her sleeping bag one-handed, keeping the gun trained on him with the second.

"You wanna come back to camp with me?" the man offered.

"*Hell* no!" Rat snapped. "*Leave*."

"I looked at the bodies back there," he went on blithely. "Most of them were a knife or a kick to the head. Even starved. You're really good at killing stuff, ain'tcha, Whiskers?"

...*Whiskers?* Rat stopped and scowled at him over the gun. She stared at him blankly for several minutes. The stranger merely waited, watching her calmly.

"Tell you what," Rat said finally.

He raised his frizzy white brow, obviously listening.

"You tell me what you want," Rat said, "and I'll tell you how fast you're gonna have to run to survive the next twenty seconds."

"Honestly?" The man laughed. "I'd like to convince you to join us."

"Not gonna happen," Rat snapped. "I don't associate with rapists."

"Tyson would agree with you," the man said. "Me, I find it rather impossible to get it up, so that's not a problem."

Rat scowled at him. "You're not running."

"Correct." He beamed a winning white smile at her. "I'm convincing you to join my army."

Rat cocked her head at the puffy-haired creep. "*Your* army?" She put her right hand back on the gun, tense. "So those guys were under *your* command?"

"Indeed," the man said. "I hacked the computer to break them out of a spiritual penitentiary. The guards locked the place down when Judgement started and were going to leave us all to die. How very Christian of them."

"I'm not joining you," Rat snapped. "*Git.*"

"You're hungry. I have food."

Narrowing her eyes, Rat snatched up her bag, threw it over her shoulder, and tucked her bedroll under an arm. "Don't follow me. More will die." She turned to go.

"If you don't come back willingly," the man sighed, "I'm going to have to acquire you as a prisoner."

Rat, who had started to walk away, stopped and turned back to him slowly. When he just grinned at her, she cocked her head at him in bafflement. When he didn't retract his statement, she raised her rifle scope to her eyeball and blasted off the poof of curly white hair in a *whoosh* of explosive, star-making energy. The man screamed.

"Acquire that," she told him. Then she turned and, grabbing the last of her things, stalked off in the other direction.

• • •

Slade returned to camp bleeding from the eyes.

Well, not quite, but blood was trickling down his scalp and forehead and getting *into* his eyes, so it was still annoying and made people scream.

Tyson's mouth fell open as Slade entered the camp, the ever-present piece of straw falling from his lips in shock.

"I want her," Slade said, his chest still throbbing with something between glee and awe. He'd gotten a hardon. The moment he'd met her cold gray-green eyes. Like goddamn wrought iron. Fuck *yes!*

"Uh," Tyson said slowly, "Ghost, your—"

"My hair is bleeding," Slade snapped. "Yes, I know." He swiped another irritated forearm across his brow, and it came back crimson.

He wiped the blood off on his pantleg in annoyance. "We're catching the Congie."

Tyson's mouth was still open, his eyes fixed on the wriggling white filaments that had woken up sometime after half of them had been blown off. "But your hair is—"

"Writhing?" Slade grunted. "Wriggling? *Squirming*, Tyson? Yes, I know that too. They'll stop once they get over their panic."

Tyson cocked his head at Slade for so long that it almost looked like some sort of mental cog had cracked in half. "Are you Human?"

"Not exactly," Slade said. Then, forestalling Tyson's next question, he said, "It's complicated. Tell me how we're gonna catch this girl." He walked over, yanked a towel from his personal accoutrements, and began scrubbing the blood out of his eyes.

"Uh," Tyson said, still blinking at him. "We don't."

Slade started wiping at his face. "I want her, Tyson. That's final. How do we do it?"

"You want her...dead?" Tyson offered. He was still staring at the top of Slade's head under the towel.

"No," Slade said, irritated. "I *want* her. As in *mine*. Your fearless leader wants to take a woman. Something to warm his bed and keep him entertained on those long winter nights. Get me?"

"You want her...crippled?" Tyson cocked his head with a frown. "Maimed?"

Slade wrapped his head in the towel and secured it to his head in a turban. "No, I want *her*. Preferably disarmed."

Tyson continued to frown at his towel. "You mean her arms cut off?"

"No," Slade said. "Removed of all weapons."

"You mean her arms cut off," Tyson said again.

Slade narrowed his eyes. "This is not debatable." Already, his boner was subsiding. Like a sinking ship. *Damn* it!

"Better make it her feet, too."

Slade squinted at his second. "Are you afraid of a *girl*, Tyson?"

"You're goddamn right, I'm afraid of a girl," Tyson blurted. "She killed twenty of our guys in like ten minutes. You ask me, we should be running in the opposite direction."

"Funny, I'm not asking you," Slade said. "We're *getting* her. Now help me figure out how."

Tyson peered at him, his eyes flickering from the bloody towel back to Slade's face. "Why you want her so bad?"

"You can say that, looking down the oiled barrel of her energy weapon, I had a personal awakening," Slade said. He bent and pulled a rifle from the pile beside his belongings. Shoving it into Tyson's hands, he said, "She's a walking skeleton. Starving. Probably gonna be dead in a couple days. I want her *now*."

Tyson shoved the rifle back. "Tell ya what. *You* go get her, and *I'll* watch the camp for you while you're gone.

Slade grimaced down at the rifle, making no attempt to take it. "I have no idea how to use a gun. Besides. I want to *capture* her, not *kill* her."

"And that," Tyson said, shouldering the rifle, "is why I'm staying right the hell here. When you die, I get your stuff."

Slade glared at his second. Then he turned to look at the rest of his flock, many of whom were staring at their Fearless Leader as if he had just grown tentacles from his head. Which he had, sort of.

"All right, fine," Slade said. "But *don't* eat my gum. I know exactly how many pieces are left."

"I want one pack," Tyson argued. "For keeping order for you while you're gone."

Slade carefully weighed the benefits of letting the orangutan eat his gum, then reluctantly went over to his case of Bubble Manium, grabbed a couple handfuls of packs, stuffed all but one into his cargo pocket, then offered the last to Tyson.

As Tyson went to reach for it, Slade jerked it back out pointedly. "Just one," he warned.

The huge Aryan gave him an irritated look, but nodded.

Slade slapped the gum down in the man's hand, then went about gathering up food and camping supplies.

"Don't take too much food," Tyson complained.

Slade paused and raised a brow as he shoved bundles of matches and rope into his backpack. "You really don't think I'm coming back, do you?"

"Uh," Tyson said, "not really, no."

Slade snorted. "Gimme a week." At that, he threw the backpack over his shoulder. "Stay here until I get back."

"A week, huh," Tyson said. "And if you don't come back by then, the gum and the Society is mine?"

"Yeah, sure," Slade said. "One week. Otherwise known as seven days. Or one hundred and sixty-eight hours. Or ten thousand and eighty minutes. Or six hundred and four thousand, eight hundred seconds. Starting right now." He hit the timer on his watch.

Tyson gave him a dubious look. "You're crazy, you know that?"

"Yeah," Slade said. "Pretty sure that particular screw came loose in my teenage years. Been a wild ride ever since." He grinned and gave Tyson a sarcastic salute with his survival handbook. "Later."

At his back, Tyson shouted, "You don't even know how to light a fire!"

Inwardly, Slade grinned. There had been...*concern*...in Tyson's voice. Poor fool had no idea who he was dealing with. Even then, Slade could feel the formidable gears in his head coming to life and starting to turn. Ghost, for the first time in thirty-two turns, had finally found something interesting to do.

24

TICKTOCK

Rat started out of a restless sleep and sat up, her heart pounding. Immediately, the wave of exhaustion returned and she had to prop herself up with an arm to stay upright.

She'd only made it a mile or two. The alien trees above her seemed to whisper at her as she sat there, blinking away her exhaustion. It was well past dawn, the strange yellow star already halfway to its zenith, and still she was tired. It had still been light when she'd fallen asleep.

Rat had been sitting there for several minutes before she noticed the bright pink square on a rock a few dozen rods off, down by the creek.

Instantly, she lunged to her feet, pistol in one hand, rifle in the other, and backed up until she had her spine against the trunk of the oak beside her bedroll. "Who's there?!" she shouted.

Silence hung around her, ringing. Only the trickle of water in the dried riverbed broke the calm.

Rat's heart was pounding, now, wasting energy she didn't have. "Hello?"

Nothing. The whole place was eerily quiet.

Looking at the gum, Rat licked her lips. That the fuzzy-headed cretin had followed her was setting off a dozen internal alarms, but the sight of *food* was completely overriding them. It was all she could do to keep her spine glued to the tree.

"What do you want?" Rat shouted into the forest around her.

No response. She waited several minutes, listening to the babbling of the creek and the breeze in the treetops, before she reluctantly moved away from the tree. She had picked another good location—she had a three hundred and sixty degree view, and again, unless the bastard was a Jikaln or a Jreet, she was alone in the camp. Very slowly, she started walking down the hill to the creek, expecting some sort of trap.

She found nothing but a piece of gum.

Her mouth watering, Rat's body responded without her agreement. She reached down, grabbed the gum, yanked the paper free, and chewed the blessed sweetness until her mouth again spasmed and she swallowed, despite herself. She finished it off with a few palmfuls of water, keeping watch on the forest as she did, then went back to her camp. It took all the effort she had just to climb the hill and return to her bedroll. She looked at the sky, thought about trying to get up and move again, but just sat there, instead, staring down at the rock where the stranger had left his gum.

She felt the stifling heat of the day already rising, baking the air to something almost intolerable without her biosuit. *And this is considered Humans' perfect habitat?* she thought, in disgust. There was no food, the days were too hot, and the nights were too cold. She hadn't seen a single large mammal since she'd landed on the planet. All she had found were bones. Bones of people, bones of animals, bones of buildings.

Rat swatted at another fly and leaned her head back against the tree beside her bed. Never before had she failed so thoroughly on a mission. Not only had she failed to locate her target, but now she was stranded and starving on the very planet that was supposed to be the cradle of Human life. What a load of Dhasha flake.

She must have fallen asleep, because when she opened her eyes, the sun was higher in the sky and there was another pink square on the rock down by the creek. As soon as she saw it, she sat up, alert.

What's his game? she wondered, nervous.

The little pink square sat there on the boulder at the bottom of the hill, baking in the sun, taunting her.

Carefully, Rat got up and went down to retrieve it, keeping an eye on her surroundings in suspicion.

When nothing sprang from the nearby boulders, no shots were fired from the treeline, no explosions threw her away from her prize, Rat reluctantly lowered her rifle and lifted the piece of gum from the boulder. Swallowing hard, she looked up to scan her surroundings. "Hello?" she demanded. "What do you want, you burning furg?"

Nothing.

"I'm not joining you!" she shouted at the woods.

Her gut was telling her to drop the gum and *run*, get as far away from here as she could, but once again, her stomach overrode her good sense. She unwrapped it, thrust it into her mouth, and chewed. She was able to keep it in her mouth a little longer this time before she swallowed on instinct.

The sweetness, however, did nothing for her dwindling energy levels. To get back to her hideaway on the hill, Rat had to get on all fours and crawl.

Panting, Rat dropped back to her bed and tilted her head against the tree. Then she simply slid down sideways and went to sleep.

When Rat woke, it was to moonlight. Like every other Congie in the Army, her eyes had been augmented to pick up ambient light to better aid her function in tunnels or nighttime assaults. The result was that, despite the fact she knew it was close to total darkness, she could still see the little pink square on the boulder.

And the note.

Rat narrowed her eyes. She was so tired that she probably wouldn't have gone after the gum if it weren't for the note. But curiosity was a Bagan itch, and it nagged at her for hours until she finally dragged herself back down the hill to the boulder.

Reluctantly, Rat took gum and note and opened the folded piece of paper—which appeared to be the inside first page of an ancient book—and was a bit startled to see it was written in perfect, spiral-form Congie.

If you'd like more, you can always follow me home. I have food. Real food, not just gum.

Rat narrowed her eyes and crushed the sheet of paper. Dropping it into the creek, she ate the bastard's gum, filled her stomach with water, and made her exhausted way back to the top of the hill.

This time, she slept until past noon.

Rat sat up, disoriented, totally unable to concentrate. *I'm dying,* she thought, more than a little stunned. In all her years working for Mekkval, she had never imagined that she would starve to death on some lonely hill on Earth. She hadn't had the energy to look for a rodent, and now she didn't think she had the energy to kill one even if it came within range.

She was just starting to nod off again when she saw the plate of food sitting on the boulder. Instantly, she sat up, every nerve in her body suddenly afire.

Food. It was unmistakably *food.* Potatoes and onions and bread and what looked like a leg of chicken.

Her heart thundering, Rat somehow found the energy to drag herself down the hill, gun in hand, then hesitated at the plate of food. She nervously looked it over for some sort of trap. She sniffed it, then poked at the plate with her rifle.

When nothing jumped out at her and another fly landed on the chicken-leg, Rat snatched up the plate and waited, nervous. Under the plate was another Congie note.

Fine, I can see you're going to be difficult. I'll feed you morning and night until you regain your strength, then we can talk.

Throwing the note aside, Rat began wolfing down the food. She ate until her stomach cramped, then followed the food with water. As the first wave of sleepiness hit her from the sudden influx of food to her system, Rat glanced up at the boulder, wondering if she could simply curl up around it to sleep.

That's probably what he wants, she thought, thinking about how indefensible the boulder position was. After all, the bastard had talked about taking her home with him.

The thought of being captured again was what finally drove her back up the hill, crawling whenever her feet slipped out from under her on the upward climb. Then, her body numb with exhaustion, she dropped to her sleeping-bag and lay down. She slept a full twenty-four hours.

When she woke, the plate was back.

Rat knew she was playing with fire, but this time, upon seeing the plate, her body overrode all her sense. She got up, stumbled down the hill, and ripped the plate off the boulder to eat.

No sooner had she lifted the plate did she realize it had been holding something down. She heard something snap in the brush across the creek, looked up just in time to see a tree snap upwards, then screamed as something caught her ankles and yanked her off her feet and whipped her out into the water. As Rat went under the rushing current, it dragged her downstream until she came up short abruptly by the rope around her feet. Then she found herself pinned there like that, trapped by the pull of the water, fighting the current, struggling just to keep her head above the surface.

As she flailed in a panic, she caught sight of the broad-shouldered, fuzzy-headed sooter wading out to her, a rope in his hands.

Ash! her mind screamed. She desperately tried to swim away from him, but the rope around her feet kept her thoroughly in place, her body tugged to its limits by the rush of the creek.

The freaky-eyed stranger was standing in water up to his thighs by the time he reached her and made a grab for her throat. Choking, struggling just to breathe, Rat couldn't stop him. He caught her by her neck and his impossibly strong arm shoved her under the water, and Rat realized he was going to drown her. Her lungs burned and she started to thrash, slamming her fists against his arms, but he didn't let go. She could hear the flood of water all around her, the air bubbles roiling against her ears. She felt herself losing control, her lungs starting to spasm in the need for air. Then, startlingly, the stranger yanked her up again and held her there, her head just above the rush of the creek, his freaky purply-blue-white eyes scowling down at her sternly. "Hold out your hands, Kitty."

"B-b-burn y-you," Rat managed.

He raised a cotton-puff eyebrow and dunked her again.

"Hands," he said calmly, when he let her back up.

"Go to...Hell..." Rat sputtered.

He shoved her back into the creek.

The third time he dragged her to the surface, Rat gave him her hands. He calmly held her head up against a knee as he started wrapping her wrists in rope, then—to her dismay—feeding rope between her wrists to tighten it.

Then, to her *worse* dismay, the bastard pulled out a lighter and, still holding her in the creek, melted the two ends of nylon rope together, giving her nothing to untie.

Casually popping the lighter shut and dropping it back into his pants-pocket, he peered down at her quizzically. "Going to behave?"

Thinking about the way the water was rushing around her on all sides, and the way that, with her hands bound, all it would take for him to drown her would be to remove the knee holding her head above water, Rat reluctantly nodded.

The stranger bent down, got his body under hers, and lifted her out of the creek. He spent a moment fiddling with the rope around her feet—*retying it*, she realized in horror—and then cut her free. Thus detained, he carried her out of the creek, past her discarded rifle, and upriver what seemed like a length or two, into a camp that with a crackling fire and a blanket. And more food.

He was prepared for this, she thought, miserable. The fact that he'd planned the whole damn thing just made her feel...stupid. And mad. Really mad.

Lowering her to the blanket beside the fire, her abductor leaned her against a tree and squatted in front of her, examining her in silence. After a few minutes, he pulled a pack of gum from his front pocket, pulled one free, unwrapped it, and popped the pink square into his mouth. Then he offered one to her.

Rat ignored it.

For a long moment, Rat and the stranger just peered at each other over the gum. Then, when it was obvious she wasn't going to take it, he sighed. "What's your name, Tabby?"

Rat looked away, eying his camp, wondering where he kept his knives.

"My name's Sam," he told her, when she didn't respond. Then he seemed to jerk and frowned. "Slade. My name's Slade."

"Sure it is, Sammy," she growled at him.

He narrowed his weird, electric-blue eyes at her. "Slade."

"You said Sam."

"It was a slip of the tongue."

"Yeah, right." She scoffed and went back to mentally locating and cataloguing his weapons. She couldn't see any. None. Not even a knife. *Damn.*

Sam reached out and took her by the chin and turned her head to face him. "Slade," he warned.

She gave him a vicious smile. "You bet, Sammy."

The big man blinked down at her, looking caught between perplexed and pissed. "I'm in charge of the food supply, Kitten." He put the gum away pointedly. "You call me Slade."

"You got it, Sam," she said sweetly.

He opened his mouth to retort, then closed it and glared.

"So what now, Sammy?" Rat demanded. "I hope you had some grand plan for all this, 'cause the moment I get free, you're dead."

He narrowed his eyes a little further. "You just became my personal servant, bedwarmer, and entertainment system. How does it feel?"

Rat laughed at him. Then, when she ran out of air, she took a deep breath and laughed at him some more. Finally, when she could find the control to speak, she said, "I'm going to rip off your balls and feed them to you." She glanced at his crotch to judge how difficult it would be to tear off the little raisins. Then she frowned when she saw the bulge and jerked her eyes to his face. "Thought you said you couldn't get it up, sootwad," she snapped.

Sam actually flushed and twisted so that his groin was out of sight. "You hungry? I have food." When she didn't respond, he cleared his throat uncomfortably. His face was so red it looked about to catch fire. "Chicken and mashed potatoes. We came across an abandoned farmstead awhile back. Good scavenging. Have been hatching chicks in this solar-powered incubator I built ever since." He wouldn't meet her eyes.

"You can take your food and shove it up your ass," Rat said, still disgruntled that he had used it to trap her like a wild burning animal. She started eying the knots on her ankles. He'd fused those ropes together, too. Ashy Jreet hells. She needed a blade.

"You don't need to be afraid, Kitten," Sam said, following her gaze to her bound limbs. He sounded almost...gentle. "I'm not going to hurt you."

"Oh come on," Rat snorted. "Why not? I'm going to hurt *you*." She smiled at him pleasantly. "'Specially if you keep calling me Kitten."

He blinked at her again, obviously not the response he had been looking for. "You're tied up."

"Yes, and?" she cocked her head at him, waiting.

He looked startled. "And I'm not."

Rat cocked her head at him. "You didn't really think this through real well, did you?"

She *watched* it cross his jenfurgling brain that she had annihilated eight of his men after they'd tied her up, then let the survivor run back to camp so she could follow him and kill his friends, too. She continued to smile sweetly. "What, did you start thinking with your dick, there, jungle-man? Bribe a pretty girl with some gum, knock her over the head, drag her home by the hair to warm your bed? Kinda forgot the fact she's trained in about ten thousand different types of murder, and the moment you let down your guard, she's gonna cut off your sooty head? That it's just a matter of time 'til you're dead?"

Sam just stared at her, his crimson becoming a near purple that made his screwed-up irises stand out an eerie white in his skull. He looked...scared. "No."

Rat laughed. "Ticktock."

25

STRAGEDY

This was not going according to plan.

No, scratch that, this was the worst idea Slade had ever had. Even worse than hacking that damn government file and dosing himself with gene-altering nanos. This was simply *brainless*.

The Congie had somehow wriggled her feet free and escaped twice already, had *almost* escaped four more, and if she hadn't been so damned weak from starvation, she probably would've kicked his ass all six times he'd run her down. As it was, he had a bruise on his temple—where the towel had cushioned a full-on kick to the head that would've crushed his skull—and his nuts still ached from their last scuffle.

He'd invented a word for times like this, when the best laid plans were doomed to fail. 'Stragedy.' A combination of strategy and tragedy. That's what had happened four days ago, when he'd been standing at gunpoint, thinking with his dick. He'd been forming a stragedy. Already, Slade wished the annoying thing would go back to sleep, but what had seemed like a blessing at first had become a distraction that was making him stupid. And Slade wasn't stupid.

It hadn't even been a plan. Just a crazy obsession to nab this girl and make her his before she could starve to death. And, now that he had her—the execution of which he was still particularly proud of—she made it clear with every breath, every look, every *smile*, that she was going to eviscerate him the moment he slept. Hell, she'd already grabbed a sharp rock and tried.

So now he sat with his back against a boulder, the Congie mummified to an opposite tree, leering at him in the dull light of the fire as Slade tried not to nod off.

"You're scared," the woman said. "I can see it in your face."

"You can't see my face," Slade said. "Shut up."

She still hadn't given him her name, but Slade had a photographic memory, and her face had been all over the news after Neskfaat and her purported attack on Mekkval. He had been hoping all the cat references would tip her off, but she seemed as dense as an ingot of ruvmestin. Typical Congie.

"They augmented our eyes," Rat said. "I can see your face." The smugness in her voice left absolutely no doubt in his mind that she was telling the truth.

Wasn't that just *splendid*. Not only did he have to worry about her breaking out of her bonds and running away, but he also had to worry about her, oh, say, escaping at night, when he couldn't find her, then coming back to hunt him in the dark with an automatic energy weapon.

"You're sweating," she noted.

"Silence, Congie," Slade said. *God* he was tired.

There was a long pause, then, "I'm not going anywhere. You can go to sleep, you sooter."

Slade snorted. "Right. Because that worked so well the *last* six times."

In the dimness, he could barely make out Rat's frown. "You can."

"Just shut up and let me think," Slade replied. He couldn't kill her. He *still* had a rock-hard boner, sweet-Jesus-praise-the-Lord, and as much as it annoyed him that the loss of blood was sapping his intellect, he wasn't about to give it up. He knew there had to be some sort of weird Congie chemical or unique pheromone involved because his little buddy seemed to jump to attention the moment he got within a few feet of her. And, with that thought, he had the sickening knowledge that if he killed her before he figured out what the chemical was, he was going to miss out on his chance to have an honest-to-God, self-induced, not-in-your-sleep orgasm for the first time in thirty-two years. He'd been itching to pound one out in his glee, but he was pretty sure that would give her the wrong impression.

And he *really* didn't want the pretty Congie with the penchant for eviscerating people and surviving ten-million-to-one odds in all-out deathmatches against Dhasha to get the wrong impression. Especially since her foot seemed to be able to reach his head without any effort at all on her part.

"I need to go to the bathroom," Rat said for the eighth time that night.

Slade frowned at her. "No. Stop asking."

"I'm stating a fact," she growled. "You leave me here much longer and I'm gonna piss myself." She hefted her bound wrists disgustedly underneath her mummified torso, then plopped them back into her lap.

Giving her an irritated look, Slade turned back to the fire, trying to figure out how to deal with this particular problem without meeting an untimely end or killing the best aphrodisiac to show up in over thirty years. She was a badass. A certifiable badass. And he had her tied to a tree and had refused her requested potty-break. Because it was dark outside. And she was a badass.

He was so screwed.

When the Congie spoke again, her voice was almost tentative. "So, uh, why *did* you go through all that effort to grab me? It's been two days and you haven't so much as tried to make a move on me."

Slade felt his face flush. Because he couldn't really come up with something better to say—and because this woman made him stupid—he said, "I was out looking for slaves and you struck my fancy."

Not surprisingly, it was the wrong thing to say. He knew it was the wrong thing to say because her pretty features twisted into a thunderhead. "You aren't very smart, are you?"

Slade laughed miserably at that. "Lady, you have *no* idea."

When he said nothing more, silence once more descended on the camp. Then she muttered, "So what, jungle-man, we're just gonna sit here until one of us passes out?"

The idea that she had taken him for a survivalist because he had made a cool snare he'd adapted from a book made Slade laugh again. She was obviously giving him *way* too much credit. Which meant, as soon as she figured out he was a computer geek, he was dead.

"You gonna just leave my rifle out by that creekbed to rot?" she finally demanded, as the night wore on.

"Why yes. Yes I am," Slade said. "Along with everything else you can kill me with." He'd made sure to leave all the sharp, pointy objects behind before bringing her back with him, too, thank God. If he hadn't, he would be dead already. Simple as that. He'd dropped his knife beside Bubblegum Boulder on his way past and stowed his pen under a rock in preparation. Hell, he'd even left behind his nail clippers. Still, the constant throbbing in his temple where he was pretty sure she had given him some sort of concussion made it hard to escape his notice that she could still kill him with her foot.

Or her pinkie. *Especially* her pinkie.

"Fuck," Slade muttered, tossing another stick on the fire. The only real option was to take her back to the Society so there were more eyes to keep watch on her, but Tyson would likely blow her head off the moment she slipped her bonds the first time. *He* wasn't an idiot.

"You could let me go," she offered. "Maybe give me some more of that chicken."

Slade gave her a wary look, then saw the calculation in her gaze. "Nice try."

Rat peered at him through the darkness. "So why don't you want anyone to know your real name, Sammy?"

Just as he had every time she'd used the name, Slade jerked in annoyance and intended to tell her to screw off. The words that came out of his mouth, however, were, "I have a very famous brother and he screwed me over hardcore." Then, realizing he'd already dug his hole, he decided to just get it out. "I didn't want to be associated with the dick anymore. I decided to use one of my aliases. That was like twenty turns ago. Haven't looked back."

She was silent a moment. Then, "You gonna let me go?"

"No. Stop asking."

"I'm asking," Rat said, "because if *I* have to let myself go, you're not gonna survive it." She cocked her head at him. "But you probably already know that."

"Hence my current conundrum," Slade said, "and why I'd like you to silence yourself while I think, okay?"

She glanced at the bloody towel wrapping his head and stayed there. "Did I miss, then?"

Slade frowned. "Miss?"

Rat pointed at the crimson stain with her bound wrists. "I was just trying to vaporize a little hair. I hadn't realized I'd hit you." She almost sounded irritated with herself. For missing, not for shooting him.

"Nah," Slade said. "You got the hair. Mine's just a little...unique."

"What *is* wrong with you?" she asked, like she were discussing the weather. "You look like a burning Huouyt."

Slade snorted. "Probably am, a little." At her odd look, he took a deep breath, let it out in a sigh, then decided to tell her his sad, sad story. "I got bored one night and broke into a top-secret government computer system, stole all the info on their experiments, and, in between sipping martinis and getting laid, found this really cool one about making people live longer, think better, and able to change form. Kind of wrote it off for a few weeks, but then I got drunk again and decided to try it on myself." He grimaced, remembering. "I don't get drunk anymore. Kinda swore off the stuff when the normal 'groan and get the trash-can' hangovers graduated to 'blind and impotent, with a liberal sprinkling of bone-crushing headaches.'"

During his story, Rat had gone utterly pale, staring at him like he'd suddenly grown mandibles. Probably because, for the last three days straight, he had had a boner so hard it was painful. And he knew she'd seen it. She kept *looking* at it. That was another thing about

Congies. With them constantly having to bare everything to put on their biosuits, they had very little modesty.

"You...some sort of super genius or something?" she managed.

Well, duh. Wasn't it evident in his brilliant, *non-violent* methods of catching a Congie?

"The Tesla of the Congressional Era, at your service," Slade said, giving a little bow.

She swallowed, hard. Like she thought his next experiment might be to impregnate her with Huouyt-Human crossbreeds. Which, of course, would be utterly awesome if she was interested. Slade could definitely handle a few little Sladelings running around, doing theoretical physics as they played hopscotch and marbles.

Well, maybe not marbles. Slade had despised marbles. He'd never had the dexterity of some of his more physically-inclined, nongenius classmates, so after trying his first game and losing—which he hated—he had decided to do something about it. His simian companions had offered him other games, practice 'freebies' with no penalty for messing up, but Slade had waved them off and gone home. Instead of screwing around trying to practice something as pointless as shooting beads of glass across an arbitrary line in the dirt, he'd taken a weekend trip to visit his MIT fanboys and, with their excited blessing, had designed, built, and programmed a tiny AI robot to play marbles for him over the course of a three-day weekend. After the thumb-mounted machine obliterated six different opponents, wiping out their bags completely, nobody would play marbles with him anymore, and Slade had felt better.

Still. What poor losers. It never said in the rules he couldn't use a robot.

Rat was still staring at him. "You don't look impotent." Like he was lying about being half Huouyt or something.

Slade sighed. "Okay, look. I *was* impotent. Like, last week."

"Last week." Like he was speaking ancient Ayhi or something.

"Yeah. But then I found *you*."

"Me." Still that blank look.

Damn, she wasn't making this easy on him. In fact, the woman of his dreams was peering at him as if he were dribbling brain matter down his earlobes. Slade sighed again. "Okay, truth is, I haven't had sex in thirty-two years." There. He said it. It wasn't that hard. It only made him feel *slightly* inadequate.

"Sounds about right," she said.

Slade narrowed his eyes. "I don't have to explain myself to you."

"You do if you want to live once I get free," she said.

"You're not getting free," Slade said.

She languidly raised an eyebrow at him, looking utterly secure in the fact she was getting free.

Slade swallowed. Though he certainly didn't intend to free her, he decided to hedge his bets. "Okay, look. I *was* impotent for thirty-two years. But there's something about you that's…uh…making it all come back. I think I could actually blow my load, you know?" Then, at her look of distaste, he blushed and said, "Listen, you're a girl, so you've got *no idea* how cool it is to get hard for the first time in thirty years. It opens up *so* many possibilities. Now I just wish I could put it to use." As soon as the words left his lips, his mouth fell open. Wow. Had he *really* just said that? He glanced down at his cock, wondering what the hell was wrong with him.

Against the tree, Rat swallowed.

Oh greaaaaaaat way to ease her mind, you dumbass furg. Holding up a hand in peace, Slade quickly said, "Wait, lemme back up. That's really not what I meant. I mean, it's great you get me hard, but I'm not really interested. It's *intellectually* exciting, get me? I want to get to the *root* of the problem. I'm a *scientist*. Basically, I just wanna use you to figure out what chemicals you're carrying or excreting and replicate them so I can actually *breed*, you understand?" Hearing himself dig an even deeper hole, watching her eyes go wider, Slade suddenly had the urge to crawl under a rock and die. "I'm not going to hurt you," he muttered again.

They shared an uncomfortable moment. Then, softly, Rat said, "You want to breed?"

Slade's heart gave a startled hammer and he swallowed. He'd heard of Congies' general promiscuity, but her offer was disconcerting coming so soon upon finding her, and the unfamiliar throbbing in his groin was making it hard to think. Still, the world could use more of him. Even genetically diluted, half-Congie versions of him. Surely *some* of his intelligence would pass on to his children. Hell, he *owed it to the world* to attempt to pass his genius on to the next generation. A lot. Multiple times a night. Yeah, he needed to make sure to do it every single night. Sometimes during the day if he could get away from his devotees long enough to do his patriotic duty.

She was peering at him like a chicken eying a bug.

Slade blushed and cleared his throat. "Um. Do you?"

"I'm not interested in sex, you jenfurgling itch," the Congie snapped. "I want to know if you're planning on having *kids*. Like, soon. *Do* you already have kids?"

Slade blinked at her. Now *that* was a leap he hadn't expected. He'd planned sex first, maybe a few years of practice getting back into the hang of things, *then* blessing the world with needy, hungry, attention-seeking Sladelings. "You're sterile," he said. "I'll have to grow you another womb."

Rat looked like she was going to bark something else at him, but then her frown faded and her mouth fell open. For a moment, she just stared at him. Then, in an uncertain whisper, she said, "You could *do* that?"

"Oh sure," Slade said, waving it off dismissively. "I'd just need to make a pit-stop in a major city and find a good lab. Easy." He raised an anxious brow at her, trying not to fidget. "Why? You game?" *Please let her be game...*

Immediately, her shock faded, replaced with irritation. "No, I'm not 'game'."

Damn. Ah, well. Disappointed, Slade went back to trying not to nod off—and therefore die—as he waited for dawn.

"You can untie me," she muttered.

"I *can*," Slade agreed, "but *you* can also kill me with your big toe. Hell, maybe even your *little* toe. You ever killed anyone with your little toe?"

She got a thoughtful look on her face. "Maybe. Depends on whether or not boots count."

Slade groaned and dropped his head into his hands. He was screwed. So totally screwed.

"You untie me," she said, "and I won't kill you with my toe."

Slade gave her a flat look.

"...or anything else," Rat added, grinning.

Yeah, right. Like *that* was going to happen. "I'll get right on that," Slade said, pointedly leaning back against his boulder. He needed to get his priorities straight, he decided. Priority One: He needed to figure out what it was about her that was making his long-lost friend rise to the occasion. Priority Two: He needed to take her home with him. Priority Three: He needed to figure out how to not die in the process.

Then Sam frowned. Priority Two had come from nowhere, but when he thought of leaving her behind, tied to a tree, while he bailed at a run, his heart started to pound like it did when he thought about running out of gum. He really *did* want her to warm his bed, he realized. Which could get...complicated.

Nervously, he looked at her again. Her face was barely visible in the dim light. She hadn't stopped staring at him like a predator.

Suddenly, Sam knew what it had to be. A predator. She was a *predator*. Since her death had been so obviously faked, she must have been working for the Dhasha Representative for the last twenty turns. He felt this little rush of glee, realizing he'd found a way to have it *all*, and not die.

"Ka-par," he said.

There was a brief flash of surprise that crossed her face before her eyes narrowed. "You can't declare ka-par. You're not a warrior."

"No," Slade agreed. "But you can."

She frowned. "That's a lose-lose situation for me. If I lost, I'd be bound by honor. If you lost, you'd just go back to kidnapping me."

Slade frowned at her. "I'd follow the rules. On my honor."

"*What* honor?" she snorted.

"*Family* honor," Slade snapped back. "I haven't hurt you yet, have I?"

There was a brief flash of uncertainty in her eyes before her face hardened again. "I don't believe you," she snorted. "You're giving me a fifty percent chance of becoming your slave on my honor… or being your slave by force. Burn you, I'm going to *kill* you. No ka-par."

Slade scowled at her, his pride prickling, now. "You don't think I'm honorable?"

Rat narrowed her eyes at him. "You trapped me like an *animal*." She jerked violently against the tree for emphasis.

Slade swallowed and leaned away from her motion, his throbbing face and nuts remembering the last time she'd lunged at him like that. "Because you scare the shit outta me."

"But you want to take me home," she growled. "As your slave."

"Well…" Slade cocked his head, "…yeah."

She squinted at him. "Are you stupid?"

"No. Ka-par."

"You *can't declare ka-par!*" she snapped.

"No, but you can," Slade said.

"Burn you, you're a criminal," she snapped. "It takes a warrior and a warrior's honor to ka-par."

"Listen, pussycat," Slade said, "you want outta those ropes? The moment you declare ka-par, I'll let you go. We won't start until you're free and clear. On my honor."

She glared at him, desire obviously warring with distrust. "I'm weak," she finally muttered. "You'd win." The reluctance with which she said it actually made Slade's heart ache.

And pound. She was *thinking* about it. This was *awesome*.

"Okay," Slade said quickly, "You declare ka-par, I'll let you go, we feed you until you're up to it, then we give it a go."

She frowned at him. "What makes you so sure you'd win?"

"I'm smarter than you," Slade said.

Rat squinted at him for over a minute. Then, "You're sootin' on, you jenfurgling prick."

Slade actually *bounced* from his seat and went over to her to start untying her. Then he paused at the ropes and gave them a pointed tug. He lifted a brow. "Ka-par?"

She squinted up at him. "You'll let me completely go and feed me to regain my strength."

"Sure," Slade said. This was going to be a *blast*.

"Are you burning insane?" she finally asked.

"Yes," Slade said. He frowned at her. "Why?"

She just peered at him, her mouth still slightly open in confusion. "Ka-par," she finally said, looking almost curious, now.

"Ka-par," Slade agreed, barely able to contain his glee. Then he realized that his rock-hard boner was getting painful from the proximity, and he said, "Okay, no offense, but before I let you go, I've gotta smell you first. Just in case you turn me into your depraved slut and won't let me near you again—or you kick me in the head, take my food, and run off, okay?"

Her face darkened in a scowl. "I'm not going to run off." Then she leaned as far from him as possible and gave him a wary look. "What do you mean, 'your depraved slut?'"

"What else would you do with a six-foot-seven hunk of a certified genius?" Slade said.

"Make you carry my gear."

Slade grinned at her. "I'm *much* too pretty for that."

She narrowed her eyes at him. "You look like a fucked-up albino."

"Details," Slade said, waving it off dismissively. "Now seriously, don't bite me or anything, but I need to smell you. You wear perfume?"

She just peered at him.

"Are you going to bite me?" he asked warily.

She was still giving him that wary look. "Possibly. Smell me where?"

In reply, Slade warily lowered his nose to her shoulder and inhaled. He was pleased when she just continued to stare at him rather than sever his jugular with her incisors.

"Are you really a genius?" she demanded.

"Certified by the California State School Board," Slade said, groaning at the way his body suddenly seemed to spasm in response to her scent. He trailed his nose down her arm, intrigued. "Then MIT, then the government investigators, then the Congie Peacemakers, then the California Department of Corrections, then—"

"You can stop smelling me now," she growled, as he neared her breast.

Slade blinked, then reddened and sat up. "I'm pretty sure it's on your clothes. *Do* you wear perfume?"

She just scowled at him. "Perfume draws predators."

"Okay," Slade said, "what about laundry detergent?"

"I've been wearing the same clothes since Koliinaat."

That was...nasty. But with Congies, who had different body chemistries from all the drugs they fed them, not unheard of. Slade grimaced. "Okay, what about places? You go into any pleasure-houses before they sent you back to Earth? Anything like that?"

He saw a moment of recognition flash in her eyes, but she just continued to scowl at him like she expected him to try and give her an STD. "Maybe."

Slade's heart gave another leap. "Which one? They use a lotion? A salve?"

Rat gave him a long look. "Release me, feed me, ka-par, and then, depending on who wins, you'll find out."

Slade's mouth opened to argue, then he sighed. He raised a brow at her. "On your honor?"

"Yeah," she said. "On my honor. Sam..." she hesitated at his last name, "Jungle Man. By the blood on my paws, I challenge you to ka-par." Hell, she almost seemed to be looking *forward* to it.

Oh, the poor, deluded little kitten. Keeping his grin to himself, Slade started unwrapping her from the tree. Then, when she didn't kick him, punch him, or otherwise try to stab, maim, or strangle him, he got out his lighter and started working on her bonds.

"You realize I'm going to win this, right?" she said, eying him. "And you're gonna serve me or die."

"Sounds like fun," Slade said, prying the melted rope apart. He hissed and blew on his fingers as he burned himself in his haste, then started unwrapping her bonds.

When her hands came free, she still just stared at him. "You're a few charges short of a full magazine," she said, still peering at him dubiously.

"Generally," Slade said. When her hands came free—and she didn't try to kill him—he went to work on her feet. She watched him in interested silence.

"You know," she said as the bonds around her ankles fell loose and she uncoiled like a panther, "you never accepted the ka-par."

Slade froze, his mouth open to object, the horrible realization that she was right hitting him like a size-nine boot to the side of the head.

"And you're *really* a super-genius?" she asked dubiously. She crossed her arms and tapped her boot on the ground, peering down at him.

"The Tesla of the Congressional Era," Slade managed, his eyes warily on her polymer-encased toes.

She continued to tap her foot.

"Well?" she finally demanded.

Slade swallowed and glanced up at her. "Well?"

Her gray-green eyes were amused. "Are you gonna accept? Or should I just make you my slave and get it over with?" She cocked her head at him, eying his lower body a bit too carefully, a little smile crossing her full lips. "You're right. You *are* sexy. I think I'll put you in a thong."

Slade's heart gave another startled little hammer. "Uh."

She started tapping her fingers on her bicep. "Well?"

"I accept," he squeaked.

"Ka-par rak'tal. It's your formation, asher." She immediately turned and walked over and started rummaging through his things. Yanking a piece of stale, mostly-not-moldy bread from his backpack, she regarded him over the fire as she took a bite. "We'll pick this back up in…" She cocked her head at him. "Three days?"

"Sounds good," Slade managed.

"And Sam?" the Congie said.

Slade swallowed. "Yes?"

She gave him a pleasant smile. "Don't run. I can find you." At that, she took his backpack—and everything in it—and walked from the camp, into the darkness. Towards her rifle.

Slade sat there and watched her go, so thoroughly turned on he was having trouble breathing. *This*, he thought, over the blood rushing in his ears, *is going to be so much fun*.

26

WARRIOR TROUBLES

"**Y**ou," Joe growled, stalking up to the morning campfire in his underwear, "are getting on my nerves."

Sometime in the night, Shael had *re*-stolen the pair of energy-resistant pants he had hung up to dry outside his tarp that night, cut a good chunk off the lower legs, and had wound them to her waist using *all* of his thirty-thousand-lobe survival line. Thirty-six rods of it. Her knotwork, apparently, needed work, because both ends were trailing loose and it was even then unraveling at her feet, tangling in scrub and grasses when she tried to walk. And now, a look of utter concentration on her face, she was crafting a spear using his favorite combat knife, more of his survival line, and a really big, somewhat-sharp rock. Joe could tell just by looking at it that the endeavor wouldn't go well for her.

As if he were an annoying child, as soon as he came to a stop beside her, Shael said, "Now you see what a real warrior's weapon looks like, Voran." Her brow creased in concentration, she went back to hacking a split into the end of her crude 'spear.'

Amused, Joe crossed his arms and leaned back against a tree to watch.

As predicted, Shael kept cutting herself, the huge rock kept slipping due to its weight, she couldn't get the survival line to stay in one place, and despite her best attempts to knot it, the line kept slipping loose, tangling at her feet.

Eventually, she let out a scream of frustration and hurled spear, rock, and twine to explode together in the trunk of a eucalyptus on the other side of camp. The tree groaned, then slowly fell over in an arc, cut in half by the garrote of near-indestructible wire. Nine-G looked up, curious, but then went back to picking little red berries into a crude grass bowl, with Alice directing.

After taking stock of yet another demonstration of How Flake Could Go Wrong with forty mind-furgs that could scramble brains or pulverize boulders at a whim, Joe bent down to collect his knife. He had another pair of pants, but the loss of his survival line would be irritating. "Tell ya what," he said, hefting the knife.

Shael gave him a look of irritated incomprehension.

"You let me *cut* you a small *piece*—" he gestured with the knife to her unraveling 'belt,' "for you to use, and I'll teach you how to *tie*," he pulled off the bandana he had taken to wearing after his hair grew in and held it up so she could clearly see the knot, "a *knot*." He tugged on it.

When she continued to give him a blank look, Joe sighed and said, "Twelve-A, translate."

The minder gave a mental sigh. *Must I do all the work around here, furg?*

"What 'work'?" Joe cried. Even then, Twelve-A was propped on a leafy mat of vegetation provided by a doting Alice and Eleven-C. Several of the People were sprawled around him to keep him warm, and one had even lain down near his feet so his toes wouldn't get cold.

I'm still recovering. Recovery takes energy. You said yourself I should rest. The telepath coughed weakly, then tilted his head sideways a little so one of the People could feed him another of the little red berries that Alice and Nine-G were collecting.

Joe narrowed his eyes. "I hope they make you sick."

They probably will, but it makes them feel good to help me. Twelve-A accepted another berry from a doting, concerned-looking experiment.

"Yeah, you're taking a real hit for the team, there," Joe growled.

Maybe you would like to trade places with me? Twelve-A offered. *I could always ask Shael to beat you until you were dizzy and coughing blood.*

Thinking that the experiment in question would probably jump at the opportunity, Joe quickly changed the subject. "I only want my survival line back. I'm willing to trade a knot-tying lesson."

To her. What are you willing to trade to me, sooter? My chest still hurts to move, so I can't sit up and make another hat like I want to. I'm bored.

"You have forty people waiting on you hand and foot!" Joe snapped.

That's boring.

Sensing a bartering session that was *not* going to fall in his favor, Joe growled, "What do you want, you pointy-eared Jahul?"

Something interesting to pass the time while I heal. He coughed again, weakly.

Meaning he wanted to delve into Joe's memories again in exchange for translator duties.

"You're not tricking anyone with the invalid act," Joe growled. "I gave you nanos and battledust. You're healthier than the rest of them."

Good luck telling them that. The smug bastard accepted another berry.

Joe thought about relieving himself in the furgling's cider bottle the next time he napped.

Try it, furg. Perhaps you'll wake up scratching your ear with your foot and licking your own asshole.

A muscle in his neck twitched. Joe turned back to Shael in a wave of disgust. She was still staring at him, pert chin lifted in challenge, like she was waiting for him to try to take his stuff back—and was going to put him solidly in his place if he tried.

Remembering the garroted eucalyptus, Joe cursed. *Fine, Pointy. What do you want to know?*

Immediately, Twelve-A said, *I'm still curious what that woman was doing to you when you were tricking me into telling you who to shoot. That memory where she was bouncing on top of you and you were both screaming. It looked painful.*

Grimacing, Joe thought about telling the furgling to bumble back to his sootpile and eat Dhasha flake, but then realized he really wanted his survival line back.

"Fine," he muttered. "Two tics."

Five, Twelve-A argued.

"Three," Joe retorted. "And you convince her not to mess with my stuff while I'm sleeping."

Four, and you help Alice make me another hat.

The very *last* thing Joe was going to do was weave grass like a flower-loving peacemunch freak, but he kept an even voice and said, "Sounds fair, leafling."

I can read your mind, simian, Twelve-A said flatly.

"Fine!" Joe cried, throwing up his hands. "Fine. Four tics and you keep her out of my stuff."

And you help make me another hat.

"Have Eleven-C *mojo* you another hat," Joe retorted.

It means more if someone makes it for me.

"She *would* be making it," he snapped.

It's the thought that counts. The telepath gave a little, pathetic whimper as one of the People repositioned his head to better accept their offerings. *Besides. Weaving grass would do you good. You're too violent.*

Joe narrowed his eyes. *Five tics, I make you a hat, you keep her out of my stuff, and you translate what I say to her whenever I need it.*

Twelve-A considered. *Six.*

"Fine. Six. But you take it *after* I get my survival line back and I'm done showing her how to tie knots."

Twelve-A sighed deeply. Then his brow creased in a tiny wrinkle of concentration—easily mistaken as a gesture of pain by his attendants, many of whom immediately started petting him and cooing.

Joe turned back to the mover wearing his stuff before he vomited up last night's pork roast.

Shael's head cocked slightly to the side and her eyes flickered toward the minder. A moment later, her eyes flared wide and she jerked back to look at Joe, her face tightened with deep suspicion and...anger?

She says you can dance on her tek, Twelve-A told him.

"What did you tell her?!" Joe demanded, realizing that was *not* the reaction of someone who'd just been offered a lesson in survival techniques.

I told her you wanted to tie knots together.

Realizing that was a colloquial term for Jreet sex, Joe groaned and dropped his face into his hands. "You know what?" he groaned, giving up entirely. "Never mind. Just never burning mind. Go back to eating berries and stay outta my head. No deal." Shaking his head, he just turned to go safeguard what gear he had left.

Wait...you don't want to tie knots together? Twelve-A demanded, sounding disappointed.

"No," Joe said, going to dig a spare pair of pants from his backpack. "I definitely do *not*." He dressed, found something to eat from one of the pits, and tried to pass time as the People lazily went about their morning routine. Except, now with bumps and bruises to nurse, it was taking ten times as long. Progress—which was already glacial—had ground to a complete halt.

"What's the chance of moving this operation along?" Joe finally demanded of the minder. "I'd like to make it to our destination sometime in the next millennium, you know?"

I'm not sure I'm fully recovered. Twelve-A coughed pitifully again, to more sympathizing moans from his fan club.

"Burn you," Joe growled. "You're fine."

True, but the other People have bruises. It will hurt them to walk.

"Are the bruises on their *feet*?!" Joe demanded, desperately trying not to lose his cool.

No, but they don't want to walk. They want to rest and feel better.

Joe inwardly counted to ten. He was a former PlanOps Prime. For someone like him, watching the furgs laze about in self-pity was, for lack of a better description, like picking cankers from his ass in the bowels of Hell. As pleasantly as he could, he said, "Those guys are still out there. You want them to come back?"

You and Shael killed all the mean ones, Twelve-A responded, almost accusingly.

Already, the naïve little furg had forgotten his lesson about hungry people and good intentions. Joe muttered a curse to the Sisters, found a good lookout spot, and hunkered down to watch forty-four full-grown adults busily doing absolutely nothing. Because it was so maddening—and because he was about to start yelling and waving Jane around—Joe decided to reacquaint himself with his favorite drinking pal and pulled out his canteen to spend the next three hours reminiscing with good ol' Jim Beam.

He must have fallen asleep, because he awoke screaming, clawing for Jane. All around him, the tunnels of Neskfaat were closing in, and Dhasha were hiding down every hole, waiting to sink their monomolecular black talons into his liver. Corpses were strewn everywhere, lining the tunnels like ragged, clothes-covered hunks of meat laid out in a butcher's shop.

It took Joe several deep breaths to realize that the corpses that he had seen weren't a dead PlanOps regiment on Neskfaat, but rather, the *live* sleeping bodies of his friends. Several had sat up, looking startled, as his final scream echoed across the mountainside.

Twelve-A was crammed into his mind in an instant, a mountain squeezed into a cardboard box. *Why are you screaming? You're scaring the People.* He sounded more concerned by the fact that Joe was scaring the experiments than by the fact that he was screaming.

Groaning at the pressure in his skull, Joe doubled over, holding his temples. "Just…a dream…Soot. *Stop*, you long-eared furgling asher! Go back to your sootpile."

Twelve-A reluctantly pulled back, returning the controls.

Joe swallowed and straightened, shivering in the cool mountain air. His body was still soaked with an icy sweat, his heart hurting from pounding, his throat still rough from screaming.

Another Neskfaat dream. Joe felt a pang of dread hit him like a round to the chest. He hadn't had a Neskfaat dream since flashbacks had forced him to leave Der'ru, when he had spent the next seven rotations—and several million credits—letting a shrink tinker with his head. He'd thought he'd *fixed* it. Joe thought of all the screaming fests, the cold sweats, the insomnia-induced rages he had inflicted on his groundmates during his final days on Der'ru. He thought about how his Second had finally come to him with the private code to a Jahul head-doctor. He thought about going back to that, berserking over nothing, once more unable to control himself or his temper, inflicting that on the People, and his left hand again started to shake.

Yet *another* thing that he had thought he'd gotten more or less under control. Immediately, Joe balled his hand into a fist and tried to clear his mind like the Jahul had tried to teach him. Instead, the fear of losing what little civility he had managed to regain dropped him into a cold sweat, and he felt his heart speeding up, his mind starting to race, dragging him back to distant battles, to the faces of people he had failed, wounds he had taken, weapons he had fired.

Not again, Joe thought, realizing he was on the verge of something he'd managed to stave off for three turns. *Sweet Mothers' talons, not again.* He closed his eyes and pressed his fist against his forehead, trying to clear it of the images that were trying to climb out, demanding to be seen.

As if summoned by his own anxiety, the very thing he feared began to spread out before him in vivid, three hundred and sixty degree color detail. A field of death, Dhasha princes carving swaths of blood through moving slabs of meat, friends that had fallen, pickups that never came...

His panic must have carried to Twelve-A, because the telepath grabbed Joe's mind in a vise and squeezed, yanking him back to the present. *What happened? What are you doing?*

When Joe looked, the minder had sat up fully, all pretenses of being sick gone, giving Joe a deeply anxious look.

Nothing, you control-freak furg, Joe muttered, dropping his eyes to his shaking left hand, suddenly very ashamed. *Flashback. I get them.* In that moment, he would have given anything not to be in the meadow with the People, but alone in some bar, drowning his sorrows in whisky and strangers.

Twelve-A cocked his blond head slightly. There was a slight pause, then, *You want me to make the flashbacks stop?*

The simple words hit him like a Dhasha paw. Joe had the startling realization that, after seventy-four turns of drugs, therapies, and visits to Ooreiki shrinks, all to no avail, Twelve-A was utterly serious. And utterly capable. With a thought. And it terrified the soot outta him.

Don't you dare, Joe thought in sudden anxiety, realizing he was about to become some sort of drooling, gun-toting zombie. *You need those memories. They're what are keeping you furgs alive.*

But I can fix them…

No, goddamn it! Joe snapped. *You're not going to 'fix' them. Get out! My mind, my rules.*

Twelve-A held his mind for a moment longer, in which Joe was acutely aware that the telepath was thinking about doing it anyway, then reluctantly released him. Joe let out a huge, shaky breath, realizing how close he had come to being just like the drooling, happy-go-lucky, crotch-groping idiots around him.

Across the camp, Shael was watching him with confusion. Unlike her challenging stare from earlier, when she was stealing his stuff, now her Dhasha-green eyes looked almost…worried for him?

Time to get back on my meds, Joe thought, sweating as he uncapped his canteen and took a long swig. *She'd rather shove a knife through your guts and leave wild animals to eat you alive for being 'weak' than worry over a used-up Congie Prime.* Once he'd steadied himself, he tucked the flask back into his chest pocket and, taking courage from liquid oblivion, took a moment to return her stare, looking her completely over with what he hoped was the same disdain she had shown him earlier.

It probably wasn't. She was utterly gorgeous and topless and Joe hadn't gotten laid in six turns.

Her emerald gaze was startling in its intensity, and made his heart pound oddly to meet it. The vivid green eyes were set under a growing fringe of curly black hair, above a delicate, sunburned nose. Her full lips were pursed in amusement, her pert chin lifted in challenge.

She still *thinks she's the better warrior,* Joe thought, stunned and irritated. Seeing that, after all the ass-saving Joe had done in the last few weeks, was the last little itch that set off the Dhasha.

Buoyed by Beam, Joe took out Prime Sentinel Raavor's ovi and decided to *show* her just how inept she really was. He got up, cut a spear-length sapling, whittled it down, notched it, then used pieces he salvaged from her abandoned project to fasten a more reasonably-sized stone to the head of his spear, all in the space of sixty-six tics. Finished with something that he was half proud of, he held it up, looked at her, looked at the scattered remnants of her own spearmaking attempt, and smirked.

Shael, who had been watching intently, flushed and quickly found something else to do.

Joe blinked as she retreated, realizing he had quite unexpectedly won some sort of little war between them.

A moment later, Twelve-A took his mind in a fist and squeezed hard enough to make Joe stagger. *You made Shael cry.* Twelve-A sounded as if he felt he should return the favor, with interest.

And Joe, realizing he had just bested a naïve and ignorant 'Jreet' genetic experiment with his infinitely more vast knowledge of death and warfare, suddenly felt like a sootbag. "Ash." Disgusted with himself, Joe dropped his spear. One of the young men who had been watching the operation immediately picked it up and carried it off, to stick the pointy end in the fire.

Is she still crying now? Joe demanded.

Yes, furg. She was trying very hard to impress you, earlier.

And once again, after being repeatedly groped, thrown around, his belongings pawed, his psyche thrown into all-out war flashbacks, and his mind outright assaulted, *Joe* felt like the inconsiderate asher. Realizing he needed to make amends, he sheathed his blade and went after her.

He found Shael seated on a hillock overlooking the valley, her arms crossed around her chest, chin on her knees. Seeing she wasn't going to run off, Joe slowed and approached her with all the caution one would use on an angry Dhasha. He knew she heard him, because she stiffened.

"Look, I'm sorry," Joe muttered, once he got close enough to be heard. "I didn't mean it. All the standing around is leaving me in a sooty mood. I was just trying to make you feel a little bad."

Well, it worked, Twelve-A said, obvious disapproval in his voice.

Shut up and shove off, furg, Joe growled. *I'm taking care of it.*

Twelve-A gave a derisive mental snort, but then left him alone.

Very carefully, Joe lowered himself to the hill beside her. "That was a really cool spear you made," he said lamely.

She refused to look at him. He could see tears trailing down her cheeks. And, no matter how much Joe tried, he couldn't say something she would understand. *Doing* something comprehensible had been easy enough, but *saying* it was like growing wings. Even now, she was huddled over herself, quietly sobbing into her knees.

"Sorry," Joe muttered. "Sisters, I don't belong here. What did I think I was gonna do, really? Kill kreenit until I died of old age? Just so they could...what...repopulate fifty turns after I'm dead? You know how utterly *worthless* my entire life has been?" He dropped his head into his utterly stable, robotic right hand and stared out at the valley. With his shaking left, he dragged J.B. from his pocket, uncapped it, and took a swig. "Just a dumb ol' Congie waiting to die," he said, on a burning exhale of whisky fumes. When tears continued to leak down her face and she showed not a twitch of recognition, he just sighed and took another swallow, sharing their moment of mournful silence.

Looking down into the valley, he briefly found himself in another place, on a windswept hill on Rastari, watching Jikaln lead his best friend off to be interrogated.

That's what happened to his friends. They got killed, some by his own damn hand. It was like some cruel conspiracy between the Sisters, where Life took those who meant anything at all to him and murdered them in the most brutal way possible. Hell, with the People, an incompetent band of idiots had already tried.

And, once again, he hadn't been able to save his friends.

Wondering what would happen when the People ran up against someone with more skills and fewer scruples, Joe took another swill in silence.

The shaking in his left hand was now bad enough to make it hard to put the cap back on the flask. Remembering the dream, the flashback, his behavior afterward, he wondered if, now that the Congie drugs were wearing off, all that alien death and dying he had stuffed into his subconscious was going to start to resurface in ugly ways.

God I hope not, he thought, watching Shael whimper to herself. *They're too innocent for me to go psycho Congie on them.*

"Sorry," he muttered again.

Shael gave him a sideways look through tears.

"I'm a furg," Joe said, gesturing to himself with his flask so she couldn't take it the other way around.

She knew what 'furg' meant. He used it enough times, generally when the People were doing something lazy, slow, or mind-numbingly stupid, that the word had stuck. Still, she shuddered and glanced back out at the valley.

"Look," Joe said, "I don't know what happened to you, but whatever you think you are, you gotta start over. Learn it all from scratch, you know? I'll teach you, if you want to learn." At her tentative look, he leaned the flask against his ankle, pulled one of the salvaged lengths of survival line from his pocket, tore up a handful of grass, and knotted the line around it so she could clearly see how he did it.

Shael's eyes widened.

Seeing that he'd caught her attention, Joe gingerly laid the survival line and its bundle of grass on her knee. "Now you try." He mimed untying it and starting over.

Surprising him, she immediately did. And, with startling accuracy, she was able to replicate what he had done. Then she untied it and re-tied it several times with the acute concentration and precision that Joe recognized from PlanOps shooting ranges, weapons drills, or species debriefings. He frowned at that a moment, but then shrugged it off. *She just* thinks *she's a warrior,* he told himself. *Of course she's going to concentrate like one.*

"How about we start over, Shael?" Joe asked. It didn't escape his notice that 'Shael' was the name of the famous Welu folk-hero—probably one of the only Jreet names the majority of Humanity even recognized. "Hi. I'm Joe. I'm a big, badass Congie vet with an attitude problem. You're innocent and ill-treated and I've been a furg."

She gave him a blank look, then, in Welu-flavored Jreet said, "How about we start over, Voran? I'm a hardened warrior. You're obviously unsuited to the strains of battle, so from here on, I'll protect you, and someday, you'll give up your tek and take my spawn."

Joe blinked at her, jaw going limp. "What?"

She gave a satisfied nod of her head. "Good. Agreed, then."

Joe continued to peer at her. Straightening, he insisted, "No, *I'm* protecting *you.*" He pointed at his chest, then hers, for emphasis.

She scowled. "No, *you're* taking *my* spawn." She did the same.

Joe knew from his time with the Jreet—first Daviin, then Edrin and Wiirik—that when a Jreet found another Jreet he was interested in, those two had to decide which of them would trigger the hormone change, drop their tek, and become female. It was usually decided by a battle-to-surrender, which, with a Jreet, often meant a battle-to-the-death because they didn't surrender. Yet another reason their numbers were so few.

Twelve-A, Joe thought hurriedly, *now would be a good time to convince her I'm not trying to get her pregnant.*

Why? I'm amusing myself, watching the two of you. Everything else is so boring.

Six tics, Joe blurted, seeing the fire returning to her eyes.

Seven. You reneged on our deal.

Joe narrowed his eyes. Ignoring the minder, he said, "Look. Shael. You obviously got brainwashed by some really bad men somewhere along the way. You are *not* a Jreet. You can't impregnate me. That's what I do to you."

As soon as the words left his mouth, he realized it was Jim Beam talking and definitely the wrong thing to say. Thankfully, though, he'd said them in Congie and she couldn't understand a damn one of them. Saying a little prayer to the Sisters, Joe opened his mouth to come up with something better.

I translated for you, Twelve-A said. *When do I get my six tics?*

Joe's heart gave a startled hammer at about the same time he flew off his seat on the boulder and went rolling down the hill in an awkward, tailbone-crushing somersault.

"*I am more Jreet than you will ever be, Voran!*" Shael screamed at him from somewhere up above.

In the back of his mind, he heard Twelve-A's mental pause. *Can I start my six tics now?*

Why sooting not, Joe thought, ending his roll on his back, staring at the sky. *The day can't get much worse.*

Sure it can, Twelve-A said. *You could be beaten until you wheezed blood because your chief of security was sleeping on the job.*

Joe narrowed his eyes. *You* made *me sleep, furg. My vote was to kill them all!*

Twelve-A ignored that.

Sometime later, Joe limped back to camp, found that his stuff had been again rooted through by grabby female hands, considered snagging what was left and wandering off, then crawled back into his tent to sleep it off, instead.

● ● ●

Twelve-A got them moving again two days later, thankfully giving Joe enough time to recover from his merry jaunt down the mountain before having to go back to his routine of keeping the leafmunching furgs alive.

They hit the road again at Speed of Slug, giving Joe plenty of time to jog ahead, scout around, jog back, check their backtrail, jog ahead again to ensure they were all going in the right direction, then go back to again make sure they weren't being followed. All that before the People made a single ferlii length. The entire time, Shael either cast him furious looks or refused to look at him altogether, though pointedly kept up with him wherever he went, as if he had turned guarding the People into some sort of contest. And Joe, being bigger, stronger, faster, and carrying all the weaponry, was happy to oblige.

Let the little furg stew on that, Joe thought, easily outdistancing her yet again.

She could crush you with her mind, Twelve-A noted casually.

She's gotta catch me, first, Joe retorted. Then he crested a rise and stumbled to a halt, seeing that the People, in between his last trip to the front, had stopped forward progress altogether and were sitting around on the empty roadside, piling rocks or chasing lizards. *Are we stopping* again? he cried, disgusted.

Alice was hungry.

Which meant they had halted everything so an eight-year-old could have a cookie break. Great. Joe fought yet another overwhelming urge to drive his forehead into a pine tree. "Tell me when they start moving again. I'll be watching the rear."

There's nobody dangerous around, Twelve-A said.

Remembering Twelve-A's idea of 'dangerous,' Joe went to the rear and found a comfortable vantage on an abandoned car anyway. Shael nonchalantly followed him, lowering herself to a boulder a couple rods off, pointedly ignoring his existence completely.

Joe glanced over at the woman, who was patiently scanning the surrounding landscape with all the intensity of a border-patrol bot. He could only imagine what would happen if she decided she wanted one of his automatic energy weapons to complement his pants, knife, and new bandanna, which she had tied to her head with the knot that

Joe had shown her. To that end, Joe now slept with *all* his weapons in his tent with him, stuffed under immovable body-parts.

They sat like that, neither having anything to say, totally silent except for the occasional slapping at horseflies or mosquitoes.

When several hours passed without Twelve-A alerting him they were resuming their march north, Joe got up and went back to find his friends to figure out what was taking so long. Shael, nonchalantly pretending the idea had been her own, got up and followed him, pointedly taking a seat completely opposite him in their latest 'camp' at the edge of an abandoned road—a place that Joe, had he been given his way, wouldn't have come within ten lengths of, much less walked *on*.

The People, however—who still utterly refused to let Joe dress them—didn't like walking on sticks and pebbles and brambles with their bare feet, so, in the mornings, before the sun heated things up, they walked on roads, instead. When Joe complained, Twelve-A told him that security was *his* job, and why should the People worry about where they walked if he was doing his job? Hence Joe's frantic jogs back and forth each morning, just to make sure they weren't about to run into any rampaging gangs or kreenit jaws while Twelve-A was busily picking flowers or raptly mind-reading bugs.

Besides, all the jogging worked up an appetite, and he might as well get something to eat while he waited for the furgs to work up interest in walking again. The fruit that Eleven-C had made at the start of their 'lunch' break was almost gone. He took a banana and sat down against his backpack with a sigh. The People were not very enthusiastic about walking long distances, despite his frustrated attempts to speed them up. 'Urgency' simply wasn't part of their vocabulary, and they traveled at the same slow walk regardless of how high his blood pressure skyrocketed—if he could get them to walk at all.

For someone like Joe, who was used to his every order being obeyed immediately and without complaint, having to watch them creep along like stubborn, carefree children was almost as painful as a plasma shot to the gut. He endured it, but only because there wasn't a damn thing he could do about it. Several times in the past, he'd even gotten frustrated enough to pack his stuff to leave, but each time, he stopped and thought about that Congressional nuajan machine.

Wasn't *that* a nice thought.

We're not killing anyone, Twelve-A warned him.

Stop listening in on thoughts that don't belong to you, oversized leprechaun, Joe snapped.

You told me I could look, Twelve-A retorted. *You didn't tell me I had to stop.*

Joe narrowed his eyes, realizing the telepath had just spent three days ogling his mind and memories in exchange for translating something that had gotten him thrown down a mountainside. *Stop.*

Twelve-A gave a mental mutter, but Joe felt the tell-tale retreat of his psychic presence like a sudden pressure releasing in his mind.

You're like a goddamn peeping Tom, you know that? Joe demanded, gesturing with the banana. *I give you half a chance and you're climbing in my window.*

You're interesting, Twelve-A muttered. *And I have no idea how long six tics is. You never told me.*

Joe opened his mouth to argue, then glared. *You intentionally never asked.*

It slipped my mind.

Which was like saying a Dhasha forgot to eat. *I'm about to put a boot up your ass,* Joe growled. *Not without my permission.* Joe finished his banana and surveyed the camp. Eleven-C was sitting with Alice and Nine-G. The little brat was jabbering away at her adoring masses from atop the giant's shoulders, weaving yet another necklace of flowers and grasses as her followers struggled to do the same. Nine-G was busy picking seeds from the outside of a strawberry while Eleven-C seemed to be interested in drawing a picture in the dirt.

Joe had to grit his teeth not to let his aggravation show. The People were so *lazy!* Sure, they didn't have the rigorous military training—or the subsequent war flashbacks—but they didn't seem to have any drive whatsoever. Now that the 'mean' people were dead and Twelve-A had given Joe the task of getting them to safety, the minder had seemed to lose interest in management altogether.

To Joe's frustration, even before their run-in with Mike and his gang, it was the best he could do to get the People to walk ten lengths a day. That wasn't good enough, and yet, every attempt he made to speed them up resulted in them slowing down. He felt like tearing his hair out in frustration, but he still didn't have enough to get a good grip.

Sometime around the point when Nine-G had picked the strawberry clean, Joe got up and walked over to Twelve-A, who seemed to be quite enthralled with a purple flower he had harvested along the roadside.

Joe squatted beside Twelve-A, having had several hours to plot out how to get his point across without killing the pointy-eared bastard. "Look," Joe said, as evenly as he could while wanting to wring the telepath's scrawny neck. "We need to get moving. The *kreenit* aren't going to stay in the cities forever, and sitting along the road like this makes us penned Takki."

Then you can kill them with your rifle, furgling, Twelve-A told him cheerfully. *Do you know what this flower is called?* With the drugs Joe had given him, the minder's bruises had faded completely, leaving him looking better than most of the rest of the group. Unfortunately, that meant he was once more taking extra time to do stupid things like picking flowers and weaving hats.

Joe tore his eyes from Twelve-A's again-pristine face and squinted down at the flower, having to fight down the urge to rip it from the telepath's hand and hurl it into the woods. He had learned, from experience, that the minder didn't react well to that. "A posy."

Twelve-A frowned at him. *For some reason, you continue to lie even though I can read your mind.*

"It's not lying," Joe growled. "It's sarcasm. I lived most my life off-planet. What the hell would I know about local flora?"

You're not telling the truth, so you're lying, Twelve-A told him firmly.

"I'm not the one who was locked up for the first twenty turns of his life," Joe retorted. "In fact, I'm seventy turns older than you. Come back to lecture me when you get out of your swaddling clothes."

I have other people's experiences to look through, Twelve-A told him, sounding almost defensive. *If I wanted to, anything you know, I could know.*

"Then you know sarcasm is good for the soul," Joe retorted. "And *no*, that wasn't an invitation to go back to digging through my mind," he said, refusing to take the bait.

Twelve-A, the wily bastard, made a disappointed sigh and turned back to his flower. Watching him, Joe had to give the telepath one thing. He hadn't outright broken their bargain, despite all the loopholes he kept trying to put into it. Joe's mind, it seemed, really was his own domain—as long as he caught the caveats in time.

"What *isn't* good for the soul is getting eaten by a kreenit or getting caught in a blizzard," Joe went on. "Winter *is* coming, you know. I don't know what the local weather's like, but I do know it's gonna be unpleasant."

Twelve-A ignored him and turned the stem of the flower in his hand to glance at it from all angles. Twelve-A let out a little breath of pleasure. *It's so beautiful.*

Because it was obvious another gun-waving tantrum would only get him put back to sleep, Joe squinted at the thing, reluctantly trying to figure out what the furg saw in it. "It's probably poisonous."

Twelve-A flinched and looked up at him in blue-eyed shock. *Something so pretty could be poisonous?*

Joe couldn't hold in his laugh. "You don't judge a Dhasha by his scales."

Twelve-A glanced at the flower and, after giving it a long, careful examination, slowly put it down. Then he stood. *I will get the People moving again.*

Joe almost hugged the pointy-eared freak out of gratitude. "Thank you."

All at once, every one of the forty-four naked men and women lifted their heads toward Twelve-A. Then they stood obediently and Eleven-C started leading them north again. Their pace was a little faster, which was an improvement, but it would still be several rotations before they reached the place in the mountains that Joe had marked on his map.

• • •

Twelve-A became aware of another group of minds gathering near their hill sometimes towards midnight, four days after Joe had rescued Eleven-C from the Humans who had stolen her. He frowned, realizing that, as Joe kept predicting, Mike and his twenty-three friends were following them.

That...wasn't good. His first instinct was to tell Joe, but then Twelve-A realized what Joe would do to them if he did. Even then, the Congie was plotting out how to kill a few of them in the most horrible way possible, scaring the rest of them into running away and never coming back.

But he'd already done that once, and if it didn't work the first time, why would it work the second?

Besides, Twelve-A could *see* the goodness in Mike-the-Politician; the desire to feed his family, his love for his children, the feeling of brotherhood that all the terror and hunger and dying had instilled in him towards his band of friends. They, like the rest of Humanity, were broken, not evil.

They also hated Joe for what he had done. Joe and Shael, both. They wanted to kill them. They had lost companions to Joe's brutality, had been forced to leave friends behind to die, unable to bring the maimed along through an apocalypse, unable to spare the supplies to keep them alive after they left.

They were not, however, when Twelve-A looked closely again, evil. Just...broken. Sad and broken. And determined to take Eleven-C away from them again because they were desperate. Starving. Afraid. They knew their own limitations, they knew they'd lost their best fighters to Joe's violence, and now they knew they weren't going to survive. Mike, who was used to making decisions from his old job, had been the one forced to make the call to leave their mutilated friends behind and salvage the stuff they could use for the people who were going to live through the apocalypse. Though they had begged and pleaded with them to stay, Mike had to think of the future. Of the *children*.

Twelve-A settled into their thoughts as Mike sat down to boil water over the fire that night, several lengths away. Everyone was hungry, tired. They had run out of food that day, and were now boiling grass and twigs in water to make it taste like it wasn't just water. One of Mike's boys had shot a squirrel with a slingshot, and it was now boiling in the pot with the twigs. The smaller, hard-eyed group spent the time watching the squirrel cook talking about how they would ambush the People's group the next morning, when Joe got off shift and took his nap. The minder, they agreed, was too soft to hurt them, and with the proper distractions—

I can help you, Twelve-A offered gently.

Fuck, he's in my head again. Fuck! Just how far can he reach?

As far as I want to, Twelve-A said. Which was true—he could reach to the ocean in any direction, and he didn't want to reach beyond that. The emotional misery on this continent alone was overwhelming, straining Twelve-A's ability to see anything but the sickness every moment of every day.

"Change in plans, guys. That freak can sense us coming." **God. Tammi's gonna starve. She's already sick...**

Nobody has to starve, Twelve-A said. *We can share.*

Could he be serious? Then a wash of disgust. **Yeah, right. Nobody would share that. They're walking around with a cornucopia, and we already tried to take it once. We'll just have to take it again, and not leave the fucking Congie or his foreign bitch alive to stop us.**

We'll share, Twelve-A assured him. *We have more than enough.*

"Guys, we need to get out of range. I think we walked into the bastard's head-space. Let's pack up. Head out. Wait 'til the freak's asleep."

Listen, Twelve-A insisted. *You don't have to take her. We'll give you food. You could bring things to trade. Alice likes beads. Joe keeps saying we need rubbing alcohol and antibiotics—*

We're not giving you our goddamned antibiotics, you ailo freak.

He began to think about how they would have to find a way to figure out which of the experiments were useful after they killed the leaders. The little girl had said there was more than one of the experiments who could pull the magic trick. They'd have to ask her which ones, then they could kill the rest. Maybe lure them off with beads and trinkets while Mike slaughtered the rest of the cattle. Then they'd have to find a way to hide the makers from the rest of Humanity. Let those ignorant ailos die off, squabbling over cigarettes while Mike and his folk lived like kings. They'd need somewhere secluded, somewhere *quiet...*

Twelve-A was taken aback. He saw the goodness in Mike, but now it was masked, hidden behind a wall of hardness. If anything, Judgement had made Humanity's sickness worse. Fear was a common thread, everywhere he looked. Fear and *greed*.

I didn't mean you should give the antibiotics to us, Twelve-A said. *Once Eleven-C can get a look at something, she can make it. We can give you ten times as much back. We just need a pattern.*

Mike hesitated. **She can make antibiotics?** His group was running low because Joe had met their violence with more violence and taken out his anger on their friends—and Mike had had to use up over fifteen doses of antibiotics before he had been forced to cut his losses. Two had died. The one without a foot had lived...but only long enough for Mike and the others to have to abandon him in their search for food. Even then, that man starved to death in a stagnant mental pond of loneliness and despair.

You want...to give us food? For nothing? It was hesitant, uncertain. Mike began to think of happy thoughts, like playing with his daughter in the park and taking his son to the merry-go-round before Judgement.

Yes, Twelve-A agreed, excited over Mike's mental shift. *There's no need for you to starve. There's enough for everyone. I plan to collect even more people everywhere we go, to help the whole world see I've got a better way for them to follow. If Eleven-C gets tired, we can all eat a little less.*

That soft, deluded rat fuc—Mike thought of his engagement to his wife, the way he had given her silver, instead of gold, because it was all he could afford. He thought of how his son had been failing in middle school, and how Mike had slipped the principal a few hundred bucks to fudge some scores. He thought of his daughter's first puppy, and how she had tried to feed it chocolate chips instead of Kibbles.

I think we can work together, Mike said. He thought of holding his wife, watching a sunset. He thought of the birth of his first child. **But nobody here likes that Congie. Or the foreign girl. You think we could meet somewhere they won't bother us? To do a little trading, then go our separate ways?**

Twelve-A felt a little twinge of alarm, thinking of meeting with outsiders alone, but then he remembered what Joe and Shael had done to scared, helpless, hungry men and women *last* time and he decided that Mike was right. They were too violent. Twelve-A and Eleven-C could give Mike the supplies he needed and then send him off, with neither of them being the wiser.

I can arrange that, Twelve-A agreed.

He's so naï—The man thought of his last trip to Disneyland with his family, and their last weekend in the waterpark. He thought of his littlest boy, before the kreenit ate him. Happy, smiling, full of laughter. He thought of his daughter riding her first pony. **Okay, when do you want to meet?**

Tomorrow, Twelve-A told him, thrilled that the goodness was pouring out of the man again at the thought of someone finally being *kind* to him. *See?* he wanted to tell Joe, *They* can *be healed.*

When are you going to sleep? the man asked. Mike thought of his daughter's first words, his son's first peek under a hood with him, his wife's first 'baby-belly'. **Maybe we can do it tonight.**

No, Twelve-A immediately told him. *Joe watches the camp at night. I'll have to distract them both tomorrow so you can come do your trading.* He yawned. *Besides, it's past midnight. I should go to sleep now. Joe wakes me up early.*

If we think of something you might like us to bring, could we contact you in your sleep? Would you hear us? Maybe just by thinking loudly? Mike thought of taking his boys to shoot turkeys on his grandfather's old farmstead and playing Old Maid with his little girl.

No, Twelve-A said, getting tired. *I wouldn't hear you. Just wait until morning. We have plenty of time.*

So stupid. Twelve-A flinched at the bitterness and triumph of Mike's thought, once more getting the eerie feeling he should tell Joe about the proposed meeting, anyway. **"Guys, we're gonna go trade with them in the morning. They'll give us food and antibiotics, no hard feelings."** Then Mike added, *You know, if you keep being nice to everyone like this, I might just have to start harboring hope for the Human race. Start bringing it back from the brink, ya know?*

I hope so, Twelve-A said, plaintively. *I can't live with all the pain. The world is filled with* so much misery. *It hurts. I have to find a way to fix it. I can barely stand it.*

He sure won't have to stand it for very long.

Twelve-A frowned. *I won't?*

Mike hesitated, and Twelve-A felt a weird pang of panic before Mike quickly added, **No. I mean, if you keep doling out bits of food to hungry people, you can heal them. You could fix everything. You could get everyone to follow you and help you build the perfect society, with you teaching them all how to love each other and live in peace. You would have thousands of disciples hanging on your every word. You could travel the whole damn globe and teach people the right way to live.**

Twelve-A blinked. He had hoped for as much, but he'd never heard it spoken aloud by another before this. *You really think so?*

Sure, Mike went on quickly. **Right now, we're liars, we're thieves. We're greedy and hurtful and arrogant and uncaring. You take away the stuff we're afraid of, though—like starving to death—and all we need is a little love and compassion. You change the whole, ugly, backbiting Human race into something beautiful again, something where everyone loves their fellow man, shares everything, doesn't covet their neighbor's happiness...You could change it all.**

Twelve-A felt his suspicions die in the wake of hearing his own desires from another mind, unbidden. He let out a relieved sigh. *I was hoping I could do that.*

Come talk to me tomorrow, Mike said. *I have all sorts of ideas on how to save the Human race.*

Twelve-A felt his heart begin to pound, because he could sense that Mike wasn't lying. *You do?*

I do, Mike said, *but I spent my life speaking face-to-face for a living. I think better out loud. I'll have to show you in person.*

Excited, now, Twelve-A could barely contain his glee. *You could tell me out loud right now...*He would do anything—*anything*—to end the agony he heard all around him.

No, I need to see you, Mike said.

Twelve-A's disappointment almost crushed him. *Okay,* he said, unhappily.

*So...*Mike said, sounding uncertain,...*are we still on for tomorrow? Zero and the foreign girl stay home?*

I'll find something to distract them with, Twelve-A replied, grateful beyond words that there was at least one other soul on Earth who *understood,* who could see how sick the Human race was, and how easily it could be fixed with a little kindness and compassion. He knew, just by Mike's simple words, that the two of them could be friends.

It worked, Mike thought, on a wave of amazement. *That was easier than I thought it'd be. The old job actually paid off.*

And, in that moment, Twelve-A realized that Mike was hiding something from him. Sensing that, Twelve-A got another strong pang to tell Joe of the proposed meeting between himself and Mike's group, but the temptation of asking Mike if he had any ideas on how Twelve-A could help the Human race, in *person,* was too tempting to ignore.

Unlike Joe, who was buried in the bad, trained to be violent and insensitive his entire life, Mike could *see.* He recognized that people were sick, and just needed a little help to heal. Perhaps the two of them could work together, converting other Keepers, forging friendships and happiness wherever they went.

See you tomorrow, Twelve-A told Mike, his heart singing for the first time in his life. *Maybe, over time, you can teach me how to be a politician, too.* Of anyone, it was the *politician* that understood the needs of the many over the needs of the few, of the need for change, the need for self-sacrifice and cooperating with one's fellow man in order to create a better world. Twelve-A had never been so happy in his existence, and he wanted to learn what this man knew, to study him and change the planet with him.

Uh...sleep well, Mike replied.

And Twelve-A did.

• • •

The next morning, when Joe was ready to get moving again, Twelve-A delayed them. Again. When Joe demanded to know why they had to be such lazy burning Takki, Twelve-A told him he could take his Test Tube and shove it up his ass.

Which meant that Joe was *still* being punished for teaching Shael their intricate 'clan names' when he was bored because everyone else was sitting around playing with grass like leafmunch furgs. Joe sighed and, realizing they weren't going anywhere fast, slipped out of camp to check again for Mike and his gang. He was pretty sure that they were going to make an attempt to get Eleven-C back, and he wanted to be ready when they did. Twelve-A could spew all the mind-vomit he wanted about peace, happiness, and the goodness in people, but Joe knew there was no better deterrent than a freshly-charged Nocurna plasma pistol sizzling against the earlobe. He also suspected that this time, Mike's crew wouldn't leave survivors when they hit. He knew that Shael's little tree-topping spectacle—and his own penchant for shooting off body parts—would have been as good a reason as any to shove Mike and his followers over that razor-edge of civility, from the Tie You Up And Leave You To Die merry band that had fallen on a string of bad luck to the outright backstabbing, murdering kind whose eyes danced as you died from their bullet wound.

By the time Shael caught up with him atop the hill, Joe was trying to figure out how long a group of starving survivors would follow them before they struck again. He figured it would be around the same time they ran out of the scant piles of food that Eleven-C had made for them in their gold-encrusted camp. Probably tonight or tomorrow.

Seeing Shael pretending to ignore him as she fell into stride beside him, Joe sighed. He had tried to slip out of camp without being seen, but lately, she'd been sticking to his side like a Rashurian ground-leech. "Nice day for a walk," he said, not expecting a response. She hadn't said more than a few manly grunts to him in days, though he got the odd feeling she was watching his every movement, analyzing it, *learning* from it…

Soot.

Shael gave him another manly grunt and hefted her club. Lifting her chin high, she continued to pretend to ignore him, walking side-by-side up a path that was barely big enough for one.

Joe sighed again. He had to fight the urge to challenge her to a fight-to-keep-your-tek duel right then and there, because he was down to his last pair of non-shortened pants and he had the feeling she was quietly eying his grenades. He hadn't told her what they *did*, but he'd caught her fondling them that morning, and he was pretty sure that she'd registered his screaming fest and underlying panic afterwards as indicating that whatever they were, they were Very Cool and Ultra Desirable To Have, and therefore *hers*. Ever since, he had been struggling with the dilemma of digging a very, *very* deep hole and leaving them behind for some Ooreiki archeologist a thousand turns from now to dig up and pee himself over, or continuing to carry them around with a bunch of grabby powder kegs who liked to paw through his stuff and steal his favorite bandanna.

He needed to bury them, he decided. Too much could go wrong if she went snooping again. All it took was a *twist*…

Twelve-A, I need you to call Shael back to camp, Joe insisted. *We really don't want her to get her hands on grenades.*

There's that lake we passed, Twelve-A suggested. *You could throw them in the lake.*

Joe winced at that. If he *buried* them, he at least had the chance of getting them *back*. *I'm going to bury them*, he told Twelve-A. *I just need you to distract her for a bit.*

I don't think it's a good idea to bury them, Twelve-A replied. *Who knows who might dig them up?* Meaning, of course, that the posy-picking peacemunch mind-furg had gleefully jumped on the chance for Joe to irrevocably lose his grenades.

You know, Joe growled, *if I didn't know better, I would suspect you're pulling a Neskfaat on me.* Which, since the Geuji's masterminding of the intricate plot ending in the Huouyt banishment from the Tribunal, had become a colloquialism for setting someone up to spectacularly fall, pulling their strings to make them dance to your tune, and then disappearing back into the void of space like an Ooreiki ghost.

Twelve-A gave a moment of mental hesitation. *What makes you think I'm pulling a Neskfaat?*

Joe groaned. Like most every other colloquialism he'd ever used on the leafling, Twelve-A couldn't see past the literal meaning of the saying itself. Which, taken plainly, meant he was setting Joe up for the biggest war Congress had ever seen.

Deciding it was too early in the morning to lecture science experiments on the finer points of Congie language and culture, Joe just ignored him. He didn't *want* to go to the lake, which was at least ten lengths from camp, but he knew damn well what the result would be if he buried his grenades with Shael out here to witness it. Besides, without Joe to pull their scales and get them moving, Twelve-A and the People would probably still be wandering around catching bugs and picking posies somewhere within the same two-length radius if he didn't bother to come back for another ten turns, much less ten hours.

Still, looking out over the mountainous, twisting road they had taken past the lake, Joe realized he *really* didn't want to leave the People alone for that long.

You should go, Joe, Twelve-A said. *We'll be here when you get back.*

Joe snorted at the peacemunch minder's crude attempts to get him to give up perfectly good weaponry and pulled out his binoculars to scan the valley for signs of Mike and his gang. It had been a thriving residential area, before Judgement, but now it was just clusters of silent houses, many of which had been either bombed or clawed into oblivion. He saw a lean-looking person here or there, furtively scavenging the wreckage with half-full knapsacks slung to skinny bodies, guns or knives at ready, but no large groups.

Had Mike and his tribe given up? It was a pleasant thought. Somehow, though, having seen the lined desperation in their faces, the bitterness, the *greed*, Joe had trouble believing they would simply let Eleven-C walk away, even if she was being guarded by Zero himself.

Joe lowered his binoculars and caught Shael eying one of the many guns he now kept strapped to his person at all times. She looked away quickly, but not before Joe caught a covetous gleam in her eye.

First the grenades, now the guns…

Joe sighed. "You wanna learn to shoot?"

Immediately, Twelve-A babbled, *What are you doing? You can't teach Shael to use guns. She hates guns. She hates to fight.*

Could've fooled me, Joe said, thinking of their 'epic battle' with her flailing against his outstretched arm. *Now get out of my damned head, you nosy little leprechaun. I said I'll train her how I want to train her, and unless you want a trigger-happy furgling running around with expensive Congie weaponry, you're gonna let me handle this.*

…which will result in a trigger-happy furgling running around with expensive Congie weaponry, Twelve-A argued. *Just go throw the grenades in the lake. I'll make it so she doesn't care about the guns.*

Joe narrowed his eyes at the minder's hypocrisy. *So you'll ward her off my guns, but not the grenades, huh?*

Twelve-A hesitated, obviously not having considered that particular train of thought. *I, uh…*

Who is Chief of Security? Joe reminded him.

You are, came Twelve-A's mental mutter.

That's right, Joe said. *And I just recruited our first secondary officer. This is my job. Let me do my job, and you go back to mind-melding field mice and leading your eleven o'clock hugging practice.* "You," Joe said, visibly startling Shael, who immediately gave him a guilty, defensive look. He pulled one of the guns off his shoulder. "You wanna learn how to use this?"

Shael's pretty eyes widened and she swallowed.

"Do you want *me*," Joe pointed to himself, "to teach *you*," he pointed to her, "to use *this*?" he gestured at the gun.

Shael's breath caught and she nodded.

"All right," Joe said, shoving it at her. "It's on safety. *Don't* fiddle with any buttons until I tell you to."

I'm not translating for you, Twelve-A warned.

"You don't have to," Joe said. "I'm speaking warrior-speak. It's universal." Indeed, Shael had dropped her club like the badly-whittled stick it was and was reaching out to take the laser rifle with all the reverence of an Ooreiki oorei. Once her fingers touched it, she swallowed hard and froze like she was afraid that, by moving suddenly, she would destroy a sacred object of the Black Jreet herself.

"Now," Joe said, taking on the famous bark of a Prime. "This gun is your *life*, you understand? This gun means *everything* to you out there in the blood and the diamond dust, when you're dealing with bad guys who poke their heads out of shadows to shoot you in the face when you're trying to take a crap."

If Joe had learned one thing from his time giving lectures as Commander Zero, it was that *tone* carried almost as much meaning as *words*, and even then, she stared at the gun in open-mouthed awe.

"Now," Joe said, "this here's the trigger. Pretty obvious. You pull it, it goes boom. *Don't*—" he barked, startling her into a full-body jerk, "—pull the trigger until you're *absolutely sure* you're ready to shoot whatever's on the other side."

Shael swallowed and nodded.

"This here is the charge clip," Joe went on, pointing. "It comes out like this." He demonstrated. "This is the *ammo*." He said the word slowly and waved the charges so she could see them, then made an exploding gesture with his hands. "A standard Congie laser clip is six hundred sixty-six charges. A standard plasma clip is a hundred and thirty-two charges, 'cause they take up more space. This is what's called a tunnelbuster." He pointed to the hundreds of additional charges. "For those times you get stuck underground and you spend a few days in a firefight. One thousand, nine hundred, ninety-eight charges. Three times the normal. See?" He pulled a standard clip from his other laser rifle and showed her the difference.

Shael squinted at the two a moment, her brow tensed as her mouth worked. "One packs more punch," she offered.

"Not quite," Joe said. "Laser is pretty standard. They got them as good as they could get about a million and a half years ago and the tech really hasn't advanced much since. It'll burn through two rods of anything not energy-resistant in a nanotic or less and can shoot pretty much as far as you can see as long as there's no atmospheric interference—which there always is."

Shael made a face at the rifle. "You speak the tongue of skulkers and cowards as if you expect me to speak it back."

There she was again, calling *him*, *Commander Zero*, a skulker. Joe scowled. "Well, if you don't want lessons, I'll just take that back." He reached for the gun...

...and his hand ran into an invisible wall that could have been glass had it not shoved him backwards a dig.

"I never said I didn't want lessons," Shael grumbled, as Joe muttered a curse and shook out his knuckles. "I said I wanted you to stop talking in the language of weaklings. I...like talking with you, Joe Dobbs ga Badass. Though he is as honorable in his words as he is in his actions, Twelve-A ga Test Tube ga Pointy Ear ga Flaxen Hair continues to try to convince me that my true nature is one of peace, and the rest of the furgs drool or babble nonsense. It's...refreshing to find another who can speak the tongue of warriors. Doctor Philip ga Uppity Sootwad was not a great warrior like you."

Joe grunted, feeling infinitesimally guilty for teaching her the litany of 'clan names'. Then it passed. He crossed his arms over his chest, flexing as unobtrusively as he could, and peered down at her. "What happened to Beda ga Vora, your worthy opponent and lifetime arch nemesis, 'middling warrior of the upland clans', over nine rods of rippling crimson muscle?" The Jreet habit seemed to be working again, so he wasn't surprised when she stiffened.

"I..." Joe could see the confusion in her eyes, because this is where her theory began to fall apart. Her eyes dropped to his legs and she swallowed.

Joe waited.

"They..." She swallowed. "You must have been abducted, as well."

Joe lifted a brow.

"They abducted me," Shael blurted. "Stole my body and gave it to Humans to fight their enemies. They must have done the same to you."

"Oh, is *that* the story today." Joe sighed and dropped his arms. "Look, Shael—"

Her pretty green eyes darkened instantly. "If you don't wish to teach me, no one is forcing you, Voran." She shoved the gun back at him and turned to go.

"Hey, hold on!" Joe cried, grabbing her by the arm.

Normally, Shael would have simply crushed the offending appendage for the transgression, but this time, she stopped and looked down at his hand, then reluctantly lifted her eyes to his face, anger still pooling in the emerald depths. Anger, and...Something else. Fear? Confusion?

Then Joe imagined what it must be like, stuck believing you were something you were not because some scientists decided to try tinkering with your head as a doctorial coup, and he felt an instant pang of empathy. "Look, Shael..." he began softly.

"I don't understand what I'm doing wrong," she blurted, on a whimper. "I do everything just as I remember it, and it comes out *wrong.*"

Of course it did. Because someone had brainwashed her into thinking she was Jreet, who could punch their fists through the hull of a ship or strangle a Dhasha if it struck their fancy. Jreet survived on brute force, not finesse. And, at barely five digs in height, if she was *ever* going to hold her own in a fight, someone needed to teach her finesse. Badly.

"Everything is harder than I remember," she went on, oblivious. "I've spent *weeks* trying to figure it out. It's not the gravity of this place, because it doesn't affect anyone but me. It's not drugs, because they would have worn off. It's not that Humans are bigger than Jreet, because I've seen them compared to kreenit. It is not a superior new fighting technique, because even the most unknown, clanless Human warriors seem to know it. I just don't *understand*!" she cried again. "My scales haven't grown back. My coils are misshapen. My strength still escapes me. My tek refuses to unsheathe. I just don't understand what *happened*. It's like…" She swallowed hard, and her voice became a whisper. "It's like I'm not actually Jreet." Tears were welling in her pretty green eyes and her lip was trembling. "So what else could have happened, Voran? All I can think is that they stole my body from me. Put me in the body of a…" She hesitated and swallowed hard. "Put me in the wrong body," she finished, her voice breaking.

Joe sensed an opportunity to open her eyes staring him in the face, and, for a moment, he thought about telling her the truth of what she was. Then self-preservation nipped that thought in the bud and he coughed and looked away, uncomfortable.

"You've seen it too," she whispered, horrified. "You've *noticed* my shame."

Joe thought of all the times she had cursed his heritage, the uncountable instances she casually dismissed his fighting-skills, thrown him around, or scornfully demeaned his manhood, and realized this was a stellar opportunity to deal that all back to her, in spades. Then he thought of being trapped in a tiny brainwashing bed as cold, inhuman doctors fed him whatever memories they wanted him to have simply because he'd had the bad luck of being conceived in a test-tube and not a Human mother, and, instead, Joe bowed his head in a Jreet symbol of respect and said, "I will teach you everything I know. It would be an honor."

Shael blinked, her mouth falling open slightly as she stared at him in shock. "An…*honor*?" she whispered. "But I barely…"

She swallowed, her face flushing as she looked away. "I...lose. At everything."

Joe snorted. "Then you didn't have a very good teacher."

She swallowed again. "You'd...*teach* me?" Almost like she were terrified she'd misheard.

"*Somebody's* gotta protect those Takkiscrew furglings," Joe said, jabbing a thumb over his shoulder at the People, "and these all-night shifts are taking their toll on me. Not only are you the only person who's showed even the slightest interest in learning what I know, but you've got the warrior spirit. I've even seen you put that pointy-eared bastard in his place. Hell yes, I'll teach you."

Shael doesn't want to be a warrior, Twelve-A insisted, at the same time Shael spontaneously threw her arms around Joe and started sobbing. At first, Joe thought maybe the minder was right, and that Shael was somehow terrified of the idea of soldiery, but then he pulled back enough to get a look at her face and realized they were tears of *happiness,* not despair.

"Uh," Joe said, acutely aware that the act of hugging was un-Jreetlike and very likely to get him squished later, once she came to her senses, "you okay?"

"I tried *so hard,*" she whimpered into his chest. "*So hard,* and it all came out *wrong.* Thank you, Joe Dobbs ga Badass ga Male Model ga Chiseled Pecs. I owe you everything for your generosity, but my clan has abandoned me on this planet, so I can only offer my friendship and my spear beside yours in battle."

Okay, so maybe Joe felt a little bad about the clan thing. Maybe. He had, after all, just been thrown down a mountain.

"I should have known you had greatness within you," she went on. "Your kindness in teaching me your clan names after I'd exploited your weakness and threw you down a hill using nothing but my war-mind is a generosity only a *true* Jreet prince would give to an ignorant weakling like me."

Joe winced. "Uh, Shael...?"

"Thank you, Joe Dobbs," she said again. "After you offered to tie knots, I was too cowardly to ask for your help remembering my training. I thought you would take it as an invitation to battle for my tek. And, after coming to a draw with you, then losing to a *Human*…" She was crying again, and this time, he was pretty sure it was not happiness.

"Aw, Shael," Joe whispered, drawing her close. He put his chin on the top of her head. "You don't deserve what's happened to you."

She went still in his arms, but, surprisingly, she didn't struggle to break their 'ridiculous biped touching ritual'. Silence reigned; one where Joe could hear nothing except her soft breaths against his chest. "What do you mean by that?" she finally said softly.

Joe flushed and felt his heart start to pound. "I, uh…"

Shael pulled back, old tears reddening her eyes. She was frowning, now. "Do you know of what happened to me, Joe Dobbs?"

His heart wrenching at the anguish in her face, Joe winced. He'd never been good at telling a direct lie. "I have a pretty good idea," he admitted.

She cocked her head, her pretty green eyes scanning his face. "But you don't want to tell me."

"Not especially," Joe said. Then, to pre-empt her next question, he quickly added, "It's just a theory, like yours. And, since you actually *lived* through it, I'm sure you have a better idea than I do what happened to you."

Shael made a face, her pert chin scrunching adorably. "I do, but until I can retake my rightful place as prince of Welu and war-leader of the equatorial swamps, I'm willing to listen to any and all ideas how I can get my body back, however useless you think they might be."

Joe met her gaze for several long heartbeats, again having the knowledge that she was close—*very* close—to realizing the truth of what had happened to her in Doctor Philip's dubious care. All it would have taken on his part, at that point, was just a gentle nudge, a simple phrase pointing her in the right direction. Something within Joe strained to tell her, ached to help her realize the truth, screamed to give her the answers she so desperately needed.

Be very careful, Twelve-A said. *That could go poorly for you.* With his words came a very vivid image of Joe's head exploding like an overfilled zit.

Reddening, Joe cleared his throat and said, "So how about we get you trained up in modern weaponry? I suspect you've been… interred…long enough that a lot of these weapons are new to you?"

She gave his guns another suspicious look. "Early iterations were known to me before my move from Welu. That's a laser weapon. Can puncture a warrior's scales in under a nanotic."

"*If,*" Joe said, "they're on the visible spectrum. If you've gotta take out Jreet, plasma or grenades work a hell of a lot better. Part of what a Jreet's energy-field does is redirect light, and a laser is just light."

Shael made a face. "It is the weapon of cowards."

Joe shrugged. "Maybe. But it's cool to shoot. Watch this." He slapped the clip back in place, then brought the rifle up to his shoulder, aimed his superpowered Congic laser at the gas-tank of a rusting ground vehicle, and squeezed the trigger. A second later, the crude antique in the valley below exploded, scattering the Human scavengers into cover.

"Wow!" Shael gasped. "That was *amazing,* Voran!"

Joe found himself a bit stunned at her open excitement. It was such a nice change from the typical Jreet condescension and arrogance that he had to blink at her a moment to determine if he'd been hearing things.

"Again!" she cried, gesturing excitedly. "The blue one, over there." She pointed, grinning.

Blinking at her, wondering which Huouyt had come to snatch her body and replace the Shael he knew, Joe reluctantly brought the gun back to his shoulder and took out another one.

Shael actually *giggled.*

Hearing that delighted sound, so unlike the imperious threats or insults he was used to hearing from her, Joe felt his chest start to heat up with the desire to hear it again. Without her asking, he peered through the scope and took another shot. Then another.

Then another. Human survivors in the valley below began scattering like terrified hordespawn as each vehicle went up in a cloud of flames and billowing black smoke.

"My turn!" Shael cried, when he lowered the gun.

Joe, who was still stunned at the idea of Shael *giggling*, numbly handed her the rifle in a mute daze.

Shael didn't seem to notice his shock. "And this," she gestured from a safe distance at the trigger, "fires the weapon?"

Joe shook himself, realizing he'd given her a high-powered rifle, fully charged, with no instruction on how to keep from blowing her own foot off. He quickly moved in to guide her hands, show her the correct way to hold it. "Grip it like this," he offered, sliding her hand down the stock to a firmer resting point. "Shoulder here. Cheek here. Legs like this." He adjusted her stance with a foot.

And Shael, so swept up in the act of learning to fire a rifle, didn't even seem to notice their closeness, the way Joe was breathing against her neck...

The sound of a car exploding in the valley below yanked Joe out of his reverie and made him blink at Shael in surprise. "I didn't tell you how to aim..." he blurted.

"Seemed simple enough." Shael grunted and turned to locate another one through the scope. Without asking, she fired again. Like the first, it was almost six lengths away, at the very edge of the rifle's useful range without an AI to make interference adjustments.

"Uh..." Joe managed. "Lucky shots."

"Luck?" she snorted. "What you see is *skill*." Indeed, when she took out three more vehicles in rapid succession, Joe had to agree. It was almost like someone, somewhere, had taught her all of this before...

Then Shael said, "Try to best me, Voran." She took out a bus, then lowered her rifle to grin up at him in challenge. "That is, if you think you have the tek."

Joe, not one to turn down a marksmanship challenge from a pretty lady, said, "Oh, I've got the tek, sweetie," and shrugged his second laser rifle from his shoulder and switched off the safety. "What's the target?"

She squinted out at the valley. "The red land vehicle beside the gaudy yellow biped dwelling along the field."

Joe brought his rifle to his shoulder and glanced out over the valley in question, finding the target in question approximately three lengths from their current position. The sleek red vehicle obviously belonged to a wealthy Human, before the Judgement. Now, the yellow house was half caved-in, the remnants ransacked, and he could see the bone-piles of kreenit droppings littering the road outside.

A cluster of motion at the edge of his scope caught his attention and Joe trained his rifle on the dark shapes trudging through the knee-high alien grasses at the center of the cluster of houses. He frowned when he saw the group of ragged survivors crossing the field toward them—at least twenty of them. And, though it was almost six lengths out, some of the faces seemed almost familiar…

"Only Takki stand there for hours, quivering before they make their shot," Shael snorted. She exploded the Voran-red vehicle in question, and the group of survivors scattered back toward the trees.

Feeling a little pang of unease, Joe swung his rifle around to glance behind him at the little river gulley where he'd left the People. He couldn't see any of their naked forms standing out against the rock and scrub, but that wasn't unusual. A lot of the time, when Joe left to do his scouting missions, when he came back, it was to find them all weaving grass under a tree, attempting to get out of the heat. Still, something didn't seem right. There were very *few* trees they could be hiding under. Half of him wanted to drop everything and sprint back to camp. *Everything okay over there?* he finally asked the minder.

We're doing just great, furgling, Twelve-A said. *You can go back to playing with your guns.*

I don't see you along the river where I left you, Joe insisted.

Eleven-C decided she wanted to pick flowers on another hill, Twelve-A replied.

Joe shuddered at the idea of standing around watching forty-four under-dressed adults aimlessly wandering a hillside, pawing at plants. Definitely *not* in his job description. Besides, this was the first time he'd had a chance to shoot anything since hooking up with the experiments, and he was looking forward to a good marksmanship challenge.

"What are you doing, Voran?" Shael asked, suspiciously.

"Just checking on our charges," Joe said, swinging back to look out over the valley behind them. The last couple members of the group out in the field were slinking back into the forest, the burning car throwing up huge plumes of smoke nearby. Joe zoomed in on the stragglers, but they weren't carrying the lumpy, rope-filled bags of Mike's gang. He allowed himself to breathe easier, though there was still a knot of unease in his gut for leaving his friends behind.

I should be down there with them, he thought, prepping to end his scouting session early, despite Shael's interest in a shooting match, and go back to guard the experiments. It was immediately followed by, *They've got the telepath with them, and he wouldn't do anything stupid. He's the most rational, responsible person I've ever met, and he can take care of them while I'm gone.*

"And how do they fare?" Shael demanded, sounding worried.

"They're fine. They've got Twelve-A watching them," Joe said, raising his rifle again.

Shael snorted. "Twelve-A is a naïve furg." Then she seemed to twitch. "But he is the most rational, responsible person I've ever met, and he can take care of them while we're gone."

"My thoughts exactly," Joe said, sighting in on another car. "How's that blue land-roamer at the end of that cul-de-sac with the white tower sound?"

Shael lifted her own rifle to peer at the vehicle in question, looking a bit dubious. "The one by the big tree?" She gave him a little frown. "That's…far."

Of course it was. Because he was showing off. "Yeah," Joe said, as casually as he could. "Looks like a hydrogen job. This should be fun…" He sighted in and pulled the trigger.

Indeed, when Joe exploded the piece of machinery in question—at the very edge of the six length limit—the ball of flames took out a good portion of the street around it. Lowering his scope, he raised an eyebrow at Shael and said, "The yellow one right beside it. If you've got the tek."

Shael grunted, raised her rifle to her cheek, peered through the scope a moment, then fired. The yellow car did not explode. Joe raised a fist to his mouth to stifle his chuckle.

"I shot it!" Shael cried, sounding betrayed. She raised her head from the scope in fury. "Look at it! I *shot* it and the jenfurgling thing *sits* there!"

Seeing her adamancy, Joe frowned and raised his scope. Indeed, he saw that there was a pretty new hole through the vehicle, exactly where the gas-tank or hydrogen cells should have been. He grunted. "Probably one of those electric deals."

"Or one of those scavenging furgs stole the fuel," Shael growled, watching the retreating Humans through her scope.

Joe swallowed, realizing that now would be a *very* good time to teach the Jreet wannabe not to start picking off Humans like insignificant skin parasites. "Um, Shael…"

But off in the distance, the car crumpled with a tortured shriek of metal that echoed over the mountainsides, carrying to them even at the distance of their vantage point. When Joe looked again, the former car had been condensed into a perfect sphere about the height of his knee, even then rolling down the slightly-sloping street at the pace of a slow walk.

Seeing that, Joe froze. *She doesn't even* need *the rifle*, he thought, stunned.

But Shael had already pulled the trigger again. Joe's heart gave a startled thump when he at first thought she'd just taken out one of the figures running from the explosions, but when he raised his own rifle to get a better look at the damage, he saw no bodies, only a smoking tree at the base of a telephone tower.

"Hit the top satellite dish," she commanded.

Joe, who instinctively balked at the idea of destroying the remnants of Earth's soon-to-be-nonexistent technology, nonetheless wasn't about to argue with a woman who had just reduced a sports car to a glorified marble. He put the rifle to his shoulder and pulled the trigger. The dish took a hole the size of his thumb, which wasn't very impressive, so he began making a face. One corner of the lips came out a little lopsided, 'cause hey, he was basically twitching a nanodig at a distance of six lengths in order to create a three-foot swath of destruction, but other than that, it was perfectly recognizable as a diamond-headed Jreet smiley...If the Jreet would ever demean themselves enough to come up with a smiley face for their species.

Shael, who was watching through her scope, grinned. "You're not bad at this, Voran."

Well, I should burning hope so, Joe thought, considering how those same skills had kept him alive through just about every alien Hell in which Congress had ever decided to throw Humans. Knowing how delicate her 'Jreet' pride was, however, Joe instead said, "The compliment is yours. For someone who just picked up their first gun, you've got the favor of the Black Jreet."

Shael froze and glanced down at her rifle. Joe watched as she suddenly paled, then swallowed, her face changing as she stared down at the thing in her hands like it had suddenly morphed into a Dhasha hatchling. Without another word, she dropped it, the sensitive equipment clanging against the rocky ground as she started to wipe her hands against her borrowed pants.

"Hey," Joe said, reaching out to her carefully—carefully, because he recognized the symptoms of one of her weird flashbacks, and she had the penchant for obliterating everything in twenty-dig swaths when she was in the throes of a flashback.

Hey, Pointy, Joe said quickly, watching Shael start to back up, staring down at the gun in what looked like horror, gasping. *I think we got a problem.*

I'm busy, was Twelve-A's distracted reply.

Well, un-busy *yourself,* Joe cried. *Shael's having another breakdown! In broad daylight!* Indeed, she had fallen onto her ass and was panting, tears beginning to form in her eyes.

Twelve-A did not answer him. Shael's hyperventilating did not slow, and she was starting to whine like a terrified thing. Already, the ground around her was beginning to shudder and crumple, pushing outward in a sphere…

"You're safe!" Joe cried. "Safe, burn it. I was just teaching you to use guns!"

"*I don't want to use guns!*" Shael shrieked, in Human Congie. She was staring at the thing in his hand like it had been dredged from the worst, most fearsome, razor-fanged depths of the Jreet hell of Dro.

Joe blinked at her, then at his guns. Slowly, carefully, he lowered it to the ground. "That better?" he asked.

"You're a *soldier*," Shael whispered, wide-eyed. Again, in Congie.

Twelve-A, I really *think we have a problem,* Joe said, seeing the terror and unconcealed hatred in her face.

I'm taking care of something else, Twelve-A said. *Find a way to handle it, furg.*

I don't think that's an option! Joe shouted back. *Help me, burn you.*

Can't. Stop interrupting me. Busy.

As Joe stood there, gritting his teeth, trying to urge the stubborn minder into cooperating, Shael held up her hand towards him in a perfect imitation of Nine-G's tree-flattening trick.

"I'm not a soldier!" Joe cried, dropping to his knees and flinging the rest of the weaponry off his shoulders to scatter the ground around him. "I'm a Congie." He held up both arms in peace, then yanked off his glove to show her the glowing PlanOps tattoo. "See?"

Shael was shaking all over, shivering so hard her teeth were chattering. "They want…us to…fight the…Congies."

"Not anymore," Joe babbled. "Those ashsouls are dead. All dead." He was acutely aware that he was walking a razor edge between keeping her talking and getting utterly crushed to pulpy, liquefied death.

"C-Colonel C-Codgson?" she whimpered. She still spoke perfect Congie.

"Dead," Joe insisted, taking a wild-ass guess that when Twelve-A said he killed *all* of the people who knew about their lab, he meant *everyone.*

"W-who k-ki-killed him?" she whimpered. Then, in plaintive terror, "Me?"

"Twelve-A killed them," Joe replied. "No, you're fine. You didn't kill anyone."

"Yes I *did*," she whispered. The fingers of her left hand were gripping the dried grass with such intensity that the knuckles were white. "So they killed Charlie."

Aside from the machete-carrying furg and the unnamed guy still topping that pine tree behind them, Joe didn't remember her killing anyone. "Uh," he said, "Was Charlie your brother or something?"

Her face instantly contorted in pain. Then, in a childish wail, she sobbed, "Charlie was my raaaaaaaaabbbiiiiiit."

Hearing that childlike grief, so heart-rendingly intense, made Joe forget about the danger he was in. "Aw, Shael…" he said, easing himself towards her. "Come here…"

"No!" she screamed, scrabbling away from him, hand up again. "I don't want to be a soldier! I hate soldiers!"

"*I'm not a burning soldier*!" Joe bellowed back, realizing he had to startle her out of her terror, now, or he was about to lose a head. "They *dumped* me here to *die*. I'm not even a Congie anymore."

She gave him a nervous, uncertain look over her splayed fingers, but didn't lower her hand. "You're not a soldier?" She was still panting, sweat standing out in a glossy sheen on her forehead.

"No," Joe insisted. "I'm *nothing* like those pampered Takki."

She swallowed and started to shake again. Slowly, she lowered her hand to grip her knees to her chest, instead. "They tried to make me a soldier."

"They're gone now," Joe insisted. "You're safe. You're *never* going back."

"They put me in that *machine*," she whimpered. "Doctor Philip stuck a needle in my arm and *locked* me in there and wouldn't let me out when I screamed." Her voice was barely above a whisper, her eyes unfocused and distant. "They were gonna cull me, but they put me in the *machine*, instead. There was a black Jreet and she was telling me I needed to save the Humans…"

Seeing her total desolation, her vulnerability, her deepest terrors laid bare, Joe had to do something to help her. Slowly, so as not to spook her, he moved close enough to put his hand on her arm. Then, when she didn't kill him for the effort, he gently—like a man handling a wild Dreit—pulled her into his embrace. Shael reacted stiffly, her eyes wide and uncomprehending, but when she did not try to struggle free, he wrapped his arms around her. For a long moment, she was utterly still in his arms, like she was afraid to move. Then, after what seemed like an eternity, she began to relax. They sat like that for several minutes, Joe awkwardly perched on the ground, Shael pulled up against him, the two of them saying nothing.

After a while, Joe had the startled realization she was whispering against his arm. He had to lean down to make it out.

"Please don't let me forget," she whimpered.

Joe felt another ache in his chest. "I won't," he said. "I promise."

That seemed to quell her fears, because she relaxed fully, her head slumping against his chest, her arms going limp on his thighs.

Joe settled his chin against the top of her head and let her sleep. For upwards of thirty tics, he sat there like that, listening to the soft whispers of her breath against his bicep, the sound of Earth-insects buzzing around them. And, given ample opportunity to sit there and think about it, Joe had the strange realization that the feeling felt...right. Like he'd finally found his favorite plasma rifle, for years stuffed just out of sight under his bed.

Joe was just starting to nod off himself when Shael jerked in his arms. "Why do you hold me, furgling?" she snapped, thrashing out of his grip and hurtling to her feet. "Where is Eleven-C? Why are we not at our stations?"

Realizing he had to think quickly or forever lose the opportunity, Joe managed, "You don't remember? We engaged in a duel, but we fought each other to exhaustion."

Shael's eyebrows went up and she gave him a surprised look. "We...did?" Then she seemed to re-evaluate his impressive Congie musculature and managed, "I...*did*?"

"To a *draw*," Joe agreed. "We'll have to try again some other time."

She swallowed and licked her lips, obviously not looking forward to that. "Yes," she said hesitantly. Then she lifted her delicate chin in Jreet challenge. "Yes. We can't leave that unsettled."

Joe felt a familiar twinge in his crotch, thinking of taking her up on an honest-to-god wrestling match. Then he thought about exploding head-pimples and gigantic car-marbles and quickly squashed the idea. He was still reddening and rubbing the back of his neck, staring embarrassedly at the ground between his knees, when Shael imperiously collected a rifle from the ground, threw it over her shoulder, and said, "Until then, you will continue to train me in modern weaponry, Voran. It will serve you well when you are forced to give up your tek and become my brooder."

Joe choked. "Uh. Right." At her sharp look, he said, "I mean sure. It would...serve me well...to have you trained...in weaponry."

She grunted and started walking back the way they had come.

Joe scrambled to get his guns back over his shoulders, then jogged after her. "You know, Shael," he said, coming abreast of her, "I wanted to talk with you about those things you pulled from my pack this morning."

Shael gave him a sideways look. "Those things Twelve-A told me to pull out?"

Joe frowned. "He *told* you to pull them out?"

She shrugged. "He said they were some great Earth-weapons and I was interested in seeing how they worked."

Joe blinked at her, unable to decide if she'd just told him that the minder had tried to get her *killed*, or if he'd tried to get her to 'relocate' his grenades so they could be left behind with the next move. Cautiously, he said, "Those things you took from my pack. They're called grenades. They're *extremely* dangerous to play with..."

Shael's derisive snort was all he needed to know that she would therefore play with them at the nearest opportunity.

"No, listen..." Joe grabbed her by the shoulder and stopped them both. He quickly retracted his hand at Shael's dangerous scowl, but quickly went on, "If you set off one of those things in camp, it could kill everyone. Not just you, but *everyone*."

She gave him a dubious look, then sniffed. "Show me."

Joe opened his mouth to argue, saw that to argue would result in her immediate acquisition of said grenades and her studious attempt to figure it out for herself, then sighed and shrugged off his pack. As she watched with an obvious attempt at detachment, Joe pulled one of the more impressive grenades from its hallowed spot buried at the bottom of his gear. He held the ovoid blue sphere up for her to see. "This is called a thunder egg. One guess as to why."

"It draws down the wrath of the gods," Shael said.

Joe grinned. "Pretty much. It's the biggest one they've got for hand-throwing. A lot of guys don't lob it far enough and it ends up taking them and all their friends out with it." He let out his breath. "Okay, you ready for this? I'm gonna throw it down the mountain, but you should still get behind cover."

Shael made a noncommittal snort, but he could tell she was interested.

Joe twisted the grenade to the ARMED position, then quickly heaved it down the hill and ducked low. The explosion that followed a few nanotics later was enough to pound the air in his lungs and make his ears ring. It took trees, rocks, and a good section of the mountainside out in a massive blast of the most powerful hand-held Congie explosives in the Planetary Ops arsenal.

When it was over, there was a ten-rod-wide circle of destruction, a few utterly obliterated trees, and an ominous, ringing silence in which not even the Earth insects had the courage to go about their daily business. Joe felt a rush of satisfaction, knowing how impressive it must have looked to a science experiment who had never left her lab before this.

For her part, Shael had never twitched from where she was standing, facing the explosion, a frown on her face. She continued to stare down the mountain like a kid waiting for a magic trick. Eventually, she turned the frown on *him*. "That was it?"

Joe blinked, the smug satisfaction completely draining from him in the face of her confusion. "Uh," he said, "yeah?"

Shael snorted. "You can keep your grenades. I can do such things without them." Then, to illustrate, she casually raised her hand and imploded a ten-rod section of mountainside, completely pulverizing everything caught within until there was nothing left within the bubble but dust. She raised an eyebrow at him, waiting.

"Uh…" Joe found himself staring at the swath of destruction she had just wrought. It looked eerily like what his thunder egg had done.

Except better.

"So like I said," Shael said, re-hefting her rifle over her shoulder, "keep your toys if you need the crutch, Voran. A *Welu* doesn't need tricks to defeat his enemies." At that, she began marching back in the direction of the People.

Joe blinked at the two obliterated areas of mountainside, then at her departing back. That morning, she'd stolen one of his black Congie shirts, as well, and it hung over her body in a ridiculously baggy display that would have been funny had it not been for the fact that it was his *favorite* shirt and she would probably kill him for taking it back. Because he really didn't have anything else he could do, he ran to catch up with her.

• • •

That dickcheese Congie just shot at us!

They weren't shooting at you, Twelve-A assured him. *They were just doing some target-practice on some old cars. If they'd been shooting at you, you would all be dead right now.*

I still say you should put him out. What if he interrupts us? Mike had been arguing for this all morning. He still, however, continued to feel great happiness and excitement about their future, remembering all the happy moments he'd had in his lifetime, all the joys of fatherhood, all the thrills of his glory years as a young Global Police officer before he became a politician.

He won't interrupt us, Twelve-A said. *I'll put him to sleep or something.*

Good. Do that. I don't want to lose anyone else because he gets pissed we decided to trade with you.

It's not going to be a problem, Twelve-A insisted. *He's distracted.*

Distracted or asleep? Mike demanded.

Twelve-A hesitated. He hated to lie. Hated it. He also knew, however, that Mike was thinking about calling off their meeting, and he *needed* to talk with this man who understood the Earth's deep-rooted need for change and experienced the same drive to work towards a better tomorrow. His very *soul* craved it, craved having someone to share his concerns with, his desires, his fears.

Yet, at the same time, he wasn't about to leave both Shael and Joe alone, unconscious, on a hillside for whatever Human or kreenit decided to wander by.

Asleep, Twelve-A said, in a little white lie that really didn't hurt because Mike would never know. *Everything's safe.*

How long will he be out? Mike insisted. *How far away is he? Where?*

He's on the hillside overlooking the road to the east, Twelve-A said, offering Mike a mental picture. *See? Plenty of distance from us.*

Have to send someone—good! Let's go get this over with, then. If we're gonna change the world, it starts one step at a time, right?

Right, Twelve-A agreed, though he was frowning. Not only had he, in that instant, caught something odd in the underlying happy thoughts that Mike had been projecting ever since Twelve-A had offered to help him, but Mike's followers were all thinking...strangely. Instead of happy that they were about to pool their resources for the betterment of mankind, they were incredibly anxious, so nervous that it permeated Twelve-A's mindspace like the smoke even then settling over the valley from the objects Shael and Joe had set on fire. Though some were trying to hide it, they thought Twelve-A was going to try to kill them.

Hey, Pointy, Joe's mental spasm of fear shot down their connection. *I think we got a problem.*

I'm busy, Twelve-A replied. Now that he was looking for it, he could see that *all* of the small mental spheres collected around Mike like a colorful constellation within the void were vibrating with nervous energy. When he grew close, they were thinking things like, *Shoot the blond ones. Just the blond ones.* Or, *That big guy's first. Mike said he's first.* Or, *That brunette's the one. Gotta make sure she doesn't get caught in the crossfire.*

Mike, Twelve-A said, frowning, *the other members of your group are worried they're going to have to shoot the People. Can you please tell them nobody's going to get hurt? What they're thinking is dangerous.*

Oh shit, those stupid fuckers. "Listen up, furgs!" Mike snapped. "**We are going to play** *nice* **today, right? Nobody shooting any- one. The escaped lab rats are our** *friends.* **We're going to be giving them a better future.** *Get* **me?**"

Twelve-A's frown deepened at the use of 'lab rats'. Even though Mike was emanating images of happiness and caring, the word itself felt weird, almost as if it were a derogatory dismissal, and not a friendly one like Joe liked to use. Even then, several of Mike's gang were chuckling to themselves, or rolling their eyes.

Well, **un-busy** *yourself,* Joe cried in his mind, the intensity of his panic almost jolting Twelve-A away from the dozens of minds that, if anything, seemed more bent on doing harm to the People. *Shael's having another breakdown! In broad daylight!*

Indeed, Twelve-A could feel Shael's panic driving itself down their own connection, but she was in her mind-space, where Twelve-A couldn't touch her, and something he didn't quite understand was happening with Mike and his gang, something that he instinctively knew was a thousand times worse. Leaving Joe to deal with Shael as he had almost a dozen times in the past, Twelve-A concentrated on the minds around Mike, trying to glean what he could from their rougher, less organized thoughts.

While Mike's thoughts were clear and distinct—and still singing of the beauty of love, children, and marriage, as well as his desire to build a better future for all—his followers' were much more garbled. Many were scared. Or resigned. Or thinking about stealing Eleven-C for themselves.

When Twelve-A frowned and narrowed his focus to those thoughts, he found *several* young men that looked like they were planning to run away with Eleven-C after everyone else went to sleep. Or shoot everyone, including Mike, to keep her.

*Twelve-A, I really **think we have a problem**,* Joe interrupted in a panic, almost shattering his concentration.

I'm taking care of something else, Twelve-A said, struggling to maintain his hold on the thoughts drifting through Mike's group. *Find a way to handle it, furg.*

I don't think that's an option! Joe shouted back. ***Help me, burn you.***

Can't, Twelve-A snapped. *Stop interrupting me. Busy.*

Unlike Mike's crystalline, perfect thoughts of happiness and joy, most of Mike's group, Twelve-A realized, were nowhere near his level of mental harmony. Instead, they were adrift in greed and selfishness. Their hearts burned with malice. Their stomachs twisted with avarice. They wanted Eleven-C for themselves. And several were willing to kill for her. No, more than willing. *Plotting to kill…*

Mike, Twelve-A said, concerned, now, *there are several men in your group who plan to take Eleven-C from us. They…*he hesitated, because it seemed so strange to him, after he offered to give them anything they wanted,*…plan to kill people to take her.*

He felt a spasm of panic on Mike's mind-link. Then, ***Who are they planning to kill?***

You, Twelve-A said, confused. *They think they have to kill you to keep her for themselves. Why would they want to kill you to keep Eleven-C, Mike?*

He felt Mike's mind harden. ***Because I would keep them from hurting you. Give me names. Which ones plan to take her?***

Twelve-A hesitated, not liking the brief blast of fury he felt before Mike's normal happiness returned. *Why? What are you going to do to them?*

Convince them to stop, Mike replied.

And, because he could sense that Mike was telling the truth, Twelve-A, relieved, concentrated a little. *Daryl, Roland, and Jerome.*

Mike continued to portray happy thoughts of his true love, killed by cancer two years ago, and his kids, most of whom had died in

Judgement, and his elite home on the San Diego coast, a multi-million credit property on the coveted island of Coronado.

When the first mind floating around Twelve-A winked out, he twitched, confused. When the second and third vanished, their lights succumbing to the Void, Twelve-A began to feel a deep, nagging sense of dread. *What did you do?* he asked softly, afraid of the answer. He knew that they had somehow mysteriously died, but he hoped for any answer—*anything*—other than Mike had killed him, because the kindred spirit Twelve-A sought would *not* have killed them.

Those despicable cowards were going to try and run away with Eleven-C, Mike said. A flash of fury interrupted his thoughts of hearth and home before the wall of happiness slammed back into place. ***They did not deserve to live.***

And that's when Twelve-A realized that it was, indeed, a wall. Frowning at it, now, he began to push the happy images aside, slipping under them to see what lay beneath.

A field of corpses rotted within Mike's mind, buried behind the smiling faces of his wife and kids, the cheerful jingle of the merry-go-round, the cheers of his constituents as the last vote was counted, the rush of pride as he put his ring on his wife's hand...

He plans to kill us all, Twelve-A realized, with a start. The idea that he had not seen through the guise, that the kindred spirit he'd been looking for had turned out to be a murdering psychopath, that he was really that *naïve*, was so horrifying to him that, for long minutes, Twelve-A could only stare at that field of corpses in Mike's mind, still diligently hidden by a wall of fake happiness.

And, now that he was looking, the happy images themselves weren't real, but rather, were gaudy creations, hollow fabrications that had been put in place to obscure the truth. The perfect marriage to his wife, when Twelve-A touched it, dissolved into a wretched existence of screaming fits, closed doors, cold beds, and whores, followed by a silent meeting in the night, an exchange of money, and his wife's tragic death on the news, the exceptional pictures of him mourning over her casket, the boost in poll numbers, the unexpected comeback, the surprise victory. The happy thoughts of his children at the park or the Ferris wheel, upon inspection, disintegrated into bitter custody battles, unhappy goodbyes, and simmering hatred. The only *true* happy thoughts, of any of them, were the ones surrounding his elections, and even they were stained with greed, triumph, and gloating. And, underneath those, the images of a new rise to power, one in which he controlled the only steady supply of food and resources. In time, Mike aimed to be a king. A prince of the people again, generously doling out small portions of food to people in need—too small to satisfy, but just enough to keep them obedient to his every word...

He didn't kill them because he was protecting us, Twelve-A thought, slipping into despair. *He killed them because they were going to take the People's side and try to join us.*

Faced with such selfishness, such *greed*, Twelve-A wondered again why he didn't just silence the Human race. His hopes, raised so completely by the idea of having someone that truly understood him and his purpose, now crashed to lifeless, broken things, bashed against the jagged rocks of reality, crushed by the images of death walled behind a façade of brotherhood.

He saw his own face amongst the dead in Mike's mind and stopped to stare at it. He steeped himself in the malice he felt there, reveling in Mike's hatred for him. Mike not only wanted him to die, but he wanted him to die in *pain*. In *fear*. Because Twelve-A had challenged his power over his little group. Threatened his right to lead. Because Twelve-A controlled something that Mike wanted, resources that Mike could use to rule. But it was more than that. He despised Twelve-A because he had such power, but refused to use it. He despised what Twelve-A could do, because *he* couldn't do it. He contempted him because he was harmless. Because Twelve-A was soft, weak. Because Twelve-A *believed* him. Because he *trusted* him. Because he didn't see it coming.

Swallowed by that pit of disdain for him, personally, Twelve-A floundered. Lost in his own misery, paralyzed by the sickness of the Human race, he struggled in the ether, caught between the urge to give up and the urge to get even.

He lied to me, Twelve-A digested, ashamed that he had fallen for the deception, ashamed at his own naïveté, ashamed of his *hope.* For a brief instant, he wanted to kill Mike for it. He wanted to show him every pain he'd wrought upon others throughout his lifetime, every humiliation, every act of greed and avarice, every hurt and cruelty in his jostling for position. Then, just as quickly as it had come, it passed. Mike, like everyone else on Earth, was broken. Twelve-A didn't want to break them more.

He decided he needed to send Mike and his band away forever, make them forget...

The cold barrel of a gun touched the back of Twelve-A's head. In a sneer, Mike said, "And they thought *you* were the greatest weapon ever made?"

• • •

"I'm sorry for pushing you down the mountain, Voran," Shael said. "You are weaker than me and it was not a fair fight."

A few minutes ago, they'd reached the place where they'd left the experiments, only to find the furgs had wandered off, back in the direction of the lake, the exact *opposite* direction that they'd been headed the last rotation. Joe had tried to attract the minder's attention, to tell him to turn them the hell around, but Twelve-A had not responded. Joe was even then showing Shael how to track an inept Human's passage through the dry grass and parched shrubbery.

Weaker than her, huh? Joe grunted and glanced down at Shael. At one and a half digs shorter than him, she wasn't exactly a spawning Hebbut.

Then again, she could crush every bone in his body with a thought, so perhaps she had a point.

"I think we have different strengths," Joe said, as diplomatically as he could.

She gave him a challenging smirk. "You have a *strength*?" Like it was definitely news to her.

Joe pointedly ignored the obvious—that he could pound her dainty female body to a pulp with his elitely-trained pinkie—and said, "I've got more extensive combat experience."

"Ha!" she cried. "You're no older than me."

And *that's* where she would be wrong.

His snort must have carried his meaning across, because Shael blinked. "You *are* older than me?"

"Oh, only about seventy twists of the Coil," Joe replied. She, like Twelve-A, and Eleven-C, looked to be one of the youngest of the group, probably in her twenties, at most.

She blinked confused green eyes up at him. "But you look younger than Doctor Philip."

"Congie tech," Joe said. "They don't like their soldiers to wear out on them before they've had a chance to serve out their terms. Means the data-crunchers have to spend money training new ones."

"Oh." She seemed to consider that. "Well, nonetheless, it was beneath me to sully my tek on half a warrior."

"Half a…" Joe stumbled to a halt. "Do you even know who I *am*?!"

She stopped and lifted her head in supreme challenge. "You are Beda ga Vora, second prince of the upland clans. A middling warrior, at best."

The same thing, almost verbatim, that she had said to him about twenty times before. This time, instead of letting her simply go with it, Joe squinted at her. "I'm Joe Dobbs," he said. "Some people call me Commander Zero. Otherwise known as Hu-man." He pronounced out the species name slowly, for her easier understanding. "I'm Human, not Jreet."

"And yet you speak to me in a language fouled by the Voran tongue," she retorted, crossing her arms over her chest.

Joe opened his mouth to object, realized he really had no way of arguing with that, and started walking again. When she caught up to him, she said, "It's all right, Voran. I understand. I was in your same position, weeks ago. I found my body stolen, my strength abandoned me. What you are experiencing is just a result of what they did to you."

Joe stopped again. "No," he bit out, "I'm Human. I'm not Jreet. I have *never* been Jreet."

"Then why do you speak Jreet?" she demanded.

Joe scowled at her for long minutes, trying to think of a rebuttal. How *did* he speak the Jreet language, when he'd never even *seen* a Jreet until he was fourteen? *Could* he have gone through something similar as her? Maybe something the Congies did to him, en route from Earth after the Draft? *Could* he have been brainwashed? Then, shaking himself, he said, "No," and kept walking again.

"You are just as Jreet as I am," Shael said, catching up again. "I can sense it within you, Voran."

Joe groaned, but didn't stop walking. As they continued to track the well-off-course experiments, he tried to think of something definitive, something completely undeniable that would clearly prove to her that she was not, indeed, a Jreet.

"Okay, how about this?" Joe said. He'd heard enough about Beda and Shael from his starry-eyed Sentinel that he was sure he could go more in-depth into the legend than any Human researcher. "When you captured Beda on Vora and took him home with you to stake before the masses, how did he escape?"

Immediately, her eyes grew guarded. "You hijacked my personal ship and took me home with you to dismember before your people for the insult."

Ah, a good ol' Jreet love story. Joe nodded. "All right," he said. "So why'd you end up fighting Dhasha with the Vorans?"

She scowled at him. "The Dhasha insulted the Jreet on Vora by breaking a blood-pact, attacked us during a festival with their slaves using grenades and gasses. I am Jreet first, clan second. I fought with my brothers."

Joe blinked. He had expected her to say, "I fell in love with my Voran captor and we decided to make babies," just like any good brainwashed Human would say. A little confused, he said, "And you helped save the Voran homeworld."

"And my own!" she snapped. "We got there in time to stop the second wave headed for Welu. The cowards were attempting to rid themselves of their only barrier to conquering Congress, using the tactics of skulkers and deserters, hiding behind their slaves like the dishonorable vermin they are. We annihilated them, then led the attack on the Dhasha homeworlds and obliterated six of them before the cowards surrendered, and the Regency could stake itself when it told us not to." She snorted in the complete contempt of Congress's most powerful politicians that only a Jreet prince could manage.

Joe peered at her. "And then you allowed yourself to be impregnated by a Voran...why?"

She scowled at him. "That didn't happen."

"History says it did," he challenged.

She stepped up and grabbed his jacket collar in a petite fist. "It didn't." She jerked him to eye-level. "Happen."

Interesting. So the brainwashing hypocrites only gave her half of the story. Great.

But, since the pretty woman had a penchant for mentally frisbeeing people, Joe kept his mouth shut until he could reliably prove otherwise. "So what did happen?" he asked.

She grimaced. "I went back to Vora."

Of course you did, Joe thought. *Because Shael ga Welu wanted to breed.* Why *else* would she have latched onto Joe as her arch-nemesis, a long-dead Voran folk hero? It *had* to have been part of the story somehow.

"And why would you do something like that?" Joe asked, innocently.

"Because you and I had unfinished business," she growled. "We still had to fight to the death."

"On Vora."

"Yes. I had been a prisoner there. It was my duty to return to my place of capture before the Dhasha intervened and face my fate with honor." Which was true to the legend.

"And who won?" Joe asked casually. Every fool knew Beda had won. That was the fabled love story.

"I did." She lifted her head. "I pumped you so full of rravut that you couldn't move, and it would have been an easy thing for me to slice you open and be done with it. You put up a good and honorable fight, though, so I wasn't about to dishonor you in front of your own kind."

Joe frowned. That was definitely *not* how the story went. Beda won gloriously, made her surrender, and took his bested opponent to mate. "So what did you do?"

At that, she gave him a blank look. Cocking her head, she said, "I, uh…" Looking befuddled, she said, "I'm not sure. It gets fuzzy there."

That seemed an odd thing for brainwashing crew to leave out, considering it was the pivotal point of the legend. Joe frowned. Maybe they just wanted to leave her thinking she was a badass. But if so, why give her the part about Beda ga Vora at all?

"And now you're Human." There was still that one, teensy, tiny detail she seemed to be overlooking.

The statement seemed to puzzle her. "I'm Jreet."

"But your *body* is Human."

She squinted at him like he was speaking ancient Shadyi, though this time, Joe *knew* his Jreet habit was working. Again, he decided perhaps it was best to lay out the facts and let her make her own decision. "You're hairy."

She looked down at herself blankly.

"Your body is covered with skin, not scales."

She made a face.

"You have no tek."

Immediately, her green eyes flashed like emerald lightning and he felt the air solidify around his body with a *whoosh*. "I have more tek than you'll ever have, Voran!" she snapped back at him, mentally linebacking him into the abandoned asphalt road.

She then turned and walked away, leaving Joe staring at the sky.

Watching the horseflies buzzing around his head, listening to the woman he'd held and comforted through yet *another* random flash-back walk as unconcernedly away as if he were one of those insects she had just swatted, Joe narrowed his eyes.

"You know what?" he demanded, sitting up. "You *are* tekless. And scaleless. And tiny. And *soft*. The only thing you have is teeth, and those aren't even very sharp." He lunged to his feet, glaring.

For her part, Shael had gone utterly still, back to him.

"You wanna fight me?" Joe demanded. "Then fight me, weakling. Kick me, punch me, gimme a good old-fashioned ass-whupping without your sneaky, underhanded tricks. I *dare* you to fight me like a Jreet." Joe walked up to the woman-who-now-wore-his-pants, bringing them chest-to-chest, scowling down at her, daring her to throw the first punch so he could legitimately kick a girl's ass and win that little duel she kept talking about once and for all.

Instead, somewhere between her fiery green eyes, flushed lips, and her pert chin tilted in challenge, Joe forgot what he was angry about. That weird heat was expanding in his chest again, and his heart was pounding erratically. Just being close to her felt...thrilling. As short as she was, Joe towered over her. She probably weighed half what he did, if that. She wasn't what he was used to in a woman—a lot more curves, less muscle—but something about that just made his heart pound harder.

As she narrowed her eyes and opened her mouth to no doubt lecture him on his ill-documented ancestry, Joe put his arms around her, dragged her mouth to his, and kissed her.

This time, when she put him on the ground with enough force to make his ears ring, Joe laughed. "Tricks!" he shouted at her. "You use tricks!"

Her face flushed and hair disheveled, she turned on heel and walked away.

Joe lifted his head to grin at her backside, admiring the sexy way her hips swayed in his much-too-baggy pants. He thought about how spirited she was, how adorably naïve, how intriguingly stubborn. Then he thought about how easy it would be for him to ruin that innocence forever, just by being near her, and his smile faded.

What was he *thinking*? He was Commander Zero, the sole survivor of just about every war he walked into. Everywhere he went, he found a storm of misery and death, with him walking through it, untouched at its eye.

Sobered, Joe sat up and stared at his feet, watching the flies crawl across his boots, the Earth insects no doubt still smelling the blood from the man he'd castrated to get them back.

Seeing the tiny black insects licking his Congie polymers with their proboscises, Joe felt worse than he'd ever felt in his life. He'd castrated a man over a pair of boots. Now he marched with a merry band of innocents, trying to make them dance to his tune. *Kissing* them.

Eventually, Joe got back to his feet and started forward at a walk, a sinking feeling in his gut.

He got people killed.

His shit rubbed off and he got people killed.

He was still brooding over this when a loud bang echoed over the hillside, followed by three more, rolling almost like thunder. Joe stopped and frowned, trying to figure out what could the People could have gotten themselves into to make a sound like—

Heart lurching, Joe yanked Jane from her holster and broke into an all-out run. Having spent so much time on advanced planets, dealing with impenetrable biosuits and advanced weaponry, he had forgotten to associate that sound with death.

Within minutes, he recognized Alice's thin scream up ahead. Two more gunshots went off, closer, now.

Pointy? Joe demanded. *What's happening? Are you okay?*

He got no response.

Twelve-A! Joe snapped.

Joe, Twelve-A's panicked mental voice babbled, *I made a mistake. I was going to erase Mike's memories and send them away, but Nine-G started a fight! I can't stop him in his mindspace. I need help, Joe!*

Mike. *Soot!* Joe lunged up the hill and burst through a copse of trees to see two dozen men and women hip-deep in grass, taking aim at a startled-looking group of People. Nine-G had put Twelve-A behind him, and no matter how much the minder tried to get around him, the mover kept the much smaller man firmly in place, scowling at the row of guns like they were spears, instead.

Even then, one of the gun-bearers squeezed his eyes shut and fired at the giant's big chest. Nine-G grunted and stiffened, then he and Twelve-A went down together in a heap, the minder crushed beneath the much bigger man. A few rods away from a bawling Eleven-C, Shael was in a twisted pile on the ground, obviously having fallen from a similar wound.

Help! Twelve-A screamed. *Joe help!*

Seeing the People huddled there, naked and helpless, a row of guns even then aimed for their exposed bodies, Joe didn't think—he just started firing. He took out men, women, children—he didn't care. Anything carrying a weapon became a target. And Jane, the sadistic, psychotic bitch that she was, sang with glee each time she sent another soul off to meet its maker.

By the time he finished, the field was littered with bodies and, yet again, Joe was the only one with a gun still standing. It had taken only seconds.

He went to Nine-G first, because Nine-G was still breathing. Alice was holding the giant man's sobbing head in her lap, her eyes glued to the blood spilling over his chest. An Earth-gun lay on the ground nearby, along with the would-be shooter. Seeing Mike's twisted, caved-in torso, his legs and arms wadded up like crumpled paper, Joe knew he was dead.

Nine-G, however, wasn't much better off. Joe fell into a crouch beside him, viciously fighting down his fears that he was too late.

The mountain of a man was hyperventilating, his eyes round with pain and shock. A spreading pool of blood was soaking the ground around him, staining it dark red. He was sobbing, his huge hands feebly trying to keep all the blood inside.

"Did I get them all?" Joe snapped. He held Jane at ready with one hand, scanning the trees as he tried to determine the severity of Nine-G's wound with the other. When the minder didn't answer him, he swiveled on the telepath and screamed, *"Are there any more out there?!"*

You killed them all, Joe, Twelve-A said softly. *One kid is still alive, but he's running away.*

Joe tucked Jane away and went into battle-medic mode.

"Twelve-A, get over here!" he snapped, ripping his jacket off. He tore his last shirt from his chest and started shredding it.

Twelve-A appeared at his shoulder, eying the dying man warily.

"Put Nine-G out."

Why? He's dying.

"*Now!*" Joe snapped. He started wadding up the shirt shreds. Nine-G didn't want to move his hands, so he had to pry the massive fingers away one by one. Fighting a giant, especially *this* giant, didn't get him anywhere. "*Now, the Ayhi damn you!*" Joe shouted at Twelve-A, desperately tugging at the man's huge, blood-slickened fingers.

Suddenly, Nine-G went limp.

"*Thank* you!" Joe cried. He pushed Nine-G's hands away and wiped at the wound. More blood flushed out over the skin, pumped out in a weakening flood. It was a full-on chest wound, not a shallow graze as he had hoped. The asher had shot him in the heart. He had nanotics to work.

Joe pressed the shirt wads against Nine-G's chest. "Hold these here and press hard!" he snapped, roughly dragging Twelve-A down to kneel beside the giant.

Without waiting to see if the telepath would do as he was told, Joe ran back to his survival pack and withdrew several tubes of battlefield powders from his kit. He rushed back and spread tiny amounts of battledust over the wound in succession, the final one staunching the flow of blood for good.

"You don't need to hold those anymore," he said curtly to Twelve-A as he withdrew a long needle from his medipack and opened a fist-sized jar of silvery liquid. He dipped the needle in the liquid and carefully replaced the lid on the jar. He packed it carefully back into the medipack before he turned back to Nine-G. Without ceremony, he flipped Nine-G's bloody wrist over so he could see the vein, then jabbed the needle into his arm. He withdrew the needle and waited long enough to make sure it wouldn't bleed too badly, then replaced the spine in his medipack.

Snagging up his supplies, he rushed over to Shael and dropped beside her. Despite what he had feared, he couldn't find any blood, no wound of any sort.

I put her out before she could enter her mindspace, Twelve-A said. The minder had followed him over to Shael's body, looking down at her in white-faced horror. *All I wanted to do was trade them some food, Joe. They needed food. I didn't want to hurt anyone.*

Joe spun, grabbed Twelve-A by the shoulders, and hauled him onto his tiptoes. As Twelve-A blinked up at him startledly, Joe leaned down into his face and shouted, "You *knew* these sooters were near the camp and you didn't *tell* me?!" He motioned at Mike's crumpled body, not releasing Twelve-A from his white-knuckled grip. "Even after you saw what they did last time?!"

Twelve-A started to look away and Joe shook him. "You're supposed to be *protecting* these people!" He dug his fingers into his shoulders and dragged him until their noses were almost touching. "Nine-G took that bullet protecting *you*. They were aiming at your *head*." Into his face, he bit out, "You. Would. Have. Died. Do you even understand what that means?! Nine-G could have *died!*"

Twelve-A gave him a startled glance. *You mean he won't?*

"I caught it in time," Joe growled. "Though, eventually, we should try to get that damn bullet out."

Relief washed over Twelve-A's face in a wave so innocent and naïve it was painful.

Joe shook him again, making the telepath's blue eyes widen startledly. "You don't get it, do you?!" he snapped. "The rest of the people we meet aren't *like* you! They're like those three ashers who kicked you until you were hemorrhaging inside. They're going to shoot first and ask questions later. If you want your people to live, you have to keep the bad guys *away* from here. And if *you* don't wanna do the dirty work, tell *me* to do it. Understand? I *will* take care of the problem." He pointed at the field of corpses that were even then still twitching in the evening sun.

Twelve-A had tears in his eyes when he nodded. *I understand, Joe.* The rest of the experiments were standing around in nervous clusters, looking like skittish melaa, obviously having no idea what had just transpired, visibly wondering why Twelve-A wasn't vegetablizing Joe for yelling at him. At their feet, Shael was sitting up, looking as startled as the rest of them. Clearly, none of the others had made the connection that their Fearless Leader could have prevented *all* of their misfortunes, every single one of them, had he simply pulled his peace-loving, posy-sniffing head out of his ass and realized that the world was a hell of a lot darker than it was light.

...and then Joe realized that he was still trying to make the minder think like a bitter, war-hardened Congie and he released Twelve-A's wiry shoulders in a spasm, feeling dirty to the core.

His shit rubbed off and he got people killed.

Feeling sick of himself and death and Life in general, Joe turned away from the teary-eyed minder and muttered, "Tell everyone to settle in for the night. We're not going anywhere until Nine-G is better. From now on, you tell me the *moment* anyone gets close. *Anyone.*" Joe turned back to face Twelve-A, his voice going cold. "Or I'm *leaving*. You understand? I swear to the Jreet Sisters and I swear it to the Dhasha Mothers—you let strangers walk in on us without warning me again and I'm *gone*." He jabbed Twelve-A in the chest. "And I *won't* be coming back."

I'm sorry, Joe. Twelve-A sounded miserable. And...cowed.

Which made Joe feel ten times worse.

"I'm gonna go move some bodies," Joe muttered. "And keep the People the hell away from them! No need to give them nightmares. Hopefully they won't attract kreenit until we can get out of here."

Twelve-A nodded, and the People immediately moved away from the field of corpses, sinking back into the treeline, dragging Nine-G into the forest with them, leaving Joe alone with the chaos he had wrought.

Joe couldn't bury them—it was too much effort and already too late that night—but he could go and look at every single dead man, woman, and child and wonder what their lives would have been like if he hadn't pulled the trigger. He wondered how many other kids had been left behind, too little to carry guns, now starving wherever their parents had left them, waiting in vain for their families to return.

Seeing the small, scrawny corpses, a much-too-big rifle or pistol beside each tiny, limp hand, never before had Joe wanted so badly to be alone with Jane.

Instead, he pulled his twenty-three victims into rows, sat down in front of them, and drank.

When he had run out of whisky and tears, he walked over to his pack and lay down, propping his head up against it, stewing in the silence. Then, a few rods off, he heard the tentative sound of sulfur striking as Alice built a fire with the book of matches he'd given her, while every one of the People looked hungrily on. Like little kids, none of them liked the darkness. If anything, they feared it more than they feared spiders or snakes or bad guys with guns. Or death. Especially death.

In the distance, he heard several of them pounding on a hollow log with sticks, giggling at the sounds it made. Alice was blathering in her professor's voice about how important it was to save matches, even though Eleven-C could make enough matches to light the world on fire. Her devotees, of course, nodded as if she spoke the Sisters' Scrolls.

None of them seemed to realize or even care that twenty-three corpses lay in the weeds a few hundred rods off.

They didn't understand. None of them did. But Joe, having seen it a thousand times before, understood it all too well. And it was something, as he lay there thinking about those twenty-three bodies, listening to his giant friend snore under a pile of doting experiments, that made Joe even more aware of how different he was. He was dirty. *Tainted.* Unlike Joe, these naked furgs he now ushered around through the woods like carefree children, were *pure.* Even Twelve-A, the mind-numbingly naïve sooter he was, was *pure.*

…And Joe was all that was standing between them and society crushing them, remaking them in its image.

Yet, only moments ago, wasn't *Joe* trying to do the same damn thing? Hadn't he tried to force Twelve-A into that same bitter distrust of his fellow man? Hadn't he *wanted* them to shed that purity, to take on the same hardness that Joe carried in his soul? Hadn't he just spent the last rotation trying to 'toughen' them? What had been his goal, really? To turn them into jaded, unhappy Joe Dobbs simulacrums?

Lying there, listening to them laugh and giggle, Joe wondered if he could afford to be around the People any longer. He wondered if he could even stay without destroying their innocence.

For long minutes, Joe stared up at the ever-darkening, oddly-blue sky as the People started bringing Alice sticks and pinecones to burn as night descended on them, thinking about what would have happened if he hadn't gotten there in time.

"You burning *tell* me," Joe shouted into the silence.

I'll tell you, Twelve-A replied, sounding as deeply swallowed by despair as Joe himself felt. *I'm sorry, Joe.*

"Dumbass pointy-eared sootling," Joe said, feeling the tug of tears again.

You'll know as soon as I know, Twelve-A assured him. Then, almost gently, *Furg.*

Joe knew that the minder was trying to cheer him up, add a little levity to drag him out of his despair, but when he closed his eyes, he saw Mike's crumpled body, the pale, lifeless head of his little girl lolling in the grass, his little boy with a circular ring of white ribs showing along the edges of his hollowed-out chest cavity.

Death. Everywhere he went, his shit rubbed off and people died.

Under his leaden right palm, Jane was singing his name.

27

TO GRAB A CONGIE BY THE
HAIR...

When Slade returned to camp, Tyson looked up from sharpening his big Zero-lookalike Prime Sentinel replica ovi that Slade had always found particularly gaudy and distasteful. "You're still alive," Tyson said. As if he expected otherwise.

"Thanks for the vote of confidence." Slade grabbed a half-eaten burrito from the plate beside the fire as he passed and started stuffing it in his face, staring at the fire, trying to plan out exactly how he was going to win a staring contest with a Congie. If he cheated, she'd kill him. He really didn't want to die, but he didn't especially want to be her slave, either.

"Where's my stuff?" Tyson asked, frowning.

"She took it," Slade said distractedly. "What sorts of things would you do to prepare for a staring contest with someone of your own species?" He had thought about getting naked as a distraction, but had decided against it when he realized that a Congie had a lot more experience being naked than he did, and it would probably just make him uncomfortable.

And, it seemed, if he was within twenty *feet* of her, certain… facets…of his anatomy were going to be embarrassingly…willing. Which she would certainly use to her advantage. Dammit.

It took him a moment to realize that Tyson hadn't answered his question. When Slade turned to look, Tyson was staring at him.

"You realize," Tyson said, "you came back here *without* my stuff, covered in bruises, head wrapped in a bloody towel, with a black eye and a swollen face, grabbed my burrito, started *eating* it, and asked me how to win a staring contest as if it were a life-or-death problem?"

Around the burrito, Slade said, "Yeah, so?"

Tyson gave him an odd look. "What kind of staring contest?"

Slade grunted. "The one where you can't lower your head or look away."

"Can you blink?" his second asked reluctantly.

"Yes, otherwise your eyes would dry out and you would go blind," Slade said, frowning at the stupid question. "These things can last for *days*."

Tyson stared at him for much too long. Then, "If I were to tell you that your mother was on some really interesting medication when you were conceived, what would you tell me?"

"Seemed to work out pretty well for her," Slade said, swallowing another mouthful of food. "Why?"

"No reason." Tyson cocked his head at him. "Why do you need to win a staring contest?"

"Because she'll put me in a thong if I don't?" Slade gestured vaguely with the burrito. "Or something. We haven't worked that part out yet."

Another long silence. Then, "I'd ask you if maybe you got a little too much sun out there," Tyson said, "but you're always like this."

"Oh come on," Slade demanded around a mouthful of some unidentified meat, "you never heard of ka-par?"

Tyson sat down on a fallen long beside him and pulled a knee up into his laced fingers, raising a brow.

"It's an alien dominance ritual started by the Dhasha. Whoever wins gets to do whatever he wants to do to the loser."

Tyson stared at him. "Or she."

"Huh?" Slade took another bite.

Eyes on his burrito, Tyson said, "You said 'he' gets to do whatever he wants to the loser. You're gonna try to stare down this Congie?"

"Yes," Slade said, frowning at his tone.

"You're fucked. I get your gum."

"I'm not gonna lose," Slade said, offended.

"Your case of gum says you do," Tyson said.

Slade snorted. "You don't have anything I want." He took another bite of Tyson's burrito, finishing it. "See?"

Tyson narrowed his eyes. "So let's say she wins," his second said. "Then what?"

"She won't win," Slade laughed.

Tyson gave him a flat stare. "I get your gum."

"Fine, whatever, sure," Slade said, waving him off. "I won't lose, so it's not an issue."

• • •

Rat spent two days sleeping, eating, and generally preparing to whip the soot out of Zero's brother in ka-par. She still wasn't sure what she was going to do with him once he had him, but she'd get to that when they came to it. She was relatively sure that he wouldn't try to renege on his ka-par because 1) he was terrified of her, 2) he seemed utterly insane, and 3) he actually seemed to get turned on when she kicked him in the face.

Rat grinned, bemused by the powder-puff. She knew she was going to have a hard time actually killing him when the time came. Though, she thought with a frown, if he swore to serve her, she supposed she could effectively keep him from breeding, which was what concerned Mekkval. Or she could cut off his nuts. That would solve the problem, too.

Before she did anything, though, she was going to get him to tell her everything he knew about the experiments he had discovered.

He supposedly had a photographic memory, so he should be able to provide her with some maps, or at least some physical coordinates. It was the best lead she could have hoped for. Now she just had to figure out a way to win a burning staring contest against a Dobbs.

• • •

When the Congie strode into his camp at noon on the third day, Slade had to do a double-take because she wasn't dressed. In anything. At all.

As in, not a stitch in sight. She wasn't even wearing boots.

Slade quickly discovered that the weird sphere-of-influence aphrodisiac wasn't clinging to her clothes. Reddening at the sudden heat in his groin, all he could think to say was, "You're naked."

She grinned at him. "You noticed." She walked over and leaned against a tree. "You ready to do this thing?"

Slade sputtered. "You're *naked*."

"Yeah. And?"

That just wasn't…fair. Because he thought of it first. And dismissed the idea because it would give her the advantage.

Slade found himself with the sinking feeling he was right smack in the middle of another stragedy unfolding before his very eyes. He swallowed hard. "Uh. Maybe you should put some clothes on. There's mosquitoes."

"Bugs don't bother me," she said, eying him flatly. "You ready for this, slave?"

Slade blinked at the sudden rush of excitement he got from the challenge. "You're seriously going to ka-par me naked."

"Yep." She smiled at him. "Why? Does it make you uncomfortable?"

Yes. Very. Slade was pretty sure the seam of his crotch was about to explode. "No, not at all. There's nothing wrong with the human body." He allowed himself a slow, languid look, then winced as the heat in his groin tried to set his pants on fire. What the hell was *wrong* with him? He alternately felt his face flush when he thought about how disconcerting it was going to be to stare down *breasts*, then pale when he realized what she was going to do with him if he lost, then flush again when he realized he might like it. She watched the whole thing with her arms crossed over her perfect boobs, a smirk on her face.

"Having second thoughts?" she asked.

"Oh screw you, lady," Slade said. He started tugging off his own shirt, then his pants, then threw his underwear and boots aside. She raised both eyebrows as he did so, obviously impressed.

Yeah, take that, Slade thought, giving her a good look.

"You know," she said, "they're smaller than they looked in your pants. Do you stuff?"

Slade flushed furiously. "No."

"Really." She gave him a flat look and raised a brow.

"Ka-par," Slade blurted. "You're not supposed to talk in ka-par."

"Have we started, then?" she asked, honey-smooth. She pushed herself off the tree and strode over to him. Looking up into his eyes, she said, "Or do you need a few more minutes of freedom?"

Slade's mouth just fell open and he didn't know what to say. It was like all the blood in his brain, after going unused for so long, suddenly took up residence in his cock, and all he could think about was grabbing her by the hair at the nape of her neck, tilting her head back, and kissing her until she kneed him in the crotch to relieve him of the problem.

"You're..." He swallowed hard. "Annoying."

"'Mistress' has a good ring to it, don't you think?" she asked, peering up at him pleasantly.

It did, at that.

Then Slade realized what he'd just thought and he froze, his eyes widening.

The Congie had totally just psyched him completely out, shaken him so badly he had already tipped his mental hat. Before the game even started. *I'm going to lose*, he realized.

The thought was so utterly startling—and foreign—to him that, upon having it, Slade bolted.

He was actually pretty pleased with himself for outdistancing a Congie—and was most of the way back to camp—when something grabbed his arm, spun him, knocked his feet out from under him, and threw him violently to the ground in a sprawl of dirt, twigs, and painful abrasions.

"No!" Slade shrieked, kicking at her. "Goddamn it! Ka-par didn't start! It didn't start!"

In an instant, the Congie had his arm twisted behind his back and had her knee squarely lodged in his spine. "You ran," she panted, "from ka-par. That makes you *mine*."

"I'm sorry, fuck, *fuck*!" Slade screamed as his arm started to dislocate from the upwards pressure she was putting on it.

"You run again," she said, twisting it in warning. "I win."

"Ow ow ow ow," Slade babbled.

"*Okay?*" she demanded. "You *get* me, you criminal itch?"

"I get you!" Slade cried. "Yes!"

"Then mahid ka-par," she growled into his ear. "Let's do this thing."

She let him up, putting herself between him and the Harmonious Society of God, muscular arms crossed, callused fingers tapping biceps that put Slade's thighs to shame. Warily, Slade crawled to his feet and backed away, swallowing.

"Backing away," she said calmly, "is losing."

Slade swallowed and stopped. Very carefully, he began brushing dirt and pine-needles from his stomach and knees, trying to stragedize out how he was going to get out of this particular cluster. He was pretty sure that if he yelled loud enough, Tyson would hear him. Whether he would come to *help* him, however, was another matter altogether.

"Delaying," she said, staring at him like a cat with a mouse, "is losing."

Slade felt a rush of adrenaline arc through his veins. He reluctantly lifted his eyes to meet her cold gray-green stare and felt another rush of panic. Somehow, he forced himself to straighten and return her ka-par, his heart hammering painfully in his chest. As he met her eyes, though, he suddenly remembered a fortune-teller's tent, over eighty years ago, with enough force it almost knocked him over.

"Your soul mate's name is Leila. You will ensnare her with a pack of gum, then drag her home by her hair, much to your chagrin. You will meet her in your attempt to take over the world, and once you find her, you will stop at nothing to obtain her."

"Ka-par?" she asked, her gaze utterly cold.

Slade's heart was pounding painfully against his ribs, the sound blocking out everything else. He'd made himself impotent. The dog had died. Joe had fought aliens. "Is your real name Leila?"

She twitched, but it was enough. Slade was caught between a sudden rush of joy and absolute terror.

"Are you going to ka-par?" she demanded again.

"I want Tuesdays," Slade blurted.

Her brow tightened in a small frown. "Excuse me?"

"Tuesdays," Slade said. "I want them."

"What is that?" the Congie asked, her frown deepening. "And I said delaying is losing."

"I'm not delaying," Slade said. "You win. I surrender. You get Wednesdays through Mondays."

She squinted at him suspiciously. "What are those?"

He thought she was being coy, then realized, as a Congie from the very first Draft, she probably hadn't had to use them in over seventy turns. "Days of the week," Slade said quickly. "There are seven on Earth. Monday, Tuesday, Wednesday, Thursday, Friday, Saturday, Sunday. You get six. I want one. Tuesdays."

The Congie squinted at him. "What day is today?"

Slade grinned back at her. "Tuesday."

He saw the faint ghost of a smile twitch across her face. "You're surrendering…but *I* have to go first?"

"Damn straight," Slade said.

Any normal woman in the world would have told him to get lost, kicked him in the face, and then proceeded to fit him with a thong. Instead, the Congie just eyed him over her crossed arms, a little quirk of interest on her lips. "One day out of seven?"

"Sounds good to me," Slade said.

"Starting now."

"Starting right now," Slade agreed.

For eons, she just stood there, watching him. Then, giving him an unreadable look, she inclined her head. "Then, by the rules of kapar, Samuel Dobbs, I accept your surrender."

Slade gave her a nervous look. "Then I can do anything I want?"

She continued to watch him over her crossed arms. "Is it Tuesday?"

Looking at her, Slade licked his lips. His heart was pounding like a jackhammer in his chest. He was finding it hard to breathe. "You won't kick me?" he asked finally.

Her look was totally unreadable. "Is it Tuesday?"

Meaning, of course, that on Wednesday, he was going to get obliterated.

Slade swallowed again, hard. *God hates a coward*, he thought. Then he took two steps forward, grabbed the Congie by the hair, wrenched her startled head back, and kissed her.

28

TUESDAY

Slade walked back to camp trailing his docile Congie with a rope around her neck, her gun slung over his shoulder. It made every single member of his flock stop what they were doing and stare. No doubt, they had heard about his intent to subdue the Congressional soldier, and no doubt, most of them had expected him to die horribly.

Especially his Second.

"Hey Tyson," Slade said, saluting with his survival manual. He walked over, the Congie's rope knotted loosely around his belt, then sat down beside his second at the fire. Rat seated herself calmly on a nearby log and started trimming her nails with her wicked alien combat knife.

Tyson just stared at her, then at Slade. The grass popped from his open mouth. "But…how did you…?"

"Snare," Slade said.

"You did that with a *snare*?!" Tyson cried. Then when Rat raised a brow at him, he belatedly said, "No offense, lady." He lowered his voice. "You did that with a *snare*?"

"Told ya it would work," Slade said.

"Don't bullshit me," Tyson snapped.

"Snare," Slade said, grabbing a hunk of bread. He offered it to Rat, who paused in trimming her nails to take the bread and stuff it in her mouth. Then she went back to running her monomolecular knife across her fingertips.

Tyson peered at him for several moments, then turned to Rat. "He caught you with a *snare*?"

"Yep," she said. Slade could have kissed her. Again. But the last time he'd kissed her had lasted several hours, and he was pretty sure his flock would pull up chairs to watch. And there was something about this woman he wanted to keep...special. Secret. Between them.

Tyson glanced at her combat knife. Then he glanced at the rope running from her neck to Slade's back pocket. Then he looked at her face. "Why isn't he dead?"

"It's Tuesday," she said. She stopped cutting at her nails and blew on them. Catching Slade's gaze, she smiled evilly. And...blushed?

"So," Slade said, around his own hunk of bread. "What did I miss?"

Tyson slowly tore his eyes from the Congie and back to Slade, but it was still a long time before he shook himself and spoke. "There's a group that's following us. Big. Well-armed. They picked off a couple of guards in the night and ate them. Jeb and I went looking for them this morning and found them picking off the bones. We're talking a *big* camp, Slade. Bigger than ours."

Slade's heart gave a startled thump. At last count, they were at seven hundred and forty-two members of the Harmonious Society of God. He'd come to think of them as having enough numbers to be invincible. "Well," he said, "that's not good."

"Want me to kill them?" Rat asked, calmly examining her nails.

"Yes," Tyson said, at the same time Slade said, "No."

At Tyson's funny look, Slade said, "Plasma wastes meat."

Rat immediately made a sound of disgust. "I'm not eating people."

"We'll find you something else, pussycat," Slade said distractedly.

He could feel her glaring at him. "Wednesday is coming," she said.

"And I'm looking forward to it," Slade said. He winked at her.

In reply, the Congie grunted, picked up her rifle where Slade had left it leaning against the log, and started checking it for dust.

Tyson watched the exchange with undisguised curiosity, then his eyes flickered over Slade's shoulder to glance out over the grassy hills beyond their stand of pines. Instantly, his face dropped. "Oh shit."

Slade turned to look behind them just in time to see a man stumbling towards them up the hill. He vaguely recognized him as Klyde Masons, a priest of the Back Order, who guarded their rear, as opposed to a priest of the Front Order, who wandered ahead and combed the terrain in advance of the group, seeking followers and supplies.

The man was weaving drunkenly and had a big energy burn across the front of his chest, a glancing blow that had vaporized most of his shirt.

Behind and beside him, Slade felt Rat and Tyson get up and ready their guns. *God* it was good to have decent bodyguards. Slade stood with them, and gave the approaching, burned man his best disapproving scowl.

"Attackers, Great Leader!" Klyde gasped. He doubled over, panting, holding his burned chest.

Beside him, he saw Rat raise a brow. "'Great Leader'?"

"It's just a formality," Slade said dismissively. "How many?" he demanded of the man.

"Hundreds!" Klyde cried. "They killed everyone in the back. They're headed our way..."

Rat immediately sliced through the rope holding her to Slade's belt and shouldered her rifle, turning to stalk out towards the grasslands. Slade held up his arm to stop her.

"I can kill them," Rat growled.

"Stay here," Slade said. "I'll handle this."

Both Rat and Tyson looked at him as if he'd lost his mind. Well, *more* of his mind. Carefully, like he was a cerebrally-challenged infant, Rat said, "I need to find a good sniping position."

"I said I'd take care of it," Slade said. "Just stay here and protect the Society."

Rat cocked her head at him and looked like she was going to go stalking off into the grass anyway.

"Tuesday," Slade reminded her. Something about the idea of the Congie putting herself in danger made Slade's gut clench. Of course, he was smart enough not to tell her as much.

"So what's your plan?" Rat reluctantly asked.

Slade stuck his finger in his mouth and lifted it to check the direction of the wind. Seeing it was was headed out over the dry, brown, amber waves of grain, Slade grimaced, "Wind's headed in their direction. They can probably smell us."

Tyson and Rat frowned at him.

"It's in the book!" Slade cried in, thumping his survival manual in exasperation. Then, returning his attention to Klyde, he said, "Okay, so let me guess. You saw a big party hanging out in the countryside and you didn't bother trying to round them up to join our Order, or—God forbid—doing any reconnaissance. You just started shooting. Because you were hungry."

"There were too *many* to round up," the man complained. "I mean, it would have taken ten of us to even get half of them."

"So you started shooting at them," Slade said disgustedly. "And at what point did you realize they were armed? When one of you received a plasma shot through your chest?"

The guard bit his lip and did not respond.

"We'll talk about this later," Slade said, dismissing the man as his attention was drawn by a surge of armed men rushing over the grassy ridge, obviously having followed Klyde back to his source. They slowed down once they realized the size of Slade's band, then braced themselves against the dry earth and opened fire.

Slade recognized the skull-and-dagger emblems on their ripped and dirty jackets and muttered a curse. It was the remnants of one of Los Angeles's most notorious street gangs, Satan's Creed. They must have headed towards the mountains once they realized that they'd once and for all been kicked out of town by something bigger and badder and hungrier than them. Just his luck.

"Oh *shit* that's a lot," Tyson said, backing away.

There were at least a thousand of them, and all were carrying weapons of one form or another. Several carried plasma or rifle pistols, and were currently mowing through the HSG's ranks. Everywhere in the grass, people were exposed and screaming.

"Get everyone over the hill behind us!" Slade shouted at Tyson. "Get them into cover in the trees!"

Rat calmly ignored him, stepping forward to get a better firing position. Slade grabbed her arm and she glanced at his hand with a frown, then lifted her gray-green eyes to his face.

"Get behind me," Slade said. "Over the hill with everyone else."

Her eyes darkened. "This is the best firing position. We run, we die."

"Tuesday," Slade reminded her.

She gave him a long, irritated look, then shouldered her rifle and said, "Wednesday will be fun. If you live." Then, like the calm killing machine she was, she turned and jogged after Tyson, who was shouting orders to the terrified masses fleeing the oncoming gang.

Slade took a long look at the dirty, weapon-toting masses flowing over the hills and swallowed down a rush of panic at the sheer numbers. Already, they were starting down their hill, chasing down the fleeing survivors. He took a breath, steeling himself, and thought, *God hates a coward.* Letting it out in his best impression of a war-cry, Slade ran forward, toward the maniacs with guns. As soon as he got past the last retreating members of his Society, he pulled out his lighter and, trusting the wind at his back to take the fire to his foe, lit the grass at his feet.

After several decades of drought, the grass burst into flame as if it were made of jet fuel. Slade grabbed a handful of grass, lit it, and ran along the ridge, touching his torch to the golden ocean. Then he dropped the grass and ran to the safety of the other side of the ridge, ducking down behind a fallen pine to hide with Tyson and Rat.

His tactic worked better than he had expected. The fire ripped through the landscape, sometimes moving so fast that it left patches of unburned grass behind it. Within minutes, Satan's Creed had gone from being a mob of well-armed jerks to a mottled patch of smoking bodies. Those who survived were running south ahead of the growing wall of flames, most not fast enough to be overwhelmed by the fumes.

Once the fire died down, Slade climbed to his feet and dusted himself off. All around him, people were staring. Even Rat. Which made him grin like a furg…on the inside. On the outside, he kept his cool, gave them all a smooth, confident smile. Surveying the field of smoking bodies, Slade said, "And *that*, my less fortunate friends, is why *I* am in charge."

When none of the awed masses around him argued with that, Slade began walking down towards the blackened corpses. He felt the Congie follow him, keeping pace like a curious predator.

"Well," Slade said, stopping at a charred body and nudging it with his foot, "at least we won't go hungry for a while."

"We will not be eating people on my days," Rat said. She shouldered her rifle casually and gave him a flat look of finality.

Slade grimaced. "This is a lot of food."

"This is a field of corpses. Not food."

"People are food," Slade argued.

Rat studied him a moment. "You have a seamstress in your group?"

Slade frowned. "Probably a dozen of them."

"Good. I'm going to need them to make me a thong. Six of them, actually. Change things up a bit."

Slade swallowed, hard, into the silence that followed.

"Looks like we'll eat good, at least," Tyson said a couple moments later, jogging up to survey the destruction. "*Look* at all that food! Wonder if we could dry it."

Rat raised her eyebrow at Slade, waiting. For a moment, Slade had an insane urge to ka-par her again. Then he remembered what had happened last time. And that this time, she was carrying an energy weapon.

"Fuck, fine!" he muttered. Twisting his face, Slade turned to Tyson and said, "I've just received a divine epiphany that the Harmonious Society of God will be forbidden from eating the flesh of his fellow man on the days of Wednesday through Monday."

Tyson's beaming smile, which had widened to cover his whole face at their unexpected bounty, slid off his face. He turned, very slowly, to cock his head at Slade. "Say what?"

"Wednesday through Monday. Human flesh. Off limits."

For several minutes, Tyson just stared at him. Then his second glanced at Rat. "What about you? You let us eat long pork on Wednesdays?" he demanded. And in that moment, Slade realized that he was, very easily, in danger of losing his position to Rat and getting left for the flies. Or eaten. Probably eaten.

"If I were in charge," Rat said calmly, "you wouldn't eat it at all."

Tyson made a face and glanced at the heavens for several moments, then turned back to Slade. "Fine. But *you're* telling the flock that one." Then, as if he hadn't just offered Slade's position to Rat, Tyson reached down with a rag and picked up the hot plasma pistol that the man had been carrying. A goofy grin was spreading over his face. "I've always wanted to use one of these things."

"Wait until you need it," Rat replied. "It packs a lot of punch, but has a shitty recharge rate. They've only got a twelve-round capacity before they need to recover or be exchanged for a different clip."

Tyson gave her an impressed look and tucked his new weapon under his belt. "What about the survivors? Want us to chase them down?"

Slade moved through the scorched grass and found another plasma pistol lying only a few yards away. He nudged it out of the ash with his foot, then picked it up with his shirt. It amazed him how easy it was for the scum of the earth to obtain that which Congress had been hard-pressed to supply to even its most elite forces. He glanced up at the column of smoke moving south and decided that the former gang members weren't worth his time. He had enough problems with felons. Sooner or later, he'd like to start acquiring some normal people. If 'normal' people had survived Judgement. He found it somewhat doubtful, considering.

"Nah," he said, standing. "Gather up whatever weapons you can find, then let's get this show back on the road."

"What about Klyde?" Tyson asked, reminding Slade of the priest who had drawn the gang's attention.

"Bring him here," Slade replied, turning his new plasma pistol in his hand. "Our priests of the Back Order have been failing in their duties, lately." He caught Rat's gaze and winked at her. "I need to make an example of him."

Tyson grunted and stalked off toward the rest of the HSG, most of whom were standing anxiously on the edge of the blackened terrain, watching their leader with horror and fascination.

"What kind of example?" Rat asked, still standing beside him with her rifle slung over her shoulder casually.

"I'm gonna have Tyson eviscerate him, then I'll eat his heart in front of the entire congregation a la the Aztecs circa the 14 and 1500s," Slade said. That would show them.

Rat eyed him. "Wednesday is coming," she said.

Slade peered back at her. "Is that you asking for leniency or wanting to get in on the action?"

She gave him a sweet smile. "It's a statement of fact."

The smooth way she said it gave Slade a little thrill of fear. He swallowed, a mouthful of raw heart suddenly losing its appeal. "Uh. Yes. Huh." Seeing her continued smile, Slade swallowed again, finding himself once again the proud owner of some rock-hard human flesh of his own, and was sweating by the time Tyson returned a few minutes later dragging his recalcitrant priest.

He had Klyde's gun in his hands, two guards hauling the man between them, despite his loud protestations. The Aryan came to a halt in front of Slade and shoved Klyde toward him. "Here he is, Ghost. Tried to sneak off while you were distracted."

"Oh?" Slade asked, examining the panting, tearful man. He still itched to tell Tyson to pull out his knife, but the Congie's threat was enough that he was able to keep it under control.

Klyde swallowed hard as he fearfully met Slade's electric-purple eyes. "Sir, I thought I saw a stream and was gonna go get some water…" He trailed off, licking his lips.

"You saw a stream," Slade said flatly.

Klyde nodded, though his face had lost all its conviction. Instead, he was as white as a ghost, sweating like a stuck pig, his eyes glancing nervously from side to side like he was waiting for an opening to bolt.

"I have a dilemma, Klyde," Slade said, turning the blue metal of the plasma pistol in the sun so it sparkled. It was six pounds of a ruvmestin alloy that hadn't even been singed in the fire. In truth, it was a beautiful object. Almost as easy to appreciate as a good steak. He glanced down at Klyde pointedly. "Ask me what's my dilemma."

"What's a dilemma?" the man whispered, terrified.

Slade rolled his eyes. Plebs. "It's a quandary. An impasse. A predicament."

"A *problem*," Rat said, when the man continued to stare at him blankly.

Slade paused, waiting for the information to register in Klyde's wet brown eyes. When it did, he said, "So ask me what's my problem, Klyde."

"What's your problem?" Klyde asked in a very quiet, very frightened voice.

"My problem is that normally, in a situation like this, I would have Tyson shoot you and use your meat to feed us." Klyde gasped and started to shiver. Slade ignored him and motioned out at the field of charred bodies. "*However*, since I have been commanded to end the eating of human flesh between the days of Wednesday and Monday, and since we have enough meat here to last us a year of Tuesdays, killing you would be a waste." He paused, leaning closer so that Klyde got a real good look at his freaky eyes. "And I am not a wasteful man, Klyde."

Beside him, Rat made an amused snort.

Klyde, however, was so frightened that he peed himself. The guards holding him jeered, but Slade continued to hold Klyde's gaze, eyes boring into his skull. "I don't want to kill you, Klyde, but I also don't want future members of the Harmonious Society of God to be corrupted by the genes of morons."

Klyde was shaking all over, like one of those miniature dogs that delusional people liked to raise as pets.

"So I'm going to ask you to swear to one thing, in payment for your actions and the consequent deaths of our members." Slade continued to hold the man's gaze.

"Anything," Klyde gasped.

"I want you to promise never to have sex with any fertile women for the rest of your life," Slade told him. "If you do, I will be forced to eat you *and* your ill-begotten progeny. Do you swear?"

"I s...sw...swe..." The man couldn't seem to get the word past his chattering jaw and he swallowed again, tears streaming down his face.

"Good," Slade replied before he could start stuttering again. "Now go clean yourself up in that stream you saw, then report to Tyson for your gun."

Klyde's eyes went wide. "You're giving me back my gun?" he whispered in disbelief.

"You are still a priest of the Society," Slade said simply. "This debacle has prolonged your promotion to cleric, but in time, you might still earn it."

The relief in the man's face was so intense that Slade was afraid the man might attempt to hug him, piss-soaked pants and all. He was relieved when Klyde simply bowed as deeply as he could go and ran off to the north, doubtless to take clean pants from a member of the flock.

"You went easy on him," Tyson told him after Klyde was out of sight. "If it were me, I'd have killed the bastard."

"I think that one might've actually deserved to get eaten," Rat said.

Slade gave her an irritated look. "Well, I was perfectly willing."

"Then again," Rat said, casting his camp a disgusted look, "if it were me, I probably would've already killed most of the guys here." Her eyes stopped on Tyson and she looked him up and down, then made a grunt of what almost sounded like approval. "You play cards?"

"What kind?" Tyson asked, showing no fear at the Congie's perusal.

"Jahul Sixty-Six or Takki-Toe."

Tyson cocked his head slightly. "I play spades."

"Don't play spades with him," Slade said. "You'll lose."

But Rat said, "You'll have to teach me to play spades so I can kick your ass."

"You're on, Congie."

Slade ignored them and started to follow Klyde's path up the slope. He reached the crest and searched the clusters of people for Klyde's face. He located his wayward priest running up to the group furthest from any of the others, away from all law enforcement.

Tyson and Rat followed him to the ridge, talking about spades. When Tyson saw what Slade was looking at, he grimaced. "So what are we gonna do about him, seriously?" Tyson asked, following the man's progress with his Aryan blue eyes. "I mean, he's a despicable shit in the first place if he'd just start shooting at people for the hell of it, like they're target practice or something."

"Some people need to be target practice," Rat said. She was scowling out over the field at Klyde.

Indeed, the man slowed at the last cluster of HSG followers. As they watched, he shoved a gray-haired man to the ground and started kicking him.

Narrowing her eyes, Rat said, "Excuse me." Shoving her rifle at Slade, she started off down the hill.

"A *snare*?" Tyson demanded, as the Congie broke into an easy jog toward the scene.

"Among other things," Slade said distractedly.

"*What* other things?"

Before Slade could answer, Rat smoothly stepped between Klyde and the bleeding old man on the ground, then twisted and delivered an alien-kung-fu kick to the side of Klyde's balding head that made Slade's own head ache in recognition.

And, apparently, without a towel to shield his brain, it really *would* have killed Slade. He blinked when the man collapsed like a rag doll and didn't get back up. In the meantime, Rat bent and started helping the old man back to his feet.

"I like her," Tyson said.

Slade felt himself grin, despite himself. "She's warming my bed tonight."

Tyson peered at him. "Why?" As if Slade had just told him the Congie would be sharing bedspace with an undead, brain-eating leper.

Rat finished righting the old man, then turned and started back towards them, a swath of flock quickly getting out of her way on both sides. Seeing the tides part before her, Slade's grin just widened. "Because it's Tuesday."

29

WEDNESDAY

Slade woke with a groan, his cheek pressed in a puddle of slobber on his pillow. Sex. *Good* sex. He'd had it. *Lots* of it, unless he was completely delirious—or he'd been dreaming. But he didn't think he'd been dreaming because Mr. Woodrow was back and reporting for duty.

Blearily, Slade rolled over to check on the Congie, then grunted in surprise when he found her side of the bed empty.

It was then that he heard the distinctive *shink, shink, shink* of a whetstone being pulled across a blade.

"Good morning, slave."

Slade swallowed. Nervously, he rolled back over to see her sitting in a fold-out canvas camp-chair, fully dressed in her ominous black gear. "Uh. Morning."

She continued to hone her wicked Congie blade. "Sleep well?" Hanging from the arm of her chair, Slade realized, was a purple thong.

Slade's eyes widened and he tried to think back to whether he had done anything untoward the night before. There had been a little rope, but as far as he could remember, she'd enjoyed herself. A lot. "Uh…"

Her gray-green eyes sharpened and the whetstone stopped moving. "I asked you a question."

"Yes," Slade managed.

She gave him a lingering, dangerous look and went back to sharpening. "Tell me about this experiment that fucked up your hair. I want to know everything you know."

Slade frowned. "Why?"

She lifted a perfect, delicate brow and peered at him over eleven inches of monomolecular death.

Slade started to talk.

When he finished, she said, "We're not going to Nebraska. You're taking me south to look for this lab."

Slade peered at her. "What the hell do you care about those experiments? Congress wiped them all out."

She gave him a long, deadly look and said, "Are you questioning me on a Wednesday?"

Eying the thong, Slade said, "No, Ma'am."

"You can start by cooking me breakfast," Rat said, examining her knife in the hazy dawn light filtering through the thin tent walls. "Then you will gather your flock and tell them that there will be no slaving on Wednesdays through Mondays. Anyone who has taken a slave by force shall release them on those days."

Slade frowned. "Except you."

She gave him pleasant smile over her blade. "You surrendered in ka-par."

He had *known* that was going to come back and bite him in the ass. Groaning, Slade slumped back against the pillow and stared at the ceiling. "I can't tell them they can only have slaves on Tuesdays."

"If you don't, and I catch anyone slaving on my days, I will release their captives of their bondage and give their former slaves guns."

Yeah, *that* wouldn't go over well. "I mean," Slade muttered, "I can't tell them only Wednesday to Monday. They'll think I'm insane."

"You are insane."

Slade sat up and scowled at her. "Only a little!" he objected.

She raised a delicate eyebrow at him.

Slade groaned, deeply. "So what, I just tell all my priests there's no real benefit to being a priest anymore?"

"Further," Rat said, "you will not be calling them 'priests' and 'clerics' and your 'flock' anymore. It's blasphemous."

Slade narrowed his eyes. "On Wednesdays to Mondays."

She just smiled at him.

"I don't believe in God," Slade growled. "So there's nothing to blaspheme."

"Oh really?" Rat asked. "Have you ever visited an Ooreiki temple, Sam? Walked the halls of the dead?"

"Holographs," Slade said dismissively. "They do it with holographs."

She gave him a look that told him what he had just said was so utterly stupid it did not deserve a response. Slade reddened. "They're not holographs?"

"No."

"So you want me to free the slaves *and* change the very makeup of my Society?" Slade demanded. "That's asking a lot."

"Further," Rat said, "you will institute a no-sex-without-consent rule, starting today. Those who violate it will lose their dicks."

And, he realized, she was utterly serious. Slade narrowed his eyes at her, because that was just sexist. "And the *females* who violate it?"

"Ka-par doesn't count," Rat said.

He felt his eyes go wide and he swallowed, hard. And Willy, loveable little bastard that he was, ate it up, making it once again almost impossible to think through the sudden lack of blood supply. "Uh."

"I've also noticed," Rat said, "that you have no women carrying guns. Why is that, Sam?"

Slade made a nervous sound. It had generally been agreed upon by the founding members of his society that women would be slaves. He had, after all, been trying to form a perfect society.

The Congie continued to give him a cold gray-green stare.

"We can give them guns," Sam managed.

"Good. I have some picked out. I also have some males picked out who will lose their gun privileges or they will disappear. Are we clear?"

Slade made a face. "Crystal."

"And last…" Rat slipped the tip of her wicked blade through the thong and tossed it at him. "Put that on. It'll accent your eyes."

Slade snorted. He flipped it back at her and crossed his arms over his chest. "Make me."

He realized too late that that was the wrong thing to say to a Congie, because she did, in fact, make him.

Afterwards, still red-faced and breathing hard, she made him do more sit-ups than Sam had done in his entire life, followed by enough push-ups to make his arms fall off. After that, she took him jogging in the thong, then, after Sam could barely struggle back up the hill to the fire, made Sam cook breakfast in it. Sam wasn't sure if it was his creepy eyes, the fact he'd just killed a couple hundred armed men with a lighter, or the utterly straight-faced, gun-toting Congie, but nobody so much as mentioned it to him that he was making breakfast in a purple thong.

That both delighted and dismayed him. Delighted, because it meant he was more or less untouchable. Dismayed, because it meant they didn't think it was out of place enough to mention. Even Tyson just raised his thick blond brow and went back to what he was doing. The Congie, for her part, sat on a log and watched, cleaning her gun, looking absolutely unfazed by what had to have been a five-mile run.

Things started getting tricky, however, when he explained the Congie's demands to Tyson.

"So let me get this straight," Tyson growled. "We're not only *not* going to Nebraska, but women are free, there are no more slaves, no more rape, and you're changing the name of the Society to the Survivor's Guild."

"You forgot 'Taking the guns away from the assholes,'" Rat noted.

Tyson gave her nod of acknowledgement. "And you're taking the guns away from the assholes. Have you found your mind?"

Slade, who had expecting Tyson to say, 'Have you *lost* your mind,' had to do a double-take when it sounded funny. "Excuse me?"

"Found it. As in, the opposite of lost." Tyson peered at him like he was trying to look into Slade's formidable brain. "You know, like you collected some of your missing marbles. Came back from around the bend. Got back *on* your rocker."

"Tightened a few screws," the Congie added helpfully.

"Yeah," Tyson said, gesturing at Rat gratefully. "That."

Slade scowled at them both. "I don't know what you're talking about."

Tyson met his scowl in silence for several moments, then his eyes slid pointedly down to his crotch, which was even then covered in vivid purple spandex. Slade *refused* to look. "That was not my fault."

His second gave him a flat look. "My point is, you ask me, you should've done it a long time ago. What changed?"

Across the fire, the Congie started to loudly sharpen her knife once more.

Watching her, Slade said, "One could say that I had a…divine… awakening."

"Divine, huh?" Tyson gave him a flat look. His gaze flickered towards the Congie and back. "How divine?"

"I was…stirred…to action, filled with a dizzying new awareness I never thought I'd have."

Tyson gave him a flat look. "You got your rocks off."

"Oh indeed," Slade said, delighted. "More than once!" He sobered instantly at the way the man with the gun's eyes narrowed. His second stared at him so long that Slade started stirring the oatmeal pot to keep from fidgeting.

Finally, Tyson said, "If it was anyone else who just smiled and told me that he'd made socio-economic decisions for an entire society based off a recent oiling of his pleasure piston, I would pull out my gun, shoot him in the head, and leave him for the crows to find." He cocked his head at Slade. "But for you, I somehow think it's an improvement."

Slade felt his face heat. "We need to call everyone together, spread the news, and head south."

Tyson grunted and got to his feet. "The Congie and I are gonna go disarm a few folks first. You stay here and..." he glanced back down at Slade's crotch, "...cook." Without another word, his second grabbed his gun, turned, and started down the hill.

"I'm an *excellent* cook!" Slade shouted at his broad back. Then, muttering under his breath, "Bastard."

Rat had stopped beside the fire, her wicked blade sheathed and her gun slung over her shoulder. She was grinning at him.

"What?" Slade demanded, his mood deteriorating.

"Day One," Rat said. Then she went to follow Tyson down the hill.

30

SHAEL

You will remember again. I promise.

Shael sat up, his heart pounding, the minder's words still ringing in his ears. It had been another of the dreams of Six Six Five, just as intense as the other ones, and his chest still ached in terror. Over near the fire, Joedobbs ga Badass ga Male Model ga Chiseled Pecs was talking to Alice in hushed whispers, the rest of the camp sleeping.

"No," Joedobbs said in the Earthling tongue, "I'm *not* interested in telling you a sootin' bedtime story. Go burning lie down before I knock your annoying ass out."

"My mommy told me bedtime stories when I couldn't sleep."

Joedobbs ga Badass turned to scowl down at the little hatchling with the full power of his warrior glare. "Do I look like I've got burnin' *breasts* to you?"

Alice pouted. "But my mommy—"

Joedobbs leaned down to put his face an inch from the little girl's and yanked a thumb towards the blanketed People, obviously in a foul mood. "Go. Sleep."

Pouting, the little girl did, but not before Shael frowned, wondering what 'breasts' meant. It was the second time Joedobbs had mentioned them, and he seemed to have been indicating the fleshy lumps standing out from Shael's chest, revealed from the descaling. The way he had said it, though, had suggested—again—that Joedobbs ga Badass already thought Shael had given up his tek.

Shael glanced down at his chest, then at Joedobbs. He had gone back to polishing his gun at the fire, and didn't see Shael sitting up, watching him. There were distinct differences between their bodies, now that Shael was looking. Joedobbs ga Badass seemed thicker in the upper body, though did not carry the fleshy lumps. Further, Shael's lower torso, just before his coils, was wider—much wider—than Joedobbs' similar area.

Shael's eyes caught the two long appendages beneath his lower torso and his vision seemed to twist and he got a headache as he looked. *Coils*, he immediately thought.

But his head burned. They looked…like Twelve-A's. And Twelve-A was Human. And Joedobbs had not only claimed he was Human as well, but he had *also* had two bony appendages that worked as limbs. Over time, watching his movement carefully, Shael had come to the reluctant decision that they had to be legs, and therefore could not be coils, which therefore meant Joedobbs was not Jreet.

But if they were Human, did that mean that Shael, too, was…

Immediately, Shael's headache came back in full force and he tried to think of something else.

Human. The telepath's voice entered Shael's head like a clear, ringing bell, and Shael flinched and turned. Indeed, Twelve-A was sitting up amidst the sleeping throng of People, watching him carefully. *It means you're Human.*

A Human body, Shael agreed.

No, Twelve-A told him. *You were always Human.*

Immediately, though it had been something he had come to suspect since weakling-Mike had easily knocked him down, Shael balked. Human? How could that even be possible? He was Jreet. He *remembered* being Jreet. He remembered his great victories, his staking of his enemies, his strangling of Dhasha.

Then, unbidden, Shael once again got a flash of Six Six Five, forced to watch an image of the Black Jreet, begging her to help the Jreet people by teaching Humans to fight…

Shael's breath caught in his throat. "Oh no," he whispered.

Sometime within the minutes he sat there, staring out at the night in horror, Twelve-A got up and walked over to crouch beside him.

"What the soot are you doing awake, Pointy?" Joedobbs snapped. "I'm on night shift. Get your ass back to sleep so I can get some shut-eye in the morning." Again, it was in the Earthling tongue, not Jreet.

Twelve-A ignored the Congie completely, focusing on Shael. *You remember what I said to you as Doctor Philip shut the lid?*

Shael felt a full-body dread hit him like a wave of ice. He knew, without asking, that Twelve-A was talking about something horrible, something buried deep within, something he didn't *want* to dredge up.

"Twelve-A, goddamn it!" Joe snapped, throwing his polishing cloth aside and getting up. "I *told* you I *only* get to sleep when your lazy ass is awa—"

The Congie slumped to the ground with a startled grunt and began to snore.

Twelve-A hadn't even taken his eyes from Shael. *Remember?*

Shael swallowed, hard. His hands were shaking, his heart was hurting, his throat aching. His mouth felt dry, and at the same time, he was sweating all over. It felt like a dam within his mind was about to burst, strained beyond capacity, and it was about to sweep him along with it.

"I'm scared," Shael whimpered. His body felt like he were dying of cold in the frigid ice-crusted mountains of Welu. He couldn't stop shaking.

Twelve-A reached out to touch his shoulders with his slender fingers, steadying him. *I'm here. Nine-G's here. Joe's here. You're safe.*

"But," Shael whimpered. "I'm Jreet."

I'm sorry, Twelve-A replied softly. *You're not.*

Shael flinched. Twelve-A had never lied to him. Twelve-A *didn't* lie.

And, in that moment, the dam, even then stretched to capacity, burst in his mind, flooding his brain with sensations and images that left him gasping, clawing at the earth in front of him to stay upright.

"They wanted to make Six Six Five into a Jreet." Suddenly, it felt as if Shael's throat constricted, allowing nothing but a whisper. "They wanted to make *me* into a Jreet." His heart was pounding out of control, now, and it was hard to see through tears. Everything was rushing back, everything, and it left him breathless, feeling as if his confident, self-assured world had been swept away, replaced with a world of pain, terror, fear, and the unknown, leaving him no anchor, nothing he could hold onto.

Then Twelve-A's arms wrapped around her and he lowered his chin on her shoulder. Totally overwhelmed, Shael closed her eyes and cried.

They sat like that long into the night, until Shael's heartbeat had slowed and the awful images of her past were obscured by a haze of numbness. Then, as the shock fell away, she began to feel humiliation that she had been so thoroughly convinced of something so ridiculous. Humiliation and *anger*. Many times, she had heard Doctor Philip talking with his superiors. Many times, he'd had her 'demonstrate' for them her 'warrior prowess,' allowing her to smack around a 'weakling lieutenant,' but now, looking back, she knew their grins and snickers for what they really were. A human girl, thinking she was Jreet, and a lieutenant who was being paid not to fight back.

They used me, she thought, utterly shamed to the core. *They looked at me like I was an* animal. The shame and total degradation of that knowledge was so great that she had trouble breathing.

Only after she had stopped sniffling did Twelve-A finally pull back.

Remember what I asked you, when he shut the lid? Twelve-A asked again.

Shael thought back to those final moments of fear, when Twelve-A first spoke to her. She couldn't remember anything he had asked—all she could remember was her terror. She said as much.

I asked you if you wanted me to kill them, Twelve-A said, meeting her gaze, his blue eyes intense in the firelight. *I need to know your answer now.*

Shael felt her eyes widen, her gut sinking at the idea that Doctor Philip could be alive. "I thought you killed them already," she whispered.

I mean the rest of them, Twelve-A said. *Humans.*

Shael balked. "*All* Humans?" she whispered.

Things like what they did to you are not new or uncommon, Twelve-A said. *They hurt each other as easily as opening their mouths. They're selfish. They're cruel. They think about only themselves, and take when they should give*

Shael swallowed, hard, still feeling that burning humiliation in her stomach that she had been forced to think she was Jreet. "What about Joe?" she asked softly.

Twelve-A hesitated, looking uncertain. *He's like the rest of them. Broken inside.*

Shael felt a rush of sympathy, knowing exactly how that felt. "Then fix him," she whispered.

Twelve-A gave her a long, careful look. *I can't fix them all,* he said softly. *Mike was proof of that.*

"You don't need to fix them all," Shael growled, remembering Joe holding her as she cried, his strong arms braving a mind that could crush him to dust to give her the solace she needed on the mountaintop. "Just fix him."

Twelve-A considered. *And kill the rest?*

Shael thought about it. She thought about how they'd hurt her, how they'd humiliated her and given her no compassion at all for her terror. She remembered the brutality, the mental agony, the death. She thought of Colonel Codgson and his mind games. She thought of Doctor Philip and his dispassionate face as he locked her into the machine. She thought of the soldiers, calling her 'robot' and 'automaton.' She thought of the techs, wiping up blood.

Then she thought about Doctor Molotov, giving her Charlie.

"They're not all bad," Shael whispered.

Twelve-A's face strained, and as she watched, tears began to reflect the firelight against his eyelids. *I know.*

"Then just keep the hurt away," Shael said. "You can do that, right?"

Twelve-A shuddered and blinked, shedding the drops that had been welling in his eyes. Softly, he said, *I can do it for the People.*

"Just keep everyone at a distance, like Joe's been telling you to do," Shael insisted.

Twelve-A dropped his head to stare at his slender hands. *I can do it for the People*, he said again.

Shael watched the anguish in his face. "But not you."

No. He didn't look up. For long minutes, they sat like that, facing each other, with Twelve-A refusing to lift his head. Then the minder stood, still refusing to meet her gaze. *No, not me.* And then, without another word, he went back to his place with the People and lay down.

Shael turned to glance at the Congie's limp form beside the fire, still snoring. He had saved her life, back when she had been too blind to recognize it, and she had done nothing but hurt and scorn him in return.

"So…" Shael said softly, glancing back at Twelve-A, "you can fix Joe?"

Twelve-A was silent for much too long. *I can make him stop hurting*, he finally said.

And, to Shael, knowing Joe was someone who had risked his life to save her time and time again, who had helped her when she could only mock him back, that was enough.

• • •

Sister.

Shael flinched and opened her eyes.

The fire was dark. Beside it, the Congie continued to sleep where the minder had left him. Twelve-A and the others had gone back to bed, leaving Shael alone. Shael, who had decided to stay awake to watch the fire and guard camp so Joe could sleep, had instead fallen asleep against a log, the day's events too much for her.

Sister Jreet, the voice came again.

Immediately, Shael thrust herself into her war-mind, wrapping it around her as a shield as she sat up, tense.

What she saw in her second sight made her gape. The stars were surging around her, moving in rolling waves of galaxies.

No, Shael realized, *not waves...coils...*

The entire camp was wrapped in sliding, twisting *coils*. Coils the color of the night sky, thicker than she was tall, surrounded them, the starry blackness twisting against itself as the coils slid against each other, with the fire and its sleeping charges at its core.

Sister Jreet, we have a message for you, the voice said again. Shael twitched, realizing that, unlike Twelve-A's mental voice, which sounded from all sides, this mental voice had a direction, and it was coming from directly above her head. When she looked, the undulating, starry blackness coalesced into a diamond-shaped head many times more massive than any Jreet she had ever seen. Its eyes were larger galaxies within the star-specked head, whose twinkling pin-points seemed to change color with the movement of the coils.

The Black Jreet, Shael thought, stunned. Immediately, she remembered the little bed, the Black Jreet on the screen, asking her to save Humanity...She frowned and pulled herself straighter. "Twelve-A?" she called, frowning. She glanced at her friend. He still slept soundly. "Twelve-A!" she hissed, keeping one eye on the gigantic apparition.

He can't hear you, Sister-Jreet, the starry void told her.

"Twelve-A!" Shael shouted, fighting a rush of panic. "*Joe!*"

The great mass of starry coils slipped closer, all but swallowing Shael in their embrace. *Sister Jreet, hear our warning. Within a turn, you shall have met Seven Sentinels. You already share a fire with the Horned Sentinel and the Sentinel of the Vaghi. In your travels, you will meet five more—the Void-Sentinel, the Hunted Sentinel, the One-Eyed*

Sentinel, the Sentinel of the Rock, and the Golden Sentinel. Combined, their actions now will determine the success of your new race.

"I..." Shael wasn't sure what to say. What she *could* say. She wasn't entirely sure what she was seeing wasn't a result of the dam breaking in her mind, a way for the brainwashing to reclaim her...

Mercy is the key, Sister-Jreet, the apparition went on. *By showing yours, you unlocked the door. It is now for the Seven Sentinels to open it, and to face it together.*

Shael swallowed, hard. "I'm not dreaming, am I?"

You Dream, the Jreet told her. *But it is not a dream.*

Shael's heart was pounding. She was talking to the Black Jreet. The *Black Jreet*. The Jreet's only Seer. "You want me to show mercy?"

You began the chain. Now you are supposed to remember, and to guide. As the Black Jreet is to Vora, you shall be to Earth. Mercy is key. Yours is a path foreseen throughout the ages, and it only has two outcomes. One of death, for all. One of peace, for all. Each Sentinel must now show mercy, but only after it has been given to them. Guide them well, Sister-Jreet, for a single break in the chain will end it all.

Then the stars were collapsing in on themselves, the void-black coils with their galactic sprays slipping together, crushing inward, compressing, growing more compact until the stars and galaxies seemed to be a pinpoint of light within a tiny speck of black, and then it was gone completely, leaving Shael alone in the camp, surrounded by sleeping experiments, only the painful wash of goosebumps and the cold sweat on her body to prove to her she hadn't imagined her ethereal visitor.

"Joe?" Shael whispered hoarsely. She wiped her hands on her borrowed pants. "Twelve-A?"

They didn't stir. Shael swallowed and looked up at the sky. For a brief moment, she thought she saw a glimmer, there, a serpentine shadow moving against the night, then it was gone.

END

To Be Continued with ZERO4: Zero's Redemption!

ABOUT THE AUTHOR

My name is Sara King and I'm going to change the world. No, seriously. I am. And I need your help. My goal is simple. I want to champion, define, and spread character writing throughout the galaxy. (Okay, maybe we can just start with Planet Earth.) I want to take good writing out of the hands of the huge corporations who have had a stranglehold on the publishing industry for so long and reconnect it to the people (you) and what you really want. I want to democratize writing as an art form. Something that's always been controlled by an elite few who have (in my opinion) a different idea of what is 'good writing' than the rest of the world, and have been feeding the sci-fi audience over 50% crap for the last 40 years.

To assist me in my goals to take over the world (crap, did I say that out loud??), please leave a review for this book! It's the first and easiest way for you guys to chip in and assist your friendly neighborhood writer-gal. And believe me, every review helps otherwise unknown books like mine stand up against the likes of the Big Boys on an impersonal site like Amazon.

Also, I have an email! (Totally surprising, I know.) Use it! (Don't you know that fanmail keeps writers going through those dark times when we run out of chocolate???) I love posting letters on Facebook—gives me something fulfilling to do with my time. ;) Shoot me a line! kingnovel@gmail.com

You can also ask to SIGN UP FOR MY MAILING LIST! Seriously, I give away free books, ask people to beta-read scenes and novels, and give updates on all the series I'm currently working on. Stay informed! J

And, for those of you who do the Facebook thing, check me out: http://www.facebook.com/kingfiction (personal) or http://www.facebook.com/sknovel (my author page) or stay up to date on continuous new ZERO publications with The Legend of ZERO fan page: http://www.facebook.com/legendofzero

MEET STUEY

Meet Stuey. He's our mascot here at Parasite Publications. Stuey is a brain parasite. Stuey burrows into people's heads and stays there. He takes over your body. He shuts you away from your senses. He talks to you in the darkness. He makes you do things you would never do while you can only watch in horror.

But he's an understandable little monster.

Imagine your favorite action-adventure story. Your favorite romance. Your favorite epic sci-fi. Your favorite thriller. Each one of them is going to have a character that left you breathless, one that had you at the edge of your seat, rooting for, screaming at, and pleading with. Those are the *only* stories that Parasite publishes.

Our goal at Parasite Publications is twofold: First, we want to produce memorable, sympathetic characters that readers will still be thinking about years after finishing our books. Second, we want to create a team of creative minds whose work can be trusted by readers to produce the same kind of character stories they love, time and again. We're forming a club. A logo. A place for readers to go to read books about *people*, not places or machines. A place for character writers to band together and create a brand that means quality to readers. Readers of Parasite books will no longer have to wonder if they're throwing their money away on novels that, even in 150k words, never really get into a character's head.

They never have to wonder, because that's what we're *about*. Getting into the character's head. And, if we do our job right, Parasite will get into your head and stay there. Just like Stuey.

Check us out on Facebook at http://www.facebook.com/ ParasitePublications/info to read more about Stuey's mission to change publishing for your benefit.

SARA RECOMMENDS

If you're looking for another great character novel, try Changes by Charles Colyott. This thriller writer grabs you by the balls and doesn't let you go until you beg for mercy. Colyott is a character writer supreme. Seriously, I haven't had a novel hold my attention this thoroughly since George R. R. Martin. Colyott is an independent author that blows most traditionally-published authors completely out of the water, and he deserves your money. (GIVE HIM YOUR MONEY!!) Ahem. J

OTHER TITLES
BY SARA KING

Guardians of the First Realm: Alaskan Fire
Guardians of the First Realm: Alaskan Fury

Millennium Potion: Wings of Retribution

Outer Bounds: Fortune's Rising

Terms of Mercy: To the Princess Bound

The Legend of ZERO: Forging Zero
The Legend of ZERO: Zero Recall

COMING SOON

Guardians of the First Realm: Fury of
the Fourth Realm ~ Sara King
Guardians of the First Realm: Alaskan Fiend ~ Sara King
Guardians of the First Realm: Alaskan Fang ~ Sara King

ZERO: Zero's Redemption – Sara King
ZERO: Zero's Legacy – Sara King
ZERO: Forgotten – Sara King

Aulds of the Spyre: The Sheet Charmer ~ Sara King
Aulds of the Spyre: Form and Function ~ Sara King

Outer Bounds: Fortune's Folly ~ Sara King

MINI GLOSSARY

(I.E. THE SO YOU DON'T LOSE YOUR MIND TINY VERSION)

—CONTAINS SPOILERS TO ZERO 1 & ZERO 2—

DHASHA-SPECIFIC

Itch (alternately: Bagan itch)– a nuisance/pain in the ass. To add 'Bagan' to the front indicates it's a huge pain in the ass, as the Baga are known for their painful pranks, infuriating intelligence, and general gleeful sabotage when bored.

Ka-par (ka-par) – The predatory game of wills that older Dhasha play with worthy prey creatures or other ancient Dhasha. A stare-down until one contestant submits.

Ka-par inalt (ka-par in-alt) – 'I submit.'

Ka-par rak'tal. (ka-par rak*tal) – 'duel accepted.' *is used to denote a guttural, back-of-throat, almost hacking sound.

Leafling – As the Dhasha are carnivores, as are their Takki and their greatest threats, 'leafling' is used to describe anyone who is utterly useless for anything but food.

Leafmunch – Used by the Dhasha to describe herbivores with disdain. Generally indicates derogatorily peaceful and physically weak beings. Alternately used with 'peacemunch.'

Mahid ka-par (ma-heed ka-par) – 'may it begin.'

Mothers – The four mythic beings who weave the lives of all creatures into a tapestry upon which the Trith can gaze. Considered the Dhasha gods by many.

Peacemunch – See leafmunch.

Slavesoul – Derisive word for anyone unworthy for anything but slavery. A Very Bad insult, and when used on another warrior is cause for a fight to the death to appease the insulted party's honor. Much worse than saying 'coward.'

Vahlin (vah-lin) – the legendary leader of the Dhasha, prophecized to be 'dark of body' and lead them to independence from tyranny.

HUMAN-SPECIFIC

Ailo - A derogatory word coined on Earth after it was conquered by Congressional forces, used to describe a person unlike oneself; i.e. an outsider. Derived from 'alien' during the resentful days of the occupation.

HUOUYT-SPECIFIC

Breja (bray-shjah) – the quarter-inch long, downy white cilia covering a Huouyt's entire body. Extremely painful to be pulled or mutilated, as it is basically raw nerves.

Ze'laa – (zay-lah) – one of the most powerful Huouyt families in Congress. Both Jer'ait Ze'laa, the current Peacemaster, and Rri'jan Ze'laa, the last Huouyt Representative, were from this wealthy family.

Zora (zoh-rah) – the red, wormlike, many-tentacled appendage that exits a Houyt's forehead. Much like a fleshy form of coral in appearance when fully extended. It is the zora that allows a Huouyt to digest and analyze genetic material to take a new pattern.

JAHUL-SPECIFIC

Oozing furg – dumbass. Someone who's young, stupid.

Sivvet (siv-et)– the sensory organs within a Jahul's head that allows it to sense the emotions of other sentient creatures.

JREET-SPECIFIC

Beda's bones – used alternatively as a curse or exclamation of surprise. Beda ga Vora, who was originally Beda ga Welu. A great warrior who led Congressional forces in a heroic multi-species civil war, but who was abandoned by his own people for falling in love with a Voran, only to be saved and claimed by the Vorans as the only gray-scaled (Welu) clan-member in history, one who was eventually held in such high esteem that he was given breeding privileges. *(See Beda and Shael)* Considered the epitome of a Jreet warrior.

Skulker – one of the strongest insults in the Jreet vocabulary. Suggests a creature too afraid to fight, one that hides in the shadows rather than facing his enemies.

Softling – Someone who is too weak or weak-willed to fight. Another word for coward.

Tek (tehk) – the appendage sheathed within their chests that extrudes poison instantly deadly to any other species in Congress—but not Jreet. Can produce several thousand lobes of pressure in a single strike. The tek's sheath is also commonly used as a storage area for Jreet to carry things like credit stubs and ovi, usually in a leather carrying case.

Lesthar (less-tar)– the favored intoxicating drink of Voran Jreet. Smells like burning tires. Small sips will kill most other species.

Melaa (may-lah) – Large, blubbery herd animals that are a Jreet's favorite food item.

Ovi – the transparent, razor-sharp, glasslike knife that is used in every important Jreet ceremony. If a Jreet dies and his body cannot be returned to his clan, it is expected that his tek be removed with his ovi and carried back to his clan for burial.

The Ninety Hells – The ninety levels of pain and unpleasantness that a Jreet warrior must pass through upon death in order to reach the afterlife. (See The Legend of ZERO Additional Materials.)

Rravut – the poison extruded by a Jreet's tek. The most powerful poison in Congress. Causes instant death in all living creatures except other Jreet, who only get numbed or drunken from it.

The Black Jreet – The Jreet version of a prophet. Considered by all Jreet to be sacred, an embodiment of one of the Sisters. Only one is born or is in existence at a time, tekless, and she grows much faster than all other Jreet, becoming several times larger than the largest prince over the course of her lifetime. She sees and interacts with the future in a shamanic manner. Guarded by retinue of special/highly esteemed female Jreet warriors who agree to drop their teks in order to spare the Black Jreet from intrusion of any male presence/possibility of impregnation.

OOREIKI-SPECIFIC:

Ash/soot – a disgusting, unclean substance
Asher – much like 'asshole,' but with an aggressive, fighting connotation
Ashsoul – the most extreme insult in the Ooreiki language. Also translates to 'lost one'
Ashy – shitty/gross/disgusting/awful
Burn/burning – used much like Human fuck/fucking
Charhead – dumbass, someone stupid, alternatively: someone with an unclean/dirty mind
Furgsoot – bull, bullshit, horseshit, crap, yeah right
Niish Ahymar (nish ay-a-mar) - An Ooreiki ceremony to determine caste where a red-hot brand is pressed into a child's skin. Vkala do not burn, and are then cast to onen. The traditional Ooreiki ceremony of adulthood.
Oorei (oo-ray) – the Ooreiki term for 'soul.' It is the name of the crystalline sphere carried within every Ooreiki and removed by Poenian yeeri priests at their death. Emotional/psychological experiences throughout life change color of crystal. Considered to be the highest crime of Ooreiki society to harm an oorei.
Shenaal (She-nahl) – Mark of the Pure. The burn left when Ooreiki niish are tested during the Niish Ahymar.
Sootbag – someone disgusting, unprepared, unequipped
Sooter – disgusting, unclean person; bastard
Sootwad – degrading, denotes disrespect, a useless person

PLACES:

Aez – the fallen Jreet clan of the Aez's destroyed homeworld.
Der'ru – a lush, sub-tropical Huouyt planet that rebelled on the 15th Turn, 860th Age of the Jreet. Joe fights there for two turns.
Jeelsiht – the staging-planet for the war on Neskfaat.
Kaleu – An Ueshi pleasure-planet known as a vacation destination. Any request will be accommodated.

Koliinaat – The artificial planet conceived of by the Geuji and funded by the Ooreiki one and a half million years ago, to celebrate the 100th Age of the Ooreiki. Is the home of the Regency, the Tribunal, and the Sanctuary. It is manned, in its entirety, by the artificial sentient life-form called the Watcher, also a Geuji construction, who conducts all Koliinaati affairs with supreme precision.

Levren – the Peacemaker planetary headquarters. Also home of the Space Force Academy.

Rastari – A rebel planet where Joe fought Jikaln, Hebbut, and Dreit after giving up his Corps Directorship to return to the front lines in the mid 11th Turn, 860th Age of the Jreet.

Regency – The sphere-shaped center of Koliinaat, where all the Representatives of Congress gather to discuss new laws or political conflicts.

Sanctuary – The one area of Koliinaat—about the size of a large city block—where the Watcher has no effect. Was claimed by Peacemakers almost immediately after Koliinaat's creation, though it was originally constructed as a place for delegations of non-members of Congress to gather to discuss treaties, trade, and other matters of diplomacy. Since Congress has swallowed every society it has come across, unlike the intent of its original charter, there are no non-members to require separate quarters.

Telastus – Ueshi karwiq bulb planet where a minor Huouyt family took over control of government with lookalike Huouyt plants to skim profits. Joe sent help remove the Huouyt for three turns, beginning the 21st Turn, 860th Age of the Jreet.

Torat – a Congressional Ground Force training planet. It is where PlanOps trains its operatives.

Vora – The original Jreet homeworld. Now home to the Voran clan, of crimson scale.

Welu – One of two Jreet worlds, due to Jreet reproduction rates being so low. Home to the clan Welu, of gray scale.

UNIVERSAL WORDS:

Ekhta (ek-tuh) – Planet-killer. The most destructive bomb in the Congressional arsenal, one of the many great inventions of the Geuji during the Age of Expansion. Like all Geuji technology, the manufacture is so complex that it is un-reproducible by any other mind, and Congress simply follows the steps outlined by the Geuji to create it. (For more info on the Geuji, check out 'The Moldy Dead' and 'Breaking the Mold' in The Legend of ZERO Additional Materials.)

Ferlii (fur-lee) – The massive alien, fungus-like growths covering Ooreiki planets whose reddish spores turn the sky purple. Used as a unit of measurement: One ferlii-length is similar to a human mile.

Forgotten – a mythical Geuji mastermind that roams the universe, the last of his kind to maintain his freedom. Responsible for the fall of Aez, the Jreet rebellion of Neskfaat, and the Huouyt's banishment from the Tribunal.

Furg – A short, squat, very hairy alien that is as ugly as it is stupid. A tool-user, but too primitive to use anything other than sharpened rocks. Think a stocky, 2.5-foot-tall Neanderthal who breeds fast enough to replace numbers lost to stupidity. Darwinian law does not apply.

Furgling – A younger version of a furg. Shorter, hairier, and stupider than its parents.

Haauk (hawk) – skimmer, the floating platforms used as personal planetary transportation

Jenfurgling – One of the most blatantly stupid creatures in Congress. An evolutionary offshoot of furgs arriving on an island where the population underwent a severe bottleneck and had no predators. They delight in beating their hairy faces against the ground and playing with their own excrement.

Kasja (kas-jah) – Highest congressional war-medal. Awarded to a very few, very highly esteemed. Usually comes with a three million credit reward.

Kkee (ca-ca-ee) – yes

Kreenit (cree-nit) – massive scaly predators that evolved on the same planet as the Dhasha and share their monomolecular talons and energy-resistant scales, but not their intelligence.

Nkjan (naka-john) – war; also: "Evil"

Nkjanii (naka-john-ee-ay) – "Evildoer" – battlemaster

Non-sent – colloquial/shortened way to say non-sentient, usually used in a derogatory manner.

Oonnai (oon-nigh) - hello

Oora (oo-ra) – "Souled one" - sir

Peacemakers- the governmental, semi-military authorities who are autonomous in judging, monitoring, and policing the populace. Their main task is to make sure nobody has seditious thoughts, symbol is an eight-pointed star with a planet balancing on each tip. Their base planet is Levren, but they also maintain the Sanctuary on Koliinaat, which is the only place on the planet that is inaccessible to the Watcher.

Planetary Ops (also: PlanOps) – symbol is a single sphere, half red, half blue. Tattoo is of a green, single-moon planet with a head-com, a PPU, and a species-generic plasma rifle leaning against the debris ring. The tattoo glows slightly, a cell-by-cell gene modification that causes the tattooed skin to bio-luminesce.

Ruvmestin (ruv-meh-stihn) – A whitish, extremely heavy metal with a greater density than gold. The most valuable metal in Congress. Used in Geuji technologies, esp. nannites, like biosuits and spaceships. Does not oxidize in air. Mined on the government planets of Grakkas, Yeejor, and Pelipe. Once ruvmestin is discovered on a planet, Congress immediately claims the planet for the common good, removing it from the Planetary Claims Board queue.

Sacred Turn – Time period. 666 turns.

Sentinel – the elite Jreet warriors who guard every Regency member.

Tribunal – The three members of the Regency chosen to represent and make judgments for the whole of Congress. The Tribunal are the power-members of the Regency, usually occupied by members of the Grand Six. Aliphei is First Citizen, and has maintained a seat on the Tribunal for the entire duration of Congress. The symbol of the Tribunal is three red circles inside a silver ring, surrounded by eight blue circles formed into two sides facing off against each other.

Vaghi – a small, nuisance pest-animal that eats and breeds uncontrollably. Once introduced to a planet, the entire planet must be killed in order to remove them. Which, unfortunately, is often necessary because the vaghi leave no vegetation or small animals behind.

Zahali (za-ha-li) – I'm sorry

SPECIES:

Baga (Ba-guh)– Small, one-foot beetle-like fliers with iridescent green carapaces and faceted red eyes like a fly. Have *abbas*, which are the glands that produce their infamous glue, a compound that instantly becomes whatever it touches. Are afraid of *miga*, their natural predators, whose wings break the sound barrier with every stroke. Can't count effectively beyond 6.

Bajna (Bajh-nah)– The 'bankers' of Congress. Black, ten-legged spider-like creatures approximately eight feet wide at rest—twenty if stretched out—who are extraordinary good with numbers.

Dhasha (Dah-sha) – One of the Grand Six. Very dangerous, violent beasts with indestructible metallic scales that shine with constantly-shifting iridescence. Big, crystalline, oval green eyes, long black talons, stubby bodies, sharklike faces with triangular black teeth. Their nostrils are set beside their eyes. Females are golden instead of rainbow, males have two layers of scales, indestructible metallic on top, gold underneath. Gutteral, snarling voice. Laugh by clacking their teeth together. Grow continuously throughout their lifetimes.

Geuji (Goy-gee)– a form of sentient mold whose entire body structure is composed of microscopic biological nanotubules capable of exchanging, storing, and processing information. If allowed to grow, they are easily the most intelligent species in Congress, with computing capacity far exceeding every artificial machine built by Congressional minds. Were the creative genius behind the ekhta, Congressional nannites, biosuits, and flowing-state ships. Bodies are glossy black that ripple in the light as information is passed throughout. Originated on Neskfaat, but were uprooted by Huouyt sabotage. *(See The Moldy Dead.)* Then imprisoned by Trith betrayal. *(See Breaking the Mold.)*

Grekkon (Greh-kuhn) – a creature that looks like a gigantic brown jumping-spider, but with a bulbous rear that extrudes a substance that will immediately decay/dissolve any substance, including otherwise indestructible Dhasha scales. As a species, do not have emotions. A burrower by nature.

Hebbut (heb-uht) – large humanoids with lizard-like skin, small eyes, huge toothy mouths, and massive strength. Think alien ogre.

Huouyt (sounds like: White) – One of the Grand Six. Three-legged, ancestrally aquatic shape-shifters. Bleed clear mucous. *Breja* – downy white fluff covering body. Tentacle legs and paddle-like arms. Cylindrical torso, enormous, electric-blue eyes, and a triangular, squid-like head. *Zora* – red, wormy gills in upper center of Huouyt heads that allow them to take the genetic patterns of another creature. Huouyt have a bad reputation in Congress. They are cunning, sneaky, adaptable, and excellent mimics. Considered to be psychopathic by most species in Congress.

Jahul (Jah-hool)– One of the Grand Six. Sextuped empaths with greenish skin and a chemical defense system of releasing their own wastes over their skin when they are frightened or stressed. *Sivvet* – the sensory organs that allow Jahul to feel emotions.

Jreet (Jreet) – One of the Grand Six. Red, gray, or cream-colored serpentine warriors who guard the First Citizen and the Tribunal. Have the ability to raise the energy level of their scales and disappear from the visible spectrum. Use echolocation to see.

Have great concave depressions in the sides of their heads to focus sound, much like bat ears. Believe in ninety hells for cowards, and that each soul splits into ninety different parts so they can experience all ninety hells at once. Their rravut within their teks is the most powerful poison in Congress. Bluish blood. Short, engine-like *shee-whomp* battlecry. Cream colored bellies. Diamond-shaped head. Tek- the talon protruding from their chests.

Nansaba (nan-sah-bah) - Sentient creatures with large black eyes, pointy ears, and four dexterous hands. Smooth, almost lizard-like skin. Highly prized as Dhasha slaves.

Ooreiki (Ooh-reh-kee) – One of the Grand Six. Heavy aliens a lot like boneless gorillas. Five hundred pounds on average. Four tentacle fingers on each arm. Big brown ostrich-egg sized snake-eyes, brown legs, skin turns splotchy when frightened. Huge mouths. Wrinkle their big faces to smile. Grunting rattle of speech. Five feet tall on average. Laugh by making a guttural rapping sound in the base of their necks like a toad croaking. Average age is 400. Outnumber humans ten thousand to one. Only the Ueshi are a more populous species.

Shadyi (Shad-yee) – The species of the First Citizen, Aliphei. There is only one surviving member of this species. Shaggy blue alien, walks on four feet, elephant-sized, black tusks, red eyes.

Takki (Sounds like: Tacky) – The ancestral servants of the Dhasha. Reviled throughout Congress as cowards and betrayers. Purple scales, very dense bodies, upright humanoid lizards. Crystalline, blue, ovoid eyes.

Trith (Trith) – Small, skinny-limbed, bulbous-headed aliens that see every aspect of the future all the time. The 'grays' of early Human mythology.

Ueshi (Oo-eh-she) – One of the Grand Six. Small blue or blue-green aliens with excellent reflexes and rubbery skin. Aquatic ancestry. Headcrest.

MEASUREMENTS:

ST – Standard Turns 9 standard rotations (1.23 years, 448.875 Earth Days to a Standard Turn)

SR – Standard Rotation 36 standard days (49.875 Earth Days to a Standard Rotation)

SD – Standard Day 36 standard hours (33.25 Earth Hours to a Standard Day)

SH – Standard Hour 72 standard tics (55.42 Earth Minutes to a Standard Hour)

St – Standard Tics (1.299 tics to an Earth Minute, .7698 Earth Minutes to a Standard Tic)

Standard Ninth-Dig (colloquially 'ninths') – approx. 1.3 inches
Standard Dig- approx. 1 foot
Standard Rod- approx. 9 feet
Standard Length - approx. 4,000 feet
Standard March- approx. 9,999 rods (90,000 feet)
Standard Lobe- approx. 2.5 pounds

RANKS:

Multi-Specieal Galactic Corps – Prime Corps Director
18-unit Galactic Corps – Secondary Corps Director
3-unit Galactic Corps – Tertiary Corps Director
Single-Species Sector Corps – _____(species) Corps Director Single solid silver eight-pointed star with a solid black interior.
Sector Unit – Prime Overseer. Silver eight-pointed star and four inner circles of a Prime Overseer
Solar Unit – Secondary Overseer. Silver eight-pointed star and three inner circles of a Secondary Overseer
Planetary Unit – Tertiary Overseer
Force – Petty Overseer